BY JONATHAN FRENCH

The Free Bastards
The True Bastards
The Grey Bastards
The Exiled Heir
The Errantry of Bantam Flyn

THE
FREE BASTARDS

THE
FREE BASTARDS

A NOVEL

JONATHAN FRENCH

NEW YORK

The Free Bastards is a work of fiction. Names, characters, places, and incidents are the products of the author's imagination or are used fictitiously. Any resemblance to actual events, locales, or persons, living or dead, is entirely coincidental.

Copyright © 2021 by Jonathan French

All rights reserved.

Published in the United States by Del Rey, an imprint of Random House, a division of Penguin Random House LLC, New York.

Del Rey is a registered trademark and the Circle colophon is a trademark of Penguin Random House LLC.

Hardback ISBN 978-0-593-15668-1
Ebook ISBN 978-0-593-15669-8

Printed in Canada on acid-free paper

randomhousebooks.com

10 9 8 7 6 5 4 3 2 1

First Edition

For Mom.
Your endless strength and inexhaustible love
could only be equaled in the pages of a fantasy.

THE
FREE BASTARDS

ONE

THERE WERE TIMES OATS ITCHED to shave his beard.

Never mind that he'd begun to grow the damn thing the year before he became a slophead. Never mind that without it he'd look a damn full-blood orc, all huge and hairless and near black. Never mind that he liked the way it thrust from his jaw, a challenge without words. There were still times he wished it wasn't there. Vomiting, for an instance. Never want a beard when your guts are fountaining out of your mouth, especially if there's bits. Licking quim sometimes too. Trying to provide a woman a sure path to spending but she keeps giggling on account of chin thatch tickling her thighs, that's a frustration.

Sure as shit, there were times in life Oats wished he'd taken a razor to his face the day before.

Right now—a dying man's gauntleted fingers tangled in his whiskers—was one of them.

To be fair, Oats had hold of the frail too, hand clamped over his mouth to keep him from making a noise. Or breathing at all. Still, he wasn't going all that quietly. He kept struggling.

And pulling Oats's fucking beard!

The stinging hairs, snarled in the segmented metal of the gauntlet, were more irritating than a kick in the cods. The strongest frail would have been hard-pressed to move Oats, but his beard wasn't made of muscle. He was forced to give, leaning into the man's pull, or else allow a denuded patch to adorn his jaw. He'd fallen victim to this strategy before, at the pink hands of a little girl on Fetch's shoulders during a game. Never suspected a full-grown fighting man to try it, even as his last act. He dragged the man close, encircling the entire helmeted head in his arms, and wrenched it around until the bones crunched. Always a weird thing, breaking a neck. Oats was never sure if that grinding was something he heard or felt. Either way, it was fucking unpleasant. Made him a bit sick, every time.

Not enough to vomit, thankfully.

Two backward steps brought the new-made corpse into the deep shadows beneath a high arch set into the side of the temple. Careful not to look up at the statue looming within, nor dwell on whatever judgmental god it depicted, Oats deposited the body behind the plinth and crept from the arch, giving the shrouded glare of the statue his back. He went across the alley, preferring the shadows cast by the portico of the adjacent house to the darksome embrace of the temple.

Oats hated temples. Hated their spires, all barnacled with hideous adornments. Hated the walls, all carved with images of leering devils and dwarfed people. Built like castles, they defended nothing but their own creepy mysteries. Well, that wasn't entirely earnest. Their bell towers were well suited to rousing armed men, should a murdering half-orc get himself spotted by a sleepless priest.

But that's what a mongrel faced when leaving the Lots. That was the risk taken when setting foot in Hispartha.

Damn walled towns and their horrid fucking religions.

Ellerina's cobbled square sprawled at the feet of the temple, silent and empty. None had seen Oats nearly make a pig's ear of killing the guard. He waited, watched, listened, rubbed at the sore skin beneath his beard. A day ago this town had been nothing to him but a map traced in the dust. The house sheltering him had been a rock. One of

Jacintho's daggers thrust into the ground served as the temple, a cup for the well at the center of the square. As the stillness drew on, Oats hoped the other frails on watch were dying quickly and unnoticed. No cry had yet broken the night. Likely all was done. Jacintho and his cutthroats weren't in the habit of fumbling a murder. Or twelve.

The wind kicked up again, enough chill in its breath to make Oats grit his teeth. Winter was dying, spiteful in its final days. Down in the Lots it rarely found much of a grip, contenting itself with spitting rain over the mountains. But here, on the north side of the Umbers, the cold could find a foothold when the sun went down. Oats worried it would keep the guards alert, though his man hadn't exactly been a hawk, the beard-yanking fuck.

The wait stretched on. Oats could feel himself getting nervy. He clenched his hands, resisting the urge to crack his knuckles. He couldn't wager how long he'd been lingering. Time was nothing but a queer stretched instant between the plan going right and going to shit.

Then he saw the sparks. Tiny motes of brightness across the square, birthed in the shadows between the farrier's shop and the ... the ...

Fuck.

Oats couldn't recall what the structure was. It had been a lemon rind on the dirt map. Anyway, the signal was appearing right where it was supposed to, the sparks bursting to life and dying just as they began to fall. Oats surveyed the square one last time before hurrying across its exposed width.

Jacintho melded further with the darkness when he arrived, tucking the measure of flint he'd used to strike the sparks back into his rags, but not the knife. Oats wedged himself into the alley next to the man. They did not speak. There was no need. The sentries were dead, their bodies hidden. The easy part of the plan.

Jacintho made for the alley's opposite end, pausing for a heartbeat at the mouth before creeping into the street. Oats stayed on the rangy frail's heels, feeling every bit the lummox. Simple to convince himself he was deft at sneaking when alone. Towering over a scrawny little weasel like Jacintho made Oats feel as furtive as a farting bull fucking a sack full of empty wine jugs. Still, the town remained undisturbed by their presence.

Ellerina was the largest settlement Oats had ever set foot in that wasn't a ruin. Jacintho was confident in their path, however, despite only having part of a day to scout the place. He'd dressed as some kind of wayward penitent, barefoot and clad in sackcloth, a guise he still wore. Odd to see him without his ugly flop of a hat, held together by more filth than cloth. His lank, greasy hair was tied into a tail that fell near to his ass, a lure that pulled Oats along through the murk of sleeping streets and reeking alleyways.

They came to the broken stirrup. That's what Jacintho had used to represent the place. In truth, it was a square two-story building of stone. A small arched portal set with a door of iron-studded wood was the only entrance. Jacintho had not been able to gain access. The only way in would have been at the rough invitation of Ellerina's bailiffs. And such an entrance would have made it damn unlikely he would ever come out again. So he'd resorted to idle gossip among the most loose-lipped sots of the tavernas. Their wine-soaked tongues had confirmed this was the spot.

Getting in without bringing the entire militia down upon them hampered their planning.

Until Jacintho had placed a small sack down on the miniature rendering of the town and said, "They also have a powder mill."

The broken stirrup was near Ellerina's center. The sack of blackpowder rested close to the scratched line denoting its western wall.

And it was from the west of town that the explosion now thundered, the sky flaring over the rooftops. Dogs began barking, disturbed babes wailing. Ellerina woke, her people's dreams blasted apart. The powder mill's stores were brimming, Jacintho had said, and Oats now heard the evidence. Felt it too. The building next to him rattled, render falling away from the bricks as the distant barrels continued to burst in an unsteady rhythm of startling concussions.

Hoping the explosions would mask the coming ruckus, Oats sprinted from the alley, charged the door to the fortified building, and bashed it open with his shoulder. He broke the beam barring the door . . . as well as the man behind it.

Oats hadn't known he was there. Perhaps he'd a mind to come out and see what the commotion was. Piss luck for that frail. He lay unmoving beneath the shattered wood. Oats stepped over, wasting no time to see if he still breathed. Jacintho would see to it he wasn't for long. Oats was more concerned with the man who appeared in the arch to the right, rushing into the cramped entry room, mace in hand. His steps stuttered when he saw Oats, the creases of determination in his ruddy face smoothing with the slack of sudden fear.

Men often needed a moment to put a fresh tally on their courage after setting eyes on Oats, he'd found.

This one came up short. He halted, spun to flee.

Grunting with aggravation, Oats lunged, caught the coward's jerkin and flung him back into the vestibule. The man tripped on the spars of the door and went down hard on his ass, made an "oof" noise that Jacintho transformed into an airy gurgle by sliding a forearm's length of sharp steel into his heart by way of a lung. The bandit had already dispatched the bailiff beneath the door.

Oats swallowed a rising unpleasantness in his throat. He wished the men had offered a fight, at least. Still be dead, but . . .

"These lead down," Jacintho hissed, leaning into the arch opposite where the coward had come.

Oats signaled for him to hold and went the other way.

The next room was larger, its stone expanse cut almost in half by a partition of hewn beams, standing flush together and running floor-to-ceiling with three doors set within its face, all reinforced with iron. Whatever this room's purpose, it had not been designed as a prison, necessitating the construction of this cumbersome wooden block of cells. Each door held a squint. Seizing a lantern from the guards' table, Oats went to the cells and unlatched the squints, peering into each in turn. Only one held an occupant, a confused and cowering frail. Just some drunkard rousted off the streets by the look—and smell—of him.

Cursing, Oats slapped the squint shut. Another arch led to an ascending spiral of stairs. The scuffle and scrape of movement could be heard through the ceiling, drawing Oats's eyes upward. There were more guards on the floor above, likely preparing a defense.

They could fuck around up there all they wanted. Oats had no need to go up. Up meant windows, fresher air. Mongrels would be held below. In the dark, the dank.

He returned to the entry chamber, handed the lantern to Jacintho as he strode past the bandit to take the downward stair.

The stink within the spiraling shaft had weight. Oats had taken in some evil smells in his life, but this tested his grit. For each step his feet took downward, his guts took one up. Soon, he was swallowing stuff he didn't remember eating. A grunting heave and a splash on the stairs behind him signaled Jacintho chose a different way of coping. The man retched twice more before they reached the bottom.

An iron grate, mossy with mold and rust, rested in the floor. It was barred and locked. Still gagging on the stench, Jacintho went to work with his picks, almost as quick with that task as he was with ending helpless men. Soon as he was finished, Oats hauled the grate aside. Five faces stared up at him from the pit, each just above the surface of a loathsome sink of human filth. Their wide eyes, filled with relief, were painful spots of bright white within the shit. They were too far down to reach, even for Oats's long arms, but a heap of corroded chain nearby provided the captives a way to salvation.

The three unfamiliar half-breeds climbed out first. Two males and a female, though beyond that Oats couldn't discern much due to the stinking muck coating them to the jawline. Hells, he barely would have recognized Sluggard when the mongrel clambered from the cesspit were it not for the ragged surface of his scalped head. Thresher came out last, the old scars cross-stitching her face nearly caked over with foulness. She and Sluggard both tried to speak, to offer thanks, ask a question, give a report, something. Neither of them managed to do more than croak and toss their guts on the floor. Oats grit his teeth against the hard sight and waited for all five of the freed to finish being sick.

"Please . . . let's . . . go," Jacintho said, swallowing hard and pressing the back of his hand against his mouth.

Oats cocked his head at the stairs, sending the man scurrying ahead with the lantern. If the bailiffs on the upper floor had found enough bravery to come down, Jacintho could be the first to meet them. Oats liked the weedy cutthroat, but not enough to take a thrumbolt or spear in the guts for him. Glancing back, he gave the other mongrels an encouraging nod, focusing on Sluggard and Thresher, but his words were aimed at the three strangers.

"You're free. But not safe. Not yet."

Oats went to the stair and followed the lantern's swiftly receding light.

At the top, the entry chamber remained empty save for the bodies of the two bailiffs. If their comrades had come down, they had not lingered long. Oats hesitated. They might have gone for help, or they could still be holed up on the second floor. He'd like to know before they set off, but checking would waste time, especially if they had remained and forced a fight. Jacintho knelt at the building's entrance, spying out from around the empty jamb. He'd extinguished the lantern, cloaking the vestibule in gloom. Outside, the powder mill was done erupting, the best of their diversion spent. But all was far from quiet. The night was filled with the clamor of bells. Ellerina's boldest would be fighting the fires caused by the explosion, as well as those set by Jacintho's men on their way out of town. Still, there would be wakened and wondering eyes at the windows of the houses now, likely a few folk in the street called out by the tumult but too timid or lazy to offer aid. Such could be frightened back indoors, but if the bailiffs had run to alert the town's militia, that would be an entirely different breed of bad.

Up? Or out?

Thresher made the decision for him. She emerged from the arch and crossed the vestibule, stooping on shaky legs to pluck the dead bailiff's mace from the floor.

"Dacia!" Sluggard hissed, either forgetting or foregoing her hoof name in his alarm.

She did not heed him, and strode into the room with the wooden cells. Oats went after her.

"Wait," he said, but she paid him as much attention as Sluggard and continued toward the upward stair. Growling, Oats shoved her away from the arch. She was weak from the ordeal of the cesspit and he misjudged the blow, knocked her into the beams of the cell block. Thresh cursed, nearly spilled to the ground.

"If you're going up, use your head," Oats said, more upset with having to bully her than with her stubbornness.

Going to the table, Oats seized two of the legs, flipping it as he lifted. The craftsmanship was simple, but solid. Held in front of him, the rectangular tabletop shielded Oats from the chest to nearly the knee.

"Stay behind me," he told Thresher, and started up. He'd not worn his tulwar, nor brought his thrum. Dangling swords and slung stockbows have a habit of clacking against city walls during a climb, their metal catching even the scantiest of starlight. He had a knife in each boot, but at the moment he preferred the legs of the table to fill his hands. As he reached the last turn of the stair and saw the glow of light from the upper room, Oats raised the table to cover his face and rushed up the last few steps, hoping he didn't have a sudden spat of clumsiness and trip, hoping whatever men were waiting would be too unnerved by the speed of his entry to notice that his legs were vulnerable.

Bursting through the arch, Oats braced himself for thrumbolts to strike the table, spearheads, axe blades. Hells, he didn't want to take a mace to the knee. But the only thing that struck the table . . . was another table. This one was upended too, turned over so it faced the arch. Like him, the bailiffs had the idea to use it as a shield. Unlike him, they were no longer behind their barricade.

"They've fucking gone," Thresher spat. She sounded disappointed.

Oats dropped his table. This room was larger than the one below. No, same size, just lacking the wooden cells. There was a fireplace instead, the black logs within still aflame.

"They're gone," Oats agreed, taking in the overturned furniture and lone dropped lantern. "Means we can't linger."

"Means we're better off with weapons than without," Thresher replied, rummaging through a heap of saddlebags, blankets, and brigands in the far corner. She made a triumphant noise and straightened, holding her chain mace and wearing a grin. "Besides. I wanted this back."

"Hand me that slicer," Oats said, pointing to the one sword in the pile.

"It's Slug's," Thresher replied.

As if summoned, Sluggard came into the room.

"Jacintho says he's leaving without us if we don't come now."

Oats grunted, gestured for Sluggard to get his blade. There was nothing else. Not surprising. The bailiffs would have taken the stockbows. Likely Ellerina's regidor didn't allow them to be kept here at all. Thresh handed both maces to Oats, peeled out of her befouled shirt, and dropped it to the ground, donning her brigand over bare flesh. Sluggard followed her example. Both were barefoot, their boots lost to the sucking embrace of the cesspit. Oats kept hold of the bailiff's mace and handed Thresher her chained weapon.

The three of them hurried back down to the entry chamber.

"Do you relish the notion of the noose?" Jacintho complained. "Because I do not!"

The bandit slipped out the doorway, swift and silent. Oats directed the rest to follow him, using his hands like a drover. He nudged Thresh out, next the three new bloods. A small swat sent Sluggard after them. Oats took his own position at the rear of the line.

The town was alive and fretting, but the destruction of the powder mill continued to be an ally. The streets were mostly clear. Oats spied the backs of a few folk hurrying toward the pulsing glow of the fires, buckets jostling at the ends of their arms. Jacintho raced across the lane, abandoning all attempts of concealment in favor of speed. Fucker was fast as a hare. The weakened mongrels between him and Oats were struggling to keep up. Still, it would be folly to call for him to slow, for the only thing swifter than Jacintho's feet was his mind. He read the growing turmoil of the town on the run, darting down alleys, sometimes pausing at their mouths to let passels of shouting townsfolk pass by. Other times he rushed headlong, seemingly careless of discovery, yet they crossed paths with none and no cry was raised. His instincts were uncanny. Somehow, the bandit folded his gaggle of trailing mongrels into the currents of Ellerina's distress, melding with it so as to be invisible.

Yet the plan was fraying. Oats didn't know the town cold the way Jacintho did, but he saw the bandit's teeth flash once, bared in frustration, a heartbeat before he hustled the mongrels beneath a mercer's stall. The goods had been removed for the night, but the tables and racks provided tenuous cover when a group of armed men rushed by. Blinded by their haste and the light from their own torches, they passed within a mule's cock of Oats and his companions, all belly down and holding their breaths.

When Jacintho judged it safe to leave the uncertain shelter of the stall he doubled back for the first time.

Oats tamped down his growing agitation.

Their plan contained only two points of egress from the town. And the bandit had just deemed one of them closed; the private, now neglected garden of a failed spice merchant abutting Ellerina's wall. According to Jacintho's report, it would make an easy, secluded climb thanks to the screening hedges and unmanaged vines. But it seemed the militia had made that route too risky. That was the trouble with likely means of escape: they were well known. So, they couldn't go over the walls. That left going under, through the old Imperial sewers. Jacintho had discovered only one way to reach them.

He led them back to the alley he'd used to signal Oats, ducking patrols the entire way. The temple square was before them. The bells were silent, gone back to sleep after ensuring the town would not. Their plan had reckoned the temple's well would be too far from the powder mill to be any use fighting the fires. They'd been right. But the square was not entirely empty, and this time it was occupied by more than some damn cat.

"Shit," one of the new mongrels hissed.

Thresh silenced him with a look.

A mother stood outside her door on the edge of the square across from the temple. She had a babe in arms and another child—a young boy—at her skirts. Her attention was fixed westward, as if she were trying to peer through the spires of the temple to witness the fires.

No. She was keeping vigil, worrying for neighbors and loved ones gone to battle the blaze, leaving her alone.

"A moment," Jacintho whispered, his voice sharp as the blade in his hand.

Oats bulled past the others and caught the man before he could slither from the alley. It was no effort to push him against the wall and hold him there. Frails didn't have a half-orc's sight in the darkness, but even if Jacintho could not see the warning in Oats's glare, he damn well felt it in the strength of his arm.

Jacintho loosed an aggravated breath. "She will cry out unless—"

Oats pressed him further into the wall. "No." He could feel the man's ribs bend beneath his splayed hand. It would be an easy thing to kill him, easy as it would be for the bandit to kill the woman and her children.

"No," he repeated, and let Jacintho go. He turned to the huddled mongrels. "We're going to make a run for it. With luck, she'll shut herself away at the sight of us. If she hollers, keep moving. Straight into the temple."

"What about the friars?" Sluggard asked.

"If a bunch of quim-fearing old frails are fool enough to stand in our way we'll go through them," Oats replied.

"But they—"

"*Move.*"

Scorning further delay, Oats led them out of the alley at a run.

Jacintho outpaced him after a few strides. The bandit's rush grabbed the woman's attention. Boots pounding the cobbles, Oats craned his head to watch her. She didn't cry out, nor flee inside. Instead, she stood frozen, more perplexed than afraid. It must have taken her mind a moment to reconcile the sight of a bedraggled pilgrim sprinting ahead of a half dozen mongrels. She still hadn't found her voice by the time Oats raced beneath the temple's central arch. Jacintho had one of the great doors open; by chance or skill, Oats hadn't seen. He didn't care. The others bulled through the portal within a few heartbeats. Jacintho shoved the door closed, muting the burst of the woman's stalled outcry.

Oats looked for a way to secure the doors.

"You will find neither bar nor beam, soot-skin," a confident voice declared from behind him. "We have no need to fear any that would enter here."

Oats whirled, finding his companions already turned, stiff with alarm.

The priests waited within the vaulted hall of their sanctuary, nearly a score in number. They had indeed decided to stand in the half-orcs' way. With swords in their hands.

TWO

OATS HAD THOUGHT TO ENCOUNTER some choir of frails in cassocks with watery eyes. A cringing, indignant cluster of soft-bellied, jowly scribes and splinter-legged, liver-spotted hermits. The men barring his way were all wearing cassocks, but beyond that they refused to mold to his imaginings.

Steel was in their stares as well as their hands, one as hot as the other was cold. Their sword blades were straight, wide at the crossguard and tapering toward the point. Those weapons would cut well and thrust quick. Each was paired with a steel buckler. Like the swords, the small, round shields were held with steady confidence at the ends of forearms corded by their use. The priests had the spare forms of men who indulged only in training. Their ages ranged from bald coots to thick-haired swains, but none were weakened by too many years or too few. All wore a beard down to their cods.

Oats threw a glower at Jacintho. "Who the fuck are these goats?"

The bandit gave nothing but an uncertain gurgle.

"We are the Salt of Amarsaphes. Oblates of the Twin-Crowned Lord."

Oats looked at the stern speaker, a balding man of middle years, the ruddiness of his dangling beard blanched at the jaw. The priest's pronouncement, like his eyes, burned with pride and threat. He seemed to think he'd given some important answer.

"Uh-huh," Oats replied.

"They're Steel Friars," Sluggard said. He sounded shaken. "Tried to tell you."

Oats nodded, still not truly understanding, but men with swords didn't need deep thought to comprehend. "You did."

It wouldn't have mattered if he'd taken the time to listen to Sluggard's warning. The town had been closing around them. This was the only way out of Ellerina now. The hard way in the plan. Just harder now was all.

"Don't reckon you'd stand aside," Oats said to the head goat, careful not to glance at the big wrought-iron candle trees standing at the threshold of the antechamber and the temple proper. "Tell your brethren to let mine pass so this don't come to blood?"

"Blood was required the moment you half-breed swine shattered the sanctity of our home with fire and skullduggery."

"That some kind of vow?" Oats asked, giving the mace in his hand a little wag, testing its weight.

The man opened his mouth to respond. Oats threw the mace at his head. To his credit, the priest got his buckler up in time. His reflexes were honed, but he wasn't prepared for the power Oats could put into flinging a piece of heavy metal. The head of the mace slammed into the buckler, crumpled the edge and sent the bent shield rebounding into its wielder's face. The priest reeled, spitting blood and broken teeth, but he regained his footing quickly.

Damn. Oats had hoped to drop him. Felling the mouthiest fuck in the room can sometimes take the grit out of the rest. Sometimes.

These Steel Friars had mettle. They wove around their injured brother, eager for the fight.

Oats darted and snatched up one of the candle trees, forcing the goats to arrest their charge by swinging it in great, reaping strokes. His own companions had to dance back to stay clear. The frails weren't fools. They gave ground in tight ranks, none risking the reach of the whirling iron. Oats was strong, but he couldn't keep them at bay forever. Besides, the priests were likely to receive help long before his arms gave out. The militia would be coming through the doors at his back any moment. The Friars had but to wait. And they knew it.

Oats forced them deeper into the temple. The lofty hall of the sanctuary widened as he passed from the antechamber. Whatever god these frails grew their beards to please must have frowned on loafing, for the place was free of furnishings. Still, Oats had to shorten the width of his swings to keep from striking the sculpted columns marching down the length of the sanctuary. The Friars fanned out, loosening their formation to allow a few of their number to move around the columns, intent on using the side aisles to flank Oats.

Sluggard hurried to cover the right, Thresher the left. Behind, Oats heard the scrape of iron and frantic cursing—Jacintho trying to secure the temple doors with the other candle tree.

The Friars were coming two abreast down the aisles, four on each side. Nine remained facing Oats in the center, the broke-mouth leader among them, looking mighty surly. Two of the unfamiliar mongrels were standing with his fellow Bastards, one of the men with Thresh and the woman with Sluggard. Oats couldn't see the third mongrel. Helping Jacintho, perhaps. Little good it would do. Save for Sluggard's slicer and Thresh's chain-mace, the freed half-orcs were armed with nothing but the stink from the cesspit.

Oats let loose a growl as he continued to herd the priests with vicious swipes of the candle tree. He had come to save his captured brethren and he'd just led them blindly into a fight they couldn't win. What would the chief say? That he'd been too hasty in his planning and too hesitant during its execution. That he should have known who defended this temple. That he relied too much on Jacintho and the other mountain bandits. That he shouldn't have left his thrum behind.

No. She wouldn't say any of that. Leastways, not that he would hear. Because Oats would suck cock in all the hells before he'd fail to bring his brethren home and live to report the shame.

With a roar to rival the exploding powder mill, he waded into the

Steel Friars. The candle tree pummeled the air as they scrambled away, but Oats surged forward and caught one hapless priest on the backswing. The man tried to catch the blow, using both his sword and buckler, but the hurtling branches of the iron tree broke his guard. And at least one wrist. The yelping priest toppled sideways into a few of his fellows, upsetting their balance and their ordered ranks. Oats went to work widening the breach, chopping downward with the candle tree, scattering the Friars in its path. One wasn't quick enough and the snap of his leg resounded in the sanctuary an instant before the clang of iron striking the stone floor. An agonized shriek drowned out the strident echo.

Oats bulled to his right, sweeping the tree back up to plant its wax-coated tines into the chest of the nearest Friar. Didn't have enough force to skewer him, but he was good and snared. The others were rallying, a flood of brown robes and flashing steel seeking to eclipse the black boulder that had dropped into their midst. Sharp edges slashed, bright points darted to draw blood. Oats charged through the pain, shoving the priest caught on the end of the candle tree backward until he smote a column. The man's skull smacked the stone and his eyes went glassy. Oats dropped the candle tree, grabbed the dazed priest's face, and gave his head a second helping of the column. This time, blood dashed an arm's length up the face of the stone. Oats spun behind the column, letting it deflect the vengeful strikes of the pursuing Friars. Most of them. He was slashed twice, at the shoulder and forearm, and another blade pierced the side of his ass.

Why did the pain of being cut feel hot while being stabbed was cold?

Grunting, Oats reeled into the side aisle and stumbled into the priests attacking Sluggard. He hadn't expected it, but neither had they. And he weighed a heap more. He brought two of them down as his own footing failed, one falling beneath him, the other tripping in the tangle. This man struck at Oats, but succeeded only in swatting him with the flat of his blade. Tucking his elbows, Oats rolled. This time he meant to collide with the priests. The log of his body hit the pair still striving to kill Sluggard and took their legs out from under them. They spilled over his spinning bulk, expelling words in their alarm Oats would have thought unfit for holy men. Sluggard and the female mongrel were nearly knocked over themselves, but they managed to scuttle backward in time.

Oats gained his feet as the six remaining Friars he'd assaulted with the candle tree came swarming to aid their fellows. They flowed around the columns and eclipsed the sprawled priests, a tight trio forming a screen of thrusting swords to keep the half-orcs back while the rest bent to help the fallen stand. If they'd chosen aggression for their foes over concern for their comrades, they'd have butchered Oats and his brethren. What fools didn't press for the kill just to help their downed . . .

Brothers.

Oats didn't understand their god or their temple or their statues, but now he understood *them*.

Springing forward he clapped his palms against the flat of the central Friar's blade, wagering he'd trained hard to keep a firm grip. It was a good wager. The priest didn't let go as Oats yanked the blade, jerking the man forward. Releasing the sword, he punched the man in the throat. Not enough to crush his windpipe, but more than enough to cause panic. All the training under the sun couldn't prevent him from dropping his arms now. Blade and buckler clattered to the stones as the priest grasped his own throat. As if touching it would cause his air to return. Strange how everyone always did that.

Spurred by the violence, the other Friars attempted a rush, managing only a single step before Oats had their choking brother spun around and seized, pinning the man's head in his great arms.

"Think twice!" he bellowed. "I'll tear his head from his shoulders!"

The men before him froze, their steely stares wavering.

Oats jerked a look to his left, saw Thresher keeping her own foes at bay with relentless swings of her chain mace.

"Tell them to leave off!" Oats cried, turning his attention back to the head goat with the busted lips.

The man hesitated.

Oats squeezed on his captive's head until his wheezing ceased. He couldn't see the priest's face, but he knew from experience the man's eyes were beginning to pop. Ever an unpleasant sight, that. The other goats certainly saw. More than one visibly paled.

"Cease!"

The Friars engaged with Thresh halted at their master's barked command.

The feeling of relief lasted all of a heartbeat, dispelled by the sound of the temple doors being battered from without. The militia had arrived, demanding entry with shouts and shuddering blows. The thick wood muted both. For now.

Oats set his jaw and ignored the banging behind him, as well as the pitiful slaps on his arms from the trapped priest. The man couldn't have broken a thrice's hold prior to being throat-punched; he sure as shit had no chance now. About as much chance as the half-orcs had of escaping this fucking temple.

"Sluggard," Oats said, gaze still locked on the head goat. "What do they call their chief?"

"Abbot," came the reply.

"Make a choice, abbot," Oats told the man. "We want to leave. You can prevent that, but you'll lose this brother here. Or you can lay your blades down and we're on our way with no more dead. But once those doors give way . . . ain't either of us left with a choice."

The Friars nearest the abbot gave him imploring looks. Whether they wanted to save their brother or kill the mongrels, Oats couldn't guess.

The drumming at the doors was joined by the sharp accompaniment of splintering wood.

"We have little time!" Jacintho proclaimed, voice whetted with panic.

The abbot's mouth was half-open, eyes wide and bright as his buckler.

"You ever been tossed a man's head?" Oats asked him, tensing to wrench his prisoner's neck.

The abbot took half a step forward. "The tenets of our order prevent us from laying down swords in the presence of adversaries."

He'd tried to keep the plea from his voice, his face. He succeeded with the one, not the other.

The angry shouts of the militia were coming clear through rends in the door, ever widening beneath the plunging bites of axe heads.

Oats made another swift wager and a swifter offer. "Them slicers can stay in your hands so long as they stay out of our hides."

"Very well."

"Give me your fucking word!"

"You have it!"

Without wasting another breath, another precious moment, Oats hauled his captive toward Thresher. She was breathing heavy, eyeing the four priests standing less than a decent spit before her. The freed mongrel who had stood with her was also panting, but not from exertion. He was sitting with his back to the wall, trying to hold his guts in. One of the nearest Friars' swords was red to the crossguard. Oats felt a rising wrath, a powerful itch to kill the man in his grip before moving on to the one who'd run the poor mongrel through.

"We must leave him," Jacintho said, appearing at Oats's elbow.

"Just find the damn tunnels."

Oats thrust the captive priest at Sluggard and stooped to lift the gutted mongrel. His hissing breaths transformed into agonized screams as he was moved.

Turning with his suffering burden he found the abbot had drawn nearer with his herd of bearded swordsmen. For a moment Oats feared the man had decided to toss shit on his oath. No need to keep his word to a half-orc. The doors would soon give way.

The abbot raised his arm and pointed to the rear of the great hall. "The old tunnels can be reached from the undercroft."

Oats nodded. "We'll leave your man once we're below."

The abbot's face held no belief in those words. Only hope.

Jacintho had already vanished through the low portal at the far end of the sanctuary by the time Oats and the others reached it. Beyond they found a circular alcove with two further arches. And no sign of the bandit.

"Which way?" Sluggard demanded of their captive priest.

The man lifted his chin. "There."

"If you're lying—"

Sluggard's warning was cut short by Jacintho emerging from the shadows of the indicated archway. "He speaks true."

With that the bandit fled back the way he'd come.

Oats jerked his head for the others to follow, putting himself at the rear of their line with his armload of groaning, shivering half-orc.

A single candle illuminated the entrance to the stair. Jacintho took it from the wall and descended the spiral without breaking stride. If anything, his pace was only slowed by the desire to keep the candle from being snuffed.

They emerged into the cool of the undercroft, tailing the meager light as it scurried around and between the stacked casks of the temple's larder. Oats ducked hanging meat, the pungent odors of cheese and fresh butter managing to reach his nostrils even through the stink of the befouled mongrel he carried. Jacintho paused only once, directing the mongrel woman to pilfer a bundle of resin torches from the priest's supplies. The bandit drew up in a cramped corner where a trapdoor stood open, a stairwell running straight from its mouth into even lower depths. He lit one torch from his candle and distributed its greater flame among the ends of the rest. Soon as each mongrel had a brand they were urged down the stair by a word from Oats and the insistent revolutions of Jacintho's free arm. When Thresh and the two new mongrels were gone, the bandit tarried a moment, his flinty eyes flitting to the captive priest in Sluggard's grip and the wounded half-orc in Oats's arms.

"Go," Oats told him, answering the question that resided in those brief glances.

Leaving the candle atop a cask, Jacintho plunged into the old tunnels.

"You can't take him down there, Oats," Sluggard said. "Going to be low and cramped enough as it is. Especially for you."

"There's no need to take him down." Slowly, Oats knelt and laid the mongrel on a bed of grain sacks. "He's dead." Standing, he found both Sluggard's and the priest's eyes locked on the body. Sluggard's jaw bulged.

"Get going," Oats told him, breaking him out of his haze.

Blinking, Sluggard seemed to shrink. Letting go of the Friar he lit a torch from the candle and fled the cellar.

Left alone with Oats, the priest began to panic.

"Y-you said you'd let me go," he stammered.

The hollow sounds of distant raised voices were funneled into the cellar from the far stair. Oats could see the first stirrings of light coming down through the arch.

"Best run and warn them boys," Oats told the Friar, lighting the last torch. "Tell them it's fool-ass to come charging into a burning cellar." The priest watched in horror as Oats touched the blazing torch to the wheat sacks cradling the dead mongrel. "'Course, I reckon word—and these flames—will spread quicker if you take them both with you."

Oats snagged the man by the cassock as he turned to run and flung him down atop the body on the makeshift pyre. He stamped down on the screeching frail with his boot, held him there until his robes were alight. Once the man was a living torch he let him up, allowed him to flail and flee, spreading the flames among the provender as if sharing it would diminish its hunger for his flesh.

As the man leapt with unintentional vigor to his destructive purpose, Oats turned for the stairs, leaving the larder—and the honor of half-orcs—to go to the hells.

THREE

THEY NEED TO FEAR US . . .

Squatting in the mouth of a lightless tunnel, back to the clammy stone, knife in hand, Oats tried to keep his ears open for sounds of pursuit, but the chief's words kept crowding his attention.

We're animals to them. Cattle they can pen. Bears they can hunt . . .

She wasn't wrong. Half-breed swine, the Friars' abbot had called them. So Oats had roasted his man.

We need to be something they can't hunt, can't cage . . .

It wasn't to be cruel. It was . . . tactics. The fire was necessary to keep the frails from their heels. The flames and the fear had done the job. Plus, Ellerina had now lost more than its powder mill. The ample stores of some militant zealots with stiff cods for fighting mongrels were up in smoke too. The chief would approve. Give her something to feed the other hoofmasters' ever-increasing demand for results. Another tally mark toward victory. Gunpowder and wheat, better to deprive Hispartha of them than it was to kill their men. Tonight, Oats had done all three. And added to the chief's cause of convincing the kingdom that mongrels were more than beasts.

We need to be monsters.

Not cattle, or bears. Or swine. No. They were devious brutes who took captives with promises of mercy only to set them on fire. Hells, not even the thicks did that and Hispartha was terrified of them. So what did that make tonight's deeds? Worse, maybe. What did that make him?

The shuffle of movement snapped Oats out of his own head, but it was only Jacintho, scuttling over to his side for the fourth time.

"I tell you, this is folly."

In the complete blackness the man existed as nothing but his passionate whisper. Not even thrice-blood eyes could see in the deepness of the Imperial tunnels once Oats had halted their flight and ordered the torches extinguished. That had drawn disbelieving stares from all, but he'd chosen the spot carefully; some manner of junction chamber where the mouths of three tunnels converged. It was the first such place they'd come upon after hurrying along narrow, arched passages with nothing but instinct to decide their path. Not even Jacintho, the shortest among them, could stand much above a crouch. A channel ran through the center of the tunnels, carrying the cold, reeking waste of Ellerina that managed to worm its way down into the ancient sewers. The junction provided enough room for them to gather, stand a little straighter, and to fight if their luck continued to resemble the contents of the drainage channel. Mostly, it was a good place to wait . . . were it not for the smell, and the rats, and the pitch-dark.

"We should keep moving."

And Jacintho's ritual pestering.

"You know the way out?" Oats whispered back. "Because you didn't last three times I asked."

"No, but if you would just give me leave and light, I could discover us a deliverance."

"Starting to reckon it might be best to find the militia? Trade us for your life?"

There was a little intake of breath. "Big Bastard, you wound me."

"Do more than wound you if you try sneaking off alone."

In truth, Oats trusted Jacintho far more than that. And he shouldn't. Leastways that's what the chief told him. So Oats said what he reckoned she would in his place and left it at that. If the bandit was affronted, he didn't let it keep him silent for long.

"We may not know where these tunnels go, but we would be fools to believe the men hunting us do not. Your fire thwarted them from following, *yes*, yet what—I ask you—prevents them from cutting us off? We cannot win such a race by sitting still!"

"Can't get lost down here and die in the dark either."

"Do you understand that the temple was the only access *I* discovered? That does not mean there are no other avenues to this antique ant hill. There could be men scouring for us even now."

"And they'll have light. Means we'll see them coming." Oats had placed himself on watch at one tunnel. Sluggard and Thresh covered the other two. Still, for all that caution, he was holding on to a hope that the wrathful men of Ellerina weren't going to be the first to find their position. It *was* a race, but Oats and the others weren't the runners, they were the prize. "We hold to the plan. We wait."

Jacintho refused to buy his confidence. "What if they don't come? What if they never found a way in? Or never tried?" The distrust in his voice, the thinly veiled contempt, and the heavily draped fear revealed he wasn't referring to the militia.

"Barsius won't leave us to die."

"You can't be certain of that."

Oats didn't bother to answer. He could be certain. And was. He just couldn't tell Jacintho the reason. So he made no reply at all.

His wounds were troubling him. The Friars had made more of a mess than he'd felt at the time. Before the torches had been snuffed he'd seen the way the others looked—tried to avoid looking—at his slashed and bleeding limbs. But it was the stab in his haunch that worried him most. He'd tried to stay on his feet, but the low ceiling made it a torture before long. He succumbed to squatting, hoping his ass's new closeness to the sewer's horrid creek didn't invite some ravenous rot into his blood.

He never heard them coming. Wouldn't have even if he weren't lost in grim thoughts of dying in some raving, sweating, pus-oozing fit. He didn't hear them coming, but he did see them. But only because the halflings wanted to be seen.

Vision returned as a grey specter, carving the black into curved edges. The trio of tunnel mouths appeared to yawn as pale light within crawled nearer. Stretched shadows preceded stout figures. They came with ghostly lanterns and drawn swords, their dark faces blue in the eldritch glow. Three each emerged from Thresh and Sluggard's tunnels. Oats made room for the four that came his way, one detaching from the rest to stand in the center of the junction chamber.

"And I worried we would have little to do this night," Barsius said, surveying Jacintho and the half-orcs with his smile flashing bright. The leader of the halflings sheathed his leaf-bladed sword without bothering to wipe the blood from the bronze.

"So. They sent men down after us," Jacintho said, cocking a displeased eye at Oats.

"More than a few," Barsius replied, though it hadn't truly been a question. "Unlike you, they will never again see the sun."

Frozen worms wriggled down Oats's spine at the thought of meeting his end at the hands of the tunnel fighters. He wasn't the only one disturbed. The two new mongrels eyed the halflings warily. Oats wasn't sure what their experience with waddlers was, being from Hispartha, but Barsius and his bunch took some getting used to. With their unkempt garments, well-tended weapons, filthy hair that resembled the plaited wool of a black sheep, and ritual scarring that left swirling rows of puckered half domes upon their faces, these halflings were far from the serene pilgrims who often represented Belico's devoted. It was a queer feeling, fearing someone that was waist-high, but one Oats had long accepted.

Jacintho, however, continued to mask his intimidation with aggression.

"You could have come sooner," the man groused. "Aided us in the temple."

Barsius ran a thumbnail across his lower lip, making a show of consideration. At last, he grinned at Jacintho. "But that was not the plan."

The bandit lifted his mouth in a tight, insincere smile. *Fuck you*, that smile said.

Oats had to swallow his own frustration. Barsius and his killers could certainly have aided against the Steel Friars . . . had anyone besides Sluggard known such men guarded the temple. Even if they had, it was unlikely the halflings would have committed themselves to a fight aboveground. Oats had quickly learned that what Zirko's disciples were capable of doing was often a far ride from what they were willing to do. Besides, they weren't here to help fight the war, despite their unconvincing claims and limited usefulness. They were hunters, hoping Oats would lead them to their secret quarry. To Xhreka, and the tongue of the god she bore. Long before he'd known Xhreka's connection to Belico—and her importance to Zirko—Oats had seen nothing but a halfling, alone and fighting to survive in the Pit of Homage. He'd vowed to protect her then, though she needed him little, being earnest. Perhaps she didn't need him now, either, but Oats aimed to test her pursuer's patience to the hells and back.

"Can we get the fuck gone?" Thresher demanded.

"Yes," Oats replied. "Barsius, lead us out."

The halfling gave a swift command to his fighters in their own clicking tongue. They melted back into the tunnels, leaving only their leader behind. The plan was for them to remain in the sewers, both to thwart any further pursuit and keep the halflings from being caught on the surface where they were more vulnerable.

Barsius dipped his head at the tunnel Sluggard had guarded. "That's our road."

The sewer tunnels were no less sinister and confounding with the small man guiding them. His lone lantern provided light enough to see, but did nothing to illuminate Oats's sense of direction. He became convinced that the tunnels spread far beyond the limits of the town above. Perhaps the Imperial settlement had been much larger, or maybe the old emperors and their subjects were so full of shit they required such expansive works to carry it all away. Regardless, Oats was glad he'd chosen to wait. Twice they had to tramp on the bodies of slain men clogging the passage, those sent down to kill the fugitives only to be butchered themselves. Oats had no notion how the halflings managed the slaughter. Little as they were, these remained cramped quarters for a fight and an ambush would be all but impossible. But the waddlers had been striving beneath the earth in search of their god's relics for hells-knew-how-many years. Dark deeds underground were something of a birthright. And for some, a burden.

At last, a sigh from Sluggard signaled the end. After the closeness and hollow echoes of the tunnels, the expansive glow of the night sky—though still smothered with clouds—was a dizzying relief, the roar of the wind endless and threatening. They emerged from what appeared to be the base of a hill, but Oats spied traces of crumbled masonry among the choking scrub and tumbled boulders. Whatever this structure had been, it was reclaimed by the land long ago and now stood outside Ellerina's walls, maybe even beyond the knowledge of her defenders, for their escape was met with nothing but the scratching sway of the surrounding broom shrubs.

Refusing to squander time or good fortune, Oats gave Barsius a grateful nod and Jacintho a permissive swat on the back, sending the man to scout ahead.

"I will see you back at the Pit," the halfling said as he returned to the shadowy embrace of the tunnels.

Oats directed the mongrels to follow Jacintho.

They fled Ellerina in the manner they'd come, on foot, in the dark, favoring good cover over speed. Yet they'd had the entire night to reach the town, and now only its last gasps to leave it behind. They would not reach the mountains before dawn. The sun would betray their path if the men sent to track them were even half competent. Perhaps none would follow. Perhaps Oats had sowed enough dread that they would not dare chase the monsters. But it was a fool-ass that planned on perhaps.

Morning came, and with it the order to run. Their pace was hampered by the rescued mongrels, lacking boots and weak from their ordeal. Encouraging words and reminders of pursuit only got them so far. The light growing with every lost moment, Oats had no choice but to allow them to rest. They went to ground in a thicket of fig trees and oleander, both shriveled from winter's cold neglect.

"We won't linger long," Oats told the half-orcs as they slumped to the ground. Even Thresher succumbed, a testament to their exhaustion. Oats pulled Jacintho aside. "Find some high ground. I want to know if we got anyone hounding us."

The man left the thicket without making a sound.

"Is there any water?" the new female mongrel asked.

Oats shook his head. They had traveled light.

The mongrel sitting beside her growled and shook his hanging head. Oats watched his gnarled hands clench until the female nudged his ribs with an elbow. He settled but did not look up. He was a decent-sized son of a thick. Might have been a concern if he weren't a cunt hair from collapse.

"You two got names?" Oats asked.

"Rant," the female responded. She tilted her head to the side. "This is Roar."

Oats snorted. All these mongrels coming south thought themselves legends already. The first hundred or so that Sluggard and Thresh led into the Lots were the worst. Oats had lost his patience at the third fuckwit calling himself "Deathrider."

He shook his head at this latest pair of kingdom-bred hopefuls. "You'll get your hoof names when you earn them. Until then—"

"Until then the names our father gave us will serve fine." The mongrel woman pointed a thumb at her chest before hooking it at the slumped, sullen ass beside her. "Rant. Roar."

"Father?" Oats frowned. "Master, you mean."

"She means our fucking father!" Roar raised his head to fix a burning stare at Oats.

"Fruit of his loins and all that," the female said.

"You're . . . brother and sister? By blood?"

Rant clicked her tongue. "Rare, but true. Our mother was fertile for a half-breed. And before you make another wrong assumption, she was loved by our father. *Loved*, not owned. They were wed, by their loyalty if not by the king's law."

"You two are mighty big for frailings," Oats said.

"Papi wasn't a small man," Rant replied with a fond, sad smile. "And the greatest shipwright to ever live."

"Shipwri—?" Oats cast a look at Sluggard and Thresher. Both wore weary grins.

"Means he built ships," Roar barked. "And we would be continuing his work if half-orcs were allowed to inherit."

Oats ignored him, continued to stare at his hoofmates. "They know boats?"

Sluggard's smile widened. "They know fucking boats."

"Ships!" Roar protested.

Oats felt a smile forming on his own face, but a sudden thought made it wither. He strode over to Thresh and Sluggard, grabbed an arm of each, and hauled them to their feet, half dragging, half carrying them a few paces away into a forced huddle. He spoke in a hush.

"The other one—the one got himself killed—tell me he wasn't some genius with siege weapons and shit."

"Slave to a mule-skinner," Thresh assured him.

Oats let out a deep breath. "Aw, thank all the hells."

"You did good, Big Bastard," Sluggard said, squeezing his shoulder. "Thanks for coming after us."

"Thank Jacintho," Oats replied. "It was his men that heard you'd been caught."

"Spying and rescuing are leagues apart," Thresher said. "You didn't have to risk it."

Oats looked her square. "Yes. I did. You're True Bastards." Kneading the backs of their necks, he turned them loose and lifted his chin at the hopefuls. "We need to get them two to the Cradle. A pair of shipwrights? That's fortune we never saw coming."

"Reckon chief'll spend in her breeches once she hears," Thresher said.

"Need to reach the Lots first," Sluggard pointed out.

"And we won't do that sat here. Anvil is waiting at Ul-zuwaqa with mounts."

Sluggard shot a glance through the thicket at the sun. "Ul-zu—Oats, that's directly east! We need to go—"

"The frails expect us to go south," Oats cut in. "They'll be riding hard for the Smelteds, try to block the passes. Ul-zuwaqa is closer. And they might not think to look for us there."

Sluggard shrugged. "You know best."

Oats gave no reply. He didn't know fuck-all. But it was important he was convincing. "Rant. Roar. On your feet! We're moving on."

Jacintho burst into the thicket. "And I would suggest doing so at some haste."

Oats felt a shit coming. A runny one. "Frails?"

"Cavaleros."

"They see you?"

Jacintho shook his head. "Riding measured for now. But they are headed this way."

Oats swept his arms forward. "Everybody move! We got a start. We just need to hold it. Go!"

Strong words. And total hogshit. They would never be able to outpace those horses. Not with four barefoot mongrels who hadn't eaten in days. But neither could they make a stand. There was nothing to do but run, try to keep out of sight for as long as possible. Once the cavaleros spied them, they'd put spur to horse, and the chase would end.

North of the Smelteds the land was a garden compared to Ulwundulas. The plains were filled with grass, not dust. Trees dared to gather in stands rather than survive the barrens alone, greedy for the scant water. But it was still winter. The garden was dead, and spiteful for the fact. There was little to shield them from the horizon. Perhaps that was best. Fewer temptations to give up and hide. Or perhaps that's what they should do. Scatter. Hunker down. Cling to the fool-ass hope that the hunting party would pass them by. He didn't damn know. So he kept running, followed Jacintho, trusted the cutthroat's fleet steps and uncanny instinct for self-preservation. They cut a direct course east, the new sun spearing their eyes. Oats cursed the blinding glare when he stumbled, bashed his toes on unseen rocks, and praised it when he realized the horsemen faced the same impediment. As the sun climbed higher it ceased to be an enemy. And an ally. Distant, cold, uncaring, it was nothing now but a witness.

The morning faded. Along with their strength.

Sluggard was the first to fall behind. His feet were in tatters. Thresher went back for him.

"Come now, you scalped eunuch," she said, throwing his arm over her shoulder. "You ain't ever lived up to your name. Not going to let you start now."

Oats waited on them to catch up, fearing with every heartbeat the cavaleros would appear. He took Sluggard's tulwar. "Just going to carry this for you a span."

At the end of that span, Oats was still carrying the sword. And Sluggard.

With the mongrel slung over his shoulder, Oats's own limits were swiftly approaching. His legs were leaden, vision plagued by tiny, floating pinpoints of light. Breathing was a greater burden than Sluggard. Oats had to focus on drawing in air, had to concentrate on moving his limbs, lest both cease without permission. He could no longer tell how fast he was moving. Was he rushing headlong like some crazed damn goat or slogging ahead like a crippled turtle?

He fell.

Sluggard cried out as he struck the ground. Someone was cursing. Thresher. She came into view, kneeling to check Sluggard. Beyond her, Roar stood with the limp form of his sister yoked across his shoulders. Oats's eyes kept clenching shut against his will. His skin itched with the crawl of sweat, but he felt chilled to the bone. Pain in his arms. Shit. He'd cut himself on the rocks. No. Those were the slashes given him by the Friars.

"Hells overburdened."

Thresher again. Now at his side. He couldn't quite see her, but knew where she was looking. The stab wound in the side-meat of his ass. It was angry with him for ignoring its protests. Tripped him up to stop any more running.

He needed to . . .

"Need to . . ."

Stand.

"stand."

"Oats. You shouldn't."

"Like hells."

He pawed the air until Thresh took his hand. He had to climb a mountain of stiff agony to reach his feet. Fuck, there were times he hated being so big. Sluggard lay on his back, dazed but conscious. Oats limped a step, grit his teeth against the sticky warmth running down his leg beneath his breeches. Bending, nearly pitching over, he took hold of Sluggard. The mongrel fought his help, but Oats grappled him into submission.

Thresher was still protesting.

"Just help me get him up," Oats growled, his words made of dripping spittle.

Together they wrestled Sluggard back onto his shoulder. The returned weight rooted Oats. For a moment he could do nothing but stare through bleary eyes.

"Where's . . . Jacintho?"

Thresher gazed east. "Gone."

Oats could only grunt. He took a step, another, dimly aware of the others moving with him.

He wondered if the cavaleros would bother taking them back to Ellerina. He'd like to avoid the shit pit if he could. Rather just die out here, given the choice. He wouldn't likely get one. If they figured out who he was there'd be torture. To get his tongue wagging. About the chief. Where she was. Her plans. Tactics. *If.* They'd know. Only one bearded thrice-blood holed up in the Smelted Mounts leading raids into Hispartha at the orders of the Hoof Queen. Hells, that was a fucking stupid name! Frails at their worst, needing to place some damn title on everything so they could, what, hate it with more ease? Pretend not to fear it? He wouldn't tell them, anywise. Just like with Barsius, Oats would reveal nothing. Simple to keep secrets that you didn't know.

"Oats!"

Thresher's strained warning brought the world back. The cavaleros had come, but Oats didn't much care to turn around and see. They could do what they liked. Until then, he was going to keep moving. Only . . . Thresh wasn't pointing behind. She was pointing ahead.

There, several thrumshots from her outstretched finger, stood a hill.

Ul-zuwaqa.

The Skull Heap.

Once just a hill, it gained a name during the Great Orc Incursion and marked the deepest the thicks had ever intruded into Hispartha. Hard to see from where Oats stood, but the hill was crowned with the closest the orcs could conceive of a wall. They were crude builders, but strong. A few score orcs could erect a pile of boulders and uprooted trees, even hauling them up a steep slope, with frightening speed. And that's what they'd done at Ul-zuwaqa when the frails had them surrounded. Fewer than a hundred orcs, but they'd held out for months, making the frails bleed for every assault made upon the makeshift defensives. The story went that the thicks threw the head of every man they slew down the slopes as a warning to the rest. By the time the last orc was killed, the entire hill—from base to summit—was covered in skulls.

Oats had been told that story since he was a boy, a lesson in the strength of the enemy that he would spend his life fighting.

And so he'd chosen Ul-zuwaqa as the meeting point. Mostly because it was close to Ellerina. And because Jacintho said the Hisparthans shunned it. But also because they'd known they would never reach the mountains before dawn. So they'd needed a place to hole up, a place they could defend. A lair for the monsters.

A thousand or so more steps. All that was left.

They were less than halfway when the signal horns blared from behind, mocking their closeness.

Oats's legs revealed an untapped well of fervor. His boots pounded the earth. Sluggard became weightless. Hells, Oats's entire body was numb. He was imprisoned within it, trapped by its frightening motion, by the speed born from the need to survive. It was a final surge, one way or another.

The hill before his eyes quaked with the fierce rhythm of his stride, but did not appear to draw closer. Somewhere upon its summit he hoped someone was watching, keeping an eye for their approach. Were they near enough to see? The air whipped his face from the force of his charge, concealing the true direction of the wind. He didn't know if his scent had reached the hill.

Please . . .

Oats drew in a great breath.

Anvil wouldn't hear him. But that's not whose ears he was counting on when he cried out at the top of his burning lungs.

"UGFUCK!!!"

FOUR

MORE UNSIGHTLY THAN AN OLD whore's quim.

Hideous as a hairless rat fucking a kitten's corpse.

A bag of farts wrapped in warts.

Seeing him made you want to pluck out your eyes. Smelling him made you wish to die.

All of this, and far worse, had been said about Oats's hog.

It was all true.

Ugfuck was a lumbering mass of sagging pig flesh covered in rashes and stiff patches of louse-ridden hair. One eye was red and bulging, the other small and often clogged with mucus. Born a misshapen runt, he should have been killed on the day he first drew breath. Were it not for Oats, he would have been. He'd saved the hog's life that morning.

This morning, Ugfuck came running to repay the debt. For the hundredth time.

Today, like all days, his laboring gait and repugnant face were a welcome, beautiful fucking miracle.

Oats trundled to a halt, eased Sluggard to the ground, and turned. The cavaleros were coming at full gallop on well-bred horses, likely the pride of some castle's stables. The movement of those animals, liquid muscles driving fluid limbs, was impressive in the early sun.

Ugfuck reached Oats first. Well, his reek was first, but Ug was a close second. The hog came to rest beside Oats, snorting and stinking, and butted him with the curved side of a yellowed tusk.

"Right."

Oats climbed into the saddle, biting the inside of his mouth to keep from crying out against the pain in his pierced rump. The cavaleros were closing, the eager yells of the riders now joining the rolling thunder of their steeds. Oats reached to untie his stockbow from his tack, but stopped. His hands were shaking so damn much the use of a thrum would be less than a bad jest. Still, he had to do something. Thresher and Roar were still stumbling for Ul-zuwaqa. If he didn't act, the horsemen would ride them down.

Oats filled his hand with the tulwar tied to Ug's back and tensed to kick the hog forward.

Anvil spared him the effort. She came barreling past on his right astride Big Pox, loosing bolts, the wind barely stirring the stiff black mop that adorned her head and near-eclipsed her face. The rest of the Bastards followed in a tight arrowhead. Well, not the Bastards. They were nomads and Skull Sowers, Shards and Thrice Freed, Cauldron Brothers and Tuskers. Nearly thirty mongrels on barbarians, greeting the cavaleros with fury and thrumming bowstrings.

A mongrel hoof made from the mongrel hoofs.

The cavaleros weren't cowards, they surged through the volley, shedding their losses. They weren't cowards. But they were frails on foals. Two score men formed a wedge of lowered lances. And broke against the Anvil. She led the hoof in a headlong charge toward the tip of that living spear, burst it apart with a final, culling wall of hurled javelins. The half-orcs plunged into the gap, shattered the cavaleros' formation with cleaving tulwars and goring tusks. Men and horses filled the air with screams.

Unnoticed, unnecessary, Oats sat his hog above Sluggard's prone form and watched as the cavaleros were tusk-fucked to a bloody grave. All but two. These Anvil allowed to live, to flee on their frothing mounts, to carry the tale and spread the fear. More of the chief's tactics. A damn mistake, if an earnest one. Anvil would not have heard the signal horns. She did not know that more men would be making their way here. They would arrive sooner—and better prepared—with two survivors to guide them.

Oats loosed a wordless bellow to gain the hoof's attention and gestured for them to give chase, put the remaining pair down. He had his breath back—and Sluggard up on the saddle behind him—by the time they returned.

"You get them?" he asked Anvil after she reined up in front of him. He made sure to voice the question after her hog had stopped so that the motion didn't upset her ability to read his lips.

"Yes," came the dull reply. "Did they signal?"

Oats nodded. "We need to get up the Heap."

Anvil offered no pardons for her blunder, for her deafness. None were expected. She turned Big Pox and led the hoof toward Ul-zuwaqa, stopping to pick up Roar, Rant, and Thresher on the way. Anvil pulled Thresh up on Big Pox. Seeing the two of them riding double, Oats was struck with how far they'd come. Slops to sworn riders in just a few seasons. The old ways were rotting swiftly in a fresh grave, dug and filled by the chief. This war demanded the years-long, arduous training of slopheads be abandoned, she'd declared. What mattered now was courage, usefulness, loyalty. Grit. Dacia and Incus had all that coming out their ears, so they'd been made True Bastards. Chief herself had given Dacia her hoof name. Incus's seemed obvious enough, a name already earned as a barefisted arena fighter, but the thrice woman had curled her lip at keeping the Anvil's Bride.

"Never had a mind to be wed," she'd announced. Easy enough to amend.

Oats shook the musings out of his muzzy head as Ugfuck began ascending the slope of Ul-zuwaqa.

Despite its orcish name, there was no heap of skulls. Whatever charnel pile had existed at the end of the Incursion was long cleared away. Thankfully, the thicks' wall was not. Boulders and entire unearthed trees had been piled to form the barricade. A few decades' worth of age had only caused the snarl to settle. It was mortared by time, decay, and blood. The orcs had lasted months behind their crude and effective works. Oats just needed them to hold for one more day.

There'd been several gaps in the wall when he'd left the hill for Ellerina. All but one were closed up now. That had been the hoof's task, but seeing Thoon looming above the wall, Oats reckoned Anvil and the boys had received some unexpected help. The cyclops waited for all the riders to come through the remaining gap before levering the corpse of an oak into place, sealing the enclosure. He wasn't supposed to be here.

"One-eyed fucker showed up not long after you left for the town," Malcontent said, seeing Oats's grimace. The Shard rider sneered and shook his head as he reined up inside the wall. "Reckon that's a love that won't be denied."

"Reckon not," Oats replied.

He watched as Thoon followed close behind Anvil, two heads taller than the thrice even when she was astride her hog. She'd told him to remain at the Pit, but clearly, he'd followed anyway. Thankfully, the lands north of the Smelteds were sparsely settled. Bandit raids were common even before the chief declared war on Hispartha, so most folk stayed well away from the border of Ul-wundulas. Still, Thoon was damn lucky he hadn't been spotted by cavaleros, hunted down, and slain during his lonely march from the mountains. Though, in earnest, it would take more than a few brave men—or damn fools—to risk attacking the cyclops. Oats had fought several Aetynian giants in the Pit, but they were either old, crippled, sick, or all three. Thoon was none of those things. How the slavers managed to take him, big and hale as he was, remained a mystery.

Turned out, Thoon wasn't the only unexpected face.

After Malcontent and several of the other boys helped Sluggard down, Oats found Jacintho waiting behind them.

"Thought you ran off," Oats said, easing himself off Ug's back.

"Ran *ahead*. There is a small, but very important, difference."

The bandit had shed his pilgrim's rags and once again wore his squashed mushroom of a hat, along with a bandolier filled with more knives than a butcher's block.

"You warned Anvil we were in trouble," Oats realized aloud. He huffed a laugh and rubbed Ugfuck's snout. "So much for you."

"Truly, your . . . *incomparable* beast beat me to the warning. He was barreling down the slope as I came up. I merely provided detail of the plight. Though how he smelled you through his own significant aroma . . ."

Some of Jacintho's men had also made it back. Oats counted eleven of the bandits milling about behind the barricade. They'd taken twice that many into Ellerina, but if Jacintho was concerned over any absences, he gave no sign.

"Well, whatever you merely did, it got us here alive. I'm grateful."

Jacintho gave that smile that made him look even more like a ferret. "What was it you said? 'Free but not safe'? The blare of the cavaleros' trumpets says we are far from out of this cookpot."

"Likely got another fight coming," Oats agreed.

The hoof didn't need to be told. Across the hilltop, preparations were being made. The hogs were corralled in the center, their riders taking position in the best spots they could find on the barricade, stockbows trained through the gaps.

"Are you certain it would not be better to ride straight for the mountains?" Jacintho asked.

"Not certain of shit," Oats replied, too tired for the coddling games of leadership. "We might make it. But we don't know how many men have been marshaled to hunt us. Fair wager Ellerina has sent word to the nearest castiles. Could get caught out there by three, four times our number. More. Rather meet them here."

"Where the enemy can surround us?"

"We're in Hispartha, Jacintho. The enemy already surrounds us." Oats glanced at the cuts on his arms. "Need to get these sewn up."

Leaving the cutthroat, he found Caltrop.

"Better to douse these in boiled wine before I stitch," the Freed rider said, inspecting the wounds. "Wait here."

Oats's ass hurt too much to sit, so he leaned on a convenient limb sticking out from a felled tree within the barricade, favoring the not-punctured cheek.

The enclosed portion of the hilltop was about half a thrumshot across. It provided enough room for the hogs to be kept well away from the perimeter, but wasn't such a large area that they couldn't defend it with the mongrels here. Still, Oats couldn't help but wonder if they should just mount up and get gone. His hope was that the nearest cavalry would take too long to muster and the hoof could slip away during the night when their half-orc vision would give them an advantage over the frails. But waiting out an entire day on such a wager was starting to seem like a fool-ass course. He decided any decision could wait until after his injuries were tended.

Half a turn down the barricade to his left, Ellerina's other fugitives were getting what measure of succor could be found on the hill, scrubbing themselves clean with rags soaked from waterskins. As the muck was banished from the stripped forms of Thresher and Rant, some of the boys on the wall grew distracted. Oats wasn't the only one to notice the stares.

"Shake your head, cunt, your eyes are stuck!" Roar barked at one of the mongrels ogling his sister.

The sight of several blooded hoof-riders—fully armed with brigand, tulwar, and stockbow—being spooked by a single city-born mongrel standing with nothing but his cock hanging down made Oats let go of a silent chuckle. His mirth didn't last long. Soon, there was a new spectacle drawing the hoof's attention. This one even encouraged a few whistles.

"Fucking hells, Caltrop, would you fucking hurry!" Oats complained with his breeches around his knees. Half bent over the limb that had been his perch, he couldn't really see what the Freed was doing, but from the feel, he was making the stab wound in his haunch worse. "Ow! Fuck!"

"Sorry, Oats. It just . . . won't . . ."

"We can stitch that if you'd like."

Oats craned his neck to find Rant and Roar, still damp from their rag baths and wearing borrowed clothes, standing behind the kneeling Caltrop. The brother's scowl hadn't washed away with the shit. The sister's grin seemed to have thrived beneath the fertilizer.

"What makes you think you can do better?" Caltrop demanded,

sounding as if his pride suffered a wound deeper than the one he was failing to close.

"We were mending sails before we could talk proper," Rant said. Her gaze shifted to Oats. "So which one?"

He didn't like the glint in her eye. "Which one what?"

"Which one of us do you want to do it?"

Oats smelled a trap. "Him . . . I reckon."

"He wants a *him* to mend his ass," Rant mused.

"Whichever one ain't going to take offense to me asking the other, how's that?" Oats exclaimed. "Just someone get in here and have done so I can pull my damn breeches up!"

Most of the hoof was laughing now.

Roar all but shoved Caltrop aside and took hold of the needle.

Oats turned back to the wall. He hardly felt the pain through the hot throb of embarrassment.

"Done."

It was over so quick, Roar was on his feet and walking away by the time Oats turned around. He was so surprised he'd left his breeches where they were.

Rant hadn't left with her brother. Bold eyes lowered, she clicked her tongue. "Oats, was it? I'd have made an argument for Yard Arm, I was you."

Oats jerked his breeches up. "Hells!"

Laughing, Rant took the barber's satchel from Caltrop without asking.

"Here. Sit," she told Oats. "I'll do the rest."

Lips drawn tight with displeasure, Cal walked off.

"He sweet on you or something?" Rant asked, merriment still in her voice as she poured the boiled wine over Oats's arms.

"No," Oats replied, trying not to flinch and failing. "Not that I know anyway. Just likes to be useful is all."

It was more than that. Caltrop, like all the Thrice Freed, had been a slave to the Orc Stains. Despite his liberty, the old habits died hard. Serving a thrice-blood with absolute devotion came to that mongrel like breathing. It made Oats damn uncomfortable at times. Other times it was a welcome change from the prideful resistance to his leadership he got from the other hoofs' riders. Oats hadn't asked Caltrop to stitch him up because of that, though. It was because he was the best with needle and gut. Until now. . . .

"What's the story with the brand on his forehead?" Rant asked, pulling with a deft hand on the threaded needle. "Those three lines?"

"It's a hoof mark," Oats said, not wanting to truly explain.

"Like these tattoos? You keep getting cut up, this ink will be nothing but scars."

Oats had never thought about that before. But Rant was right. By war's end what would he look like? Like Hoodwink, maybe, hoof ink all puckered over and marred. Hells, he was well on his way. Would folk mistake him for a nomad soon? Would the battles erase all sign that he was a Bastard? Did that even fucking matter anymore? The chief had said the way things were would not win them this war. The hoofs, the Lots, it was all part of Hispartha's cage. And that cage needed to be broken, melted down, forged into a weapon that could pierce the heart of the kingdom. Free mongrels could do that, not the hoofs. She'd said the True Bastards still mattered, though. They were the few she could trust, her eyes and arms.

T'huruuk. "Arm" in the orc tongue. And the name for the leaders of their raiding bands.

"You not going to tell me?" Rant was done with one arm and moving around to the other.

Oats's eyes were very dry. He blinked hard. "Pardons. What?"

"I asked about the cyclops."

Thoon was across the hilltop, strengthening the wall at Slim Shanks's direction with Anvil acting as translator.

"You ask a heap of questions," Oats said.

Rant's steady hand faltered. Just for an instant, but it happened. "Just trying to get my bearings."

Her voice remained light, but Oats detected the fear. Hells, she'd just abandoned a life for what she must have reckoned was a better one. And what had been the result? Caught by the frails, starved and imprisoned, nearly caught again. Now she was stitching up a grumpy brute behind a barbarous wall. Surrounded by monsters.

"Thoon's harmless," Oats said, trying to soften his voice without sounding like he was talking to a child. "He'd have to be or he wouldn't be here. You know the Pit of Homage?"

"Heard tell of it."

"Well, we took it over, the hoofs. But it was awhile before the slavers got word, so a few came with a mind to sell without knowing we'd shut the fights down. Thoon was in the last batch to come. He took a fancy to Anvil. Like a huge, one-eyed puppy. Bit unfair, being earnest, considering it was both of us that struck his chains. Shows he's smart, though. Given a choice between Anvil and me? Reckon Thoon would rather a *her* mend his ass."

He gave a big smile, but Rant was too focused on her work to notice. Fuck, he was trying too hard. Wanting to smooth over his ill temper and ending up sounding a fool-ass.

Oats cleared his throat. "Anywise. Like I said. Harmless. If he didn't fight them slavers when they came for him, I doubt he'd hurt anyone."

Rant shrugged. "Well, he's copper cursed."

"He's what?"

"Copper cursed." Rant paused her stitching and gazed across at the cyclops. "That red hair of his. The one-eyes always banish their kind with heads like that. It's possible he was given to the slavers and went willingly."

Oats was baffled, but impressed. He felt a grin growing. "How do you know that?"

"Shipwrights and sailors keep company. I've even seen Aetynia, the cyclops' isle. Never set foot on it, but saw its shores once. But that's when I heard the story. Copper cursed is just what the sailors call it. Martyred Madre-only-knows what the giants say. Or the reason."

"Huh," Oats grunted. "Wonder if Anvil knows. She can talk to him. Only one of us that can."

"She must speak Aespardoric, then. Only tongue that comes close to how the Aetynians talk. And you're an idiot."

Oats gawked at her. "The hells?"

Rant tipped the needle in Anvil's direction as she was tightening a stitch. "She's the only one that can talk to the cyclops and you think he's attached to her because she's a woman?"

"No! That's not . . . of course I knew . . . I was just trying to . . . Hells! Never mind."

Rant was laughing again so he let it go. No need to defend his bad jest now that she'd lifted her own spirits. At his fucking expense.

Biting through the gut string, Rant slapped down on his thigh. "You're ready for the next full wind." She stood, dropped the barber satchel with a gentle toss. "Any food to be had?"

"Should be," Oats told her. He looked about for a moment before pointing. "See that mongrel there? With all the charms and shit around his neck? That's Knuckle Child. Generous sort. He'll share some salt meat, whatever else is in his saddle bag."

"Thanks."

"Thank you," Oats replied, indicating his stitches by a slight rotation of his arms.

He made a point not to look at Rant's backside as she walked away. Wasn't hard with Roar trying to boil him alive with a frown from a stone's throw away.

Oats waved, pointed down at the side of his ass. "And thank you!" Then, under his breath, "Ornery boat-fucking fuck."

He sat for a span, knowing there was a choice to be made and not wanting to make it. The sun wasn't hot, but it still blanketed the bald hilltop in a glaring light. The orc wall was of uneven height, but in places tall enough to provide a little shade. Oats spied a likely spot and began to amble over on stiff legs, kidding himself that the ephemeral shelter would speed his decision.

He didn't make it.

A sharp whistle from the north side of the wall yanked him away from shade and delay.

Jacintho stood balanced on the wall's many natural footholds alongside Malcontent, Cut Wolf, and Duster. Stepping on rocks and trunks, Oats clambered up to join them, then looked overtop the wall and down the slope of Ul-zuwaqa to the grassland spread below.

He set his jaw.

The comfort was, he'd been right not to leave. But it was a comfort made of cold...

"Shit," Duster said. "How many is that?"

Oats remained silent, but he knew the answer without having to count the cavaleros riding hard for the hill.

More than enough.

FIVE

"THE FUCK ARE THEY WAITING on?" Batshit complained.

There was one mongrel asking that question at every strongpoint along the wall.

"Infantry," Mope said.

And one sage with a ready answer.

Though, in this instance, Oats agreed with the hangdog nomad. It was possible to ride up Ul-zuwaqa, but not with any speed. The cavaleros would only make themselves bigger targets during the ascent. Those who reached the wall would have no advantage while ahorse. It was too high to be leapt, even at its lowest stretch. There was a reason the orcs had lasted as long as they had. Cavalry was the only thing that gave the frails a chance in battle against thicks. Take that away and each attempt on the walls had done little but replenish the orcs' source of meat.

Still, Mope was right. If Hispartha was going to try to take the Heap again, it would be conscripted peasants tasked with the job. The cavaleros below were just a means to keep the hoof contained. They were waiting on the poor peons to arrive. Oats was waiting on the sun to set. Another damn race, one that required the hoof to sit still.

It was only now noon and patience was beginning to fray.

"Wish them blue bloods would dig their manhoods out of each other's assholes, get down off their nags, and have a go themselves!" Batshit shouted down the slope, but the distance swallowed his taunt.

Dry Gulch spat, the gob barely clearing his receded chin. "No, you don't."

Oats was glad the old Skull Sower had said it so he didn't have to. He stared down at the cavaleros, the view so unchanging he had to force himself to really see it. For a moment he wasn't certain which way he was facing. The midday sun gave him no aid. Who was here? Mope. Batshit. Gulch. That Shard whose name he could never recall. Cuirass? Cured Ass? Something like that. Pommel was here. And Worth-A-Damn. This was the western strongpoint, then. Oats had crisscrossed the hilltop between the defenders so many times he'd lost track. He'd carve letters in the logs to remind himself if he didn't know the boys would think him brain-baked. No way he was. The day wasn't even hot, just bright, the sun amplified by the haze. Made the watching tiresome. Didn't help that the view was the same in all directions. Blocks of horsemen connected by picket riders, ringing the hill. Three hundred and fifty cavaleros trapping his forty-one mongrels, twelve bandits, and one cyclops.

Oats peered up at the sun.

Sink, you fucker. Sink!

He could only hope Hispartha's peasants marched as slowly.

Climbing down, Oats didn't bother with parting words of encouragement or reminders to stay vigilant. That would only insult these hardened mongrels and make him look soft. Reaching the ground, he hesitated. Where to go? Where hadn't he been in a while? Nowhere. Damned hill wasn't that big. He decided to give the boys a break from his tedious pacing and went to the remuda.

Sluggard was among the hogs, brushing Palla down. He and Thresh had been forced to leave their barbarians behind on the last two excursions into Hispartha after the Crown decreed any half-breeds found on the backs of hogs would be put to death on the spot.

"Should you be on your feet?" Oats asked, pushing his way through the grunting current.

"I don't need to be nursemaided, Oats," Sluggard replied without looking up from his chore.

"You see my tit in your mouth?"

He meant it as a jest, but Sluggard didn't even smirk. "No, but your shoulder was in my gut. You didn't need to carry me."

"You'da done the same for me."

That did get a laugh, though Oats hadn't been jesting and the sound was bitter.

Sluggard met his eye, shaking his head. "No I wouldn't. *Couldn't.* I'm not as strong as you, Oats. Don't have feet toughened by a life working the fields like Thresh either. Hells, even those shipwrights have got thicker soles."

"Ain't no shame in needing a brother's help after what you been through."

Sluggard's face darkened. "What I've been through?"

Shit. Oats should have known better. Sluggard's pride had grown prickles since the Orc Stains gelded him. Mead had gotten like that after losing his hand. Oats had often pondered which he'd give up if the awful choice were put before him. Not having two strong hands was an unpleasant thought, but having your seed sack cut off? He could hardly think on that at all.

Oats decided it was best to keep his teeth tight.

Sluggard, however, had more to say. "Think I don't know why you have me minding the remuda?" He lifted the flap of his saddle-bag and put the brush back. Every hog remained tacked so the hoof could ride at any moment.

"Slug, someone has to."

"May as well be the nutless, scalped gritter with feet that turn to deer jerky when he doesn't have boots. No, it makes sense."

"It makes sense because of how you spent your last few days. Just need to get your strength back is all."

"Truly?" Sluggard craned his head in an exaggerated way toward the southern strongpoint. "Where's Thresher?"

Fuck. "You know she and Anvil are insep—"

"Anvil is with the northern watch."

Ass fuck! Oats took a long breath, rubbed his face.

"You even got Rant and Roar on the wall," Sluggard said, voice low and hot.

"They know ships, not hogs. And I need every eye on them cavaleros. Still need a mongrel here too. But yes, in earnest, it's you because you ain't fit for much else at the moment. If it makes you feel better I wish I could trade with you."

"Not even a bit. And I said I didn't need nursemaiding."

Oats held up an apologetic hand. "You did. But being here won't spare you from the fight, Sluggard. You're keen enough to know that. Won't matter what's going on with your feet or your fruits if those frails charge this hill. You'll stand with the rest of us. Die with us too, more than likely, especially if any infantry arrives before nightfall."

He watched his words cool Sluggard's temper. A bucketful of cold truth would do that.

"Pardons," Sluggard said with a sigh. He made an annoyed gesture to his ragged scalp. "Lost my hat when they took us. This sun beating down, just . . . puts me out of sorts."

Oats removed the kerchief from his own head, offered it out.

"Take it," he insisted when Slug tried to wave it off.

Sluggard gave a grateful nod and tied the kerchief over his scars. "Thanks."

"So," Oats said, "think they will?"

"Who? Will what?"

"Infantry. Arrive before night."

Sluggard considered. "This is the Outmarch. The barons here take pride in being the wardens of Hispartha. They keep strong castles, loyal cavaleros, and large levies. So yes, it's very possible an army will arrive before we can get away. We can hope the regidor of Ellerina was quarreling with the nearest lords and they're dragging their heels out of spite. The nobles delight in their petty rivalries. But they love killing rebellious soot-skins more."

"And what would Thresh say if I asked her the same question?"

Sluggard gave a perplexed shrug. "She'd say . . . let the thumb-cocked bunch of them come and we'll see who's better at killing."

Oats nodded. "Near enough, I wager. Ain't exactly helpful, though, is it? Her feet may be tougher than yours, but none of us know the kingdom like you. You've seen it, ridden it, you weren't stuck reaping grain on some blue blood's damn thife."

"It's . . . fief."

"See there." Oats let his point sink in for a moment. "You ain't weaker than us, Sluggard. You've survived shit that would kill the toughest mongrels. More than once. So, if you don't want to be nursemaided, stop fucking squalling for a tit to suck on."

"Hells." Sluggard gave a wry chuckle. "You know you sound like her."

Oats knew Slug didn't mean Thresh. "I know," he replied, letting out a rough sigh. "Best go sound like her in these other mongrels' ears."

"Oats," Sluggard said, stopping him. "The infantry may come, but there's something that should worry us more."

Not liking the sound of that, Oats frowned.

"Cannons," Sluggard continued. "Not saying they have any close by. Not saying they'd bring them if they do. It would only slow them down. But. If they haul any bombards to this hill, we *will* have to run, sun or no. This place would have a very different name if the frails had guns during the Incursion."

Oats encompassed the remuda with a gesture. "Then this duty just got more important. Make sure these hogs are ready to straddle. I don't want to give the order to ride and find half tangled up and the other half ruttin'."

"Understood."

"You hear that, Ug?" Oats said, stabbing a finger at his hog. "Keep your sow tamer sheathed."

Ugfuck blinked at him and pissed hard in the dirt.

The day limped slower than a one-legged mule. Impatience

turned to boredom, the hoof lulled by inaction. Jacintho's cutthroats were the first to begin napping, some coming down off the wall for greater comfort. Rather than fight it, Oats arranged a rotation. Why not? They'd need the rest and his own eyelids were drooping, every third breath a yawn. He put himself among the second batch and reclined against the most comfortable boulder he could find. But he couldn't fucking sleep. His stab wound was barking and the mongrels on the wall above kept jawing.

"Knuckle. *Psst*. Knuckle."

"He ain't gonna heed you, Brow."

"Just wanna ask him a question. Knuckle? *Knuckle*."

"Oh shit. He's clutching his necklace gods. You done it now, Hardbrow."

Spills of laughter.

Baiting Knuckle Child was a favorite foolery of this blended hoof.

"Shows he's listening." Hardbrow gave a shit-eater's chuckle. "So, Knuckle, you think if the frails come and all seems doom for us, you think your mother will appear from the clouds and save us? Think she'd do that for us? That among her powers?"

This time it was Manacles who played the part of the uninformed.

"Wait?" he asked with unconvincing ignorance. "She's got powers?"

Hardbrow was a far better mummer, but no less a cunt. "You ain't heard? She's a right walking miracle."

"How's that?"

"Well, Manacles, I ask you, who was your sire?"

"Some thick. Raped a woman."

"Yours, Rabid?"

"Same."

Hardbrow concocted a mournful sigh. "Mine too. Orc had his way with my unfortunate mother, whoever she may have been. I suppose that's the sad tale for us all, eh mongrels? An orc raped my madre, Rabid's madre, Manacles's madre. And... Knuckle's madre."

"Lies!" Knuckle Child's furious protest was high-pitched and shaking. "My mother was a virtuous woman, constant and chaste! Confronted with the threat of the orc's violent lust she prayed!

Prayed to Blessed Magritta, prayed to the Yoked Sisters, prayed to Endramari, prayed to Herathos Lionclad. And so was delivered from harm! The orc could not touch her for her piety and was forced to sate himself with his own hand!"

The infuriated mongrel's voice was nearly drowned by howls of laughter.

"And such was the strength of the thick's seed that she got a swollen belly from just looking at the spend dripping down its hand!" Hardbrow hooted, nearly breathless.

"It's true!" Knuckle Child exclaimed. "She would not lie to me!"

"Oh fuck, that never tires!"

Oats disagreed.

Faced with a choice between the gnawing discomfort of lying down while listening to this fool-assery or the grinding fatigue of standing, he got up and moved away from the merriment. He could have called for the mongrels to put a cock in it, but their jibes were keeping them awake, providing something to do beyond gripe about the waiting. Besides, Knuckle Child may have been a kind mongrel, but he was also the stupidest fucking son of a thick Oats had ever known. He courted the insults with his beliefs, goaded their repetition by refusing to ignore them. He'd be better off embracing the slights. Hells, if Oats had been saddled with that hoof name he'd have milked his cod every time a brother made sport and punched him in the mouth with a hand covered in spend. Strong wager the jest wouldn't live long once that began.

Leaving Knuckle Child to his own defense, Oats walked the perimeter of the wall. Well, *hobbled* the perimeter of the wall.

He'd set six mongrels at each strongpoint with the remainder strung along between, bolstered by the bandits. The watch rotation allowed a third of their number to sleep at a time. He passed the shipwrights, Roar's head resting in Rant's lap while she slept upright the way Oats had tried to do. Jacintho too was on his back a few strides farther on, hat covering his face. Thoon squatted on his heels, his sprawling shadow keeping the glare from Anvil's closed eyes. The cyclops was dozing, the lid of his large eye languidly drifting a short span from closed.

It snapped open when the cry came from the northern strongpoint.

"BIG BASTARD!"

Oats hurried over, the hilltop rousing as he went. Gritting his teeth against his straining stitches, he climbed up beside Slim Shanks. The older mongrel's arm was outstretched. Oats didn't need to follow the pointing finger to see what had raised the alarm. The slightest difference in the long day's unchanging scenery was as obvious as a young thrice-blood's first erection.

It wasn't an army. Wasn't cannons. It wasn't even a few dozen infantry.

It was one rider.

Oats shielded his brow with a hand. "A messenger?"

"On a mule," Mile Eye said.

Oats squinted harder, leaned out a bit. As the rider drew closer to the line of cavaleros he saw the earnestly named Tusker was right. The smaller animal moved through a break in the horsemen and continued toward the hill without slowing.

"Talk to me, mongrels!" Oats bellowed to his encircled defenders. "Any movement?"

He got answers from the other strongpoints, confirming all around what he could see from his own vantage; the cavaleros were staying put.

The mule kept coming. Alone.

It reached the slope of the Heap, began a steady, plodding ascent. The rider bore a spear and round shield, and was encased in burnished armor. Not the scale shirts and half helms of the cavaleros, but a suit of bronze-chased steel.

"What we got, Oats?" Thresher called from her post at the south.

Oats didn't give an immediate answer. What *did* they have coming? Some kind of herald?

To his left, Cut Wolf answered for him. "It's an ass on an ass!"

This drew some chuckles along the wall. But Sluggard wasn't laughing as he came darting from the remuda.

"A woman?" he asked, face disturbed as he craned his neck up toward the strongpoint.

"Nah," Cut Wolf replied. "Not in all that plate."

Sluggard was not eased. "The shield! What's on the shield? A heart pierced by a banner?"

Oats couldn't quite tell.

"Aye," Mile Eye said.

Sluggard's eyes went wide. Wider. "Kill her!"

"Wha—?"

"Oats, kill her! Now!"

"Lad's lost it," Slim Shanks said. "Feather some messenger and them frails will charge for certain."

Sluggard was running toward the wall now. "Bring her down! She's a Maiden Spear! Kill her!"

Oats cast his gaze back to the rider, halfway up the hill now.

"Don't let her get close! Give the order! Oats!"

One warrior on a mule. And Sluggard near panic. Slim wasn't wrong. The cavaleros would attack if the hoof killed this rider in cold blood.

"Dammit! Loose! Before it's too late!"

Oats could see the rider clearer now, steel-clad and heavy astride the mule, though not a large figure for all that. It might be a woman. The helm's visor hid the truth. What would make her so dangerous? Some manner of wizard? Oats didn't damn know. Just like he hadn't known about the Steel Friars, the danger they posed. Sluggard had. If Oats had listened then . . .

"LOOSE!" he screamed.

The mongrels at the strongpoint hardened their aims and, a heartbeat later, thrum cords hummed.

The mule brayed as the volley struck, its harsh cries cut short as bolts buried in its neck and chest. The rider swung clear of the dying animal, hunkered behind its shield and kept coming. Oats ordered the volleys to continue. Bolts snapped against the shield, the curved metal surface ringing with the assault. A few penetrated. A handful of the keenest aims managed to hit the exposed portions of the warrior, striking legs, the shoulder, and the arm bearing the spear. The shafts bounced away, splintered on the armor plates.

Half a thrumshot away now, the brazen figure continued to climb, weathering the storm of bolts, using the scrub and boulders for cover when possible. Another few dozen strides and it would reach the level stretch of hill before the wall.

Sluggard scrambled up beside Oats, shoving Cut Wolf to make room.

"No. No, no, no . . ."

"Your post is the remuda!" Oats barked, glaring at his stricken brother.

Ignoring him, Sluggard brought his stockbow to his shoulder and sent a bolt at the warrior, cursing as it made no difference.

"We have to stop her," Sluggard proclaimed to no one, to everyone.

"What is she, Slug?"

"A Maiden Spear! A Chosen of Magritta! If she reaches us . . ."

Sluggard didn't finish. He was casting about the surface of the hill in some frantic search.

"Could lead a sortie," Slim Shanks said. "Four riders t'would be enough to tusk-fuck that frail all the way down the Heap."

"No!" Sluggard snapped. He froze and waved at the southern strongpoint. "Thresh! THRESH! Tell Anvil we need Thoon here! Now!"

Thrice and cyclops reached their strongpoint in moments, both remaining on the ground.

Sluggard explained what had to be done and Anvil repeated the instruction to Thoon in his own tongue. Oats wasn't sure he'd even do it. The cyclops had never shown any capacity for violence. Yet, he hoisted a stray boulder from the hilltop. Damn rock was bigger than Ugfuck by half. Tucking it into his hip with one hand, Thoon seized the top of the wall, planted a foot on the curve of a downed tree in its middle, and hauled himself up. Balanced there, he stood over the defenses and lifted the boulder in both hands above his head.

The armored warrior was an arm's length from the flat ground when the cyclops made his cast. He'd risked overthrowing at that angle, but the boulder smote the ground in front of the warrior, bounced, and collided. Oats winced. Metal crunched and shrieked as the rock smashed into shield and armor, bowling the warrior over.

Rolling now, the boulder took the limp form with it down the hillside until they were both lost from sight behind rocks not hurled by an Aetynian giant.

Looking up at Thoon, Oats saw no pride, no thrill in the act. The cyclops appeared . . . sorry.

"They ain't moved," Slim Shanks declared, voice low and raspy. His gaze was fixed upon the cavaleros, still arrayed below. Those screening the northern side could not have failed to see what befell their holy warrior, yet they continued to sit their steeds without action.

Oats looked to Sluggard. "Now, what had you worried? Why was that one so dangerous?"

Sluggard did not respond. His stare was locked on the place the warrior had fallen out of sight.

"Slug, answer me!"

"No," Sluggard hissed.

Oats felt his anger rise at the refusal. But it wasn't a denial meant for him.

"Hells overburdened," Cut Wolf said. "Ain't no way."

More oaths and curses were muttered by the mongrels along the wall. Movement among the rocks had them all fixated.

The armored figure crawled up over the rocky tumble, rose on shaky legs. And began to walk forward. The shield was bent all to hells and was dropped after a couple of drunken steps. The armor too was ravaged and dented, the helm gone.

"Shit," Mile Eye said. "It is a woman."

Oats didn't have the Tusker's vision, but there was no reason to doubt him. Each step brought the details closer. Fair skin, blazoned with red smears, the largest running from the mouth across the cheek. Oats knew that decoration well, the sure sign of one wiping blood from busted lips. Dark hair, cut short and severe, matted with sweat. The spear was unbroken, as were her limbs, despite the crushing embrace of the boulder. Unbroken, but not unharmed. Oats could feel the pain in her progress, his eyes were seduced by those laboring strides up that pitiless slope.

A bolt struck her shoulder plate, sent her reeling, and snapped Oats out of his awe.

Sluggard was reloading, cursing and agitated.

"Help me, damn you!" he cried at the surrounding mongrels.

None moved. Most were still staring at the woman. Those who looked at Sluggard did so with bald disgust.

"Ain't putting down some loon-brained lass," Slim Shanks declared. "She can crawl up and be a prisoner."

"She won't!" Sluggard raised his stockbow once more. "She'll kill you. All of us!"

Oats wanted to believe him. He slapped Sluggard's thrum down instead.

His brother's incensed stare whipped up. "You're being a fucking fool! She must die!"

"Slug . . . look at her."

The woman's steps were nothing but inching slides now. Her head was hanging, blood pouring from between her lips in a steady rope. She was close enough now to hear the wet rattle of her breath. Or perhaps the hill was just that quiet.

She stopped at the lip of the slope, head rising to gaze at the wall. Hells, she was so young. Oats expected to see hatred in her face, but there was something else. Something . . . calm, yet vibrant. Water in a cauldron just beginning to boil.

She'd been using the spear as a support. She lifted it again as if to move it forward to aid another step. But she half-turned, thrust its butt end into the slope behind her at a sharp angle, wedging it between some rocks.

"No!" Sluggard snatched his stockbow up and loosed before Oats could stop him. The bolt took her in the side of the neck, coming down at an angle to lodge between her yoke bone and the edge of her armor. She lurched, gurgling, choking. And fell upon her spear. There came the shriek of rending steel. Oats's spine crawled as the woman's body slid down, the spearhead punching through the plate at her back, blossoming from a garden of flesh and metal, watered with gore. Her body came to a shuddering stop. She hung upon the spear, toes touching the earth, the rest of her suspended above the slope. Oats could hear the patter of blood upon the rocks.

"And so, upon that field of death, did the blessed Madre, fearing for the life of her son, thrust his banner through her own breast."

Oats looked over to find the source of the strange recitation. Knuckle Child stood just beyond Sluggard. Oats didn't know when he arrived. He was supposed to be on the eastern watch. Gazing down at the grisly totem of the woman's body, the devout mongrel clutched one of the many charms about his neck.

"Upon her body it stood. Within her heart it rooted."

Oats nearly told Knuckle to get back to his fucking post. Nearly.

But the impaled woman twitched and the words died upon his tongue.

"With her sacrifice was victory assured."

The hoof expelled shocked breaths as the woman began to lift from the spear, raised by some gentle, unseen force.

"For her son and his stalwart brethren did rally around that woeful pennant, that sacred, selfless woman. Blessed Magritta, Martyred Madre."

Borne aloft, the woman was delivered from the transfixing pike and set down upon her feet on the blood-soaked stones. Her head raised, her arm reached out. She took hold of the spear and pulled it free from the earth. Slowly, though not weakly, not timidly, she turned, once again fixing eyes upon the mongrels. No longer calm, her gaze was a livid, living thing.

"And beneath her protection the faithful companions of her son, for whom she had died, could not be slain, though they were grievous set upon by hordes of their foe. They were all her sons now, Men of the Mother, and woe to all who dared give them battle."

The Maiden Spear came toward the wall, and behind her, in the plain below, the cavaleros rode forth.

SIX

OATS DIDN'T NEED TO GIVE the order. The boys at the strongpoint snapped out of their disbelief by pulling the ticklers on their stockbows, sending a scattered rain of bolts at the woman they'd just witnessed rise from death. Shielding her head with an arm, the Maiden ran through the flights, hurling her spear as she came. It burst through the body of a log, struck Slim Shanks in the chest, and launched him backward. The impact upon the haphazard wall caused a section to tumble. Oats lost his balance and was dragged down amid a scatter of logs and rock, sliding more than falling.

Anvil rushed to his side, directing Thoon to lift the limb that had Knuckle Child pinned. Sluggard was sprawled nearby, but appeared more spooked than harmed. Together, they scrambled away from the crippled barricade. Oats hurried to where Slim lay. The old mongrel was on his back, the spear sticking straight up from his body, eyes quenched and staring. All around mongrels were hollering, warning of the cavaleros' advance.

Oats took a deep breath, preparing to shout for them to stand firm, but his words shriveled.

The spear in Slim's corpse twitched.

Knuckle Child gasped as the weapon took flight, streaked upward, and slapped into the waiting hand of the Maiden, now standing atop the sag in the wall.

Mile Eye, still perched within spitting distance of the woman, loosed a bolt for her head. The Maiden ducked, twisted, and thrust, sparing herself and lancing Mile Eye through the gut in one motion. Cut Wolf and Duster were moving in from opposite sides, swords in hand, but the jumble of spilled wood and stone was too precarious to rush upon. Slowed by the snarled footing and the sight of Mile Eye clutching his gushing belly, they hesitated.

Oats waved them away and caught Anvil's arm as she stepped to challenge the woman. They both knew their training, from different chiefs. Their hoof was surrounded and a foe had broken through their line. Dealing with that foe fell to one mongrel.

Oats kept his eyes on the Maiden, knowing Anvil could discern his words even from the side of his lips.

"Cavaleros are coming," he said, drawing his tulwar. "We'll need Thoon and he needs you. Hold the wall."

Anvil did not hesitate. She rushed off, shouting commands, the cyclops lumbering in her wake. The hilltop was already alive with snapping thrums.

The Maiden stood less than a stone's throw away, eyeing him, but she hadn't moved. The bolt in her neck forced her head to remain slightly cocked as she gazed down. The posture made her appear at once confused and intrigued. It was damn unsettling. Knuckle Child had sunk to his knees, clutching at strands of beads and metal chains about his neck, a flood of impassioned mumbling escaping from his lips.

"O Blessed Magritta, protect me, your faithful son. I submit to your mercy, Martyred Madre, plead your forbearance, beg your . . ."

"What's she waiting on?" Oats asked Sluggard.

"Don't know."

"Know how to kill her?"

"Once a Maiden falls on her spear . . . it's too late."

"Could have said."

Sluggard leaned to look down at Knuckle. "Would've sounded mad."

"Fair point." Oats had seen all manner of queer things. Sorcery. Devils of various kind. And still he'd found it difficult to believe this woman a danger. He wondered if that were part of her holy hoodoo. Didn't matter now. "Get to the wall, Slug. Kill some frails."

"Luck, Big Bastard."

Oats nodded. "You too."

Sluggard hauled Knuckle Child to his feet, dragged him to the defense of the hill.

The Maiden Spear remained where she was. Oats suspected she wanted to be seen by the frails, fulfill her purpose as their living inspiration. Well, perhaps not exactly living, Oats was still unclear on that part. But certainly walking, certainly something that had come to give the cavaleros a stiff cod for battle. He was less concerned with that and more worried about the stretch of wall she occupied. With her there, his boys couldn't form a proper ring, leaving an opening for the frails to swarm. He needed to get her down. Oats didn't know much about religion, but he knew believers were a touch prickly when it came to their gods being slighted.

"I knew a Magritta once," he called up. "Huge whore. *Loved* it in the ass! Sounds a heap like your Madre."

The Maiden dropped from the wall, armor clacking as she landed.

"Figured that might do it," Oats muttered as she charged. Hells, he didn't want this fight.

Never mind this woman had impaled herself then risen, actually fucking *risen* in the air. Never mind that she'd thrown a spear clean through a log the size of a rain barrel and then the damn thing had returned to her hand on its own. Never mind that he was tired, cut, and stabbed all to shit. Oats didn't want this fight because he never did relish fighting women. Made him feel more of a brute. More of an orc.

The Maiden Spear didn't care a shit.

She sent the spear darting out ahead of her. Didn't throw it this time, just thrust with a mighty hatred. Oats had been watching closely. He wasn't the most nimble mongrel even at his best, but neither could he trust in his strength entire. He opted for a bit of both, sidestepping the spear while slapping it away with his tulwar.

It worked. He saved himself a skewering and whipped a counterstroke at her even as she spun. His sword scraped against her backplate. The spear was coming again, tucked tighter to her body now, ready to kill soon as it completed the circle. She was encased in metal, but Oats still outweighed her. Bulling forward, he slammed his body into hers, knocked her flat. Any cavalero would have been dead the next instant, finished with a swift chop, but the armor and the spear made that an unwise pursuit. Oats held back, dug through the morass of fear and rage that flooded him during a battle to find that elusive kernel of patience. Hardest thing to do in a fight is not to act. Dread could force it sometimes, leave the muscles frozen. But choosing to keep still when every drop of blood flowing through a pounding heart was demanding another blow, *that* was a damned feat.

One Oats managed.

He watched as the Maiden rolled, stood. She wasn't all that fast, but she wasn't sluggish, either, for all that harness. He'd knocked her down easily enough, but the attempt had been a risk born from lack of choice. Could have easily been like throwing himself against a castle wall for all he knew of her god's blessings.

Magritta was certainly giving her chosen a will to fight.

The spear nearly caught him when she lunged, but he jumped back in time. She kept coming, thrust again, too close for him to get away. He batted the spear down with his tulwar, tried to twist clear, but the point clipped his outer thigh and dug a trench through the leather of his breeches, a lesser one through his flesh. Snarling, Oats sent a hacking cut at the Maiden's head. She ducked, shrugging behind her pauldron so that the shoulder plate took most of the blow. The deflected blade bit into her scalp, peeled back a flap of hair and skin. A crimson fall washed half the Maiden's face. Dead or not she was still bleeding, not that she gave voice to any pain. Her expression was twisted, stricken, though it was fury contorting her youthful features, not agony. Oats hammered at her with his blade. She interposed her arm, let the tulwar fall on segmented steel. He knew his own strength. The armor should have been dented, but he accomplished nothing save the blunting of his blade's edge.

How?

He'd seen the spear penetrate. It had come through the plates at breast and back as if they were made from a babe's blanket. The puncture hole was visible on the cuirass; a ragged black fissure widened into a circle when the Maiden's body had sunk an arm's length down the shaft. Yet a proven sword at the end of a strong and trusted arm was useless.

His third blow fell and the Maiden twisted her shielding arm, snatched at his tulwar with a gauntleted hand. She nearly succeeded in tearing the weapon from his grip. Juggling to keep his sword, Oats allowed his foe to hop back. The Maiden swiped with the spear as she retreated to prevent pursuit.

Now it was she who waited, watching him with bright eyes, one embedded in a field of red.

On the stretch of wall visible beyond her, Oats could see the hoof striving to defend the hilltop. Mongrels were loosing bolts fast as they could reload, calling out to their comrades. Somewhere out of sight, Thoon let out a lowing cry followed by the thud-crack of a boulder and the shrieks of horses. Close enough to hear now. The hoof had ridden to Ul-zuwaqa with bulging quivers, four to a rider, for just this purpose. Still, at three hundred and fifty strong the cavaleros were going to reach the wall. And soon.

"Not too late," Oats told the Maiden. "You can go your way. Spare a pile of lives."

He could only hope she hadn't heard how much his offers were worth from the Steel Friars' abbot.

She tried to answer. Her mouth worked, lips moved, but the bolt in her throat ravaged what little sound emerged. The woman's brow wrinkled. Confused, she raised a tentative hand, felt the protruding bolt. Oats saw her confusion grow a film of panic. The next heartbeat that panic was curdled by rage. Jaws open in a silent scream she rushed him. Oats flung his tulwar at her, overhand. The Maiden hunkered and covered her exposed head as she'd done before. As Oats knew she would.

In the instant her eyes were averted, he surged forward, grabbed the spear in both hands. Pulling, lifting, he pivoted and heaved the Maiden into the air. He revolved once and her grip came loose. Tossed, she hit the ground.

Oats, still in possession of the spear, snapped the shaft over his knee. At least, he tried. It was his leg that felt closer to breaking. He frowned at the weapon, at the featureless wooden shaft. It was oddly hot.

A howl burst from his lips as the spear ignited.

He gnashed his teeth against the pain of the licking flames, resisted the need to drop it long enough to cast it over the wall. He'd no doubt it would return. He only hoped he could kill the Maiden before it was back in her hand.

Flexing his burned hand, he charged, smashed his uninjured fist into her nose as she was rising. The blow sickened him, his vision shrinking to the woman's face. Without the spear, the armor, she looked only a few years beyond her girlhood. Hers was the face of the maidens of Winsome in better days when the town still stood. A face that should suffer no more than a sunburn while tending an orchard flush with fruit. It was a face to be protected, cherished, not battered by the hard, cruel knuckles of a desperate thrice-blood.

Feeling this in his churning gut, Oats kept hitting her.

He broke her nose, teeth, even the shaft of the stockbow bolt. He turned the flesh around her eyes to puffy mush. He was wailing now, spit and tears falling with every punch as he erased the source of his torment.

And, damn him, beneath the distaste rising to sour his tongue he found enjoyment.

The Maiden may have been a corpse before, but Oats didn't stop hitting her until she looked the part. Limp, broken. Still.

Recoiling from his grisly labor, Oats stumbled away from his murderous work on wobbly legs. He was panting, a short growl riding on each breath. Both his hands hurt.

"Breach! West! Breach!"

Oats whirled toward the cry.

It was Dry Gulch, yelling, standing with the other mongrels at the southern strongpoint. Thrums abandoned for slicers, they fended off cavaleros coming over the wall. Oats saw at least a dozen on foot crest the pile of logs and stone. He cast about for his tulwar, saw the situation to the north was little better. Anvil led the defense of the partially collapsed wall, keeping the cavaleros from breaking through with the aid of Thoon and a handful of half-orcs. Retrieving his blade, Oats ran to the south. He watched Pommel take a lance in the neck before he could cross the distance. Four men came scrambling over to fill the gap left by the slain mongrel. Only one remained on the wall, the other three dropped down into the interior.

Oats rushed straight at them, stuck a finger and thumb in his mouth, gave a whistle. That drew their attention. One cavalero had retained his lance, the others held swords. They all braced for the attack, the lance-wielder leveling his weapon. Oats screamed at the top of his voice and raised his tulwar high over his head, whirling it in great circles. It was a furious display. One that kept the frails so fixated on him, they never saw Ugfuck coming.

The hog hit the men from the left, tusks and hooves churning them into a pile of broken bones and trampled meat with such speed they didn't even cry out.

"Good boy, Ug," Oats said, hopping to the wall.

He stabbed one frail in the groin on the ascent, seized the ankle of another and ripped him off the wall. Ug gave an excited squeal when the man hit the ground. Oats climbed into the gap he'd made just in time to split the face of a man coming over the barricade.

The sight of the hillside beyond froze Oats where he stood.

"Hells take us."

The slope was flooded with horses and men. Many dead, even more alive. The orcs' wall was bolstered by a mound of the slain. Oats had gazed down at these men all day, knew their numbers, knew they'd pay buckets of blood if they attacked. And hoped that his hoof might hold out. Now, the moment was upon him, and the nagging specks in the field below had grown into a moving mass of reckless, hungry bloodlust. He felt a fool for ever believing his mongrels could survive, cursed the frails for fools for continuing to slaughter themselves. The hoof had killed dozens, scores. The Heap of Skulls was earning its name for a second time and yet the cavaleros would not cease. They swam against a current of thrumbolts and berserk horses, boulders and blood, dead and dying comrades. All so they could reach the wall and kill the ash-colored rebels, a tenth of their number.

Along the stretch of slope beneath Oats's eyes the men were climbing quicker now, spared the withering volleys thanks to their fellows engaging the defenders up close. Oats knew his brothers here had only moments to throw the cavaleros back or the strongpoint would be overrun and the entire hilltop flooded with frails.

He cut a man down to his right, leaned and hacked the fingers off another below. The maimed man fell screaming into those coming up behind. On the left, Mope was closest, bleeding from several cuts to his arms and face, his own blade slinging blood with every stroke. Beyond him, Batshit held a snapped tulwar, hurling furious insults and the helmets of dead cavaleros at the scalers. Worth-A-Damn was on the right, along with Jacintho and three of his ruffians armed with spears. The Shard with the forgotten name was on the outer side of the wall, lying tangled with the other corpses.

Cursed Ass? No. What the fuck was it?

The cavaleros didn't give him time to figure it out. It was a queer thing, seeing men so eager to reach the wall where half-orcs awaited them on higher ground ready for the butchery. Perhaps after the long climb, the hail of bolts, the sight of so many dying around them, the wall didn't seem all that threatening. Or perhaps they'd been driven mad by the simple fact that they were still alive. Within that hideous barrier they found some strange sense that this would all end if they could but reach it. Oats didn't know what drove them. He'd prefer they turn tail and flee, but they had the scent of death in their nostrils. Theirs or their foes. That's all they knew now.

He gave them what they sought.

Oats cleaved men, kicked them, shoved them, picked up their fallen lances, and threw them into the faces of their comrades. He stabbed, beat, bled. He slew. And still they came, on and on.

Until . . . one man didn't. He was scrambling up the slope among the dozens, stepping on bodies more often than ground. Oats watched him come, saw the moment he looked up. Their eyes met. Oats could have spit and hit him in the forehead. The frail's fixed, blind resolve faltered. Melted away. He saw his end in the hulking thrice above. Oats made certain he saw it. A small, childish whimper escaped from the cavalero. He took a tiny, tripping step in no real direction, which seemed to startle him. The next moment, he was crawling backward down the slope, too afraid to turn his back.

Batshit was the first to yell, whooping in victory.

The one man started an avalanche. All the grit drained out of the frails and dragged them down the slope. Oats wanted to add his voice to the cheers, but his tongue was a tanned hide. He didn't have the breath.

From the southern strongpoint, Thresher did.

"BREACH!"

Oats's heart fell and nearly took him to his knees.

He turned, saw Thresh and her crew battling against a rising tide, a wave of men that threatened to break them. He had to go. Someone had to go. He had to go.

Oats snatched a look down the slope, made sure the frails on the western hillside were truly done. They were still running. He could spare some mongrels from here.

"Mope, you and—"

The spear burst through Oats's chest.

He rocked forward, almost lost his footing. Would have pitched face-first over the wall if he had. But it hadn't been much of an impact. He looked down, saw the entire head of the spear and a hand's length of shaft sticking out of his right breast. Fucking queer sight. Sharp. Fast. He reckoned that was why it hadn't knocked him over. Was that also why there was no pain? He reached with his left hand, considered pulling it out, but his hand seemed hesitant, confused. It sort of floated there, dallying, making small, false grabs. Oats felt drunk. Faint.

The spear jerked him off the wall.

And the pain arrived.

Screaming, he didn't fall. He flew. Weightless in a world of agony. He struck the ground, nearly blacked out. The ground raked him.

He was being dragged, a huge fish on a line. But the hook was a spear and the line was the invisible pull of a god.

He heard a familiar squeal. Well, not all that familiar because Ug was rarely afraid. Oats forced his eyes to focus, saw the big hog beside him, keeping pace with the torturous tug of the spear. Oats tried to tell him to get away, couldn't speak. His jaw was seized shut. Wouldn't have worked anyway. No command would force Ugfuck from his side. That loyalty was often the death of hogs. At least Oats wouldn't have to watch. The Maiden Spear was going to kill him first.

He saw her through boiling tears, standing, waiting as the spear—and her catch—returned to her. Perhaps someone would see, come to help. Maybe Thoon—

No. The giant was keeping the frails out, Oats saw as he skidded across the hilltop. Saw the hopelessness of that fight. Of every fight. The wall held more frails than mongrels now. They were coming over. In.

He came to a stop at the Maiden's feet, the pain of halting somehow worse than being dragged. Ug bumped him with his snout, grunted at him to get up. Oats didn't have the strength to push him away. None of his limbs had feeling. He'd come to rest on his side, could feel the pressure of the spear shaft behind him pushing into the ground.

The Maiden took a side step, came into his view.

She fixed him with the eye not swollen shut, the rest of her face a discolored horror. As he'd done with the cavalero on the slope, she made certain he knew his end was coming.

He appreciated being too weak to do anything about it.

The Maiden reached for the spear shaft. This was going to hurt, but it wouldn't last long. Oats kept his stare fixed on her face. And so he saw the winged shadow burst through the haze in the sky above.

The rokh shrieked as it dove, snatching the Maiden's attention. She looked up in time to see the figure leap from the great bird's back, but she wouldn't be able to see who it was. Oats couldn't either, but still he knew.

The chief had arrived.

SEVEN

FETCHING SMOTE THE GROUND, CAME charging out of the kicked-up dust barehanded and furious. She would have seen Oats from the air, he knew. Her sharp eyes were better than they'd ever been. Eyes that were now screaming with the rage her throat kept silent. She came running and the Maiden Spear braced, trusting in her armor, fooled by the chief's lack of weapons.

Oats didn't know if the woman was dead or not, but she was about to be.

Fetching struck the Maiden with all the force and savagery of a riled hog. With none of the grace. Armor plates rattled as she slammed into the woman. Her momentum carried them from Oats's view. His upended periphery didn't provide much but a sliver of the wall. Still, it was enough to make out the rokh swooping to knock cavaleros from the top of the barricade, seizing a pair of unfortunate men in its large talons before climbing into the sky once more. Oats watched the great raptor release the helpless men in flight. Their limbs whirled as they fell, their screams higher pitched than those of the terrified men still on the ground. The rokh was banking for another pass, but Oats felt an engulfing sleep rising from the back of his skull, coming forward to drag his eyelids, and his senses, down into darkness. Ugfuck squealed at him from some deep pit. Oats tried to move so he could go to his hog, pull him out, but his body would not respond. *He* was in the pit, not Ug, and sinking deeper. Blind now, he felt Ug's cold snout, a shrinking mote of life in the black, drowning slaver of oblivion.

The spear jerked him from the lulling waters. Back to light. And excruciation. The weapon pulled free from his body with such violence it flipped him onto his face. Teeth clenched so tight, Oats could do nothing but sob into the ground and wish to die. Ug saved him from being smothered by the dirt, rolling him over so he could bleed to death instead. It wouldn't take long. Oats was already shivering, the quakes a disquieting mixture of pain and panic.

At least the chief was here. She'd see to it the survivors made it home.

The shivers ebbed. Ugfuck's head blocked the sky, complaining, insistent that Oats rise. He couldn't. Couldn't even lift an arm to ward off the dripping stench of the hog's snout. Hells, the barbarian truly was hideous. Oats hoped he smiled. He certainly tried, but his body felt dull, detached. With a clipped squeal, Ugfuck was pushed from view. There weren't many that the hog would yield to willingly. He was replaced by a far prettier face. Prettier than any mongrel had a right to be.

"Oats!" Jackal yelled, slapping his cheeks. "Wake up! No, brother, you're not doing this! Dammit, look at me!"

Oats *was* looking at him. How come he couldn't see that?

The swats were relentless. "Focus, brother! Need you with me. You're not dying on this fucking hill."

Jackal was wrong. Oats had already determined this was exactly where he would die. He'd made his peace. But somehow, seeing the fact contort his friend's face put a cold dread in his chest. Or maybe that was the spear hole. That hogshit, god-enchanted, backstabbing spear.

Oats growled.

Jackal grinned. "There you are."

He snatched a sash from his garb, the desert robes he'd adopted in the east and refused to put aside. Holding the ends, he whipped it into a roll.

"Bite down," he instructed, holding the roll to Oats's lips.

Oats did as he was told, not loving where this was headed.

Jackal drew a vial from his pouch, pulled the cork, and poured a syrupy substance into the wound. Oats thought the stuff was black, but as it stretched and caught the light he saw it was a dark emerald. He tensed for the pain, but none came. Jackal already had another vessel in his hand, this one a jar. He dumped silver powder into his cupped palm. Using his hand as a funnel, he deftly let the powder follow the ichor. The wound began to itch something awful. Jackal did the next part so fast, Oats didn't see the third ingredient, only the flame that burst from the hole in his chest. The burning agony engulfed his entire body. Oats screamed through the cloth in his mouth, hot tears running into his ear canals as he convulsed. Jackal held his arms down to keep him from tearing at the smoldering flesh. When the worst subsided, Oats had the smell of his own cooked meat in his nostrils.

Jackal removed the sash, gave him some water. Oats choked on the first swallow, but got the next one down. The sounds of fighting were all around.

Oats shoved some words onto his tongue. "Get. Me . . . up."

Jackal grabbed his shoulders, lifted him until he was sitting up. "I don't think you should try to stan—"

"*Up.*"

It hurt. It fucking hurt, but Jack hauled him to his feet. Ugfuck huddled up on his other side, used his bulk to keep him propped. Oats leaned against the pig and swept the barricade with the eyes of a drunkard.

Thresh and the boys to the south were holding, bolstered by the murderous dives of the rokh. Not one frail had come through the sag in the north, thanks to Thoon and Anvil. The fighting was thickest at the eastern strongpoint.

"Jack," Oats croaked, and lifted his chin at the wall.

Jackal nodded and rushed to aid the defenses. He must have flown in with the chief, though Oats hadn't seen him dismount. Of course, he couldn't just jump down the way she could. Or maybe he could. Hells, Oats didn't know anymore. Jackal could certainly throw himself into most any danger without fear. He entered the fray atop the wall, cut down four frails, and dropped to the other side, out of sight. The cavaleros attacking the eastern slope were now discovering the terror of a mongrel that was a devil with a sword, cunning as the son of a snake and fox, his wounds knitting quicker than they could be inflicted. The frails may have brought Magritta's Chosen to this fight, but now they faced the Arm of Attukhan.

Poor fucks.

As for the Maiden Spear...

Oats turned his gaze to the one foe who stood within the walls. The woman had lasted longer than he expected, but it was nearly over. Her armor was dented in a dozen places, the work of Fetch's fists. The chief herself was bleeding from several small cuts and punctures, something Oats had thought was no longer possible. Reckon all it took was a weapon blessed by a goddess. Still wasn't enough. The Maiden was reeling, spear held limp and useless in her hand. Fetch's punches were endless, crunching the steel plate. She avoided hitting the woman in her exposed, unprotected head. It took Oats a moment to realize why. The chief wasn't trying to kill the Maiden. She was punishing her. Again and again her knuckles pounded metal, sending the woman stumbling only to be redirected by the next strike. Fetch was savoring this kill. She thought it was vengeance. Oats could do nothing more than stand—and barely that—as he waited for the chief to see he wasn't dead. It was a few more moments, a score more resounding blows, before she did. Fetch halted her onslaught, relief smoothing the wrath in her face.

The Maiden Spear used the opening to thrust.

Fetching had been distracted, eyes averted from the attack, yet still she twisted, seized the spear just below the head and yanked it from the woman's grasp. Fetch had the same notion Oats did; to snap the haft. Only, she succeeded. And didn't need her knee. With a downward jerk, Fetch broke the weapon in two. Flames spewed from the sundered wood, licked up her arms, but the chief's flesh was not burned. She cast the blazing pieces aside with a sneer of contempt.

Seeing this, the Maiden Spear collapsed to her knees, the strength and the will to fight visibly fleeing her body as the fire guttered to smoke. Her remaining eye looked up at Fetching, bewildered. She knelt, slumped and slack-jawed. Oats didn't hold with religion, but he knew what faith in a strong leader was. He watched that faith abandon the Maiden Spear, as obvious and elusive a sight as life leaving a body. Lost, betrayed, she beheld the mongrel who broke her. Her lips moved. She said something Oats couldn't hear over the tumult of the battle on the wall, but it looked to be a single word. Whatever she spoke, it was said with her last breath. Her eye rolled to white and she pitched over onto the earth, the finely wrought armor nothing now but a jumble of battered scrap lying on the hilltop.

Fetch didn't waste time basking. She picked up the body and went to the sag in the wall. The defenders holding the breach fought harder as she climbed the pile of fallen debris and hoisted the Maiden over her head. She stood there for a moment, allowing the frails to see the ruin made of their holy warrior before casting the corpse over the wall. Oats couldn't see the cavaleros beyond the barricade, but he saw the mongrels cease fighting, saw Anvil tell Thoon something that caused him not to hurl the boulder in his hands. A moment later, a cheer went up from the defenders.

"Save your breath!" Fetch barked. "Send them off with bolts! You heard me, feather their backs!"

Thrums began snapping and fleeing men began dying. Oats was grateful he was spared the sight.

Fetch came off the barricade. "Anvil, Thoon! With me!"

Thrice and cyclops followed the chief, bypassing Oats as they hurried across the hilltop. With Jackal at the east and the rokh at the south, the only strongpoint still unsupported was the west. The cavaleros Oats had helped repel must have regrouped and found the courage for another assault. The chief was yelling at the men and mongrels along the wall there, commanding them to leave the defenses. Jacintho and his bandits were eager to obey, but the half-orcs were reluctant.

"Unless you want to die, get the fuck down!" Fetching hollered.

The wall was clear of defenders by the time she reached its base.

"Tell him to help me," Fetch said to Anvil, pointing at Thoon.

The chief squatted, worked her hands beneath the massive log at the bottom of the barricade. Thoon did the same a few strides away. Together, they started lifting. Cavaleros were coming over the top of the abandoned wall, but their advance was arrested as the rude construction began to rise. Men cried out, the wall coming apart beneath their feet. Many fell backward, others scrambling to flee the way they'd come. Straining, straightening, Fetch and Thoon tipped the orcs' barricade over, sending an avalanche of logs and rocks crashing down the hillside. None of the men in its path would have been swift enough to escape.

By the time the echoes of the destruction faded, Jackal and Thresh were signaling victory from their strongpoints. The frails were all slain or turned tail.

It wasn't enough. Not for the chief.

"Mongrels, mount up!"

Riders ran to their hogs, assembling swiftly in the center of the hilltop. When all were in the saddle, Jackal swung up on an unclaimed barbarian. Hardbrow's animal, Oats saw. He hadn't seen the mongrel die, but hells knew how many they'd lost.

"Ride them all down!" Fetch commanded.

Jackal led the hoof out the ragged hole she'd created.

Oats counted the remaining hogs, those left behind because their riders were dead or too injured to straddle the razor. Nineteen. Nearly half their numbers. It would have been all of them before much longer. Lasting until nightfall had been a fool-ass hope.

"You should sit down before you fall down."

Jacintho, though Oats didn't turn to look at him.

"Truly," the bandit insisted. "I won't try to catch you, and from that height your head will not thank you for the drop."

Oats increased his grip on Ug's saddle horn and stayed where he was. "Any of your men survive?"

"Four. Perhaps five. Gonzalo's wounds are . . . well, time will make the tally."

Oats did not respond. He was watching the chief. She stood within the churned earth of the empty remuda, still and tense as if deep in thought. Oats knew better. She was communing with the rokh, guiding it, commanding it. When last he saw her, she hadn't yet mastered the trick of seeing through the bird's eyes. Looking at her now, he was certain she had. None of the cavaleros would escape. The rokh would lead Jackal to any who had gone to ground.

Movement beyond the chief drew Oats's eye. He let out a heavy breath of relief. Rant and Roar were coming down off the barricade, supporting each other. Both were wounded, that much was plain. How badly Oats couldn't tell, but they were alive. Rant still had the spear she was given and used it to support their descent. Soon as they reached the ground they slumped down, resting against the wall and each other. Rant's hand came up to settle on her brother's face, an assurance—for both of them—that their ordeal was over.

Oats hoped she was right. He also hoped that one day he would receive the same touch, the same assurance, from his sister.

As Fetching strode toward him, he knew it wouldn't be today.

Unlike Jackal, she still dressed like a hoof-rider, though hells knew she didn't need a brigand for protection. She was hiding behind an unchanged appearance, showing the mongrels she led that she was one of them. Oats didn't reckon it was fooling anyone. She never wore a sword these days, preferring the strange fist knives given by Tarif, weapons she had not even bothered to draw to fight the Maiden.

Fetch stopped an arm's length away from Oats, but they only shared a glance before her eyes drifted away. She pretended to take in the hilltop, took a long breath.

"This was a cunt hair from a disaster, Oats."

He kept his mouth shut.

"What were you thinking?" Fetch asked, still not able to look at him.

Jacintho took a careful step forward. "We learned that—"

"Did I ask you?" the chief said, voice flat. Jacintho held up placating hands, rocked his step back. Fetch jerked a thumb at him. "Go see what can be done for the wounded."

As the man walked away Fetch shook her head. Oats could see the corner of her lip turn down.

"He reminds me of a dog's cock," she muttered. "Thin, pink, and shiny. Only pokes out when it wants something."

Oats didn't waste his breath in the bandit's defense. Jacintho had proven himself a worthy ally time and again, but there was no getting past Fetch's distaste. She didn't approve of Oats's silence either.

"Well? You got an answer for me?"

"Got word that Thresh and Slug had been taken. Came to get 'em."

"I learned that news at the Pit, Oats. My question is what were you thinking standing against the frails on their own soil?"

"No choice."

"You could have kept riding. You *should* have kept riding. Not trapped yourself and given them the chance to surround you."

Again he said nothing. She weren't wrong, but she was looking at a cat that had already scratched. Oats didn't much feel like voicing either point, though. He asked his own question instead.

"Why'd you come up to the Pit?"

Fetch looked at him, managed to endure it for a few heartbeats before turning away again. "Doesn't matter now."

"Reckon it does. You brought Jack. Has to be something."

Fetch exhaled, looked down at her boots. "Where's Barsius? I was told he came with you."

The mention of the halfling muddled Oats. "He . . . he was part of the plan. He and his tunnel boys. Helped get us out of Ellerina. They'll meet us back in the mountains. Why?"

"He still think you know where Xhreka is?" Fetch hit him with the question first, her eyes next.

Oats nodded. "Shit at hiding it too."

"Did you tell him?"

"Did I . . . ? Fetch. Can't tell what I don't fucking know." It came out with every last grain of the bitterness he'd tried to hide.

"You've been looking."

"I've been in the damn Smelteds where you sent me. Again. And you know it."

"You've been asking," Fetch said, a fire stoking in her voice. "Hiding it, but you've sent word with every merchant and nomad that will listen that you're looking for Eva, a favored whore from Sancho's. That you want to know where she is and need to talk. Trouble is, that's a woman we both know to be dead. Figure since you told Xhreka about every shit you ever took it's a message she'd know is for her."

"Sounds like Zirko's not the only one got a spy nested with me."

"Only spying if the deeds are hidden," Fetch replied, sounding bitter herself now. "I'm given reports by those loyal to me. You used to know something about that."

Oats felt the pain and fatigue boil away. "I should knock you on your damn ass. Loyalty? How about fucking trust, Isa? I haven't had yours for miles now or you would have told me where she's hidden from the kick."

"We going to chew this leather again?" Fetch pointed rapidly at her chest. "*I* know, Oats. Me. That's it. Not Jackal. Not you. No one. Hells, you still refuse to hear! I was trying to make damn certain if Zirko got desperate enough to hurt us he could only come after me. I was trying to protect you."

"Protect me? It's a war, Fetch. One you forced Zirko to help you fight, with Xhreka as the threat if he didn't. And they are helping. Barsius—"

"Is sniffing you for Xhreka's scent. Our alliance with Strava will end the moment they find her."

"Then your plan is safe, chief, because I got no notion where she is. Your tactics are working."

Fetch's jaw bulged. He'd riled her. Done it on purpose too. She scratched at the shaved sides of her head beneath the Tine plume, took a breath.

"No, Oats, they're not. We think . . . Zirko may be closing in on her."

Oats went cold. Since he and Xhreka had met in the Pit he'd known how fervently she wanted to avoid ever going near Strava again. He'd not known why until later.

"How?" he managed.

"I don't know," Fetch replied. "Not even certain I'm right. All I know is that she's gone silent. Haven't heard from her in a month."

"Then get on your damn bird and go see!"

"You think I haven't? She's not where she should be."

"And where's that?"

The shameless, silent way she looked at him, refusing to answer, made him want to chew rocks. Or force feed them to her.

"I don't know where she is," he said through grinding teeth. "Neither does Barsius, else he wouldn't still be around, would he?"

Fetch shook her head. "No. No, I don't think so. But that's what I needed to know. Why I came . . ."

Oats saw all the little clues, blatant because she tried to conceal them. "You're lying."

Fetch's face softened. "I am."

"Trying to protect me some more. Don't."

Fetch accepted that with a nod. "We need to find Xhreka. A reunion between Zirko and his god can only spell shit for the Lots. If Belico destroys Strava out of vengeance we lose the Unyars, and they're the largest force among us. If it goes the other way and Zirko wrests control of the Master Slave from Xhreka he'll be powerful enough to oppose us."

"Us," Oats echoed. "You mean you and Jackal."

"To start. But that priest may seek a reckoning against all the hoofs. He may even side with Hispartha. That happens and we've lost. So we have to find her, keep her safe. I came because I knew you'd want to help, but—"

"But fucking nothing. I'm coming."

Fetch took a step closer, lowered her voice though the intensity grew. "Oats, look at you. You can't go riding across Ul-wundulas on a hunt like this. The first day would put you in the ground."

"You may be stronger than all of us now, Fetch, but that don't make me weak."

"Weak? *Jacintho* could knock you over with one arm right now. You've never been weak, Oats, but you've never been this close to dying either. You need time to heal and this can't wait."

"Neither can this war. Winter's over. The passes are thawing. The frails will be marching in numbers we ain't yet seen. Seems to me you'll be needed."

"We need to find her quick," Fetch agreed. "Jackal may have to shoulder the search alone if we don't."

"The Arm of I-Choke-On-Cock? You forgotten where he got that power? Zirko starts yanking on his magic arm bone again and Jackal will be helping *him* find Xhreka, not us!"

"Jack's free of Zirko now and you know it."

"Still a risk. Better if I go."

"The only place you're going is the castile."

"Like hells."

Fetch leaned in. "I'm not asking. There is no one at the Pit that can tend you, not like the Zahracenes. You go back to the mountains your injuries will fester and you'll die. You go searching for Xhreka, you'll die. You don't have my permission to kill yourself. Understand? You have to recover, Oats. I'm not giving you a fucking choice."

All he could do was let his silence agree.

Fetch turned to go. To check on the wounded, most likely, or just to be away from him.

"What did she say?" Oats called after her.

"Say?" Fetching stopped, turned around. "Who?"

"The frail with the spear. At the end."

Fetch squinted at the ground, fished the detail from her memory. "'Devil.' She called me a devil."

They burned their dead on the hilltop. Tuskers, Sons, nomads, Shards, they all became the same smoke. Languishing with the other injured, Oats hadn't been able to help construct the pyre. Rant and Roar volunteered, but the others wouldn't allow it. This was a task for sworn brethren. Anvil had to forbid Thoon from aping her as she dragged wood from the wall to the pile. Both Jackal and Fetch labored alongside the riders until the pyre was big enough for all the bodies. When Thresher brought the torch to Fetching, Oats got to his feet, though he needed help from Roar and Sluggard. Jackal skirted the rear of the gathering to stand beside him.

The chief held the brand for a long while, staring at the dead. At last she turned.

"I'm wondering if this was worth it," she began. "Some of you likely are too. Perhaps you're not wondering. You've decided it wasn't. That this was too high a price to pay to save four."

Sluggard shifted uncomfortably. Oats glanced at Rant and Roar to find both siblings looking at him. He gave them a reassuring nod and turned his attention back to the chief.

"If you have a hoof-brother laying up here, one you came up with in the slops or a newer bond forged since we started riding together, I reckon it's hard not to believe this was a waste."

Fetch paused and locked eyes with every last one of those before her. Oats was last and the next two words were delivered directly at him.

"You're wrong. Today, on this hill, we showed Hispartha that they can kill us, but they cannot cage us. We showed them that we will accept death before we will return to chains. We showed them that we will come for our own and slay armies to liberate a handful. Remember that. The frails will. After they find this hill and their hundreds of unburied dead, they won't ever be able to forget. Now, let's send our fallen brethren on and thank them for doing what we all better be willing to do for our freedom."

Turning, Fetch lit the pyre.

Oats watched the smoke rise against a clouded, remorseless sky. He didn't thank the dead. He asked their pardon.

On his right, Jackal placed a hand atop his shoulder, gave a squeeze.

"Don't say it, Jaco," Oats told him softly. "Don't tell me not to blame myself."

Jackal didn't say it, not with words, but when Oats looked at him it was writ across his face.

Fetch ordered the hoof to make ready and the Bastards to gather. Things were decided quickly.

Anvil would take over for Oats at the Pit. With Thoon and Jacintho to support her, the Smelteds could remain under hoof control. Hispartha would have to bring considerable men to push them out and even then it would take months of tedious searching and hard fighting in the mountains. With the recruitment rides now too dangerous to continue Thresher requested to stay with Anvil. Fetch agreed. Sluggard would return with Oats, bringing the rescued shipwrights with them. Half the mixed hoof would come as escort. The other half would go back to the mountains with Anvil, but the chief said she would have them replaced with a fresh rotation as quickly as possible. Best not to keep the mongrels who endured this battle at the forefront of the war for too long. She had Oats make the split and he conferred with Anvil to ensure she had the best of the bunch.

The farewells were hurried and Oats soon found himself alone with Jackal and Fetching. The rokh had landed on the hilltop, croaking and preening as it awaited its master. Ugfuck was still a little nervy around the great raptor, but Oats's need of the hog as a crutch supplanted his instinct to avoid the winged predator. Oats wasn't all that comfortable with the rokh either, being earnest. He did his best to avoid looking into its golden, eerily perceptive eyes, each as large as one of the Steel Friars' bucklers.

"Still think you should let Fetch take you to the castile," Jackal said, concern etched upon his face as he peered at the layered bandage binding Oats's chest. "All I did was close it, but that hole could open again in the saddle. Let me take Ug for you while you fly."

"Last time I'm saying it—no," Oats replied. He put a smile on his face to soften the denial, but it was the third time Jackal had put the idea forth and his patience was wearing raw. "I ain't going up on that vulture. Not now, not ever."

Jackal tried not to, but he shot a look at Fetch. Oats set his jaw, dared her to order him.

"Ride safe," she said, and climbed up on the rokh's back, though the motion was more of a jump.

Jackal looked crestfallen as he embraced Oats. "Heal up, brother."

"Thanks for saving my hide, pretty mongrel."

"What was it you told me that day in the marsh? We will until the day we don't."

Releasing him, Jackal mounted up behind the chief. The rokh had no saddle, a fact that made Oats shiver. He couldn't imagine being that far up with nothing but feathers to hold on to.

Jackal opened his mouth.

"Uh-uh," Oats cut him off. "You start the creed and then I'm going to have to say 'Die on the overgrown buzzard.' And that just don't sound right."

Jack shut his grinning mouth.

There was a span of silence.

"We'll find her, Oats," Fetching said.

"I know."

The rokh turned, took a trio of increasingly lighter steps, and was in the air. Oats watched his friends ride into the sky. They were far out of reach within a single heartbeat.

EIGHT

ONE DAY IN THE SADDLE didn't kill Oats. Seventeen nearly did.

The push through the mountains in the first week he completed out of spite, the angry coals in his skull burning away the long, rough miles through the weeping passes. His wounds leaked in sympathy with the shrinking snow. He ignored them, sullenly suffering the bandage changes at every rest. There was little food but he didn't have much of an appetite. Whatever was pressed into his hand he ate without so much as a grunt of thanks to its deliverer. The fourth night he tried to aid with the camp preparations, but was too weak to handle the hogs, too shaky to strike a fire. So he sat, motionless as a saddlebag and far less useful. Neither could he stand a watch. The cold ate into him, or maybe the warmth flowed out of him, sailing away on his escaping blood. He was forced to abandon the effort, flee back beneath a shameful pile of furs and blankets. Even with such covering, even with Ugfuck pressed close, he shivered through each arduous night. He heard them whispering, Sluggard and Malcontent and Cut Wolf. They feared he wouldn't make it, weighed the wisdom of pushing on against sheltering in one of the caves the bandits used as hideaways. Each morning Oats made the decision for them. He was in the saddle when they awoke. He couldn't tend the barbarians, couldn't scavenge wood, couldn't hunt, couldn't even sleep. But he could ride. Well, not ride so much as grit his teeth and remain upright while Ug did the rest. Still, he whittled away at the miles.

It wasn't the mountains that almost killed him. It was the open plain.

His band came down from the Smelted Mounts on the morning of the ninth day, leaving the cold farther behind with each step away. Cut Wolf set a hard pace, knowing they could not stop for rest so near to Kalbarca.

The restored city was Hispartha's sole foothold in Ul-wundulas, garrisoned by two thousand soldiers. A quarter of that number was cavalry, and though they didn't often risk leaving the protection of their walls and guns to patrol in numbers, they did pepper the land with scouts. Should one of them catch sight of an encamped band of ten mongrels, several clearly injured, it could bring the cavaleros out in force in hope of avenging themselves on the half-orcs who had kept them on the brink of starving all winter.

Moving to cut off Kalbarca's supplies was one of the first moves Fetch made. In those first weeks of the war, she'd lacked the numbers to take the freshly fortified city, much less hold it. It had galled her to leave the frails unmolested, but her forbearance soon produced a benefit. Hispartha kept the city resupplied using barges coming down the great Guadal-kabir. Though the river was too wide to block, Fetch managed to assemble a force of wreckers and pirates to raid the shipping lane. The most heavily defended flotillas still made it through, but the goods ended up in hoof hands far more often than the bellies of Kalbarca's soldiers. In the end, supplying their own men proved of less importance to the Crown than denying the pilfering sootskins, and the shipments ceased by mid-autumn. The city's garrison had suffered since. The reports from Zirko's halflings in the tunnels beneath spoke of men eating little but boiled wheat and what cats could be caught.

The city still needed to be taken before Hispartha marched an army south. Oats didn't know if Fetch would carry out her plan to attack at the end of winter, but he didn't know much of anything, isolated as he'd been these last months.

Fortunately, there still hadn't been open fighting in the Lots. Hispartha's response to Fetch's declaration of war were a handful of heralds delivering threats, but no armies came south. Notch—who spent time as a scout in the Crown's armies before becoming hoofmaster of the Shards—told the chief the frails would take the winter to muster and, when they came in the spring, they would come with a thunder.

Fetch hadn't wasted the time.

While Oats and Anvil secured the Smelteds and the hoard within the Pit, Jackal went back east, taking the promise of that coin to the most notorious of Traedria's mercenary captains. He'd returned with ships and the freebooters to crew them, enough to protect the southern port at Mongrel's Cradle. The Lots had only one other useable harbor at Urci on the eastern coast, but it was little more than a cove for smugglers. The chief decided not to split her sellsword fleet, trusting the nearby fortress of Thricehold to keep the east secure. Marrow, his Thrice Freed, and the Bastards' slops held the citadel, training for the coming conflict. The Bastards' sworn brethren were scattered among the other hoofs, giving Fetch trusted eyes and ears across the Lots. Perhaps she had left the planning of Kalbarca's siege to Notch or Tomb. Oats didn't reckon she'd abandon the move even for Xhreka. Whatever was to happen, at the moment Kalbarca remained in Hisparthan hands, which meant it had to be skirted on the ride east to the castile.

No longer a slow-moving line of hogs in the rocky confines of the mountain passes, Oats's band hit the flats at a trot. He was dizzy within moments and took his first fall before noon.

Wounded pride got him remounted before the others could make much of a fuss, but the deepest cut in his arm had opened. He felt the warmth of blood welling through the pulled stitches. It wasn't long before Slug noticed and called a halt. Oats was too weak to put up much of a fight. The others sat their hogs with loaded stockbows, keeping an eye for horsemen while Rant sewed his arm up. Her brother had taken a nasty slice to the hand during the battle on the Heap, leaving her all the stitching chores.

"That hurt?" Oats grunted, looking at the mottled welt above Rant's eye.

She shrugged, concentrating on her work. "Don't feel great."

"What did it?"

"Don't know." Rant chuckled. "Never saw it coming in that shit squall. Edge of a shield, maybe. Would have felt a fathom worse if it had been a blade, though, I know that. I also know the frail that did it weren't so lucky. Roar made a mess of him."

Oats tried not to focus on the unpleasant pulling of the gut string. "Reckon he'd do that to anyone that hurts you."

"Gonna get him killed. Nearly did. So busy thrashing a man he'd already butchered he didn't see the living one coming up on him."

"But you did."

Rant swallowed hard. "We . . . always look after the other."

"That's good. You're going to need that down here. A trusted brother is about the most important thing you can have."

"Sounds like you believe that."

Oats frowned. "Why wouldn't I?"

Rant leaned and bit through the string. "Because you're about the most solitary mongrel I ever seen. Save that ugly hog, to look at you, I'd wager you didn't care to get close to nobody and call it a keen bet."

Oats opened his mouth to respond, but found he had nothing to say.

Rant stood up. "It's a queer thing, seeing a man split from himself. Sad too, because there ain't enough needle and gut in the world that can mend him."

Weren't enough to keep him on his damn hog either.

At least he didn't have to suffer the shame of the second fall. He was unconscious before he hit the ground.

THEY'D BUILT THE FIRE TOO close. Oats was drenched when he woke. Then he saw there was no fire. None on the outside of his skin anyway. Fat beads of sweat bubbled up from the hot pan that was his flesh. The drops slug-crawled down his face, each leaving an itchy trail. Someone was knelt beside him, head bowed and mumbling.

Knuckle Child.

The annoyance must have made it out of Oats in a groan, for the devout rider looked up from his fistful of charms. The joy on his face, the certainty that his pleas to hells-knew-how-many gods had been heard made Oats want to die. That would show him. He regretted the thought as the darkness granted his wish.

HIS EYES FLUTTERED OPEN TO the sight of huge, pendulous testicles. Ug was dragging him on a litter. Damn improvement over Knuckle's prayers.

Oats drifted in and out that day. Maybe two. The nights remained the worst.

On the litter he led the pain on a chase, but at rest it caught him and made him pay. The stab to his rump, the cuts upon his arms, the hole through his entire fucking body, they reveled in his discomfort. All he could do now was lie like a corpse and even that was torture. He tried not to cry out, did not want to disturb the others, bit down on his tongue. And still the whimpers escaped. Encouraged, the moans followed, with raving screams on their heels.

Rant was there, her bruised face comely above him. She put a cool hand to his brow. He blinked and she vanished. Sluggard gripped his hand, told him not to worry, that he would endure. The ragged scars on the mongrel's scalp shone angry in the firelight. More words. Knuckle Child's prayers. The others shouted him down. No, those were challenges, warnings tossed into the shadows. Voices. Calmer now, discussing if he would live. They didn't bother to whisper, thinking him senseless. Movement above. Oats rolled his eyes to look. A face, small and dark. The smell of earth.

"I look upon a hero. A brave warrior. Perhaps at his end."

Oats knew the voice. He squinted and the fire's glow sharpened Barsius's black features, etched with brazen swaths.

"I say such a one will ride beside Great Belico," the halfling proclaimed. "A proud addition to his war host. A lion among men. Do you hear his voice, lion? Do you heed his call? Tell me, from where does he speak? Where is the Voice of Belico?"

With Xhreka. In her head.

Barsius smiled. "Yes. Where is she?"

A chill gripped Oats, sent him into a violent spasm. He'd only thought about her, hadn't he? He didn't say her name aloud. He *wouldn't*.

"Where?"

Barsius was leaning closer now, his teeth flashing and hungry.

Where were the others? Why weren't they pulling him away?

"Tell me where and please the Master Slave. He will greet you with a feast without end, women without shame. Unburden yourself of secrets so you may sit light upon the magnificent steed he will grant you."

Oats set his jaw. For the first time in days his muscles responded. Reaching up, he seized Barsius by the front of his crusted robes.

No.

The halfling did not resist. His face betrayed no alarm.

"You are confused. There is no need to fear. You may trust me."

Lies. But Oats could wield them too.

She's fled to the Dragonfly Islands.

His attempt only widened the halfling's smile. "We know she remains in Ul-wundulas. Somewhere your chief has secreted her. Where?"

Kalbarca.

"No."

Up my hog's ass, then. Crawl in and look.

"There is no kindness in protecting her. The Hero Father only wishes to help her, to relieve her of the burden she carries."

More fucking lies. Zirko didn't care a shit for Xhreka. He'd rip Belico's tongue out of her skull if given the chance. Oats didn't know what would happen to Xhreka after that and neither did she, but it wasn't only for her own life that she hid. Belico was a god long kept fettered, and he wasn't pleased with those who enslaved him. Xhreka knew his wrath would be terrible should he ever get within spitting distance of Strava. The halflings and the Unyars would not celebrate their divine warlord's return. They would pay for it with their lives.

Zirko knew it too, and yet still he hunted her. Still he would not leave her in peace.

And here was Oats, dying on the ground with the priest's pet vulture circling.

The chief was right to hide Xhreka's whereabouts. He might have told here in his last moments, too stupefied with pain and fever to help himself. Too weak and vulnerable not to fall prey to Barsius's final effort to wrest the secret from him. It was the last chance for both of them.

Oats couldn't tell what he didn't know. Fetch was clever, as always. But there was something he *could* do. He could deprive the priest of one of his hounds. He could make sure Xhreka had one less nose sniffing for her trail.

Straining, Oats pulled Barsius close. The halfling began to struggle. Oats raised his other arm, got a hand around the small neck. At his best, he could have cracked the spine with a flick of his thumb, but his grip was feeble. Barsius was pulling at his fingers, about to squirm free. Oats released the halfling's robes and put his other hand over the first. He squeezed, the darkness at the edges of his sight constricting at the same pace. The effort was killing him, but not before it would kill Barsius. They could go to the hells together.

Hands seized his arms, broke his hold with pathetic ease. Barsius slipped from his murdering grasp and, in the last island of sight remaining, Oats saw a woman reel back, gasping and clutching her throat. Her coughing chased him into his final dreams.

SOW'S PISS.

That's what his mouth tasted like, welcoming him back to the world. The unpleasantness kept his eyes clenched shut for a long time. That and the light. His skull ached. So did his body, though it lay upon a cushioning bed. Not a pallet or a cot, but a bed. He could tell from the feel. Damn thing was wide too.

Oats opened his eyes in fits. They kept closing against the glare from the triple-arched window. Lead grates held diamond-shaped panes of glass smaller than a frail's hand. Oats knew that window. It was the only one like it he'd seen, an extravagance for the bedchamber of one of the most worthless men ever to draw breath, though he was good and dead now.

Realizing where he lay made Oats want to flee the bed. He tried and was felled by dizziness. Closing his eyes against the spinning, the throbbing, he languished but did not sleep. The sound of the door opening encouraged him to risk the light again.

The relief he felt was reflected in the face of the woman who entered.

"You back among us, Oats?" Thistle asked, setting down the washbasin on a trestle at the foot of the bed.

He tried to answer, but his dry tongue delivered nothing but a click.

"I need to get Hafsa," Thistle told him gently. "I won't be gone long. Stay awake."

Oats nodded and the woman hurried from the room. She wasn't gone long. Behind her came a smaller, older woman, possessing the swarthy complexion and headscarf of a Zahracene. Oats recognized her as the woman he'd throttled and his shame sent his heart rolling into a queasy gut. Small wonder she was escorted by two big men from her tribe. They stood aside, watchful, as the woman approached the bedside without hesitation. Thistle went back to the trestle and gave Oats a reassuring smile. A final familiar face entered last.

Ahlamra's graceful steps brought her to stand beside, and slightly behind, the Zahracene woman, who immediately began speaking in the tongue of her people.

"Hafsa asks if you know where you are," Ahlamra translated.

Oats worked up enough sour spit to rattle an answer. "Castile." Fucking Bermudo's bedchamber, to be more exact, but that was pushing his voice to limits it didn't possess.

Hafsa spoke again, directly to him, her face placid and eyes sharp.

"Do you feel you can take some water?" Ahlamra asked.

Oats nodded.

After a permissive nod from Hafsa, Thistle came around to the other side of the bed with a cup and helped Oats lift his head to drink.

It washed away some of the sow's piss, but turned his stomach into a churning sack of eels. He wasn't allowed a second mouthful. Hells, he was feeling worse with each passing moment, the pain and weakness waking with him.

"Do you have any numbness?" Ahlamra asked after further words from Hafsa.

Oats started to shake his head, but stopped as the question forced him to consider.

"Right . . . arm. Foot."

His answer caused him more alarm than any of the women.

Hafsa said something that Thistle must have understood, for it was she who spoke to Oats, not Ahlamra.

"We need to change your bedding now, Oats. Get you clean."

It was only then that Oats realized he'd soiled the linens. The embarrassment nearly cut through the pain.

Ahlamra absented the room while Hafsa directed the Zahracene men. Didn't seem like they needed to be told what to do as they shifted Oats onto his side with practiced ease and held him there while the bedding was stripped. Thistle took a wet rag to him like some damn babe. His tenders worked quickly, but it was still an eternity. Oats wanted to rage, to throw them off, to drive them from the room with shouts and heaved furniture, but all he could do was suffer the indignity and try not to add to it by letting loose the building tears.

Once he was bathed and resettled, Hafsa saw to his injuries, removing the bandages to scrutinize each wound with judging eyes, sniffing nose, and carefully probing fingers. Oats was rolled onto his side once more so she could tend his rump and the hole in his back. Salves were applied that stung something awful. Hafsa replaced his bandages with some assistance from Thistle, though her involvement had the look of tutelage not necessity.

At last, it was over.

Hafsa called Ahlamra back in and gave her a swift string of instruction before leaving the room, the men at her heels.

"She says you are to sleep if able," Ahlamra related.

"How . . . long?"

"More would be better than less, I think."

Oats shook his head. He tried to repeat the question, but his parched throat thwarted him.

Thistle came to his rescue with water and understanding. "How long have you been here?"

Oats grunted what he hoped was an affirmative as he sipped.

"Four days," Thistle said, doling the water with care.

"How . . . bad?"

The question brought a compassionate twist to the blond woman's mouth. "Some of your wounds were festered. You had blood fever. It was close, Oats."

He held Thistle's steady, caring gaze. She'd put on weight since last he'd seen her, looked more like herself.

"But you are going to be fine," she added. "Hafsa's a marvel."

The mention of the Zahracene woman made Oats wince. He rolled his head to look at Ahlamra. "Tell her I'm sorry?" He made a choking gesture at his own throat.

"She was not harmed," Ahlamra told him, placing a hand on his forearm. If she were lying Oats couldn't tell, but that was the manner of this small woman with just a drop of orc blood. She was artful. Like her orc heritage, she could conceal a thing to the point that it didn't exist and still use it to her advantage.

"You were out of your head, Oats," Thistle put in, pardoning him.

"Tell her. Please," he told Ahlamra.

She dipped her chin. "I will. Now you should sleep."

"Rather eat," Oats said. He wasn't hungry, but it seemed queer that he wasn't after four days. Besides, he was never going to get out of this bed if he didn't put some food in him. Hafsa may be a marvel, but Beryl was a terror, and Oats knew well what his mother's requirements would be if she were here.

"Honey only," Ahlamra said, though the words were a reminder for Thistle.

"I heard, Rue."

Ahlamra smiled. "Your Urzhar is improving."

"Got a good tutor," Thistle replied with a wink.

Ahlamra removed her hand from Oats's arm, but he managed to catch it again before she could turn to leave.

"Any word from the chief?"

"No. I will tell you as soon as there is."

Oats did his best to put some gratitude on his face and let her go.

"Let's see if the two of us can get you propped up," Thistle said.

They managed. Barely.

Oats had to close his eyes for a spell until the worst of the tide receded from his skull. When he opened them Thistle was sitting on the bed beside him, a wooden bowl and spoon at the ready.

Oats wrinkled his nose. "Anything else?"

The look he received was admonishing. "Noooo."

"At least let me do it."

Thistle placed the bowl in his hands. The numbness in his right arm extended to the fingers and he fumbled the spoon. He switched to his left, but that was quaking before halfway to his mouth. Oats dropped the spoon back into the bowl and swore.

Thistle took them from him without a word. She waited.

"I'm sorry," Oats mumbled.

"For?"

"For . . . this."

She leaned down, forced him to look at her. "For being injured? Oats. You know that's no cause."

What he knew and what he felt weren't riding the same hog, but he didn't try to explain. Instead, he nodded.

Thistle raised the spoon. "Now I can't promise this won't wind up in your beard, but . . ."

Carefully, she guided the spoon past his lips.

The sticky sweetness of the honey made Oats grimace. He swallowed it down and made a noise. "Never mind. I don't need to eat."

"One more."

"What about . . . just bread and gravy?"

Thistle narrowed her eyes at him.

"Porridge?"

The spoon lifted.

Oats opened his mouth and survived the next assault.

"Now . . ." Thistle stood, went and put the bowl down. "I can give you two choices for the pain. One is a tea. Bitter as a widow's stare, but it will ease the aches and make you sleep. Or"—her eyes brightened as a smile spread across her face—"I can allow you a visitor. Someone who is very keen on seeing you."

Oats's heart lifted, but he stamped it down and murdered his own smile before it could form.

"No. Seeing me . . . like this. It would only scare him."

Thistle's smile faded into concern. "He's more scared you're going to die, Oats."

"Then tell him I'm not."

"We've been telling him that for four days."

"Just . . . let me get on my feet first. Tomorrow I'll—"

Thistle took a patient breath. "Oats. You're not going to be out of that bed tomorrow. Might not be for a span. He needs to see you. He's . . . he's having nightmares."

Oats unclenched his jaw. He'd been grinding his teeth. "I don't . . . I don't look scary?"

Thistle shook her head and replied softly, "You don't look scary."

Oats nodded. Took his own steadying breath. "All right, then."

"I'll get him," Thistle said.

She was gone a little longer this time. Oats made sure none of his wounds were visible, that the bandages weren't bled through. He smoothed the sheet, his beard, best he could.

The door opened again.

"Oads!"

Muro rushed across the room. The little boy wasn't afraid. He didn't even pause before jumping up onto the bed and flinging himself into Oats's arms.

"You here! Not dead!" Muro said, his muffled voice high with glee and thick with tears. "You here! Not dead!"

Oats stroked the back of his dark head. "I'm here. I ain't dead."

He hugged the boy tight and rocked him, kissed his hair. The weight of the embrace pressed his wounds, but he didn't care. Oats looked up at Thistle, watching with a quivering smile. She was right. This was the antidote to all pain.

NINE

MURO FAVORED HIS MOTHER. HE had the same lopsided grin that conjured a lone dimple. The same ears, pinching at the lobes toward the jaw. Likely she would have remained alive in the boy's eyes, as well, but one was cocked now, making his stare entirely his own.

Oats wondered if there was any of Muro's father in him. He'd never seen the man. Some traveling minstrel ousted from the courts up north, Muro's mother claimed, though it was doubtful she knew for certain. The whores always tried to have a likely poke ready to name when Sancho asked. If the elected man ever came back through, the whoremonger was quick to press them for more coin "to aid in the child's upkeep." Funny how the men that put babes in whores' bellies always seemed to be those weak enough to be bullied by the likes of Sancho. Not that the mothers ever saw a single piece of the coerced shine. Muro's certainly didn't. Her singer never came back to the brothel far as Oats knew, and she was dead within a year of giving birth, one of two laid low by a tinkerer from Guabia flush with coin and some hidden putrescence. The other woman had lived, though the disease had left her face so hideously scarred that Sancho cast her out, uncaring that her mind had been eaten away along with her nose.

Oats had been freshly sworn back then, a Grey Bastard, still riding his first hog, Gorgeous. Queer to think that Muro was older than Ugfuck. Sometimes he remembered it wrong, familiarity with the present infecting the past. He'd think back on that day he'd first held Muro and recall Jackal being with him, when, in truth, it was old Creep.

They'd ridden up and found no one in the stable to take their hogs, the brothel shuttered. Sancho only unbarred the door after they'd threatened to break it down. He'd already driven the disfigured whore into the badlands. The dead one was shut up in a room, her squalling child inside with her. Sancho feared the boy was afflicted and refused anyone entry. Two of his girls had split lips and black eyes from trying to get to the boy. Delia was one of them.

But the fat whoremaster couldn't send Oats off with a strop.

He'd burst into the room, lifted Muro away from the corpse, and wouldn't put him down. Not when Delia offered to take him, not when Creep asked for help burying the mother, not even when the boy finally stopped crying.

They stayed a day longer than they were supposed to. Oats didn't want to leave until he was certain Muro would be safe. He'd been so green back then, hardly more than a slop. He had size and strength, but what good were those once he was back at the Kiln? Creep sorted it, in the end. The old mongrel was already blind in one eye, his hearing was going, and his joints creaked louder than the thrumcord when he pulled it back. Still, he'd made Sancho open his mouth, put the head of the bolt right inside.

"You think that child ain't going to live, you best tell me to pull this tickler now," Creep said. "Because I can promise you, fat man, that getting throat-fucked by this here quarrel will be a kindness compared to what my young thrice-blood brother will do to you if'n he don't. My days of whoring are just about done, but this'un? Full of spend. So you can well wager he'll be here frequent. That babe ain't hale, hearty, and plumper than you every single time Oats comes to get his iron wet, well... you think that's an eventuality nod your head and I'll mercy-murder you this damn instant."

Muro was thriving when Oats returned the following month. And he was thriving now.

For a week he rushed in and out of Oats's room with a new treasure to show. A coin. A leaf. A flute whittled for him by one of the Zahracenes. The husk of a cicada. Thistle said he had an entire collection of wonders tucked away in their chambers, but Muro wouldn't bring the entire basket at once. Each had to be presented one at a time in a specific sequence only the boy knew. Oats feared Muro was going to wear himself out with all the running up and down the stairs of the keep, but there was no bottom to his vigorous need to share all he'd discovered.

"He'll sleep well again tonight," Thistle mused after Muro raced from the room to fetch the third wonder of the day.

Oats shook his head and chuckled. "Wish I could summon that much joy over a broken bit of chain."

"He came back with an arm's length of match cord about a month ago," Thistle said. "*That* had to go missing in case he stuck it in a candle flame."

"And how'd that go? It going missing?"

Thistle continued to tear the latest batch of fresh bandages. "He hasn't noticed yet. But in another month he could be crying over it."

Oats laughed again. "He looks good with his hair grown."

"Well, he gets a bath regular now, so the lice aren't a concern like they were in the sta—"

Thistle stopped herself, used the ripping of the linen to cover the sudden halt in her words.

Oats pretended not to notice. The castile's stablemaster had been a cruel fuck to all his charges, but he heaped the largest pile of abuse on the simpleminded boy.

Muro was free of him now. He had a mother again and, to his knowledge, for the first time.

"No surprise you've done so well with him," Oats said, and felt a sudden need to clear his throat. "No surprise, but I reckon it still needs to be said."

Thistle kept her eyes fixed on the growing stack of bandages, but her industrious movements slowed a little. "He's a joy."

Oats watched her from the pen that was Bermudo's massive bed. "If I didn't say before I left . . . thank you for taking care of him."

"You said," Thistle replied with the touch of a smile.

"Good. But that was . . . before. Now that you done it, been through the winter and all, reckon it bears repeating. So . . . thank you. Again."

"I volunteered, Oats. You don't owe me anything."

"Certainly didn't deserve having me to look to on top of him."

"Volunteered for that too." Thistle moved around to the bedside. "Come. We can get your arm dressing changed before he gets back."

Oats complied. He could actually raise his arm to aid with that task now, though the feeling hadn't entirely returned to his fingers.

"I just don't want you to think I'm an ingrate," he said as Thistle worked.

"I don't think that." Her hand movements quickened, removing the old bandages. It could have been simply that she didn't want Muro to come back with the wounds exposed. He was sensitive to such sights. But Oats worried there was also a spark of irritation in her hurry. Had he upset her somehow? He hadn't meant to. Perhaps it was like her not wanting to mention the stables, thinking it would anger him. Perhaps he'd trodden on a tender matter, mentioning her taking charge of Muro. She'd sacrificed much to do it.

All Winsome's orphans had been hers to shelter, and now she had just the one boy. Fetch had sent the rest away, knowing the castile would be in the eye of the storm when Hispartha brought their armies—and open war—to the Lots. Mongrel's Cradle, on the southern coast, was as far removed from the border as they could get, with the sea as an avenue of escape should it come to the worst.

But Muro had refused to go.

He'd flown into a fit at the notion of leaving the castile. The place had been a hell for him, but it was his home. He didn't remember the brothel, far as Oats knew. He'd been but four when he left there and injured besides, skull broke and hardly alive. So, the castile was what he knew.

"Where you find me, Oads! Where you find me!"

That was all they could understand through the wailing.

Beryl had said they should simply put the boy in the wagon, that he would get beyond his grief long before they reached the Cradle.

And that had made Oats's mind. Muro should stay.

Oats loved his mother, but she had . . . her ways. They weren't always altogether kind, not on the surface leastways. Raising scores of mongrel foundlings, Beryl's tough-as-hide discipline worked. Part of her duty was to groom them for the hoof. Oats had no complaints about the way he came up. The way Jackal and Fetch and Culprit and dozens of others came up. But for Muro? No. There was no future in a hoof for him and not only because he was a frail. He had difficulties that Beryl would think she could cure by ignoring them. She'd never mistreat him, not ever, but neither would she treat him differently than any of the others. Oats reckoned there was a better way, though he didn't know what exactly it was, and neither did he know how he was going to confess it to his mother's face. Fortunately, like Creep had done nearly nine years before, Thistle did it for him.

She wanted to stay, she'd said. The Sons of Perdition would have a wet nurse at the Cradle for their foundlings and her milk was dried up regardless. With Beryl back there was no need for her to go, not when she could be of use here. Muro could stay at the castile under her care.

Still, it had not been an easy parting. Milk or no, those children had all been Thistle's to look after during the toughest shit Winsome's people had ever endured. And yet she bade them all farewell, kissed them, and helped lift them into a wagon so they could ride through the gate and out of her life, possibly forever. All for one boy she barely knew. One boy who didn't care a fig that she stayed because he only wanted Oats.

For as hard as Muro cried at the thought of leaving the castile, for all the shouted, unintelligible protests, it was nothing compared to the earsplitting sorrow that racked the boy upon hearing Oats was going away to the mountains. Nothing said could penetrate that pure, wild anguish. All Oats could do was bite down on the inside of his mouth, drawing blood to ward against his own tears, and mount up while Thistle kept Muro from following, suffering the blows of his thrashing limbs.

Oats hadn't known what to expect when he returned, from either of them. He tried not to think of them at all during his time in the Smelteds. It was easy at the start, during those first weeks when he and Anvil took over the Pit of Homage, spewing threats and spilling blood. After, when the slavers were gone, and Jacintho's men were escorting mule trains of ancient Imperial gold into the Lots, Oats had little to occupy his mind. Muro's screams woke him on the nights he managed to sleep.

But this morning, and the six before, it was the boy's laughter that snatched him from slumber.

"Is he only happy because I'm back?" Oats ventured. It had been a gnawing worry.

Thistle was finishing with the fresh bandage. Good thing too, because his arm was faltering.

"He's happier," Thistle answered. "But no, he's not been wholly miserable these last months."

"And you?"

Thistle shrugged as she tied the bandage off. "I'm well."

"You look better than you did," Oats said. The way Thistle's eyes jerked up made him regret the words the next instant. "I mean . . . you, *we*, none of us had had much to eat since last I was here, so you were thin."

"I was thin?"

"Right. But now you've filled out again. Like the way you were before. So you look . . . good."

Oats realized with horror that he'd made a certain double-handed gesture there at the end, one that could be best described as miming ample handfuls of something.

"Just saying I think it's good when people look the way they ought!" he blurted. "Like themselves. You seen Jackal? All them dune-lover robes and scarves. And the chief with her Tine coif. They . . . don't look like they ought. Like how I think of them in my head from the past. So if they were to change back. If Jack were to wear a brigand and breeches again like a damn mongrel should and Fetch were to quit razoring the sides of her scalp, then I'd say to them 'You look better.' Same as I did. Just now. With . . . you."

Thistle stared at him blankly for a long, *long* spell.

Muro came running to his rescue brandishing a falcon's feather.

OATS DIDN'T GET TO SEE the bird itself for close to a fortnight. Turned out not to be a falcon at all, but an eagle, the pride of Tarif Abu Nusar, *shaykh* of the Zahracenes. The man exercised his hunter in the spacious yard of the castile, sending it from his gloved wrist to soar and swoop, calling it back again. Muro laughed and clapped, marveling openmouthed and tensing with excitement. He'd not been able to remain seated next to Oats on the stairs of the keep once the eagle took wing. Though his body was incapable of sitting still, the spasms and tics that ever played upon his face were calmed by his rapt attention to the bird's flight. He could have watched all day, fervor never flagging.

Oats nudged the boy with his knuckle. "What did you think of the chief's big bird? The one that she rides?"

Muro jerked away as if he'd been scalded, his eyes going wide, arms drawing close to his chest. He shook his head. "Nooooh."

Oats was careful to keep his reaction small. "Too big? Too scary?"

A frantic nod.

"I liked to have filled my breeches first time I saw it too," Oats said. He pointed back to Tarif. "Look. He's going again."

Muro turned and the next instant his fear was forgotten.

Oats took a long, slow breath.

The halting plod down the stairs had nearly done for him. But Hafsa had declared him ready after days of finding his legs in the corridor. The Zahracene healer still insisted Oats lean upon her pair of burly assistants, however, and made certain Ahlamra's translation properly conveyed she was not to be trifled with on the matter. Oats wasn't about to fight her. The sight of his own feet beneath a coverlet had grown tiresome weeks ago and he was determined to be rid of Bermudo's damn bedroom, to see Ugfuck. He'd accomplished the first, but even with aid, Oats was sweating after half a dozen steps and the descent took an age. He'd needed to rest a span, so he'd ended up on his ass at the bottom of the stairs. Sitting on stone was far from a comfort, but at least he was closer to the ground should his light head send him into a fucking swoon.

The Zahracenes waited behind him. Oats would have felt less judged if they'd made some jests at his feebleness like his hoof-brothers would have done. Instead they were silent and patient as spiders. Oats didn't have a word of Urzhar, and Ahlamra had other duties than to dog his decrepit outing. Thistle knew some of the tongue, but she had used his absence as an opportunity to clean the chamber. The woman never took a moment of ease.

Unlike Oats. His life was molded by sloth now.

Tarif's hawking did little to distract him from the pain, the quivering, and the weakness. Still, it was pleasant to sit in the breeze of the afternoon. It struck him, cruel as a punch to the cods, that he wouldn't be able to see Ug today. This was as far as he could go. What strength he recovered would be needed for the return up the stairs and even that he feared would conquer him. The Zahracenes might need to employ a litter. The only thing worse than that thought was the knowledge that he was growing comfortable with the necessity of such help, grateful for it, in earnest.

Oats looked to the sky. The rokh may have frightened Muro, but Oats yearned for a sign of the chief. There was still no word from her or Jackal.

He blinked when Tarif stepped into view, his hooded eagle perched on his hand.

"Hafsa tells me you are healing well," the *shaykh* said. "I am heartened to see you risen."

Oats grunted a laugh and cocked his head at the stairs. "Not quite."

"Neither are you dead. Be grateful for this blessing."

"Grateful to you," Oats said, remembering to show some of the courtesy the Zahracenes prized. "I know you gave up the bedchamber for me, and that Hafsa is your fagician."

"Physician," Tarif corrected without a hint of mockery.

"That," Oats said, pointing at nothing. Like courtesy, it wasn't a word much heard in the Lots. "You'll have 'em both back soon. I'll be hale again before another week's turn. Ain't that right, Muro?" But the boy was fixated on the eagle and paid him no mind. Oats shrugged. "It'll be soon."

Tarif shifted his weight. "You are what is named in your tongue a thrice-blood?"

Oats peered up at the man, a bit puzzled at the question. "Uh-huh."

"Thrice is a way of denoting three instances of a thing."

"Reckon so."

"I hope I do not give offense when I say this is an odd name."

"No," Oats said. "Got three kinds of blood in me. Frail. Thick. And mongrel."

"Yes, but half-orc blood is already that of human and orc. Surely you remain a product of two, orc and man, only in different measures."

Oats sent a hand running over his bare scalp. "Well, I weren't there when they gave name to it, but I wager whoever it was figured mongrel blood is its own beast."

Tarif smoothed both sides of his mustaschios with the back of a finger in two deft strokes. "I see."

"Been bothering you awhile, has it?" Oats asked, grinning.

"Yes," Tarif admitted, returning the smile. "Thank you."

Oats nodded. "Any news on Hispartha?"

"They continue to send heralds with entreaties that we abandon this place. No. 'Entreaties' is not true. Their words became threats long ago. All offers of mercy for our renewed fealty have been withdrawn. We see more of their scouts now. With the nights warming and the days returning to hot, I foresee the first of their armies before two moons turn."

Oats knew better than to ask if he was prepared for that arrival. The Zahracenes had been storing provisions all autumn. Fetch had made sure that the castile's larders, armories, and powder stores were filled, using the coin from the Pit to buy from Traedrian merchants. The goods were brought by ship to Salduba, the port protected by Mongrel's Cradle, then hauled north in caravans. With its high walls and guns, to say nothing of the several thousand seasoned Zahracene warriors they sheltered, the castile would be an ass-fucking nightmare for Hispartha to take by force.

Didn't mean they wouldn't try.

"You ever regret siding with us, *shaykh*?" Oats asked. He didn't know if the question was courteous, but it was an earnest one.

Tarif's hawkish face became a mask of consideration. At last, he answered. "My people know what it is to be mastered by a conqueror. The Tyrkanian Empire came to our mountains and claimed them with the sword. We became slaves in our own land. Then, warriors for our new masters. I would not have my people be the sword that falls on another again. For *that* I would regret." Tarif regarded his bird of prey for a moment and stroked its breast. He looked to Muro. "Did you see how I touched him? Gentle. Do you think you can do it so?"

Muro nodded.

Slowly, Tarif lowered his arm so that the eagle was within the boy's reach. Oats saw Muro's excitement, his limitations, would get the better of him. He caught the boy's hand before it reached the bird and steadied it, guided it once down the fluffy breast. Muro was awed, flinching a little when the eagle twitched a wing in response.

"Thank him," Oats prompted as Tarif straightened.

"Thank you," Muro said.

The *shaykh* gave a small bow. He looked at Oats. "And if I may offer some words to you. Three times in life I have been wounded in battle to the precipice of death. Never was my recovery quickened by haste."

Oats accepted that with a grunt. "Just don't like being useless is all."

Tarif's gaze shifted briefly to Muro. "If you believe yourself to be useless, perhaps we should have Hafsa check your sight."

With a parting smile for them both and a final bow, the man turned to go.

"*Shaykh*," Oats called. "You nearly been killed three times?"

Tarif winked. "Thrice, yes."

As soon as the bird was lost from view, Muro began tugging at

Oats's arm. "Bears and moundtans. Play bears and moundtans, Oads."

Hells, the boy was actually managing to budge him.

"Muro. I . . . can't."

"Bears and moundtans!"

"Not today," Oats said, freeing himself from the boy's grip as gently as he could.

Muro let out a howl of frustration. It took some time to calm him, but Oats was able to convince him to sit down once more. He didn't have a kerchief, so he wiped the boy's tears and dripping nose with his hand.

"I'm hurt, Muro," he said. "And I'm angry about it too. Wish I could lift you up and play. In earnest, I do. But . . . it's going to be a while before I can."

"T'morrow?"

"Not tomorrow."

Muro sniffed. "Because you hurt?"

"Yes. But Tarif is right. We need to be glad I ain't hurt worse. I'm going to be better and that don't always happen. Sometimes folk get hurt and they never heal."

"Me."

"You?"

Muro touched above his right ear. The hair there didn't grow in fully, a crescent marking the dent in his skull. "I hurt. Ever heal. Ever."

Oats stilled. "Do you remember how that happened?"

"Yes."

"How?"

"Bad mule."

Oats tried to let his breath of relief out slowly as he put an arm around the boy and pulled him close. "That's right. Bad mule."

THE ROOM. THE BED. TWO halves of the same prison for weeks. Tonight, a welcome sanctuary. Oats had yearned for them during the arduous climb up the stairs. By the time the Zahracenes half carried him over the threshold it was full dark. At least they hadn't needed a litter.

Thistle saw him settled before taking Muro to their chambers.

Alone, Oats gave himself to the floodwaters of exhaustion. His body was done in, but his mind rebelled. Oats's eyes snapped open.

It was Sancho who made up the story about the mule. Four years after Creep's threat, the whoremaster had come to the Kiln on a nag, alone and in desperate need to speak to the chief. The Claymaster, not Fetching. Oats could live a hundred years and be a drooling dotard and never switch those two in his memories. Wasn't long before the Claymaster called Oats into his solar and ordered him to ride back to the brothel with Sancho. The fat fuck was sweating more than usual and wouldn't look at Oats directly. They were barely free from the Kiln's shadow when Sancho reined up and spewed a confession.

Muro had been hurt, but it wasn't he who had done it, he swore. Oats had never heard a man speak so quickly. He'd come to deliver the news to Creep and Oats personally, prove he was innocent. Creep was dead by then, fulfilled his oath against an *ulyud* the year before. But Oats had seasoned and he didn't smell a lie on the whoremaster. His nose proved right. Sancho hadn't hurt the boy. But neither had a damn mule.

The whores had the guilty chained up in the brothel's wine cellar.

Oats could still see that mongrel's face, every detail, though the light from the candles had been poor. That one broken fang, the unhealthy yellow stain in his callous eyes. He was a big son of a thick, the scars over his Cauldron Brotherhood tattoos marking him a nomad. Sancho had laced his wine with *ghan,* chained him once he was witless. To be certain this wasn't a ruse put on by the whoremonger to save his hide, Oats made sure the captive free-rider was clearheaded before questioning him.

He gave his name as Lucon, said he'd left his hoof-name behind when he was ousted from the Brotherhood for fucking the chief's bedwarmer, droned out the whole damn story. Oats heard little of it. He let the mongrel talk, let him think the Grey Bastard standing before him was his way out of the chains.

Words spoken in a brothel cellar traversed the years and echoed in Bermudo's bedchamber.

"Why'd you hurt the boy?"

Oats's jaw was clenched, then and now.

"Caught him going through my saddlebag, thieving."

Oats had brought the bag down with him. It had dangled in his hand, adding to the myth that Lucon was about to be on his way. Reaching beneath the flap, Oats drew out the doll made of straw and old cloth.

"This is his giant. Giants live in caves. Saddlebags make good caves."

Lucon barely glanced at the doll. He'd fucking shrugged. "Only struck him once."

"His skull's caved. Blood in his ears. He's dying."

"Well . . . they are *frails*."

Oats swallowed, set the saddlebag down, tucked the doll beneath his brigand. Above his heart.

He was a long time in that cellar. When he emerged, stained and sticky, the whores all offered to bathe him, reward him. After what he'd done to Lucon, Oats had no stomach for such temptation.

Oats squirmed in the bed, roiling in the linens, the recollection. His fever was back, though the monstrous visions were not phantoms born from a heated brain. He'd done it, mauled that mongrel, barehanded and frothing. Made sure he was a long time dying. He was enraged, but not berserk, wielding his wrath like a weapon. Vengeance required control, else Lucon would have been dead by the same single blow he'd given Muro. A thoughtless, uncaring, *easy* blow.

There was nothing easy about the ways Oats sent Lucon to the hells. And he created a fresh one in the doing.

Bathed in sweat, the bedclothes clinging to him, Oats returned to that cellar. He drifted in and out of sleep, but dreaming or awake he was there.

At last, he broke free, sat up with a jerk. His breathing filled the room. Someone else was there too. He heard them moving in response to his waking. Hafsa had said he no longer needed watching at night, but must have returned to the practice knowing the day would tax him. He wasn't certain who it was, hoped it wasn't Thistle. No, the shadow was too big. One of the physician's assistants.

"Is there water?" Oats croaked in the dark.

He heard the pitcher fill a cup, which was guided into his hands. He took a drink.

"Thank you."

"It is my pleasure, friend Oats."

Oats froze. He knew that voice.

The fat lamp on the trestle sprang to life.

The little flame glinted in Crafty's golden smile. "I hear you have been looking for me."

TEN

OATS SET THE CUP ASIDE.

"It is not poisoned," Crafty told him, smile steady as a hog's piss stream.

"Didn't figure it was," Oats replied. He swung his legs over the bedside. "Hand me my breeches."

The portly wizard glanced about the room, found the garment on the back of a chair.

"Took your damn time," Oats groused.

"Truly it is a large chamber."

"You know that ain't what I mean."

Crafty only chuckled.

Flinching, trying not to hiss against the pain, Oats got his legs into the breeches. He went to stand so he could pull them up over his ass, but only lifted a cunt hair before falling back.

Crafty stood regarding him patiently, his pudgy, ring-laden fingers knitted and resting against his paunch.

"Help me here," Oats said.

"Of course," Crafty replied, and moved smoothly to stand in front of him. "How may I best assist?"

"Just stand firm, offer an arm, and keep weighing a heap."

"I can do that."

Oats took hold of Crafty's hooked arm and pulled himself off the bed. The wizard did more than his share of the work, stronger than his fleshy body would attest. Once steady, Oats gestured at the chairs by the cold fireplace. He made his way over on his own shuffling power and sat.

Crafty lowered himself opposite and pointed at the stack of prepared kindling. "Shall I light this?"

Oats shook his head. He was still sweaty and uncomfortable from the bed. Bermudo's hearthside chairs were large and cushioned, coaxing Oats to lay his head back for a moment. He closed his eyes and breathed deeply.

"I'd offer you wine, but my fistician doesn't allow me any."

"It is to keep your blood from thinning. And the Zahracenes hold abstemious beliefs."

Eyes still closed, Oats grunted. "Forgot how backy you talk."

"Cunting swaddleheads reckon the milk of the grape's swollen teats make fucking devils take up residence in a mongrel's fucking head bone," Crafty announced in the worst impression of a hoofrider Oats had ever heard.

"Aw, hells," Oats said, laughing. "Why don't you stick to what you're best at and use your damn sorcery to turn some water into . . . the milk of grape's swollen teats."

"I fear going against the instructions of your physician would belie my assertion that I am not here to harm you."

Oats opened his eyes. "I ain't afraid of you, Crafty."

"It pleases me to hear it," the wizard said with his customary smile. "Though I did not believe you were. Indeed, sending word that you wished to speak points otherwise. It intimates so little fear, in truth, that it was I who feared."

"Worried Jack and Fetch were going to be leaping from under the bed?"

Crafty looked wistfully about the room. "I confess not to have imagined *this* as the setting of an ambush."

Oats snorted. "So that's why you took a damn pig's year."

He'd figured Crafty would think it was a trap and be cautious. It was telling that he'd waited until Oats was half-dead and isolated before showing himself.

"It took some time for your clever messages to reach my ears," Crafty said. "After, I had a long way to journey."

Oats didn't respond. He believed only half that statement. The wizard had ears everywhere, he'd wagered. As to his long journey, that could also have been hogshit, but Oats was careful not to ask where he'd been. He knew better than to match wits with Crafty. Besides, Oats wasn't interested in his hiding holes.

"Yet here I am, at last," Crafty said, raising his hands. "Eva! The whore you have been so desperate to find."

Oats felt a mote of pride. It had worked. Perhaps he'd never truly believed it would.

Jackal had scoured half the earth and been unable to run Crafty down. Oats knew he'd have no chance himself even if he'd been willing to abandon his hoof and his chief to go on the hunt. The only hope of finding the wizard was if Crafty wanted to be found. So Oats had put word out with anyone and everyone, using Eva's name as his quarry. Eva, a woman who could never be found. She'd been executed not far from where Oats now sat by order of the man who once occupied this very room, along with the rest of Rhecia's whores. Eva, a woman Crafty had once lied about fucking on the night that he, Oats, Jackal, and Fetch had fled Sancho's brothel. Fetch had been suspicious, as always, and right to be. All Oats had done was wonder about Crafty bedding a woman since he'd reckoned him backy. They'd shared a fool-ass jest—"Any ass in the night"—and laughed about it for half the ride to Strava.

It was all Oats could fathom might summon the wizard yet hide who he was really looking for. The scheme had nearly been the hog that gored him. The chief caught wind of it. If she hadn't mistaken the recipient of the message for Xhreka . . .

Oats didn't know what Fetching would have done if she'd discovered his true intent. She'd come so close and still erred. Jackal too.

They'd had the same clues Crafty did, yet missed the mark. The reason hurt to dwell upon. It was unthinkable, what Oats was doing. So unthinkable it had rendered his siblings blind.

"You ain't changed any," Oats said, stating a fact.

Over two years since he'd seen Crafty, but the wizard retained his weight, his easy smile. His desert robes were still festooned with rich and varied sashes, his head still topped by an immaculate turban.

"It pains me I cannot say the same of you, friend Oats."

"Times haven't been kind since the Kiln fell. And fuck *you* for that."

Crafty offered no apology, but neither did he gloat. His face remained carefully guileless. "If it is not to seek revenge, perhaps you would tell me why you sought my presence."

"You're the cleverest son of a thick I ever knew," Oats replied. "Don't sell me you ain't worked it out."

"I must not hold my intelligence as high as you."

Oats gave a sigh with a growl wrapped inside. "I'm too damn tired, too damn hurt for games, Crafty."

The wizard leaned forward, smile still affixed. "Then let us not play any. Speak your reasons. Don't sell to me that any amount of wounds have rendered you too weak to give your desires voice."

"I want the plague."

"Not something often uttered on this earth."

"Don't you mock me!"

Oats stilled, forced himself not to turn toward the door. Thankfully, no one entered the room to see what had caused his outburst. He needed to get his temper wrangled or risk waking the entire keep.

Crafty's face fell and he held up a contrite hand. "Forgive me. Yes, you are right. This is not a jesting matter. Yet I cannot do this. Hispartha's plague is a work of sorcery both slippery and cumbersome. Mastery of it is perilous. It would doubtless resist me as it has the Tines."

"Liar. You moved it from the Claymaster to me, then tossed it into Wily like a pair of spare breeches into a saddlebag. You can move it again. I want it out of Warbler. Out of Wily. The elves may not be able to wrangle it. But I *know* you can. Easily too, I'd wager. You broke the Grey Bastards for me to bear it. So, I'm giving you the chance to have what you fucking want."

"I am curious what you believe that is."

"Thought we agreed? No games."

Crafty stroked the arms of his chair, the motion lighthearted. "The throne of Hispartha, yes? For that was my aim. Then."

Oats felt a stir of alarm. "You don't...? That can't have changed."

"If your desire is to mount a hog and you succeed, you may call yourself satisfied. However, if your desire is to ride a far distance, then there is more that must be done. If the hog will not be tamed there are other ways to reach your destination. Slower perhaps, but much ground can be covered in two years, even without strong hoofs."

Oats shook his head. "I ain't met a mongrel yet that would walk when he could ride. You may not have been sittin' idle and waggling your cod, but that don't mean your old plans are useless."

"My old plans required the orcs invade grand Hispartha so that I—and the new plague-bearer—could arrive as savior. The orcs will not stir themselves again for some time, longer than I can wait."

"So don't be Hispartha's savior. Be its damn conqueror."

Crafty's smile broadened. He toyed with the single braid of beard dangling from his chin. "I believed you to be the gentlest of your brethren, friend Oats. Such a proposal sounds more in the voice of dread Fetching. She may not be under the bed, but I wonder if she is not hidden beneath your tongue."

"She don't know that I'm talking to you. We wouldn't be talking if she did. Were she here, you'd be dead and there ain't no sorcery you got that would save you, and that's earnest."

"*Asily'a kaga arkhu*," Crafty said. His elvish, like his Hisparthan, was accented, but Oats thought he heard a note of sadness in the words.

Ruin Made Flesh.

The wizard had just revealed he knew not only about the chief's new power, but also its source. He did have ears everywhere.

Oats grimaced, shifting in the chair to make it seem it was his wounds that disturbed him.

"The chief's got no notion to have you for an ally, Crafty. However the fuck you think I sound, these words are mine. I want that filthy shit out of the two that are cursed to carry it in my stead. An old man and a little boy! I'm asking you to finish what you started and I don't give a heap of hogshit whether that fits into your plans or not."

"And Hispartha's imminent invasion of the Lots?" Crafty posed. "Am I to believe such impending peril does not weigh your desire to possess the plague? To deliver a potent weapon to Fetching's war?"

"All I care about is that others ain't suffering on account of me."

Crafty studied him for a moment. "I believe this. Yet it is not wholly the truth. She will wield you against them, friend Oats."

"I'd be fighting the frails anyway. What does it matter?"

Crafty stood, paced away from the fireplace. His back was turned when next he spoke. "Truly, for the . . . cleverest son of a thick . . . you have ever known, you must think me a fool."

The wizard whirled before Oats could respond, eyes bright with a wild amusement.

"Your brother is the Arm of Attukhan. Your sister an *uq'huul*. And you would bid me make you master of a magic so potent that even the orcs fear its bearer? Shall I hand the three of you the known world?"

"We don't want the fucking world, just the Lots. Just our home!"

"And once you have it?"

"We . . . live. In peace."

Crafty gave him a pitying look. He returned to his chair. Oats struggled to look at him squarely.

"Do you see?" the wizard said. "Even one with a heart as great as yours cannot speak those words and believe them. Empires expand, friend Oats. In this you must believe me, for I am an instrument of that growth. Would I be here if Tyrkania did not wish to consume Hispartha? Would we be speaking if the sultans did not cast their eyes westward and hunger for their borders to reach the Titan's Ocean? I tell you, no."

Oats set his jaw. "That would be on your head then. Once they have Hispartha, if your masters need Ul-wundulas too—"

"Fetching will allow my rule?" Crafty said, cutting him off. "Truly? She will trust her neighboring mongrel leader to the north? Will purge herself of the venom of grudges past? Did you not say she will never have me as ally?"

Oats clenched his fist, thumped it against the arm of the chair. "Whatever grudges she bears, you fucking earned them!"

"The very reason I am not eager to strengthen her further."

Oats hauled his aching bulk forward. "One way to see it. The other is that you're strengthening someone who could help keep her from your throat."

"Betrayal does not suit you, my thrice friend."

"I ain't said a word about betrayal," Oats said, anger flaring. "That's your trade, and I'll watch your hands for knives the rest of my life. But you help me now, I can help you later, convince the chief to leave you be so long as you never come south. She'll be more apt to hear with the war won and you part of the reason why."

"And if my masters deign I must come south?"

"Then I'll be there standing with my brethren, ready to shove the plague down the throats of every swaddlehead that comes with you."

Crafty spread his hands. "Honesty leads us to an impasse."

"Then I'll ask you for the same. Tell me, truthfully for fucking once in your life, does Tyrkania want the Lots?"

"At present, no."

Oats stared hard at the wizard for a long span. "Fuck. You look and sound same as ever."

"You were hoping my nose would change color when I speak truth?"

"I was hoping to get the same feeling in my gut I get when speaking with my sworn brethren. I was hoping to see a fellow Bastard in front of me. Not a fork-tongued half-orc with the Black Womb's arm up his ass."

Crafty's brow knitted, hearing that. Just slightly. It was brief, but it was there. Pain.

Oats refused to chew on what was likely nothing but the wizard's constant mummery.

"Would you bring that cup over?" he asked.

Crafty rose and retrieved the vessel, filled it from the pitcher before returning to the hearth. Oats took the cup, sipped. It was wine. The surprise forced a small measure to go down wrong. Oats coughed the wine out of his lungs.

"Could have fucking warned me," he growled, clearing the burn from his throat.

"I am sorry," Crafty replied quietly.

Oats glared at the wizard and drank again. Still wine. *Good* wine. It was the first he'd had since before leaving the Pit for Ellerina. Or had he had some at the Heap when his wounds were being stitched? Hells, he couldn't remember. However long, and whatever Hafsa might have thought, in this moment it was the cure to every cut, stab, ache, and fever in the world.

Crafty raised a cautioning hand toward the cup. "Please, go slowly."

Yielding to good sense, Oats kept himself from draining the cup.

Crafty did not let the silence last long. "I feel you should know, were I willing to grant you what you ask, still I could not. Placing the current vessel—"

"Wily," Oats snapped.

"Placing Wily in the domain of the Tines put him beyond my reach. I cannot intrude upon Dog Fall."

"Hogshit. Jackal did. Whatever he learned hunting you in the east, I reckon you know better, else he'd have caught you. Don't throw a lasso looking to catch a pardon from me." Oats took another drink. "You've said why you won't help. Spitting on your iron to ease the ass fucking ain't going to make me thank you for it."

"Perhaps you would thank me for not killing you."

Oats threw the cup into the fireplace and sat forward. "Told you, I ain't fucking afraid of you. It don't take a wizard to kill me, condition I'm in. That little Zahracene physician could smother me with a rag for all the strength I got. And have an easy time of it too. Queer thing about being this weak? I don't fear anyone to harm me 'cause everyone can. So fuck your threats, and your sorcery. And fuck you."

Crafty sighed and looked away. "You will not grant me pardon, but I ask for it all the same. You mistake my words. They were not meant in threat. It is the very weakness you mention that would slay you were I to be so cruel as to grant you the plague. Wounded as you are, you could not bear it. You would only perish."

"So the fuck be it," Oats said through gritted teeth. "So long as it's out of Wily."

"No."

"Why, dammit? Dead I'm no threat to you. Fetch wouldn't be stronger, wouldn't have a weapon."

"And Muro wouldn't have a—"

"Don't you say his name!"

Oats shot to his feet. His head, bewildered at the sudden change in height, contrived to bring him back down. Swaying, Oats toppled. Crafty caught him, strained beneath his weight, and wrestled it into the chair. Oats felt a cup pressed into his hand.

"Water," Crafty said.

It took some time for Oats to be steady enough to drink.

Crafty hovered over him. "Better?"

Oats nodded, relinquished the cup, not trusting his grip.

Crafty sat down once more. "It took courage to summon me to you. To defy the will of your chief and risk the trust of your brethren. I wish you to know this truth does not escape me. So I will attempt similar courage and risk a promise. If ever there comes a time when it is safe for me to grant your request, I vow to do so. But I grieve to say it, that time is not now."

Feeling dull, head lolled on the chair back, Oats could only stare at the duplicitous wizard. He was too damn feeble for the easily spilled lies to birth even an ember of anger. "I'm going to kill you for what you've done. One day . . . I'm going to kill you."

"I fear you will have to fight Jackal and Fetching for the privilege," Crafty replied.

A bitter chuckle rose from the distant cavern of Oats's chest. Not long ago, that wouldn't have seemed any chore at all. He would have knocked their heads together and done as he pleased. Not anymore.

Crafty rose and carefully set the cup on the arm of Oats's chair. "Since it is not a contest I wish to foment or witness, I must go, lest sunup—and your hot-blooded siblings—find me here."

That made Oats frown. His head was muzzy, but he could have sworn the wizard said . . .

"Sunup? Jackal and Fetch—"

"Will be here at dawn," Craft said, cutting him off with a smile. He made a grand, swooping gesture with his hand. "Descending from the morning sky, frustrated by their failure to find what they sought."

"How do you know . . . ?"

"That they did not find surly Xhreka?" Crafty winked. "Oh! Because I have her."

ELEVEN

OATS DIDN'T KNOW MUCH ABOUT carpentry. He wasn't certain what wood the campaign table in Bermudo's solar was made from, didn't know if it was expertly joined or if the intricate carvings were done with skill. He did know it was a monstrous and heavy piece. Likely took half a dozen men to carry it into the room, the captain clucking over its worth as they labored.

The chief snapped the table in half with a single downward blow.

Oats had made a silent wager she would. She'd been staring at its surface for too long, thinking, seething.

Ahlamra startled at the sudden violence.

"My men standing sentry will be punished," Tarif declared. "Allowing an intruder into the walls is shameful, to say nothing of one reaching the keep only to leave unnoticed."

"May as well blame them for not seeing the wind," Jackal told him, arms crossed as he leaned against the wall. "Crafty is well named. Believe me. There was nothing your men could have done."

Tarif continued to look embarrassed.

"Fetch," Jackal said, prodding her to pardon the man.

Ignoring him, the chief looked up from the collapsed table and set her eyes on Oats. Of the five of them, he was the only one seated.

"He said he'd be back to trade for her?" Fetch asked.

Oats nodded. He figured she'd struggled to listen during his account. Hells, *he* could almost hear the roar of her blood, it must have nearly deafened her.

"When? Where?"

"Didn't say," Oats replied.

"And not for what either," Jackal put in, heading off the chief's next question. It was an attempt to redirect some of her ire, Oats knew, but it was hard to be grateful. Fetch wasn't the only one angry. Oats would have thrown his chair at her if he didn't need it to sit upon, a fact that boiled his guts further.

"He said she was safe," Oats repeated, refusing to throw his words in place of the furniture. "That she was unharmed."

Fetching scoffed. "And you believe him?"

"I believe Xhreka is damn hard to harm," Oats replied, teeth clenched.

"What about Hood?" Jackal asked.

Confused, Oats shot him a look. "Hood?"

Jackal hesitated, got that sheepish look he always did when he'd been caught at some mischief or said something he regretted. His eyes darted to Fetch.

"Hoodwink was with her," she said, pacing away from the table's remains.

"Where?"

"Nowhere."

"Dammit, Isa!" Oats allowed his voice to rise, but kept his body in the chair.

She spun on him, angry at his outburst, at the use of her name. Oats met her burning stare and didn't blink. She cooled before he did, took a breath. Her gaze flicked to Tarif, then to Ahlamra. Wondering if she could trust them, Oats realized.

Hells.

Fetch took another breath, this one deeper, resolved. Oats waited to see who would answer, the chief or . . .

"Xhreka was nowhere because she was everywhere," Fetching said. "She told me that Belico did not allow her to leave Ul-wundulas, that he made it painful if she tried. I figured Zirko knew that and if he sought for her, he'd send hunters to all the likely spots. That limited our choices. So we broadened them the only way we could, by keeping her on the move. No one can find Hoodwink when he doesn't want to be found, especially if he's free to roam. No mongrel knows the Lots better. Even I didn't know where they were for most of the winter. Just messages that they were still out there, alive and undiscovered."

"What manner of messages?" Tarif asked.

"Hood would kill us both if I revealed that," Fetch replied.

Oats heard in her voice that she wasn't jesting. For all her might, she believed that the pale mongrel could find a way to kill her if he chose to. Oats couldn't convince himself she was wrong.

"It proved to be the right course," Fetch went on. "You weren't the only one to have a halfling embedded close, Oats. I got word that warriors like Barsius were showing up all over. At the Bone Smiler's, the strongholds of the other mongrel chiefs. Hells, even Kul'huun reported waddlers tracking the Fangs. Always in the guise of allies, helping us prepare for the coming war at the orders of the Hero Father. And I couldn't tell the chiefs to run them off. We asked for... *I* forced Strava's aid. Scorning it now would not strengthen the hoofmasters' trust in me."

The confession caused her to falter. Eyes lowering, she slipped into a brood.

Ahlamra pulled her out of it. "May I ask, chief, why you have not made good on your threat? You proposed Xhreka—or rather the god to whom she acts as vessel—would lay Strava low if the Hero Father Zirko pursued his desire to reclaim her. If you knew he flaunted your warning, why show restraint?"

"I should make him *Rue* the day?" Fetch replied, a small smile cracking her grim face.

Ahlamra rarely betrayed her feelings, but the use of her hoof-name still made her brow wrinkle. She hadn't completely accepted it, though it was fitting, for the castile had come to regret ever letting her within its walls. Still, it hadn't stuck. Ahlamra was ... what had Sluggard called her? Self-possessed. Some backy word used in civilization, Oats reckoned. But Self-Possessed made an even worse hoof name than Rue-the-Day, so the chief's suggestion had won out. Still, the beautiful barely-mongrel woman didn't know how lucky she got, in truth. Polecat had suggested they name her Wet Dream.

Fetch shook her head. "It's not my threat to make good. It's Xhreka's. That choice would be hers if it came to it. But even she doesn't know what a clash between Zirko and Belico would bring. The destruction of Strava? More? It wasn't something either of us wanted to find out and we wagered Zirko wouldn't either."

"But he called your bluff."

Oats had tried to keep that from coming out so hateful. And failed.

"He did," Fetch replied, temper wrangled. "But he didn't find her. We were winning the chase. Until ..."

"Fucking Crafty," Jackal said. His body looked relaxed, but Oats saw the tension in his jaw. He wasn't just trying to absolve Tarif of letting Crafty slip through.

Fetch noticed too. "*Shaykh,* we're going to need a detailed report of last night's watch. And a sweep of the castile. It's doubtful Crafty left any sign or trail, but we'd be fools not to look."

"It will be done," Tarif said.

"Ahlamra, I need birds sent to Polecat, Shed Snake, and Culprit. Tell them Crafty is back in the Lots, but say nothing of Xhreka. Tell them to mind their hogs. That jowly wizard has a habit of turning them against us."

The "hogs" were the hoofmasters the remaining Bastards were tasked with watching. Culprit was with the Cauldron Brotherhood, Polecat with the Shards, because Fetch marked Pulp Ear and Notch as the most fragile in their support of the war. Shed Snake was at the Wallow with the Tusked Tide, not because Boar Lip was untrustworthy so much as his large hoof was vital to their cause. Frequent reports from trusted brethren were a necessity from all three lots. Fetch was right to place eyes and ears among them, same as she was that Crafty might try to manipulate the other chiefs. As for Marrow,

Father, Kul'huun, and Tomb, the chief considered them stalwart, but Oats wondered if she might have to take further steps to safeguard their loyalty now that Crafty was scheming once more.

"Go now," the chief told Tarif and Ahlamra.

There was a long silence once they were gone. Oats and his siblings avoided looking at one another. At least, he thought so. Hard to be sure with his gaze directed at the floor.

"You invited him," Fetch said at last, quiet and sharp.

Looking up, Oats found a mixture of pain and anger on her face. Fetch went on, her words clipped and measured.

"Those messages to Eva. You weren't searching for Xhreka. You were looking for *him*."

"Yes," Oats said.

Fetching gave a strangled sound of frustration at his admission and turned away. She scrubbed viciously at her hair. "Hells, how did I not fucking see it!"

"Why, Oats?" Jackal grabbed a chair, pulled it close, and sat next to him. "Why'd you do it?"

"For Wily, Jaco. Why else?"

"You can't believe he'd actually help."

"Well, there wasn't a damn choice left was there?"

Fetching turned around. "You mean other than the fucking Tines?"

"They ain't helping! I was there too, Fetch. I heard what Warbler said, same as you. The elves can't get a grip on the plague. Said it seemed to have its own mind. A knot that couldn't be undone except by the one that tied it. Crafty!"

"What spider you ever seen unravels its own web, Oats?"

"Did you reckon I was gonna keep waiting? Let that little boy suffer and do fuck-all?"

Jackal put a hand on his shoulder. "Oats, we—"

"No, Jack. No. I ain't going to hear any comforting words. Any more hollow pledges. I been listening, and what's it done? I let Wily go to the Tines. Let Warbler go with him in my place. Let you ride off after Crafty. And I waited over a year for the point-ears to work their hoodoo, for you to come back with the wizard or at least a way to undo his fucking magic. I waited for nothing. The plague is still in Wily because we didn't face what needed to be done from the start. So that's why, Jack. *That's why.*" Oats shook his head. He could feel the blood in his body turn to bitter bile. He was filled to bursting with the stuff. "For all the fucking good it did. Crafty won't move the plague. Only reason he came was to deliver his message about Xhreka."

Fetching gave a rough laugh. "You think that's why? Hells, you don't know the way he thinks."

"How does he think?" Jackal asked, bristling a bit and unable to hide it.

"Quickly!" Fetch answered. "Knowing Oats was looking for him, wanting to talk, that spurred his mind to a gallop. Taking Xhreka? That was born from Oats's message. He was offered an opening and he took it. A way back in!"

Oats didn't like what he was hearing. "You're saying she got took because of me? *You* left her wandering the badlands unprotected!"

For once his anger wasn't logs tossed on the fire of Fetch's own. Tightening her lips she stepped and squatted down in front of him.

"You know Xhreka can protect herself. It frightens me to think that Crafty was able to subdue her, but he wouldn't have taken that risk unless he'd conceived of a way to reap a whole heap of benefit. Why not take someone less dangerous? He could have easily ransomed Culprit or Snake. But Xhreka? That's about getting to you. And you invited him to do it. So yes, Oats, this is because of you. You need to face that so you can get past being furious at me. We gotta decide how we are going to tackle this. We. The three of us. So you wanna scream, call me a cunt, go on. But after, I need you thinking clear."

"I ain't never called you that," Oats said.

Fetch peered at him. "Not even when I couldn't hear? You certain?"

"I'm certain." Oats grinned. "Certain as I knew you were going to smash that table."

"Called that too," Jackal said, raising a finger.

"Were you hoping to fuck tonight?" Fetch asked him.

Jackal shrugged. "Sure, but Rue hasn't said where yet."

Oats let a genuine laugh come out as Fetch's hand darted forward and flicked Jack in the cods, just enough to make him flinch.

Fetching placed her hands on Oats's knees, waited until the awkwardness of their shared stare was banished by a lifetime of affection. "We're going to get her back."

"I know, chief."

She studied him, looking for the truth in his response. Satisfied, she squeezed his legs as she stood.

"Sorry I didn't get him, brother," Jackal said.

Oats could see he meant it. He reached over and knuckled Jack's leg, accepting the pardon and asking for his own in one touch.

"Jackal," Fetch said, "you got any notion how he did it? Overpowered Xhreka?"

Jackal ran a thumbnail along the line of his jaw. "I never got close enough to ever fight him directly. What we saw him do against the Sludge Man wouldn't have been enough, though. Not against the Voice of Belico. But he has allies, servants. The Black Womb kept me off him at every turn."

"Anything that could take Xhreka, though?" Oats asked.

"Some of the *djinn* they've bound, maybe," Jackal replied. "But in earnest? I doubt Crafty needed more than his tongue."

"This ain't the time for Polecat jests, Jack," Fetch said.

Jackal's face was grave. "No jest."

"You think he just talked to her?" Oats said. "Convinced her to become his prisoner?"

"It is more his way," Fetch put in. She looked at Oats. "If he threatened something she cared about . . ."

Oats blew out a hard breath. Fuck, he was a fool-ass. He really did bring this upon them.

"But . . ." Jackal went on with more than a little reluctance. "To talk to her he'd have to get close. No way Hood would have let him, not . . . without a fight."

Fetch and Oats shared a glance, both knowing what Jack was trying to say. The thought of Hoodwink being killed was tough to fathom, but Crafty hadn't mentioned him, avoiding a fact he knew would cause no small amount of wrath.

"I ain't counting any Bastard fallen until I've seen it," Fetch declared. "Especially that Bastard."

"Damn right," Oats grunted.

Jackal nodded, though there wasn't much fervor in it. "Trying to figure out what he'll ask in trade is the same as trying to find his trail. It's folly, but I reckon we should try."

"Likely he don't want to trade anything at all," Oats said.

Fetching frowned. "You think it's a trap."

"He knows what you are, chief. He made that plain. I won't say he fears you, but I wouldn't discount it either. He made sure to tell me he wouldn't make us stronger by moving the plague. Asked if he should hand us the world in the bargain."

Jackal huffed.

"Still, why Xhreka?" Fetch asked. "He could lure us with a dozen others."

"Well, it's sure as shit *us* he wants," Oats said. "Just before he left he said, 'It will be pleasing to see the three of you once again.'"

"He's fucking with us," Jackal said. "It will be plots wrapped in schemes coated in lies. Same as before."

"With just enough truth to keep us off balance," Fetch added, face beginning to smolder once more. "Fuck, he may not even have her at all."

"We can't trust in that hope, Fetch, and you know it," Jackal said.

She let silence agree.

Oats tugged his beard. "So what do we do?"

Fetch and Jackal answered in the same moment.

She said, "Before he can speak, we tear him apart."

He said, "We cut his fucking head off soon as his mouth opens."

"He knows you'll try," Oats told them. "He's expecting it. *And* we don't know when he'll show himself again. He just said we'd be together."

They all three looked uneasily at the door.

"Suet-stuffed cunt," Fetch swore. "He's already got us squirming."

Jackal stood. "Sure way to fix that."

"What are you thinking?" Fetch asked.

"He was here just hours ago," Jackal replied. "For all his sorcery he can't have gone far. Chasing him for a year taught me that much. He's no faster than anyone. Let me go after him. I may finally get my hands on him. Even if I don't he'll know I'm hounding him. Might make him less bold. At the very least it keeps us apart so he can't do whatever he intends."

"For all we know he said that just to separate us," Fetch said.

"And if not that leaves Xhreka in his hands longer," Oats added.

Jackal bared his teeth in a silent snarl of frustration. "What then?"

The door flew open. Ahlamra crossed the room at a run, arm extended.

"Chief," she said, breathless.

Fetch took the small fold of parchment from her and unfurled it, eyes darting across the small script. Her face fell, causing Oats to stand.

"Chief?" he asked.

Jackal took a step closer.

"It's from Marrow," Fetching said, eyes locked on the message. "Hispartha landed a fleet at Urci. They're marching on Thricehold."

Oats swallowed. "How long before they reach it?"

"Not faster than we can fly," Jackal said. "Let's go, Fetch."

He nearly collided with Tarif in the doorjamb.

Fetch looked up from Marrow's note. "*Shaykh,* your men find something?"

The man shook his head. "No. My northern outriders have returned with tidings."

The room seemed to be holding its breath. Oats certainly was.

Tarif delivered the news to Fetching with the bluntness of an experienced warlord. "An army is moving through the pass you name the Mother's Whip. My men estimate three thousand light horse in the vanguard. Half that number of heavy horse follows with infantry of uncertain numbers at the rear. The van will reach us in less than two days."

Oats felt his heart quicken. The frails were in the Lots, and now so was the war.

TWELVE

MORE THAN A DOZEN BIRDS took flight from the roof of the keep, bearing messages across the Lots.

Fetch took to the sky with them. Alone.

Oats stood beside Jackal and watched the rokh carry their chief east, toward Thricehold. She too bore a message. It was the answer to Hispartha's invasion, but it was not scrawled on a sliver of paper. It would be written in the frails' blood.

Jackal had not liked being left behind. He'd made arguments. The chief gave orders.

Oats could see his friend's irritation fading as Fetch shrank from view. By the time she was swallowed by glare and clouds, Jackal's bulging jaw had ground his rancor to dust.

"We've a heap to do," he said, turning for the stairs.

The climb up had not been easy on Oats, but within the aches there were muscles waking and his breath returned quicker than it had fled. He kept up with Jackal during the descent and didn't feel a need to collapse into a chair when they reached the bottom. Still, Thistle was waiting with an expression both admonishing and concerned. Muro was at her hip, though he was excited at Oats's return from the roof, where the boy was forbidden to go. Oats was grateful there was at least one person in this damn fortress who didn't fret about him being killed by a flight of stairs. As Muro ran to embrace Oats's leg, Jackal stepped toward Thistle.

"Darlin'," he said, and leaned to greet the woman with a kiss on the cheek. "Sorry we rushed by. The chief—"

"I know," Thistle cut him off with a gentle clasp on his forearm. "You're forgiven."

Jackal kissed her again and turned to Oats. "I'll see to the hogs. Can you gather the others?"

"I can." Oats put a hand on Muro's back and pointed at Jackal. "Do you remember who this is? My friend?"

Muro regarded Jackal for a moment, his twitches growing spirited with concentration. "Chackle."

Thistle snorted a laugh she tried to hold back. Oats didn't bother to suppress his merriment and beamed at Jackal. "That's right. I need you to help him in the stables. Make sure Ug doesn't gore him. Can you do that?"

"Yes," Muro said, happy with the task. He loved Ugfuck almost as much as he loved Oats. For the hog's part, it was possible he favored the boy over his rider.

"Chase me, please, Chackle!" Muro cried, and bounded out of the keep.

Thistle pressed a hand over her mouth and shook with laughter.

"What am I missing?" Jackal asked as he moved to follow the boy.

"'Chackle' is the same word he uses for his cock," Oats was pleased to tell him. Thistle was turning red.

"Wish he'd have been there the day I became sworn, then," Jackal declared, walking briskly backward. "That's a much more fitting hoof-name!"

"Considering your cod and the boy's are about the same size, I reckon that's true!" Oats called after him.

Thistle let loose when he was gone, laughing so hard she had to clutch Oats for support.

"Oh," she said when she caught her breath. She wiped at her eyes. "I won't be able to look at him now."

"Good," Oats grunted. "About time at least one woman can't."

Thistle stared at the door to the yard, sobering. "You're leaving, aren't you? Jack's going to the stables because you're both leaving."

"Not just us," Oats replied.

She looked up at him, eyes wet from laughing, but clouded with sudden worry. "Who else?"

Oats cocked his head at the door. "Tell you as we walk."

Out in the yard, the castile was queerly calm. The garrison moved along the battlements, their pace measured. That spoke to Tarif's leadership and the discipline of the Zahracenes. There was no need to run about making frantic preparations for the coming enemy. They'd known this would happen. The men had been ready for months.

"You're coming with us to Mongrel's Cradle," Oats told Thistle as they passed a group of men pushing a cartful of gunpowder. "You and Muro."

Thistle was thoughtful, silent. At last she nodded, looking a pebble's toss in front of her feet.

"Too dangerous to stay," Oats went on, feeling a powerful need to fill the silence. "Crown's going to want their stronghold back. Past time you two were with the others. With me along to take him, reckon Muro won't fuss. Hoping he won't anyway."

Hells, he was just spewing the obvious.

"Jackal weren't happy with it," he said, forcing laughter into his voice. "He wanted to go with the chief, help her fight the frails at Thricehold, but she needs him to speak with the Traedrians. Their boats need to do more than haul goods. Fetch needs them to join the fight, destroy Hispartha's fleets or at least make it tougher for them to land. Anywise... Jack will be with us, so you don't need to worry about nothing. You and Muro will be safe."

She gave him a chastening look for discounting himself. He shrugged, knowing the truth. Thistle placed a hand on his arm and a look of sympathy on her face. She gave no comforting words of denial, no false encouragement. She merely recognized that he didn't feel like his old self, accepted his diminished strength. Rather than anger blossoming from bruised pride, Oats felt only gratitude.

Thistle surveyed the battlements as they walked. "Tarif can't hold out forever. Not against what's coming."

Oats grew disturbed. Thistle had been so vital to the hoof, such a part of them for so long, it was easy to forget that she'd lived in the kingdom. Hispartha was her home in some painful, unspoken-of past.

"How long do you reckon?" Oats asked. Tarif had promised the chief the castile would stand at least a year.

"Depends on what else the Crown brings other than men," Thistle replied. Her voice was flat. She looked up at Oats, haunted. "What hurt you isn't the worst of it."

The face of the Maiden Spear entered Oats's mind. His wounds began to throb, stirred by the memory. But it was the recollection that the risen woman's weapon had been able to harm the chief that set his skin to crawling. Oats looked to the sky, wondering what awaited Fetching at Thricehold.

"All the more reason to get you away from here," he told Thistle.

She nodded again, but Oats could see the thought of leaving the Zahracenes to fight Hispartha alone troubled her. It troubled him too, being earnest. Being more earnest, neither of them would make a difference if they stayed. Tarif had his men, loyal and seasoned, as well as the castile itself. Strong towers, thick walls, and the guns they hosted would prove enough to hold the Crown back until help arrived. That's what Fetch had said. Oats could only believe her.

He and Thistle made their way to the large breaking paddock within the yard where the castile's cavaleros had once drilled and trained. The Zahracenes, fierce horsemen to a man, used it to exercise their own animals now. Today, however, it wasn't occupied by men and horses, but mongrels and hogs.

Sluggard was astride Palla in the paddock's center, turning the hog in place to shout instructions at Rant and Roar as they ran their own mounts in a pacing circuit.

"Roar, sit straight! You're mane munching again! Rant, stop letting Gorria slow! Keep that sow at a good trot!"

Oats had seen little of the other mongrels since reaching the castile. Fetch had sent Cut Wolf, Knuckle Child, and the rest of his escort either back to the Pit or to their respective hoofs. Sluggard had remained to ensure the rescued shipwrights had the skills their new life required. From the looks of it, he'd had . . . difficulty. Rant and Roar both looked uneasy in the saddle. The brother's balance was poor, and the sister was struggling to keep firm control of her hog. Both wore determined expressions, but neither would have made it out of the slops in days gone by, not with years of instruction.

But the chief didn't need them to ride into battle, just as far as the Guadal-kabir.

Oats called out to Sluggard and leaned on the paddock fence. Thistle stood beside him, watching as the three mongrels rode over.

"We out of time?" Sluggard asked as he reined up. It was barely a question.

"We are," Oats replied. He looked at the mongrel siblings. "You two ready?"

Roar glowered and nodded.

Rant cocked a thumb at Sluggard. "Ask him."

"They're ready." Slug was a good liar.

Oats noted there were no stockbows on the new bloods' backs, which meant they hadn't even attempted thrummery while mounted. He wondered if they could hit the wide side of an elephant while standing still on their own feet, but decided not to ask. No sense shaming them.

They departed the castile beneath the afternoon sun.

Ahlamra and Tarif bid them farewell at the gatehouse. The *shaykh* insisted that two score of his warriors escort them to the river, but Jackal protested. The men sent risked not making it back before the Hisparthan vanguard arrived. Tarif's honor and Jackal's good sense waged a small skirmish. They settled on an escort through the first night and clasped wrists.

The Zahracenes utilized stallions as well as mares, the first for their heavy cavalry, the second for their lighter equipped—and faster moving—outriders. It was the swifter mounts that went with them, the unarmored men on their backs carrying bows and scimitars.

They rode west at an easy pace. Muro sat in front of Oats, squirming and squealing at the thrill of being astride Ugfuck. Thistle rode double with Sluggard, an arrangement that hindered one of their seasoned fighters, but it was better than putting her with the inexperienced shipwrights. She wasn't strong enough to handle a barbarian, and horses and hogs didn't always make the best company, preventing her from having her own mount. The Zahracenes were careful to ride a stretch removed. Jackal led their tiny hoof atop Mean Old Man. The black hog had languished at the castile while Jack was off with Fetch on her damn buzzard. He was burning to throw some dust, but Jackal held him back, heeding Oats's plea before they departed that he would stay close.

"What do you think I'm going to do, Oats?" Jackal had asked with a smile as they made the traditional final adjustments to their tack. "Ride off and abandon you?"

Oats had wrestled with saying anything and quickly regretted it. "No. I . . . want to be sure is all."

"Of me?" Jack was still smiling, but Oats could see the first sprouts of agitation breaking the crust of his good humor.

"Not you. Of them. Muro and Thistle."

Jackal fastened another full quiver to his saddle. "That boy will be fine so long as you are close. As for Thistle . . ." Jack leaned over his hog's back and winked. "Reckon she could handle you being a cock's length closer."

"I ain't jesting here, Jack."

"Neither am I," he replied. He had that bright, brotherly look on his face. The one that could always make Oats smile. Not then.

"I need you to do what I can't."

His stern words caused a dispirited ripple to run across Jackal's face. It was there and gone, but Oats caught it. Jackal knew what he was asking and had a choice. He could face the truth or ∴.

"Sure. But even if Fetch wouldn't kill me, Thistle was used to Roundth, so I think your third thrice-blood leg would serve her better."

"I AIN'T PLAYING, YOU SMIRKING CUNT!"

His voice burst through the new stables, those Fetch had constructed just for the hogs. Ugfuck startled and shied. Even Mean Old Man squealed in alarm. Thankfully, Muro was off helping Thistle collect their few possessions. A few stalls away, Sluggard, Roar, and Rant looked up, their own tasks frozen.

As Oats fumed, Jackal slowly stepped around the partition between their stalls. Oats was taller than just about everyone he'd ever known, but it was rare he felt so big in front of his friend. His fury made the difference almost dizzying. But as Jack reached to place a hand on his shoulder, fix him with a piercing, caring stare, he was shriveled by shame.

"They're going to be safe, brother," Jackal told him. "I'll see to it. And so will you. You're more recovered than you think."

No, brother. I'm less recovered than you want to believe.

He should have said it. Instead, he'd swallowed and nodded, wanting the confrontation—and his harsh words—snuffed.

Now, with the sun setting, Oats helped Muro down from the saddle and gathered himself to dismount. They'd only ridden a piece of a day, but it was enough to leave him sore and stiffened. Camp was swiftly made in the ocherous plains near one of the streams stubborn enough to survive this far from its source in the Amphora Mountains. The Zahracenes kept a quarter of their number ahorse and on watch in shifts, forming a protective picket. The remaining men rested at a courteous but noticeable distance, their language as foreign as the smells from their cookfires.

Oats sat on the ground, chewing the last of a date. Muro was at his side, singing tunelessly to himself and drawing in the dust. Across their fire, Jackal rose and ambled over to the Zahracene camp, effortlessly crossing the distance and the invisible divide. He claimed his Urzhar wasn't perfect, but Oats never got the sense he struggled to make himself understood among the swaddlehead tribesmen. Hells, at a distance it was hard to tell him apart from the desert frails, dressed as he was. A little taller, broader, but the strict manners of the Zahracenes toward outsiders relaxed when he was among them.

Easy laughter soon followed his arrival. Looking on, Oats couldn't recall the last time he'd seen his friend laugh surrounded by the Bastards.

"Gold-shitting cat."

Oats looked over Muro's head at Rant, seated just beyond her already-sleeping brother. Her gaze was fixed on Jackal.

"Pardon?" Oats said.

Rant's knees were drawn up, encircled by her arms. She turned her head and smiled at Oats. "That's what my papi called men like that one." She tilted her head Jackal's way. "A gold-shitting cat. Welcome anywhere. At home anywhere."

Sluggard's back was to the Zahracenes. He twisted to look and gave a hum before turning back to the fire.

"He walks like he's doing the earth a favor," Roar grumbled without opening his eyes.

Oats glowered, but Rant spoke up before he could tell the sleep-feigning fuck to mind his tongue.

"You're just jealous he can have any woman he wants," she needled. "Unlike you, uglier than an old sailor's nut basket."

"She ain't wrong," Oats put in. "On either account."

Roar raised a hand off his stomach long enough to give a dismissive wave.

Sluggard too, appeared done with the subject. He tossed a bread heel into the fire and stood, not looking at anyone as he walked away. Oats felt a pang of guilt. All that talk of Jackal's prowess with women must have been like a kick to the cods for Slug. Cods he didn't fucking have anymore. And it weren't all he lost. The castration had softened his body, adding a fleshy layer over once hard-etched muscles. To look at him now, none would suspect Sluggard's name had once been a wry jest.

"Oats," Thistle said from behind. He turned and found her holding a jar the size of his fist. She raised it slightly. "We should get this done."

He grimaced. "Reckon I can forego."

"Oh no," Thistle exclaimed, shaking her head. "Hafsa's instructions were firm. She made Ahlamra repeat them to me four times. Come. No grousing."

Oats bit back a noise that would certainly have been considered a grouse and pulled his shirt over his head, dragging the kerchief off in the doing. He hadn't even worn a brigand, unable to bear the weight of the armored vest against his wounds. Thistle knelt behind him and went to work removing his bandages. When she pulled the stopper from the jar to apply the salve within, Oats bit down on the inside of his mouth. It wasn't the pain of the stuff being applied, though there was some, it was the damn smell. He didn't know what the medicine was made from but it reeked worse than vinegar.

Oats saw Rant try to sneak her nose into her cupped hand. He could hear Thistle continuously clearing her throat, quiet as she tried to be. Roar coughed and turned on his side, facing away. All tried to hide their discomfort for his sake. Almost all . . .

"Hhelch! Stink!" Muro shouted. "Oads, you stink!"

It was Jackal and the Zahracenes' turn to look over as the littler camp erupted with laughter.

Oats laughed loudest of all.

FOUR DAYS AFTER LEAVING THE castile, their band of five hogs reached the banks of the Guadal-kabir. Jackal had been careful with their course, making certain they struck the waterway well south of Kalbarca. Oats was always amazed at the size of the great river. You could loose a thrumbolt and fail to hit the opposite bank.

"Ever been on the water?" Jackal asked Muro, his smile widening encouragingly as the boy shook his head. "You will today. We'll take the river all the way to the sea. Then we sail east along the coast to Mongrel's Cradle."

Roar squinted hard against the sun's glare coming off the river's surface. "Unless these hogs float better than I realize, all that's going to be damn difficult without a ship."

"Fetch sent word," Jackal replied, unruffled. "Someone will be waiting for us before the confluence of the Alhundra. We'll ride downstream until we find them."

It didn't take long. Fourteen men and a moored vessel greeted them within a few miles.

Roar wasn't impressed. "That's more barge than boat."

"Enough," Rant chided as she dismounted, though Oats saw her own critical eyes never left the vessel.

Oats knew shit about ships, but this one had a single mast and broad deck. A ramp at her middle connected ship to shore. A wiry-limbed man with a keg for a belly disembarked to greet them.

"You Burgos?" Jackal asked.

"I am," the man answered.

From beneath his salt-stained leather skullcap, Burgos took them all in, sun-narrowed eyes lingering on the hogs. His weathered face was branded on one cheek, a puckered white scar forming an X-shaped island amid coarse grey stubble. Oats reckoned he was well into his sixties. Too old to be pirating as a means of survival, but former prisoners had little choice.

"I'm captain," he said, hooking a thumb at his chest. The gnarled hand swung in the direction of the deck. "That's the *Mariposa*, and those are my boys aboard. Several of them have had their tongues split, so don't take offense if they neglect to get acquainted."

"Boys" was generous. Of the thirteen crewmen, nine looked of an age with Burgos, all similarly branded. Of the younger men only one was untouched by the jailer's iron. Their baldrics were weighted with knives, swords, and hatchets.

"Our hold won't fit all them swine," Burgos said, still sizing up the barbarians. "I'd advise we put the more spirited below and them you deem more docile on deck. Still be cramped, but we'll manage."

"Good," Jackal said. "Mean Old Man will need to go below."

"Palla can handle the deck," Sluggard said. He looked at Roar's mount. "Blue Snout too. But I'd suggest Gorria be confined."

"Oats?" Jackal said. "What do you reckon for Ug?"

Burgos cocked a dubious eye at Ugfuck and clicked his tongue. "That one will take up most of the hold."

"He'll be fine above," Oats said.

Jackal guided all the hogs on board, one at a time. It was a good dose of caution. Never did know how a barbarian would react to such things and if one decided to get stubborn, better for Jackal to get ripped by a tusk than someone whose flesh didn't knit in the time it takes to have a piss.

The crew helped load and secure their saddles and other belongings, the coffin dodgers as deft as the younger men, and they were soon under way.

Oats followed Burgos as he led Thistle and Muro to the canvas canopy at the rear of the ship beneath which were a few pallets. The crew clearly slept in shifts when necessary, the *Mariposa* requiring nearly all hands to navigate the river. Burgos dipped a tin cup into a water barrel and drew a drink for woman and child.

"Bring you some food in a small while," the captain said. "You can rest here until."

"Thank you," Thistle said.

The old pirate ducked out from beneath the canvas and began giving orders.

Muro was exhausted and Thistle bade him lie upon one of the pallets. He didn't fight her and, with her hand gently rubbing his back, he was soon asleep.

"You should sleep too," she whispered at Oats.

He shook his head.

"Oats. No one will think less of you."

Oats took a drink from the barrel, downed a second cup and then a third. The fresh water in the tin, the shade of the canvas, and the motion of the boat were a lulling relief after the long ride. Time was he could have stayed out for weeks and thought nothing of it. But he was damn tired.

"What can you do out there?" Thistle pressed, lifting her chin toward the deck. "You're no sailor. It's a task for Burgos and his men now."

Outside the canvas, Rant and Roar had melded fluidly with the crew's labor; she climbing the mast with a rope in her teeth, he doing some mystery with the sail. Burgos and two of his men were looking on, impressed grins on their faces. Sluggard was finishing a rope paddock for the hogs on deck. Jackal must still have been below.

There truly was nothing for Oats to do. He loosed a breath of defeat and eased himself down on the pallet next to Muro's.

Thistle smiled at him.

Next instant, Jackal was gently shaking the toe of his boot.

"Food," he said. Beyond him the sky was purple. No one else was beneath the canvas.

Oats sat up. "Shit." He hadn't meant to sleep so long. "I'm up."

Jackal offered him a hand. "Not yet you ain't."

Oats accepted the help and they went out on deck together.

Dusk was upon the river, the dark water streaked with harsh blazes beneath a bruised sky. The sail was full, the crew mostly at ease. They took their food standing, watching the crawling shoreline as they cradled their bowls, slowly pushing steaming spoons past their lips.

Oats joined the others at the front of the ship, giving Ugfuck a rubdown as he passed. Muro sat on a large coil of rope, Thistle hovering over him, occasionally helping him take bites. The boy struggled sometimes and the growing darkness wasn't helping.

"You had anything yet?" Oats asked Thistle.

She shook her head. "I will when he's done."

"I got him." Oats hunkered next to the boy and took over. "Any good?"

Muro didn't answer. He never spoke during meals. The castile's stablemaster used to beat the boys if they did. Try as Oats might, he couldn't convince Muro that would no longer happen. Slowly, together, they got to the bottom of the boy's bowl. Thistle took it, passing Oats his portion.

He ate so swiftly, he could not have said what the stew contained. It was hot. It was cooked. It was worthy of worship.

Standing beside him, Jackal silently offered down his half-finished bowl. Oats huffed a laugh. It was an old jest from childhood. "Give Idris your supper if you don't want to lose your hand."

"Grateful, but no," Oats said. "Appetite ain't what it was."

Jackal went back to his far more measured pace of eating, tapping the spoon softly into the center of the bowl between mouthfuls.

Burgos strolled over. "Everyone fed?"

There were sounds of assent and expressions of gratitude. Oats made sure Muro thanked the captain as well.

"Good," Burgos said. He looked to Jackal. "Unless you say otherwise, I've a mind to moor us for the night. We can run her in the dark, but I prefer to court risk only when there's no choice."

"Very well," Jackal replied. "But it's important we get to the Cradle swiftly."

"We'll have you at the mouth in two days. Take a span longer to reach the Sons' port even if the Gut is kind."

"Understood."

"That warm stew in your bellies is going to pull your eyelids down in a hurry," Burgos declared. "You're each welcome to the comfort of the stern. Me and my boys will be just fine on deck, those of us that still sleep. Age tends to keep one restless."

Thistle gave a sigh of relief at the captain's invitation and stood. "Guess I'm not too old yet, then."

Burgos doffed his cap. "No, fair woman, I attest you are far from that."

Thistle smiled at the flattery and gave Oats a questioning look.

"Go ahead," he told her. "I'll see Muro to sleep."

"I'm with you," Jackal said, falling into step behind Thistle.

"Only if you dream about me, Jaco," she teased as they walked for the canvas tenting together.

Burgos chuckled. "Those two might feel they reposed a touch early. Guillelmo!"

The man called arrived with a bottle.

Roar perked up. "That wine?"

Burgos pulled the stopper. "Hisparthan to boot."

Roar all but snatched the offered bottle out of the man's hand. Oats could hardly blame him. The Zahracenes shunned wine, and the castile's stores had been distributed between the mongrel hoofs at Fetch's order. A barrel had even reached Oats and Anvil at the Pit during the winter.

"Like hells you're drinking it all!" Rant declared, wrestling the upturned bottle away from her brother's lips. She took a barely more moderate swig and gave the bottle to Sluggard. He did not drink. His eyes bored into Burgos. Oats now noticed his stew was also untouched.

"Didn't figure the Crown's prisons would foster such generous kindness," Sluggard said to the captain.

Burgos wobbled his head in consideration. "Crown's prison didn't. Mother's knee did. If I'd remembered that upbringing as a younger man, may not have ever been a guest of His Majesty."

Sluggard didn't blink.

The old sailor took a step, reached over, and retrieved the spoon from the suspicious mongrel's bowl. He ate a bite. Next, he gently pinched the wine and took a long pull.

Placing the bottle back in Sluggard's hand, he gave a nod. "Porridge in the morning won't be poisoned either. Well . . . not on purpose."

The next morning, the wind was less kind, less generous.

The crew took the *Mariposa*'s oars, six to a side and pulled with the current, hastening their progress toward the sea. Rant and Roar took a turn on the benches, sitting opposite each other and casting insults. Soon their bickering competition put them off the rhythm and their mongrel muscles were sweeping at near twice the pace of the other men, forcing Burgos to relieve them of the duty.

At midday, the captain ducked his head beneath the canopy where Oats and Thistle sat while Muro napped.

"Ever seen the city of Sparthis?" Burgos whispered.

Oats shook his head and the man made a coaxing gesture. Thistle and Oats crept away, joining the others astern. The broad waters of the Guadal-kabir spread out before them, banishing the notion that Ul-wundulas was a barren land. Burgos pointed ahead.

Oats knew the once prosperous city of Sparthis was destroyed during the Great Orc Incursion, but the ruins sat upon an island in the middle of the Guadal-kabir, far from the Bastards' lot, and near impossible to view from the saddle besides. The river provided a far better view. The island drew closer by the instant, dead ahead.

"My grandfather used to tell us Sparthis was founded by Herathos Lionclad himself," Burgos said.

"Our father said the same," Roar replied as Rant nodded wistfully, the wind playing with her hair.

Soon, they came up on the island and swung starboard—a word one-eyed Ferran, the ship's pilot, had recently made sure Oats knew—for the port fork was blocked by the massive sundered arches of a collapsed bridge. What was left of Sparthis could be glimpsed through ragged holes in the outer wall. Oats could not make much of the place beyond buildings of white stone abused by war and neglect so that now they resembled old dingy bones. Whatever it had been in its glory, the only virtue left was its size.

Burgos leaned on the railing, watching as the pocked wall continued to dominate the view. He grinned at the mongrel shipwrights and wagged a finger between Jackal and Oats. "Likely these Lotborn heathens never heard tell of ole Lionclad, eh?"

"Can't say we have," Jackal replied, smiling at Oats. "But I know an old man who wants to tell a story when I hear one."

Thistle wrapped her arms around one of Oats's as the captain cleared his throat and gave Jackal a good-humored shit-eye.

"Son of a god, was Herathos," he began. "A great hero from before even the Imperium. Journeyed here from Al-Unan, though it was known by another name then before Tyrkania came a'conquering..." Burgos's face scrunched with concentration, soon relaxing with regret. "Gone and forgotten what it was called. My grandfather knew... damn."

"Lapithia," Sluggard and Thistle offered at the same moment.

Burgos snapped his fingers as if the answer had come to him, soliciting laughter from his audience. "Lapithia! Anywise, Herathos came on some great quest, founded this city here, Sparthis, and when he left he went south to the Gut. Now, there was no sea then, just this deep basin filled with a great forest. Who did Herathos meet down there? The elves. So he tarried a time, likely because he was defiling countless point-ear maids—Shit." His sheepish eyes went wide as they darted between Rant and Thistle. "Pardons. That was rough talk."

"Don't shrink from the best details, old man!" Rant declared, beaming.

Burgos rapped his knuckles on the railing. "Stuck his cod in every hole he could get! Gods are lusty as goats."

Even Roar couldn't help but laugh at the amount the captain was enjoying himself.

"So! When it comes time for old Lionclad to take his leave, he decides to go south. But the elves warn him there is nothing that way but death. Herathos says he doesn't fear death. Elves say death is like a hungry dog. It will bite the fearful man, but follow the brave one. Of course, the rustskins being naked savages living in the wilderness, Herathos damns their warning and goes south, climbs up out of the basin on the other side and there he discovers . . ."

"Dhar'gest," Jackal said after the expectant pause.

Burgos winked. "Reckoned even godless half-breeds would know that part. Yes. Land of the orcs! And for the first time this great hero, this slayer of lions and monsters, this son of a god faces something stronger than he. Maybe not one orc, maybe not even ten, but *the* orcs—all of them—*that* he cannot defeat. So he flees. Back down into the elves' deep wood he goes. And as they warned, death followed him. Herathos, realizing he could not prevent the destruction of the elves' home, smote the side of the basin and cracked the earth, allowing the ocean to flood the great forest. He and the rustskins climbed out to safety, believing they'd drowned the orcs and created a barrier with the Deluged Sea that would prevent them from ever invading again." Burgos lifted his chin at Sparthis. "We know how wrong he was. Took the orcs a few thousand years, but they got revenge on Herathos."

"No." Thistle shook her head. "They didn't. This city was just some monument to his vanity. Might as well have been a statue of his cock. You think he cared about this place, if he existed at all? I don't. This wasn't his home."

"True," Burgos grunted. He looked at the passing ruin for a long time in silence. "But it was mine."

Oats thought of Winsome, now burned and abandoned. "Must hurt, seeing it this way."

The old river pirate stood up from the rail.

"Nah," he lied. "It's been knocked down for more years now than I lived in it as a free man. Besides, I got to see the thicks run out. That was balm enough for me."

Oats and Jackal shared a look. There was a tale they *did* know, and knew to be true. Hispartha could not dislodge the orcs from Sparthis during the Incursion and gave it up for lost. It was the Claymaster and the half-orc hog riders that would soon become the mongrel hoofs that finally drove them out. Creep and several of the other Bastards Oats remembered from childhood had been there, though they never spoke of it. Mostly, he begged the story from Beryl, who heard it after Warbler got drunk one night and his tongue loosened.

As a slave, the Claymaster had been a sapper, forced by Hisparthan nobles to undermine castle walls in their wars against each other. He knew how to bring a fortress down and used that knowledge to crack Sparthis so he and his riders could get to grips with the orcs. That was what Oats had known as a child. Now he knew that the Claymaster not only breached the walls but rode in with the other eight plague-bearers to unleash the vile sorcery chained within their bodies. The orcs were huddling behind captured walls to avoid the plague, the only thing they feared. And it came in after them.

"Those ash-coloreds did us a great service that day," Burgos said as they floated by the last of Sparthis.

Oats had never heard that slur uttered with respect, but somehow the captain managed it.

As the island and its ruins receded, here and there on both banks the ship began to pass a procession of fallen castles. The broken teeth of watchtowers came next. Soon, the river was hemmed by a cemetery of fortifications.

Burgos made a rude sound in his throat. "Hispartha! Tried to protect their precious port." He waved a hand at the shores. "All this to keep the wealth of Sparthis safe from everyone. Anyone! The Traedrian fleet, the Tyrkanian fleet. Pirates from Kyrneolis. They even feared raiders from Calmaris would come back in their longships to pillage as they'd done hundreds of years before. And what happened?"

This time it was Jackal and Oats who answered in unison. "The orcs."

This time, there was no laughter.

"The orcs!" Burgos exclaimed. "On foot! Perhaps if the Crown had built all this at the Gut, eh? We would have been spared the Incursion."

The defenses ended with two great towers standing sentry on opposite banks of the river. As the *Mariposa* passed beneath them, all the elder crewmen stood away from their oars. Burgos and the old men scowled at the tower on the east bank. Almost as one, they spat. Only when the boat had drifted beyond did they take up rowing once more.

Burgos shifted uneasily. "Might seem a touch churlish to you. That display. But we swore we'd never labor beneath that damned place again. And we meant it." The old sailor cast a hand over his shoulder, dismissing the towers without giving them a backward glance. "That was their greatest defense. A chain that could be raised across the river, block passage to the port. Towers to protect the winches, prisoners to work the winches. No warring fleets ever came upriver, but we raised that chain four times a day all the same, to ensure we were fast enough if the time ever came to do it in earnest." He gave a bitter, wet chuckle and shook his head. "Our prison became our sanctuary when the thicks came. The city fell, but not us. We held that tower. For months. The lower levels leaked, so we had water, but . . . the things we ate . . . Still, we wouldn't have made it if the Claymaster hadn't come. Never did repay him, so now I get my chance with the next great mongrel warlord. Your Fetching is going to finish what was started and free Ul-wundulas from the Crown. May not live to see it, but I'll die to aid it."

Oats felt Thistle's grip tighten around his arm. In that squeeze he felt her hope that it wouldn't come to that and her knowledge that, for many, it would. Perhaps that was simply what lay eating at his own heart.

Roar leaned forward sharply, putting a hand to his brow as he looked far downstream. "You may get your chance, old man. Today."

Everyone followed his gaze. Sluggard cursed.

Oats couldn't make out much. He didn't have Fetching's vision, or even Roar's apparently. Squinting hard, he could just make out another, larger, ship on the river. No, three ships. Or five?

"Lionclad's balls," Burgos swore. "Tell me those aren't . . ."

"A dromon and six war galleys," Rant said with grim certainty. "It's a Hisparthan fleet."

THIRTEEN

BURGOS LEFT THE PROW TO give orders, swift yet calm. The *Mariposa* began to turn, quick at the first and then sluggish as it cut across the wind. Holding to the side with one hand, Oats placed his other on Thistle's back, straining to aid their balance. He heard the mast creak, the snapping voice of the sail, but kept his eyes on the Hisparthan fleet for as long as he was able. Soon enough, the *Mariposa* came around and began to crawl upstream. The old river pirates bent to the oars.

"Is there even a chance we can outrun them?" Sluggard asked.

Roar made an ugly noise in his throat.

Rant was more elaborate. "The dromon, maybe. But not the galleys. Not for long."

"They may not give chase," Jackal said. His voice was steady, but Oats could see him tensing with the growing danger. It wasn't fear, but excitement. "One little boat. Why bother?"

"Because we ran."

Thistle's numb reply drew the gazes of the half-orcs. The woman's eyes lifted and fixed on the stern shelter, where Muro stood peeking out, roused and confused by the lurching vessel. Slipping free of Oats's touch, she made her way toward the boy.

Oats let her go, wanting to follow, but . . . not enough, it seemed.

"So we pull them damn oars," he said, gesturing at his fellow mongrels. "*Us.* Let these old frails tend the sails and jibs and shit."

"This ship doesn't have a jib," Roar told him.

"You know my fucking meaning! Not a frail alive that can match a half-orc at such labor, even if they was young."

"Those galleys will have two dozen oars per side," Roar said. "With two men per bench. And they may not even be men."

Oats didn't like the sound of that. "The hells does that mean?"

"He means Hispartha loves to use half-orcs as galley slaves," Sluggard said. "Was almost one myself before the carnavales."

"You were fortunate, then," Rant told him. They shared a look and Sluggard replied with a weighted nod.

Oats felt his jaw clamp down. He could no longer make out the ships. He hoped it was because they had chosen not to pursue and not because his eyes were shit.

"If we can't outrun them on the river, we surely can on land." He turned to Jackal. "Let's get to the shore, straddle our damn razors, and get gone."

Jackal's face went slack. "Oats. We can't just flee and allow them to come unchallenged."

"Unchall—? Hells overburdened, Jack, it's seven fucking ships! And that's what we saw! Could be twice that many!"

"Could be *half* and you'd still be insane," Rant said, gawking at Jackal as if his mind were already beyond saving.

"Seven ships, a dozen, what does it matter?" Jackal pointed upriver. "However many, they are coming to resupply and reinforce Kalbarca. They do and our chances of retaking it are dust. Our wreckers are watching for ships from the north. There is nothing to prevent this fleet from sailing right to the city's port. Just us!"

Jackal got that look, the one Oats had known his entire life, the one that said he was about to do something brave and fool-ass. Before Oats—or anyone—could wrangle him, Jackal darted off, calling for the captain.

"Here we fucking go," Oats grumbled, shaking his head as he followed.

"The river chain," Jack was saying as he caught up. "How many men would it take to raise?"

Burgos shook his head before all the words were out of the mongrel's mouth. "Can't be done. Even if we were willing to go back in that damn tower—which we aren't—too damn old and not enough of us. And you'd need twenty more men in the tower on the other shore. Besides, the gears have sat untended for over thirty years. The workings will be rotten. No, lad. That chain will stay abed in the muck at the bottom of the river."

Jackal accepted that with a nod and clenched teeth. His eyes glazed, his jaw bulged, his mind searching for another way.

Oats grabbed his arm, yanked him away from whatever scheme was beginning to seduce his thoughts. "We need to make land."

"He's right," Burgos said. "They'll be on us by the time you're unloaded, but—"

"What?" Jackal demanded. "We put heel to hog and leave you to them? You want a second brand on your face, old man?"

"Crown don't give a second. Branded outlaws are put to death." The grizzled captain's eyes twinkled. "And we wouldn't have another fate."

Oats hated the notion of these men dying for them, but he knew in his guts it would be folly to suggest they abandon their ship and run. The deck was their saddle, the boat their hog.

Rant's shouting voice snatched their attentions.

"One galley pulling ahead! They're giving chase!"

"Whatever you reckon to do, best do it fast," Burgos said, chin and eyes lifting toward the prow.

Ahead, Sparthis and its island loomed out of the water, an axe blade of earth and stone cleaving the river in two. Both passages appeared clear, but Oats knew from their trip downriver that the right fork was blocked at the north end. The left contained no such impediment, but if they took it and disembarked they'd find themselves on the western side of the river. The wrong side. There was no crossing the Guadal-kabir this close to the delta. Riding south would only bring them into the sucking embrace of the Old Maiden Marsh. They'd be forced to turn back, ride north until they could ford the river. *If* they could ford the river. The frails would likely have all the crossings watched by then. The fleet behind them was bringing enough men for the job. Even if they could avoid being caught, it'd be weeks in the saddle before they reached the Sons' lot.

Jackal clapped a hand on Burgos's shoulder and pointed toward the right fork. "Will Hispartha know about the fallen bridge?"

"Likely," the captain replied. "Unless the man in command is some blue blood given a ship by the queen just 'cause of who his padre was. Wouldn't want to wager he's an ignorant, regardless."

"Take us in," Jackal decided without pause. "Take us right."

Burgos didn't balk. He hollered the orders to his crew and the pilot angled the steering oar. The *Mariposa* swung for the eastern channel.

Oats didn't find the same ready acceptance of Jack's decision, but Roar beat him to the challenge.

"You *are* fucking moon-brained!" the big frailing exclaimed, stomping across the deck to yell full in Jackal's face. "Taking us in where we can't escape! You'll get us all killed!"

Jackal's calm outmatched Roar's fury. "You know we can't outrun them. Either way we go we're caught. This forces them to make the same hard choice. If they know this side is impassable, they won't bring the whole fleet. Might not even risk one ship."

"And if they don't know?" Roar demanded. "If they all follow? You'll have led us into a very shit position."

Jackal grinned, the folds of his headscarf flattened to one side of his face by the wind. "We'll have led that entire frail fleet into a very shit position too."

Oats watched his friend's bald confidence soften Roar's scowl. It was a reaction he knew well. Truth was, Jackal possessed a bit of sorcery long before he was given a god's blessing. There was a reason Oats had gone along with his daring hogshit since childhood.

They came up on the island's southern tip. The river shrank as they slipped into the eastern channel, yet remained wide enough for a further four vessels their size to sail comfortably abreast. Still, Oats could see Burgos and the crew grow wary, the spills of jagged rubble upon both banks thickening with each stroke of the oars.

Without being bidden, Rant climbed the mast, fast and fluid and barefooted. She held one-handed to the top and hung out, looking behind.

There was a long moment. Even the wind seemed to hold its breath.

Rant looked down at the deck, pitched her voice so they could hear but refrained from shouting.

"They're coming."

"How many?" Burgos asked.

"Two."

Oats glared at Jackal, but found not even a ripple of doubt. He was looking intently ahead, scanning the ruins. To their left the shadow of Sparthis darkened the water. Oats was more focused on the opposite shore where there remained likely spots to moor and make landfall. It wasn't too late. Not yet. Was he craven? Wanting to run? Was that what the Maiden Spear had done to him? If so, it was a worse wound than the skewering. But Oats saw he wasn't the only one with an eye for the right bank. Sluggard's gaze kept darting twixt there and Jackal, hoping he would change their course, growing more agitated with each moment he did not.

"They're beginning to gain."

Rant's report shredded Sluggard's patience. He stepped to Oats, stood beside him, but turned about so he did not face Jackal.

"You can stop this," he hissed.

Oats stared at him. "Me?"

"Give the order to make land."

"I'm not—"

"In command?" Sluggard's eyes blazed as he leaned closer. "Oats. You're the chief's right hand. Jackal's just her hard—"

"Slug," Oats said, quiet and firm. "Don't."

Sluggard took a breath, his face cooling, but only enough not to heat Oats's own temper. "The only one on this boat that sees him as above you . . . is you."

"Jack knows what he's doing," Oats said. It wasn't much of an answer.

"Why? Because he can take on an entire fleet alone? He's not alone, though, Oats. We need off this boat." Sluggard stepped fully in front of him, blocking his view of Jackal. "Thistle and Muro need off this boat."

A tether Oats hadn't known was there snapped. He bulled past Sluggard and reached the prow in four strides.

"Jaco, this ain't right. We need to—"

"There!" Jackal said, pointing ahead with a fierce joy. "Thought there was another."

The corpse of a bridge stood before them. Unlike its tumbled twin upriver, this one still partially spanned the river. Once supported by three great arches, only those in the center and on the eastern bank were intact. A gap of sky shone bright between Sparthis and the bridge's ravaged left end.

"Well, fuck me if I hadn't entered my dotage unawares," Burgos said, hurrying over. "I'd forgotten she still stood. Hello there, Isabet, my lass."

Oats cocked an eye at the captain. "Isabet?"

"Named for the highborn lady that leapt from her," Burgos replied, eyes not leaving the bridge. "Imperium likely had another name for her, but she's been Isabet since before my father's time."

"A good sign," Jackal said, giving Oats a wink. He pointed at the center arch, wider and larger than its surviving, flanking fellow. "Can we make it through?"

"Weren't meant to," Burgos said. "Vessels were supposed to use the western channel."

Jackal smirked. "But can we?"

"Aye. Aye, we can, being careful." The captain hustled off to tell his crew.

Jackal called Roar over.

"The Hisparthan galleys," he said. "How tall are their masts?"

"Nine vara to the pulgada," came the answer without hesitation. Oats didn't know his measures the way he should, though Beryl had tried to drum them into his skull. Roar sounded damn certain, though.

Jackal nodded at the approaching bridge. "Reckon they can navigate that?"

The mongrel shipwright squinted hard at the top of the arch.

"You're having to ponder it," Jackal said with relish. "Which means so will the frails. I don't know much about ships, but a fool can see they'll have to come through slower than us. And one at a time."

"Yes, but sending two ships means they suspect a trap," Roar said.

Jackal's smile threatened to split his face. "The second ship *is* the trap."

Oats opened his mouth to ask Jack what the hells he was planning, but was cut off before he voiced the first word.

"Which of you two is the stronger swimmer?" Jackal asked Roar, pointing up to the mast.

Roar's scowl deepened. "Rant. She's a damn eel. Why?"

Jackal didn't answer, the question abandoned and forgotten as their prow pierced the shadow beneath the bridge.

Burgos issued small, encouraging commands to his crew as they guided the vessel through the gullet of the arch. Oats reckoned the tips of their oars were a spear's length from the stone walls. He looked up and saw Rant still perched atop the mast. Boosting herself higher—a move that made Oats's asshole clench—she stretched an arm up toward the curved roof. She couldn't touch it, but the angle made it impossible to see how short she was.

She slid back to a less gut-tingling spot on the mast and called down to the deck.

"Frails'll make it," she said, the words directed at her brother.

Roar huffed. "Have to ship their oars, though. Pole through." His stare lowered to rest on Jackal. "That's if they come through at all. They could lay anchor and wait us out. Smartest course, especially if they know there's nowhere for us to go. Even if they don't know about the block ahead, they'll expect the rest of the fleet to head us off. They believe they have us pinned and, one way or another, they're right."

"We won't know what they'll do until they do it," Jackal said, watching the tunnel's walls pass with languid ease. The *Mariposa* was over halfway through. "Whatever it is, we'll have bought enough time."

"Time?" Oats grunted. "For what?"

"To get you, Thistle, and the boy on land," Jackal told him.

Oats felt his guts sink. More like they were punched, down into his cods. He hadn't expected that. Jack had read his damn mind, or overheard Sluggard, or . . . just knew it was what had to be done. He wasn't crazy. Never had been. Oats should have known better, trusted in all he knew of this mongrel, not just what Slug thought he knew from a far, far shorter brotherhood. Oats should have been relieved, but it was a colder, cutting feeling that seized him. Jackal was going to take on the frails. And he was going to do it without Oats. It had never occurred to him to do it another way. Before setting loose whatever wild hog he'd bred in his canny mind, he was first seeing to the safety of the innocent, the vulnerable. The weak.

Oats strode back to Sluggard.

"Get Palla and Ugfuck ready to disembark," he said. His next words murdered the relief in Sluggard's face. "You're taking Thistle and Muro away from here."

"Me? What about y—"

"I'm going to make sure these frails don't reach Kalbarca."

Appalled, Sluggard shook his kerchiefed head. "Oats, don't—"

"Don't what, Slug? Forget who I am? I'm the chief's right hand. And I just gave you a command."

FOURTEEN

MEN'S VOICES SAWED THROUGH THE bridge tunnel. Orders were barked. Commands yelled. Responses shouted. They sounded strained, maneuvering their ship through the confining arch.

Mostly, they sounded close.

Oats feared they would hear his stuttered breathing. The climb had sucked a sow's tit. He was winded, shaky in his limbs and lungs. Eyes clenched, he tried to hold his breath, but it only made things worse. Flat on his back atop the bridge, he waited, the sun warming him and his bed of ancient stones. His stockbow was across his crotch, drawn and loaded, held with care to prevent the tickler from touching the ground. Last thing they needed was Roar getting feathered by mischance. The shipwright was farther down the bridge to the left, hopefully breathing softer than Oats was. He'd certainly completed the climb faster, the surly fuck.

Oats had positioned himself near a break in the bridge's northern parapet so he could peer down to the river if the time came. Wasn't difficult to find such a spyhole. The crumbling span had more gaps than a hag's smile. For now he stayed still and out of sight, listening as the frails' first galley pushed unseen through the arch beneath him. He knew the second ship was somewhere on the other side of the bridge, but whether it would follow the first or wait he didn't know. Neither did Jackal, so he'd planned for either outcome.

When the *Mariposa* came through the arch and made for shore at speed, Jack had told them their parts in an unbroken stream of instructions, continuing to speak even as they moored on the eastern bank to offload the hogs. Oats had listened closely, bustling about the deck with everyone else, getting Ugfuck down the ramp and onto shore, using the hurried labor to avoid looking Thistle in the eye. He'd helped her into the saddle and lifted Muro up to sit before her.

"You take care of them until I join you," he'd told Ug, knuckling the hog between the eyes. It was all the parting words he dared offer. Not wanting to give Muro time to figure it out, to panic, to fuss, Oats turned and hustled down the bank to the bridge abutment. Roar was already clambering up. Grabbing the first likely handhold in the old, pitted masonry, Oats tensed to begin the climb, but paused to give the backsides of the swiftly trotting hogs a look. Sluggard rode at the front, leading the riderless barbarians. Mean Old Man, an aging and seasoned animal, followed without need of a tether. Ug bore Thistle and Muro at the rear. By the time Oats had reached his third handhold, they were gone from sight.

Fuck that climb. He was still panting.

The voices broke free of the tunnel. They came sharper now, clearer, no longer constrained by the hollow stone vault. Oats kept his eyes closed, but he knew what the frails would see. What Jackal wanted them to see: the *Mariposa*, moored at the eastern shore, less than a thrumshot from the bridge. Burgos and his crew would be going about their sailor business on deck, putting on a good show of resting for the day.

Soon, a call came from the war galley. A single voice, louder than any so far. Someone—a captain most likely—hailing the smaller vessel, a vessel that contained nothing but a gaggle of sun-cured coffin dodgers. No mongrels or barbarians in sight.

Burgos answered, though distance and Oats's own breath muddled the words.

He didn't need to hear the exchange. The Hisparthans' demands were as certain as a mongrel's morning erection.

Who are you?

What's your purpose on the river?

Why did you run?

All the same arrogant, blue-blood hogshit those who figured they were born to power had spewed since the first frail wore a crown.

Burgos's answers hardly mattered.

We're nothing but swampers, lord.

On our way down to the Maiden, lord.

Thought it best to yield the river, lord. Not for us to impede Her Majesty's ships, lord.

Didn't fucking matter what was said, but how. It was the "lord" that was most important, dribbled from a downcast chin. If Burgos had doffed his skullcap and wrung it in humble, nervous hands the noble captain on the galley was like to spend in his breeches. With luck, the man's eyes weren't keen enough to see the outlaw brands on the pirates' cheeks. If so, he might get freshly flushed and need to harass Burgos a bit longer.

So long as they were merely speaking, Oats could do nothing but lie there and wait.

His mind drifted to Thistle. To Muro. Did they understand why he'd not gone with them? Fool-ass thing to wonder. Of course the boy didn't. He'd have only the thrill of the ride and whatever comforts Thistle provided to keep him from fearing that Oats was gone for good. And Thistle herself? She'd served the hoof nearly as long as Oats. She knew the life, the creed. She'd lost a lover to it already. And Oats wasn't Roundth. The only time he'd spent with Thistle in bed was as a fucking invalid. Her feeding him, changing his bandages, his soiled and stinking sheets. Hells, he was another child in her care. An ass to be wiped. She cared for him, but in the same way she loved the orphans. That was all. How could it be any other way? Besides, he was a Bastard, Grey and True. More than that, he was Jackal's brother. And not because their skin bore the same tattoos.

They were bonded by more than ink and oaths, the two of them. It would be that way until one of them went to the dust.

Fair wager it wouldn't be the fucking Arm of Attukhan first. That was fine by Oats. Spare him the pain of surviving, of watching those he loved fill a grave or fuel a pyre.

What was taking so long?

The frails should have moved on or tried to take the pirates prisoner by now. Jackal had said they'd do one or the other. Those were the outcomes they'd planned for, not languishing all the length of the day while some captain tried to reckon the beginning of the fucking world with Burgos.

Oats lifted his chin far as it would go and craned his neck to peer through the hole in the parapet, careful not to move anything but his head. This whole scheme would go to shit the moment some falcon-eyed son-of-a-cunt on deck spied movement on the bridge and shouted a warning. Oats's view was uncomfortable, limited, and inverted, but he could make out enough to worry.

The Hisparthan war galley sat in the middle of the channel, its prow drifting a bit toward the bank. Double-masted, it was well over twice the length of the moored *Mariposa*, and wider by half. Its banks of oars had been drawn into the belly of the beast, the rowers hidden from sight by an upper deck. Was it men or mongrels on those unseen benches? No way to tell. But it wasn't his job to find out.

The upper deck held no such mystery. It was covered with armed frails. Had to be a hundred men or more. Swords and bucklers filled most hands, but Oats saw about a third carried stockbows. More than enough to kill Burgos and his crew in a single volley. Amidships, a group of ten or so armored men with halberds surrounded the source of the voice droning at Burgos, standing on his own deck perhaps a javelin's toss away. His cap wasn't in his hands, but his posture was meek enough as he listened to whatever was being said. Oats's neck was cramping by the time Burgos spoke. His words didn't reach the top of the bridge, but he made several gestures upriver and to the east. When his hand waved up at the bridge Oats snatched his head away from the hole.

Sweat itched in his beard and fear chewed at his gut.

Had the old outlaw given them up? There was nothing in Jack's plan for that.

The hum of voices on the war galley increased. Oats stared at the sky as he heard the creak of wood, the groan of rope, the smack of oars. The ship must have come about—and faster than he would have thought for such a big boat—for soon enough, it was passing beneath once more.

Oats let his head loll left and met Roar's gaze. The mongrel was a stone's toss away. A silent understanding sent them rolling onto their stomachs. They began to crawl, crossing the width of the bridge to the opposite parapet, low and slow, for the second galley was far enough removed downriver for them to see its masts. No doubt the supporting vessel had men keeping watch on the bridge. It was a fine perch for an ambush after all.

The first ship completed its return crawl through the tunnel. Oats and Roar stayed hidden, eyes locked as if the squinty looks they exchanged confirmed what they were hearing. It sounded like the frails were moving on. Oats cursed himself for a faithless fuck for doubting Burgos. He swallowed hard, his throat apple grinding inside his tense neck.

Maybe Jackal would just let the ships sail on without—

Cries of alarm erupted from the unseen deck below.

So much for that.

Oats signaled Roar with a thumb bobbed skyward. They rose slowly, peeking over the bridge's parapet to see what had the men below so riled and pointing toward their sister ship. There was a tumult on the far vessel, the men aboard surging toward the stern.

Toward Jackal.

He stood alone, dripping from the river, sword already throwing blood and water into the air as he met the first of the onrushing sailors. Rumors of the dread mongrel that couldn't be slain must have spread deep into Hispartha for the crew did not send a handful against him, they came as one, a teeming line of raised voices and blades. The width of the galley allowed perhaps five to face him at a time, but they were more than twenty ranks deep. It would have overwhelmed a full-blood thick. But not Jackal. Tulwar flashing, reaping, cutting men down, cleaving several over the side to redden the river, he did not just stand. He advanced.

Beneath Oats's nose, the confused men on the nearer galley hadn't yet reckoned what was happening aboard their fellow ship. The captain was spitting orders to close with the other vessel, to lend aid. The oars slid out, turning the galley into some many-legged insect.

No more waiting.

Oats stood fully upright, raising his stockbow. He had the captain marked, tracked him as the man strode toward the stern yelling at the ship's pilot who was wrestling with the wheel, cursing that it would not spin. That was Rant's doing. Hidden in the neighboring arch, she'd been tasked to slip beneath the water and chain the rudder during the ship's second, slow passage beneath the bridge.

The captain was still stomping down the deck, growling at the pilot, when his eyes happened to come up and rest upon Oats. The man's eyes barely had the chance to widen before the bolt punched through his noble face.

Roar feathered the pilot the next instant, hitting him in the back just above the hip. It wasn't a killing shot, but it sent the screaming frail to the deck in writhing agony.

"Down," Oats ordered, and they both ducked back behind the parapet, immediately crawling along its length, changing their position. The voices below boiled in a soup of startled anger and repressed fear.

"The steering oarsmen next," Roar told Oats as they hunkered and reloaded. "Even without the rudder they can still come about. Two men on either side at the stern."

"At the only pair of oars not below deck," Oats said. "I remember. Don't fucking miss."

They popped up again as one. Oats settled on his target and jerked the tickler just as the crew began shouting warnings at the mongrels' reappearance. He killed his oarsman. For his part, Roar didn't miss. But he shot the same man.

"I had the fuck on the left!" Oats growled when they were safely behind the parapet once more.

Roar winced as the first return volley from the crew's stockbows splintered against the bridge with empty vengeance. "Said I would take the one portside! You agreed!"

"Hells-damned backy boat talk that don't no one understand proper," Oats complained as he reloaded. He pointed down the bridge toward Sparthis. "You go that way a good piece. Show yourself and loose if you can. I'll stay here. They won't expect us same place twice."

A few bolts cracked into the stone and whistled through the gaps as Roar crawled off, shots meant to keep the ambushers down. It was fucking working. As Oats waited for Roar to get into position, Rant appeared on the opposite parapet, closer to the shore. She hauled herself over the stones, soaked to the skin and a little out of breath. Oats wondered what she was doing making the climb. She hadn't been able to take a thrum on her swim to chain the rudder, so she was no use up here. She was supposed to have returned to Burgos. What was she about?

The answer was in her face. Looking beyond Oats, Rant stared at her brother, concern writ across her entire, drenched body.

Oats drew her attention with a wave and motioned for her to keep low and stay put.

Roar had stopped, ready and waiting for a signal.

Damn.

Oats had been prepared to let the ill-tempered shipwright take the greater risk and show himself first. He was an unsure hand with a thrum and it seemed fair to let him provide the distraction while Oats killed the remaining steersman. But if Roar took a bolt through the neck while his sister was looking on . . .

Oats waved his fingers in front of his throat in a cutting motion, hoping Sluggard had taught these city-born mongrels the hoof signs. Pointing at himself he raised one finger before pointing at Roar and raising a second.

"And that don't mean we tack the keel and larboard the mizzen, you sailor cunt," Oats muttered just before he jumped up and trained his thrum.

He shot the steersman and was down again, just in time. The

answering thrumbolts struck with such fury bits of masonry popped over the parapet and rained on Oats. He'd only been up for a couple of heartbeats, yet he'd seen . . . something. Hadn't he? Best check.

Oats crawled quickly to the nearest fissure and risked a peek.

The oars were still. The current had brought the galley farther from the bridge. With its rudder chained and the steersmen dead it had begun to drift at an angle, but not enough to bring the ship broadside to the bridge.

The oars were *still*.

Even with their captain dead, wouldn't these men want to flee the bridge and the attacks from above? Just then, the answer to the unknown portion of Jackal's plan struck Oats. It wasn't men at those oars. It was slaves. Mongrels. Rebelling in the only way they could by doing nothing, leaving their taskmasters stranded. The ambush was a chance for vengeance, for freedom. That had been Jackal's wager.

And he'd just won.

The far ship was coming, oars sweeping. Jackal remained on her deck, but he weren't the only half-orc any longer. A gaggle of mongrels stood around him, free from their chains and now brandishing the weapons of their captors, whooping as their fellows below continued to row, goaded not by the lash but by hunger for a reckoning. The galley's crew had been left in the river, nothing but bobbing corpses and a few floundering survivors.

Some frails on the crippled boat below saw what was coming and cried out in warning, but it served only to sow further calamity. Caught unawares between two threats, most panicked. A handful turned their stockbows to the approaching ship, but not enough to loose an effective volley. Oats rose and began planting bolts in exposed backs. Roar lent his thrum to the effort. They no longer sought cover, but simply loaded and loosed as fast as they could. It was heartening and terrible what two thrums on higher ground can do to men already rattled by bloodshed and lack of leadership.

But every band had its Hoodwink. That one cold fuck that kept his head no matter the depth of the shit . . .

Oats saw him; a small man with a widow's peak. While his comrades stumbled about in a vain search for the scant cover on deck, this frail scurried purposefully toward a chest secured beneath the raised pilot's platform at the stern, stooping to retrieve something from the captain's corpse on the way. Oats didn't know what he was intent on retrieving, but reckoned it was best he didn't succeed. He took aim. A thrum on the deck loosed before he could, sending a bolt shattering into the parapet just below Oats's cods. He was pelted with splinters and mortar, forced to duck behind the stone. There was still fight in some on that doomed boat. Fortunate they didn't have better aim. Oats crab-crawled to a fresh position and found himself next to Rant. She had crossed the width of the bridge.

Oats scowled when he reached her. "Told you to stay put."

She didn't reply, her gaze still fixed on her brother.

Oats took a steadying breath. He rose again, ready to kill Widow's Peak, but froze when he found his target. The man had gotten the chest open and was now placing a round object larger than his palm into a sizable leather sling.

A fucking sapper's pot.

Goose-flesh sprouting, Oats snatched his stockbow to his shoulder and jerked the tickler. He rushed the shot. The bolt took Widow's Peak in the leg. Tough little fucker's stance buckled, but he remained upright and—with a quick whirl of the sling—sent the pot arcing up toward the bridge.

Oats dove, falling atop Rant and covering her with his body. The pot shattered behind him, setting free a hollow roar and a blast of scorching heat as the Al-Unan fire ignited. Rolling, Oats looked and found the bridge's span nearly blocked by emerald flame.

"Move!" he yelled, hauling Rant to her feet and pushing her away from the blaze. Another pot broke on the spot they fled, spilling more sticky flames. Oats and Rant grunted at the sudden painful heat, but escaped without any of the hellish substance splashing upon them.

Rant was shouting her brother's name, fighting against Oats as he half carried her to the other parapet. Roar's side of the bridge was blocked from view by an ever-growing wall of green fire and black smoke.

"You need to get gone!" Oats told Rant, struggling to prevent her from rushing down the length of the burning bridge.

She continued to try to bull past him, squirming to break his grip. "I'm not going without him!"

"The hells you won't!"

Oats picked Rant up and dropped her over the parapet into the river. She came up sputtering. Turning, Oats studied the bridge. There was a small gap between the inferno and the parapet on this side, barely enough to ride a hog through, but it was there. Oats ran for the gap before he could think himself out of it. The heat seared his flesh, sucked the air from his lungs. He smelled his beard singe. He slowed only at the narrowest point, leaning away from the licking flames, trying not to think about Shed Snake's arm and failing. The urge to flee the writhing hell, to fall backward over the parapet and escape to the cool haven of the river's embrace was almost too much to resist.

But then he was through . . .

. . . just in time to see Roar drop his stockbow, dash the width of the bridge, vault the parapet, and cut a perfect dive into the water.

Oats snorted and shook his head.

One brother safe. Time to see about the other.

It was all but over below.

Jackal's liberated mongrels had already boarded the other boat, delighting in the slaughter. Jackal took on the captain's guard, the ten men in plate armor. The reach of their halberds stalled him for about a heartbeat. Jack had always been quick, but these days he was the son of a panther. He slipped through the warding polearms and cracked the men's close formation, cutting the first few down and pushing the rest over the side, allowing the weight of their harness to murder them.

With no hope of mercy if they surrendered, the frails fought to the last man. And that last man proved to be Widow's Peak. Limping from the thrum-bolt in his leaking leg, the man kept his back pressed to the pilot's platform. The chest next to him was open. Oats couldn't see how many sapper's pots remained, but Widow's Peak held one in his hand, poised over the chest. The marauding mongrels stalled, seeing the danger. They formed a panting, blood-soaked ring around the man that could send them all to hells in one swift motion. But they refused to fear. They merely stood, watching with sullen eyes, waiting to see if the man had the spine to make good his threat. No pleas spilled from Widow's Peak. He didn't try to bargain for his life. He was dead, and knew it. Perhaps he wanted a few more breaths, a few more moments. That's why he waited. Perhaps he wanted to savor the knowledge that he was going to burn the mongrels with him, wanted that knowledge to take root in their minds. Whatever his reasons, he was content to linger on a skewered leg, arm hovering.

Jackal pushed to the front of the mongrels, broke the ring to stand one step closer than the rest. He stayed as tight-lipped as Widow's Peak. They regarded each other just out of spitting distance.

Oats pulled the tickler. It was a shot worthy of the chief, right in the man's ear.

The sapper's pot fell from his hand.

And slapped into Jackal's, a cod's length from the chest. Hells, he was quick. But Oats had known that, counted on it.

"Nice catch!" Oats called down.

"Better shot!" came Jack's grinning reply.

Several mongrels broke from the group and went down to the oar deck. Oats could hear them striking the chains from the galley slaves, swelling the numbers of the freed. Soon, the deck of the crippled ship was filled to bursting. The half-orcs spat upon the dead, turned tear-streaked faces to the sky, and lifted their voices. They cheered for vengeance, for victory. They cheered for Jackal.

Amid their adoration, Jack kept his gaze on Oats. They exchanged a nod before Oats turned away from the parapet. Lingering any longer was likely unwise. He was fairly certain the heat from the Al-Unan fire was going to cause the ancient bridge to collapse.

FIFTEEN

RAIN LASHED THE DECK AS Muro emptied his guts over the side. Oats rubbed his back with one hand, held on to him with the other. The river had given the boy no trouble, but the open sea was another matter. He was turning color not long after the *Mariposa* left the delta of the Guadal-kabir.

"Welcome to the Titan's Ocean!" Burgos had exclaimed, and Muro responded by spewing upon the captain's boots. This drew laughter from the old pirate, but the boy burst into tears. Between wails and heaves, he kept apologizing.

"I'm sorry. Sorry! I'm so sorry!"

Thistle and Oats tried to explain he had done nothing wrong, that none were angry with him, but the pitiful pleas continued unabated along with the retching. Thistle was laid low not long after as the weather worsened and the waves grew spirited. Dizziness forced her to lie down beneath the aft shelter, so Oats stayed at the rail with Muro, trying to keep his gaze away from the sickening sight of the undulating waves. They made him queasy, but so far he'd avoided fouling his beard. Burgos and his men went about their sailoring, immune to the roll of this new, wet world.

Oats stared at the galley ahead and wondered if Jackal was tossing his stomach ale. Likely not. He'd spent time on ships. Captain Jackal the Backy Seafarer. That's what Polecat had called him when he returned home from the east. Oats smiled at the memory.

The liberated galley slaves had certainly accepted Jackal as their captain and he'd remained aboard one of the galleys, putting Roar in command of the other, now trailing the *Mariposa*. Rant had groused about being left on Burgos's little ship, but three hundred half-orc men who hadn't seen a woman in hells-knew-how-long was too much of a risk to take. Oats had told Jackal he was pretty enough to be in danger too, and been only half-jesting. Whether they wanted to bugger him or not, the newly freed mongrels' gratitude toward Jack didn't stretch to blind devotion. Try as he might, Jackal had failed to convince them to attack the rest of the fleet. Even with surprise and the Arm of Attukhan on their side, the galley mongrels declared the dromon impossible to take. The big warship was rowed by freemen, not slaves, boasting nearly four hundred men-at-arms; a prow-mounted cannon above its steel ram; "devil cocks"—syphons that shot streams of Al-Unan fire, Rant explained—and someone aboard they called the Starving Man in hushed tones. Jackal couldn't get any more out of them about whoever that was. Wisely, he didn't press the matter. Those poor abused fucks didn't need another taskmaster bullying them into submission. Better to temper their loyalty by allowing them to bask in their freedom. And give them a new home.

Jackal gave the order to sail for Mongrel's Cradle.

Oats knew it chafed him, allowing the remainder of the frails' boats to reach Kalbarca. Men, horses, gunpowder, food, all were going upriver to resupply the city, strengthening the Crown's foothold in Ul-wundulas. To say nothing of this Starving Man, who sounded for all the hells like some damn wizard. Who else has such a name that full-grown half-breeds won't speak above a whisper?

Rant approached, as surefooted on the soaked, tilting deck as a goat on dry, flat land. On her way she patted the bent back of Sluggard, the gesture more goading than supportive. The gritter was having as bad a time of it as Muro. Worse, even. When Rant reached

Oats, her mouth turned down in genuine sympathy as she watched Muro struggle through another bout of dry heaves.

"The weather's going to be worse by sundown," she said, not taking her eyes off the boy.

Oats could only grimace and try to put more affection into his rubbing hand. Earlier, Thistle had expressed hope that Muro would be over the seasickness soon, but Burgos informed her in gentle tones that those with skull injuries—even old ones—often stayed stricken until they reached land.

"You shouldn't have done that," Rant said. "Tossed me off the bridge."

Oats looked up to find her eyes now on him and all sympathy gone. Like all of them, she was soaked by rain and spray, but where it turned Sluggard, Thistle, even Burgos and his crew into sodden wretches, Rant was made more vibrant by the ocean's touch. Oats found himself fixating on a drop along her cheekbone, tracing that hard line as it was blown by the wind.

"So . . . sorry," Muro moaned.

"You don't need to be," Oats said, hunkering in. He straightened, looked at Rant. "Can't have you killing yourself for—"

"My brother? Fuck you. You don't get to decide that."

"Orders are part of hoof life, Rant. You need to get used to that. Chief won't suffer you choosing Roar over her commands. She'll do a heap worse than toss you off a bridge if you pull that shit."

Rant's jaw hardened. "Then she must not have a brother."

"She does." Oats snorted. "A twin, but he's . . . well, they're not like Roar and you. But all hoof-riders got brothers. A few sisters now too. It won't help to favor one over the others."

"Sure," Rant scoffed, and her head turned away from him to look in the direction of the lead galley. "I'll be certain to give credence to that gullshit."

Oats opened his mouth, but she strode away before he could speak.

Whatever Rant thought, Oats didn't favor Jackal over the others. Loved him more, but that was different. That was time at work, a childhood of games and fights, hurts and shared triumphs. That was memories. But if the chief said Oats should ride to Culprit's aid, or Thresher's, or any Bastard he'd known shorter than a lifetime, he wouldn't disobey even if Jackal were in danger. Only . . . he had. He'd abandoned the Bastards entirely, defied the Claymaster, and left the Kiln. He'd fucking deserted, a death sentence under hoof code, to stand with Jackal at Strava during the Betrayer Moon. He had other reasons, truths that bolstered his courage. There was the agreement with Zirko to uphold, that a rider go to help defend the Unyars' holy place against the horse-cocks. There was the Claymaster's growing madness. At the time, Fetch herself had seemed an enemy. So he'd saddled Ugfuck and abandoned his hoof, his fellow Bastards, his brothers, for Jackal. He'd gotten lucky, was spared reprisal because the Claymaster had lost his mind and the hoof stood against him, voted a new chief. No need to punish a mongrel for deserting the Grey Bastards when that hoof was as dead as its leader.

Oats couldn't fathom going against Fetching for Jackal's sake. But was that only because he loved her equally? That her being chief, and not some other mongrel, somehow balanced the scales and squared his loyalty? Being earnest, he reckoned it was likely. Rant certainly wouldn't ever have the depth of affection for the chief as she did her own blood. The same would be true for Roar. Perhaps it was asking too much of them to dilute those bonds with oaths to a bunch of mongrels they did not know or love. Being more earnest, it didn't matter if they did. Fetch needed a fleet. She had mongrels she trusted to do the hard fighting, but not one who knew how to build warships. It was likely Rant and Roar would never be separated. They could remain at Mongrel's Cradle together, the war at a distance, and never be forced to choose between family and hoof.

Oats wished that for them.

Muro's body had calmed, even if the waves had not. He was listless in Oats's clutches, though he continued to mumble his apologies.

"You got nothing to be sorry for, sweet boy," Oats whispered as he gathered him up, letting him rest a moment in his arms before carrying him beneath the shelter. Thistle stirred as he ducked beneath the awning, rain drumming against the tight canvas.

"Need to get him dry," she said, her voice tight with discomfort.

Wincing, she made to sit up, but Oats put a hand on her knee, wordlessly assuring her he had the task in hand.

He got Muro stripped and dry, the exhausted child swaying the entire time. Oats pulled a fresh shirt over the miniature drunkard's head, steeling himself for the possibility that the boy's vomiting would return the instant he was dressed. Fortune spared them both.

At last, Oats laid Muro down. He wasn't exactly resting comfortably, the occasional whimper or moan keeping Oats at ready with a bucket, but it was a damn improvement. He kept vigil while Thistle and Muro slept, trying to ignore the motion of the ship and biting down on the inside of his lip.

Fuck. Wasn't working. He had the bucket, but this was going to be loud. Innards beginning to pulse, Oats hurried out on deck. He was a stride from the rail when he popped, but the force of the stream covered the distance. At least the rain helped rinse his beard. He hung over the side, spitting the last awful traces into the chop. Felt like maybe that was it.

"Damn good timing." Oats looked up to find Burgos standing beside him. The weathered outlaw directed Oats's attention with his squint.

The sun remained imprisoned by clouds, yet to the north a great spur of dark rock could still be seen, thrusting up from the teeming sea, king of a grey world.

"The Tower of Herathos," Burgos said, his rough voice adding deserved weight to the name.

Oats had never laid eyes upon the massive promontory that marked the southern tip of Ul-wundulas, even from land. Through the occluding curtain of rain and spray, he could still spy the vestiges of the castle built upon—and carved from—the rock. Oats couldn't reckon how long it had stood, but Hispartha once thought the fortification would deter the orcs from crossing the Gut. The Great Incursion proved them wrong and the thicks razed the castle. Now it was nothing but a roost for gulls.

Sluggard slid down the rail to join them, awe chasing some of his misery away. "Never thought I'd see it."

"Then you won't want to miss this," Rant called from the ship's other side.

Oats knew what it was before he turned. If the Tower of Herathos was before them, the view south could contain only one sight.

Dhar'gest. The Dark Lands. Home of the orcs.

At this distance the coast was but a foreboding shadow, yet the storm seemed incapable of hiding the twin peaks of Ruukam Ul'nuul, the Broken Woman. Said to have once been a single mountain cloven by sorcery, the jagged formation stood opposed to its northern adversary. Seeing them now it appeared to Oats as if the Woman had once intruded too close and been chastised by the Tower, smote and split in two before retreating across the narrow strait.

"The Gut's what, two leagues?" Sluggard asked, chin tucked to keep the act of speaking from emptying his stomach.

"More," Burgos replied.

Sluggard choked down a small belch, glared at the leaden, roiling waters. "And the thicks swim it. Hells."

Oats felt his throat tightening and not against a need to be sick. Orcs weren't the only ones to swim that menacing expanse. His mother had done it. Twice. The first time carrying a babe in her arms. The second, carrying another in her belly. Oats stood on a pitching vessel between the land of his creation and the land of his birth and was very grateful that the storm hid his unexpected tears.

The weather turned hateful as they sailed eastward through the strait. The sky hanging above their prow was a mass of brooding thunderheads.

"This'll be rough," Rant declared.

She wasn't wrong.

The rain slapped the decking in sheets. Waves pounded the hull as the ship crested and crashed through the turbulent swells. The seamen knew their art, hustling about in the downpour and wrestling with the rigging. The winds thrashed above, punishing the sails for their effrontery, but the men fought back with rope and knot, each bearded face a waterfall. They were blown closer to the rocks of Ul-wundulas than was comfortable. Burgos and Ferran strove mightily at the steering oars, recruiting Oats and Rant to aid them. The Tower of Herathos loomed above now, its jagged foundations poised to break the ship should it stray farther. The churning clouds and the lurching motion of the deck conspired to form the illusion that the Tower was descending, a headman's blade beginning its irrefutable arc.

Oats tore his eyes away from the dreadful sight. Beneath the shelter, Thistle clung to Muro. The boy was sick again, half-hidden by the bucket. Oats held up a hand, telling them to stay put. Fool-ass thing to do. Thistle would never attempt to reach the rail, where the sea's dragging paws were eager for the sudden tilts that would spill the hapless overboard.

A sudden cheer went up from the crew, boisterous enough to defy the storm's roar. Burgos shouted something, but only Rant caught the words.

"We're through!" she exclaimed, smile flashing in the gloom of the squall. "We've reached the Deluged Sea!"

The rains harried them for the remainder of the day. The night was sleepless, sick, and storm-tossed. The coastal mountains allowed no safe harbor, so the ship remained upon the waves. Oats remained awake, splitting the long watches between his ailing companions beneath the aft shelter and the unhappy hogs in the creaking hold.

At last, past midday, the storm died, leaving the sun entombed in a charcoal sky.

It broke through the next morning, just in time to brighten the view of Mongrel's Cradle.

"The Sons of Perdition are poorly named," Sluggard said, taking in the broad bay, the milky sands of the beach. "This is a fucking paradise."

Oats gave an appreciative laugh. "Reckon they knew what they were about. Who would join the Skull Sowers or the Shards when you can be a Paradise Boy?"

Beyond the bay and the cock-hardening beach, the Sons' port town of Salduba beckoned. The buildings sat the land rising away from the coast, a haven of tiled roofs nestled behind a strong wall. Above them, on the highest rise, stood the Cradle itself. The castle's curtain wall ringed the wide promontory, square watchtowers adding to its height. Behind the fortress, the landscape continued to sprawl, sloping toward the foothills that eventually grew into the Hoar Tops, invisible at this distance. Those peaks were so tall it was rare that they were without their snowy caps despite the hellish climes of Ul-wundulas. Still, they were most often called the Whores, mongrels being who they are. Mountains protecting a castle, that castle guarding a town, that town with its own wall, all of it with access to the sea. The Sons' home was more than a paradise, it was a sanctuary and a bastion. There was a reason Father's boys had a reputation for being a bit soft. Still, this would be the last place to fall . . . so long as the frails came by land. By sea was another matter, but Fetch had taken steps early.

Seven Traedrian galleys patrolled the bay; two more were docked. The other four were farther out, ranging the Deluged and watching for the Crown's fleets. A pair had come upon the war galleys and the *Mariposa* earlier in the day, spotted their white flags, and approached with caution. A few shouted words from Jackal sent them on to deliver advance word to the Sons. The corsairs had been paid with coin from the Pit of Homage, secured by Oats and Anvil before Hispartha had quite wrapped its head around the fact that the Lots were in revolt. It was all Jackal's notion. He had made some friends among the freebooter captains during his travels. The type of friends who needed a steady stream of coin, but it was better than leaving their asses exposed.

Oats had to swallow a moan of relief when he stepped onto the dock. The stable wood felt queer beneath his boots, gave him a moment's light-headedness, but it swiftly passed. Carrying Muro, he smiled at Thistle and puffed out his cheeks.

"Glad that's over."

She squeezed his arm in agreement and caressed the back of the boy's head.

"I need to see to Ug," Oats said.

Thistle held her arms up to receive Muro. "I'll take him."

With Sluggard's help, the hogs were unloaded without incident, despite their eagerness to quit the confines of the hold.

Oats paused a moment at the end of the ramp, holding firm to Ug's swine-yanker.

"Thanks," he called up to Burgos, still on deck.

The man gave a strange little gesture, something between a wave and a salute. It was almost dismissive. Almost.

"What will you do now?" Oats pressed.

Burgos leaned on the railing and surveyed the beach. He took a slow, deep breath. "Fucking retire."

Oats laughed as he walked away.

Thistle waited at the end of the pier, leaning back against the sleeping weight of Muro.

Father stood with her, a gaggle of men and mongrels a little removed. Oats had had few dealings with the Sons' aged hoofmaster, but Fetch trusted him far as she trusted any of the other chiefs. Coming from a neighboring pier, Jackal reached the little gathering a dozen strides ahead of Oats. He exchanged a few words with Father.

"She wants to see us," Jackal told Oats as soon as he was near.

"She's here?" Oats wasn't sure why it surprised him, or why the fact filled him with a sudden, gnawing worry. Something in Father's craggy face, perhaps. By the hard set of Jackal's jaw, he felt it too.

"I'll have my boys see to your mounts," Father said, motioning for his mongrels to come forward.

Oats put a hand on Thistle's back. "They need to be shown to my mother."

Father nodded. "I'll take them myself."

"Before you do," Jackal said, cocking his eyes at the Hisparthan war galleys, "make sure you have adequate numbers to watch over our new blood. They're grateful and glad to be free, but it could turn wild if they're loose in the town."

"I'll have tents erected on the beach," Father replied. "And a dozen stewpots. Slaves will desire food over women and wine, at least for this first night. We get their bellies full, give them a night's sleep free from chains and the splinters of a rower's bench, I wager we'll avoid incident. Give us time to spot any troublemakers in the bargain. By noon tomorrow, I'll have a more permanent place arranged."

Satisfied, Jackal turned to Oats. "Let's go."

Oats handed Ugfuck over to a waiting Sons slophead and gave Thistle a parting look before following Jackal's quick strides toward town. It felt good to walk after the voyage, even if the pace was causing his muscles to burn. Jackal took the stone steps leading up from the wharf three at a time. Oats settled for two.

A parade of merchant stalls awaited them at the top. Fishmongers and tinkers, costers and rope-makers plied their trades in the shadow of Salduba's wall. It was more folk in one place than Oats had seen in a long while. Not since his days fighting in the Pit, in earnest. He barely had time to take in the sight. Jackal rushed past a clutch of cooing dockside whores without a glance, surging up the cobbled slope toward the town gate. He waited beneath the arch for Oats to catch up and was off again, unchallenged by the slop sentries posted with spears. Father was wise to take their barbarians. Folk risked getting trampled if Jack had been ahog.

Inside the walls, Oats discovered that the Sons of Perdition weren't the only thing ill named in the Lots. The Bastards' old town of Winsome was a ramshackle clump of hovels compared to Salduba. The merchant stalls from outside solidified into the storefronts of craftsmen. Many of the whitewashed structures proved to be from the time of the Imperium, but unlike those in Sparthis or Kalbarca, these had not fallen completely to ruin. Columned porticos were melded to the newer buildings with brickwork, dwellings of timber and render added as second stories atop smooth, white marble foundations. The shops and homes of Salduba were as mongrel as the hoof that protected them, but they'd been maintained with such care that, as a whole, they formed a harmonious, lively, and prosperous picture. Father's love for his hoof as well as his reputation for being a scrupulous old fuck was impossible to miss even at an ass-cramping hustle.

Jackal clearly knew the way. He hurried them through town, threading their path around the busy market square using clean little side streets, the houses on either side joined by lines of hanging wash. They passed roving bands of playing children, the laughing, shouting swarms dodging around their unrelenting progress. Old folk tended small gardens of succulents in the cozy spaces behind their homes, pausing to watch Jackal and Oats bull by. They came to a dormant fountain and, beyond, an ancient little bridge crossing a dry channel, both the bloodless survivors of the Imperium's lost water-moving lore. Four strides took them across the span and into deep shade. The fortress of Mongrel's Cradle was near enough now to intrude upon the sky. Jackal swung back to the main thoroughfare, less crowded this close to the castle. Again they hiked a slope and Oats was sweating a bit when they reached the Cradle's gatehouse.

They were stalled only long enough for Jackal to announce himself. He was well known here, he and the chief having split their winter between Mongrel's Cradle and the castile, flying between the two on the back of Fetch's ensorcelled rokh. Oats realized that was the reason he had been surprised Fetch was here. She hadn't flown out to greet them. Word would have reached her well before they docked.

As soon as they entered the castle yard, it was the sight of the great bird that forced Jackal and Oats to a halt.

"Hells overburdened," Jackal hissed.

The huge raptor lay atop a thin pile of straw, foul with blood and whatever dark, sticky humors seeped from its many wounds. Most of the bed was made of the bird's own feathers. Molting, the rokh's head was all but denuded, as was its neck and broad patches along its back. The exposed flesh, pale and dimpled, transformed the once fearsome creature into a pitiful, loathsome thing. Worst of all, it was still alive. Its head moved languidly, while its sprawled wings jerked with sudden, occasional convulsions.

Slowly, Jackal and Oats approached, passing a pair of slopheads standing watch well removed from the beast with kerchiefs tied about their faces to blunt the stench. Up close the damage was a living horror. The wounds weren't cuts or punctures. They were suppurating sores. Even as Oats watched, a long, narrow blister along the rokh's neck writhed and burst, disgorging a wad of pus.

Oats recoiled, seeing the ichor played host to a mass of wriggling larvae. He'd thought the kingdom of flies cavorting in the yard had been attracted by the soiled straw, but now he realized they were birthed from the rokh's tortured body. The suffering beast's eye managed to emerge from beneath the swollen, maggot-caked lid. For half a heartbeat that yellow, feverish orb reflected Oats's and Jackal's appalled faces.

"Why hasn't it been put down?" Jackal demanded of one of the slops.

"War chief says no," came the kerchief-muffled reply.

Jackal spun and hot-heeled for the keep.

They passed several sworn Sons on their way up a corner tower. None even uttered a greeting. The air of the place was one of tense uncertainty, no doubt brought by the chief's arrival.

Two doors stood opposite each other at the top of the stairs. Jackal went to the right and nearly pushed straight through, but caught himself at the last moment. Taking a breath, he knocked. "Fetch. It's us."

"Come."

They found her leaning over a table carpeted with maps, quill moving with a fury. She was grimy with old mud, soot, and blood. The room stank, but Oats was relieved it was only the odor of an unwashed body and not the reek of corruption that filled his nostrils in the castle yard.

"What happened?" Jackal asked.

She didn't answer, kept writing until she finished. Scrawling out messages for carrier birds always took an age because you had to write so damn small. And in code, these days. Tossing the quill down, Fetch straightened, rolling the missive. She picked up another, already in its tiny bone case, and moved toward the door.

"Thricehold has fallen," she said as she passed between Oats and Jackal. Throwing the door open, she yelled down the stairs. "I need a runner!"

Fetch waited in the jamb for the Son to arrive. She held up her right hand. "Strava." Her left. "Notch. Know where he is?"

"Shatterhand, war chief."

Fetch handed the small cases over. "Go." Her hand darted out as he was half-turned and caught his brigand. "Wait!"

She marched back to the table. Oats saw the anger in her, that special kind only born when she had forgotten something. Fetch retrieved a waxed leather satchel and went back to the Son.

"This needs to get to Kul'huun. Tell Father I want Meddler to take it, and two other nomads of his choice. Go."

When the runner was gone, Fetch swung the door closed.

"Frails had moved faster than we thought. Thricehold was surrounded by the time I arrived," she said, returning to the table. "Six hundred cavalry. Three times as many infantry. They'd brought bombards by ship, but the gunstones couldn't reach the walls."

Oats felt a fool-ass. He'd had a moment of relief, hearing that, before remembering she'd already said Thricehold had fallen. It wasn't the most formidable stronghold, but it had been constructed atop what was said to be a dormant volcano with only one path of ascent for man or beast. No surprise Hispartha's siege guns didn't have the range, but what good was that? This story already had an ending.

Fetch's report continued with blunt rapidity. "They were going to have to assault us. With those numbers, they would overwhelm the walls as soon as they reached them. I had Marrow send birds to the Skull Sowers and the Tide, ordering Tomb and Boar Lip to bring their riders. Wouldn't be enough to break the siege, but they'd offer enough to make the frails fear they were about to be caught between Thricehold and all the mongrels in the Lots." Fetch's nostrils flared. She wasn't looking at them. "I figured I'd discourage an assault, buy us some time, let the frails know what waited for them at the top of the peak. I flew in, hit their infantry lines hard, and flew out before the cavaleros could arrive. Did it five . . . six times, always aiming for where they were spread the thinnest. But that's what they were counting on."

Fetch leaned and rested her knuckles on the tabletop, bent by the memory.

"There was something . . . *wrong* with the men I struck next. I saw it, right at the end of the dive, but too late. A third of the men fled, but the rest just stood there. They were already dead. Corpses dressed in armor and propped by boards. The rokh tore into them before I could stop it. The bodies burst. This fucking . . . storm of flies poured out, more than those men could have contained. I knew it was sorcery. A damn trap. We were blind, caught in the swarm. It blocked the sun. I tried to flee, but the flies kept us down. Millions of weightless pests were crushing us, choking us."

Fetching's voice was steady, but her arms had begun to quaver against the clenching of her fists.

"How'd you escape?" Oats asked, hoping his question, his voice, would nudge her out of reliving that hell.

"I wouldn't have," Fetch replied through clenched teeth. "If she hadn't come to gloat."

"She?" Jackal's voice was flat.

"The cunt conjurer. She walked through the swarm, so thin she looked to be starving."

Oats and Jackal shared a disturbed look. The galley slaves had mentioned a Starving Man. Hells, how many of these fuckers were in the Lots?

Fetch only had eyes for the table, didn't see. She barked a laugh. "She carried a fucking spade. Sharp at the end like some kind of gong farmer. Filthy enough to be one. Even through the buzzing I could hear her. She was humming, like a child would with a song they haven't learned the words to. The rokh was dying. I could feel it. I managed to dismount. Fucking sorceress had the grit to motion at me, coax me to come at her. So I did."

Fetch's eyes came up, bright and hateful. "I fought her in the eye of that loathsome storm. And cut her fucking head off."

"Damn right," Jackal said.

"It was close, Jack," Fetch said, head giving the smallest shake. She huffed. "Skinny little gash with a shovel almost sent me to the hells. Her flies died before her head hit the mud and I was surrounded by men eager to finish the job their wizard began. The rokh got us out by a cunt hair. But the frails must have sounded the assault the moment I fell for their trap. They were already coming up the slope and in thrum range of the gates. The Thrice Freed held them off long enough for me to get there, but even with the narrow approach there were too many to repel. At the end, Marrow insisted on the creed. He ordered his boys to mount and had the gates opened. And ours, our boys, insisted to ride with him."

The pain in the chief's words knifed Oats in the heart.

Ours. Our boys.

Gosse. Lopo and Bekir. Touro.

The Bastards' slopheads.

"They rode out," Fetch pushed on. "Charged right down the throat of the frails, hit them with a tusker like I've never seen. I did what I could to aid them and damned if they didn't make it down that slope. Seventy-two mongrels when they started out and most reached the flats. After that . . . the cavaleros were too many. The wizard hadn't killed me, but I was weak. Something carried by those flies. I was feverish, limbs like melted tallow. I tried, but . . . I couldn't, couldn't be everywhe—"

For an instant, the chief broke. One choked sob and a pair of tears. She bit back and swallowed the one, wiped away the two, and her grief was over.

Oats let his own tears fall.

"The rokh was ailing worse than I," Fetch went on, clearing her throat. "Still, I managed to meet the Skulls on their way to help and turn them back. The Tide were a day behind them. I continued on here, but the rokh almost didn't make it over the Hoar Tops."

"Why haven't you killed it?" Jackal asked, succeeding in keeping the question from being an accusation.

Fetch straightened, took a breath. "I was hoping it would recover. I have. Ruin shared his resilience with his dogs, but . . ."

"I killed those dogs with magic," Jackal admitted.

Fetch gave a grim nod. "And the rokh isn't getting better. Whatever power it shares with me may just be keeping it alive and suffering. But I don't know what will happen if it dies. It could spew that rot halfway to the harbor. It can't fly or I would have taken it far from here. I didn't know it was infested with that shit or I wouldn't have brought it at all. The sores didn't appear until after."

"None here have fallen sick?" Jackal said.

Fetch shook her head. "But we know Hispartha gets a stiff cod fucking about with magic plagues."

The thought made Oats's skin crawl. He scratched at his beard to hide it.

"I'll go have a look at the rokh," Jackal said. "There's a chance I can figure something out."

Even Jack's bone-deep bravado didn't lend that statement much weight, but Fetch dipped her chin.

"Do it."

Jackal didn't move right away. When he did, it was to come around the desk, place a hand on the back of Fetching's neck and rest his forehead against hers. That was it. A swift, necessary comfort.

"Just need to get some things from our bedchamber," he said, letting her go.

Jackal went out the door. They heard him enter the chamber across the landing.

"You look better," Fetch told Oats. "Not great. But better."

"And you look like shit. Isa, when's the last time you—" He was cut off by a thumping in the other room. "Hells. He decide to milk his cod or someth—"

The second, heavier thud stopped his words and sent Fetch rushing out of the room. Oats was on her ass. The door before them was ajar. Fetch drew a katara and charged through, skidding to a stop. Looking over her head, Oats felt gooseflesh crawl up his scalp.

Jackal was down. And the pale, scarred, hairless, dead-eyed mongrel standing over him was very, very familiar.

"Told him he wouldn't best me twice," Hoodwink rasped.

SIXTEEN

OATS WANTED TO LAUGH.

Hoodwink wasn't known for his jests. Hells, he wasn't known for *speaking*. What he was known for was being a snake-blooded killer. Famed and feared for it, in earnest. His name was perhaps the most famous in the Lots prior to the chief's rise. Sworn riders and nomads alike had told stories about him for years. He'd ridden with just about all of them at one time or another, his body bearing the scars of his oustings from half the hoofs. Brother-slaying was just one of the offenses he was rumored to have committed. Jackal didn't look dead, though, just out cold. Proper comeuppance for taking Hoodwink unawares in Dog Fall after Winsome fell. Hood hadn't been pleased with that, him being renowned for having the stalking skills of a leopard's ghost. So, as jests went, this was a damn good one.

So why wasn't Oats laughing?

The chief wasn't, for one. Her katara remained poised and she was carefully still. Hood may as well have been a raised cobra for all the calm he brought to the room. There was no weapon in his hands, but he'd never needed one to be lethal.

But the real reason Oats wasn't laughing was because a question blew past his lips first.

"Where the fuck is Xhreka?"

"Behind you," Hood replied, filling the chamber with a whisper.

Oats spun, confusion mounting. The landing was empty. The chief had fallen for it too, and cursed when they turned to find Hoodwink gone.

"The hells . . . ?" Oats said. "That's not . . . fucking possible."

Fetch's jaw was locked. The way she remained ready, listening more than looking, didn't ease Oats's brimming disquiet.

Their eyes had been off Hood for a heartbeat and he'd vanished. The room's window was little more than an arrow slit. Not even their four-limbed serpent of a Bastard could have slithered through. He had to be hiding. But there was nowhere, just a couple of chests and the bed. The most celebrated killer in the Lots wouldn't have dived beneath the mattress like a guilty child. Still, Oats stole a glance to make sure when he knelt to rouse Jackal. Yet calling his name and slapping his face didn't even get a groan.

Oats looked up at Fetch. "What do you think we—"

"WAR CHIEF!"

The cry came up the stairs, followed by a panting slophead. His eyes were wide in his blanched face.

"What?" Fetch demanded.

"It's . . . I don't know. In the yard."

The slop pointed a quivering hand out the door.

"Stay with him!" Fetch ordered, nodding at Jackal, before rushing out of the room. She might have meant Oats too, but if so, he defied her and left the duty to the slophead. Thank the hells they were going down, for he managed to keep up. They ran out of the keep and found the yard full of Sons. A dozen slops held lowered spears alongside half as many sworn brothers with trained stockbows. All were silent, all eyeing the . . . *thing* holding the big golden axe.

It was of a size with Oats, equal in height and muscle. Well, equal in muscle before Oats had lost some meat to injury and idleness. The flesh covering its corded thews was blue, blue as a clear sky. And there was plenty of that flesh to see, for the big creature wore nothing but a wrap of white linen about its waist. Looked like the bottom half of the backy garment Oats had seen on those ancient, armless Imperium statues. The mane growing from the thing's head was also blue, but so dark it was near to black, bronze bangles winking at the end of the odd braid scattered among the mass. A pair of horns curved out from the hair, looking like an animal's save they were made of brazen metal rather than bone. Oats couldn't tell if they were growing from the creature's skull or some kind of headdress. Seeing that its feet were cloven and the hooves were also bronze settled the doubt. Hells, there was even a tail, fleshed and muscular as the rest of this demon.

The face was broad, the bones beneath sharply defined. Intelligent eyes regarded the surrounding mongrels and their pointed weapons with fearless disdain. Its own weapon—that great exotic axe—looked forged from a single piece of metal, and was held in both hands, resting low across the thighs.

The Sons were alarmed by its presence yet none were shouting challenges or demands. They stood silent, wary, seeing the danger yet mesmerized by its appearance. The blue devil demanded the eye, left the beholders awed . . .

Until the tubby shape kneeling behind it stood up from the rokh's side.

Crafty turned and flashed a smile.

"Greetings, dread Fetching," he said, wiping his ring-laden hands with a richly embroidered kerchief. "I desire we should speak."

The chief launched herself at the wizard, legs covering the distance in a single pounce. The demon sidestepped to intercept her, shoving the haft of its axe crossways into her hurtling body. Twisting at the moment of impact, the beast moved to toss Fetch onto the stones, but she gripped the axe haft with her free hand, pulling with the motion, dragging the demon down with her and planting a boot in its stomach. Rolling, the chief kicked. The demon found it was the one being tossed. Its heavy form bashed the yard.

Oats heard it issue a grunt. Fucker could feel pain, then.

Fetch charged Crafty once more, but, seeing her, the demon snarled. Scrambling to its ... hooves, the creature swept its axe up in the same motion, the golden blade cutting a trench in the cobblestones as it ripped into the air. Fetch wasn't near enough to be struck by the sparking edge, but there came a sound akin to thunder and an unseen force hit the chief in the back. Punched off her feet, she smote the ground face-first.

"Feather that blue fuck!" Oats yelled at the Sons. His own stockbow was still strapped to Ug's saddle because he was a damned fool-ass.

As the thrums sang, the demon sneered and struck the butt end of his axe haft into the ground, unleashing another clap of thunder. The bolts burst before they could touch him, shattered by an energy that rattled the yard. And Oats's teeth.

Fetch was picking herself up, blood leaking from her nose. Hells. That axe—or whatever sorcery it unleashed—could hurt her. Just like the Maiden Spear.

She reached her hands and knees, visibly trembling. Crafty stood a pebble's toss in front of her, the pitying expression on his plump face transfixing her fury. So muddled by hatred, Fetch ignored the demon moving in behind her. Oats needed to stop it, to rush that blue fuck and aid his chief, his sister. But he couldn't move. Damn him, he couldn't fucking move! And it wasn't some damn spell. It was fear that rooted him. Fear of living dead women and horned devils with their enchanted spears and axes. Fear of taking another grievous wound. He wasn't afraid to die. It was surviving that terrified him. The sick bed was worse than all the hells.

"Truly, Fetching, I implore you. Let us speak."

Crafty's smug voice ignited Oats's own anger. It was a candle flame compared to what blazed within the chief, but it was enough to get him moving. He took a step. The second came quicker. Ten more and he would have the wizard by the throat. A hand touched Oats first, strong fingers gripping his shoulder lightly from behind. He turned to find Hoodwink. The pale mongrel shook his head. The slight motion could have been a warning. Or a plea. Who could fucking tell from that blank, cadaverous face? Oats pretended to consider, kept his eye from drifting beyond Hood to the door of the keep, where a silent form emerged.

Still, Hoodwink whirled the instant before Jackal struck, uncanny speed tearing his tulwar from its sheath to whip Jack's thrusting blade aside. Oats fled their scraping swords, left them to their viper's dance.

The devil had Fetch seized in a choking hold, his axe haft wedged beneath her chin. She'd been dragged away from Crafty. Impressive, knowing what it took to move her these days. The Sons were tracking the struggle, too afraid to loose lest their bolts strike the war chief.

"You can't hurt her! Fucking shoot!" Oats bellowed as he bulled toward Crafty.

His shouting succeeded in getting bowstrings thrumming, but it also alerted the wizard to his oncoming rush.

Crafty pivoted to face him, face betraying no unease. He reached into his robes.

Oats braced himself against whatever sorcery was about to flay his flesh or boil his eyeballs. Nothing. Head tucked, eyes clenched, Oats collided with the wizard, got fistfuls of his garment, and bore him to the ground. They landed in the putrid straw of the rokh's bed, Oats atop Crafty. He sat up, straddling the wizard's broad gut, and raised a fist. Eyes brimming from the reek of the nest, Oats saw something blocking the face he meant to pulp.

A glass jar. Something within was wriggling, flopping over itself.

Oats froze. It was a tongue.

"I bear her words, as well," Crafty said, his other hand offering up a folded parchment, sealed with wax.

Unable to tear his eyes away from the jar's squirming contents, Oats snatched the parchment.

The world had gone mad. He sat astride a Tyrkanian sorcerer next to a dying, monstrous bird. A stone's throw away one brother fought another in the swiftest clash of blades the world had ever seen. On the other side of the castle yard, a demon wrestled with the chief, using her body as a shield against a storm of thrumbolts and flung spears. Most broke against Fetching, but a few found their mark. The blue monster was now bristled and bleeding, but still held fast to the strongest mongrel in the Lots. All this madness and yet, maddest of all, Oats held a letter in his hands. Madder still, he opened it and read.

I'm safe, Idris. Safer than I've been in a long time. You must get that pair of gorgeous hotheads to listen. Uhad's schemes are fatter than he is and he's a conniving son of a cunt, but you can trust him to help himself. In doing so, he helped me. You can save Wily, Idris. But you have to listen. They have to listen. Tell Isabet if she doesn't forgive Hood, I'll never forgive her.

Idris, the bear's been fed.

It wasn't signed. Was this her hand? Oats wracked his brain, but couldn't recall if he'd ever read anything she'd written. But the doubt was forced, a caution against his immediate certainty. From the first line, he knew it was her. Wanted it to be her. It was the last that proved it, though.

The bear's been fed.

That's what she used to say back in the Pit, before he'd earned enough to keep her free from the arena. She was always marked for the Pit of Bait, a fucking hole where small and weak combatants fought animals for the amusement of the crowd. Last to survive was always hauled out and declared the winner. If you had coin enough the beastmaster could be bribed to feed the animal just before the contest. Not much, but enough to take the edge off its hunger, enough to make the beast more focused on survival than food. Make it more likely to kill the desperate men attacking it with sharpened sticks or broken bottles, rather than run down the little halfling woman keeping well out of reach. Of course, fed or not, what danger was she ever really in? The voice of a god could drive off any animal. Kill it, even, without effort. But that would have exposed her, given Barsius and Zirko's other hunters a trail to follow. Worse, it would have made her a fitting prospect for the Pit of Greatness. Why toss a helpless halfling in with the animals when you can pit the tongue in her eye socket against a centaur or a cyclops? Or maybe the Big Bastard? Oats didn't know all that back then, about what she carried. He thought he was helping her. And quickly found her to be wise. Someone he could trust.

Now she was telling him that Crafty was dangerous, but he wasn't out to kill them. He would, though, if forced and given no choice.

Oats looked up from the letter. Fetch and Jackal were still fighting. Witnessing their struggles from without, Oats saw what they couldn't from within. Hood and the demon were there to counter the violence Crafty had known was inevitable. He wished to talk, but he must have suspected there were no words from his lips that would ever reach Fetch and Jackal's ears. And they'd both become so powerful . . .

Oats looked down at Crafty. The wizard gave him a knowing grin. The next instant, he was crying out in pain from the punch Oats delivered to his mouth before standing up.

"Doing this because Xhreka says to, not fucking you!"

He strode toward Jackal and Hoodwink, stopped at the edge of their duel.

"AY! Fuck-skulls!" he yelled, reaching into his breeches. Both mongrels flicked a glance his way at the call. But it was the sight of his exposed and dangling cock that arrested their combat.

"I win," Oats told them. "Now put the slicers up."

Jackal gawked, darted a side-eye at Hood. "He's—"

"Trying to make sure you don't murder Crafty," Oats said, tucking his cods away. "At least, not until we've heard what the fat fuck has to say. We don't like it, we'll all help the chief kill him." He eyed Hoodwink hard. "*All* of us. Right?"

"We can try," came the thin reply.

Wasn't exactly satisfying, but Oats had to accept it. He turned away.

"Enough!" he bellowed at the Sons on his way toward Fetch and the demon. The stockbows ceased flinging bolts at the struggling pair.

Fetch continued to fight, tried to say something, but the axe strangled her words.

"Chief," Oats said, stepping close. "This hells-spawned fuck is going to let go. But you need to let this rest."

He wasn't sure if Ruins Made Flesh could shoot flames from their eyes, but Fetch attempted it.

"There's word from Xhreka, Fetch," Oats pressed, holding up the parchment. "Sucks a poxy cock, but we need to make peace." He gave the demon a warning frown and got close enough to whisper in Fetch's ear. "Isa, you keep this up and there's going to be blood. Once these mongrels here start dying it's too late. This is Crafty. No chance we put him down without losses. We'll lose Father if his boys get cut down in a fight that didn't need to happen. You know it. Got a choice here, sister mine. Fetch may need a reckoning, but the war chief needs to palaver."

He drew back enough to look her in the eye. The bond of a lifetime allowed him to convey the last bit without words. *We can always kill him later.*

Nostrils flaring, lips pursing, Fetching nodded, her chin grinding against the metal axe haft.

"Let her go," Oats told the demon.

The creature only glared at him, teeth bared.

"Fuqtus!" Crafty called. "Please, release our host."

The monster relinquished his hold. Fetch turned slowly, eyed her adversary up and down.

"To be concluded, Fook Toos," she promised.

The demon made no reply. It was pierced by four bolts, nicked and sliced by twice as many others. Its blood was red, and Oats saw the bulge in the jaw, the tension in the throat that betrayed a warrior attempting to ignore considerable pain.

"Perhaps," Crafty said, still pitching his voice as he'd come no closer, "you would invite us inside."

Fetch stepped around Fuqtus, making the demon tense, but she leveled no aggression toward the wizard beyond a fiery stare.

"Say what you came to, Tyrkanian."

Crafty dabbed at his busted lip with the end of a silken scarf. He made a small, humored noise. "I came to say many, many things.

But, as I was prepared for your and friend Jackal's impetuous natures, I also came prepared to be brief."

"That's a bad start for brief, Crafty," Jackal said, impatience taking a whetstone to his voice.

"Hispartha's king is dead." The wizard's words were quick, slapping the frown off Jackal's face. Crafty squinted at the blood on his scarf. "A grievous fall from his horse."

"Meaning the Black Womb killed him," Jackal said.

Crafty chuckled. "There is no assassin more deadly than the tragic blend of pomposity and cowardice that formed the late king. A man who has never seen battle leading the parade of a freshly formed army while sitting the back of a balky and ill-tempered warhorse invites his own peril. No. Truly, his death was his own making, brought by a peevish need to prove to his queen and her kingdom that he was more than the king consort, a title that always chafed upon his vanity and was seldom heard in an attempt to spare the court his tantrums. Though perhaps it is you, friend Bastards, that deserve the honor of being named his killers, as he was inspired to incompetent martial pursuits by your rebellion. A rebellion I have come now to help you win."

"No chance we will accept your help," Fetch declared.

"Well," Crafty sighed, "then we are all of us blessed that you need not accept it in order to receive it."

The wizard made a show of giving the rokh a coy glance before walking purposefully toward the keep. Fuqtus guarded Crafty's back, watching Fetch and Jackal closely. Once they were both inside, Fetching marched over to the downed bird. Oats and Jackal were only a step behind. The rokh was asleep, breathing deep and steady. The maggots had fallen from its eyes. Free from pestilence, its wounds bled clean.

Oats could hear the chief's teeth grinding as she beheld the beast. She took a breath and turned to face Hoodwink. It was a command to approach. The colorless mongrel obeyed. Fetch met his silence with her own, demanding with steel eyes that his explanation came before her question. It was a contest she lost.

"How did this happen?" the chief said when her patience snapped.

"I did as you ordered," Hood answered without feeling.

"I told you to keep her safe!"

"Yes. She is safe."

"Where?" Oats barked.

Hood's black eyes shifted to him. "I will not betray her trust to gain yours."

"She would want me to know!"

"No. She does not."

Oats had to pace a small circle to keep from throwing a punch.

"You tasked me to keep her safe," Hood told Fetching. "You also said in matters concerning Belico, Xhreka's own commands were to be taken over yours."

Oats could see from Fetching's expression that Hoodwink spoke true. She held her hand out, flicking her fingers at Xhreka's note. Oats handed it over.

"I abide by Xhreka's wishes to remain hidden," Hood went on while the chief read. "As I abided by them when she asked to meet with Crafty."

"Why would she do that?" Oats said, trying to keep the growl from his voice.

"The wizard will explain."

"What, have you reached the limit of your words for the year?"

Hood did not respond.

"How did you find him?" Jackal asked with no small amount of heat.

"I let it be known I wished to speak."

"Too much of that going on in this hoof," the chief said, shooting a sour eye at Oats. "That was a fool-ass risk, Hood. Xhreka's wishes or not, you could have brought Zirko's hunters right to you."

"I was careful."

Fetch turned from them all to stare at the keep. She shook her head. "And now that smug sack of suet is sitting in there, waiting for a palaver."

"What do you want to do?"

It was Jackal who asked, but Oats was wondering along with him.

Fetch turned and handed Xhreka's message back. "She asked us to listen, so we'll listen. Xhreka earned that much. But when the time for talking ends . . . Hood, I need to know where you'll stand."

"Beside you, chief."

Fetch nodded. "Good enough. Let's go."

SEVENTEEN

THE SONS OF PERDITION'S VOTING table could have hosted a feast. There were a hundred chairs if there was one, but Oats's attention was too diverted to waste on a count. Small wonder Father's brood of sworn brethren had to assemble in the keep's great hall just for a hoof-meet. There were more axes on that table than Oats had ever seen in one place. Where the Bastards had cast their dissenting votes into a stump, the Sons used an entire gatehouse door suspended by chains behind the table's head.

Despite the glut of chairs, no one sat.

Oats and Jackal stood flanking Fetch on one side of the table, Crafty and his demon on the other. Hoodwink waited at the foot, far removed, favoring neither side. Oats tried not to put too much weight on the choice of Hood's position, but it was impossible.

Fetch and Crafty started speaking at the same time.

"Why did Xhrek—"

"You are losing this wa—"

With any other two mongrels, it might have been humorous.

The chief took a breath. Oats waited for Crafty's smile, the smile that would turn this hall into a battlefield. It didn't come. Instead, face placid, the wizard set the jar containing Belico's tongue on the table.

"She wished to be free from this." Crafty indicated the jar with a dip of his head.

Fetch's jaw muscles bulged. "You removed a god from her head without killing her." It wasn't exactly a question. More an aggravated acceptance of what this foe was capable of.

"Let us say I brokered their separation," Crafty replied.

"Hells," Jackal said. "You made a bargain with Belico. What?"

Crafty cocked an eyebrow. "Friend Jackal. Does it vex you to know we are, both of us, beholden to the Master Slave?"

Jackal didn't answer.

"Be at ease," Crafty said, waving the matter away. "Xhreka wished to depart Ul-wundulas. Belico did not. I merely cut a path for their divergent desires. As to where she went after, I am ignorant. It was not I serving as the halfling's confidant." The wizard's eyes cut briefly to Hood. "Now, let us return to your inability to win this war."

"Why did you help her?" Oats demanded.

Crafty's smile arrived, wide and warm. "Why did you?"

"You fat fuck!"

Fetch threw an arm out, barring Oats from charging over the table. Fuqtus tensed, brandishing his axe. Somewhere on the way to the great hall, the demon had plucked free the bolts piercing his body, though the wounds remained open.

The chief spun, got in Oats's face. He didn't need her glare to tell him he was being a fool-ass. And a two-tongued one in the bargain. It was he who'd convinced her to talk, to at least hear what Crafty had come to say. Now here he was, trying to vault large-ass tables to wring the pus out of cunt-faced wizards and their devil pets. Over what? One baiting smile he knew Crafty kept loaded at all times?

"Sorry," Oats said, taking a lesson from Muro. He backed off. "Sorry."

"It is I that should offer apologies," Crafty said. "And I do, friend Oats. I find myself in a room where I know nothing I say will be trusted. However, I should not allow flippancy to replace truth, even if they are equal in their waste of breath. I ask your pardon. And I will give you an honest answer, though you will be hard-pressed to accept it as such." The wizard gestured at the jar. "This is a shield. I return to Ul-wundulas knowing I am neither welcomed nor loved. It would be foolish to come unclad against reprisal. And so, as Fuqtus serves as shield against dread Fetching, so too does the tongue of Belico shield me against Zirko the Hero Father. They are the powers in these Lot Lands. I had to ensure they would not stand in the way of what I have come to do."

You can trust him to help himself.

Xhreka's letter was now tucked beneath Oats's brigand, but its words sprang to his mind.

In doing so, he helped me.

Oats found he was struggling with the awful notion that Crafty had just given them a truthful answer.

"I can't speak for Zirko," Fetching said, "but you're wrong, Uhad, if you trust that horned fuck and his shiny axe can protect you."

"You are welcome to test me," Fuqtus replied, his accented Hisparthan rolling rough and deep from his prodigious chest. His head swiveled to take in the room. "You are *all* welcome to test me. And let Bhadra count the dead."

Crafty laid a hand on the demon's forearm and gave it a ring-weighted pat. "No need, I hope. Fetching, we are enemies. That was my doing. In this, you know I do not lie. So I would beg your patience for a moment to hear me speak other words that have no need of trust to be true. Winter is ended. Hispartha has come. An army surrounds the castile and so your Zahracene allies are cut off. Another force took the eastern port of Urci and besieged Thricehold. You lost the fortress, the lot, and the entirety of a hoof. You faced *one* of their sorcerers and were nearly slain. At least one other with such craft has entered your lands, come up the Guadal-kabir with a fleet that also served to reinforce Kalbarca, already in the Crown's possession. You managed a blockade in the north, but lacked the foresight and the ships to protect the delta. So, Hispartha needs but to set sail from their western ports, bring ships down the length of this great peninsula, and invade from the south, unimpeded."

"Not unimpeded," Jackal declared.

"As ever, brave Jackal, blind luck and daring rewarded you. Yet what of the next fleet, set to depart Galiza in four days?"

Crafty spoke the news without care, but he may as well have dumped a bucket of cold hog piss over their heads. None called him a liar now. They'd be fools to discount such tidings.

"More men, more horses, more provender to feed them. You killed a single sorcerer, Fetching. More are coming. I am pained to say, you and Jackal are not enough to stop them. Hispartha has their own champions, with armies to protect them."

Oats's hand drifted to rub at the aching scar gifted to him by the Maiden Spear.

Crafty continued to address them in swift, steady tones.

"I have no doubt you will fight fiercely, make a valiant stand, feed woeful numbers of frails on foals to the vultures. Alas, I also have no doubt that you will be defeated. Hispartha has, at this moment, three footholds in the Lots. I suspect it will take all of the strength you can muster to defy just one of them. In that time, the Crown will not be idle. A year, perhaps two, and you will wake to find yourself trapped here at Mongrel's Cradle, forced to choose between dying with what remains of your loyal mongrels and fleeing across the Deluged into exile. And I cannot imagine you would run, chief Fetching."

Fetch sneered. "This is the part where you offer to help us."

Crafty shook his head. "I have already helped you. Now comes the part where I ask if you will help yourself."

Jackal growled. "Give the word, Fetch. I can't stomach any more of his spewed shit."

The chief held up a staying hand. "Speak plainly, wizard. And quickly."

"The schemes of empire are never plain and rarely quick, but let us say that the sultans of Tyrkania do not wish to see your rebellion crushed. Once the mongrel hoofs are gone, Hispartha will resettle Ul-wundulas in earnest, bring it back under the full weight and shadow of the Crown. This the empire wishes to prevent. Already they have strived to bolster your cause. The corsairs protecting your harbor would long have been wrested away by Hisparthan coin if the sultans had not tipped the scales—and the loyalty—of the Traedrians with larger sacks of gold. And before you dub me a liar, look to Jackal. He may have shared some wine and ribald jests with the freebooter captains, but they will never love him more than their own enrichment. He knows the Guild Princes of Traedria well enough from his travels, as well as the wealth of the sultans. You would not have one without the other, not with the meager hoard dug from the Pit of Homage."

Jackal's mouth had drawn into a lipless line.

Crafty picked a piece of straw from his robes and let it fall. "Tyrkania's own fleet is not so fickle. They will put enough ships in your service to guard this harbor and set up a cordon at the mouth of the Guadal-kabir. The river will be closed to Hispartha from both ends and Kalbarca will again find itself without reliable supply. As for the army surrounding the castile, I am confident the Crown will be less disposed to attacking when our envoy reaches their camp. The Zahracenes remain subjects of the empire and any violence against them will be considered an ignoble spilling of Tyrkanian blood."

Both Jackal and the chief twitched with annoyance. Oats didn't know Tarif and his men as well as they did, but one of the first things you learned about the Zahracenes was their hatred for Tyrkania. Likely not even Fetch could have stopped them from leaping over the table, scimitars drawn, if they'd been here to listen to Crafty's claims of continued bonds with their conquerors. Tarif had led his tribe out of the empire at great peril to seek a new life. The *shaykh* risked that life when he threw in with the mongrel hoofs. To have that stance used as a bluffing wager in Crafty's writhing snake pit of a mind was an insult the Zahracenes would not suffer.

Yet there were no Zahracenes in the hall. Just a hand count of half-orcs and one . . . whatever the hells Fuqtus was. But the devil didn't matter. Neither did most of the mongrels. The words that mattered came from only two, the wizard and the chief.

"You'd have us trade Hispartha's bootheel for Tyrkania's slave collar?" Fetch hissed. "We should begin calling you Simpleton if you thought I'd ever accept that."

"The sultans do not want these lands. If it were so, you would be in chains even now."

"Tyrkania wants the world," Jackal said. "Try again."

"Tyrkania wants Hispartha," Crafty admitted. "It would behoove the Lots to help them take it."

"You trying to sell us they'll leave the Lots alone after?" Oats put in. "I ain't been there, but that don't sound like Tyrkania's way to me."

Jackal grunted. "It's not."

"And we'll have invited them in," Fetching said, eyes piercing Crafty. "At *your* insistence." Slowly, the chief drew the kataras from her hips. "I have an answer for your sultans. You'll deliver it in a basket filled with your own head."

Jackal's sword filled his hand. So did Hood's, though he made no move to either side of the table. Fuqtus smiled with relish, hands twisting around the haft of his axe. Oats had his tulwar, but he left it sheathed. Compared to the occupants of this hall, a thrice-blood with a sword was about as dangerous as one of the chairs.

"Wait," Crafty said, holding up a hand. His voice remained calm, but Oats thought he detected the barest quiver in the wizard's fingers. "Beyond myself, Tyrkania will not set foot in Ul-wundulas. Such an act would bring immediate war with Hispartha."

Fetch's brow arched. "But aiding the Lots with a blockade will not?"

"It dares Hispartha to aggression, yes. Yet they will have to strike the first blow. They will not take it, this I assure you. The queen shall not risk conflict with the empire while the mongrel hoofs are in revolt. Your rebellion provides opportunity for the sultans to offer themselves as mediator, to wage a war where ink is spilled instead of blood, where the entreaties of envoys replace the anguished cries of the dying."

"With you as their general," Jackal said with distaste.

Ignoring him, Crafty implored Fetching. "Hear me! Tyrkania will do as they wish. Your acceptance is not required. They paid off the corsairs so you would see this. I am bound for Hispartha, chief Fetching, and you would be foolish to attempt to stop me, for you know well the discord I bring to those that take me in. Slay me in this hall to slake your lust for vengeance and you crush a scorpion that would crawl into Hispartha's bed."

"The throne, you mean," Fetch replied. "Rather kill a fork-tongued tun of shit now than a usurping sorcerer-king later."

"My chance to wear Hispartha's crown passed when you thwarted the orc incursion. The frails would only accept a half-breed as their ruler if he had saved them from the thicks. Now they are at war with the hoofs, cursing the name of the Hoof Queen by day and fearing she will come north to redden her hands with their children's blood by night. Their hatred for half-orcs is a river deeper and wider than ever."

"Sounds like that makes you a shit ambassador to send, then," Fetch said.

Crafty shrugged. "I am well versed in being hated. But I will also be feared. It is important that Hispartha sees the strength of Tyrkania's sympathies toward the hoofs. Who better to display such but another ash-colored half-breed?"

"With his *djinn* slave at his side," Jackal said.

Fuqtus's lips curled back. "I am no slave."

Jackal held the demon's glare unflinching. And sniffed.

Crafty leaned over the table toward Fetching. "But also with those at my side that you choose to represent the hoofs."

The chief frowned. "You would have me send riders into Hispartha? With *you*? So they can be taken prisoner and executed?!"

"The Crown will not be so foolish. Hispartha will know us for what we are, envoys of Tyrkania and the Lot Lands, come to discuss the future and wisdom of this growing conflict."

"And offer them what? They want nothing from us save our obedience. We won't be fucking dogs!"

Crafty arched a brow. "If you wish to win the meat that is Ulwundulas, you must be. As we speak, this land is clamped between the jaws of Hispartha and Tyrkania, pulled at and fought over. It tears and bleeds. You think the mongrel hoofs are in that fight. I tell you, you are but maggots clinging to the prize. And you will be devoured by whichever dog wins. I offer a chance to place yourselves truly within the contest."

Fetch hesitated. Oats could see she wasn't pleased by the wizard's words, but still she considered them. Crafty saw it too, and pressed.

"There are many ways to fight the Crown, and it now rests unsteadily on the queen's head. The king consort's death has seeded the court with uncertainty. Ursaria Trastorias is the most powerful ruler Hispartha has seen in a century and even she, for a fortnight, made the false claim her husband was merely injured. Their union is childless, and she is surrounded by grasping dukes and capricious barons whose ambitions are now turned from fighting half-orcs to becoming the next king consort. Many within the nobility do not share their sovereign's appetite for war, not for a dusty piece of gristle infested with orcs and the progeny born from their raids. There is a chance, likely the only one you will ever see, to forever rid Hispartha of its desire for Ul-wundulas. You have shown willingness to wage war on dusty plains. Show them you have the courage to offer battle in their courts, as well, and you can only help your cause. You can offer the ruling frails proof, through their own eyes, that half-orcs are more than uncouth marauders."

"More?" Fetching said, her voice dropping to a dangerous hush. "They would have us be even less. They have mongrels in Hispartha, Tyrkanian. Pit fighters. Field hands. Whores. *Slaves*."

Crafty did not shrink from her simmering gaze. "Yes. But not hoof riders. Not free mongrels."

The calm truth of the wizard's words slapped against the hot iron of Fetch's anger.

"There are allies to be found in Hispartha, dread Fetching. Powerful allies. You cannot win them by remaining nothing more than a distant rebel. And you will not help any of our fellow mongrels still in bondage by dying down here and allowing the history of this war to be written by the queen's chroniclers."

Oats could see the bulge of Fetch's working jaw. The katara hanging in her right hand rocked against her leg as her wrist twisted back and forth, reflecting the faster working of her conflicted thoughts.

Oats held his breath, waiting for her to choose. His eyes drifted to the table, resting on the nearest axe before moving to the massive door. The Sons may not have had the hardest reputation in the Lots, but from the midpoint of the table, where Oats now stood, any mongrel had to be a sure arm to make that cast. A strong arm. Oats wondered. Could he make that throw? Would he make that throw? If Fetch chose blood in this hall, in this moment . . .

"I'll go."

The words left Oats's mouth, urged by those in Xhreka's letter.

You can save Wily, Idris.

Every eye in the room was upon him, but Oats looked only at his chief.

"I'll go," he said again.

EIGHTEEN

THERE WAS SOMETHING WRONG WITH the pie. Oats could tell by looking at it. The crust was gummy and underdone. He took a bite. The filling was over-salted. Oats kept eating. The sauce was a touch curdled. Oats hummed in appreciation. The speckle beans were pebbles, resisting his chewing and rolling beneath his teeth. He swallowed them whole. The onions and mushrooms had congealed into an unpleasant jelly. Oats choked it all down. And when Beryl offered him a second helping he held out his empty bowl with a smile.

Many an orphan had been raised on her barbarian pie. More than a few slopheads—and at least two sworn Bastards—had snuck back to Winsome on occasion in hopes of begging a portion. Oats had never known Beryl to serve a bad one.

But there was something wrong with this pie. There was something wrong with his mother.

Oats hadn't believed it when Jackal told him she'd given up the daily care of the foundlings, but the house she occupied in Salduba was silent, the trestle hardly large enough to accommodate Oats, Thistle, and Muro. Sitting upon a stool a little removed from the table, Beryl watched the boy.

"He's barely eating," she said, the veil of concern not quite covering the judgment.

Muro was waging a dutiful war with his meal. He didn't complain or make faces. Such antics weren't known to a child brought up under the cruel hand of the stablemaster. Muro had gone hungry enough in his life to eat whatever he was given. But he wasn't having an easy time with the hard, barely cooked beans.

"You're used to mongrel appetites, Mother," Oats said.

"His stomach's been sour since the ship," Thistle added, stroking the back of Muro's head.

The boy looked up. "It's not. No. It's not. Now."

Earnest little cub didn't know when he was being rescued. Oats felt a swell of pride and put his spoon into Muro's bowl, digging out a healthy chunk and shoving it in his own mouth, making an exaggerated animal noise. Muro and Thistle laughed. Beryl's weary mask was cracked by the thinnest of smiles.

"Jackal hid a cicada in his pie once, to teach you not to do that," she said.

Oats nodded, chuckling. "Worked too. Though it weren't Jaco, it was . . . aw, hells. That other mongrel, one with the crooked legs. Can't believe I forgot his name. What was it?"

Beryl frowned at the question. She thought a moment. Slowly, her head began to shake. "It was Jackal, Idris. He hid the cicada in his stew so you wouldn't eat it anymore. Isa put him up to it. I wouldn't forget that; I was so angry."

Oats went back to eating. He didn't mention the fact that Beryl was now saying stew when it had been pie a moment ago. And it *wasn't* Jackal. The name of the other boy came to Oats now. Diogo. Fetch never put him up to anything. Nor was Beryl mad when he'd done it. She'd always encouraged Diogo to be clever, knowing his crippled legs would keep him from the hoof. How could she forget him?

Muro laid his spoon down in his empty bowl. "I want a norange, thank you please."

Beryl's brow knit. She looked at Oats. "A what?"

"It's a Zahracene fruit, Mother. I can't really say it either."

"*Nāranj*," Thistle offered, her carefully pronounced Urzhar making Beryl's scowl deepen.

"Whatever that is, there's none here."

"No, of course not," Thistle said with a genuine smile. "It was our habit at the castile."

"Why don't you two go down to the port," Oats said. "I wager there will be something tart and pulpy to be found."

"Don't be crude, Idris," Beryl said.

"I meant fruit!"

"And don't speak when your mouth is full."

Thistle helped Muro slide off the bench and whispered in his ear. He went around the table to Beryl.

"Thank you for my food," he said. Before Beryl could answer, Muro embraced her, heedless that she stiffened.

Thistle leaned down and kissed her cheek as the boy withdrew. "We'll return."

Beryl nodded. "Good . . . good."

"Find me a pet monkey," Oats instructed Muro as he crossed to the door. Thistle squeezed his arm on the way out. Oats returned to his food, delaying what needed to be done.

"She should look in on the foundlings," Beryl said, eyes still on the doorway. "That wetnurse Father's employed looks like a *ghan* addict."

"We've been," Oats said. Truth was, the Bastards' orphans were fat and happy, as were all three of the wetnurses in the Sons' service. Salduba-by-the-sea would have been a paradise for anyone. After all the terrors the Bastards' children had suffered, it was a dream. Oats had hoped his mother would find succor here too, but Beryl looked sallow and unkempt. Diminished. "You see them much? The children?"

Beryl's head drew back on her neck, affronted. "Every day."

It wasn't true. None at the Sons' orphanage had seen her in weeks, but it would do no good to confront his mother and risk her wrath. According to Jackal, the chief had placed a serving girl with Beryl when she first began to withdraw. The poor frail had fled the house weeping before the first morning was over. When Jackal had asked her about it, Beryl told him she didn't understand why she couldn't have Sweeps. Jackal was forced to remind her Sweeps died in Winsome. Beryl shouted him out of the house, casting blame and a water pitcher at his back.

"With Thistle returned, I'll take our own back in hand," she declared now, her face daring Oats to challenge the claim. Her strength, once forged to her spine, was now exposed, flailing in the air as a threat against anyone, everyone. Wielded so brazenly against those who meant her no harm, Beryl's steel became a frightened display. A show of weakness.

Oats nearly didn't tell her. It would have been a simple thing, keeping his mouth shut. And a shameful act of disrespect. Beryl hadn't raised a coward.

"Mother . . . I might be going away."

Annoyance kindled upon Beryl's face. She stood, gathering up the bowls. "You all think I've entered my dotage. I *know*, Idris. Who you are, where you've been, where *she* will keep sending you. I've lived in the Lots longer than any of you have been alive and I still know the direction of every mountain range in Ul-wundulas. Including the Smelteds! So don't treat the woman that taught you how to eat with a spoon like a fool."

Oats repressed a sigh, knowing the sound would only rile her further. "I don't think you're a fool. Wasn't how I meant to sound. It ain't the Smelteds, where I'm going . . . where I might go, I reckon is more earnest. It's Hispartha."

Beryl turned and deposited the bowls in the wash bucket. Oats waited on her reaction. She cocked her head at the bucket.

"You forgotten how to scour?"

Oats jumped up. "No, Mother."

His hands entered the water, snagging the floating brush on the way.

Beryl returned to her stool. "Tell me."

Oats talked while he scrubbed. He told her all of it, slowly and carefully to make sure she understood. It was selfish, but Oats needed her guidance not her confusion. Yes, she was forgetting things and not caring for the orphans and the pie was bad, but this was still

Beryl, still the wisest person Oats had ever known. The person who taught him whom to trust—how to trust—not only through stern lesson but by proving to him every day of his life that she could always be trusted.

The chore didn't take near as long as the tale.

When he was done, Beryl's jaw was set in a way that never boded well.

"Fetching agreed to this?" she asked.

"Not yet," Oats replied. "But she's considering it. Let Crafty and his demon leave in peace."

"And Hood?"

Oats let out a hard breath. "He stayed. Chief was shut up with him for a long while."

"Without you."

"Without anyone. Not even Jackal."

"There's not another chief in the Lots that wouldn't view what Hood did as a betrayal."

"And were it any other mongrel, Fetch would have too. But . . . there are bigger things than loyalty to a hoof these days. She's said that herself. I think Hood was trying to make sure she listened. I'd wager it was Xhreka, not Crafty, that asked him to help prevent blood."

Beryl's mouth twisted. "That wizard still enjoyed watching Bastards pitted against each other."

"Reckon so."

Beryl stood. "You should go down and meet Thistle."

Oats was perplexed by the sudden dismissal. Hells, had she forgotten what he'd just told her?

"Come with me," he offered, thinking to remind her on the way. She needed out of this lonely dwelling.

Beryl shook her head. "No. I hate the smell of the sea."

Oats felt his heart sink. She would, wouldn't she? Not that anywhere in Salduba offered an escape from the briny air.

"Go on," his mother insisted. "Thistle will not thank you if that boy finds a monkey and she's left to deny him alone."

"I can't leave until you understand that—"

She chopped his words off with a sharp wave. "Idris, you're not going to Hispartha. I understand you believe that you might. I understand you think me a fuddled old crone who can't hold on to the last thing she was told. I understand what *you* don't—that Isabet will never agree to anything that wretched Tyrkanian puts forth. You're not going because your chief will not send you. Not for all the gold in Sardiz, and certainly not at the urging of an enemy with more faces than he has chins. So. Enough with this fretting over me and leaving for Hispartha. You're staying in the Lots, Idris. Where you belong."

Oats made no reply. The truth had taken him unawares, delivered a scoundrel's punch to the guts. He'd sought his mother's incisive clarity, but was unprepared for the direction it cut. She wasn't the befuddled fool in this room.

Beryl peered at him, saw something she didn't like, something Oats couldn't hide.

She took a step closer, face turning grave. "You *want* to go."

Still, he said nothing. He didn't need to.

Beryl's eyes became bright. The fury in their cores caused the tears at their edges to shine.

"Now you can explain to me something I don't understand," she said, teeth tight.

"It's because of Wily . . ."

"Don't."

"And Warbler."

"Don't!"

Oats struggled to keep his voice low in the face of his mother's growing agitation. "I have to help them. If I travel with Crafty, I can convince him to undo what he did. Bargain for it. I don't know how yet, but I'll make him remove the plague."

Beryl's hands came up, tensed into quivering claws. She rattled them in Oats's face.

"Leave them in peace! Why can't you fucking Bastards not simply leave them in peace?!"

She seized the wash bucket and flung it, scattering water and shards of shattered bowls across the room. The violent motion forced her back to turn. Oats moved to calm her, but Beryl spun on him, face twisted with hateful, ugly grief.

"What more must they suffer for your meddling? Banishment and wizards! Plagues and agonizing magic! He's a boy! Only a boy, but his life is a hell! And you would make it worse! Will Warbler be torn from him next? Will he be left alone with those hiding, useless rustskins? Or will none of you be satisfied until he is dead?"

Oats could have stopped himself. He didn't want to. Seizing his mother by the arms, he pushed her back a step, shook her as he screamed into her face.

"I AM TRYING TO SAVE HIS LIFE!"

He was larger, stronger, louder. He'd long known how to transform his voice into a bestial cudgel. It was a mistake to try to beat Beryl down with such a crude weapon. Oats had known that before impatience and the unjust lash of her words had goaded him into selfish cruelty. Yet still he'd done it. There was no undoing the painful pressure of his bruising fingers, the threat in his shouting, the shame of laying hands on a loved one in pain.

Beryl met his ferocity with a glazed look, cold and dispirited. For a single hellish heartbeat something, everything, between them broke. Oats felt a lifetime of affection extinguished, saw the sparks scatter upon winds of regret and die in the agonizing silence that replaced his outburst.

Denying that death, Beryl rekindled the flame in the next instant. Her hands came up to rest upon his face, even as his own fell from her arms. In that touch, Oats felt the chains that bound them return, hot from fires of forgiveness. Beryl's thumbs rested near the corners of his eyes, the heels of her hands pressed into his cheeks, channeling his tears into his mouth. She waited, with all the patience he had lacked, until he could look her squarely.

"Never reckoned I'd curse the day I saw myself in you," she said. Her words rippled with constrained emotion. "Perhaps this is why mongrels were not meant to know their mothers."

Oats shook his head, pressing his cheeks harder into her hands. "Don't say that."

She shushed him. "Listen to me. You need to kill that part of you.

Right now. Damn me to all the hells for giving it to you, but I am telling you to rid yourself of care for that child. Wily is lost to us. You cannot save him. Try, and you will only bring more pain. To him, yourself, all those around you." Her voice broke. She mastered a rising sob, choked it down. "You're all so afraid I've lost my senses. That my memory has fled. Then tell me why I still remember every moment in the hands of the thicks. Tell me why age hasn't given me the mercy of forgetting that orcs only laugh when . . ."

Beryl's mouth clamped shut. She grimaced, the muscles in her stricken face squeezing out the tears. She looked away, though Oats felt her thumbs rubbing his face.

"I know what it is to want to save a child," she said. "What it is to suffer for it. And I know what it is to have that child return, to learn it too suffered greatly despite all you tried to do. To know that baby lived only to become a monster."

"Mother . . . Wily ain't Ruin. He ain't a monster."

Beryl raised her head to look at him once more. The tears had tempered her eyes, restoring their old steel. "Wily is the plaguebearer. What's your memory of the Claymaster?"

Oats struggled to answer.

Beryl's hands fell from his face. She wilted onto the stool.

"Give this up, Idris. There are no words you can say, no bargain you can make, that will ever, *ever* make Crafty help you. Go down to the harbor, be with the boy you *could* save, and figure how you can survive Fetch's war long enough for that to matter. Do it for me. I already lost Avram trying to help Wily. I can't lose you to the same folly."

Oats swallowed. "You saying we shouldn't have even tried to cure him?"

The question leeched what little strength Beryl had left. Her answer could barely be heard in the little room.

"I should have seen there was no difference between taking one child by wagon to Dog Fall and swimming the Gut with another."

Jackal stood waiting for Oats outside the house. His dark desert robes contrasted sharply against Salduba's cobbled streets and whitewashed buildings.

"Chief reached a decision?" Oats asked.

Jackal shook his head. "Just reckoned I should be here. After you saw her. Didn't go in because . . ."

Because it's your fault she was banished from Dog Fall.

Oats didn't say it. This day didn't need any more bitter words.

"I brought this," Jackal said, holding his arm up to display a jug dangling from his finger.

Oats stepped to him and grabbed the vessel. He removed the stopper and took a pull. Brusque wine flowed over his tongue. It was good. The best he'd had since . . . well, ever.

"How is she?" Jackal asked, glancing at the door to the house.

Oats took another drink before answering. "You know."

"I'd hoped that seeing you would help."

Oats laughed. The day wasn't done with bitter sounds, after all. He started walking, but stopped when Jackal fell into step beside him.

"A favor, brother?"

"Name it," Jack replied.

"Go down to the harbor. Find Thistle. Tell her . . ." Oats fumbled for the right words.

"You needed to be alone," Jackal said, forcing his voice to remain light and easy.

Oats gave him a grateful nod. "That. And that I'm sorry."

"Don't think she'll need the second part, Oats."

Jackal clapped him on the shoulder and turned away, his measured stride carrying him confidently toward the docks.

Oats was less certain of his own destination.

He found himself in one of Salduba's wine sinks. Then another. And a third. Fourth?

It was a fool-ass pursuit for an afternoon, getting drunk. It had become a habit during his first turn at the Pits. The only thing he had to dull the pain of the fights, the only way to drown the screams of the crowd. Xhreka had put a hobble on it before he became just another sot forcing the wine and the fights into a race for what would kill him swifter. If she were here to see him now she'd have pinned him with her one-eyed scowl. Oats could hear the admonishments.

Sure. Get drunk. That's what the world needs, another swilling, slurring thrice-blood.

Oats chuckled into his flagon. This wine wasn't as good as Jackal's, but that had been exhausted before he left the street.

A man sitting farther down the bench looked over, his gaze drawn by the lonely laughter.

"Sometin' in m'beard?" Oats challenged.

Shaking his head, the frail went in search of a better place to sit.

An angry thrice looking for a fight now. Yes. That's a much better choice!

"I'd tell you t'shuttup," Oats muttered, tilting the flagon for the last fingers, "but you ain't here. You got what y'wanted n' fucked off. Where to, Zz-reeka? Calmaris? The Drag—*ugh*, that tasted better a'first time—the Dragonfly Isles?"

A hand slithered up Oats's arm and didn't stop until it reached the side of his neck. The hand was attached to a woman, near as drunk as himself. She kept twisting at the hips as she touched him, giving that offer of a smile used by whores who learned long ago that words were a waste of time.

"Hells!" Oats exclaimed, louder than he'd meant to. "The fucking Sons! Yer wine is good. Whores is comely. The castle hasabeach!"

His laughter stampeded out of his chest. The whore took it for encouragement and moved to sit on his lap. Oats bumped her awkwardly as he stood, nearly knocked her down.

"Pardons," he said, and stumbled out the door.

The woman followed him out, called something at his back. An insult or a final temptation, he couldn't say. The tide of wine was all he could hear. No, that was the surf. Oats's ass was in sand.

When had he reached the beach? When had the sun set?

The sea was queer at night. A shifting, inky void between countless, stark stars and the pale, glowing swath of sand. It might have been beautiful, but Oats couldn't focus on it for long without getting dizzy. He laid back, the sound of the waves blending with the pleasant drifting sensation in his head. To his left, he could hear the distant camp of the former galley slaves. They were singing. The words were lost, but Oats reckoned their voices sounded cheerful enough. At least some had found Salduba to be a place of happiness.

He might have slept. It was still dark when he sat up. And he was still fucking drunk. Nice enough for now, but Oats could feel his skull preparing to craft a few iron spikes of agony by sunrise. The mongrels in the camp were silent, most of their fires out. Dawn was a fair span away yet, Oats reckoned. A much smaller light approached him first, coming down from the docks. A lantern, borne by a lone figure.

He didn't want company, considered moving on, but the wine mocked the notion of him going anywhere in a straight line and in a hurry. So he stayed planted, a besotted beach turnip.

The light made directly for him, its nimbus shielding the intrusive bearer. The figure stopped a few strides away and lowered the lantern to the sand.

Thistle stepped around into the pool of light. She looked down at him for a moment, hair tugged by the incessant breeze. Oats turned back to the water and waited for the chastisements to fall.

"I'm so sorry, Oats."

The tender compassion in Thistle's voice washed warmly over him. Guilt delivered a hammer blow in the same instant. Why was she always so kind? He'd never done anything but saddle this woman with burdens.

Thistle lowered herself down next to him. They sat together in silence for a long while. Oats nearly asked who was looking after Muro, but knew it was an unworthy question. Thistle would have made certain someone would be near if the boy woke.

"How'd you find me?" he asked instead.

"A drunken Big Bastard leaves quite the trail," Thistle replied with a hint of tease.

Oats grunted a laugh, shook his head. "Fool-ass way to carry on."

"Certainly is. If it's every night. Every day. Not with what you've suffered these last months." Thistle bumped him with her body, forced his attention. She titled her chin at the discarded bottle near his feet. "Anything left in that?"

Oats wasn't sure. He managed to snag the bottle after a few failed attempts, but the weight proved a disappointment.

"Just dregs and a little sand," he said.

Thistle clicked her tongue with regret as Oats flicked the bottle back to the beach.

"It's beautiful here," Thistle said after a span.

"Makes a mongrel hate the Sons a little," Oats replied. "The Lots are supposed to be made of misery. I reckon the Claymaster must always have been mad. Can't see how he didn't end up with this during the allotment draw, elsewise."

"Perhaps he feared what a refuge like this would do to him. Or how it would make him appear. He never did want to show weakness."

Oats often forgot that Thistle's tenure with the Grey Bastards was almost as long as his own. She'd stayed most nights in the Kiln, hearing the gripes and confessions of a sworn brother for years. Likely those included the old chief more often than not.

"You ever miss him?" Oats asked.

Thistle cocked an eye at him. "The Claymaster?" She let the jest hang for a moment before grinning, showing she knew his true meaning. Her face became somber, the starlight illuminating a fondness in her eyes. "Roundth was . . . loving. Lusty as Polecat, which was fucking exhausting. It was rare that after a day of tending babes I wanted to break the bed, but Roundth had this—"

"Keg of a cock."

The wine made Oats say it and fueled the laughter that followed. He knew it wasn't respectful, but he was watching a mummer's show of himself, a powerless spectator to his own braying japes.

Thistle clicked her tongue again, but there was no regret in the sound now. "He *was* named for it. But it didn't drive him. Unlike Cat, who would fuck anything, Roundth wasn't ruled by his lust. He wanted . . . me. That's how he made me feel. Desired, even when I didn't want to be. He could be dimwitted and selfish—I think you all get that when you don the brigand—and, yes, it was often a relief when he was on patrol and I was spared going up to the Kiln, and there were many, *many,* nights I considered not going up even when he was there. But. That mongrel could look at me and I saw this . . . awe, as if he couldn't quite grasp how fortunate he was that I chose to share myself with him. That's what kept me going back. That and the shame that I didn't feel the same."

The confession took a moment to puncture Oats's dulled brain. He didn't have a response. Thankfully, Thistle didn't appear to need one.

"I was wed," she continued, talking at the sea. "Before all this. A mother. When that life died, I didn't. I made a new one in Winsome. I was a wetnurse and, later, a bedwarmer. You hoof-riders are honest in your titles. I reckoned I knew what was required. Your mother warned me against it, but after a while I needed something other than the orphans. I was already letting mongrel babes suckle from my body, why not let a mongrel man use it for another purpose? Beryl told me if I was to do it, I should choose Hobnail. She said Roundth was too moon-eyed when he looked at me. I know now she was trying to spare me what she suffered. Loving a rider only to lose him. Well, I lost him, but I never loved him. Truth is, I can't say for certain I miss him either. Those days seem so far gone I can't imagine him here. It's as if he's tethered to that time. I don't know how to yearn for something that never was. Too busy hoping for what might be."

"And what's that?"

Thistle tossed her head back and loosed a nearly silent, mirthless laugh at the sky. "They say the gods don't have a place in Ulwundulas, but at least one found its way here to laugh at me."

Oats had upset her. He just wasn't sure when. "I'm sorry, Thistle. I'm drunk and—"

"Upset. I know. Jackal said you wanted to be alone. I should have listened." Thistle stood, brushed the sand from the back of her skirts. "Truly, Oats, it pains me about Beryl. Know that I will look after her."

"You don't have to do that."

"I'm not looking for a reprieve from you. Or gratitude. Beryl has always been kind to me. She is my friend. We spent years together with Sweeps and Cissy. She and I are all that is left now. I would care for her even if I hated you."

"Do you? Hate me?" Fuck all wine to the ending of the world. Why couldn't he keep this foolery locked behind his teeth?

"I hate that you won't look at me."

"That ain't true," Oats said, aware that he turned his gaze back to the surf when he spoke.

"You look at me like you fear you'll never be able to repay a debt, not—"

"All worshipful like Roundth?"

"Not like a woman you would raise a child beside."

"I'm a Bastard, Thistle. A half-orc sworn to a hoof. I ain't ever going to raise a child beside anyone."

"Then why save him? Muro? Why care?"

"Because . . . I love him. I won't say it was from the moment I first picked him up, got him out of that brothel room reeking with his mother's corpse. But before I put him down, I loved him. When he got hurt, when it looked like he was going to die, I knew it would kill me too. If not the pain of it, then the anger of it. The injustice, the rage, it'd make me . . ."

"What?"

"Into something too hateful to let live."

Muro had survived and still Oats had committed unspeakable acts. Lucon had died hard, died ugly. The pitiless nomad struck Muro once. Oats made him pay with anguishes that stretched half the night, rendered him powerless as a child. And sobbing like one long before the end. Oats knew the castile's stablemaster had beaten Muro too. It was a mercy for the man—and for Oats—that he'd died during the fortress's fall.

Thistle's voice reached through the sinking morass of black, bloody thoughts.

"Oats. Look at me."

He shook his head, knowing it would hurt her, but worried she'd see. See straight down into the dark of Sancho's cellar. By the time he reburied the truth and found the courage to face her, she was gone.

THERE WAS NOTHING BEAUTIFUL ABOUT the beach in the morning. The stench of low tide set Oats's guts churning. The sun besieged his eyes. He wanted to murder every gull that wouldn't cease trilling, which was all of them.

Worst of all was the toe of the chief's boot burrowing into his hip.

Oats growled in complaint, but managed to sit up.

"Find your legs," Fetch said, tossing a wedge of bread into his lap. "There's a heap to do before we depart."

Oats took up the bread, rolled it around in his hands while he repeated the words in his pounding head until they made sense. It didn't happen.

"We?" he echoed. "You're going to Hispartha with me?"

"No one is going to Hispartha," Fetch replied. "It's time to attack Kalbarca."

NINETEEN

RANT AND ROAR PROVED THEIR worth in a week, offering the chief priceless guidance on the preparation of her fleet. They hadn't the time to build any ships, but those they possessed were repaired, reinforced, crewed, and loaded under the direction of the mongrel shipwrights. The fleet included both the captured Hisparthan war galleys, two merchant vessels outfitted to carry hogs and supplies, and three Traedrian corsairs. The mercenaries would sail as escort as far as the Guadal-kabir, then return to the Cradle. It was vital the harbor remain protected. To that same end, Fetch ordered Father and the Sons of Perdition to stay behind.

Still, the force setting sail from Salduba numbered nearly four hundred. The former galley slaves comprised the bulk. Oats feared many would rebel at the prospect of taking up the oars once more, especially since they would now be rowing toward battle. But Fetch spent time among them as the ships were made ready, placing Jackal in their camp when she was needed elsewhere. The pair of them might as well have been gods.

The liberated mongrels marveled at their presence, laughing at Jackal's jests and setting their jaws in iron when Fetch was near. Oats could conjure memories of Jackal shitting himself on their first patrol ride as slops, his nerves were so frayed. And Fetching used to be so afraid of scorpions she wouldn't step on one even with a booted foot. But these freshly unshackled half-orcs knew none of that. To them, Fetch and Jackal had begun as stories, rebels in faraway Ul-wundulas spitting at the Crown, slaying its cavaleros, and taking its castles. They couldn't be killed, it was said. Even the thicks feared them. They had sworn vengeance on Hispartha, offered a haven to all half-breeds. They were powerful, unconquerable. Free.

By the time Fetching put weapons in their hands, every one of those mongrels was ready to die for her cause. They renamed the ships that once held them in bondage *Crownbreaker* and *Queenslayer,* and set to the oars with a fervor that bordered on frenzy. Fetching traveled on *Crownbreaker* and put Jackal on *Queenslayer*. The new mongrels were eager to prove themselves, but they were untested and would need their beloved champions nearby should the fleet encounter any Hisparthan ships on the way to Kalbarca.

"Didn't we just do this?" Sluggard japed, moments after they were under way. He stood next to Oats on the deck of *Fatback*. The *Stylark* sailed to their starboard. Slug and Jackal had made a contest of naming the hog transports. The chief called them both fool-asses.

"Ain't exactly joyed to sail through the Gut again," Oats replied. "Once was enough."

"'Scream on the poop deck. Die crashing against the rocks,'" Sluggard proclaimed with mock bravado. "Doesn't stir the blood in quite the same way."

Oats couldn't force the laugh Sluggard sought. He kept his gaze fixed on the dwindling harbor.

Thistle had not brought Muro down to see them off.

Oats saw little of them the last few days. He was tasked to help Roar affix stronger rams to the spurs of the galleys. The labor provided unexpected evidence that Oats's old strength was returning. He felt capable again, a sensation nearly forgotten. From sunrise to sunset he'd hoisted, hammered, sweated, and cursed alongside one of the surliest mongrels ever to draw breath. The work had proved a far more effective balm than the wine. His nights were equally long and arduous, staying awake into the late watches planning the attack, holed up with Jackal and Fetching.

The hoofs would be hard-pressed to take Kalbarca by storm. That fact remained as true now as it had from the beginning of the war. Cavalry made poor besiegers whether on hog or horse, and the Lots had nothing to breach the walls that could stand outside the range of the city's guns. Fetching had hoped starving the garrison would force them to abandon Kalbarca. But the frails had not lived up to their name.

The city had to be taken by guile, cracked from within.

Oats didn't know what connection Belico had to the place, but all who dwelled in the Lots knew the halflings claimed the ancient tunnels beneath Kalbarca as their own, grubbing away in the dark for something their once-human god possessed in life. Whatever it was, the stunted worshippers of the Master Slave were Fetch's only hope of capturing the city. She'd urged Zirko all winter to commit his followers to the task, but the Hero Father had remained adamant in his refusal.

He would not command his devout to open the gates. To do so, he claimed, would be a naked hostility toward the Kingdom of Hispartha. Oats reckoned sending Barsius and his killers over the border to aid Thresh and Sluggard's rescue was a worthy risk. Zirko couldn't have his perceived lead to Xhreka getting hanged, for one. Second, the halflings left no survivors beneath Ellerina.

In a city the size of Kalbarca, however, someone would survive. The tale would reach Hispartha, if only as rumor. Zirko would have difficulty denying it was his followers who opened wide the gates, allowing the mongrel rebels to enter. Despite all Fetch held over the Hero Father's head, Zirko stuck to his position. Until now.

"Why'd he change his mind?" Jackal asked, sprawled in a chair around the table in Fetch's solar.

"Because his people are dying," Fetch replied, rubbing bloodshot eyes. She plucked a missive from the table. Jackal sat up to receive it. He read quickly and passed the note to Oats.

A sorcerer has come to the city. He has ordered the tunnels be cleared. My disciples are hunted. There have been executions. Come swiftly. This must stop.

"The Crown has drawn first blood," Jackal said.

"Not in truth," Oats grunted, thinking of all the slit throats in Ellerina's sewers.

"Strava couldn't pretend to stay out of this forever," Fetching declared. She slumped into her own chair. "Zirko's folk would still be alive if he'd agreed to the plan sooner. Hispartha was always going to stomp down with a metal boot. Blue-bloods don't know another way."

Oats placed the missive back on the table. "Think this sorcerer is the one that sailed in on that big ship? The one the galley mongrels were so scared of?"

"The Starving Man," Jackal said, raising his eyebrows to show he thought it was likely. "If the Crown has given him leave to kill the halflings, he'll be formidable. They wouldn't provoke Zirko unless they thought any retaliation could be met."

Oats agreed. "Reckon that's why Zirko just hadn't told his tunnel boys to throw the gates open and let the Unyars ride in."

"Zirko may be angered, but he's never foolish," Fetching said. "No need for his own warriors to die when he knows we'll do it for him."

"We don't have to," Jackal said, drawing a stern look from the chief. "Fetch, we could let this go."

Fetch pressed a finger into the table. "We let this go and we never get another chance. It's spring, Jack. Kalbarca has already been bolstered with men and supplies. They'll only get stronger. If they find all the halflings, Zirko's reasons to help us die."

"We could wait. Force him to help himself."

"And if he decides that he'd rather lose a few dozen acolytes than lose half the Unyar horsemen? Between the river, the walls, the guns, and whatever magic this Starving Man can sling, the Unyars better pray Great Belico is on their side. And what are the chances of that, given where we know his tongue to be?"

"So you want us to ride at the magic and guns?" Oats asked.

"I'm saying Zirko *won't* risk it. But we have to. Leaving Kalbarca in Crown hands will see them win this war by summer."

Jackal leaned forward, took a deep breath. "Chief, if we all die during this attack, the Crown wins within a fortnight."

Fetch picked up another slip of paper. "Which is why I've made Zirko give his word that if we aid his people now, he'll have the Unyars take the field against Hispartha's armies. They'll ride with us to help Tarif at the castile and, after, to retake Thricehold. That's ten thousand horses, bows, and swords that would have done nothing but protect Strava otherwise."

Oats slid the kerchief from his head. It was itching something awful from the day's sweat. "Why don't the halflings flee? After what I seen with Barsius, you can't sell me they don't have a hundred secret ways out of the city."

"It's holy ground for them, Oats," Jackal said. "Somewhere down there is a relic of Belico or one of his brothers—"

"Another Eye of a Big Thick Cock?"

Jackal made a disappointed face. "You've had better."

Oats shrugged. "I'm tired."

"We're all tired," Fetch warned.

"They won't abandon that site," Jackal finished quickly.

Fetching stood. "So we seize this chance. Rant tells me the ships will be ready before week's end. We sail the instant the last nail is hammered. Or knot tied . . . or whatever the fuck. Hells, I hate boats."

"You should sleep, Fetch," Jackal said. He stood. "We all should."

Oats stayed where he was. He stared at his friends.

"What is it?" Fetch asked. The question was patient despite her obvious weariness.

"Belico's tongue," Oats replied. "You said we know where it is. What if Zirko does too?"

Jackal chewed on an answer, but didn't produce one. The room was silent for a span.

"He might," Fetch said at last. "Though I think if it were so simple, he would have reclaimed it long ago. He wouldn't need to have dogs like Barsius sniffing your crack for a trail. And I don't think

Xhreka would have relinquished it if she thought doing so would put it at greater risk of falling into Zirko's hands. She found a new guardian for it. We all know how dangerous Crafty is. If Zirko knows, let him confront the wizard. Those two killing each other wouldn't be the worst outcome."

"Fetch," Jackal said, the word a reproach. "Zirko saved me. He saved you."

The chief looked down at the table, her jaw clenching. When she looked up again there was no anger in her eyes, only more fatigue.

"Belico isn't our burden anymore. Zirko can go on thinking we're hiding the tongue or not. Right now, I could care a fuck." Fetch glanced at Jackal. "He's helped us in the past. Always with something to gain. This is no different. We help save his people, we get Kalbarca and the largest army in the Lots. Agreed?"

They had.

And now, the planning and preparations complete, they sailed.

Oats's second passage through the Gut was easier than the first. It wasn't storming, for a start, and the merchant galley, far larger than Burgos's boat, navigated the strait with less drifting. The Tower of Herathos and Ruukam Ul'nuul—pillars that marked the gateway between worlds—came and went without peril. Soon, the river delta opened to embrace the fleet. The Traedrian corsairs did not enter. As ordered, they came about and set a course back east.

Traveling upriver, the fleet plunged deeper into the estuary, flanked by white dunes keeping the salt marsh beyond at bay. Gangly water birds high-stepped along the banks and through the bogs, keen eyes and pointed beaks on the lookout for unwary fish. Oats kept his eyes on the sky, stockbow in hand. This was rokh country. It was doubtful one of the massive raptors would attack a ship, but he wasn't about to be as complacent as some damn fish.

The chief's rokh hadn't recovered enough to make the journey. Jackal had broached the idea of stopping in the Old Maiden for Fetch to master another, but she'd swiftly dismissed the notion.

"No time," she said. "I was dizzy and sick for days the first time, remember?"

"Yes, but you understand it now. You're stronger—"

"*Jack*. There's not time."

True to the chief's order, the fleet did not tarry. By dusk of the first day on the river, they reached the meeting point with the Shards.

Notch and three score mounted mongrels sat their hogs on the eastern bank, watching as the ships moored. Oats disembarked, joining Fetch and Jackal on shore. Together they tramped through the reeds toward the Shards' chief, but it was the hatchet-faced mongrel beside him they greeted first.

"There are my fellow Bastards!" Polecat said, smiling as he dismounted.

They all embraced him, even the chief.

"Heard you were nearly killed and your beard fell out," Polecat said, clapping Oats on both shoulders.

"It did. This is a whore's minge."

"So long as you gave her a good ride on that face, eh?"

There was laughter all around.

Notch came down off his hog, the river wind snapping the embroidered scarves tied about his head and waist.

"You made good time," he told Fetch.

The Shards' fortress of Shatterhand lay due east from the river, separated from the Gut by the Fangs of Our Fathers' lot.

Fetch took in the assembled riders. "No luck finding Kul'huun."

"None," Notch replied. "I sent patrols, but they came back shaking their heads. Not even a single *ulyud*."

Oats could tell Fetching was disturbed by the news of the Fangs' absence, but she didn't dwell on it long. Kul'huun and his half-naked band of thick-worshipping mongrels had kept their own queer ways since the hoof's founding. Those ways had only grown stranger with the arrival of the chief's twin brother and their resurrected elven mother. Hells knew where that gaggle of zealots and sorcerers had gone. Fetch suspected Dhar'gest. Wisely, she had not hung her planning on the Fangs' participation.

"Good to know the orcs are staying away," she said. "What about Sparthis?"

"Scouted it myself," Notch told her. "Frails have it occupied, like you reckoned."

"They see you?"

Notch shook his head. "Me and my boys know how to stay out of sight. There's four score men on the island. Arbalesters, mostly. They're clustered near the southern end, waiting for you. The city may be a ruin, but it makes for a strong redoubt. And a watch post. The frails there can give Kalbarca ample warning if you come upriver. Try to sail through and your decks will be raked with thrumbolts from the old walls. The bigger threat waits at the north end of the western channel. Three war galleys. And they've learned their lesson. No slaves on those ships; rowers are all men-at-arms. No going around because, as you know, the eastern channel is already impassable."

Polecat sniggered and pointed a pair of splayed fingers at Oats and Jackal. "Heard that was you two."

"Seem to recall it was the frails that set the bridge on fire," Oats said looking at Jack.

"Can't really take the credit," Jackal agreed with a jaunty tilt of his head.

Notch sucked his teeth. "Well, Al-Unan fire will do that. And those galleys upriver have plenty."

"This redoubt on Sparthis?" Fetch pressed. "Any cannons?"

"Not yet, but they could bring them downriver at any time." The former sellsword thought a moment, rubbing a thumb beneath his stubbly chin. "I don't think they'll make the effort, though. They know you don't want Sparthis. That pile of rock is just a good vantage with a heap of cover. Frails'll keep their strength at Kalbarca."

Jackal raised his eyebrows at the chief. "Meaning no wizards at Sparthis."

"Right," Fetching said, eyes going blank for a moment. She made a decision, nodded once. "Get Hood."

Jackal ran back to the ships without hesitation.

"What are you thinking?" Notch asked.

Fetch answered him with her own question. "You hear from Pulp Ear?"

"Yes," Notch replied, frowning at the dodge. "He's waiting at

Black Knuckle. Said the Brotherhood would be ready to ride when we arrived. Tusked Tide is there already."

Fetch pointed at the less burdened of the two merchant galleys. "Get your mongrels and barbarians loaded onto that boat."

"It's the *Stylark*," Oats said.

Fetch shot him a barbed look.

Notch expelled an uncomfortable laugh. "War chief . . . did you not hear when I spoke about the rain of bolts from the island and the blockade of ships?"

"I heard."

"So rather than load my hogs onto a boat, let's offload yours and we can ride to Black Knuckle."

"The river's quicker," Fetch said without looking at Notch. She was too busy drawing her kataras to check the edges on the blades. "And I got nearly three hundred mongrels without mounts who wouldn't know how to straddle a razor even if I gave them one."

Notch stepped closer, lowered his voice. "You'll lose most of them trying to run that channel. The rest will burn when you reach the blockade. You can't—"

Fetch turned away from the frustrated hoofmaster and moved to meet Jackal and Hoodwink as they rode up from the bank leading the chief's hog.

"None of ours are going to die, Notch," Fetching said, climbing atop Womb Broom. "Get your hoof on board. We'll be back before dawn."

The chief spurred her hog without another word, Jackal and Hoodwink at her flanks. They followed the river north at a gallop.

Notch turned to Oats. "She can't intend—"

"To clear the frails off Sparthis with just them two to help her?" Oats said. "Yes, Shard. That's what she intends to do."

Polecat shook his head and laughed with appreciation. "Hells, those three make me hard."

The sight of them riding away did something entirely different to Oats. Gritting his teeth against the unpleasant broth of worry brewing in his craw, he turned to face the Shards.

"Loading hogs ain't swift work!" Oats called out so all could hear. "Let's get to it. You got an ornery pig, I need to know now!"

It took near half the night, but in time the *Stylark* was sitting as low in the water as the *Fatback*, holds echoing with the snorts, grunts, and squeals of the confined barbarians. The Shards milled on deck. They used dice, hushed conversation, or mute vigilance to mask their uncertainty about being on the water, depending on the mongrel. None slept.

Polecat ran a hand along the rail and scrunched up his face. "I dunno. Think I'd have named her . . . *Young Whore*. Wet, salty, and filled with the pork between fifty mongrels' legs."

Oats huffed. "Then the other should be *The Leaky Cod*."

"Had that a time or two," Polecat said, tugging at his sack through his breeches. "From whores young and old. Worth it."

"Roar wanted to name one *Squealhaul*," Oats said, hoping to shepherd the banter away from Cat's poxy cods.

Polecat weighed the name, gave it a hum of approval. After a heartbeat, his brow furrowed. "Who?"

"New mongrel." Oats pointed hard at Cat. "Stay away from his sister. Believe me."

"Half-breed with a sister? By blood?"

Oats nodded.

Polecat's eyes brightened. "She comely?"

"Hells." Oats couldn't help but laugh at the futility of warning the lecherous mongrel away from quim. "Don't come whingeing to me when the brother stoves your skull in."

"Deal. What's her name?"

"Rant."

Polecat made a strained noise. "I just spent."

Oats could only shake his head, but the smile on his face wasn't forced. Strange to admit, but he'd missed Polecat.

"What'd she want to call them?"

"What? The ships?" Oats had to think. "*Drift* and *Drove*."

Cat's eyes narrowed. "I don't get it."

"Two names for a bunch of swine."

"Ah! Clever. I like them clever."

"You just like them."

"True." There was a pause. "Naming boats is fun."

They saw a glow flush the sky long before their brethren returned. It was too early yet for morning, but none would have looked for the sun to come up in the north, and no dawn had ever colored the horizon such a fuming green. The bodies came next, bobbing downriver in increasing numbers as the night wore on. All activity on deck ceased, replaced by a silent communal vigil as the mongrels leaned on the ship's rail to witness the current carry the dead past.

When the three hogs appeared on shore, Oats was relieved to see each bore a rider. Hoodwink's pale flesh was dyed with blood, none of it his. Jackal's clothes were slashed and torn, but whatever wounds had resided beneath had vanished. The chief was damp and filthy with soot. She wasted no time and gave the order to sail as soon as the hogs were stowed.

Soon, Oats could hear the pitiful thuds the corpses made against the hull.

Sparthis and her island stood against a backdrop of pulsing green light. The mongrel fleet entered the western channel. Sharing the deck of *Stylark* with the Shards, Oats watched Notch as they sailed between the ruins of the city and the crumbling fortifications of the western bank. The hoofmaster's sharp eyes peered at the shadowed walls and towers, thrum in his hands, half crouched and wary. Every one of his boys followed their chief's example.

The storm of thrumbolts they feared never fell.

The only evidence of Hispartha's men were the lifeless flotsam in the river, and one lone corpse on the island, draped facedown through the hole in the wall he must have chosen as his vantage. Oats imagined the man fighting sleep and boredom as he stood watch at that cranny. Imagined the yawn that was cut short by Hoodwink's knife. Likely he never knew that, all along the defenses, his fellows had died the same way, that others would follow. He'd awake in a hell of familiar faces with slit throats, pierced hearts, punctured lungs. The dark, nearly abandoned island had been Hood's hunting ground, Oats had no doubt. A place of the sleeping, the unaware. But there would have been too many to butcher, even for the silent ghost of a mongrel. Jackal had helped, likely hit the main encampment. Oats couldn't see it from the river, but it was there, somewhere behind the ragged walls. It would have been necessary to cause a commotion, force all the sentries to come running from their nooks. Waking to a half-orc in dark desert robes setting upon your camp would have caused the needed ruckus. Some man or another would have cried out, thinking it would bring aid, ignorant that it was exactly what the ambusher wanted. The shouts of alarm would only have increased as the lone mongrel began cutting men down, one against dozens, heedless of the blades fortunate enough to touch him before their wielders were slain.

Those cries hadn't reached the mongrel fleet far downriver, but they would have reached the human ships anchored at the end of the channel.

What remained of the war galleys now came into view.

Several Shards surrounding Oats cursed, and all were forced to squint against the emerald blaze. Two of the three ships were half-sunk, what remained above the water line awash in Al-Unan fire. The third was fully submerged. It would have been lost to the darksome river, but the tales of the alchemical substance continuing to burn underwater proved true. The Guadal-kabir held a torch entombed in its depths, a bubbling, flickering phantom. Above that unnatural sunken light, the water steamed. Oats's spine crawled at the sight, his nostrils filled with the stench of charred and boiled meat.

The crews of the doomed ships might have heard the men dying on the island, but it was likely they were already lifting their own voices in panic. They wouldn't have remained brave long once the chief was in their midst.

The mongrels at the oars rowed carefully through Fetching's work, threading their ships between the burning wrecks. *Crownbreaker* was in the lead and the tip of one oar brushed a blazing spar. The oar ignited in an instant, but the rowers were swift to cast it overboard before the hellish fire reached the ship. Aboard *Stylark* every mongrel held his breath until they were clear.

Oats caught Notch's eye. The hoofmaster grinned and held both hands up, palms forward in a gesture of pardon for his doubts.

Next to Oats, Polecat gave a strange little cough. It could have been from the smoke, but something about it sounded forced.

"The chief. She's gotten . . . I mean, she's become . . ."

"I know," Oats said as they left the fires behind to burn and the corpses to drift.

The Cauldron Brotherhood's castle was almost as unsightly as their swaybacked chief. It wasn't uncommon or unwise to build defenses on elevated ground. The castile had its promontory, Thricehold its rumored dormant volcano, but whoever built Black Knuckle had tried to put too much fortress on too little of a rise.

There was no room for a curtain wall on the knob of rock, so the castle was nothing but a bloated keep constructed in an artless triangle. Two of the walls were straight—though of uneven length—and the third curved outward. Some fool-ass had decided to attempt to cover the exterior in iron plates, but ran out of metal long before they gained sense or lost patience. Time and weather had not been kind to the perceived reinforcement. What plates remained were rusted and pocked, staining the bare patches of wall with umber tears. The travesty of a stronghold reminded Oats of the grossly fat fighter he'd briefly known at the Pit of Homage who often sat on a stool entirely too small for his bulk. The man had died on that stool. Someone went to rouse him for his next fight and found him an upright corpse with half a slack face and his pupils wide as a well.

Oats reckoned Black Knuckle was about as formidable. Thankfully, they weren't here to stay.

The blister of stone serving as the castle's perch sat at the end of a long, bald, and narrowing ridge. Oats rode toward the one and only entrance, a small gatehouse built out from the keep, connecting it to the ridge, a puckered navel on the stronghold's distended belly. He and Ugfuck were behind Fetch. Notch rode at her left, Boar Lip on the right. His Tuskers were camped farther back on the ridge, beyond the tiny village that inevitably sprouted up near a hoof's fortress. Oats didn't catch the name of the place, but Winsome hadn't been as desperate and bleak-looking even in its final days. If the Sons of Perdition enjoyed the best land in Ul-wundulas, a strong argument could be made for the Brotherhood suffering the worst.

"It's a wonder the thicks never took this place," Boar Lip muttered as they waited for the screeching portcullis to rise. Oats couldn't tell if it was derision or respect in the Tide master's voice. His massive lower fangs kept his mouth fixed in a permanent snarl and rendered every word into a rough expulsion. Whatever Boar Lip's opinion, Oats would have been content to wait on the river, but the chief had insisted he accompany her the several leagues to the heart of the Brotherhood's lot, leaving Jackal with the fleet as a precaution against any Hisparthan vessels.

At least it gave Ugfuck a chance to leave the ship's hold and run. He was snorting and farting happily in the sun until the gates opened.

Black Knuckle possessed no yard. The gatehouse tunnel led directly into the keep and to what passed as the Brotherhood's stables. It was a low, wide chamber, lit by only a few arrow slits and even fewer fat lamps. Slopheads worked diligently in the gloom to keep the stalls clean, but without the wind the stench of hogs would always prevail. But it wasn't the smell that most disturbed Oats. It was the harrow stags. A pair of them stood together in a single stall, their antlers glowing a pale eldritch blue as they stamped in agitation. A Tine woman risked being inside the stall with the great animals, hands and voice working to soothe them.

"The hells is a rustskin doing here?" Notch asked.

Fetch didn't answer, but the pained look she gave Oats as she dismounted didn't ease his confusion. She turned her hog over to a slophead and approached.

"Oats, I didn't know if they'd agree. So, I didn't tell you."

The presence of the stags, the elf, Fetch's expression, all had conspired to hold Oats in place. He was stuck astride Ugfuck, looking down at the chief. Her hand was on his knee, he noticed with a queer detachment. Why was he so dumbfounded?

"Tell . . . tell me what?" he managed. "Agree to what?"

"Crafty was right," Fetch said, her words measured. "I couldn't win this war. Because I've never waged one. I know how to fight. I can kill, better than any now. But a war isn't a fight. It's battles and sieges. It's making choices with information days, weeks old, or none at all. The hoofs haven't had a conflict like that since the Incursion. That was our last war. So, I needed someone, the *only* one who knew how it was fought. I needed the last mongrel to stand against Hispartha and win."

"The last . . . ? Fetch, the Claymaster's dead."

Fetch's hand squeezed his leg. "Every chief has a strong right hand, Oats."

There was movement in the arch leading farther into keep.

Warbler stepped from the shadows.

The old thrice stood tall, his white mane falling to broad shoulders. His eyes, long ago squinted by the sun, remained sharp as a hawk in his craggy face. He walked deeper into the chamber toward them, carried on strong limbs. The last Oats had seen him, he was limping, one leg swollen by pus to near twice its width. But there was no sign of weeping sores upon his body now. No feverish eyes or sallow flesh. No evidence of the sorcerous corruption he had attempted to absorb.

The Tines had finally cured Warbler of the plague. For a moment, Oats dared to hope. If the sickness no longer had its claws in the aging mongrel, then perhaps it was also banished from . . .

No. If that were true, Fetching wouldn't sound so strange. She wouldn't look so grave. So damned sorry.

Oats got down from his hog, the movement freeing him from Fetch's touch. He'd known. From the moment he saw the stags, he'd known.

"He's dead, isn't he," he said, forcing himself to look Isa in the eye just so she was forced to meet his.

"Come with me, son," Warbler said. The strength of that resonant voice had never failed him.

They had placed Wily in a small chamber. There was no window, just the same awful slit. He was on cot, a colorfully woven Tine blanket pulled up to his chin. It was elven practice to bequeath the dead such coverings. A grey-haired Tine sat by the boy, his voice issuing a low, melodic chant. Oats didn't know if there was any magic in that song. He hoped so. But be it potent sorcery or mere lullaby, it was beautiful and comforting. Wily's head was a misshapen lump, his face all but eclipsed by the plague's putrescent touch.

Oats began to cry. It wasn't the sight of the boy that demanded his tears. It was the sound of his wet, ragged breathing.

"It won't leave him, Oats," Warbler said, a step removed. "I could share it with him, but not hold it entire."

"So you had them stop trying," Oats said. He didn't care that it came out as an accusation, didn't care that his nose dripped.

"Only for now." Fetch's voice, gentler than he'd heard it for months. Gentle because she was trying to pardon herself.

Oats lowered himself to the floor beside the cot. He wanted to put his hand on Wily's belly, to feel it rise and fall, but worried the weight would crush what shallow breaths were left to the boy. Instead, he rested his elbows on the cot and put the knuckle of his thumb against the lobe of Wily's ear. Beryl had told him to kill his affection.

Oats remained on the floor next to the cot and swore he never would.

TWENTY

"... AND YOU'D THINK THEY'D be good cooks. It would make sense. Look at the Kiln! Well, I mean, you can't look at it because it's on the other side of the Lots and it's all fallen down besides, but *think* about the Kiln. Bastards were sappers, they destroyed castles, so it makes sense that their castle was well-built. All the Rutters were whores. Polecat is a wizard of fucking. Skull Sowers? They were gravediggers. Reason why the Furrow is underground and their brothers are all really scary. So why is it, Oats, that if the Cauldron Brotherhood started as cooks' servants, why is it that they're the worst fucking cooks in Ul-wundulas?"

Oats didn't respond.

Not that Culprit needed him to. The young mongrel hardly took a breath before continuing.

"No jest! The hogs think twice before shoving their snouts in the troughs. And I'm fair certain they ate better than us! You shoulda seen this soup. No! You shoulda smelled it! Reminded me of the time all us slops got the trots because Grocer refused to waste spoiled meat. He ever do that when you were a hopeful? Hells, I wager he did, the old miser."

Oats had to resist spurring Ugfuck to a faster gait. He liked Culprit and it was good to see him, but—much like the shits from Grocer's rotten vittles—the flow of words hadn't ceased all morning. The occasional grunts Oats conjured in reply weren't helping, forcing the younger mongrel to fill the silence. This time, Oats attempted to ignore him completely, eyeing the clouds gathering in the eastern sky. They'd darkened in quick order and looked to have a powerful need to get rowdy. Rain wasn't plentiful in Ul-wundulas, but storms in early spring made up the bulk. They'd be riding wet by afternoon.

"Anywise," Culprit went on. "Never been so glad to see the chief. These last months have been . . . I don't understand why Shed Snake didn't get stuck with the Brotherhood! Lucky son-of-a-thick's been living all comfortable with the Tide. Think the chief likes him better than me? Always reckoned I was her favorite. Good to be riding again and away from there, though. What does that say, that I'd rather go besiege a city than stay another day with Pulp Ear and his shitty food? And by that I mean he feeds his hoof *shit*."

Culprit may have been relieved to put Black Knuckle behind him, but Oats hadn't yet left. His body sat Ugfuck, leagues from the fortress. His mind, however, was still in that dim, stale-aired chamber where Wily lay.

Oats had tried to remain close, but it didn't take long for his bulk to be nothing but an impediment in the cramped room. The old Tine worked around him with the patience of a growing tree, changing Wily's dressings and bedclothes, rubbing ointments into his corrupted flesh, laving his body in the smoke of various smoldering herbs, and guiding liquids into his mouth with a hollow length of bone. No matter the act, the gentle singing continued. The elf was as unmindful of Oats as he was diligent with Wily. The child was alive and suffering, but his caretaker was devoted to his comfort. Oats wasn't made to feel unwelcome, simply unnecessary. Still, he'd lingered until the needs of war required his attendance, even if they couldn't demand his attention.

Fetch and Warbler held a private council for the meat of a day before calling the other chiefs in to palaver. When they emerged in the late watches of the night, the plan was made and orders given.

The hoofs rode out the following dawn.

The column striking out from the Brotherhood's lot was the largest concentration of mounted mongrels Oats had ever seen, well above three hundred in number. He hadn't realized, not with such clarity, how effective Sluggard and Thresher had been in their recruitment runs into Hispartha. The fruits of their two-season labor had bolstered the ranks of the hoofs. Most Fetching had sent to the Wallow for training. Next to Father, she trusted Boar Lip more than the other chiefs, and he'd swiftly turned the best of the bunch into competent, if inexperienced, hoof-riders. The Tusked Tide now counted one hundred twenty-one half-orcs, bringing them to a strength they hadn't known since their founding. The Cauldron Brotherhood had swelled to over eighty. An equal number of free-riders and Notch's sixty-odd Shards completed the assembled cavalry. Of all the chiefs, only Tomb had refused to take in new blood. Fetch had not summoned the Skull Sowers to Black Knuckle, thinking it best to leave them in the east to keep an eye on the Hisparthan army now in possession of Thricehold. Oats hoped that those two dozen mongrels—and the two hundred Sons at the Cradle—wouldn't be the difference between victory and defeat.

Thankfully, the sizable drove of hogs now kicking up a cloud of dust was only one of the forces moving on Kalbarca.

Jackal and the fleet continued their progress on the river, less than a league from the column's left. The former galley slaves had formed their own hoof, though they rode waves and not barbarians. They had named themselves the White Wrists after the stretch of pallid flesh left behind when their shackles were struck. It proved a challenge to set a proper pace between the hogs on the land and the ships on the water. The terrain didn't always allow the riders to remain in sight of the Guadal-kabir, rendering the first stretch of travel a frustrating exercise. But Fetch and Warbler had it sorted before the sun was too high, sending outriders back and forth to the river to ensure the strokes of the oar matched the drum of the trot.

Shed Snake galloped up from the latest such run and waved his scarred arm back in the direction he'd just come. "Cul. You're up."

Culprit made a face. "All these mongrels and it still falls to the Bastards to keep an eye on a bunch of boats."

"You're free to bring that gripe to the chief," Snake said.

Culprit hesitated, mouth half open, hand scratching at the shaved half of his head as he considered.

"You *are* her favorite," Oats told him, nodding toward the distant head of the column, where Fetching rode.

Culprit's mouth clapped shut and he turned his hog. Toward the river.

Shed Snake chuckled, guiding his hog into step next to Ugfuck. The easier pace allowed him to pull the half-cape he wore over the puckered flesh of his left arm. All this time later and even heat from the sun still caused the old burn to pain him. He took in the growing storm head.

"That'll be a gully-washer before long."

Oats grunted an agreement. He could feel his brother Bastard peering at him.

"I won't offer any chatter," Snake said after a moment. "Figure Culprit's filled your ears to bursting by now."

"Appreciate that." Oats let the silence rule for a dozen hoofbeats or so. "Polecat's got him convinced he's a sex wizard."

Shed Snake burst out a laugh so loud it drew backward glances from the nearest Shards riding ahead.

Oats couldn't help but let his own mirth bubble out. "Didn't dare venture to ask if he had some firsthand knowledge of that."

Shed Snake gave an over-exaggerated shiver. "Hells, can you imagine?"

"No. Thank you. I've seen Cat with a woman. Almost more than I could handle."

"Ah, enough! We all have! That fucking narrow face all . . ." Snake contorted his own features into a wide-eyed, teeth-baring mask of intensity. It looked nothing like Polecat, but was somehow perfect.

"Don't pretend you don't know!" Oats called to the spying Shards. "You've seen it too!"

"I'm amazed they didn't kill him," Snake said as the other hoof-riders turned their shaking heads forward once more. "I'm amazed *we* didn't!"

Oats nodded. "But you want to hear something queer? I missed him. Polecat!"

"I know," Shed Snake said. "I did too. Don't fucking tell him!"

Oats raised a pledging hand.

They rode for a moment in silence. Shed Snake looked ahead, his smile sobering without vanishing entirely.

"I understand why the chief split us up," he said. His scarred arm emerged from beneath the cape just long enough to wave a hand to encompass the column. "Couldn't have done this if she hadn't. I get it. But . . . a hoof, it's—I don't want to sound backy, but—"

"It's family," Oats said. The pair of words came out sharper than he'd meant for them to.

Snake exhaled. "I keep thinking about our slops. Touro was so close to getting his brigand. And Gosse—"

"It don't bear thinking on, Snake." Hogshit and dishonest advice. Oats amended it quickly. "Leastways not until all this is over."

"Oats. I know what the chief did . . . asking Warbler to come back, what that did to Wi—"

Oats cleared his throat, loud enough to cut off the rest of Snake's words. "She did what she had to. Same as she did with our hopefuls. I understand that. In earnest, I do."

"You say so . . ."

"I do."

"Because you don't—"

"Reckon we oughta tell Culprit that the Brotherhood were scullions back when? That they scoured the cauldrons, not cooked in them?"

Shed Snake shook his head, face falling as he took the hint. "Reckon not."

The clouds were pissing stronger than a drunkard by the time Oats made his run to the river. The storm provided relief from the sun, but brought its own gaggle of miseries to replace the swelter and glare. Snake was right. It was a gully-washer, transforming Ulwundulas's dusty crust into a friable morass. The going was slow, leaving Ugfuck slathered in slung mud after traversing a pair of the storm's namesake.

The hoofs had other names for this breed of rain. Frog-strangler. Ass-chapper, for nothing rubbed the seat raw like riding in wet leather. Roundth had coined "twixt-splitter" after what one such rain had done to the stretch of flesh between his seedsack and asshole. The Grey Bastards had all shared a laugh when Fetching retorted with "double gash" for the same reason. Oats recalled the humor, but not the ride that birthed it. Just one of dozens of orc hunts, notable only because it had rained and no one died. They wouldn't have been making jests, otherwise. It was rare back then for Fetch to crack wise, so the Claymaster was certainly not among them that day. But Oats knew the memory was flawed, for his mind saw Mead, Roundth, Hobnail, and Grocer there, which was likely true, but they rode alongside other now-dead mongrels who wouldn't have been. Creep and Gripper and Marrow. Dumb Door.

A hoof that never was.

Oats didn't reckon he'd live to old age. Few sworn riders did, preferring to stick to the creed. But he wondered if, somehow, he survived long enough to pass his remaining days seated on a chair instead of a saddle telling tales of his time wearing a brigand, how much truth would be left in his murmured memories. Likely little, being earnest. Brothers who never met in life would fight side by side in battles far larger and more courageous than the day they occurred. Mongrels who never smiled would laugh heartily, all the whores would be beautiful, and every war would end in victory. Perhaps that was reason enough to die on the hog. It kept a mongrel honest.

The river came into view, near to bursting its banks from the downpour. The storm had slowed the fleet some, but not enough to worry. Oats would return and tell the chief to ease the column's pace for a span. With luck it wouldn't cause a delay in her plan. The river was already beginning to bend from its northward course. In a few leagues the fleet would be sailing easterly, marking the final stretch to Kalbarca.

In the mountains north of the city, the bandits and brigands under Anvil's command would be gathering. Warbler had looked to Oats for a tally of their numbers, but was disappointed with the answer. Fact was, the cutthroats skulking in the Smelted Mounts numbered in the thousands, but it was impossible to say how many would agree to aid in the assault. Oats had no doubt Anvil had earned the respect of many, and the fear of more. Combined with Jacintho's sway among the brigands and the prospects of sacking the city, men would come, but an estimate of how many was something Oats couldn't wager.

"Count on none and be grateful for whatever you get," was all he'd been able to offer.

They'd know soon enough.

By tonight, the column and the fleet would halt, well beyond sight of the city walls. The ships would moor on the western shore and a group of mongrels would ride hard for the Smelteds. All had served there during the winter and been handpicked by Oats. They were to meet with Anvil and return to report the size of her force. So long as it was sufficient, Fetch would be able to threaten Kalbarca from three points: the fleet from the river, the brigands from the foothills above, and the cavalry from the plains to the south. All should be in position by the following dusk.

Oats waved to the ships, waited for one of the men on the distant decks to return the gesture, and turned Ugfuck's head.

He found Warbler riding to meet him.

The old thrice's headful of hair—rare for a thrice, like Oats's beard—hung heavy beside his craggy face, the drenched white locks darkened to steely grey. Fully equipped with brigand, tulwar, and stockbow, his harness heavy with full quivers and braces of javelins, he looked capable of taking on an entire *ulyud* alone. Seeing him approach, Oats realized Warbler rode better than Jackal. Untrammeled by the sodden ground, he came at a confident trot, sure in his seat and light with his guiding hand in the hog's mane. His former hog, Mean Old Man, was now Jack's and though the offer had been made to return the animal, Warbler refused. This new barbarian he'd dubbed Old Friend, a name that had caused Sluggard to comment that there was a poet hidden at the center of the scarred, grizzled mongrel. By Warbler's own admission he didn't know his exact age, but he had to be well into his sixties, older even than Father. Perhaps the weight of years never slowed a thrice-blood. Oats found the thought wearying.

Warbler reined up next to Oats, facing the river. He surveyed the fleet for a moment, water running through the creases in his face to dribble from his chin in a steady stream.

"Jaco seems to have that well in hand," he said.

"Captain Jackal the Backy Seafarer."

Warbler's wrinkles deepened as he grinned. "Know what he'd say to me right now? If he were sitting there instead of you?"

It didn't take Oats long to produce an answer. "He'd ask if you thought he couldn't handle a simple scouting run to the river and back. Otherwise, why else would you be here?"

Warbler nodded. "That's his pride. Seeing a reflection of himself in the doings of others." The squinted eyes moved away from the river and fixed on Oats. "But that ain't you. Is it? Thought like that never entered your mind."

"No."

"Why am I here, then?"

"You're aiming to get my pardon. For Wily."

Warbler stared at him for a while longer. He turned his hog. "Let's ride back. We'll go easy."

Their hogs settled into a walk beside each other. It was always worse going slow, ass grinding into the saddle rather than poised above as was done at a hard gallop. Oats could feel the abrasive scrape of his soaked breeches.

"My twixt is gonna be stinging something awful come sundown," Warbler announced.

"Just thinking that," Oats replied, repressing a small laugh.

"So are most of the mongrels up ahead," Warbler said, nodding forward at the column, though it wasn't yet in sight. "That's what hoof training does. Get us all thinking the same thing, the same way. Claymaster's notion, truth be told. And a damned canny one. That's the entire reason for the slopheads. A hoof could draw some whelp that could already ride, track, hit a flea with a thrumshot, even be some fucking terror with a slicer, he could have all the skills he needed and the Claymaster said he still had to suffer the slops. Because he wanted to make certain he thought like his brothers."

Oats gave no reply. It seemed Culprit wasn't the only Bastard with a need to ramble on this long ride.

At least Warbler's slower, sonorous voice was easier on the ears. "Once I was ousted, it surprised me how most of the nomads I'd meet weren't outcasts because of a failed challenge or killing a brother or any such deed. Most simply never earned a vote. Not because they were too weak or too stupid or hopeless in the saddle, but because they never learned how to think the way a hoof-rider ought. Did you know many hide it? They tattoo themselves or get another nomad to do it for them, then they cut the ink with their own hand." Warbler drew a demonstrative finger across the old scars crisscrossing the tattoos on his arm. Of course, his ink—and the puffy, pale tissue that now marred them—had been given by his hoof. "Better to be known as some evil fuck that got exiled than as a skilled slophead that never earned a name because he kept doing things his own way."

Most of what the old thrice was saying wasn't new to Oats. Hells, Jackal had very nearly been such a slop. Too willful and rebellious for the Claymaster's taste from the first day in training. It was Oats who got him through. He'd had to knock Jackal flat one night and pin him down to prevent him from quitting. Oats reckoned the Claymaster was cursing both their names from some hell even now for that interference, and the many that came later.

Warbler spat rainwater from his lips. "Those of us who make it to the voting table, don't matter how many years separate us, we think so damn similar it's our brains that make us brothers, far more than the brigand and the ink. We're all of us Bastards. We become kin. We know each other. From a fresh-sworn like Culprit all the way to a coffin-dodger like me. Reckon that's true?"

"I reckon so."

"Then why is it, Oats, that you'd ever think I'd need to seek a pardon from you about that boy?"

Warbler tried to swallow the anger in his voice, but it was there, an ember he'd tucked between his teeth and cheek, hidden but still burning.

"Didn't say you needed to," Oats replied without a measure of contrition. "Just thought maybe you were. I didn't demand it and I don't need it. Go ahead and tell me the reason since I'm so off the mark. Seems you need to."

"We're riding toward a battle, Oats. The biggest the Lots have seen since before they had the damn name. I don't relish facing that with a mongrel distracted by his anger at the fucking world."

"I'm not angry, War—"

"Hogshit!" Warbler reined up hard. It was so sudden, Ugfuck was several strides ahead before Oats pulled him to a stop. He turned in the saddle. Warbler's glower was hard and fierce as a hammer blow. "You're a thrice-blood, Idris. We're born angry! You can try to hide it from the others, deny it to their faces, but you won't with me. Not with me! The orc is thick in our blood, son. It's an ugly, vicious birthright that roars at us to commit ugly, vicious acts. You don't have to embrace it like Knob and the Orc Stains did—fuck them eternal in all the hells—but telling yourself it ain't there is a lie. You're a fool to tell yourself that lie. You won't make me one by feeding it to me. I know what I've done when the orc wins. What I've become. The same merciless brute as you."

The words washed over Oats's wet skin, chilling him to the bone. He suppressed a shiver. No, he didn't. He was quaking. Was Warbler guessing? Or did he know? He'd been a free-rider for years. If Sancho had let it slip once, just once . . . even a rumor would have been enough for Warbler to seek the truth. And there was no chance Sancho would ever have scraped up enough courage to keep from telling the renowned outcast from the Grey Bastards all that he knew.

Warbler nudged his hog to cover the gap between them. He regarded Oats for a moment, marking his quivering. Whether he took it for fury or fear, Oats couldn't guess. He wasn't sure himself.

"Try as I might, I can't think of you as a brother," Warbler said. "Thought maybe it was all the years away. But that ain't why. It's because of all the years before, the ones you can't recollect. When I was . . . more to you than I am now. If I hadn't spent all that time with you, with Beryl, down in Winsome and away from the Kiln, I might never have thrown my axe against the Claymaster. And had I not, I would've had more time with you both. I got some of it back, a second chance with her in Dog Fall. But not with you. It was another child I raised with your mother. For over a year Wily was ours. He called me Wubba." The old thrice's voice hitched. He looked away, baring his teeth in a silent snarl to keep the emotion at bay. "Not War Boar the way you and Isa and Jaco did. Wubba. That's what he'd call out when we were in the Tines' medicine lodge. That's what I'd hear him say when the pain was so bad it had blinded him and he feared I wasn't there anymore. I suffered with him through every ordeal the Tines put him through, put *us* through, to get that fucking magic out of him. And when banishment separated me from my hoof and from Beryl for a second time, I nearly put a thrumbolt through my own throat. Didn't matter that it was the rest of you exiled, I was left alone again. Only I wasn't. Not entire. I had Wily to care for, to live for. The elves may have hosted us, but don't think for a moment they helped me beyond their failed attempts with the plague. I've been caring for him. Feeding him. Bathing him. Singing him to sleep. When it comes to that child I owe you precisely nothing. You won't match your love for him against mine, Idris."

Oats held the older thrice's gaze. His jaw was clamped so tight his teeth ached.

"Do you hearken me, boy?!"

The outburst caused Oats to flinch, but it was more from shame than surprise.

"I hearken, War Boar. And I'm sor—"

"Don't offer a damn apology. I've tried never to be one that got a stiff cod over others assuaging my wounded pride. I ain't looking to hear pardons any more than I'm willing to speak them. But there is something I needed you to hear. Fetch didn't order me to come. She asked. Just like she asked the Sitting Young if they would allow me to leave Dog Fall. It was the Tines' choice first. After, it was mine. It fell to me, Idris, the decision to let the plague return fully to Wily. And it was the gravest of my life."

"Then why choose to let him suffer?" Oats asked.

Warbler answered without hesitation. "Because I knew he'd survive. I was there when the plague was created, Oats. I lived through every foul moment of its conception. And I knew every one of the nine mongrels that left that cave bearing it into the world. Wily is stronger than any of them. We were waging a losing war, me and him and the elves. I was willing to take the plague, but it wasn't willing to go. Just like when those cursed frail wizards shaped it, that fucking sorcery didn't want me as its vessel. Reckon I'll go to the grave never knowing why the Claymaster and not me. Why Quick Lime and Seeper and Thrum Lung and all the rest, but not me. Why Wily . . . but not me. I would have continued to try, hopeless as it was. I would have for his sake. But when the chief sent word that Hispartha was gaining ground and asked for my help, I couldn't continue to languish in Dog Fall while other mongrels died."

"You saw a war you could win," Oats said.

If Warbler begrudged him the bitterness, he didn't show it. "I saw that it was time to accept what Wily was. What I wasn't. I'm no plague-bearer, hells know why not. That poor boy is. And you know it too, or else you wouldn't have tried to strike a bargain with the Tyrkanian behind the chief's back."

"I was trying to save him."

"And I ain't given up on that," Warbler declared. "But Ulwundulas won't be a place worth living for any mongrel if Hispartha takes it away from us."

"It's barely a place worth living now."

"Perhaps not. But it's what we have. What we cut free from the frails, bleeding far more than they during the cutting. I won't ignore the call to fight for it. I made my hard choice. Time you did the same."

Oats was flummoxed. "Me? I'm here. Standing where I always stand."

"I've seen a mongrel take a dozen steps after his head was cut off," Warbler said.

"The hells is that supposed to mean?"

"Do you know what happened the day I threw my axe and challenged the Claymaster for the chief's seat? What made me do it?" Warbler shook his head. "Nothing. I didn't know I was going to do it, didn't wake with a plan or a purpose. My hand grabbed and my arm flung. Simple. Brainless. A fucking reflex. I can't tell you now what the Claymaster was saying when I did it. What I do know was that I wanted to be with the family I'd created more than the brotherhood I helped found. Reckon I thought I could have both if I was chief, but I can't say for certain. Who knows what the mongrel with no head is thinking when he's stumbling those last steps. But those of us watching him, we can see clear that he's dead and there's nothing left but reflexes."

"I'm not about to challenge the chief, Warbler."

"I might have said the same."

"I ain't you."

"No. Not yet. You'll be lucky to live as long if you ride into this battle stewing on Wily and that pair of frails you have tucked away at the Cradle. And that's why you need to make a choice, son. Them or the hoof. You can't have both. If it's them, so be it. Turn your hog and go south. You'll be branded a craven and a deserter. You'll have to live with the shame, but you'll *live*. Longer than you will if you enter this battle with your head and heart missing."

Oats huffed and shook his head. He couldn't help it. "The truest Bastard is likely to die at Kalbarca. Hells, Hoodwink's loyalties are more shredded than his hide and I'd wager he'll survive. If the shit you're selling was true, Mead wouldn't be buried on Batayat Hill. Creep used to say that wisdom was just words that were well said. Well, right now, Warbler, you're just prattling in the rain."

Oats spurred Ugfuck on. He didn't ride south. He rode toward the hoof, toward Kalbarca, and whatever end the battle would bring.

TWENTY-ONE

A RAUCOUS CHEER GREETED THE Big Bastard's return to the Smelteds. The voices of the bandits flooded the canyon, rebounded off the surrounding slopes, and filled Oats's ears with a lusty triumph. It sounded as if the hills were made from men, not stone. The outcry was so great, there was little doubt it could be heard down on the plain in Kalbarca. That was good. The chief wanted the garrison to know the bandits had amassed. Let them hear. Let them fear.

Trailed by his chosen riders, Oats guided Ugfuck through the wet canyon, urged him through the noise of uncountable throats, most unseen in the gloom of the gathering dusk. One voice managed to cut through the tumult.

"We rejoice to have you among us once more, my friend!"

Jacintho stood atop a spill of boulders, arms wide above his head.

"This fucking frail," Malcontent complained to Oats's right.

"Nay!" the merry bandit exclaimed, pumping his arms higher and spinning in place to encompass the slopes. "Nearly three thousand fucking frails!"

Jacintho's tally echoed through the canyon, giving strength to the cheers even as it was swallowed by their renewed fervor. Oats had to concentrate to keep his jaw from dangling in awe. It was far better than he'd hoped. Jacintho came bounding down the rocks, his bandolier of knives bouncing across his lean frame as he descended to meet them, surefooted as a goat.

"You in earnest?" Oats asked as soon as the greasy, smiling face of the bandit stood before him. "Three thousand?"

"At least," Jacintho replied. "It will be more since they are, even now, still arriving."

Oats turned in the saddle to signal Cut Wolf and Rabid. "Go."

The elected mongrels turned their hogs and headed back the way they'd come to deliver the news. Fetch would be relieved. Three thousand men, all eager to sweep down on Kalbarca at her command.

"You and Anvil have been busy," Oats told Jacintho.

The man doffed his soaked hat, the Ugfuck of head coverings, and cut a bow. "We played a part."

"What'd you do?" Malcontent growled. "Tell this horde of rapers that the garrison has been shitting jewels all winter?"

"There was mention made of plunder, surely. But it was our thrice-blood hero that attracted the greatest share."

Oats smiled with approval. "Anvil is persuasive."

"She is effective, it is true," Jacintho said. "But it was you that I meant."

"Me? I ain't even been here."

"Not in the Smelteds," the bandit replied with a strange little smile, "but upon this earth? The tale of your wound taken by the Maiden Spear spread. One which many who were there to witness said you should not have survived. Yet it is known that the chosen of Blessed Magritta fall upon their spears to gain the favor of their goddess. Many here believe she who skewered you upon the Heap granted you the life and power of the Martyred Madre, for it was you who truly rose from impalement while the girl was left to molder among the Hisparthan dead."

"That's the most fool-ass notion I ever heard!" Malcontent blurted.

"You ain't wrong," Oats said.

Jacintho shrugged. "And yet here you stand. As do men in their thousands. Is their faith truly misplaced? One mongrel defies the Crown and gains the blessings of Belico. Another declares war, her flesh hardened against harm by elven sorcery. And now you, companion to the others since birth it is said, transfixed by a killing blow yet alive to take your vengeance. Is it fools that name you the Immortal Bastards? Or sages?"

"Fools," Malcontent replied readily.

Jacintho winced and leaned toward Oats. "Even if you agree, it would not be wise to show it. Men that will charge high walls with cannons atop them are a rare breed. Who are we to question their reasons?"

"Fair point," Oats grunted.

The bandit bowed gratefully as he stepped back. "Now, shall I escort you to the others?"

Oats and his seventeen riders followed Jacintho deeper into the canyon, accompanied by the continuous elated howls from the silhouettes teeming upon the slopes.

Malcontent kept pace beside Oats. "A portion of me hopes you die in this battle just to prove these lackwits wrong."

Oats let the Shard's black jest go unanswered.

Dogging Jacintho's heels they made their way up the side of a slope, using a switchback trail that was easy on the hogs. Reaching the crest of the hill, they doubled back along the ridge and traveled along the canyon's edge for some time until Jacintho plunged deeper into the Smelteds' embrace. Soon, they surmounted the largest rise in the area and discovered a throng gathered on the broad plateau. Dismounting, they hobbled their hogs before weaving through the crowd of hill men.

All were bearded and unkempt, lightly clad in roughspun tunics and leather breeches, eyes narrowed against the incessant drizzle. Long knives were thrust through their belts, stout spears and hide shields clutched in their hands. The occasional steel buckler, axe, or proper sword denoted the leaders among the bandits. The men gave way for the mongrels, their grim silence a stark contrast to the jubilation of the canyon.

Anvil and Thresher stood upon the bluff, gazing down at the city. Barsius and Thoon flanked the half-orcs. The halfling was the first to turn at Oats's approach, his smile radiating more menace than the entire bulk of the looming cyclops.

"He is here," Barsius announced, drawing Thresher's attention, who nudged Anvil in turn.

Oats gestured for his mongrels to hold back and walked to the cliff's edge.

Anvil's mass of bristle-hard hair, jeweled with trapped droplets, dipped in greeting.

No one spoke as Oats took in Kalbarca. The sun was low, nothing but a smear of weak light behind the thick clouds, and served only to stretch the shadows of the Smelted Mounts over the city. The garrison may have been hungry during the winter, but they hadn't been idle. Even from a distance the repairs were obvious. The outer wall, once dotted with crumbled cavities, was now an unbroken barrier of old stone and fresh masonry. Many of the buildings inside remained in ruin, but the cliff's vantage provided a clear view of scores of newly tiled roofs. The nearest stretch of wall was Kalbarca's northwest end and hosted no gate, for the Smelteds had been a nest for raiders since the days of the Imperium. Any attackers coming down from the hills would be forced to scale the walls.

"Reckon we got ladders," Oats said.

"About three dozen hidden with men below," Thresher said, waving at the creased land at the foot of the cliff. "Not nearly enough. We didn't expect this many would come."

"Neither did the chief," Oats replied. "Which is the reason the plan doesn't rely on us getting inside."

Jacintho clicked his tongue. "Though if we do . . ."

"She won't hate us," Oats admitted. "But she will if we don't do what she *does* expect, which is give the frails a heap of distraction."

"Wait," Anvil said. "The light is gone."

"We need a torch over here!" Thresher called.

A mongrel arrived at a run. It was Caltrop, his branded forehead dipping slightly when he saw Oats. This thin, subservient rider was the last of the Thrice Freed, spared the massacre at their stronghold only because he'd remained in the Smelteds to represent his hoof. Now he held a torch to illuminate Oats's lips so Anvil could see what was said.

Oats pointed down to where the Guadal-kabir flowed to meet Kalbarca's southwestern end. "Our fleet will attack first. That'll leave the frails with a choice. To counter with their own ships or try to use the cannons atop the harbor towers to sink us first. With the sky continuing to piss, Warbler reckons they won't trust in their powder. That leaves their big ship, the dromon, and whatever galleys they have left. Jackal and the chief will deal with the dromon while the White Wrists tackle the rest. No matter what the frails do, our fleet will sling sapper pots at the towers above the harbor. When we see them burning green, that's our signal. We hit the walls with all we've got."

"Thankfully, that's a pile," Thresher said.

Oats looked to the sky. What little light remained outlined the unrelenting clog of storm clouds.

"This rain looks to linger awhile. If it gets any stronger, we may be spared the worst of the cannons. But we'll still be charging into a storm of thrumbolts, spears, and whatever else the frails decide to throw over that wall to kill us. Whatever it is, we can't falter. We need the frails' attention on us, so it's not on the other side of the city." Oats lifted an arm and chopped it over the middle of Kalbarca. "They got strong defenses at the main gate, plus the river. The bridge narrows the approach and stalls any charge. Likely they won't expect a run on it. And the hoofs would be fools to try. Unless the gates are open."

Every eye followed Oats's gaze down to Barsius.

The halfling scratched his nose with a knuckle. "So long as enough of their numbers have been drawn away, the gates will be open. We will see to it."

"We?" Thresh asked, the scars on her face knitting tighter as she frowned.

"Yes," Barsius replied. "I will be leading the effort myself."

Jacintho cocked a dubious eye at Kalbarca. "Then I suggest you hasten away. That is a long way to go on short legs."

"There is time yet. The distance you perceive is not so great to my eye, thanks be to Great Belico."

Jacintho loosed a mocking laugh. "And that means what?"

It meant that Barsius carried some relic of his god, just as Jackal did. Oats had long suspected it. Zirko wouldn't have tasked just any hunter with finding Xhreka, no matter how loyal or faithful. It would need to be someone capable of standing against her, against the Voice of Belico, should she resist. And she *would* resist. For all his skill and cunning, Barsius was far more than a skilled tunnel fighter and born killer. Whatever his god-granted gifts, they'd served well in the past. Tonight's attack could only benefit from his involvement.

"Means he knows his job and will get it done," Oats said. "When the gates are open, Warbler and the hoofs will charge from the plain. Once a few hundred mounted mongrels are inside the walls, the garrison will have a difficult time putting up an organized defense."

"A *Bastard* of a time," Jacintho declared, beaming.

Thresher made a disgusted noise.

"With pressure from us and from the harbor," Oats went on, "the frails will be hard-pressed from multiple points without and within. Warbler says panic will do the rest. But until then, we strive for the walls. Understand?"

Firm nods answered him.

"Spread the word," Anvil told Thresher and Jacintho. "When the harbor towers burn, we go. Oats, we should speak."

Taking the hint, Caltrop handed the torch to Oats and fell into step behind Thresher.

"I will away too," Barsius said, resting a hand on the pommel of his ancient sword. "Luck to you, Big Bastard."

"And you."

As the small warrior in threadbare robes moved across the crowded plateau every man and mongrel stepped out of his path.

"Can others hear my voice?" Anvil asked when only she, Oats, and Thoon remained at the bluff.

Oats looked around. None were within earshot. "No."

"Tell me if I grow too loud."

Oats agreed with a nod.

"You know what the hillmen believe about you?"

Oats gave a rueful laugh and shook his head. "Pile of hogshit."

Anvil's broad face grew grave. "You saw the Maiden Spear die. We all saw her fight on. That was no trick."

"No. But it don't mean I'm like her just because she ran me through. I ain't no goddess's chosen, Incus. Been weak as a runt. I didn't die and come back. I just didn't die at all, though it was only by a cunt hair."

Anvil turned to Thoon and spoke a string of words in a strange tongue. Oats didn't understand a lick of Aespardoric, but he wagered he knew a question when he heard one. The cyclops regarded Anvil for a moment before fixing his lone, somber eye on Oats. Curtained by long, matted, rusty locks, and lidded by a heavy brow, Thoon's eye should have been nestled in shadow, yet it seemed brighter than the torch in Oats's hand. He'd never considered the giant to be witless, but neither had Thoon ever displayed a stare of such incisive intelligence. Oats had to fight an urge to strike out at the cyclops, to blind that piercing, limpid orb.

Thoon blinked and the aggression fled Oats with a speed that left him light-headed. When the eye opened again, it was dull with shame and embedded in a face full of remorse. Thoon hung his head as his deep voice uttered something brief and sheepish.

Anvil turned back to Oats. "He asks you to forgive him."

"I . . . I ain't even certain what it is he did to me."

"Some Aetynians can see secrets," Anvil said.

A sudden panic seized Oats. "Secrets?"

"The language we share is not native to either of us, so . . . I may have it wrong. But Thoon can see what is hidden. He says it must be powerful. I think it has to be sorcerous."

"Like magic?" Oats said, breathing a little easier. There was nothing mystical about what he'd done to Lucon. That act had been simple, evil vengeance.

"I think so."

"And he saw some? In me?"

Anvil glanced back at the cyclops, still slumped and refusing to look at either of them. "He cannot tell you unless you forgive him. It is the way of his kind. I think it is part of the reason he was banished."

Oats wasn't certain he wanted to know, being earnest. But he couldn't leave Thoon so crestfallen. Seemed cruel even if Oats hadn't asked him to work any damned hoodoo in the first place.

"I forgive him. Thoon, look at me. You've got my pardon."

Anvil translated and the giant raised his head to show a face resolved if not wholly relieved. Thoon spoke, though his words remained short.

"Well?" Oats prodded.

"He says he saw . . ." Anvil faltered. Her toneless voice rarely betrayed emotion, but she sounded disturbed. "A festering wound where your heart should be."

Oats raised a hand to the scar beneath his brigand. It often ached, but beneath the pain was the throb of his heartbeat.

"Spear missed my blood pumper, Anvil. The Zahracene healer that looked after me would have noticed if it were elsewise. She knew her craft, believe me. I don't know what Thoon sees or why, but . . ." Oats huffed, frustrated. He forced himself not to cast an aggravated arm in the direction of the men on the plateau. "They can believe what they want. I can even understand it, queer as that sounds. But they're just lumping me in with Jack and Fetch, seeing miracles everywhere. Hells, I wish it were true. But I'm just me, stronger than some I reckon, even after nearly going to the dust. Belico, Magritta, the Tines, none of them put any magic in me. I'm a thrice-blood and a Bastard. Same as you. Nothing more. Likely a pinch less, if I'm earnest."

Anvil frowned, considering. At last, her shaggy head bobbed in a slow nod. "Perhaps. But—"

"But it don't do no good to tell these men. I know. Jacintho said. And he's right. You're right, both of you. I won't dispute it where they can hear."

"It would be better if their belief is true. I hope it is. Because if the chief wants these men to charge those walls, you're going to have to lead them. We risk most of them deserting if you do not."

Oats rubbed the water from his beard to hide his grimace.

Below, Kalbarca's sprawl was a hulking darkness, barely discernible through the haze of rain, distance, and nightfall. The chief had known his presence at this prong of the attack would be important. He and Anvil had lived with these men—well, a number of them—all winter. It served to reason he would help lead them again, give their courage a boost, but none had counted on Oats being received as some fucking folk hero.

"If that's what it takes," he said, at last, "then that's what I'll do."

"We all will," Anvil replied.

"No. You have other orders." They were his orders too, but there was nothing for that now. He had a different task thanks to these fool-ass frails and their fool-ass notions. "Kalbarca is hosting a whole mess of cavaleros. Warbler suspects they'll ride out against the bandits, especially if it looks like they're about to break. Cavaleros love to ride poorly armed men down. Sally forth and all that shit. There's no gate here, but there is on the north end this side of the river, where we don't have a presence. A good spot for the frails to send a sortie out. The attack on the walls is going to be a rough task, even with three thousand men. If it goes wrong and the men start to fray, then a charge from a bunch of cavalry will spell the end. Warbler fears a rout. It'll be up to you and the riders here to make sure that doesn't happen. You'll need to watch that north gate, out of range of the guns. If the cavaleros come out, you tusk fuck them into the grave."

"If it doesn't go wrong, I'll be sat back in safety with nothing to do."

Oats almost said he was envious, but that wouldn't help. He almost offered to trade positions with her, but that would be worse. Truth was, he'd been both relieved and offended when the chief had given those same orders to him. Right now, Anvil was questioning her usefulness and wondering why she hadn't earned a greater part in what was to come. At the same moment, she was realizing that her chances of surviving the night had just increased by a hundredfold. Being tugged in opposite directions made a mongrel question their grit at a time when they needed more sand than all of Ul-wundulas.

Oats leaned forward so Anvil would see he was about to speak.

"During your prizefighter days, you ever have an opponent refuse to fight because they were too scared of you?"

"Yes."

"What happened then?"

"My masters would call to the crowd. See if any were brave enough to enter the arena. They would increase the prize coin and allow three, four, even five men to fight me at once. But there had to be a fight."

"There always does," Oats said. "And it's often bigger than the one you managed to avoid. I know you'll keep those frails on foals off me, Anvil, even if it's just because they're too damn craven to face you."

HUNKERED IN A MUDDY DITCH, staring at the black barrier of Kalbarca's wall, it was impossible for Oats to fathom not dying. He'd once scaled the exterior of the Kiln and never felt the certainty of death he did now. But Jackal had been with him then. Now he was surrounded by nameless men. They existed as a disturbance of coughs, sniffs, hushed voices, and vague movement. Several of the nearest had made the swinging-cock proclamations of scared men trying to sound hard when Oats scrambled into the ditch beside them.

What they said and what Oats heard were vastly different.

"Cunts on the wall are going to shit themselves when we come running."

I'm going to lag behind and fill my breeches when the order comes to charge.

"We'll be over the parapet so fast they won't have a chance for a single volley."

Be lucky if half of us make it to the wall.

"City will break as quick and bloody as a virgin, Big Bastard."

A thrumbolt is going to kill me in my face.

Three thousand men. Not all would be braggarts or cowards. Many were silent and steel-eyed, focused. There'd be tight-knit bands among the horde, men who had fought and raided together, saved each other, trusted each other. They would act with a singular instinct, drawing courage from all the violence they'd shared and survived. Some would gain another story of death defied after this night. For others, the charge on this wall would bring the end. All it took, even for the toughest brotherhood, was that one man to go down, the one you all thought the hells would never claim. But then he catches a bolt in the eye, a spear in the neck, a sword in the gut, and that glorious, invincible son-of-a-cunt you would follow anywhere without fear is made into a gory corpse. It can take the legs out of his companions and they all start dropping.

Oats didn't have anyone here he trusted. The rest of the mongrels were with Anvil and Thresh, somewhere far out of sight, sitting their hogs. Ugfuck had been left up in the hills. No need to risk him on this charge. Oats would reach the wall on his own feet, same as the rest, or not at all.

Three thousand men. They were spread along the flats, using what cover there was. Boulder snarls, clumps of gorse, dry creek beds, tiny copses of lemon trees. Oats's ditch was the forward-most nest, roughly in the center. He could feel the army he was to lead stretching out behind him, all the way back to the foothills. Jacintho was back there somewhere, tucked up on a ridge on their southern flank, where his keen eyes would be fixed on the harbor towers, waiting to blow the signal horn and send this blood-hungry tide to war.

Likely there wasn't a tenth of their number on the walls to oppose them. But Oats had seen what determined fighters defending a prepared position can do. He'd been on the other side of it upon the Heap. He and his mongrels had thrown back many times their numbers, made the frails pay for every step up the slope. They'd made corpses by the score. And they hadn't had cannons.

No, try as he might, he couldn't imagine not dying tonight.

Worst part was that *he* was the glorious, invincible son-of-a-cunt in the eyes of these men. What would happen when Malcontent got his wish? When a gun-stone took Oats's head off, showed the bandits how wrong they were, what then? Maybe they'd keep going. Maybe the attack would have enough weight to carry them through.

Surely three thousand men didn't need one thrice-blood to get this task done. Surely not . . .

The night stretched on, the wait growing into a living, gnawing insect. And the invisible fucker had laid eggs, birthed a swarm of other little invisible fuckers to crawl beneath the skin, chew at the mind. That tickle was more vexing than the spitting rain.

Oats wagered it was well past midnight, but he couldn't be sure. The moon hid behind a wall of clouds thicker than the stone one a few thrumshots ahead. The men grew impatient, boredom causing several nearby to abandon whispering. Little pockets of palaver began sprouting up along the ditch. Laughter wasn't far behind. That was the cowards again, using their tongues to distract them from their heads.

Oats grit his teeth. It was an annoyance, but there was no cause to stop it. The men in Kalbarca knew they were here. Every last frail manning the wall could have been blind and still not missed the bandits coming down from the hills. They would have seen the sea of raiders, the spears, the ladders. Hard to imagine such a sight wouldn't have made them nervous.

That proved true when the first man wandered from the ditch to take a piss, provoking a cannon shot from the wall.

The gun thundered, shattering the complacency of the long night. Men all around expelled curses and cries of alarm as they fell on one another to duck lower into the ditch, which suddenly seemed scant protection for the mountain of meat Oats called a body. He didn't duck, because there seemed little point. Still, his spine nearly leapt out of his throat at the blast, and made a second attempt the next heartbeat when the ball impacted with the ground. The burst of mud went up more than a stone's throw from the ditch and far to the left of where Oats stood, but he felt the impact, couldn't help but flinch.

The man standing with his cod in his hand either had a buzzard's brains or a hog's balls, because he hadn't moved. Oats's orc blood allowed him to clearly see the spectacle, but only the men nearest the pisser were able to witness his brazen feat in the dark. A laughing cheer went up, quickly building into abuses shouted at the wall as the story spread along the ditch. The garrison had been spooked by one man brandishing his cock.

Oats didn't share their amusement. The shot proved the garrison was on edge, but it also proved they had managed to keep their powder dry.

There was no time to worry. Off to his right, Oats saw a green glow infuse the belly of the clouds above the city. The harbor towers were ablaze. The next instant, the signal horn blared.

Oats climbed out of the trench, relieved to escape the press and the wet. He turned his back on the wall, drawing himself to his full height as he faced the men. It was rare that he relished the orc in his veins, but if anything would survive this night, it was a thick. Oats buried what little human was within him and let the beast loose from his lungs.

"TO THE WALLS! KILL UNTIL YOU FUCKING DIE! AND MAY THE HELLS TAKE THE HINDMOST!"

The cheers he'd received in the canyon were nothing next to the ravenous roar that erupted from the plain. The bandits surged from the ditch, baying for blood. The surrounding land birthed a swarm of screaming men. The guns responded, their reports throwing feeble punches into the wave of war cries. They were discharged too soon. Oats didn't need to turn to know the gunstones fell short, pocking the ground the bandits had not yet reached. He continued to stand, urging the men on with a bellow as they rushed by in a seething current.

Oats waited for the right moment, feeling the rhythm of their charge in his gut. Only when their boiling core washed over him did he turn, joining the howling mob. He allowed his legs mastery, muscles pumping, boots pounding faster than his heart. His long stride overtook several heaving layers of men and brought him closer to the fore of the onslaught. The wall was the entirety of his shaking vision. Stockbow bolts cut through the rain, whistling as they fell, many ending their path with a slapping thud. Men cried out, fell. Oats jumped a tumbling body, ran on. The thrum volleys wouldn't be the worst of it unless he hurried. Yelling at the top of his voice, he sprinted through the rain. Hells, the wall was no closer. No, it was.

He could see the shapes of men at the top now, see the frames of the shelters built over the guns.

Shit.

The timber and canvas caves belched smoke and fury. The blasts put a hiccup in Oats's stride. His body screamed at him to drop, his mind said to halt was to die. The disagreement tripped him up. He fought the stumble, regained his balance. The gun stones pummeled the ground. He felt them in his boots and bones.

Ahead, the earth erupted. Oats saw the leaden ball bounce, come hurtling toward him, slow enough to see yet too fast to dodge. It missed his legs by a frail's cock. Others behind him weren't so lucky. He heard high-pitched screams as the ball chewed through the throng, one of a dozen making a meal of the bandits. Oats charged through a shower of sizzling earth, broke through a plume of smoke. The ground beyond was churned and blistered, littered with shattered bodies.

But there remained scores of survivors still charging the wall. These were the swiftest men, the front of the line. Thousands more were following. Oats—and hells knew how many hundreds more—would reach the walls before the cannons could fire another volley.

The swell of relief lasted less than a pair of steps, the time it took for half the men in front of him to be cut down by thrumbolts. The bandits had their shields raised, but the hard-cured hide was scant protection against the stockbows wielded by the garrison. They would be heavy affairs, the frails needing a crank to reload them. Slow, but powerful. Oats unslung his own thrum on the run. It was just as heavy, but he didn't need a fucking crank. He loaded without slowing, loosed at the battlements. Again. And again. He was a lone mongrel, slinging single bolts, but maybe it would keep one man's head down. The man who might kill him.

He reached the wall. Alive.

Joining about three dozen equally fortunate fucks at Kalbarca's stony breast, Oats sucked in air, head craned to watch for defenders. Oddly, nothing tried to kill them. They were too close for the cannons to be a danger, but nothing prevented the stockbowmen from leaning over the parapet. Yet the flying bolts—like the cannon fire—were all going over their heads. Looking down at the pocket of men, all wide-eyed and sweating, Oats realized why they were being ignored.

They didn't have a ladder. There was no threat in a gaggle of fleet-footed fools stranded at the base of the wall with nowhere to go.

Oats whirled to face the plain, just in time to catch a man barreling into him. There was no spear in his hand, no shield. All he carried was a trio of thrumbolts lodged in his torso.

The bandit looked up at Oats, his smile leaking blood.

"Made it," he said, and died.

A wave of bodies struck, forcing Oats to dump the dead man and brace against the heedless press. He was a big mongrel, tall and strong and heavy, yet a sudden panic seized him as the men piled in, the weight of their numbers growing by the instant. The first arrivals were in danger of being crushed against the wall. A man nearby lost his footing and went down. Oats saw him swallowed by the swelling morass of besiegers. He should have been heartened by the mass reaching the city, but the army of bandits wasn't overwhelming the wall. They were trampling one another.

Oats pushed back, shouldering at shields and backs, making space for himself, demanding it with shouted words and curses he could barely hear over the roar of the living surf.

Movement caught his eye farther down the wall. A ladder going up. Oats twisted to look the other way. Two more, rising in stiff, stuttering arcs. The nearest was the first.

"THERE!" Oats cried out, wrestling an arm out of the swamp of limbs to point over men's heads. He began shoving his way forward, fighting a constant pressure toward the wall. A man worked his way to Oats's left, stiffened his body behind his shield to act as a bulwark. Another joined them. Then another. Soon, Oats was surrounded by an escort, using their shields, elbows, and voices to cut him a path. There were always good men, those who kept their heads, saw what had to be done and acted. They seemed to be drawn to Oats as he moved.

He kept his eyes on the ladder. The closer they got, the thicker the resistance from the defenders. Thrumbolts and stones fell upon the men teeming there. The bandits fought back, forming a shield wall and casting their spears at the parapet, trying to buy the climbers time, but none reached the top. Even as Oats watched, the ladder was pushed away from the wall, thrust back by a forked pike to fall among the attackers.

"Let's move!" Oats told his guards, and they redoubled their efforts, plowing forward. A bolt took one of his boys through the skull. Boneless, he dropped. The rest tightened up and kept moving. By the time they reached the fallen ladder, they no longer had to push at living bodies in front of them. It was the dead ones under their feet that were the thickest impediment.

For all the slain there remained a staunch knot of bandits holding out against the withering flights from the wall. They were already wrestling the ladder back into the air. Oats and his boys joined them, seizing the rungs to hoist it higher. Drawn by the Big Bastard's presence, men ran in from all directions to help. The top of the ladder clacked against the wall and a brazen bandit immediately began to clamber up.

Oats swiftly loaded his stockbow and snatched it to his shoulder. He waited for the defender with the pronged pike to show himself. A cheer went up from the bandits when Oats shot him in the chest. Hurled spears followed his bolts, most falling short or clattering uselessly against the battlements, but it suppressed the garrison enough for the first man on the ladder to reach the top. A halberd thrust to the face ended his progress. He fell, but another was behind him, and another. The bandits formed an unbroken line, nose to ass, each driven by a mixture of courage and delusion, each believing that he would be the man to gain the wall, the man that would force a hole in the garrison, allowing the rest to follow.

Because it took only one. That was the queer truth. A high wall bristling with weapons seemed unconquerable until one man proved it wasn't. That man could rip the heart out of the defenders and grant it to the besiegers.

One man. Or one mongrel.

Oats spent his last bolt and stepped to the ladder. As soon as his boot touched the first rung he felt the surrounding bandits fight with renewed fervor. He didn't bother to draw his tulwar. Climbing quickly would serve him better than steel in his hand. He'd worry about how to kill the fuckers who stood in his way when he reached the top.

If he reached the top . . .

There were eight men climbing in front of him, connected by the precarious slant of the ladder, which seemed suddenly fragile and monstrously long. Odd, but it was the third man from the top to fall first. Oats didn't even see what struck him. He just cried out and twisted, knocking the man directly behind him off the ladder as he plummeted. The other bandits hunched and hugged tight to the rungs. Oats was still on the ground, giving him a clear view of the two stricken men landing in the muck, one with a bolt in his ribs. The other's fall was broken by the carpet of corpses. He scrambled to his feet, snatched up a spear, and hustled to stand behind Oats, taking his place in the line once more.

"They won't stop me twice, Big Bastard!" he proclaimed.

"Mad fucking hero," Oats replied. "A dozen like you and we'll get this done."

There was no time for further words. The men in front of Oats had climbed to fill the gaps. There was nothing for it but to follow, quick as he could. For a moment, he feared his weight would snap the ladder. Feared, and hoped. Yet it held. He was more than halfway up when the line stalled, leaving him suspended in the strange space between the twin hells of the bloody ground and the gnashing wall. He snatched a look in both directions and saw one other ladder far to his right loaded with a stream of grit-filled fools.

His line's delay was caused by the topmost man nearly punching through. He fought for all he was worth, doing messy work with a broken spear, one foot on the wall. The angle didn't allow Oats to see what stove the man's head in, but his valiant effort ended with a final gift. He fell forward instead of back and must have tangled up the defenders with his corpse, for the bandit behind him went over the wall without resistance. Oats kept climbing, watching as a second man went over. And a third.

That was it. That was what they needed. One bandit was all that separated Oats from the top. He and four men could hold the gap until more arrived. The ladder was full behind him, the stream that would overrun the defenses. They would fight their way down the walk to the other ladder and any others beyond. Fetch had asked for a distraction, but the hillmen were on the verge of taking half the city.

The bandit in front of Oats stiffened and froze.

"Almost there," Oats said, butting the man with his forehead. All he had to do was haul himself over. His fellows were holding firm, maintaining an island of safety at the head of the ladder.

But the man remained motionless, staring at something above him. Not the wall, he was level with that. Oats followed his gaze skyward.

And his bowels turned to putrid ice.

He couldn't have said when the rain stopped. He didn't know when the break in the clouds appeared. Yet there it was, framing the bright, full face of the moon. A moon that should have been pale and new.

"The Betrayer."

It was the man behind Oats who said it, the crazy fuck who fell off the ladder and came back eager for a second attempt. His voice was wavering now, thin and childlike.

Oats tried to convince himself it wasn't, that he'd been mistaken about the phase. But no, it was a new moon tonight. Warbler and Fetch had been adamant the lack of light would aid their siege. The cursed thing had waxed without warning—without their knowledge—while it skulked behind the clouds. Never had the fucking Betrayer so earned its name.

"Forget it!" Oats yelled. "We have the wall. Go!"

He pulled himself higher, pressing against the man before him, trying to bully him the last measure. He wouldn't budge.

"It's a bad omen," he whispered. "The centaurs, they'll—"

Oats wouldn't have heard, but he was nearly cheek to cheek with the stricken man. And so it was almost his head that got pulped when the soldier appeared before them swinging a mace. The iron flanges squelched into the bandit's skull. The brained man lurched, fell back on Oats. He tried to take the weight of the convulsing carcass, but the fucker with the mace kept swinging, bashing the shield of dead meat. Grunting, Oats snatched at the edge of the wall and caught firm. If he could just pull himself forward—

Metal rang against stone and the blinding pain in Oats's fingers shot up his arm, stole his breath.

The ladder flipped.

Oats hit the ground before he knew he was falling. Men were sprawled beneath him, at least one atop him. The fingers of his left hand were on fire. He kicked himself free of the tangle, forced himself to look. His middle finger was gone past the first the knuckle. The tip of his third was a mess of bloody, flattened gristle. Spit flew from between Oats's lips as he growled through teeth clenched with pain. Near him, a dazed bandit with a gashed head tried to rise. A falling rock smote the poor man between the shoulder blades, broke his back. He died gurgling, facedown in the carnage. Oats rose, taking up a fallen shield with his good hand, cradling the other to his chest. All around, his men were coming apart. They were shouting, pointing at the moon, many already in flight.

"No!" Oats yelled, throat thick with the mucus born from pain. He darted in the path of several routing bandits, throwing his shield forward to shove them back. "Turn! We've men on the walls!"

They scattered away from him and kept running. Every man who fled dragged a half dozen more in his wake.

It was hopeless. The bandits were broken.

The bolts fell with renewed vigor, feathering men in the back. One came for Oats, penetrated the top of his shield, and struck his bicep. It was a shallow wound. The next wouldn't be. He had no choice.

Oats joined the retreat.

Again he ran, but his legs were stubborn mules, refusing to move at the pace he desired no matter how hard he goaded them. Bolts shrieked by on both sides, cutting men down in droves. Oats knew one would soon take him in the back and the certainty made him scream with fear and shame and outrage.

It was the guns that got him. He didn't hear them discharge, just the blast as the ball struck. A hammer the size of the world launched him off his feet. He flew, carried by a wave of dirt and sound and broken men. The noise buried his ears, the dirt and men buried his body. Tears streaming, Oats blinked against the charred grit.

He couldn't move his legs. Had they been . . . ?

Fuck, he was too afraid to look. No, they were there. Pinned. He felt them now, beneath an uneven pressure. Dead men.

Oats flipped to his belly, gathered himself to crawl free. He heard the fleeing men coming, saw them, tried to cry out, but he choked on the smoke. A panicked foot kicked him in the head. His eyes flashed as more feet stomped him deeper into the mud, closer to death.

His vision cleared to see Kalbarca, the wall. Oats hadn't gotten far. He could still see the triumphant gestures of the garrison, their upraised, pumping arms. He could still see the gun shelters. One in particular drew his attention. Oats shivered, knowing it was the one that would kill him. Staring, bleary-eyed and beaten, he was seized with the same cold sensation he got when he knew there was a snake hidden in the straw of the stables. He could always feel it looking at him, waiting to strike if he got too close. Up on the wall, beneath that shelter, men were reloading their cannon. He wondered if they could see him, if they knew—like he did—that their next shot was going to tear him in half.

Oats saw the smoke punch out, heard the weighty pop.

A massive figure landed an arm's length from Oats's face. He heard a smacking impact and a throaty grunt as the figure doubled over, skidding closer toward him on bare, wide-set feet.

Oats knew that cliff-face of a back, those piercings of bone.

The figure turned to look down at him, a steaming cannonball held tight to its belly in both massive hands.

Death had just been denied.

By Ruin.

TWENTY-TWO

THE CHIEF'S TWIN HAD ANOTHER name. Some guttural, growly title in orcish Oats had heard once, but would be hard-pressed to remember even if he weren't cannon-blasted and befuddled.

Besides, Ruin served just fine.

Huge and bald and naked, he appeared for all the world like the fiercest thick ever to draw breath, his elven blood buried beneath a mountain of bulging muscle, charcoal skin, and savage, hells-birthed strength.

Teeth-bared, Ruin spun, lobbing the gun stone back at the walls. The ball hurtled through the shadowed opening beneath the canvas that expelled it. Oats heard the impact, the screaming. The timber frame shattered, collapsing the shelter, silencing the screams. And the gun.

Whirling, Ruin stooped. Oats thought the brute was moving to lift him, but the next instant he was shoved aside with such force he rolled free of the dead men. The guns continued to sound, thumping the air at irregular intervals. Ruin paid them no mind. He was too busy digging through the corpses, tossing them aside with increased aggravation. Oats struggled to get his legs under him. He'd only made it to his knees when Ruin issued a furious snarl, gave up on the dead, and darted to grab the front of Oats's brigand. Oats had lived his life at least a head taller than most and now he was hauled up with the ease of a caught trout, boots dangling off the ground as Ruin looked him in the eye. Any closer and their noses would touch.

Ruin shouted something, fast and angry. And in elvish.

Oats knew about three phrases of Tine. He wished one of them could tell this monster to go fuck his own ass.

Ruin shook him, repeated the question. This time, Oats caught something.

Ta'thami'atha.

Twin. Or near enough to it in elf parlance.

Of course he was looking for the chief. Oats could say one thing for Ruin. He was fucking constant.

Oats kept his lips tight. He wouldn't utter a word about Fetching to this hulking cunt.

Ruin had hunted her once, though the chief now claimed it was out of curiosity rather than malice. But it turned ugly and this giant son-of-a-thick had nearly killed the entire hoof. Fetch stopped him, in the end, and they'd come to an understanding of a kind before Ruin left with the Fangs of Our Fathers, but Oats wasn't about to wager on any standing peace. Not under this moon.

"Ka'siqana!" Ruin demanded, his breath hot.

"Shout her point-ear name all you want," Oats replied as the sky strained against the whistle of gunstones. "I'm not telling you."

The scowl on Ruin's slab-browed face deepened.

"Te'hanoc!"

Ruin's head turned at the shouting voice. There was another hurried string of elvish. Oats craned to see a Tine warrior riding toward them, the antlers of his harrow stag aglow with the same ghostly light imbued within the stone head of the club he bore.

It was the chief's other brother, Oats realized, recognizing the black war paint covering the top half of his face. Blood Crow. Starling's son.

The elf reined up and threw a few heated words at Ruin, pausing to swing his club, unleashing a trilling wave of sound that scattered a flight of incoming thrumbolts.

Ruin set Oats down and held on to his brigand long enough to ensure he was steady.

"Your chief?" Blood Crow said, casting keen eyes about as if he expected Fetch would be close. "Where is she?"

"Why?" Oats returned, trying to ignore the fact that he was standing on a battlefield having a palaver with a rustskin and an orc sorcerer—both kin to Fetching—while Kalbarca spat all manner of death at them.

"My brother believes she is in peril," Blood Crow replied, keeping his stag well in hand against the guns' tumult.

Oats pointed at the walls of the city. "We're all in peril!"

Ruin's primal pit of a voice said something to Blood Crow even as a thrumbolt struck the brute in the shoulder and splintered against his flesh. Whatever he said caused the elf to turn his stag. Ruin cuffed Oats on the back, pushing him toward the hills. The savage stayed on his heels, using his bulk as a shield.

They ran over swaths of dead, but it was the injured that made the field a hell to cross.

The number of poor, wailing forms without feet, with legs reduced to twisted offal, brought Oats's guts to his throat. Whatever mad fuck had conjured the notion of propelling a lead ball out of a bronze tube at such speed deserved to be torn apart by his own creation. Oats reckoned the men struck by thrumbolts were the fortunate ones . . . until he saw the man pierced through the cheek, the bolt angled so the broadhead protruded between his jaw and neck. The transfixing shaft had wedged in the man's mouth, leaving it gaping, dribbling blood. Small, throttled noises pulsed from his stricken throat as he crawled on hands and knees.

Oats could carry one man from the field. One. It was all he had the strength for, the time. He kept passing by, enduring the ignored pleas, hoping to spy the obvious choice, the man with a chance at living and not just another corpse dragging itself along because it hadn't yet realized its wounds were fatal. How many had he passed in his search who would have lived if he'd simply quit stalling and grabbed them up? A wordless sound came strangling out of him, the ugly child of a curse and a sob. He trudged to a stop, snatched up the nearest man—a man missing an arm—and continued on.

"Magritta . . . bless you," the bandit said, and went limp over his shoulder.

Ahead, Blood Crow sat his stag outside the range of the thrums and the guns. A few bandits had collapsed in ragged groups nearby, so defeated and blank-eyed that the appearance of the elf did not stir them. Most of their fellow survivors had continued on into the deeper safety of the foothills.

Oats stomped to a halt and lowered the armless man among his slumped comrades.

"Tend him," he said, "or the Martyred Madre will curse you."

Fucking fool-ass thing to say, especially now. Any belief they had in him lay butchered beneath Kalbarca's walls, but if the misguided faith of the hillmen could get hundreds of them killed, maybe it had enough blindness left to save one.

As Oats plodded the last dozen steps to Blood Crow's waiting stag, a hunchbacked shape prowled from the night and fell into step beside Ruin. Too big to be a dog, too ugly to be a wolf, Oats knew the slavering animal. It was the last of Ruin's pack of bewitched hyenas, the only one Jackal hadn't killed because it had been pinned to the earth by a javelin. Oats's javelin.

"You're welcome," he muttered at the unsightly cur.

"You must take us to her," Blood Crow declared. His Hisparthan was accented, but considering he hadn't spoken a word of it since half a year ago, it was damn perfect.

"Gonna need more reason, point-ear," Oats told him, wagging a thumb between Blood Crow and Ruin. "The pair of you don't stoke much trust."

The Tine warrior's proud face tightened with repressed ire. "Whatever has drawn Te'hanoc is capable of killing our sister."

"Drawn?" Oats said, sucking in air. He threw a grimace skyward. "Then you knew this shit was coming."

Blood Crow hardly glanced at the Betrayer Moon. "Crazed centaurs cannot challenge *Asily'a kaga arkhu*," he said, invoking the name for what the elves believed the chief and Ruin to be.

"Meaning it's fucking worse," Oats said, feeling very weary.

Next to him, Ruin paced, impatient as a caged beast, his hyena bristling by his legs. He threw a heavy arm back at the battlefield and griped at his elven half-brother before directing a bitter look at Oats.

"Speak so I can understand!" Oats barked in orcish.

"Te'hanoc no longer dirties himself with that tongue," Blood Crow said. "He says he felt Ka'siqana here, but was mistaken. He says this confusion means—"

"She was thinking about me," Oats said, needing no explanation. He may not be Fetch's blood-kin, but he was closer to her than either of her natural siblings. He'd grown up with her, helped train her, conspired with her, been hurt by her. These two may have come from the same womb as Isabet, but that didn't make her more their sister than his. He possessed a lifelong love they could never touch. She may not have confided in him for months now, but Oats still *knew* her. She was in his marrow.

The question remained—why him?

As chief, Fetch forever carried the burden of her hoof's lives. She'd confessed that fear to him more than once. You didn't need to be a hoofmaster to worry for the safety of your fellow riders, Oats knew, but he also knew leadership compounded the worry. So why would Ruin come to him above all the rest? What would frighten Fetching so much that her thoughts would turn to him so completely that it muddled whatever mystical twin hoodoo connected her to Ruin?

Oats didn't have the answer. Only Fetch would.

He started running. "Come on!"

He could have made directly for the river, but that meant cutting across the killing ground in front of the wall. So he kept his distance, skirting the hills. Ruin, Blood Crow, and that loathsome hyena stayed on his ass, all hampered by his pace.

"Ride with me," the elf said. "It will be swifter."

"I ain't straddling no damn deer," Oats replied. "Probably break its fragile spine."

He thrust his fingers in his mouth and threw a whistle. The first was a dry, feeble expulsion. The second was ill timed and eaten by a gun's report. But his third attempt was nice and sharp. Oats threw a fourth after a hundred more steps, just to be sure.

He meant to summon one hog, but nearly fifty soon caught up to them.

It was the mixed hoof, Anvil at their head, her tulwar bloodied to the hilt. Beside her, Thresh had her chain-mace in hand. They'd been in a fight. Seeing Ruin, Anvil tensed for another one. A growl from Ruin betrayed he remembered her too.

Oats got between the hogs and the naked sorcerer, lifting his voice for the benefit of the riders who weren't Bastards, those who hadn't encountered the fearsome *uq'huul*.

"Easy! He's a friend. I know he looks like the father of all thicks, but he's . . ." Hells, there wasn't time to explain it all. "He's fucking worse, so don't cross him and be glad he's the war chief's ally. The elf too." Oats cocked a thumb at the hyena. "And that."

As the assembled mongrels muttered and cast dubious looks, Oats stepped to Anvil's side.

"The cavaleros?" he asked, lifting his beard at her stained blade.

Anvil nodded.

"They rode out when our frails broke," Thresher said. "Then we broke them."

"Any losses?"

"Four," Thresh replied. "One against the cavaleros. Soon as we weren't in grips with them the guns had something to say, did for the other three." Her eyes drifted to Oats's injured hand, cradled close to his chest. "Looks like you lost the end of your clit-diddler there, Big Bastard."

"It's nothing. We need to get to the chief. Something ain't right."

Thresh cocked an eye at the Betrayer. "Can't imagine what."

Oats heard Ruin give a disgusted snort and complain in elvish.

"He says—" Blood Crow began.

"That my hog is close," Oats said, smiling at his fellow Bastards. "I know. I can smell him too."

Ugfuck came running from the foothills, forcing the hyena to scamper out of his lumbering path.

Oats mounted up, swallowing the pain as he gripped Ug's patchy mane with his mangled fingers. His stockbow was gone, but he still had his tulwar at his side and a brace of javelins strapped to his tack.

He nodded to Anvil. "To the river."

She spurred forward, leading the hoof into a gallop. Oats remained outside the column on the right, Blood Crow riding beside him. Ruin and his hyena had no trouble keeping up on foot.

"Where are the Fangs?" Oats demanded, pitching his voice over the thudding hooves.

"They fell behind almost twelve days ago," Blood Crow replied. "Te'hanoc refused to wait. Our mother could not sway him. This need to reach Ka'siqana has gripped his spirit for nearly a moon's turn."

"You've been traveling a month? Where the hells were you?"

"Dhar'gest." The orcish word sounded strange coming from the elf.

Oats wasn't surprised. What they were doing in that deadly land he couldn't guess, but the deserts and jungles claimed by the orcs were also Ruin's home. According to Fetch, the orcs hated and feared her twin, viewing him as something between an animal and a god. Even with Ruin in their midst, the Fangs of Our Fathers had taken a great risk trespassing beyond the Gut, but they'd always been a loon-brained bunch of mongrels with queer notions about the thicks. Likely Kul'huun and his boys had crossed the Deluged using their stiff cods as boats.

Riding alongside Blood Crow, Oats had a new appreciation for the elf's harrow stag. The Fangs' hogs were notoriously hardy, yet they had fallen behind long before this spindle-legged animal. Perhaps it wasn't so fragile.

There was no time for further questions. Ahead, the Guadalkabir reflected the light of the Betrayer across its broad back. Kalbarca's harbor lay upriver to the hoof's left, its towers transformed into torches by emerald flames. Beneath their lurid light, the battle upon the river raged.

Nearest the hoof, the bulk of the dromon listed in the water, its lolling hull rendering the menace of the great ship into a pathetic wreck. It had drifted away from the harbor before running aground near the opposite shore. Beyond, the war galleys grappled, close enough for Oats to see the surging silhouettes of men and mongrels fighting on the decks.

The hoof reined up on the banks. With the galleys in the grip of battle there were no vessels to act as a ferry. No part of Warbler's plan accounted for the riders in the Smelteds rejoining the main body.

There was no choice. They had to get across.

"Mongrels!" Oats called. "We're hogwashing!"

The half-orcs hurried to dismount, doffing their boots and cramming them into saddlebags. Some took off their brigands and discarded them on the sand. All began inspecting their tack, tightening girth straps and securing quivers. All but three.

Anvil, Caltrop, and Thresher aped the others, but their movements were uncertain, their expressions puzzled.

This was the consequence of mongrels not getting years of slop training. They could be full of grit, deadly fighters, skilled riders, loyal to the bone, but rushing them into the saddle meant some drills were neglected.

Oats hurried over, pulling Ug by a swine-yanker, and gestured for the three to gather.

"Your hogs can swim this," he said, making sure his face was lit enough by the moon for Anvil to see. "They can carry you across, but not if you're on their back." Oats hunkered next to Ugfuck, gripping the saddle's gullet with one hand, the cantle with the other. He pressed himself close to the animal's side. "Put yourself on their upriver side. Don't put any downward pressure on them. Just hold—loose and light as you can—and let them do the work. Stick close to their ribs, but don't pull. Keep your feet up and out behind you, like you're swimming. Kick if it helps, but don't snarl your hog's pace. If you don't drag them under or roll them, they'll make it. And remember, the current will take you farther downstream. Let it. Getting to the other side is all that matters. We'll make up the lost ground when we're back on land. Hogs'll be a touch winded after, so don't push them."

He let Thresher and Anvil continue with their preparations, but pulled Caltrop aside. The mongrel had never managed to conquer the weak frame from his days as a slave. It was as if the starvation and abuse the Orc Stains made him suffer clung beneath the skin, denying all meat and muscle from reaching his bones. It wasn't a body fit for surviving such a crossing.

"I need you to ride back to Jacintho. Tell him what's happened. See if he can rally any of the hillmen. Go."

Caltrop gave a firm nod, the triple scars of the brand on his forehead brightened by the Betrayer. If he suspected Oats was giving him a pointless task to save his life, he didn't show it. Caltrop pulled his boots back on, swung into the saddle, and made swiftly for the hills.

Oats lifted his next words for all to hear.

"We'll be well scattered on the other side, so the dromon is our muster point." He lifted a finger to the floundering ship. "That was the chief's first task, and it looks like she got it done. Need to find her, so that's where we'll start."

Blood Crow related this to Ruin in elvish and the brute's gaze snatched to the wreck. He took off running up the bank. When he drew even with the dromon, he leaped. Powerful as he was, even Ruin couldn't clear the width of the Guadal-kabir, but he damn near reached the deck of the ship in a single bound.

"Fuck me," Malcontent swore as the huge orc splashed down well beyond the mighty river's middle.

Ruin surfaced and swam for the dromon, borne swiftly by the sweeps of his massive arms.

"Our turn," Oats declared, and pulled Ugfuck into the shallows. All around, hogs and barefoot riders waded into the drink.

Oats leaned down to Ug's ear. "Let's not drown. Bargain?"

There was an answering grunt and the big pig trundled forward. His hooves soon left the silt. Oats allowed himself to float, gritting his teeth against the first bite of the river's chill. He wanted to keep an eye on Anvil and Thresh, but his view was limited by Ug's body. His injured hand went blissfully numb after a shock of pain, so he was able to grip the saddle's gullet, but he didn't put much trust in his mutilated fingers, forcing him to grasp the cantle harder than normal. Ug strove against the weight, legs milling as he pushed through the water.

The sounds of furious splashing, gasping mongrels, and squealing hogs quickly dispersed, replaced by the river's roar. Fact was, they wouldn't all make it. Crossing the Guadal-kabir by hogwash was an act even the most seasoned nomad would avoid. The strength of the current, the roaring, the uncertainty of every moment, they all conspired to unnerve a mongrel. Some would panic, Oats knew. They'd pull on their hogs, forget their training, and try to scramble onto their back, thinking it a safer perch. Like all living creatures, a barbarian didn't fancy being drowned. They'd fight to live, even if it meant throwing their mongrel off to suffer the merciless river alone.

All Oats could do was make damn certain it didn't happen to him.

It was impossible to tell how far they'd come. Oats couldn't see the opposite shore, only the undulating swell of the dark water. He knew they were going faster downriver than across, but he didn't blame Ug for that. Successfully crossing the Guadal-kabir required endurance, not speed.

Fortunately for Oats, from the day he first drew breath, Ugfuck had never known what it was to give up.

After what seemed an eternity, the huffing hog dragged them both ashore.

Oats got to his feet, relieved to see he wasn't the only one who had made it. Up and down the bank, mongrels were emerging from the river, seven that he could see. Oats made a swift inspection of his tack. Two javelins had been lost, but otherwise all had held. He retrieved his boots and pulled them on before hustling upriver, gathering the others on the way. Malcontent was among them, as well as Mope and Rabid. And Thresher. Oats had to suppress a sigh of relief when he saw her. The scarred mongrel had even managed to cross without losing her chain mace.

"Incus?" she asked, as soon as she saw Oats.

He could only shake his head.

Thresher cast a searching look in either direction.

"She'll make it," she said, breathing heavy. "She'll make it."

By the time they reached the dromon, Cut Wolf, Stoat, Knuckle Child, and a dozen others had joined their dripping company. But more than half their number was missing, including Anvil. Oats hoped they were only swept farther downriver before reaching shore. Surely that would be true of some. He suspected Anvil would catch up before long. She was strong, but—more important—she was patient. Big Pox may have been an older hog, but he was well trained. It was unlikely he'd fail to bring her across.

Blood Crow was already on shore near the dromon when what was left of the Smelted hoof arrived. Oats hadn't seen the elf begin the crossing. For all he knew, the point-ear's queer stag could run on water, but as they drew closer Oats saw animal and rider were soaked. Blood Crow's war paint was washed half away, the diluted black streaking his sharp features, turning his face into an unsettling skeletal mask.

"She is not here," the elf said.

The dromon was half a thrumshot from the bank, the deck leaning sharply toward land. Ruin stood on the slanted surface, undiminished even by the massive warship.

"He says there is nothing but dead men."

Oats nodded. He could see them sprawled on board, a few floating in the shallows.

Fetch and Jackal were to cripple the dromon together. Warbler suspected Hispartha would keep its wizards tucked safely in Kalbarca, but as a precaution he thought it best they didn't split up for this opening gambit. The only thing that had ever been able to threaten the pair of them now stood upon the sinking mass grave of their making.

Ruin jumped from the deck, his bulk hanging momentarily weightless at the top of the arc that brought him to shore. His hyena reached the hoof a moment later, drenched from the crossing. Oats yearned to give others the chance to catch up, to reduce the millstones of guilt churning away in his gut. But there wasn't time. This was the Betrayer. Every moment brought death closer on hundreds of rampaging hooves.

Oats kicked Ug forward.

The sounds of battle from the ships reached his ears. He snatched a look at the river.

The waters leading to Kalbarca's harbor were a cauldron of violence. The war galleys from both sides were locked together, ensnared by ropes and grapnels, joined by the brutal kiss of the iron rams at their prows. The Guadal-kabir was all but dammed by the fractured flotilla. Bodies fell over the sides, leaped between the decks, threw themselves at one another in pressing mobs. Cries of pain and rage escaped from a locusts' song of clashing steel. Oats could feel the heat of the Al-Unan fire consuming the harbor towers from across the river. The hellish green flames would have rid the surrounding walls of defenders, sparing the galleys from thrum volleys and cannon fire. Still, it was impossible to tell if the White Wrists were winning the struggle. They were outnumbered. The Hisparthans had two ships in the water for every one of theirs. Jackal was supposed to have joined the fight after the dromon, but Oats couldn't make him out in the crush.

As for Fetching, she was to join Warbler for the assault on the gate.

The assembled hoofs stood waiting in the plains beyond the city's main gate. Unlike the bandits, Fetch hadn't wanted the riders seen. Distance, darkness, and the far side of a rise served to conceal them. Only a few scouts—hidden by cover and cunning—waited within sight of the walls, ready to blare a signal when the gates opened. Oats led his band away from the river and away from the city, fighting the urge to ride straight for the hoof's main body and, in doing, risk giving away its position. Only when Kalbarca was lost from view did he wheel back, approaching the mustered mongrels from the south. The sentry riders let him pass, but Oats could feel the confusion and tension he dragged through Fetch's army, spread by the sight of her preternatural brothers. He spied the Bastards near the front of the throng. Polecat, Sluggard, Culprit, and Shed Snake watched him ride by. Thresher peeled off to join them, but there was no time for Oats to dally. He signaled for the rest of his riders to fold in with the great hoof.

Oats brought Ruin and Blood Crow to the hoofmasters. They sat their hogs away from the army, their council on the verge of boiling over. Notch was tense in the saddle, his usual confidence strained as he struggled not to shout at Warbler.

". . . yet we should remain? We'd be fools, old thrice! And you know it. Give the order, cease thi—"

The flustered Shards chief was cut off by Oats's arrival. Or rather, Ruin's.

"Devils and all the hells!" Pulp Ear swore, eyes going wide in his ugly face.

Boar Lip's hand slapped the grip of his tulwar.

Warbler turned, his gaze drawn by Ruin, but, unlike the others, it wasn't imprisoned by the massive sorcerer. Instead, his attention shifted to Blood Crow.

"*Iya os kaganak, N'keesos,*" Warbler said, his slower elvish allowing Oats to catch the sound of the words.

Blood Crow dipped his chin and replied.

The Tine tongue passed between thrice and elf for several moments, each exchange increasing Notch's aggravation, easing Boar Lips's grip on his sword, and doing nothing to Pulp Ear's sour grimace. Ruin spoke once during Warbler and Blood Crow's quick conversation, the vexation in his wet, rumbling elvish testing the raw nerves of the chiefs.

When all was said, Oats found Warbler's eyes on him. The look they shared was its own language.

Warbler knew at least as much as Oats now. The chief was in danger and, clearly, not here. Added to that was the Betrayer and the unopened gate. Warbler had to tread carefully in his response or he'd only strengthen Notch's argument to withdraw. But there was no time to think. He had to move fast, think even faster, and be cautious all the while. Oats didn't envy him.

"We attack now," Warbler said.

Pulp Ear's face curdled. "The gates remain closed."

"Yes." Warbler's eyes rested on Ruin. "But we have something that can breach them."

The disbelief on Notch's face split into a mocking grin. He shook his head, gestured at Ruin. "We're now putting our trust in that?"

"He's—"

Notch cut Oats off with an upward toss of his hand. "I know what he is. We've heard the stories, even if the war chief doesn't like them told. But if she wanted the gate broken by a mongrel with the strength of all the hells, she could have done it herself, not gone off with that filthy waddler to take it by guile."

Oats managed not to throw a confused look at Warbler. Fetch left with Barsius? That wasn't part of the plan that he heard. And by Notch's piss-soaked attitude, it had been a surprise to him too.

"Matters have changed," Warbler said. "Our task is the same. Take the city. We're riding to do that. Right damn now."

All ill humor vanished from Notch's face, replaced by a steely severity. He lifted a lone finger skyward. "And that? Fucking thing could have appeared hours ago behind the clouds. The night is nearly as old as you are, Warbler. An experienced nomad shouldn't need to be reminded that there's a centaur grove between here and Strava. Another to the south, even closer. Horse-cocks could be upon us at any moment."

Warbler remained placid. "All the more reason to get ourselves behind those walls and not to dawdle in the doing. Now, get to your hoofs."

Notch's eyes glinted as he pondered further dissent. Pulp Ear eyed him, waiting to see what the Shard chief would do. It was Boar Lip who broke the standoff.

"Come," the Tide's master said. "Warbler's right. We need to get this done."

Notch sucked his teeth, a slow nod building. Giving Ruin an appraising glance, he nudged his hog away.

Oats spurred Ugfuck closer to Warbler's hog as soon as the chiefs were out of earshot.

"Fetch went with Barsius? When?"

Warbler spoke quickly. They didn't have long. Behind them, the mongrels—already prepared for the assault—were tightening their formation. "He was here waiting when she arrived from the river. Said the gate was being watched by Kalbarca's wizards. The halfling claimed his folk couldn't take it unless they were dealt with first.

Claimed he could get Fetch in unseen so she could help. I urged her to wait on Jackal, but . . ."

Oats huffed. Warbler didn't need to say the rest. Patience had never been one of Isa's gifts. She'd sobered some as chief, but with the night wearing on and the attacks on the harbor and western wall in progress, she'd had little choice.

Oats tugged his beard in frustration. "Barsius springs that on her, the gates still ain't open, and the fucking Betrayer came without warning from Strava. That means—"

"Zirko fucked us," Warbler said. "His stub-fingered hand is gripping the knife in our back. Whatever this danger Fetch's in, it's that priest's doing. Fuck him eternal."

An end to the low tumult of shuffling hooves, hushed voices, and creaking harness told them the great hoof had solidified. The assembled mongrels waited now on the order to move. Oats could feel hundreds of eyes on him.

"This going to work?" he asked, enough above a whisper so he didn't sound craven.

Warbler's craggy profile stayed locked on the surface of the rise blocking their view of the city.

"Reckon it has to. Best if the Bastards ride in the vanguard, though, to prove our conviction."

Oats's sudden laugh caused the older thrice to direct a frown at him.

"Pardons," Oats said. "Second time tonight I've had to charge Kalbarca just so others will follow."

"Ought to change your hoof name to Mother Goose," Warbler said with the hint of a grin.

"And yours to Gambler."

"Join your brothers." Warbler made the smallest tilt of his head toward Ruin. "I need to speak with . . . him."

Oats rode back to the main body. The True Bastards met him in the center. Oats blew out a relieved breath to see Anvil now among them, her coarse hair still wet from the river.

"That the chief's twins?" Culprit asked, stretching in the saddle to wave at Ruin and Blood Crow. "Hello, Fetch's twins!"

None in the trio now holding council acknowledged the japing rider. It was odd, seeing Warbler so close to Ruin. The hoary-headed old thrice sat his hog and still had to look up when speaking with the naked, hulking *uq'huul*.

"They're not both her twin, fool-ass," Shed Snake said. "Just the big one."

"Oh." Culprit kneaded his half-shaved head. "Thought the point-ear was her brother too."

"He is. He's her half-brother."

"Right. The elf half. The big one is the orc half."

Snake was flummoxed. "What?"

"The chief is half orc and half elf. Those two are them."

"Are you . . . ? No! The elf and Fetch have the same mother."

"So does she and the orc, right?"

"Yes, but he's not an orc. Just fathered by one. Same as the chief."

"I know. And the chief's mother was an elf. So, she had one orc, one elf, and the chief who is half orc and half elf."

"But that's not how it . . . that would make them triplets and still make no sense!"

Thresher leaned toward Shed Snake. "You realize he's just yanking your cod, right?"

Culprit managed a straight face for a heartbeat longer, but Snake's slack-jawed uncertainty caused him to burst.

"Hells, you're such a child," Snake said, trying to slap his giggling brother's head, but Sluggard was between them, a good-natured barrier for Culprit to duck behind.

Oats smiled. It had been too long since he'd ridden with all of them. And even now they weren't whole. Oats didn't bother to ask where Hoodwink was. The chief had taken him aside during the planning at Black Knuckle. As always, he had a shadow task to perform.

"If you mongrels want to stop grabbing ass and put thrums in your hands!" Warbler called as he rode up. Ruin went the opposite direction, striding off over the rise with only his hyena. Blood Crow rode away to the west.

"Rather grab ass," Polecat mumbled, but unslung his stockbow.

"Where are they going?" Thresh asked.

"I asked N'keesos to return to our ships and find Jaco, tell him what's happened," Warbler replied.

Oats was annoyed with himself. He could have thought to do that when they passed the harbor. No doubt Blood Crow was a strong swimmer and he could leap nearly as far as Ruin thanks to whatever magic was trapped within his club.

"As for the other, he's agreed to open Kalbarca's gates."

The Bastards grew still. The thought of being aided by Ruin wasn't a comfortable one, but none were willing to gainsay Warbler.

"Scrounged this for you," Shed Snake told Oats, offering a thrum and full quiver.

Oats nodded in appreciation and took the weapon, but he couldn't quite manage to tie the quiver to his tack with his crippled fingers. Snake did it for him while Oats threw the stockbow's strap over his head and arm.

Warbler gave them all an appraising look.

"Who wants to say it?" he asked.

"I do," Sluggard replied.

Warbler gave him a permissive dip of the chin.

Sluggard swept them all with a small, fond smile. "Live in the saddle, Bastards."

Their replies were quiet, but firm. "Die on the hog."

Warbler looked beyond them, surveying the army for a long moment before turning his hog. He kicked Old Friend forward and the True Bastards fell into pace, fanning out on either side. Behind them the mongrel army rumbled to motion.

They took the gentle slope at a walk. As Ugfuck crested the masking rise, Oats felt his heart begin to knock uncomfortably against his breastbone. Again Kalbarca waited for him, farther away now than it had been at the foot of the Smelteds. The approach was longer, wider, flatter. The hoof boasted but a tenth of the bandits' numbers and could spread out, covering the distance at far greater speed. But only as far as the river. The Guadal-kabir provided Kalbarca's greatest defense from this direction. To cross its imposing expanse and reach the gate, the hoof would be forced onto the Old

Imperial Bridge. The ancient construction was wide enough for nearly ten hogs to traverse abreast, but still the hoof would be forced to cluster, to slow. They would be vulnerable at the chokepoint. Without the gates open, the bridge was nothing but a butcher's block.

The half-orcs, however, had a living battering ram.

Oats could see Ruin ahead, his hyena at his leg. Still outside the range of the defenses, they hadn't yet broken into a run. Likely the garrison could see them now too, though none of the frails would be hawk-eyed enough to pick out the details. For now they'd spy only a lone figure and a dog. Perhaps some keen man would notice both were larger than they should be. It wouldn't be long now before Ruin's nature would be revealed. Once he started running, the garrison would see what they thought to be a massive thick. If there were wizards at the gate, perhaps they'd have knowledge of what he was, try to stop him. Regardless, the guns would sound, signaling the hoof to spur their hogs into a gallop.

It wouldn't be long now . . .

The hyena snapped to a stop, ears standing erect as its muzzle swung around. Ruin halted and followed its gaze. Stark still, both looked east, staring into the distance above the hoof's right flank.

"The hells they doing?" Culprit asked.

Warbler's arm was half-raised to signal a halt when they heard it.

The rolling thunder of hooves.

Polecat's face went slack in the moonlight. "No . . ."

The tremoring sent a ripple of uncertainty through the hoof. Mongrels began pulling their hogs to a stop.

Oats watched Warbler's jaw clench. Another choice, every heartbeat closing the chance to make it. They could flee, away from the yet-unseen enemy, away from Kalbarca, from the attack, from the chief. Or . . .

Warbler stood tall in the saddle, sweeping his arm toward the city.

"RIDE!"

Oats kicked Ugfuck into a gallop, casting quick glances eastward, hoping not to see what he knew was coming. Not yet, dammit. Not yet! Ahead, Ruin charged, triggering the first spate of cannon fire. Heedless, he bulled between columns of erupting earth. He wouldn't be stopped, Oats knew. He would reach the gate. If he could smash through, open a path for the hoof, there was a chance. They only needed a few more—

The centaurs came in an avalanche from the edge of darkness.

"Shit!" Culprit screamed. "Shit, shit, SHIT!"

The size of the herd was a mind-trampling nightmare. A wall of murder-lust, birthed from the night. Oats had fought twice at Strava during the Betrayer, stood with the Unyars against hundreds of the beast-men. Never before had he seen so many as now and he knew, with sickening despair, that those he beheld were only the fore of an uncountable horde.

The centaurs were closer to the city, surging toward the hoof with ravening speed. The hogs seared the dust at full gallop, huffing headlong for the gate. It wasn't enough.

The centaurs would cut them off before they gained the bridge.

"War-boar!" Oats screamed.

"I see it!"

Warbler raised a crooked arm, signaling a shank-shot.

Oats repeated the gesture, hoping it would be passed back down the length of the column. He loaded his stockbow just in time to pull Ugfuck hard to the right.

For several horrible heartbeats they faced the stampede.

Shrill, blood-crazed shrieks poured from gaping mouths as the centaurs celebrated what they believed to be the beginnings of a slaughter, a forest of jostling spears raised above their wild-haired heads. But the half-orcs followed Warbler around in a tight wheel, bringing their left side to face the horse-cocks. As the hogs cut across the centaurs' line, the riders trained their stockbows and loosed, sending a cascading volley into the herd. Oats didn't see where his bolt struck, but it was impossible to miss the oncoming wave. Completing the wheel, he fled. As he came about, he saw the great hoof moving in a perfect, unbroken spiral of two offset columns, allowing gaps for the second rank to shoot. The rearmost riders had been forced to turn quicker, tighter, in order to prevent the horse-cocks from overtaking them, but all completed the maneuver, hurling death and defiance with every thrumbolt.

All save the Shards.

Oats could see the tails of the crimson sashes wrapped about Notch's head and waist trailing behind him as he led his band away from the fight, fleeing southwest. The Shards had cut away without risking the shank-shot. Another betrayal added to the night's tally.

Warbler kept the rest of the army moving, gaining enough distance on the centaurs for another shanker. A second volley added to the slain.

They may as well have tried to kill the Titan's Ocean for all the good it did.

The centaurs trampled their fallen without care, swallowed them up and kept coming. There weren't enough bolts in the hoof's quivers to kill even half of the maddened herd.

And it was too late to run. Centaurs beneath a Betrayer Moon possessed a dreadful vigor. Stronger and faster, they would pursue their quarry without need of rest, with no thought to mercy, and there was not a hog born that could outpace them for long.

Already the hoof struggled to keep away from their grasp. Deranged as they were, the horse-cocks weren't brainless. The herd began to spread out, their far superior numbers consuming the open ground. Soon the hoof would be swept toward the walls, toward the guns. Warbler saw the danger. Guiding the hoof with precision through the ever-shrinking eye at the center of the howling storm, he brought them around to face Kalbarca. The centaurs blocked their view of the bridge, though the gatehouse was visible above.

Warbler drew his tulwar.

And signaled a tusker.

Steel scraped into the air as three hundred riders drew swords, spurring their hogs into a charge with a belligerent war cry. Not since the Incursion had the half-orcs fought in such numbers. Oats should have felt unconquerable amongst the pounding hooves of so many barbarians, but the swarm of baying 'taurs made a mockery of their might. The hoof charged a monstrosity with a thousand faces, a collective maw that could eat the world. The riders on the wings loosed a volley before drawing tight, narrowing and strengthening the spearhead. 'Taurs went down in a tangle of flailing limbs, but the herd's counter charge was not stalled. Sword raised, Oats snatched a javelin from the brace. Staying in the saddle with nothing but his legs, lungs pouring out a scream he couldn't hear, Oats rode with the Bastards in the vanguard, the piercing head that had to break through or the hoof would not reach the bridge. Only Warbler rode ahead of him, nearly close enough to touch.

The vanguard flung their javelins at the last moment. Oats put all the strength of his arm and Ug's charge behind the throw. The felled centaurs were crushed between the earth and the hooves of the unflinching herd. Their ugly deaths were the last thing Oats saw before the impact that nearly knocked him from the saddle.

His sword was useless, the spears of the centaurs impotent. Only the tusks of the hogs mattered. They cut a bloody, bone-snapping furrow through the herd, using the horse-cocks' own speed to kill them. Following hard in Old Friend's wake, Ugfuck kept his head low, shoulders strong as he dug a tunnel through a mountain of meat. The Bastards were the front of a plow blade, the cutting edge of a wedge formed by the rest of the great hoof. The centaurs were soil soaked in blood.

Yet even the wettest ground holds stones, blunting and slowing the blade. The stones that impeded the hoof were fired from Kalbarca.

The walls boomed, tearing chunks out of the massed centaurs. Oats saw their mangled forms popping up ahead, lifted on cradles of mud and smoke. He heard hogs squeal behind him and knew the cannonballs were killing more than the enemy. The garrison had waited, damn them. The centaurs had been in range since they appeared, but the frails waited until the hoof was mired in battle before igniting the guns.

Oats didn't know how many of his brothers and sisters were dying. He couldn't look back. Forward. He had to look—had to move—forward.

Ugfuck began to tire, slowing with every 'taur he struck. Oats added his tulwar to the hog's efforts, hacking to their exposed left. His blade slashed flesh and battered the hafts of spears, keeping the roiling herd at bay, clearing the way for the mongrel behind. Culprit. It should have been Culprit. But Oats couldn't hear him. His ears were drowned by the pitched exultations of the centaurs, the deep pool of their voices broken only by plunging gunstones.

At the spear's tip, Warbler and Old Friend strove to cut a path. The old thrice's sword never stilled, his white hair stained pink with gore. At his right flank, opposite Oats, Thresher made good on her hoof-name, her chain-mace hard at work. Still, the tusker began to falter, bogged down by the immense weight of the foe. Soon they would grind to a halt. To stop was to die. Nearly three-hundred mongrels had formed this charge. Oats didn't know how many were still alive behind him, but they'd all sink beneath the relentless tide of the centaur herd if they didn't soon reach . . .

The bridge.

Through the ragged edge of the press, Oats spied the white stones. Warbler waded toward them, fighting with undiminished fervor. He lopped legs, smote skulls, baling blood. Oats made damn certain he kept up. There was no art to the fighting. It was desperate butchery, fending off a horde of deranged spear thrusts with his own wild strokes. Oats kept his sword in motion, trusting his hog and his fellow riders.

As if freed from a tethered anvil, Ugfuck burst from the crush. The night sky loomed huge above, rescued from the suffocating clutch of battle. Ug's hooves rasped upon the stone of the bridge, a confined road leading from the belly of one beast to the teeth of another.

Kalbarca's gatehouse yawned at the far end, promising death if they approached. Thrumbolts arced and hissed from the top, snapping against the stones. Oats spurred Ug on, knowing the guns would follow. They fired from the walls, the towers, but the shots howled overhead, none striking the bridge. Did the frails fear its destruction? If so, it was a foolish, fortunate caution. Oats rode hard through the scattered thrumshots, speed his only shield. He heard Thresher snarl. Glancing right, he saw her face was set in a grimace, but there was no wound that Oats could see. Like him, she pushed her barbarian, racing for the gate.

The shattered gate.

The last measure of the bridge steamed, the cobbles swamped and shiny. Murderholes in the gatehouse drooled black tar, the last lazy remnants of dumped cauldrons. The hogs jumped the noxious slick, barreling through the twisted remains of the huge gatehouse doors. They didn't slow through the length of the tunnel. Whatever the Hisparthans had waiting to meet them would be best hit hard. And they needed to make way for the rest of the hoof, those who survived. The centaurs would follow, bringing their rampage into the city. The fight within the walls would be bitter, but the frails wouldn't be helped by the centaurs' invasion. Neither would the hoof. This night's terror would only fatten.

The Hisparthans had placed a cadre of cavaleros to stand against a breach at the gate. These weren't lowborn exiles in steel caps and scale coats, but heavy horse in fitted plate. Oats couldn't guess at their numbers.

Ruin had torn them to pieces.

The wide street beyond the gate was a charnel pit of dying horses, dismembered men, and corpses crushed within dented, leaking armor. Ruin's hyena savaged a screaming horse, jaws clamped on its throat. The devil dog's back was lacquered with cooled tar, as was the flesh of its master. Ruin stood near the center of the carnage, tearing the last living cavalero from the saddle and slamming his fist full into the face mask of the man's helm. The metal caved, as did the skull beneath. The frail's armor rattled with his dying convulsions.

There was no sign of further opposition on the street, but the walls were barnacled with men. Ruin's massive body invited the thrumbolts that failed to harm him. They came haphazard from the top of the gatehouse and the walls to either side. The hoof's appearance gave them other targets.

Warbler barreled up the street, past Ruin. Oats and the others split to ride around the *uq'huul,* a river of hog flesh parting before a boulder. The street emptied into a square. Warbler used the space to turn the hoof and form up. Oats made a quick count as the mongrels pulled their hogs to face the gate once more. Two score had reached the square, perhaps less, but more were streaming through the gate, through the spitting hail of missiles from the defenders.

"Thrums!" Warbler shouted, causing blades to be sheathed, stockbows unslung and loaded.

The riders in the square loosed at the gatehouse, the walls. Kalbarca didn't possess battlements on the inward-facing side, leaving the garrison unprotected. Men dropped, some falling off the wall. A second flight sent many scurrying to escape the raking volleys. The gate tunnel spewed a torrent of hoof-riders that quickly ebbed to a trickle before ceasing entirely.

Oats looked around as the last mongrel reached the square. Too few, barely a hundred. The faces surrounding him were slack with the same truth. Too few. Not even all the Bastards were there. As Oats took in those nearest to him, his heart sank at the missing. Culprit. Polecat. Anvil.

"You see them fall?" he asked, looking at Sluggard, Shed Snake, Thresher.

He was answered with silence and head shakes.

"Some are still out there!" a blood-covered brother with Tusked Tide tattoos exclaimed. "My chief and some others. Horse-cocks surrounded them before they got to the bridge."

"Then they're dead," Pulp Ear said.

"Not all of them," Warbler rumbled. "Not yet. Or the horse-cocks would already have come through."

He spurred Old Friend forward. Oats and the Bastards and more kicked their hogs to follow. But not all. Pulp Ear remained where he was, anchoring the remaining Brotherhood and a dozen more.

"We'll not," he spat.

Warbler didn't turn. "No. You'll take the gatehouse."

"Damn you, old thrice!"

Warbler didn't slow, ignoring the hoofmaster's shouted abuses.

"I'll take the gatehouse! To have a good vantage of the 'taurs tearing you apart! You're fools! All of you that follow him! Fucking fools! The horse-cocks will rip you to pieces! You've no chance! They're animals! Nothing but vicious animals!"

Pulp Ear's protests struck Oats's ears even as his eyes fell upon the hyena, now feasting on the entrails of a horse. Ruin was nowhere to be seen. Oats slowed Ugfuck. Warbler and the Bastards were already in full gallop, entering the tunnel gate. Oats broke away, keeping to the street, ignoring the shouted rebukes from the other hoof-riders thinking he'd lost his nerve.

It took only a moment to find the bloody, bare footprints.

Oats followed the tracks down a narrower lane. He didn't worry about an ambush from the garrison. Ruin's passage would have unmanned any frails with a mind toward resistance.

Oats found him across another broad street framed with dilapidated structures razed during the orc occupation. Scrub grass grew between the cobbles. There was no sign of restoration or habitation. Like much of Kalbarca, the street remained abandoned. The perfect place to move in secret if you'd a mind to take the gate from within as Barsius had promised.

Ruin squatted by a low arch housing a barred culvert, one of many drains to the city's ancient sewers. Grasping the grate, the brute flexed and stood, breaking the stone and casting it aside in one motion. The hole left behind was still too small for his bulk. He began hammering at the rough edges with his fists.

"We need your help!" Oats shouted in orcish.

Ruin ignored him, continued to smash through the masonry. Oats gained his attention by shooting a bolt into the back of his skull. The *uq'uul* whirled around, face twisted with anger.

"She's down there," Oats said, tipping his stockbow at the sewer opening. It wasn't a question. His next words were. "Is she dead?"

Ruin glowered. He shook his head.

"Then she can wait," Oats said, the words almost choking him. "The centaurs are slaughtering us. We need you."

Again, the brute shook his head. "Ka'siqana." He turned to the hole once more, fists rising.

"YOU'RE NOT SAVING HER BY LETTING US DIE!" The raw rage in Oats's voice halted Ruin. The orcs named their warriors after the strongest parts of their bodies. *Ulyud. T'huruuk. Dulv M'har.* But the hoof-riders weren't Fetch's hands or arms or teeth.

"The half-bloods dying out there are her heart! She's their chief. What do you think will happen to her when she hears they're gone? You won't have saved her, U'ruul Targha B'hal. Not if you don't save them!"

Ruin's frown deepened.

"You've magic," Oats pressed. "Power over beasts. There's too many in that herd for you to kill. Not in time. But—"

His words were cut off by Ruin smiting the stones once more. Ugfuck balked at the flying debris.

"To the hells with you, then," Oats told the brute, pulling his hog around.

They surged back through the streets.

There was fighting along the walls. Pulp Ear and his mongrels had set to the task of taking the gatehouse.

Oats raced through the darkness of the tunnel and emerged onto the moon-bathed bridge. At the far end, his brethren hurled themselves at the centaurs. They must have forced a hole in the eclipsing herd, for wounded mongrels staggered on foot away from the battle. Oats passed the corpses of several who'd escaped the press only to be shot down from the walls. Clumps of unhogged riders took cover behind the plinths along the bridge. Once home to Imperial statues, they supported nothing now but amputated stone feet.

Warbler had left a rearguard to hold the bridgehead so they wouldn't be cut off again, but the screen was faltering against the weighted fury of the centaurs.

Oats shouted to the limit of his lungs, waving for the rearguard to make room. Ugfuck plunged through the gap. Oats feathered the first centaur in his path, loosing from so close that the bolt punched clear through the filly's head. Ugfuck knocked her collapsing body aside and gored the horse-cocks beyond. Letting his stockbow fall to the end of its strap, Oats drew steel just in time to parry an incoming spear and whip his blade beneath the bearer's arm. The limb was half sheared away, but the centaur kept fighting, kept spewing screams and frothing spit. A crosscut took his head off.

Warbler's charge had won through to the others. Oats could see them through the press of 'taurs that came flooding back to fill the swath. He cut his way through to the pocket of ground held by his brothers, a hard-pressed ring of hogs defending mongrels on foot. Seeing him coming, Thresh, Shed Snake, and Sluggard pushed their hogs forward, enough to form a gap. Oats and Ugfuck killed until they reached it, turning to solidify the ring once more. Before he did, he caught a glimpse of the hogless survivors, perhaps sixty in all. Anvil was among them, supporting a dazed and weakened Boar Lip, half her face awash in blood. Hells, she was missing an eye.

Two riders to Oats's left, beyond Sluggard, Polecat fought against the rockslide of horseflesh, ceaselessly issuing a frantic chant.

"You won't fucking get me! You won't fucking get me! You won't fucking get me!"

The ring of riders tried to move, to grind their way to the bridge and the rearguard, but the centaurs were a vise, constricting them with endless waves of berserking wrath. Even the dead were a hindrance, the large bodies of the 'taurs building a grisly barrier to bar the hoof's way.

They were trapped.

Oats's arm grew leaden against foes that did not tire. The hogs were forced back by the onslaught, collapsing the ring. Thresh's barbarian, pierced by spears in the neck, chest, and shoulders, finally succumbed. As the animal dropped, Thresh flung herself backward over the saddle and inside the ring. Oats pulled Ug back and found himself fighting side by side with a nomad he didn't know. The mongrel died a heartbeat later, torn from his saddle by the empty grasping hands of the centaur he'd run through a moment before.

"You won't fucking get me! You won't! Fucking won't!"

Again Oats gave ground to keep the ring unbroken. He no longer knew who was beside him. To look away from the herd for a moment would invite death. His arm burned to keep his tulwar aloft and swinging, chopping at a forest of spears. It would fail him soon. He wanted to die fighting, but it was likely the horse-cocks would slay a staring, dull eyed, breathless lump of spent flesh.

The centaur before him reared, the front legs of its stallion body churning in the air, spear poised to plunge.

A terrible wail split the air. The rearing centaur toppled, thrashed upon the ground, spear forgotten as the beast-man clutched at his skull, face contorted with agony. All around the horse-cocks began to buck, their war cries strangled by torment. Those that remained on their feet ran wild, scattering the herd. The wall of savagery crumbled before Oats's eyes, allowing him a view of the bridge.

Upon a plinth at the center of the ancient span, taking the place of whatever frail marble emperor had once been installed, stood Ruin. His stance was wide, torso hunched, head bowed. Even from a distance Oats could discern the slow, irregular flexing of his fingers, the muscles of his entire body tensed to the point of quivering.

The centaurs howled in defiance, fought his sorcerous dominion. They gained nothing but pain. They collapsed in the hundreds, heavy forms crashing to the mud, limbs flailing. Thrumbolts thudded into helpless hides as the hoof wakened from certain death to find an opportunity for a reckoning. Oats didn't bend his thrum to the slaughter. His attention was fixed on Ruin.

The brute fell to his knees, a hand gripping the edge of the plinth. His head began to rise. Oats saw his chest expand, his mouth opening as a scream emerged, born from the depths of prodigious pain. Ruin's cry overpowered the strained voices of the centaurs, his face lifting skyward, revealed in a concentrated beam of moonlight.

Oats looked to the Betrayer. Its fullness waned before his eyes. It happened so fast, Oats couldn't swear he saw it true, but the light fled the moon, shot down the beam, and struck Ruin, an arrow from the heavens. The stricken *uq'huul*'s scream was cut off as he was knocked from the pedestal, lifted into the air by the force of that celestial blow. Ruin's bulk was thrown over the width of the bridge and vanished over the side. The Guadal-kabir claimed him with an uproarious splash.

The centaurs struggled desperately to rise and began to flee. Many were cut down by vengeful hoof-riders before they could gain their feet. Oats startled, raising his sword as the 'taur nearest him shot up. The look on the centaur's face stayed his hand. It was clear-eyed, confused, and terror-struck. Oats let his arm fall. The 'taur took flight, joining the receding waters of the running, defeated herd.

TWENTY-THREE

A SINGLE SHOT PUNCHED FROM the wall east of the gate. The ball landed well short of the depleted hoof, churning nothing but earth and the dead. No others followed. Whether the crews were slain, fled, or simply out of stones, Oats couldn't say, but the lone shot was reminder enough that the mongrels were far from safe.

Warbler's resonant voice cut through woolly exhaustion.

"Look for wounded!"

Oats hadn't known if the old thrice had survived until that moment. The order demanded speed. To sift the injured from the slain. A grim task that needed to be done swiftly. Oats heard the movement of other hogs, the voices of his fellow riders, some calling out names of favored brothers, most lifted in wordless misery. He was too afraid to turn and behold the loss, to make it real with the touch of his eyes.

One voice, familiar but altered, provided proof that at least one other Bastard came through alive.

"Not going . . . not fucking going . . . not going to . . ."

Oats guided Ug to Polecat. He still sat his hog, animal and rider covered in blood. Hells, they all were. Cat's sword continued to make feeble cuts at the air, the barbarian beneath him sidling to keep them balanced. The eyes in his hatchet-face bulged.

"Not going to get . . . me. Not me. Fucking . . . not me . . ."

Slowly, Oats reached up and placed a hand around Cat's fist, ceasing the sluggish sword strokes. Cat lowered his arm.

"Chief didn't get a warning," he said, voice more air than sound.

"No," Oats replied.

Polecat's head swiveled to face him. His expression was leagues away.

"Did he survive?"

"Who, Cat?"

"The chief. Salts! The horse-cocks get him? Is he alive?"

Oats grit his teeth, swallowed a curse at the injustice. Salts had been the name of the Rutters' hoofmaster, killed—along with most of his brethren—during a Betrayer Moon near ten years ago.

"No, Cat," Oats said. "He's not."

Polecat's face didn't change. It remained blank. "Oh. They didn't get me."

Oats clasped his shoulder. "No."

A gormless grin twitched at the corner of the former Rutter's mouth. He'd stood firm in body. But his mind had fled.

It was only the beginning of the cost.

Culprit wouldn't allow anyone near Shed Snake's body. He sat among the carnage, slumped against a dead barbarian, hugging Snake close, weeping upon his brow.

"You have to promise not to burn him!" Culprit pleaded, toneless with tears. "He wouldn't want that. He wouldn't want to be burned!"

Sluggard crouched nearby, hand outstretched. "We won't—"

"You have to promise! The chief has to promise!" Culprit's swollen face shifted up to Oats. The young mongrel's naked despair hovered above Shed Snake's open, sightless eyes. "Oats! He's . . . he's . . . he's gone, Oats! I didn't see it . . . I don't know how it . . . HELLS!"

Oats wanted to get down from his hog, to grieve, to give himself over to the anger and the anguish as Culprit did. But there wasn't time. Warbler saved him from being the cruel fuck.

The old thrice rode up, jumped down from the saddle, and took a hard step toward Culprit.

"Time to move, Bastard. Let him go."

"You need to swear—"

Warbler squatted, thrust his face toward Culprit's with such fury the younger half-orc quailed.

"I can't swear, son. I don't know if there'll be any of us left alive to tend him at all. City ain't ours yet. And that moon may be dim now, but I won't wager against it turning again. We don't survive then we won't have a say what happens to our fallen. The Hisparthans may throw him in a pit with all these others alongside the 'taurs that killed them. Or they may burn them. You don't want that to happen, you need to get up, you need to leave him behind, and you need to help kill every last fucking frail behind those walls. Do you hearken me, boy?"

Culprit's puffy face hardened around the mouth. There was a mote of hatred for Warbler in his nod. Oats couldn't blame him.

Warbler returned to Old Friend and rode off, rumbling orders. Sluggard took Snake's weight, allowing Culprit to shuffle from beneath the body. Rubbing his eyes with the back of a hand, Culprit gave Slug a nod and took his friend once more. He eased Snake's head to the ground.

"I'll be back for you, brother."

Culprit stood and went for his hog, but stopped short. He went back to Shed Snake, knelt, and made sure Snake's half cape covered his burn-scarred arm. Standing again, Culprit faced Oats and Sluggard, though he didn't meet their eyes.

"In case the sun's up before we get back," he explained, voice growing thick.

The hoof gathered its wounded and returned to the bridge, quick as the walking would allow. They were seventy-one mounted mongrels. Of the sixty-eight on foot, barely half were hale enough to still fight. Anvil insisted she was one of them, despite half a dozen deep wounds, to say nothing of the spear thrust that took her right eye. She'd tied a rag over the grisly socket, waved off Thresh's help, and moved toward the city with a steady stride.

Oats paused at the bridgehead to look over the side, searching for sign of Ruin. There was nothing but dark water lapping at the stone foundations. He wondered, distantly, if an *uq'huul* could drown. The possibility stirred nothing within him. Perhaps that made him an uncaring cunt. Perhaps he'd simply left his capacity for sorrow a few hundred strides behind, just another dead thing discarded on a bed of gore.

No bolts or gunstones beset their passage into the city. Half-orcs stood in the embrasures atop the gatehouse in place of men. The streets beyond the tunnel were clear, save for the mess Ruin made of the cavaleros. But there was a new corpse lying among the men and horses; Ruin's hyena, sprawled on its side. There was no wound, no sign of violence. The beast had simply died where it stood, sharing the fate of its master as it shared his dread resilience.

Warbler worked quickly, directing the wounded into the nearest buildings, ordering those without hogs to stand guard and reinforce the gate. Pulp Ear came down from the wall, a bitter twist to his mouth. The remaining chiefs gathered in the shadow of the gatehouse, protected by a screen of hog-riders. Oats stuck with Warbler. He needed to get to Fetch as soon as matters were sorted here.

"The frails have fallen back," Pulp Ear declared. "Far as I can see, they've abandoned the walls."

"They'll have a strongpoint deeper in the city," Warbler said. "A place to hold out. I'd wager they barricaded the old garden palace."

"Let them stay there," Pulp Ear replied. "It is time we were away."

Boar Lip sat slumped on a barrel of abandoned gunpowder near the stairs to the wall. He'd taken a spear through the gut. He was dead soon, and knew it, but until then he was chief of the Tusked Tide.

"I won't . . . leave my injured," he said, throat clogged with pain.

If any were left behind, Boar Lip would certainly be among them, but not even Pulp Ear was callous enough to throw that truth in the expiring mongrel's face.

"Go if you've a mind to," Warbler told the Brotherhood's master. "But I'm taking this city. Else all this was for nothing."

Before Pulp Ear could answer, a call from above drew their attention.

"Got some fucks approaching, chief!" a Cauldron Brother yelled, pointing toward the harbor. "They're ours!"

Blackened with soot, smeared with blood, the White Wrists came rushing toward the gate, some atop the wall, more along the streets. Jackal led the mongrels above, his desert garb sodden and tattered. Blood Crow was behind him, afoot. In the street, Thoon towered above the Wrists, carrying a cannon barrel in his hand like a club. The cyclops had been given no role in the attack, at Anvil's insistence, but here he was, long amber locks hanging in wet twists. Jacintho hurried beside the lumbering Aetynian.

Spying Oats, the bandit ran over, cracking a smile.

"Ever clung to a giant's back while he swam the Guadal-kabir and then climbed a city wall, Big Bastard?" Jacintho asked. "Neither had I."

"Caltrop found you," Oats said.

Jacintho nodded. "Thoon set off as soon as the words left the Thrice Freed's lips. I suspect he understands more Hisparthan than we credit."

Anvil came forward to meet the cyclops. She said something to him, too quiet to hear from where Oats sat, but the jab of her finger bespoke a chastisement. Thoon remained silent. He pushed Anvil's matted hair away from her face with his smallest finger, revealing the blood soaked rag over her eye.

"It appears they share more than a language now," Jacintho said. It was a grim jest, but uttered with a quiet regret.

Jackal came down the wall stairs two at a time. Oats could see him taking in the casualties even on the move. His face was set, vexation housed in the tightness of his jaw.

"How many are you?" Warbler asked, wasting no time.

"Shy of two hundred," Jackal replied. "The frails did not want to let go of the harbor gate."

"Wizards?"

"One."

"You kill him?"

"Her. Yes."

"Reckon there'll be more. Hope your ship boys have more fight in them. We got one waiting."

Oats let them talk. Dismounting, he went to Blood Crow. The elf had come down from the wall and moved immediately to the dead hyena. His eyes never left the animal while Oats explained, as best he could, what happened.

Blood Crow's face betrayed no emotion, but Oats saw him swallow hard.

"I must find him," the Tine warrior said, turning toward the gate.

Oats grabbed his arm. "What about Fetch?"

Blood Crow stared at Oats's hand until he let go. "I am not honor bound to Ka'siqana. My pledge is to my mother and, through her, my brother."

"He's likely dead. Fetch ain't. We could use your help."

"I am helping you, half-orc. A Ruin Made Flesh is not easily slain. You say Te'hanoc was struck by the curse of the centaurs' moon. What if he lives? What if he awakes possessed by that curse?"

The thought of Ruin on a loon-crazed rampage made Oats queasy. "Aw, hells . . ."

"You must hurry," Blood Crow said. "I can stall my brother should it be so, but only our sister can stop him."

The elf turned and rushed for the gate. Jackal called out to him in elvish as he ran by, but Blood Crow did not slow, did not respond. Oats beckoned Jackal and Warbler when their confused stares rested on him.

"We need to go, Jack," he said when they came close. "Now."

Jackal looked to Warbler.

"Think I can't do this without you?" the old thrice said. "Go get her."

"We're going to need light," Oats said.

Warbler yelled for a lantern from the gatehouse. Sluggard brought it at a run, Thresher beside him.

Jackal held out his hand, but Slug made no move to hand the lantern over.

"We're going," Thresh said.

Jackal opened his mouth, but Oats spoke before he could respond.

"You're not. And there ain't time to argue it."

Sluggard's chin lifted with defiance. "She's our chief, t—"

Oats snatched the lantern from his hand. "SHE'S MORE TO US!"

Soon as the bellow left his chest, regret flooded in to replace it. Sluggard's eyes went bright with fury. Thresher looked ready to punch Oats. Jackal was careful not to look at him at all.

"I need you both here," Warbler said, taking the shit Oats had flung in hand. "Thresh, stick with Anvil. We need that cyclops, so we need her. Make sure she don't push herself to death. Thrice-bloods can do that better than any. Slug, you're with me. Same orders." Warbler's squinted stare shifted to Jackal and Oats. "Why are you still standing there?"

"Right," Jack said.

They darted away together, breaking into a run.

Oats shed the weight of his fear as he led Jackal through the empty streets. It was an old feeling, forgotten until its return. As children, Jaco had been smaller, weaker, barely quicker, yet whenever he was near Oats gained an unthinking courage fed by his friend's limitless daring. Regaining that now brought strength to his limbs, speed to his steps. His mind was no longer burdened by worry, his heart no longer mired with doubt. There was only what had to be done and the movement needed to bring Fetching back to them.

Reaching the torn-out sewer grate, they paused only long enough to put daggers between their teeth before clambering down through the hole. Beyond the culvert, a slope of masonry led to the sewer proper. Jackal went first with the light, sure and silent. The tunnel at the bottom was larger than any beneath Ellerina. Oats barely had to crouch and Jackal could stand fully upright. The sewer led away in both directions. Moonlight from the street drains above sliced through the gloom at irregular intervals.

Oats took his dagger in hand. He signaled to Jack to go left one hundred paces, indicating he would do the same to the right. Jackal nodded in agreement.

They moved off.

It wasn't long before Oats found the stonework of the sewer wall broken, a smaller passage leading down into a blackness that even half-orc eyes could not penetrate. He returned to the culvert and found Jackal waiting.

"Anything?"

"No," Jackal said. "You?"

"Another hole," Oats replied. "Looks to have been dug out. Goes deeper."

"Let's see it."

They went back together. As they approached the cavity, Oats's heart jumped to his throat. A smear of light now resided deep within the smaller shaft.

"That wasn't there before," he hissed.

Jackal pressed against one side of the opening. Oats took the other. They waited, barely breathing, snatching glances down the shaft. The light did not draw closer.

"Trap or invitation?" Jackal whispered.

"Fuck them for either," Oats replied, standing away from the wall. He sheathed his dagger, pulled his stockbow around, began to load. His wounded hand made him clumsy. He fumbled the first bolt, biting down on the pain and a curse.

"You good?" Jackal asked.

Oats didn't look up, but could feel his friend's eyes on what was left of his two fingers.

"Ask me that again and I'll shove these mangled stumps so far up your ass Belico will have no choice but to regrow them," Oats replied.

Jackal kept his mouth shut. He didn't carry a thrum anymore. These days, he killed quicker when close.

"Jack," Oats said, placing the second bolt. "Barsius may be nose-high to my cod end, but don't think that's all he is."

"I don't."

Stooping, they entered the rough shaft, Jackal in the lead. Caution and the ever-steepening downgrade made their progress slow. Oats smelled the tallow candle long before it was revealed around a bend in the tunnel, its melted base stuck to a jutting rock. A second could be seen farther on, leading them deeper.

"An invitation *to* a trap," Jackal muttered.

They kept going. Branching passages appeared on either side. Most were black, perfect nests for ambush. Jackal pushed the lantern's light into all of them, illuminating nothing but more rough-hewn stone. Still, Oats trained his thrum down every one as he passed, expecting halfling killers to come bursting forth. But only the earth's quiet weight assailed them. The sixth candle rested a few steps within a spur tunnel, the first to tempt them away from the central shaft. Jackal did not hesitate nor hurry. His steps were measured in their pursuit of each guiding light. He didn't shrink from the inevitable danger, but neither did he court it.

The candles lured them farther, deeper.

After what seemed an age, the branching passages—and the candles—ceased, leaving them once again with a single narrow road. Oats's legs were afire from the hunched march upon chiseled rock. The tunnel grew smaller, constricting as they pushed through its throat. Oats didn't look back, fearing he'd find the passage defying all nature and sealing behind them.

At last the tunnel leveled off, ending in a blister of space. Over Jack's head, Oats could see nothing but a wall of cut, fitted stone. The tunnel had been sealed with masonry.

A dead end.

Oats let his breath out. It was all he could do not to scream.

This had been a trap, but not one intended to kill. They'd been led on a chase with no quarry. Small wonder the candles had ceased. Barsius—or one of his boys—must have placed the last and doubled back. No doubt they'd all been snuffed out now, gathered up. Oats and Jackal would be hard-pressed to find their way out. Even if they did, what then? The halflings had been scuttling around down here for generations. The tunnels would be endless.

Jackal squatted.

The place was so cramped, it was only then that Oats saw an opening in the base of the barricading wall. Jackal crab-crawled aside, making just enough room for Oats to hunker down beside him. The light from the lantern reached into the opening, revealing a straight, level tunnel with no discernible end.

It was roughly the width of a coffin.

Oats looked up to find Jackal's face set in a grim mask carved into a question. *Go back or go on?*

It wasn't a fucking choice.

Oats stood, quickly shedding his stockbow and brigand.

"No chance I'm fitting through with them on," he said.

"Oats..."

"Get going. I'll be along."

Jackal's mouth relaxed. Not quite a grin, but it was something. "See you on the other side."

He dropped to his belly and slithered into the hole, taking the light with him.

Oats unbuckled his sword belt, trying to do whatever he could to reduce his girth. He didn't fancy being without his tulwar, so he removed the sheathed weapon from the belt and pushed it into the tunnel first. He considered tying it to his ankle to drag along behind, but if it came loose there would be no retrieving it. Sucking in, he crawled forward. His shoulders almost stopped him before he began, but he forced them through, flesh scraped by the stone. He could just make out Jackal's light ahead, all but blocked by the shuffling shadow of his body.

Oats had been wrong in his estimation. The channel stretching out before him was tighter than a coffin. And it would serve as one if he became stuck. He fought down a welling panic, began pulling himself along, pausing to shove the tulwar forward. His elbows were beneath him, pressed into his torso by the roof of the shaft. He quickly regretted bringing the sword. He had to nudge it forward with the fingers on his good hand, slowing down his already torturous progress. He couldn't crawl over it. There wasn't room. Oats committed to the labor, to the small exhausting motions. Nudge. Inhale. Drag. Exhale. It was too tight for him to wriggle, to employ his hips and legs. All he had were his pinned and restricted arms. Nudge. Inhale. Drag. Exhale. Mind-shattering terror crouched in the spaces between each profitless movement, waiting for the moment he failed to struggle forward so it could pounce and trumpet a helpless, prolonged death with his crazed shrieking. The light was gone. Whether it had gone out or Jackal had simply moved too far ahead, Oats couldn't say, for he could not raise his head up enough to see. His muscles were screaming, cramping. To continue on was an agony, to stop was a horror. And then he heard it.

"Nearly there."

Jackal's voice. But still there was no light.

Nudge. Inhale. Drag. Exhale.

After an eternity of compressed, interminable effort Oats heard his sword dragged away. A moment later, Jackal's hand reached in for his and helped pull him free. Oats jumped to his feet, every sinew in his body demanding to move, to shake off the grip of the stone. He took in deep lungfuls of air. His breaths echoed. He couldn't see, but he could feel the coolness of the space around him. They'd emerged into a cavern.

"Why're we in the dark?" Oats whispered.

"Knocked the lantern over during the crawl," Jackal answered in a hush. "The candle went out."

"Shit."

"Close your eyes."

"I'm blind already, Ja—"

A flash replaced the darkness with a painful glare. Oats grunted, eyes forced shut against the burning white radiance. The dazzle subsided behind his eyelids, leaving dancing blobs behind. Opening his eyes, Oats found Jackal dumping powder from a small vial onto his dagger blade. The metal was awash in ephemeral blue flames. As the harshness of the light's source softened into a glow, Oats realized they weren't standing in a cavern, but a lofty corridor.

A double row of fluted columns soared into shadow, marching away into the gloom. The white marble shone in the ghostly light. At their feet, an intricately tiled floor could be spied beneath the scattered debris of untold ages. Oats turned in place, following Jackal's stare to the wall housing their entry tunnel. Its entire broad surface rippled with embossed carvings. The stone bulged with the leg muscles of a colossal man, his stance wide. The sinuous swell of a great serpent's coil snared one thigh, wrapped about the man's bare torso. Grappling hands, huge and straining, fended off the constriction, but in that supple shaping of marble Oats beheld futility. Both man and snake had been decapitated by time, the roof of the corridor partially collapsed at this end, the raw stone of the earth patiently intruding. Oats shivered, wondering how long this structure had endured the press of burial, hoping it would not choose this night to succumb.

"We should move," Jackal said. "This light won't last long."

Oats retrieved the fallen lantern, opened the shutter. "So kiss the wick with your magic flame there."

"It's alchemy, not magic," Jackal said. "And it doesn't burn." He put his hand in the blue fire as demonstration.

"Got any more of them vials?" Oats asked with little hope.

"No."

Oats sighed, drew his tulwar. "Let's go, then." He kept hold of the lantern on the chance they found honest fire.

The corridor was as wide as the great hall of any castle, strewn with the cast-offs of its slow decay. One column had toppled and now lay broken in even segments taller than Oats. Jackal picked a path between a pair of the huge discs and proceeded on, his flame-shrouded dagger held high. The light barely reached the walls, but Oats could see more carvings cresting from the pools of deep shadow. The heads of beasts, the wings of great birds, the breasts of women. Together they melded into the twisted forms of monsters. Jackal and Oats passed through a graven parade of serpent-haired demons, bulls that stood upright, horned men with cloven feet and erect cocks. Always they struggled against the same figure, a mighty-thewed bearded man dressed in the pelt of a lion.

One vast carving of the man battling centaurs drew Jackal closer. The dagger flame splashed light over the rearing horseflesh, the wild, leering faces. It was so lifelike, Oats was forced to avert his gaze.

"I've been beneath Strava," Jackal hissed. "It's a hoard of grave goods stashed in a warren. But this . . . this is a temple. From the Imperium. This looks like the god Burgos told us about. Lionclad."

"Herathos," Oats grunted in agreement, remembering the old

river pirate's story about the founder of Sparthis. "Why you bothered, Jack?"

Jackal turned away from the carving, his slack, puzzled expression stiffening as he shook his head. He led them on without another word, but he stayed close to the right wall. Oats could see him continue to study the carvings as they moved.

Burgos had said Herathos went to Dhar'gest and ended up fleeing with the orcs on his ass. He created the Deluged Sea to stop them, destroying the forest-basin homeland of the elves in the doing. If the builders of this temple knew the same tale, Oats didn't see any evidence of it in their art, though hells knew what adorned the opposite wall. Burgos had also said Lionclad was a lusty sort and here the sculptors agreed, for violence wasn't the only act that embroiled the roving god. The carvings rendered orgies with as much detail as the battles. Herathos was entwined with piles of nubile women. And with men and monsters too.

Oats felt Jackal's wordless disquiet taking root in his chest. A man fucking centaurs, goat-men, women-faced vultures with tits. It should have been a jest spoken to a fellow rider while passing a skin of wine. It *would* have been a jest . . . aboveground and in the light. But down here, down in the dark, surrounded by these ancient carvings wrought with reverence by gifted hands, Oats found no mirth. He could not smile. Worse, neither did Jackal, a mongrel who lived to laugh in defiance of all repression. Spilled from the lips of an aging captain standing in the sun, these were stories to be heard and dismissed. But engraved in this cold yet vibrant chronicle, the deeds of Herathos gained form and menace. Walking through this temple that time had made a tomb, Oats gazed upon the undying work of the Lionclad's vanished worshippers and shivered, threatened by a devotion the earth had swallowed but could not digest.

Was this temple the purpose of the halflings' digging beneath Kalbarca or merely a chance discovery in their search for more of Belico's relics? Is this where they'd brought Fetching? Or was it nothing more than a well-decorated pit for her pursuers to wander in vain?

The answer came with the dying of Jackal's light, drowning the surrounding walls in darkness, but not vision entire. There was another light far ahead. The familiar, pulsing wash of fire gnawed at the right edge of the passage. They crept forward through the intervening pitch, feeling their way until the illumination was close enough to aid their approach. A great intersection stood before them, their passage crossing with a larger hall. Going to a crouch, Jackal snuck to the corner and peered around. Whatever he saw caused him to breathe a curse and rush into the lit hall.

Oats was a heartbeat behind.

They ran between enormous columns and plinths serving as perches for the statues of hideous creatures, but none of the stone monsters drew Oats's eyes away from the three made of flesh holding Fetch suspended at the end of the hall.

They were giants, heavy-boned and brutishly formed, larger than Thoon, though each possessed not one eye, but two. And two pairs of arms. One giant stood to either side of the chief, one upper hand grasping her arm, the lower hand her leg, holding her limbs splayed. The third massive creature stood behind Fetching, his lower hands encircling her waist while the upper had hold of her head. She was twice her own height from the floor, motionless. Most of her face was covered by the giant's fingers, but Oats did not think she was conscious. Still, her monstrous captors looked capable of quashing any resistance. Hells, those eight savagely muscled arms could likely tear the chief apart.

For now, there was no violence in their bodies, a striking contrast to the spasms of wrath playing across their faces as they bellowed in a tongue Oats did not understand. Their furious speech was spat down upon the figure standing between the great flaming bronze cauldrons at their feet, his small frame undaunted by their immensity.

Zirko.

Jackal called the high priest's name as he ran, and the halfling turned.

"Interference would not be wise," Zirko said, his voice carrying without effort over the abuses of the giants at his back.

Oats was prepared to cross the last dozen strides and cut the Hero

Father down, but Jackal halted, his boots skidding on the crusted stones.

"Zirko . . ." he said again, a low warning in his voice.

The priest's brow furrowed with regret. "I had hoped it would not come to this, Jackal of the True Bastards."

"Release her."

"I cannot."

The giants continued to spew curses, and Oats saw now that all three were blind, their eyes clouded. From the neck up they appeared to be seized by a fit, their hairless heads jerking in chaotic patterns. Though their language was gibberish to Oats's ears he began to hear their overlapping voices echo one another.

Jackal snarled and darted forward again. The next instant he cried out and stumbled as a cloud of inky smoke burst at his back, disgorging Barsius to slash the backs of his legs. Oats couldn't say where the hell he came from. Didn't matter. He bulled forward and sent his tulwar chopping down, but his blade hissed through another eruption of eldritch fume to smite the stone floor instead of the halfling warrior's skull.

"Please," Zirko said. "There need be no more blood this night."

As Oats cast about for sign of Barsius, Jackal sprang up once more. The cloud appeared in an eyeblink just above him, Barsius streaking down at an angle from its murky core with the speed of a thrumbolt, cutting Jackal across the face with such force it spun the mongrel and sent him reeling back to the ground. Barsius's feet never touched the stones. He fell into another cloud, which vanished as quickly as it formed.

Oats moved to Jackal's side and helped him rise. A gash ran down from his forehead, splitting one eye and laying his cheek open so deeply Oats could see his gritted teeth through the wound. Already, the flesh was beginning to close.

"Attukhan and Huroga oft quarreled in life," Zirko said, his face pained. "I do not wish to see their feud revived. I ask again. Please desist."

Barsius appeared at Zirko's left, the grubby killer next to the immaculate priest.

"Not while you have our chief," Jackal growled, his words wet with blood.

He tore away from Oats's support and charged again. Barsius vanished. Jackal swung his tulwar anyway. Oats reckoned he was trying to intercept the halfling's reappearance, but Barsius struck from the side, slicing Jackal's ribs. Jackal spun, sword whipping, but he cut only the eldritch smoke. He struck in every direction, his blade a striking serpent of steel. Hells, he was fast. It wasn't good enough. He battled nothing but air and the lingering laughter of his foe. The smoke birthed and absorbed Barsius time and again. He was there in an eyeblink when before there was nothing, his leaf-bladed sword tossing Jackal's blood with every strike.

Oats wanted to help, but it was fruitless. He could not anticipate when or where the halfling would appear, and Jackal's whirlwind sword made it perilous to get close.

Jackal's boots moved in a sticky pool of his own blood. Whoever this Huroga fuck had been, he allowed Barsius to strike faster than Attukhan could heal. Jackal fell to his knees, his flesh gaping from dozens of dribbling wounds.

"Enough!" Oats shouted at Zirko.

"Barsius," the priest said.

Jackal gave a gurgling grunt as the point of the bronze blade sprouted from his gut. Behind him, Barsius grinned. Pulling the sword free he fled in that damned wink of smoke, returning to Zirko's side the next moment.

The giants' furor reached a new height. For a moment Oats thought they would lash out at the halflings, but they stayed where they were, continuing their firm holds upon the chief. It was then that he saw their feet were made of marble. The veined stone crept upward, hardening their flesh. It was now halfway to their knees.

"My people have toiled for a century to keep Great Belico's relics from the hands of the Black Womb," Zirko said. "Only to have one of our own willingly hand the greatest of those relics over. Xhreka would never have done this were it not for the misguidance of your chief."

"So this is your answer?" Jackal said, voice hoarse with pain. "I'd thought you above petty vengeance, Hero Father."

"This is far from vengeance," Zirko said.

"No?" Oats demanded. "You allowed the centaurs to butcher us, waddler!"

Zirko's chin dipped. "A waste of life. The oracles of this temple only awaken with the coming of the Betrayer Moon. Yet there are few others with the strength to restrain Fetching now. I will not ask forgiveness for your fallen brothers. I know you will never grant it. But the blame lies with her. I warned against forcing my aid in this war."

Jackal spat blood upon the stones, his strength returning. "Aid! You've done nothing but send your spies, and cozen us into a trap!"

"Was it nothing to warn you against the tenebrous ways of sorcerers when first you came to Strava in the company of the one you named Crafty? Was it nothing to bestow you Va Gara Attukhan, grant you the power to fight the Black Womb's pet, an adder at the Grey Bastards' trusting breast? Was it nothing to rid Fetching of the orcish filth poisoning her, and provide food for her starving people? I have been a friend to the Bastards and was repaid with threats, my wayward follower delivered to wicked hands."

"Xhreka wasn't your damn follower," Oats said. "Not for a long while now. All we ever did was help with what she wanted. Which was to stay well away from you."

"She has sacrificed much," Zirko said. "Her travails have caused her confusion. I could have helped her if she had but returned to Strava."

"She's not confused," Jackal said, getting to his feet. "Xhreka didn't trust your help. She had the voice of your Master Slave in her head. Belico isn't pleased with you, Zirko. And Xhreka knows why. I reckon it's more than being made to serve you." Jackal cast a sullen eye around. "You've led us into a temple of Herathos. His big oracles there don't sound happy to be doing your bidding. How many gods hate you, priest? How many want you dead?"

"If only you knew the pains I have spared this world while earning such enmity."

"I don't care a fuck," Jackal said. "Give us Fetching!"

Zirko shook his head. "I tried to save her from this fate. I know something of wielding great power to protect a beloved people. The burdens of such guardianship are . . . wearying. Yet its origins are found in desperation, even elation. The road behind is strewn with pain, doubt, cruelty, every step a defiance of the death that shadows the path. When such a road ends, not in death, but with power, is there truly a choice? At last, a weapon. At last, a way! What battered, servile soul would not seize the chance to never again fear another living thing?"

As the Hero Father spoke, the petrification of the Lionclad's oracles rose ever upward. The giants' chorus of vitriol never abated, even as the stone claimed their legs entire, proceeding on to their bellies.

"Jack . . ." Oats said.

"I see it."

"I confess it was a temptation to which I succumbed long ago," Zirko went on. "Yet it is tragic how swiftly the shards of that fractured fear cause harm to all those surrounding the wielder of such power, those who remain vulnerable. Shielding them, fighting for them, it is a monstrous task."

"Fetch is no monster," Jackal declared, but Oats heard another voice—the chief's—the memory of her words whispering in his head.

They need to fear us . . .

"You no longer know what she is," Zirko said.

"I know she can break stone." Jackal smiled. "And your oracles are soon to be statues."

"And so too will she be."

We need to be something they can't cage . . .

Oats went cold. Hells. Zirko had found a way.

The priest's calm pronouncement provoked a fiery scream from Jackal. He bolted forward, tulwar extended low at his side. The instant Barsius vanished, Jackal leapt to the side. The maw of smoke disgorged the halfling killer, but his striking blade hissed through the air. Jackal spun, sending a reaping cut almost too fast to see. So fast, Barsius was forced to interpose his own sword to keep his head. Metal rang through the lofty temple, but the halfling vanished again before Jackal could strike a second time.

Oats rushed Zirko. If he could reach him . . .

Belico's high priest stood motionless, the giants above him now stone to the chest, the marble beginning to sheath their lower arms.

Oats was three strides away when the unearthly smoke burst between him and Zirko. He slashed with everything he had and felt the familiar impact of a blade biting meat, breaking bone.

The fumes broke . . .

To reveal Jackal, cleaved from the yoke bone to the belly.

Oats had killed enough in his life to know he'd cut straight through the heart. Jackal's eyes went wide, wide with confusion, wide as Oats's own horror-stricken stare, which met them.

"Jack?" he managed, releasing his tulwar to catch his falling brother. "Jaco!"

The answer was nothing but a squelching rattle that was somehow still cruelly recognizable as Jackal's voice. He went limp, the weight bearing them both to the ground.

"Don't, Jackal. Don't, don't. DON'T!"

Oats ripped the sword free from the ruin he'd made of Jackal's torso and pressed the yawning gristle together. The blood soaked his hands, causing them to slip and fumble.

"Heal! Attukhan, you fucker, heal him! Jack!"

Jackal's eyes remained open, but they saw nothing. The only twitches in his body were those caused by Oats's fevered attempts to hold him together.

Oats looked up at Zirko. "Do something, damn you!"

The Hero Father gazed at Jackal with distant disappointment for a moment before looking to Barsius and speaking a few words in the tongue of the Unyar. He reached and placed a hand on the warrior's shoulder and the smoke enfolded the high priest, spiriting him away, but Barsius remained.

The giants had grown silent. Whether it was because Zirko was gone or because their throats were now marble, Oats could not say. The lower arms were stone past the elbow. Soon, it would reach their hands and, Oats knew with grim certainty, would spread to Fetching. She had not awakened. At least she had been spared the sight of what Oats had done. What Barsius had made him do.

"I wish I could kill you," he told the halfling.

"Please, do not try," Barsius replied. The patterns of domed scars upon his face danced in the light from the cauldrons. "It would pain me to slay you, Oats, but I will if you attempt to stand in the way of what I must do."

"What more could you do," Oats growled, feeling his throat constrict and Jackal's blood cool beneath his hands.

"The Arm of Attukhan must return to Strava."

Oats found a seed a hope. "Will Zirko help him?"

"The Arm of Attukhan," Barsius repeated. "Not its bearer."

The halfling's sword wagged slightly in his hand as he tested the weight.

Oats jumped to his feet, lifting Jackal. He backed away.

"You ain't doing that."

"You cannot prevent it," Barsius said. He did not move. He did not need to.

Oats kept moving anyway.

"It was to be my next task," Barsius told him. "You saved me the effort of hunting him down. It is impressive you were able to find this place, I admit."

You led us here with candles, you stunted fuck.

Oats nearly said it, but something killed the words. It was the column to his left, the fluted cylinder gouged by time. No, it wasn't the column, but the eyes that opened upon its pitted surface of pale stone and looked at him. There was no mistaking those black, unfeeling orbs.

Oats halted and loosed a dispirited breath that was far from mummery.

"Do it, then," he said, stepping closer to the column to lay Jackal down at its base. He backed away.

The smoke took Barsius. No sooner had it disappeared than it arrived over Jackal's prone form to deliver the halfling, his back to the column.

No scorpion had ever struck with the speed Hoodwink unleashed to stab Barsius. He detached from the column, flesh retaining the appearance of mottled stone, and punched a dagger down into the side of the halfling's neck four times in the span of a heartbeat.

Barsius lurched, dropping his sword, to paw at his fountaining neck. The smoke tried to appear, but it roiled weakly, half-formed and guttering. The halfling pitched over, his wild gaze finding Hood standing over him with a dripping blade. The mongrel's pallid, scarred flesh reclaimed his body from its enchanted mask of stone.

Barsius forced out words throttled with blood and disbelief. "Va. Aris. Qarataun..."

Oats sprang and cut the halfling's head off, his tulwar sparking as it met the stones beneath the neck.

"The chief," Hoodwink said, and ran for the oracles, springing to begin climbing the giant on the left, which was more statue now than flesh.

He hauled himself up a leg and clambered to the lower arm. The hand holding the chief's leg was stone to the wrist. Holding on to the upper arm, Hood drew his tulwar and leaned to chop at the diminishing flesh.

Oats left him to it and went to the other side. He wasn't as swift as Hood. By the time he made the climb it would be too late. He cast about, his eyes falling on the great bronze cauldron. Ignoring the flames, Oats seized it by the lip, gritting his teeth against the pain of the burns and his crushed fingers. He spun as he lifted, revolving fully twice to gain momentum. The cauldron lifted from the stones, spilling fiery pitch.

Oats flung the heavy vessel, aiming for the upper arm of the giant.

The cauldron smote the marble, clanging as it rebounded. Oats dove away as the vessel and its burning contents returned to the floor. The arm was still intact, smirched with pitch. But Oats thought he heard a crack. He hurried to retrieve the cauldron.

Hood had severed the lower hand of the leftward giant and was now hacking at the top. Fetch's right leg hung free, a massive hand dripping blood dangling weakly from her boot. The oracles could no longer scream from their gaping, graven mouths, but their blind eyes blazed with a terrible agony.

Oats flung the cauldron again, knowing he wouldn't get a third chance.

The curved edge of the bronze bowl snapped the marble above the elbow, sending the upper arm falling into the lower and breaking it in turn. Slipping from the chief, the massive stone limbs struck the temple floor and shattered, forcing Oats to stumble away from the flying debris.

Hood had cut away the upper hand on his side, but there remained the giant behind Fetching. Those to the sides had held her arms and legs one-handed, but this one had her head and body ensconced in all four fists. The fingers were stone to the second knuckle.

Hoodwink climbed to the shoulders of his giant and leapt over to the other. But he was out of time.

Oats drew every bit of air into his lungs.

"ISA!"

Fetching jerked and he saw the flash of an eye between the calcifying fingers.

Arms swinging up in unison, the chief slammed her fists into the giant's. The stone fingers fractured, fell away. Fetch hammered her elbows into the last of her prison and fell free in a cloud of dust. She rose from the rubble and staggered to Oats, eyes glassy.

"Barsius..." she said, voice creaking. "He's—"

"A fucking corpse," Oats told her. "But Fetch..."

They returned to Jackal together, crouching on either side.

Fetch frowned, her searching stare and hands growing frantic as they moved over him.

"He's not healing," she said.

Oats swallowed. He couldn't look at her. Couldn't look at him.

"I know. I don't... I don't think he... Fetch. It was me..."

"You?"

"I—"

His words were cut off by a wet, tearing sound. He and Fetch looked to find Hoodwink squatting over Barsius's headless corpse, cutting its heart out.

The pale mongrel stood, his arm crimson to the elbow. He held the shiny organ over Jackal and squeezed. Blood ran in thick rivulets into the wound. Hood wrung every drop and tossed the heart aside. He drew a knife and cut his own forearm the next instant, clenching and unclenching his fist to coax more spilled blood into Jackal.

"The hells, Hood?" Fetching hissed.

"Attukhan, Huroga, and Qarataun fought and bled for Belico," Hoodwink replied. "Their spirits may draw strength from one another, as they did in life."

The blood pooled in the cleft running the length of Jackal's torso. Oats held his breath. And nearly pissed himself when Jackal began to thrash. He and Fetch wrangled his convulsing limbs until the worst had passed. When the fits died, Jackal's breathing was shallow. But he was fucking breathing.

Oats cocked an eye at Hoodwink.

"You know he was like Jackal?" he asked Fetching.

"Later," was her only reply.

Jackal's wound was just beginning to knit when his eyes finally opened. They rolled, drunken and sightless for some time before settling on Fetch. His voice was a rasp.

"You're. Safe."

"Yes," Fetching said, rubbing his face.

"Did I . . . fucking die?" Jackal's tenuous focus moved to Oats. "You fucking kill me?"

"Nope."

Jackal's grin was weak and wonderful. "Liar."

TWENTY-FOUR

SMOKE FROM THE GRAVE PITS filled the sky over Kalbarca.

Warbler's prisoners had done the digging. Nearly three hundred men had thrown down their arms when he took the garden palace and soon found their hands filled with shovels. But three hundred men couldn't dig a hole large enough for the slain. The centaurs alone would take weeks to properly bury, so Warbler had ordered the pits dug just deep enough to contain the Al-Unan fire. The captured frails were put to work, dragging bodies to the blistering edges of the pits, feeding the alchemical flames with stacks of dead.

Shed Snake was not among them.

Culprit had wanted him buried on Batayat Hill next to Mead, on Bastards soil, but the journey was too long, the season too warm. The body would never make it. So the True Bastards bore him away from the city, carried on a sled roped to Culprit's hog. They couldn't go far, couldn't be away long, but Fetch told the young mongrel he could choose the place. Culprit rode southeast, the direction of their lot.

It felt good to get away from Kalbarca, from the walls and corpse smoke. It was a shit errand, burying a brother, but Oats was grateful for the excuse to put the city in the dust of Ug's hooves. Two days since the garrison surrendered, two days since he and Jackal and Hood and the chief had climbed out of the tunnels, two days that passed as long and taxing as two years.

With the city in mongrel hands Jacintho was able to convince a sizable portion of the hillmen to return. Fetch needed them to serve as the new garrison, but they turned their focus away from the walls in favor of looting on the first night. Jacintho forewarned the chief of the ransacking. It was the price of the bandits' aid. They'd bled buckets for the chance. To deny them would only spell more blood. With no choice, Fetch allowed it, ordering the hoof-riders to quell any violence against Kalbarca's small population of innocents. It was a queer duty, riding patrol around a conquered city—little more than an ancient ruin even before the attack—and watching over men as they picked its bones. The sight of half-orcs sitting their hogs close by was enough to deter the worst of the hillmen's impulses, but Kalbarca was vast and there was no denying foul deeds were performed in neglected corners. Several patrols reported having to prevent the bandits from setting fires. Thresher beat down a trio of bandits abusing an old man, and Sluggard feathered another through the leg for trying to make off with a woman's girl-child. There were stories that cut the other way, of mongrels lending themselves to the pillaging rather than keeping it controlled. Anvil killed a pair of nomads, but refused to say what evil they were committing. Fetch didn't press it.

Harrowing as the night was, the morning delivered the greatest injustice. Dawn saw many of the men return to the Smelteds, carrying their disappointment with the lack of spoils with them, throwing curses at the fucking sootskins for keeping the best for themselves. Those who remained were little better than squatters. Fetch couldn't trust them to so much as guard the prisoners. That duty fell to the White Wrists, but the former galley slaves could not resist the chance for vengeance against the frails who'd put them in chains. By the time word reached the chief more than a dozen men had been tortured to death. The other hoofs were hardly more reliable.

Pulp Ear and the Cauldron Brotherhood were chafing to return to their own fortress. It was all Fetch could do to keep them rooted. The Tusked Tide was content to linger, but only because they hadn't yet voted a new chief. Boar Lip had climbed onto his hog's back and slit his wrists rather than die slow and screaming from a festering gut wound. Beloved by his riders, his loss had left them flatfooted. Red Nail was the most likely to be the next hoofmaster, but he too had been injured in the battle with the horse-cocks, miring the vote with uncertainty and indecision.

With few left the chief could trust, it fell to the Bastards to ensure her commands were met. They ran messages, stood watches, rode patrols—an endless rotation of duties to keep Kalbarca from slipping away from Fetch's control. Sleep was snatched, so brief it was more cruelty than comfort. Food was something to be tallied, not consumed. Oats wished Grocer were still alive. The old coin-clipper would have thrived in the unending toil and privation. But the Bastards made do without him, as they made do without Shed Snake and Mead and Dumb Door, and all the others gone to the dust. They had always been few, but never so diminished.

Polecat had come out of his stupor, but he remained listless and was oft taken with sudden bouts of confusion. Fetch kept him close, managing the city from the front of the garrison's storehouse so that their supplies were always well protected. Warbler took permanent post at the main gatehouse. Anvil had command of the north gate, Thoon with her as ever. Warbler had been right about needing the cyclops in the final assault.

The garden palace had been well defended for the frails' last stand. The greatest of their wizards, the one the White Wrists called the Starving Man, stood in support of the men behind the barricades, but Thoon proved immune to his sorcery and crushed the wizard beneath his cannon club. Their arcane champion's death broke the back of the defenders, and it wasn't long before their spears and halberds, swords and stockbows were cast down even as their voices rose in pleas for mercy. Warbler had struggled to give it. Many an unarmed frail was cut down before he quelled the fury of the mongrels. Even now Pulp Ear pressured the chief to execute the prisoners the moment they were done burying the dead. Fetch hadn't made her decision, but the whispers of speculation had sped through the city. Standing guard at the burial pits, Oats had seen several men weeping as they dragged bodies to the fire, fearing they would soon follow. The White Wrists would murder them all without question. Perhaps Pulp Ear would too. Oats reckoned Warbler could, if he thought it prudent. But Fetching? Oats wasn't certain.

There'd been no time for her to speak anything but orders since coming out of the tunnels. They'd emerged to find the city captured, but not yet docile. Pockets of resistance went to ground all over, men who didn't fall back to the garden palace and were too determined or too scared to give up the fight. Jackal might have tackled the holdouts alone, but he could barely stand after the ordeal in the Lionclad's temple. It was Sluggard who offered the notion that the men could be talked into surrender. The chief agreed and Slug did not rest until he convinced every last stubborn soldier to lay down arms.

In the meantime Fetch sent Oats off in search of Blood Crow.

By midmorning, he'd found the elf outside the walls, downriver. Ruin lay in a great heap upon the bank, still alive, but only just. Too huge to drape over the back of hog or stag, they'd had to drag the *uq'huul* with ropes back to Kalbarca, a chore that required Oats to first return to the city for more hogs. Fetch had her twin placed in the storehouse, where she could be near if he woke. So far, he'd given no sign that he would.

The last two days had required the Bastards to dredge every grain of grit they possessed just to keep chaos at bay. And now they risked it all, leaving the city as a hoof to bid farewell to one of their own.

A few leagues from the walls, Culprit reined up beneath a stand of carob trees.

"Here," he said, dismounting.

Warbler and Anvil took up picks and broke the first rocky layer of dirt. Oats wanted to help, but his hands were too thickly bandaged. The burns from the cauldrons were worse than he'd realized, and what was left of his mace-bashed fingers had to be cut away, leaving him a pair of nubs in the center of his left hand. Thresher and Culprit deepened the work with shovels. They dug in pairs until all had taken a turn at the labor, even Oats though his contribution was paltry, spelling one another not because it took more than one mongrel to dig a grave, but because the True Bastards buried their fallen as a hoof. They hadn't slept, hadn't eaten proper, had found no respite in days. They were heartsick and tired to the edge of collapse, but they shifted earth and stone without pause, all sweating, some bleeding from wounds not yet closed. Shed Snake's shriven body lay upon its sled, waiting for the completion of the last act his brethren would ever do for him. They'd be damned if they weren't going to do it right.

Too soon it was done.

They did nothing but stand for a long while, letting the miserly wind of Ul-wundulas stir the paltry branches above the grave.

Culprit took a stuttering breath. His mouth opened only to pinch shut the next instant. The young mongrel's half-shaved head drooped, then gave a small, anguished shake. Oats could see the flesh quivering around his lips. Again he tried to speak and again was thwarted. There were no words in him, only the sobs he struggled to master. Unwilling to let them loose, he looked to Fetching, shame settling in the recesses of his clenched face. She stepped to him, placed a hand upon his shoulder. Whatever words she was about to utter were cut off by Culprit's sudden, hard embrace. It shocked her—shocked Oats—the swift, nearly violent familiarity. But Fetch's reflexes allowed no pause. Her arms snapped to encircle her crumbling rider, held him firmly together.

"You loved him," she said, her words just strong enough to reach Culprit through his sharp breaths. "We all loved him."

They clung tight to each other for a span, and Oats could see in Fetch's face the gift Culprit had given her by allowing her to be not a chief but a simple rider once more. She waited until he was ready to relinquish the hold. Sniffing, Culprit climbed into the grave and Sluggard handed down Shed Snake's saddle. Jackal and Warbler lashed Snake to a board, leaving a pair of lengths at the head and foot. Oats offered a hand to help Culprit out of the hole.

"Would you help lower him down, Oats?" the young mongrel asked.

Oats nodded.

Culprit went to Polecat next. The stare in his hatchet-face was leagues away.

"Cat? Cat?"

Polecat blinked hard. He seemed puzzled by Culprit's presence.

"I think Snake would have enjoyed making you work," the young mongrel said, forcing a smile.

Polecat's eyes flicked from Culprit to the grave and back. His perplexed expression deepened before finally breaking. He molded his old self together. "Sure."

"Chief?" Culprit said. "Would you?"

"Of course."

The four of them took up the ropes and carried Snake to his grave. Steadily, they lowered him into the ground. Oats felt the coarse burn of the rope through the linen shrouding his fingers and used the pain to keep his tears at bay. Shed Snake settled onto the flush bed of churned dirt, his saddle above his head.

The Bastards filled the grave as they'd dug it, each giving effort. And he was gone.

Thresher retrieved a waterskin from her tack and passed it around while Oats secured the tools to the sled. When he returned, the hoof still surrounded the grave, some closer than others.

Warbler, ever willing to be the voice of hard truths, was first to break the silence. "Time we were back."

All eyes went to the chief, but her stare was fixed on the fresh mound at her feet.

"We're not going back," she said. "Not all of us."

The quiet born from sorrow grew taut at the chief's words.

"There's something you all need to hear," Fetch went on. She looked up. "This is my fault. We're burying a brother, and countless others, because of me."

"Because of Zirko," Jackal insisted.

Fetch shook her head. "He may have set the trap, but I led us into it. I'm the one who made him our foe when he refused to be the ally I demanded."

"You couldn't have known he'd go this far, chief," Thresher said.

"No," Fetch said, angry at herself. "But I knew in my gut there was a chance his call for help was hogshit. I took precautions, sent Hood down into the tunnels before the attack to look for signs of truth to Zirko's claims that the halflings were being hunted. He hadn't come back when Barsius said I was needed to take the gate. I knew not to trust him. But I put too much trust in myself. I wagered if there was a danger, I'd be the only one to face it. And whatever it was, I could defeat it. I was wrong. Never figured on the fucking Betrayer." She made a disgusted noise. "Well fucking named."

"Chief," Oats said. "What caution you took saved your life. Jack and I would never have found you, were it not for Hood. As to the rest, you said 'later.' I've held my tongue these last days, but . . . reckon now is good?"

The Bastards followed his expectant gaze to Hoodwink standing at the fringe of their ring. He'd removed his namesake for the digging despite the scant shade of the carob trees, leaving his milky, scarred pate and lifeless eyes exposed. He met the chief's stare and gave her the smallest permissive nod.

Fetch loosed a hard breath. "If ever there were words you needed to speak, Hood, it's these."

In all the years Oats had been around Hoodwink, he'd never known him to display emotion. And he didn't now. Yet Oats saw, for the first time, Hood suppress them. A tiny swallow, a mere tremor at the jawline, the briefest flash born and snuffed in those black eyes. On any other face, such signs would have been insignificant, imperceptible, but upon Hood's death mask they shone harsher than the sun.

"I bear a relic."

More silence. No one moved. Perhaps, like Oats, the others were repeating Hood's thin, unfeeling words in their heads, trying to reconcile them.

"I'm lost," Sluggard said, at last.

"He's like Jack," Oats told the hoof, moved by a mixture of impatience and a desire to help Hoodwink with the uncomfortable task of speaking. "Got some piece of an old Unyar warrior in him, allows him to . . . fucking blend in with shit."

"Explains a heap," Thresher said.

"What'd you get?" Sluggard asked Hood. "An arm bone like Jackal or like a rib . . ."

"The hells does that matter?" Thresh said.

Sluggard shrugged. "Curious, is all."

"Flesh." Hood's word brought all their attentions back to him. "Qarataun was found mummified. His flesh replaced mine."

Sluggard went wan. "*All* of it?"

Hoodwink nodded.

"Explains a *heap* more," Thresher said.

"You know this?" Jackal asked Warbler.

The frowning old thrice shook his head.

Jack squinted at Hoodwink. "You weren't called to defend Strava the night I was. What bargain did you strike with Zirko?"

"Va Aris Qarataun was not given me by Zirko."

"Then who?"

"The Black Womb."

"You mean Crafty," Oats said. "He gave it to you when you took Xhreka to him."

"No. It was joined to me as a boy."

"A boy?" Jackal said, confounded.

"Keep your head, Jack," Fetching warned without looking at him. "I mean it."

"You mean, he's Black Womb?"

Oats could feel his friend's fury building, so strong it nearly stunk. They'd all put their swords aside for the digging, left their thrums hung on saddle horns and tree limbs. But a good rider always had a knife stowed. Hood would have several. Not that he or Jackal needed a blade to be lethal.

"Go on."

Warbler's deep voice smothered the tension. His craggy face showed no compassion, no understanding, only a grim desire to hear the rest. Warbler had ridden with Hood when they were both free-riders, when one was ousted from the Grey Bastards and the other hadn't yet joined. If there was a mongrel in the hoof who could claim to know Hoodwink, it was Warbler. A claim he could not now make in earnest.

"They trained me," Hood said. "Granted me the relic. Sent me here with the task to learn the Lots."

"So you joined the hoofs," Jackal said, teeth clenched.

"Those I could."

Hood's body bore the scar-eclipsed ink of the Skull Sowers, Cauldron Brotherhood, Shards, Sons, and Tusked Tide. Not being a thrice-blood had kept him from the Orc Stains, and the Fangs of Our Fathers didn't exile their fallen brothers, they killed them, something Hood likely discovered during his stints as a nomad. Oats reckoned the Rutters had been destroyed before Hood got around to joining them, though he'd have been hard-pressed to fit among that notoriously lusty bunch. That left the Grey Bastards, the only tattoos he possessed not yet crisscrossed with old cuts. Not yet . . .

"Why us?" Oats asked. "Got yourself tossed from the rest. Why stick with us?"

Hood didn't answer. Oats couldn't tell if it was hesitance or unwillingness that kept his lips shut.

Jackal provided the bitter answer. "It was the Claymaster. The last living bearer of Hispartha's plague. The key to Crafty's grab for the throne. Crafty, who knew so much about us before he arrived. Because you were his fucking spy."

"No."

"And you still are."

"No."

"Small wonder you refrain from speaking, Hood. Your forked tongue is showing!"

"I have no allegiance to the sorcerer. I came here years before him. The first I saw him was at the Kiln, the same night as you. Yet I knew his masters were those that trained me. I reasoned what I had learned of the Lots had been passed to him. He knew me for what I was, but he never sought my help and I did not offer it."

Jackal made a disgusted noise.

"Why?" Thresher peered hard at Hoodwink. "If you were both Black Womb, why wouldn't you conspire?"

"I could not be trusted," Hood replied.

"He trusted you enough at Mongrel's Cradle," Oats said, his anger a few steps behind Jackal's. "Looked to me that you and Crafty were all manner of conspiring. Zirko said he's been trying to keep Belico's relics from the Black Womb. What happened, Hood? The chief sent you off with Xhreka. To protect her. To help her. Did you run immediately to Crafty with her and the tongue? Is that what you did, you blanched fucking cutthroat?!"

He didn't charge, much as he wanted to. He was too damn tired. Yelling nearly caused him to collapse. But he wished for all the hells he had the strength to get his hands on that pale, lying throat. He could strangle a treacherous cunt, even with only eight fingers.

"I brought her to him because she asked me to."

Oats found he had the strength after all. He surged toward Hood, but Fetch stepped between them.

"Oats." She halted him with a hand on his chest. "Just listen." Her other hand pointed over his shoulder. "Jack!"

Oats had his back to Jackal, but he'd felt him move in support of his stillborn rush. He took a breath. Fetch removed her hand, but did not step aside.

Still, Hoodwink hesitated. It wasn't fear of Oats or even Jackal. It was . . . discomfort. Whatever he was about to say, the chief had already heard. For a mongrel who rarely spoke, repeating himself must have been a small hell.

"Xhreka is insightful," Hood began, his words measured to the edge of stilted. "She speaks always, but it is not prattle. She fights with what she says. It was not a duel I could win. She bested my silence. And I told her about . . . myself." Hood still seemed perplexed by the admission. "She listened."

Oats glanced down to find Fetch giving him a meaningful look. He found himself relaxing, nodding. "She does that."

Hood took no notice of the empathy. "Later, she asked if I would contact the Black Womb. She knew of them from her travels. She wanted to be free of Belico's tongue and she saw in them a chance to be rid of it. She insisted that my refusal would not be an offense. She said no matter my answer we would remain friends." The last word was a marvel made from sound, both to hear and for Hood to say. "I sent word to the Black Womb, though I had not done so in years. They sent Crafty."

"Your old friend," Jackal spat.

Hood's eyes shifted. "Was he? I seem to recall he was yours."

Polecat snorted. "He has you there, Jackal-boy."

Perhaps it was the bald truth that subdued Jackal, or perhaps it was simply the return of Cat's familiar, lecherous sneer. Whatever it was, Jackal did not rile.

Warbler stepped right up to Hoodwink. The old thrice's sun-squinted eyes moved over the austere mongrel's features, sharp enough that Oats wouldn't have been shocked to see Hoodwink's flesh peel away.

"I knew you kept secrets," Warbler said. "What nomad doesn't? But I never smelled a lie on you. And you did all I ever asked of you. Perhaps I'm fooling myself with the belief that I'll see any falsehood, but I'm going to ask you plain. That wizard ran roughshod over the Grey Bastards with his schemes. Jackal weren't the only one he cozened. Claymaster fell into his web. Fetching too, despite seeing him for what he was. Yet you claim you didn't help him. Why?"

"I could not be trusted," Hood said for the second time.

"Think we grasp that part," Sluggard said with a wry smile.

"You don't understand," Fetching said.

"No. I don't," Jackal replied.

"It's because he was a Bastard."

All turned to Culprit, now squatted by Shed Snake's grave, one hand resting on the mound of dirt.

"He was a Bastard," the young mongrel said again. "Maybe not quite Grey and not yet True, but . . . he was us, not them."

"He's not us," Jackal said. "He's—"

"A powerful mongrel with queer abilities that just showed up and joined the hoof?" Culprit asked, cutting Jackal off with his words and a sharp stare.

"I was no stranger, Culprit. I was blooded and sworn. And you knew me before I left."

Culprit shrugged. "I knew how you liked Hearth brushed. That you rarely took ale during table meets, but often an entire skin of wine after. I knew you the way a slop knows a rider. Which ain't much."

"That's the way it was," Jackal said. "Same when I was a slophead."

"Same," Culprit mused. "Reckon that's so. I was raised by Beryl too, you know. Yes, we came up the same. Orphans. Slops. Bastards. You know who didn't come up that way? Every other mongrel here save Oats! Chief was never a slop. Not truly. Warbler either. Cat was, but not as a Bastard. Slug, Anvil, Thresher. You not going to trust them because they were fighting in pits, riding in arenas, or working a field instead of fetching you a fresh skin of wine? Pardons, chief."

Fetch shook her head, face flush with a somber pride.

Jackal's jaw bulged. "Never said a rider had to be a slop, Cul. And you're talking from your hind end. You got no notion what the Black Womb is."

Culprit's mouth twisted with thought. "No. But it sounds like they got their own form of slophead. And that's what Hood was. You going to fault him for having loyalty to them over us when that's what he knew first? Be like the chief blaming you for following the old Claymaster."

"I don't care a fuck what his past loyalties were, only where they are now. And I say there's no way to ever know."

"He saved both our lives, Jack," Fetch said. "He's loyal to the hoof. Same as every mongrel here."

Jackal set his jaw. He didn't defy the chief's assurance, but neither did he accept it.

"How long have you known?" he asked.

"Since the Cradle."

"Why tell us now?" Anvil asked.

When Fetch answered, she swept the entire hoof. "Because I'm about to ask you to ride into the greatest danger you've ever known.

And I can't do that if you don't trust one another. Crafty could use Hood's past as a weapon against us, but only if it's a hidden blade. By knowing now we've disarmed him from sowing division later."

Oats's scalp began to crawl. "Crafty? You don't mean . . . ?"

"He offered to help us win this war," Fetch said. "It's time to accept."

"Hells overburdened," Jackal muttered, pacing a few steps away.

"You in earnest, chief?" Polecat asked.

"I am. There's no choice. We won't withstand an attack from Hispartha. Kalbarca was our chance to blunt their invasion, but taking it was too costly. We can't hold it."

"Then we don't hold it," Warbler said. "We fall back. Make the frails hunt us. No need to throw in with the Tyrkanian to keep fighting."

"For how long, War-boar? To what end? They'd only gain ground and we'd only lose it. We'd be lucky to last a season. Without the Unyars we've little hope. Now . . ." Fetch took a slow breath. "If Strava rides against us we're through."

"Then we strike first," Jackal said, turning to face the chief once more. "We ride to Strava and rid the Lots of Zirko."

"With what army?" Fetching asked him. "Our numbers are shattered. The Shards are gone. Won't be long before the Tide and the Brotherhood follow them. The mongrel hoofs are days away from being what we were. Nothing but dwindling bands looking to their own survival. We didn't have the strength to challenge Strava before. Sure as shit don't now."

"Then *we* go," Jackal said. "Just you and I. Zirko fears you. His actions prove it. But he failed. He schemed and he betrayed and sent his deadliest servant and still he failed. We shouldn't wait. We go now and—"

"What? We take his head?" Fetch said. "The Hero Father, High Priest of Belico. Do you believe one foiled attempt to kill me has left him powerless?"

"It can be done," Jackal insisted.

"And it may come to that. One day. But revenge against Strava does nothing to stop Hispartha. They're coming, from more directions than we can watch, in more numbers than we can defy. We call them frails, but we're seeing steel in them. It gags me to say it, but Crafty was right. It took all the strength we could muster just to take Kalbarca. We've little left for what's coming. That's why it's time to accept his offer, to ride with him into Hispartha, to wage a different war. A handful of mongrels won't make a difference in the fight here. But up there? They could be the difference between victory and defeat. Especially when they're the best damn mongrels I know."

"But . . . chief?" Polecat rubbed the back of his neck. "Hispartha? That's the bull's own field."

"I won't order you to do this," Fetch said. "You've all earned the right to fight and die where you please. I'm asking for volunteers. I've already had one." Fetch looked at Oats. "Unless you've a change of mind."

Oats held her gaze. She didn't challenge, didn't implore. He'd said he would go, standing in the great hall of Mongrel's Cradle. Seemed years ago now, though it was hardly a fortnight. But much had changed. The chief looked to see if all that transpired since had affected his willingness to accompany one enemy into the realm of another.

"No," he replied. "My mind's not changed. I'll go."

Culprit stood up, taking a handful of dirt from the grave. "Me too."

"I ride where you ride, chief," Anvil declared.

"I'd hoped so," Fetch told her. "Because I'm staying here. And I didn't fancy trying to keep Thoon from following you."

"You ain't going?" Culprit said.

Fetch shook her head. "Still a war to fight here."

"Then I'm with you," Warbler said. "Wouldn't be no damn use in civilized climes anywise."

"But I am," Sluggard said. "And it will be interesting to lay eyes on this wizard you've all been cursing for so long. What do you say, Thresh? One last risky ride north?"

Thresher scowled at the ground. Her answer came through a tight jaw. "Reckoned I was full quit with the kingdom. You order it, chief, and I will, but if I'm to say, then no."

"No orders," Fetch reminded her. She looked to Polecat and couldn't quite hide the struggle in her face. The mongrel appeared to be his old self for the first time since the Betrayer, but Oats could see—and shared—the chief's uncertainty it would last. "Cat?"

Polecat scratched beneath his lip with a thumbnail. "Sluggard, you know any decent brothels up there?"

"One or two hundred."

"I'm in."

Jackal was last. He stood silent, still. His eyes darted once to Hood before fixing on Fetch. "What do you want me to do?"

"No orders," she said again.

"What do *you* want me to do?"

"Can you trust Hood?"

"No."

"Can you ally with Crafty?"

"... No."

"Then you'll serve the hoof better from here."

Oats could see Jackal grappling with the truth of it, trying not to see it as some failure in his courage. Or some folly in Fetch's reasoning. It didn't look like he fully succeeded with either struggle.

"How can you trust him?" Jackal asked the chief.

"I don't. But as Xhreka said, he will nurture his own plans. And for now, those plans aid us."

"How can you know?"

"Because they already have. A rider from the Sons arrived last night. The fleet Crafty said Hispartha sent from Galiza? It arrived at the mouth of the Guadal-kabir three days ago. And met a blockade of Tyrkanian ships. The Hisparthans withdrew. One of our Traedrian corsairs witnessed it and reported to Father. Without Tyrkania blocking the river, Kalbarca would already be back in the Crown's hands. I've also had a bird from the castile." The chief reached beneath her brigand and removed a slip of parchment. "Ahlamra says the army camped outside has not attacked. That she and Tarif were invited down to speak with their commander, a palaver that was mediated—her fucking word—by an envoy of the sultans. Three quarters of the Hisparthan force broke camp and departed the next morning. She says those that remain are tasked with"—Fetch read from the parchment—" 'honorably escorting the leader of the half-orc uprising or any of her designated emissaries safely into Hispartha.' "

Oats grunted. "Tyrkania's doing everything Crafty said. The blockade. The castile. All of it."

"He told us the empire would move ahead with its plans with or without us," Fetch agreed.

"The wizard's urging you to reconsider the without," Sluggard said.

Fetch took a long breath. "He asked if we would help ourselves. To wage war in the courts as well as the battlefields. Ahlamra volunteered to go, to act as my envoy. My voice. I've agreed. Couldn't ask for better. She knows how to handle herself with blue bloods of every hide. Likely she'll be our greatest strength up there, for this is the type of war she was trained for. But she's a True Bastard and will need her brethren to back her. This chance won't come again. Time we took it. We've nothing to lose."

"Just the lives of those that go," Warbler pointed out.

"Why I said it's the greatest danger I could ask this hoof to face," Fetch replied. "Hispartha could decide to hang you all the moment you're over the border. Or wait until the queen and a throng can watch from some palace square in . . ." Fetch looked to Sluggard. "Where?"

"Magerit. Zaxara. Vallisoletum." Sluggard shrugged up to his ears. "Hells, they might make a tour of it. Execute us one at a time at cities across the kingdom. The peons will love it."

"Fuck, I can't decide if you're jesting," Polecat mumbled, going pale.

"He ain't," Thresher said.

Fetch drew in a breath. "Crafty's assured me the Crown fears a war with Tyrkania too much to risk angering the sultans. But his assurances don't count for shit. And I won't give you any. I'll just say this. Hispartha will be the death of us all if we lose this war. I don't know why Crafty wants us with him, but it's a chance we can't turn down. Not anymore. He's casting his net at the frails. It'll be twisted and woven with lies, we know, but he'll be what he claimed. A scorpion in the Crown's bedroll."

"And somehow, he'll use us to sharpen his sting," Oats said, looking hard at the Bastards who had agreed to come.

"What if he needs squashing?" Polecat asked. "Crafty's going to take more than a bootheel to crush, and not just because he's a fat fuck."

"Only one of you is going into Hispartha with any orders from me," Fetching said, her gaze fixing on Hood. "When Crafty poses more danger than aid, he dies."

Hoodwink nodded.

"Certain you can kill him, Hood?" Culprit asked.

"Yes."

"And that blue demon of his?" Oats said.

Hood considered. "Fuqtus will kill me. But only after the wizard is dead."

"Madre," Sluggard marveled. "Not speaking was key to you *not* telling the truth, wasn't it?"

Culprit rubbed the shaved side of his head. "How will we know, chief? When Crafty is too dangerous. Who decides that?"

"If there's time, you all do, as a hoof," Fetch replied. "If not, Hood is free to act alone or if either Ahlamra or Oats orders him, without question. Understood?"

Another nod.

"In dealings with Hispartha, Ahlamra speaks for me," the chief continued. "In all other matters, Oats holds my vote."

"And mine," Jackal said.

"You get mine, youngblood," Warbler said, clapping Culprit on the shoulder.

"*Me?*"

"Reckon I'll take the Tine's way and let the future of our hoof decide its path."

"Thresh. Anvil," the chief said. "Who'll have your votes?"

The pair looked at each other for a moment. Thresher's lips moved, but she did not speak aloud. Anvil dipped her head.

"I'll be taking both," Thresher said. "We can't let Rue go up to

Hispartha alone with all these swinging cods. They'll be too entranced with her backside and not watching her back."

"I don't find Ahlamra all that comely," Culprit said.

Polecat was aghast. "Are you blind, backy, or both?"

"No! Just saying she's too thin for my tastes. So I can watch her back just fine and not get distracted. Just like any other brother."

"Careful, Oats," Sluggard said out the side of his mouth. "Culprit may not be there when you need him. He'll be too smitten with your meaty ass."

"That ain't what I said!"

Thresher gave Fetch a dull stare. "Behold my fucking point."

The chief retrieved a pair of laden saddlebags from Womb Broom. Oats had been so weary, so distracted, he hadn't noticed them on the ride.

"Supplies for the journey," Fetch said, handing the bags to Culprit.

Sluggard grinned. "You were in earnest saying we weren't going back to Kalbarca."

"No time to waste," the chief replied. "Make for the castile. Keep a sharp eye for Unyar riders. We can't trust them anymore."

"Chief, I'd like to get back," Warbler said. "My nerves are afire thinking on that city without us."

"You and Anvil go," Fetch told him. "Jack and I will be along."

Warbler took in the Hispartha-bound Bastards. "Luck to you. Live in the saddle."

Oats answered soberly for them all.

"Die on the hog, War-boar."

The old mongrel smiled. "Not today, I hope."

He mounted up as Anvil embraced Thresher. After, her single eye regarded the others from between the stiff drapery of her hair. "Fight hard, brothers."

The pair of thrice-bloods rode out of the carob grove.

"Didn't figure I'd be saying goodbye to more than one today," Culprit said, mouth twisting with regret.

Thresher put an arm around him. "Come. Let's be of use and get these vittles stowed. Cat, Slug, lend some hands."

Fetch turned to Hoodwink. "Best start scouting ahead."

Hood moved immediately for his hog.

Oats stood quietly with Jackal and Fetch for a moment.

"What will you do?" he asked at last.

"Depends what the Crown does," Fetch replied. "If they march on Kalbarca, we will be forced to leave. But if Crafty can bring a halt to the war, even for a small while, we might be able to remain, refortify. If not, there's the castile. At the least, I'm hoping we can stay here long enough for the Fangs to arrive. N'keesos says Starling might be able to awaken Ruin."

Oats shook his head. "Fetch. I wouldn't hold too tightly to him recovering. When the Betrayer . . . lashed out at him, it was . . ."

Words failed him.

"I felt it," Fetch said, her voice taut and low. "Trapped in the temple, I felt it when he was struck. It was as if a mountain of rage fell on me. That's what knocked me senseless. I've never been hit, never been hurt, like that. But for all the pain, all the fury, what I felt most was this fucking certainty that the blow was far weaker than it could have been. As if whatever unleashed it was . . ."

"Like it was holding back?" Jackal offered.

Fetch chewed on that for a moment before shaking her head. "Like it was bound."

Oats had never seen Fetching wear the apprehension that was now upon her face. She would keep fighting, he knew, defiant as ever, but she'd been shaken by the trials underground. He realized now that the physical torment he'd witnessed wasn't close to the full measure the chief endured.

"If I hadn't stopped him," Oats said. "If I'd let him go to you—"

"Then there would be a heap more Bastard graves here than Snake's!" Fetch declared. "You did right, Oats. So did Ruin."

Realization settled over Oats. The answer was so simple he couldn't stop from laughing at himself. It came out small and humorless. "You sent him to me."

"Yes." Fetching looked down, rallied something inside. When her eyes came up again, they were bright and sharp as a freshly honed blade. "Soon as we were away from the hoof, Barsius touched me. Everything went dark. Felt like . . . hells, I can't describe it."

"Like someone reached up through your asshole, used your jaw as a handle, and pulled your head down into your stomach," Jackal said.

Fetch cocked her head in agreement. "I was dizzy, sick. Those giants had me before I knew where I was. Zirko was there. He told me the Betrayer had come, that my army would be slaughtered. But I felt Ruin getting closer. I knew he was coming for me. I needed him to save the hoof, not me. So I sent him to the one mongrel I knew would make fucking certain he did."

"I ain't the only one," Oats said. "Jack would have done the same."

"I would have."

"You killed Ruin's pack, lover," Fetch told him dully.

"You did," Oats said.

"I did," Jackal sighed.

They all fought the smiles that were building, none truly winning.

"You picked the right thrice for the job, chief," Jackal said. "Then and now." He stepped to Oats and embraced him. "Don't die up there, brother. Please."

"Can't swear to it," Oats said, squeezing hard. "But I'll strive not to."

"And if you do end up killing Crafty," Jackal said, breaking free. "Piss on his corpse for me."

"After drinking an entire barrel of wine," Oats promised. Fetch had drifted close and he reached to haul her in. "If Culprit gets to do it, so do I."

Fetching kissed his cheek as he crushed her.

"Watch out for them," she said.

"I will."

The three of them stood in a rough, comfortable circle.

"You know what this reminds me of?" Fetching said, a strange look upon her face. "When the three of us would all sneak into the larder together when Beryl wasn't looking and filch all the persimmons."

Jackal's brows knitted. He glanced at Oats.

"This isn't anything like that," Oats said, chuckling.

Fetching looked at him for a long moment. "No. You're right. It isn't."

They turned to find the hogs ready, the Bastards mounted. Oats strode to Ugfuck and climbed into the saddle.

"We'll see this done, chief," he said.

Turning his hog, he led the True Bastards away.

TWENTY-FIVE

THE PLAINS BENEATH THE CASTILE were forested with banners, the colors upon the fluttering cloth lurid against the dun expanse now awash in the tents of the frails' encampment. The pavilions were worse than the pennants, garish beasts with silk skins striped in crimson and gold, blue and ivory, and half a dozen other shades Oats couldn't put a name to. Smaller tents of undyed canvas were arranged in neat rows surrounding their resplendent betters, armed men moving everywhere along the dusty lanes between.

"Fuck my mouth," Polecat swore, gawking at the bustling camp. "*That's* a small escort? Chief said most of the frails fucked off back north."

"She spoke true," Tarif replied, keeping his mare well in hand. The Zahracene chief and thirty of his tribesmen had ridden out to meet the Bastards. "Five times this number was here not a week past."

Oats hadn't taken any chances. He'd sent Thresher ahead to the castile well before it was in sight to make sure they weren't trotting toward an ambush, a task that traditionally fell to Hoodwink. Choosing Thresh instead caused a moment of silent tension. Fetch told them they needed to trust each other, and Oats knew he'd just tossed shit all over that notion, but the promise proved simpler than the practice. None said a word as Thresh spurred away, though Oats felt a hog's ass sitting in the silence. He was twice the ass once she returned with the Zahracenes' and Tarif's assurance that all was safe.

They rode together through the Hisparthan camp, every frail they passed stopping to eye them. The disdain was heavier in the air than the smell of unwashed men.

"To the hells with you too," Culprit muttered.

Halberdiers and arbalesters stood guard at numerous laden supply wagons. The men watching over the corrals were similarly armed, but double in number. Oats could now see distinct separations within the mass of men. Where the mongrel hoofs used tattoos, the humans used the colors of their lords. The azure falcon on the red banner outside one pavilion also adorned the tabards of all dwelling nearby. Past them, a bushel of some yellow crop upon a field of black took over the snapping pennants and breasts of the soldiers. Next, a sword-pierced scroll over quartered white and green. It wasn't one camp, Oats realized, but several, sharing the ground. Still, they were melded by purpose and a shared hatred of half-orcs.

The Zahracenes put the Bastards in the center of their formation, keeping a brisk pace until they reached the trail ascending the escarpment. The castile sat above, high on its frowning crag. Soon, the camp lay beneath them. The vantage only made the Hisparthan host appear larger.

"Five times all of that and they didn't attack," Sluggard mused on the ride up to the fortress. "Our Zahracene friends were fortunate."

Ahlamra awaited them beyond the gate. She was the only Bastard to wear linen instead of leathers and never bore a weapon save a sharp mind and honed civility. Her education, gained by a parade of tutors within the cloistered gardens of far Sardiz, was writ into her bearing. She stood flanked by Tarif's own bodyguards, men with massive scimitars held close across their chests, but any who didn't know better would take them for Ahlamra's own servants, warriors pledged to the service of some breath-stealing eastern princess. Standing at a slight remove was another, older, man. Dressed in rich silks, his headscarf and dark complexion marked him for a Tyrkanian. Four young women, their faces covered by veils, held poles attached to a brocaded awning over his head, blocking the sun. A faint smile rested behind his grey beard, sharp eyes taking in the hoof as they reined up.

"True Bastards," Ahlamra said, her hand making a small, elegant gesture toward the man, "this is Orhan ibn Osman, *katib* of Alaeddin Nasr al-Dīn, Sultan of the Oath-Championed Domains of Grand Tyrkania. *Katib* Orhan, allow me to present my brethren Oats, Thresher, Hoodwink, Culprit, Sluggard, and Polecat."

The old Tyrkanian patted his hands together several times in a tiny, silent show of delight.

"You honor me, *emira*," he told Ahlamra, smile deepening.

Polecat dismounted with a prolonged moan of strain and stared artlessly at the women holding the awning, attempting to judge their figures beneath their layered silks.

"Never met a sultan before," he said, pulling a foot up behind his ass to stretch.

"And you do not now," Tarif proclaimed, giving the older man a look of naked loathing from atop his horse. "Orhan ibn Osman is merely one of al-Dīn's servants, a serpent dressed as a man. It is good to see you again, my half-orc friends, but I will be delighted when you depart, for then there will be no more reason to host this spawn of a she-viper."

Expelling a word in his native tongue, Tarif spurred away, his tribesmen following.

"My apologies, *katib*," Ahlamra said. Her words were sincere, but she did not fawn nor display embarrassment.

Orhan's narrow shoulders raised a hint. "The Zahracenes are ever proud. Pride is what a man is left when all else has been taken from him. It is a pauper's treasure."

The old man's smile vanished and there was spite in his voice.

Oats dismounted. "We should speak, Rue."

Ahlamra dipped her chin. Oats was always struck by how small she was. Her mongrel blood certainly didn't show in her slight, graceful frame.

"If you will excuse my absence for a time, *katib*," she told Orhan. The Tyrkanian bowed.

Ahlamra said something to her guards in Urzhar, leaving them behind as she turned and proceeded deeper into the castle yard. The Bastards fell into step around her, leading their hogs.

"Old swaddlehead's a bit of a cock," Culprit said when they were barely out of earshot.

"He's a powerful man," Ahlamra said without feeling. "Powerful men are, I have found, shit."

Thresher snorted a laugh.

"Tarif's powerful," Sluggard said. "He's not bad."

"Tarif Abu Nusar was once powerful," Ahlamra replied. "No longer. Men who survive such a loss often gain the virtue of humility."

"What about mongrels with decently big cocks and tireless tongues?" Polecat asked, pulling his sow quickly to draw even with Ahlamra.

"They can be useful on rare occasions. If they learn to shut up and lick."

Polecat made a point of staying silent the rest of the way.

The Zahracenes had constructed new stables to replace those that burned down when the Bastards took the castile. Tarif tended his mare with the aid of a groom in the foremost stall. Oats took Ugfuck past all the horses. The fresh-cut timber could still be smelled even over the dung. Memory brought the clog of smoke to Oats's nostrils. He could still see the inferno of the old stables, still feel the panic. Untacking Ugfuck, Oats tried to put it out of his mind, but he rushed headlong into that blaze once more. Hells, he still didn't know how he'd found the boy. The smoke was an ocean, the heat a wall. Perhaps there were gods in the world and one happened to be smiling on him. No, it would have been smiling on Muro. He hoped it still was. After what he'd endured in his short life, the boy deserved to be happy and thriving down in Salduba. Oats also hoped Thistle was not still angry. The castile had birds trained to reach the Cradle. Perhaps there would be time to send a message.

"And say what?" Oats asked Ugfuck softly.

Apologies for leaving you both. I'm now going even farther away. Into Hispartha. Reckon I'll get killed. Muro, wish we could play. Thistle, shouldn't have ignored you that night, but I'm a fool-ass. Oats.

Shaking his head, Oats knuckled Ug between the eyes and left him snuffling in the stall.

The Bastards gathered around Ahlamra in the central aisle of the stable.

"I know you need rest," Ahlamra said. "However, it will be best if we do not tarry long." She lowered her voice. "Tarif's hatred of Orhan ibn Osman risks grievous offense with every moment."

"Hogs need until morning," Oats told her. "After that, we leave when you say."

"Good. Now that you have arrived I will speak with Duke Hernan. He is envoy for the Crown. As yet he has not been forthcoming on which of the lords camped upon the plain will be accompanying us across the border."

"Where are we bound once in Hispartha?" Thresher asked.

"Orhan insists that we will ride directly to meet Uhad Ul-badir Taruk Ultani," Ahlamra replied. "He has declined, in his slippery way, to reveal exactly where the wizard resides despite much pressing from the duke."

Culprit raised his hand. "Uhad Ool-a-deer bla-blook oolala. That's Crafty, right?"

"Yes," Ahlamra said, her patience a castle wall.

Sluggard shook his head. "I don't like it. We need to know where first."

"Agreed," Oats said.

Ahlamra cast a look between them. "Why?"

"Why?" Sluggard repeated with a breathy laugh. "Because it could change everything. Hispartha is vast. It would help us to know how long a journey we're facing. And that's the least concern. Rue, you're keen and well trained, but you don't know Hispartha. There are bitter rivalries between the nobles, old feuds that go back generations. We need to know whose lands we will be crossing. In the kingdom, the 'where' matters."

"It most certainly matters," Ahlamra said. "Crafty is in Hispartha, but has not yet come to court. We know this because Duke Hernan remains ignorant of his whereabouts. The duke would not hesitate to make a choice of escort were it otherwise. If he knew which family hosted the wizard his decision would be informed, not fettered. It is an ambitious house that would offer the Tyrkanians support. Yet they are all ambitious in Hispartha, each hungry for more power, so such knowledge does not shrink the list of culprits."

"That only happens when I'm cold."

Ignoring Culprit, Ahlamra went on. "The family that has taken Crafty into its protection is brave to risk the Crown's wrath. Or desperate. Either could describe the Estravaras, who have no less than four times in Hispartha's history fought for the throne in open rebellion, and live under the shadow of crushing debts as a consequence. Yet Duke Hernan's wife is the niece of Marques Estravara, so he might feel confident to rule them out, though it is rumored the duke has not shared a bed with his notoriously cold bride in years. Perhaps Crafty has ensconced himself with one of the wealthier houses. The Tirado come to mind. They hold the fur trade in a vise, resisting the rise of guilds despite much pressure from Traedrian agitators. It could be argued they have more to lose than to gain, but there is a madness to be found in the grasping of wealth. Were Hernan to choose blindly, sending, say, Lord Froila d'Ortaza with us, it will come to blood if we set foot on Tirado land, for d'Ortaza was fostered there in his youth and ruined two of the late Baron Tirado's daughters, though it is widely whispered it was a son he was caught with and the girls' reputations were sacrificed to keep the secret. So yes, Sluggard, it does hold great import where Crafty has secreted himself. To the Hisparthans. But I will ask, again, why it matters to us. Will we refuse to go if Orhan will not divulge his location? Will we tell the chief we could not continue our task because we felt undue caution over a matter we could not control? Crafty is where he is, plotting what he will. We will never discover where he is nor what he intends from here. There is little advantage in knowing before we strike out. However, there is much to be gained from keeping Duke Hernan in the dark, for it keeps Hispartha unbalanced, which I would propose is to the benefit of the chief and our war against the

Crown." Ahlamra arched an eyebrow. "If you have other arguments, Sluggard, I am prepared to hear them."

Slug held his palms up in surrender. "I Rue the Day I opened my foolish mouth."

"Hells, I've fucking missed you," Thresher said, giving Ahlamra a slap on the butt and causing the smaller woman to smile.

"This Duke Hernan," Oats said, tugging his beard, "he here in the castile?"

"Yes," Ahlamra replied. "It was prudent to our negotiations he be shown that hospitality."

"Wasn't hospitalitous of him not to greet us, though," Culprit said.

"He is the duke of Baxscedures, one of the most feared men in the kingdom, descended from giants—"

Polecat made a rude noise.

Ahlamra paused at the interruption, took a steady breath. "Brethren, I need you to hear me. The duke believes it is beneath him to receive a band of half-breeds. From birth he was taught this and nothing in his life has belied the fact. To him you are nothing but my entourage, a gaggle of ash-coloreds sent by an upstart mongrel warlord whom he oft refers to as a hog-fucking whore and a spend-swallowing hussy." She studied them all with a steady eye. "I see Culprit bristling. Dacia, your fists are clenched. And Oats your beard cannot hide the repeated bulging of your jaw. Already, you are galled though the words come only from me, delivered without rancor. The duke will offend you by his very nature. He will not be the first. All of his ilk, every noble, their vassals, even their servants, will look down upon you. You must gird yourself against their scorn, beginning now, or we will fail. And swiftly."

Polecat shrugged. "Won't be the first time I've been pissed on and asked for more."

"Nor I," Thresher said with no trace of humor. But she shook her bunched fists until they relaxed and gave Ahlamra a reassuring nod. "Unless they come at us with bare steel, they'll provoke no fight in me."

"Right," Oats sighed.

"Abril," Ahlamra said, slipping into her habit of eschewing hoof-names. "You are still seething."

Culprit took a long breath and let it out slowly. "I know. Pardons. Just hearing a frail call us . . . those names. Boils my blood every time. But I can weather it. In earnest, I can."

"You must," Ahlamra told him. "You all must. The slights will not always be obvious. They may take you unawares. If you are uncertain if something is an insult, assume it is. But *do* nothing."

The hoof gave grunts and nods of agreement—save Hood, who remained still and silent. Oats reckoned they would all be wise to begin aping his example.

THERE MAY HAVE BEEN SOME truth to Duke Hernan di Baxscedures being descended from giants. He proved to be the biggest frail Oats had ever seen, equal in height and with a beard to rival his own. In his armor of enameled cobalt plate he was nearly as bulky, as well. He emerged from the keep not long after dawn, bearing no weapon save a long dagger at his belt. Shaped to punch through armor, it was more spike than blade. Orhan ibn Osman trailed the duke, looking pleased.

"That's a shit-eater's grin if I ever saw one," Polecat said.

Sluggard hummed in agreement.

The Bastards were already sitting their hogs in the yard when the duke arrived. Ahlamra's idea. She wanted the man harried to make a decision, frustrated by the hoof being assembled before his own men, calling his competence into question. If Hernan was vexed at all, he did not show it. He called for his horse, but his strong voice was neither rattled nor infuriated. As his pages sprinted away, the duke summoned waiting messengers to him and they spurred away after brief, sober instruction. When they were gone, the man stood stolidly. He did not speak with Orhan ibn Osman, but neither did he purposefully ignore him. It was as if the old Tyrkanian did not exist. Duke Hernan looked for all the earth that he was alone in the yard and perfectly at peace.

The stallion brought to him was a massive animal. One groom

held firm to the bridle while another placed a stepped stool upon the ground to aid the duke in mounting. Culprit expelled a derisive snort at the sight. They were far enough away that only the hoof heard, but Oats saw Ahlamra stiffen. The stool was telling. To Culprit it was a sign of weakness, but not to Oats. Hernan was a large man, made monstrously heavy by his armor. Using the stool spared his horse's back. It was a kindness, an acknowledgment that the animal had worth.

The duke rode toward them, slowing his horse enough to speak to Ahlamra.

"I will accompany you myself."

His gaze never strayed to the rest of the hoof as he passed.

Oats caught the thinnest thread of a smile pulling at Ahlamra's lips. She had barely enough orc blood to be considered a frailing and lacked the strength to handle a hog, so she sat a Zahracene gelding gifted her by Tarif.

"You're pleased," Oats said in a hush, though the duke was nothing now but the distant clink of horseshoes on stone.

"Not knowing the right man, he sends the best man. Himself. We have removed, at least for a time, his presence from the Lots. The Crown's most experienced general and he is leaving the field to serve as a guide. Yes. I am pleased."

Across the yard, Orhan ibn Osman crawled atop his own horse, aided by his serving women. Four mules waited to serve as their mounts. Oats had been surprised to learn that the Tyrkanian emissary traveled with no other protection. He wondered, not for the first time, if the sultans' envoy was another sorcerer of the Black Womb. Hood might know, but Oats hadn't found the moment to ask. No. In truth, he hadn't found the fucking spine after doubting him.

Tarif approached on foot.

"I wish you good fortune and sharp senses," he told them all. "And I implore you once again to accept some of my tribe to journey with you."

"Your generosity honors us, *shaykh*," Ahlamra said. "This is for us to do. Our tribe."

Tarif dipped his head. "As you will. I shall send word to Fetching of all that has transpired."

"Thank you," Oats said.

Tarif backed away, raising a hand in parting.

Down on the plain, Duke Hernan had mustered two score cavaleros. These weren't the penniless exiles typical to the Lot Lands. All were richly equipped in burnished armor, their tabards, shields, and the pennants fixed to their lances boasting all manner of color and devices.

"Minor lords sworn to the service of Baxscedures," Thresher explained as the Bastards watched the final preparations.

Duke Hernan's own banner depicted a great splayed red hand rising from a black chasm against a storm-grey field.

"One of them weren't who you ran off from, I hope," Polecat muttered.

"No," Thresher said. "Their lands rest on the northern coast and in the mountains there. Far from where I was, but we heard stories of the duke, even in the fields."

"Stories? Like what?"

Blaring horns cut off any answer Thresher might have given. The cavaleros began to move without word or glance given to the half-orcs.

"Come," Oats said, clicking his tongue. Ugfuck trundled forward, settling into an easy pace behind the horses. The Bastards kept enough distance to spare themselves the worst of the dust. Behind them came Orhan ibn Osman and his tiny mule train.

Culprit hooked a thumb backward. "Ain't he the only one who knows where we're going?"

Sluggard cocked his head wryly. "At the moment, brother, we all know where we're going. Hispartha." He pointed north. "And it's that way."

TWENTY-SIX

A STRIDENT, WAILING CRY JERKED Oats awake. His head did not lurch away from the saddle, his hand did not dart to grasp his thrum as they had the first night. And the fourth. The anguished voice that burst through the Bastards' slumber was no longer alarming, only heartrending.

Oats rose and moved toward the ruckus in the dark. Sluggard grappled with Polecat's flailing arms, tried to quiet his screaming with soothing words.

"We have you, brother. Calm yourself. We're here, Cat. We have you."

Culprit and Thresh stood nearby, ready to jump in should the fit be too much for one mongrel. Polecat's face stretched in terror, mouth agape as it threw his stricken voice into the sky. His eyes were sightless and rolling. Sluggard continued to contain the worst of his thrashing, but there was no blunting the screams. The dark produced other voices, angry words from the frails' camp, shouting abuses. As always there were encouragements to end the fuss with a thrumbolt. The hoof never responded.

At last, Polecat calmed, slumping in Sluggard's arms, feeble moans tumbling from his lips. They all stood for a moment, waiting to see if he would kick up again, but he succumbed to a twitching slumber.

"Not as bad as last night," Culprit whispered, desperate to find some good.

The Bastards ambled back to their bedrolls.

Oats needed a piss first. He moved away from their little camp to find a likely tree. Best thing about Hispartha, pissing against trees. He went toward the cavaleros' camp. If he couldn't holler back at them, he would at least loose his cock and water in their direction.

The Umbers were a day behind them, the broken, rocky valleys giving way to sparsely wooded uplands. They were now well beyond the border demarked by the mountains, reaching the fortress of an Outmarcher lord just before dusk, the first sign of settlement since leaving the castile. The baron of the place invited Duke Hernan to spend the night within his castle, a courtesy not offered to Orhan ibn Osman or Ahlamra. The Tyrkanian envoy was spitting mad at the injustice, disappearing into his pavilion after staring daggers at the departing duke's back. He enacted a small revenge on the cavaleros, tormenting them by having noisy sex with his serving women.

The Bastards had shared a laugh at his barbed pettiness.

"Old coot still has some iron," Thresh said.

"Helped by an herbalist's powder, no doubt," Ahlamra replied in the dry tone that was as close as she ever came to jesting.

Polecat had an expert ear cocked intently toward the pavilion. He shook his head. "He's only cracking one of them. And she's doing the work. The others are just making sounds. Old fraud. What do you say, brethren? Should I strip down, stride in there and show him how it's done?"

"Hells no," Oats said at the same instant as Thresher.

"Please do not," Ahlamra added.

"Or I could go in there and bugger *him*," Polecat offered. "Save those poor women the effort."

"And if Orhan wishes to be the plow?" Ahlamra challenged.

Polecat put on a mummer's coy face. "Well. He is *very* dignified..."

Ahlamra's famed composure shattered into a genuine smile that she quickly tried to conceal with a hand, igniting a bout of fresh laughter among the hoof.

"Oh!" Cat exclaimed, pointing. "I got her! I got her!"

Hells, that was the great pain of it. He was so often the old Polecat. The journey had banished the bouts of mute, leagues-long staring, the sudden confusions. But what was buried in the daylight came sprouting up with the night.

It had nearly come to blood the first time.

Cat's screams had brought the men posted to sentry duty rushing into their midst with swords and maces in hand. Thankfully, Hoodwink struck first, disarming three of the cavaleros in an eyeblink, giving the remaining two cause to ponder the odds. When their eyes and torchlight fell upon the writhing, senseless Polecat, the men relaxed. It was obvious that the source of the outcry wasn't a threat. They departed with disgusted looks.

"You half-breeds sleepwalk as well as screech like children?"

So captured by his own thoughts, Oats hadn't noticed the cavalero standing watch. The man didn't have a torch, though the starlight in this high country bathed the surrounds well enough.

"Where you headed, sootskin?"

The cavalero was half a stone's toss ahead of Oats and a little to his left.

"Here's good," Oats replied, and unlaced his breeches. His stream covered most of the distance, falling just short of the cavalero's boots. The man held his ground. Oats looked him square in the face during the entire piss.

THE DAYS IN THE SADDLE were many, but often short.

The duke, more interested in sleeping beneath a roof than covering ground, ordered the cavalcade to halt at every town, manor, and castle. Sometimes the column would be done traveling before noon. The crawling pace scoured the Bastards' patience raw, an irritation further chafed by the duke forbidding them entry to any settlement. Polecat had groused, but Ahlamra remained insistent they offer no protest. The slow procession, insisting they sleep rough, it was all a calculated drip of disrespect, meant to erode Orhan ibn Osman's endurance, force him to reveal their destination. Yet the Tyrkanian envoy was as stubborn as he was venomous. Each morning the duke sent a man to ask Orhan where they were bound and each morning the sneering coot would answer with a single word.

North.

And so they rode, the border keeps dotting the Outmarch slowly giving way to vast, ocherous plains filled with reddled sheep, threaded with the crystal waters of descended mountain streams, thick with trout.

Oats didn't know land could be so vibrant, so beautiful. He said so and Sluggard laughed.

"Just wait," the smiling mongrel replied, breathing deep of the fragrant spring air.

"Just wait." Thresher echoed the words, but not the tone, and her scarred face bore no joy.

They traveled upon the ancient, invincible roads of the Imperium, the bend of their course remaining unshakably northward. Orhan's continued mulishness caused Duke Hernan to adopt new dalliances. He tarried a full two days in one town as the guest of its mayordomo because—according to Ahlamra—he found the local wine to be exceptional. That had been Oredal. Or perhaps it was Madre's Crossing, though that may have been where they languished for three days beside yet another wheat field so the duke could romance one of the serving maidens at the taverna. Oats couldn't recall. The names were beginning to blur, just like the towns themselves. All he'd seen of them was what could be spied as they passed through to begin another spate of easy, tedious riding. The villages close to the border had been little more than outposts, a few mean hovels huddled around a well. Only the furtive, hard-eyed stares from behind cracked shutters betrayed the places weren't abandoned. Past the Outmarches, civilization began to bear less shriveled fruit. The hovels became proper houses and the folk risked coming into the sun to cast their mistrustful stares.

The hogs grew restless by the second week, yearning to leave the sluggish confines of the road, to flee the flat stones and surge into the rolling country. They wanted to run. Given the chance, Oats reckoned, the barbarians would turn south and gallop with a desperate speed back to dry Ul-wundulas, back to the dust and the seared rocks, back to the war. Back home.

Well, perhaps not all of them.

Palla appeared content to trudge deeper into the kingdom, needing no guidance from Sluggard, who sat languidly in the saddle, weaving a garland of yellow broom and blue cornflowers gathered at their previous, none-too-distant camp. When the wreath was done, he drifted back to Ahlamra and placed the decoration upon her horse's neck.

"Think our gritter's glad to be back," Oats muttered to Ugfuck. He'd adopted a habit of riding at the rear of the hoof, removed from the others with only the trailing Tyrkanian envoy and his servants behind him.

"He's afraid."

Oats startled at Hoodwink's thin voice, his head darting to the left to find the pale killer riding beside him.

"You do that on purpose?" Oats asked, annoyed. "Or can you simply not fucking help it?"

There was a long silence.

"Xhreka suggested I should wear a bell," Hood said at last.

Oats couldn't stop himself from huffing with amusement. "Lucky you didn't creep up on her and get a telling-off from Belico."

"That happened once. I was unconscious for two days."

Oats looked hard at Hood's profile. He couldn't tell if he was jesting. No, likely not. Oats let out a grunting giggle.

Hood peered at him. "I do not jest."

Oats was belly-laughing now, near to bursting. Through watery eyes he saw the others turn in their saddles to stare. He carried on more than was warranted, but it felt too good to restrain. Each time he tried to compose himself, the thought of Hoodwink knocked heels-over-ass by a spooked Xhreka sent him into fresh gut-shaking peals.

"Oh," Oats managed, between an unsteady drumbeat of chuckles. "Wished I'd seen that."

"It nearly killed me."

Oats erupted again, feeling a cunt, but unable to help himself.

"It was after I awoke that she asked to be taken to the Black Womb."

That put a cork in Oats's mirth. He stuttered to stop and cleared his throat.

"Shit."

In Winsome, Xhreka had made a lark of expressing an attraction toward Hoodwink. At least, he'd thought it was a lark, for what woman would ever be drawn to a hairless, scarred, dead-eyed mongrel the color of a dead frog's belly? Or, as Oats now knew, the color of a long-dead man's skin. One woman, at least, he realized. Oats didn't know if it was a gift granted by Belico or birth, but Xhreka did have a way of seeing deeper than what was there.

"Hood," Oats ventured, "can you . . . tell me where she went?"

"No."

"Wagered not. Now. What's this about Sluggard being afraid?"

"He steels himself with smiles. Lies to himself that the beauty of this land is a welcome sight. He is afraid, hiding behind a face long lost to him."

"Well, losing . . . all he's lost, that would have killed most mongrels," Oats said. "I'm not going to judge him harshly for a little fear. Hells, I got more than my share, being earnest."

"Are you?"

"Am I what?"

"Being earnest. Or is your fear the same as Sluggard's smiles, a thing displayed from habit, but no longer real."

Oats's didn't answer. He didn't need to. Because there wasn't even a hint of a question in Hood's heartless voice.

The first windmill was a delight to behold. Oats had heard of them, but the only one built in the Lots was on the Tusked Tide's land and burned down when he was still a slophead. He'd only seen the charred skeleton. This one, standing above the golden fields, sails turning with a lulling speed, was a welcome distraction during the plodding span it was in view. It held him queerly captivated. There was something marvelous, even menacing, about the way the latticed blades perched atop the tower, turning against a backdrop of clouds shot through with spears of sunlight.

"Elaekton's Arrows," Sluggard had named those heavenly bursts. "They're only so bright in spring. And only in the heartlands of Hispartha."

There was no pretty name for the folk toiling beneath the revolving shadow of the mill. They were too far away to be more than stooping shapes among the wheat, but it wasn't long before the column passed a group working closer to the road. The scythes were wielded by men. They wore sandals and straw hats. The half-orcs sweating behind them, gathering and bundling the reaped stalks, were barefoot, heads and backs exposed to the demanding sun. There were five of them, one only a boy with the paler skin of a frailing. The grown male looked nearly as old as Warbler, though he was no thrice-blood. The three females were younger, one sticking close to the child. Her son, Oats knew in his gut. He wondered which of the two human overseers sitting on their mules with coiled whips in their fists had fathered the boy. One of the men looked up and saw him staring. The surprise at seeing a hog-mounted, hoof-inked, armed half-orc quickly crawled into a scowl. His arm came up, jerked down, the motion almost lazy. The old mongrel grunted as the whip lashed the back of his legs. His pace quickened and he dumped his load in the wain, rushing back for another bundle.

Oats pulled Ugfuck to a halt, his sudden fury causing the hog to snort in complaint.

"Oats."

It was Ahlamra, the use of his name a reminder. Hells, he didn't care. Damn all vows and restraint. The whip-cracking fuck was one blow from Oats's fist removed from a broken skull. He could already feel the satisfaction in his knuckles, his mouth watering at the prospect of swift retribution.

Thresher rode up and blocked his view of the overseer. Her face, hatched with livid scars, was stern.

"Don't fuck us," she said. "If I can ride away, you damn well will too."

Oats swallowed the bile in his throat and nudged Ug on.

The slaves were left behind, the duke abandoned the column for the comfort of his next host, and the hoof lazed for the remainder of another day as the hot sky paled to citron, then to lilac. The cavaleros were resupplied at every town and village. The Bastards were left to fend for themselves. Fortunately, they had Hoodwink, who rarely failed to find game even in pitiless Ul-wundulas. In teeming Hispartha, their cookfire never went without a brace of hare or clutch of fowl.

It was Culprit who asked the question.

"Why do they suffer it?"

His voice was meek, sincere. The chewing slowed, every glance falling upon Thresher. The meat in her hands hovered in front of her mouth.

"There's little choice," she said at last, answering the fire. She took another bite.

"They could run off. Like you."

Thresh grunted. "On foot, with nothing, men on horses with cudgels on the trail. With hounds too, most times. You can hide, run, but hunger catches you no matter how fast you go. All the gods worshipped here and not one temple will offer succor to a half-orc. Peasants will turn you over out of fear, out of hatred. There's not a friend for a runaway anywhere in this kingdom, Cul. Running's a choice. But it ain't much of one."

Culprit frowned as he grappled with that cold truth. He made a strong effort to brighten. "Well. I'm glad you made it, then."

"Yes," Thresher said with a humorless chuckle, looking around at the dark beyond the fire. "Because I managed to get really fucking far."

Oats stared down at the nearly stripped bone between his fingers. Since before he could feed himself he'd known the orcs wanted to conquer Hispartha. As a hoof-rider he learned that Tyrkania too coveted this kingdom, yearning to make it part of their empire. He was now possessed by the same desire as the thicks and the sultans, to bring steel and fire to this land. Not because he wished to seize its beauty, but because he needed to rid the earth of its ugliness.

"FUCK ROADS AND THE HIND ends of all horses."

Polecat uttered the words, but it had become something of a second creed to all of them.

Nearly a month in the saddle. Nearly a month and still they were nowhere. The Bastards could have walked the length of Hispartha if not hampered by the peevish game between Duke Hernan and Orhan ibn Osman.

Another day of chewing on the cavaleros' grit. Another day of passing peasants forced off the road by the cavalcade, making way for the blue bloods even if it meant their wagon breaking a wheel or their flock scattered. Every herdsman, farmer, family, and merchant yielded the way without complaint, heads bowed, eyes downcast. Only when the cavaleros were past did they look up. Perhaps on any other day they might have risked a rude gesture or a barbed stare, but any small displays of resentment that might have surfaced were smothered by the sight of the hoof. Half-breeds riding hogs was outlawed, and the flaunting of that decree never failed to widen the eyes of the peasants, slack a few jaws. And there were more than enough insults flung from the bravest, gobs of spit from the most vicious.

"We ain't the reason you're standing in the ditch!" Culprit shouted when a particularly daring shepherd boy pelted them with goat shit.

On it went, their progress marked only by subtle changes in the countryside. Stands of pine and blankets of pink oleander decorated the fields, here and there backed by distant hills. But Hispartha's comely climes ceased to hold Oats's attention. His mind kept turning back to the Lots. He'd spent a month on a tedious trek, but time for Fetch would not have passed so dully. Did she still hold Kalbarca? Had Starling arrived? Ruin awoken? Was the Crown's offer of a temporary peace in earnest or were they merely stalling so fresh armies could arrive and finish the weakened hoofs? Hells, there was no way of knowing. Whatever messages the duke received were not shared. Ahlamra had succeeded in meeting with him only a handful of times during the journey and the man was never forthcoming, voicing only his contempt for Orhan and demanding Ahlamra convince the *katib* to reveal their destination.

On the thirty-third day since leaving the castile, there was a change.

Orhan ibn Osman paused at a crossroads. The heedless Duke Hernan and his neglecting cavaleros continued northward. Without word or warning, the Tyrkanian and his women took the branching road to the northwest.

Oats was the first to notice and whistled at the hoof. They all turned in the saddle, pulling their hogs to a halt upon seeing the departing envoy.

"Reckon we should follow him," Thresher said.

Oats grunted in agreement.

Polecat cocked a head at the heedless cavaleros. "And them?"

"They will realize their error before long," Ahlamra said. "I tire of supping on their dust."

She spurred her horse to follow the Tyrkanians.

Oats grinned at the others. "You heard her. Let's ride."

The hogs needed little encouragement. Given their heads for the first time in weeks, they surged up the road, catching up with Orhan swiftly. Oats signaled the hoof to ride past him, drawing whoops from Cat and Culprit. He'd be damned if they weren't going to churn some ground before the duke caught up and hobbled them with his dying cow's pace. If the cavaleros wanted to reclaim the front of the column they could fucking earn it. They strung out in a long single file, Sluggard in the lead on Palla, the fastest barbarian among them. Culprit and Polecat made a contest of second, Thresher content in third. Oats and Ugfuck were next, Hood behind them. Ahlamra remained with Orhan, no doubt making an effort to calm his ill humor at nearly being trampled by a half dozen thundering barbarians.

Sluggard broke away from the road, pulling Palla left to jump the bordering ditch and plunge into the neighboring field. The hoof, trained to the instincts of the lead rider, followed without hesitation. As Ugfuck bounded over the ditch, Oats caught a glimpse of something in the road ahead. An oxcart. Sluggard had led the hoof off the road so that the travelers wouldn't be forced to give way. Something in that small kindness, that defiance of the very nature of Duke Hernan and his ilk, kindled a fire in Oats's heart. Coupled with the speed of Ugfuck running free, that fire propelled a joyous shout from his lungs. Rough ground, open country, those were the realms of the hoof-rider. To all the hells with paving stones and the whims of noblemen.

And Sluggard, that glorious Bastard, sensing the need of his brethren, didn't swing back to the road, even after passing the cart. He led the hoof into a full gallop, cleaving a trail through tall grass and wildflowers. The race between Polecat and Culprit matured from a lark to a true contest. Charging abreast, close enough to throw elbows at each other, they laughed as they rode. Leaning, Oats shifted Ug's course with nothing but the weight of his body, angling farther away from the road. He caught up to Thresher on his right, Hood drew even on his left, and the three of them fanned out across the field, banishing the constraints of the last weeks.

They did not let up until their hogs were nearly spent. Slowing their huffing mounts to a walk they clustered, sharing satisfied grins and pulls from their waterskins. They were in the middle of an untended wheat field heavy with nodding poppies. The hogs pushed through the bristling heads, the stalks whispering as they bowed over.

"Any notion where we are?" Polecat asked, wiping his newly wetted lips with the back of his hand.

"None," Thresher replied, squinting ahead at a dark line of encroaching pine.

Sluggard shook his head.

It wasn't long before the woods forced them back to the road. The trees grew thick to the left, shading the path. The sound of water heralded a bridge, the road arching over the back of its aged, sturdy stones. It proved wide enough to accommodate four riders abreast, spanning the gentle currents of a healthy river. As the Bastards reached the center of the bridge, Hood raised an arm, pointing above the tree line, where the top of a tower, swollen with bartizans, was just visible.

"We should wait," Oats said, reining up. "Ahlamra ain't going to like us blundering toward some castle."

"Should we get off the bridge?" Culprit asked. "Might look like bandits sittin' here in the middle. Like we're gonna waylay travelers."

Thresher made a face. "We're six half-orcs with thrums and swords who ain't washed proper in a long while. Where the fuck *wouldn't* we look like bandits?"

"Naked in that river," Polecat suggested.

"Have to admit, there's some wisdom to it," Thresh said after a moment's pause.

Oats nodded. "We'll go back across and down to the bank. Water the hogs. Those with a mind to wash, do it."

Culprit, Thresh, and Polecat shed their breeches and brigands the moment their hogs were tethered. Hood, never one to be vulnerable, remained vigilant up on the road. Sluggard tarried on the bank. Oats knew the shame of his mutilation kept him from the water. Nothing could be said to remedy it. Oats took his boots off, his brigand, but he merely sat on the bank and dangled his feet in the water. Soon, Sluggard came and sat beside him. Feet floating in the cool current, they watched their brethren swim.

"Thank you, Oats," Sluggard said quietly.

Oats leaned and nudged him in reply.

The others were fresh out of the river by the time Ahlamra arrived with Orhan. The old Tyrkanian cast a glance down, but did not slow his horse.

"Come!" he called, striking the bridge. "This bedamned march is almost done and I'll not wait while you rid yourselves of the stink of swine."

Sluggard snorted. "Remember when he was honored to meet us?"

"Barely," Oats replied, his feet sloshing out of the river as he stood.

Leading their hogs back to the road, the mostly dripping Bastards mounted up and followed the mules. Not long after the bridge, the pines thinned and the road turned farther west, leading through rocky pastures to a walled town. The Hisparthans delighted in building their castles upon promontories, and the tower Hood spied from the bridge was revealed to be the central keep of a fortress resting upon a bluff, anchoring the western end of the walls. Despite its daunting perch, the stronghold bore little resemblance to the brutish bulk of the castile. Its lofty towers of honey-colored stone basked in the coaxing sun, reaching skyward as if nourished by the light. Glorious as the castle was, it was unfinished. The smaller towers were still bedecked with scaffolding.

The gate nestled in the walls was open to their approach. Little more than a large door, it boasted no defenses of its own. Oats had needed a ladder to scale the walls of Kalbarca. These he could surmount with a running jump and a boost from a strong companion. There was no sign of a garrison, and the Bastards rode through the gate unchallenged.

A huddle of houses waited in the square beyond, watched over by the growing castle. Sweating men covered in masonry dust ambled down a cobbled lane from the bluff. Their steps hitched for a moment upon noticing the hoof, but they raised no alarm, and seemed careful not to stare as they skirted the square and moved off deeper into town. They couldn't go far, however. The place wasn't what Oats would call sizable. Bigger than Winsome had been, certainly, but not by much.

Orhan ibn Osman proceeded without hesitation up the street toward the stronghold. Led by Ahlamra, the hoof went along after him, passing several long, open-front buildings housing women hard at work behind looms and spinning wheels. Like the masons, the weavers had a moment's pause at the appearance of the riders, but made no fuss. The road narrowed as the slope increased and the Bastards were forced to go single-file the last measure, passing beneath an archway before leveling out onto the crag's plateau. The castle sat back upon the bluff, leaving room for a courtyard fronting the keep, the stone cut to form a gap between them. A drawbridge, already lowered, connected the fortress to the yard. And still there was no sign of any men-at-arms.

"At last." Orhan sighed. Wincing, the old man started to dismount, but the sharp striking of swiftly approaching hoofbeats from the road behind stopped him. Four cavaleros shot through the arch, followed by a fuming Duke Hernan, sweaty from the hard pursuit.

A further five horsemen entered the courtyard behind him. The rest would still be held up at the bridge, Oats reckoned.

The duke spurred his huge stallion toward Orhan, reining up with such furor that the animal reared.

"Explain this!" Hernan growled.

The aged Tyrkanian did not flinch in the face of the bigger man's anger. Rather, it amused him.

"This is where I shall sleep tonight," Orhan declared. "And every night hence until I can return to my palace in Eskutar and never again sully my mind with thought of this dunghill of a kingdom."

Duke Hernan cast furious eyes at the castle. "Here?"

"Here," Orhan said with relish. "And I shall leave you to find your own lodging out in the wilderness as you have kindly showed me to be the custom."

The duke paid the vindictive remark little notice. He kept staring at the fortress, wrestling with his spirited and stamping horse.

"This is where your masters have found ally," the giant of a man said, bemused.

"It is."

The *katib*'s needling response drew the duke's attention at last. Hernan's baleful glower fell upon the Tyrkanian. Oats saw a ripple of ire, quickly cooled. The duke's face became placid before a grin formed beneath his fierce beard.

"Here," he said again, the word no longer a question.

Orhan sneered. "I—"

The duke snatched the long dagger from his belt and rammed its stake of a blade into Orhan's open mouth. The tip broke through the back of the old man's skull with a squelch as the steel disc forming the guard shattered his teeth. Orhan's horse whinnied and shied, fleeing the limp corpse on its back. It trotted away, but its former rider continued to hang in the air, a grisly fish dangling at the end of the duke's strong arm. Tipping his fist, he allowed his murdered catch to slide off the blade and crumple to the stones.

The courtyard was quiet. Orhan's spooked horse was the only one that reacted to the slaying. His own serving women did not utter so much as a gasp. The Bastards kept their hogs well in hand. Oats knew his brethren were watching the cavaleros, waiting. If the duke ordered more bloodshed, the hoof wouldn't die so easy.

The duke of Baxscedures looked up at them for the first time. And smiled. Turning his horse, he rode out of the courtyard, the cavaleros falling in behind him.

"Hells," Polecat swore, releasing a heavy breath.

Culprit ran a hand over the shaved half of his head and looked down at Orhan's body. "Really hope we're in the right place. 'Cause that old fuck was the only one who knew where we were goin'."

"We're in the right place," Oats said.

The hoof followed his gaze to the drawbridge.

Crafty spread his hands wide as he walked across, lifting his voice.

"Strong Oats! Friend Bastards! I am pleased you have arrived at last."

His plump face offering a warm smile, the wizard stepped over the envoy's carcass without a glance.

TWENTY-SEVEN

"WELCOME TO VOKASTRIA. MY HOPES it was a pleasant journey."

Beaming, Crafty swept them all with an expectant look. None answered, not even Ahlamra, her poise held captive by the sight of the towering blue devil that trailed the wizard. Oats had warned the others about Fuqtus, but hearing tell of him and beholding him were different beasts. The sun glinted off the demon's brazen hoofs and horns, the golden blade of his cumbersome axe flashing as he strode across the drawbridge.

Ahlamra regained her composure with a blink.

"It was wearying," she told Crafty.

Sluggard was far less collected.

"The fuck was that about?" he demanded, pointing at Orhan's seeping corpse.

Crafty cast an unconcerned glance back. "Oh, I suppose the duke was enraged by our choice of host. Orhan died for that offense. A brute's idea of a message to Tyrkania that the Crown will always fight to stay upon Queen Ursaria's brow. A useless act, but the man is known for his ill humor."

"Ill humor," Oats scoffed. "He'd more cause than that. Out with it."

Crafty gave a little hum. "Soon, soon, I promise. Now, forgive me, you said you are weary. Please, I will lead you to a place of undeniable rest."

"That . . . sounds like you're going to kill us," Polecat said, eyes narrowing.

"Ah!" Crafty chuckled. "No. Though you may find a paradise."

With a wink, he began to set off across the courtyard.

"Surely the castle will suffice," Ahlamra said to his back.

Crafty did not slow nor turn, waving a dismissive hand over his shoulder at the keep. "The place is often a din of hammers. Come!"

The hoof hesitated. Ahlamra glanced at Oats. He nodded.

The Bastards eased their hogs forward. Despite his bulk, Crafty's stride was steady and swift as he proceeded beneath the arch and down the sloping street. Eyes watchful beneath his heavy brow, Fuqtus stayed at the rear. Orhan's serving women continued to sit their mules, making no move to follow.

Once the width of the street allowed, Ahlamra guided her horse to walk along next to Crafty.

"Will Duke Hernan's actions goad Tyrkania to war?" she asked.

"It is more likely the sultans will send the duke gifts," Crafty replied. Oats could only see his ample, silk-swaddled back, but heard the grin behind his voice. "Orhan ibn Osman soured in favor long ago. Useful, for he was familiar with Hispartha, serving here in his distant youth. Beyond that, expendable. The sultans would not send one they feared to lose."

"Says something about you, then, doesn't it, hefty?" Polecat jabbed.

Crafty chuckled again, twisting a bit to smile at the hoof. "Truly, how I have missed your company!"

"You deflect, Uhad Ul-badir," Ahlamra said.

"In hopes my mongrel appellation will be changed to Buckler," Crafty declared, enjoying himself.

"We could start calling you Cock Sweat," Polecat said.

"Cock *Cheese*," Culprit offered.

"Shit Curds."

"Wet Fart."

A low growl from Fuqtus did nothing to cow the japing pair.

Passing the weavers' workhouse, Crafty led them down to the gate square and exited the town.

"I beg patience as I extend your journey a little longer," the wizard said.

They crossed the bridge and found the road beyond littered with piles of fresh horseshit, but there was no other sign of the cavaleros.

"Frails didn't tarry," Sluggard muttered.

"The duke will now be making haste to Magerit," Crafty said, stepping around the dung. He halted after a few dozen steps, casting sweeping looks off the roadside to the east, searching the edge of the forest. "Alas, the path ever eludes. Forgive me, friend Bastards, such a surfeit of trees conspires to confound this son of barer climes."

Hoodwink spurred forward, passing the wizard and riding a thrumshot farther south, where he stopped.

"Ah," Crafty sighed. "Trust hawk-eyed Hoodwink to have spied it. Doubtless he marked it on the way in, eh?"

If Hood had, Oats certainly hadn't. But when they reached the spot, there it was; a path in the woods, little more than a game trail of well-trodden dirt.

"It is a lengthy but pleasant walk," Crafty said as he trundled down the small embankment. "Your ease and the answers to all questions lie this way."

The trail was narrow and the wizard's pace would slow them, but Oats gestured for the hoof to remain mounted. He loaded his stockbow. The others followed his lead. Taking no notice of their caution, Crafty continued on beneath the pines.

Damn him, but it *was* a pleasant track. Oats had never been in a forest this big. Even the trees in Dog Fall had been sparse, mountain stands. Here the trunks grew tall and straight above a thick carpet of verdant underbrush. Soon, the road was lost and the forest marched on as far as the eye could see in every direction. The air beneath the shading boughs was cool, sharp with the smell of the pines. They crossed several gurgling streams, the trail taking them down into forested valleys and up again. The sun had been high when they entered Vokastria, but now it dipped from sight. A break in the trees revealed mountains to the east, closer than Oats would have expected, so tall they remained crowned with snow.

"Sierra Drakós," Sluggard said, the first words anyone had spoken since entering the forest.

"Beautiful to behold, yes!" Crafty announced. "We are quite close now."

The trail widened until it was lost altogether, replaced by a swath of level, well-trodden ground. It wasn't quite a clearing, for the trees still held dominion, encroaching upon a walled compound. Built from the same pale stone as the castle at Vokastria, the place had none of its height. The tiled roofs of several buildings peeked up over the round-topped little wall.

A pair of small, misshapen figures lounged on low benches on either side of the closed, wooden gate. They stood as Crafty approached, though it did little to increase their height.

"Hells overburdened," Polecat swore, seeing the guards up close.

Both were so hunched it looked as if their heads grew from their chests. Their ancient faces were deeply creased and distorted. One wore a shaggy black beard, but the other had nothing to shield his hideousness save the mixture of dirt and soot darkening his sallow flesh. They were dressed in goatskins, the beardless one wearing a hood made from the animal's head. Their legs were bandy and thin, their arms heavy and overlong. Knives and hatchets hung from their belts, and spears leaned against the wall beside their benches, but neither of the malformed dwarves reached for the weapons, though they stared at Crafty with obvious loathing.

"Good Britu, watchful Beiru!" the wizard greeted them. "Our guests are here, at last."

The beardless one swept the hoof with a yellow gaze and fashioned a smile.

Oats loved the ugliest hog ever to draw breath, but even he had to look away from that rotten horror of pitted teeth. Beardy performed a mocking bow, the gesture so overwrought he could have pissed on them with more respect. His bent-over back revealed a pair of withered black appendages, protruding from slits in his leathers.

"The fuck is that shi—" Culprit exclaimed, and was cut off by a slicing glare from Ahlamra.

Sluggard dismounted, amazed. "Are they . . . mouros?"

"Possibly the last two in the world," Crafty replied. "A tragedy they are both male. Their last master clipped their wings. Their tongues too, fearing they would bewitch him."

"Sounds like a cunt," Polecat said. "Who was he?"

Crafty's smile never wavered. "My father. Please, come within."

The wizard stepped between the miserable guards and shoved the gate wide. The hoof led their hogs through and entered an enclosure of wonders.

A throng of screaming monkeys greeted them from a cage of rope netting to the right. To the left, a paddock containing a stalwart stag and resting does watched them pass. Sluggard laughed in delight at the trio of bear cubs wandering free, running and rolling at play. A yowling leopard startled Culprit, hidden atop its perch behind iron bars. Diminutive goats grazed in a pen across from a larger one housing a massive bull, skin glossy black and crimson when it caught the light. Swarthy men ambled about, tending the animals and sparing hardly a glance for Crafty and the hoof. Most astounding of all were the barbarians. Four of the best-bred hogs Oats had ever seen supped from a trough within a pen near the back of the compound. An impressive stable stood beside, and it was here Crafty led them.

The building was circular, the stalls surrounding a central sheltered breaking yard occupied by a giant ram. A tall man stood beside the beast, stroking its throat with a huge hand and speaking softly. The hoof's arrival drew his attention. His unshaven face hosted a nose broken so badly it was flat.

"Mannrique," Crafty said. "Might we find room for a few more?"

The man stared for a moment, clinging to the ram. He was nearly as large as the duke, but where Hernan had been bulky and imposing, this homely frail was slouching and ungainly.

"Yes," he said, detaching from the beast. "Yes."

Mannrique plodded out of the enclosure.

"I will tend them myself," he told the wizard, though there was a hesitance in his voice.

"Most kind," Crafty said. "Please, True Bastards, leave your mounts. I assure you they could not be in more skilled hands. Mannrique, we go to the lodge for some ease and refreshment."

"Oh, yes. Good," the groom replied, taking Ahlamra's mount first, though shrinking away from looking at her.

The hoof eyed Oats. They usually saw to the care of their own hogs.

"We—" he started.

"Are eager for rest," Ahlamra said smoothly. "Thank you, Mannrique."

Stepping toward Crafty, she flicked a telling look at Oats. He still didn't like leaving the hogs, but the chief had said to follow Rue's lead. Oats gave the others a permissive nod. Unloading their stockbows, they all tied their hogs to the rail of the breaking yard and left the stable.

"Wager you a cock-sucking that moon-faced frail gets himself gored," Polecat whispered to Culprit.

"Fair certain that's not a wager I want to win or lose, Cat."

"I meant from a whore, fool-ass."

Culprit looked around the compound. "Fair certain there ain't a whore around."

"Not unless you want to get amorous with a pygmy goat," Thresh said.

They crossed the width of the compound to the largest building behind the walls. An exterior stone stair ran up the left side to an upper level, but Crafty went through the door on the ground floor. The wide room within was well appointed with trestles and benches, as well as several finely fashioned yet sturdy chairs, all resting on polished wood planking. The fireplace was set, but cold. At the rear of the room, three steps led down to a recessed, earthen-floored kitchen dominated by the bulging brick belly of an oven. Oats felt a sudden pang of loss for the Grey Bastards' meeting hall, long-destroyed along with the rest of the Kiln.

"Please," Crafty said, gesturing broadly to the chairs and benches. He retrieved one of the jugs hanging from the beams among drying herbs, taking it over to a table set with pewter cups. "The few that serve here are sworn to the comfort of the animals," he said with a grin as he began to pour. "Surely that will not present a difficulty for a self-reliant hoof. All the same, allow me to offer this first drink with my own hands."

He passed the cups around two at a time. None of the Bastards had sat. Sluggard and Polecat gave their wine longing looks, but did not drink. Lurking beside the door, Hoodwink made no move to accept the hospitality, leaving Crafty stranded for a moment with an outstretched arm. The wizard shifted the cup to Fuqtus. The demon took it and drained the contents in a single swallow.

"The time for mistrust shortens with every mile Duke Hernan rides closer to Ursaria," Crafty proclaimed, going back to the table and pouring a final cup for himself. "Shortly, we will be called to court. Days, perhaps. Not much time. Unless you have not eaten nor slept for fear of daggers and poison. Then, truly, it will seem an eternity." He sipped and sat, making a mummer's show of both actions. "You will gain much from ridding your minds of any whispers that I desire to kill you."

Ahlamra lowered herself into a chair. "In the House of Lustrous Gaze we had a name for women like you."

Crafty's eyes flashed. "I am now intrigued. Tell me."

"It does not translate well into Hisparthan."

Ahlamra said something in an eastern tongue, too swift and foreign for Oats to catch.

The laugh Crafty expelled was so loud it made Culprit jump. Struggling not to spill his wine, the wizard guffawed, prodigious cheeks offering a slope for his tears.

Ahlamra glanced up at Thresher. "It is one who touts her prowess in the bed, yet is timid at heart. A seductress who shrivels during the act of coupling."

Polecat nodded knowingly. "We call that a Whore's Corpse."

"Cod Tease," Culprit said.

Cat pulled from his cup, sucked his teeth. "No. That's a woman who promises all manner of delight, but don't ever deliver. A"—he looked at Ahlamra—"what'd you call it?"

Ahlamra repeated the word.

"*That*," Polecat said. "They'll get sticky with you, but it's like you're alone because they lay there all distant and sad. All that wantonness they showed before is snuffed out suddenly. A Whore's Corpse."

"So . . ." Crafty said, still squirming with mirth. "Which am I?"

Ahlamra leaned back and drank, looking at the wizard over the rim of her cup. "I know only that I am neither." She set the wine aside. "We are here at your invitation. So. Are we teasing? Fucking? Or are we to conspire against the Crown of Hispartha?"

Crafty's smile tightened with satisfaction. "I fear I will soon be your willing slave, Ahlamra el'Huriya."

"I would be content with a Zilsha'ir of the Black Womb with a dubious claim to the throne posing as envoy to the Tyrkanian Empire."

Crafty reclined. "My claim, dubious or adamant, is no longer of import."

"By the time we reach court, I suspect that will be true." Ahlamra looked at Culprit. "Abril. When I say, I would like you to please step outside."

"Wasn't me, Rue!" Culprit protested. "Fair certain it was the wizard when he laughed."

"Please, do as I say. But only when I say." Ahlamra returned her attention to Crafty as Culprit shot a fuddled look at Oats and received only a shrug. "What news from the Lots? My brethren will be less anxious if they hear how our chief fares."

"There has been no further fighting," Crafty said.

Oats felt a thousand snakes in his gut unknot. Sluggard slumped into a chair and breathed a sigh of relief. Thresher squeezed his shoulder.

"As promised, the Tyrkanian blockade at the mouth of the

Guadal-kabir remains," the wizard continued. "Hispartha maintains hold of the port at Urci and the fortress at Thricehold, but does not stray farther west. The last word I had of dread Fetching, she remained in Kalbarca. I confess, that news is now weeks old."

"We will need to send word to her," Ahlamra said.

"Trusted messengers are scarce," Crafty replied. "Those with swift horses scarcer still. Yet, of course, we shall arrange it."

"What about Strava?" Oats asked. "Zirko made any moves?"

Crafty shook his turbaned head. "The Unyars have not stirred."

"That all sounds . . . better than I thought it would," Polecat said, going to the wine jug and refilling his cup. Oats caught his eye and made it clear with a glare he needed to slow down.

"It is not all so glad," Crafty told them. "The barons in the Outmarch have been ordered to call their banners. Armies are assembling along the border. The greatest at Ellerina."

"Means they'll march through the Smelteds," Thresher said. "Come at Kalbarca by land."

"That'll be slow," Sluggard added. "Chief has time. We have time."

"For now, they are only making ready," Crafty said. "Though the duke of Baxscedures will bray war in the queen's ear. He will not be alone."

"Will he confess to the dishonorable slaying of Orhan ibn Osman?" Ahlamra asked. "He flaunted his lack of fear of the empire, yet I wonder if the queen shares that bravado."

"Stop," Thresher said, waving an irritated hand by her ear. "Rue, stop. The rest of us still don't understand why he knifed the old lech. I saw the duke's face. He was furious one heartbeat and pleased the next. All on account of where we ended up. Fat Cheeks here says once the Crown knows where we are then we're no longer a threat. I slaved and blistered in a lord's fields most of my life and never once heard the name Vokastria. You, Slug?"

Sluggard gave a contrite twist of his mouth. "There's a song . . ."

"Hells, don't fucking sing it!" Thresh exclaimed. "Someone just explain why we're in some forest with a mess of caged beasts guarded by ugly little fucks my madre used to tell me night-tales about before she caught a flux and died without telling me those malicious dwarf-cunts were good and real."

Ahlamra reached over and grasped Thresher's hand. "Dacia."

"What?"

"Sit the fuck down."

"Right." Thresher snatched the freshly filled cup from Polecat and planted her ass on a bench.

Ahlamra straightened in her seat.

"We are now prepared to listen," she told Crafty. "If you are prepared to cease wasting the time you claim is short."

Eyes dancing over his cup, the wizard took a drink. Tongue wetted, he began to speak.

"Vokastria and the surrounding lands, including this forest, were once the holdings of Girón Trastorias, firstborn son of King Anscaro the Third. Girón was possessed by a love of viciousness, compelled by profane appetites. Truly, I believe tales of him have reached even down to the Lots."

"The one that kept an old man on a chain, made him bite children?" Polecat said.

"The most palatable of his habits," Crafty replied. He was no longer smiling. "Girón's wanderlust, his cruelty, his attraction to sorcery, made a troublesome potion in an heir. Since its beginnings, Hispartha has bred rambunctious nobles, and no ruler among them ever sat the throne free from the schemes of jealous and grasping rivals. Yet Anscaro's entire court feared Girón, and it was rumored the king loosed him upon those he suspected of plots against his reign. The truth? The prince was ruled by nothing but madness and whim. Both king and court, however, were freed from Girón's shadow for several years when the prince went east to Tyrkania."

"Where the Black Womb hosted his evil ass and arranged for him to father a half-orc," Oats said, scowling at Crafty. "We've heard this hogshit tale before."

"It is not what occurred there that matters," Ahlamra said, gaze never leaving the wizard. "But here in Hispartha during his absence."

Crafty dipped his chin. "As you say. The queen, driven mad years before by her son's wickedness, died at last. Anscaro had a fresh young bride within the month, and a child within the year. A daughter."

"Ursaria," Sluggard said. "Now queen of Hispartha."

Crafty pointed a pudgy finger at him. "King Anscaro strove mightily in his waning years to ensure it was she and not Girón that succeeded him. The nobles flocked and fawned, putting their sons, themselves, forward to wed Ursaria from her first breath. Fortunately for the king, this scramble to entwine with the royal bloodline fractured alliances among the scheming houses of Hispartha, distracted them from the traditional pastime of taking the throne by force, a thing Anscaro would have been hard-pressed to prevent in those days. Shrewdly, he played them against each other for years, all the while arranging a match for his daughter that would ensure her wealth once she wore the crown, but would not jeopardize her power.

"Girón returned on the eve of the wedding. Whether this was design or chance is not known. If the wayward prince attempted to reclaim his birthright is not known. Anscaro had his son seized and Girón went to the headsman the following dawn."

"Laughing, the song claims," Sluggard said.

"The old king outlived him but a week," Crafty finished. Draining his cup, he stood and refilled it.

"Good story," Thresher grunted. "My eyes are misty. Still doesn't explain why us being here enraged Hernan."

"Because it is not the entire tale," Crafty said. "The duke's smile was a message for the mongrel hoofs, for you have—in the duke's mind—hitched the fate of the Lots to little more than a walking folly."

Oats drew a long breath to feed his starving patience. "Talk plain."

"Abril, go out now," Ahlamra said.

"I don't want to miss any—"

"Go now. And smile at whoever you see."

A puzzled Culprit set his cup down and left the lodge. Crafty sipped his wine, watering the seeds of a grin. His smile shone when the door opened again mere moments after Culprit left.

The big groom ducked into the room, bringing the reek of the stables with him.

"True Bastards," Crafty said with good cheer. "Let us raise our cups in thanks to our host, my uncle, Mannrique Trastorias, Prince of the Blood, second son of King Anscaro the Good and—most impressively—founder of Robledondo, this haven among the pines."

Ahlamra rose smoothly, cup held forth. "We are grateful and honored by your hospitality, my lord."

Mannrique shifted awkwardly, oversized head trying to retreat into his shoulders. There was shit on his face.

Oats downed his wine.

TWENTY-EIGHT

THE BASTARDS WERE GIVEN USE of a bunkhouse between the lodge and the stable. The hoof pelted Ahlamra with questions the moment they were alone. They came all at once, but Thresher's cut through the rest.

"The hells, Rue?"

Ahlamra went to the nearest cot, removing her headscarf and shaking out her curls on the way.

"Uhad Ul-badir has found one with a better claim to the throne than the queen," she said.

"*That* horse-toothed clod?" Polecat laughed.

Ahlamra sighed. "That horse-toothed clod is older than Ursaria. And a man."

"It's more hogshit, though," Oats said, hanging his stockbow and quiver on a peg in the wall. "Like Crafty being the mad frail's by-blow. It's a mummery."

"No," Ahlamra said. "I believe Mannrique is what the wizard says."

"How can you know?" Sluggard asked.

"Duke Hernan's face. He was struck with an earnest rage. Fear births fury in men like him. He would not have been afraid if Vokastria did not house a true threat to the Queen. And Crafty was rightly named. He would not embark on this gambit with an impostor."

Thresher folded her arms, her scarred face set in a frown. "Then why ain't he king? Mannrique. The story Crafty told didn't say shit about a second son."

"Just look at him," Culprit muttered. "Big, mopey halfwit."

"I would not be so quick to judge his wits," Ahlamra replied. "But there is truth to what you say. His nature does him little service. And he remains in the prime of his years, meaning he was born much later than his brother. I feel confident Girón's evil was inveterate by the time Mannrique was drawn from the queen's womb. The birth may well have been what undermined the last of the beleaguered woman's resolve. Whatever her state, she did not engage much with this second child, not after the tragedy of the first, of that I am certain."

"How?" Oats asked.

"Mannrique struggled to look at Thresher and myself."

Thresh scoffed. "Men haven't looked with longing at my face in a long while."

"Then they're backy fools," Polecat declared.

"You're just flattering to get fucked," Thresh said.

Cat raised his eyebrows. "Is it working?"

Thresh sized him up. "It ain't a no."

Culprit snorted and Ahlamra allowed herself a slight smirk before continuing.

"There are no women here, only up in the town. No, here the prince has created for himself a sanctuary free of anything that discomfits him."

"So he *is* backy," Polecat said, flopping down on a cot with his boots still on and putting his hands behind his head.

"Perhaps," Ahlamra said, shrugging without care. "More likely it is affection itself that he cannot abide. He would have spent his youth striving to be the opposite of Girón in all things, all the while being scrutinized by nurses and tutors for the slightest sign of his brother's perversions. His childhood must have been lonely and loveless."

"So . . ." Culprit paced a small circle. "If he weren't mad, why did his padre not let him be king?"

"Anscaro would have taken an interest in grooming the boy. Clearly, an interest short-lived. Mannrique wasn't his brother, but nor was he his father. Ursaria's very existence points to Anscaro abandoning the idea of Mannrique ever ascending the throne. He is shy, unattractive, graceless."

"He fears bloodshed," Hoodwink said.

The hoof looked curiously at their usually silent brother.

"Goats and deer," Hood explained. "Livestock and game, yet they are kept and pampered. There was no gelding knife among the tools in the stable."

Ahlamra nodded. "His talent for violence is undoubtedly lacking. He would flee all his brother's lusts, or try to atone for them. The crippled mouros at the gates. Living here in Girón's former lands. The new castle. I suspect he ordered Girón's pulled down. He is trying to wash the stain away."

"Why ally with Crafty, then?" Oats asked. "A half-orc claiming to be his brother's mongrel son. You can't find a larger stain. Why welcome it?"

"Crafty is kind to him," Ahlamra answered simply.

Polecat laughed. "That's it?"

"For one such as Mannrique, yes."

"She ain't wrong, Cat," Culprit said. "Rue told me to go outside and smile at who I saw. Damned if it didn't work. That Mannrique was waiting when I came out, kicking rocks like a damn child. Thought he was gonna run off, the way he looked at me. But I smiled like Rue said and he sorta . . . stilled. Didn't manage to look me square, but he walked by me and went inside."

"Too timid to go into his own lodge," Sluggard said, shaking his head.

"Not without invitation," Ahlamra agreed softly.

"A smile," Oats grunted. "And Crafty has those by the heap. Those and more."

"Uhad Ul-badir could easily cozen Mannrique to anything," Ahlamra said. "The man is malleable and pitifully eager to please. His reclusiveness is his only defense. Once that has been breached…" She shook her head with resignation.

"And you worked all this out in a few moments just by looking at him?" Polecat asked.

"That's what she fucking does," Thresher said, smiling with fond pride.

"Rue," Oats said. "What do you reckon Crafty's got stewing?"

Ahlamra took a breath, considering. "At the least he will use Mannrique as a distraction. Dangle him before the queen while his other hand is at work to undermine her. The obvious ploy would be to press Mannrique's claim, gather support, and usurp the Crown. Yet if any of the noble houses thought such a plot would work, it would have been attempted long ago. Ursaria herself has never thought it likely. If she believed her meek half-brother a threat, he would not be alive. No. She contented herself with forgetting him, allowing him to remain cloistered. Perhaps she thought he would prove useful someday. But Duke Hernan is galloping to remind her that others are now attempting to use the forsaken prince.

"With the king so recently in his grave, Ursaria will already be beset by the least subtle of her suitors. However, I have little doubt there will be some at court who do not relish being the next overshadowed consort. Why wed an adept and redoubtable queen when you can rule through a cringing and malleable King Mannrique? The man does not inspire rebellion, but Crafty? With one so canny using the prince as a puppet, anything is possible."

"The obvious ploy," Oats repeated. "Make himself king without the title. But Crafty's schemes ain't ever been what I'd call obvious."

"No," Ahlamra said. "I do not suspect this one will be either."

Polecat stretched noisily. "Maybe he intends to put that big, blue fucker up as the queen's next husband. Horns and hooves. Likely hung like a bull too."

None even smiled at the jest.

"The hells is that thing?" Thresher asked.

"A *jhevadi*," Ahlamra said. "They dwell in Ul-Kadim, servants to the priestesses of Bhadra who rule the city with fear. Bhadra is a goddess of death, and hundreds die each day beneath the sacrificial knives of the High Conciliatrix and her sisters. Though it resides within the Tyrkanian Empire, the sultans have no sway in Ul-Kadim, for they are wise enough to leave the Bhadran cult to its own governance. Yet the *jhevadi* are enslaved to the sisterhood. I have never heard tell of one ever leaving the temple-palace of Ul-Kadim unless it was to escort Bhadra's anointed."

"So . . . Crafty's found religion?" Sluggard said.

"Bhadra's cult does not allow men," Ahlamra replied.

"And Fuqtus got surly when Jackal called him a slave back at the Cradle," Oats said. He looked to Hood. "Anything you can add?"

"He is devoted to safeguarding the wizard's life," Hood told them. "And they are lovers."

Polecat sniggered, his eyes closed. "Buries the notion of Fuck You wedding the queen, then."

Ahlamra was pensive.

"What do you reckon we do?" Oats asked her.

"We accept that for now Uhad Ul-badir is not our enemy," she answered flatly. "We help him. And keep our eyes open."

The words had hardly left Ahlamra's mouth when Polecat began to snore.

"Get some rest," Oats told the hoof, and left the bunkhouse before any could question him.

He returned to the lodge to find Crafty sitting across from Fuqtus, moving some little carvings atop a series of wooden cubes set in an irregular pattern between them. There was no sign of the rustic prince.

"Ah, Oats," Crafty said. "I do not suppose you know Ascent of Twenty Heavens? I fear I am hopeless. Poor Fuqtus longs for a worthy match."

The demon—the *jhevadi*—didn't appear too concerned with the game. He peered hard at Oats from beneath his heavy brows. His axe stood propped against the table, close at hand, but he made no move to take up the weapon.

Oats did not answer. He walked over to the table and pulled up a stool, sitting with Crafty to his right, Fuqtus to his left. Letting his silence continue he stared at the wizard. Crafty's attention remained on the gaming pieces, a languid smile on his face.

"You appear to be waiting on something," the wizard said.

Oats grunted in agreement. "You to stop fucking around. Tell me the plan, Crafty."

Reaching over the cubes, Crafty moved a piece with his many-ringed fingers. "We wait here until it is time to journey to court."

"Then?"

"We attempt to make peace."

"How?"

"I cannot tell you."

"Seem to recall someone saying in this very room that the time for mistrust needed to end. Fairly certain that was you."

"And I believe that truth."

Oats leaned closer. "Then tell me. We came at your insistence. We're here. *Why?*"

Crafty hung a broad hand over the gaming board. "Diplomacy is much like Ascent of Twenty Heavens. It is partly a race, yet also a—"

Oats shoved the board off the table, sending the cubes clattering to the ground.

Fuqtus surged to his feet with a seething snarl, but Crafty held up a hand.

Oats's motion had been swift and violent, but he kept his next words at a slow boil.

"Hatch your scheme, damn you."

Crafty loosed a weighted sigh. "The courts of queens and sultans are nothing but artifice, friend Oats—"

"I ain't your fucking friend."

The wizard's chin dipped as he took a hitching breath and held it for a moment. When he looked up his face was armored, his stare edged.

"Then I shall speak as your foe with hopes you will hear. The scheme you wish me to confide died stillborn and is now buried beneath your Kiln. My masters were not pleased. I do not wallow, foe

Oats, nor do I blame. But perhaps you need to hear what I know to be true, whether you will accept it or not. None of what you endure now would be necessary had I succeeded when first I came to Ul-wundulas. Hispartha would be under my rule, there would be no war in the Lot Lands, the fortress of the Grey Bastards would yet be standing, and much of the hardship and death your hoof has suffered since would have been avoided. You toppled my designs, you and Jackal and dread Fetching. And yet now you harass me over the revelation of another. Shall I again allow you to stand in the way of a peace that will rid your land of human rule?"

"Why? What do you care if the frails take the Lots?"

"Does your hatred prevent you from accepting me as a mongrel?"

"Tyrkania ain't ruled by half-orcs, Crafty. The sultans' skin may be a different shade, but they're as human as any in Ursaria's court. Hispartha may want to put chains on us again, but I wager your empire enslaves more people in a day than the number that live in all of Ul-wundulas."

"It is not my empire. And when I speak of my masters I do not mean the sultans."

"The fucking Black Womb, then. Don't try to sell me they care about our freedom."

Oats stood. He would not waste his breath questioning this sack of lies further. Hells, Oats wanted to strangle him, toss his fat carcass into one of the animal pens outside.

The wizard gazed up at him with regret.

Passing the scowling Fuqtus, Oats made for the door.

"Oats."

He turned at Crafty's voice.

"I cannot overcome your disbelief. I can but hope you will hear me when I tell you that should we come to the end of this alive, you will have what you wish for."

The wizard's words were quiet. There was no mockery or amusement in them. Hells, he sounded in earnest.

Oats knew better.

Sleep proved easy to come by in Robledondo. The soft cots, the clean bunkhouse, the near silence of the woods beyond the walls, it all conspired with the heat of the day to create a lulling island surrounded by the last months of war and the long road. And there was little else to do.

After two languid days in the compound, the only danger the hoof faced was having their supper stolen by the ever-brazen bear cubs. As for Crafty, he spent his time strolling about, gazing at the animals, Fuqtus dogging his steps. He spoke merrily to the caretakers, receiving laughs and jovial responses from some, grumbles and curt nods from others. The wizard spent his nights on the upper floor of the lodge in a room beside the prince's, Ahlamra said. She'd been invited up to dine with Crafty the first morning after the hoof's arrival. Again, Mannrique had not been present. Crafty confided the prince preferred to eat alone. Otherwise, he revealed nothing about the man or his intentions for him.

A rider came before the morning was out to take Ahlamra's message to the chief. Culprit volunteered to go with him, to ensure the missive wasn't burned or put in the Crown's hands, but Sluggard and Thresher wouldn't allow it. Mongrel hog-riders were outlaws in the kingdom and any caught without proper escort would likely be killed on sight. It was too long a journey to risk. This was the greatest test of their trust in Crafty, Ahlamra said. As a precaution against Hisparthan eyes, she had written the message in Urzhar and instructed the rider to make haste for the castile. Tarif would translate the words and send his own men to bring it to Fetching. Crafty's man was to wait for a reply. Unhampered by a churlish noble's purposefully slow pace, he'd make better time than the Bastards and, with luck, be back inside of three weeks.

In the meantime, the hoof could only wait.

Oats put a duty rotation in place. One mongrel with Ahlamra, one in the stables, one outside the compound gate, one keeping an eye on Crafty whenever he left the lodge. The last task bordered on pointless. In the close confines behind the walls, not even Hoodwink could trail the wizard unnoticed. Oats also wanted to put someone on Mannrique, but Ahlamra cut the notion down, claiming it would strain the man needlessly. Robledondo wasn't large and the lumbering prince was always about. If he approached one of the animal pens, the caretakers would seamlessly give over whatever they were doing. Oats had seen him feed the leopard, shovel goat shit, clean the rabbit hutch, and brush the bull. He worked with diligence, his face contented in the presence of his beasts.

The duty at the gate proved the most taxing.

The mouros were unpleasant company. Beyond their ugliness, they smelled sour and were determined to make a hell for whatever half-orc stood watch with them. They farted with every other breath and labored noisily to drag phlegm from their throats, spitting whatever slimy foulness they excavated upon the Bastards' boots. Culprit lost his temper and kicked at the bearded one, but the dwarf danced away unhurt and capered with his fellow as if he'd won some victory. Oats reminded Culprit that the mouros were armed and it would be a fool-ass death to have an axe planted in his back by a piss-reeking creature that barely reached his ass crack. But Robledondo's odd little guards didn't limit their torments to disgusting antics.

They seemed to know things.

During Sluggard's first turn at the gates they kept leering at him while dropping pairs of pinecones from between their legs. Polecat returned from his watch fuming. Thresher finally got him to confide that the mouros spent the entire time galloping around him, one bent over behind the other while clutching its waist, mocking the form of a centaur.

"It's fucking Crafty," Polecat declared. "He's told those little shits to torment us!"

"To what end?" Ahlamra asked, not without sympathy but neither was she convinced.

Cat gave an anguished, flummoxed shrug. "To get his cock hard?!"

That night, Polecat's screams returned with fresh ardor.

In the morning, Oats told Thresher he would be taking her post at the gate.

The mouros sprang from their benches when he came out, creased faces eager and grinning. Oats looked down at them, unblinking. Maybe Crafty *had* whispered in their ears, given them stones to hurl.

Maybe they possessed some hoodoo of their own, a way of seeing like Thoon. The cyclops had said his heart was a rotting wound. Let these dwarves behold that. Whatever they knew about Oats, whatever they saw in him, he invited them to wield it against him. The smiles sloughing from their pallid cheeks, the mouros' eyes faltered. They skulked back to their benches and made no further move nor sound.

Not long after, the gate opened and Fuqtus ducked through. Oats waited for Crafty to follow him out, but the demon was alone. He came to stand beside Oats, placing the butt of his axe haft in the leaf litter, a hand resting atop the curve of the great, sweeping blade.

"What gods do you worship?"

The *jhevadi*'s sudden, rumbled question made Oats squirmy, but he refused to let it show.

"None."

"Yet you know them to be real."

"Witnessed some of their workings, I reckon. None of what I've seen needs to be worshipped. Religion is just loads of hogshit made up by folk looking to have power over others."

Fuqtus laughed, deep and throaty.

"What's funny?"

"Uhad said you hoof-orcs were a breed of flagrant heathens."

"That's us. But he don't know us as well as he thinks he does."

The demon's closed lips bulged as he rolled his tongue across his teeth. The response had galled him.

"I have oft heard your brethren swear by the hells."

"So?"

"So you hold to no gods yet believe there is existence after this life?"

"Got to go somewhere when it's over."

"And you believe what follows will be worse."

Oats shrugged. "We wouldn't fight so hard to stay alive if it were better."

"If we are bound for the hells, why not the heavens?"

"A body drops when it dies, Fuck You. It don't float away."

"It does when it is burned. Was this not the practice of your brotherhood? To commit their corpses to flame, to smoke, which lifts to the sky?"

"That just saved us the effort of digging. Besides, we had a big damn oven. The dead don't catch fire unless someone lights them. You die alone out in the badlands, the buzzards don't build you a fucking pyre. They eat you and shit you out. Your bones lie in the dirt, turn to dust. It all goes into the ground one road or another."

Fuqtus's fingers kneaded the metal of the brazen blade beneath them. "I know the gods to be real. I have seen the face of mine. This axe was hers. Bhadra wielded it in one hand, one of six calamities to match the number of her mighty arms."

Oats thought of the giants beneath Kalbarca and tried to imagine a woman with two more arms than them slinging that chopper around.

"Hope she ain't looking to get it back from you," he said.

Fuqtus's craggy face was grave. "She is long dead, her legend pilfered and perverted by those that now rule in her name. You did not err when you said religions were created to grant power to tyrants. In Ul-Kadim I was nothing, flesh chattel enslaved to the High Conciliatrix, one among many disposable thousands. Yet the Sixth Thunder spoke to me, urged me to risk the life I did not own in defiance of the priestesses. And so I liberated the weapon and escaped, hounded by slave catchers and branded by names. Fuqtus the Idolater. The Dissenter. The Untamed. One day I will return to Ul-Kadim, to the temple-palace. That day, the Sixth Thunder—with me as its instrument—will cleave the skull of the High Conciliatrix and spill the blood of all in her sisterhood, ridding Bhadra of false prophets and returning her to glory.

"Wish you luck with that," Oats muttered.

"You wonder why I tell you this. The answer is simple. You know nothing of me. Perhaps you care not to, but I would have you hear from my own lips that I despise slavers and tyrants. And I would not pledge the strength of my arm nor the love of my heart to one. You say Uhad knows your brethren less than he believes. I say you know him not at all."

"I know you weren't there when he fucking betrayed us," Oats replied. "Could be no one knows him. Even you."

Fuqtus grinned bitterly. "What precisely did he betray, half-orc? As you say, I was not there, occupied as I was with other tasks in service to the same ends. So you may tell me where I have the tale wrong. He came to your Lot Lands, presented himself to the strongest leader among your kind, and offered his puissance as well as a plan to rid you of Hispartha's grip. He never intended to betray your Claymaster, nor did he. No, the only lies told were to a trio of upstarts scheming to usurp leadership of your tribe, a scheme that could—and did—undermine all he sought to accomplish. What did he betray, save a childhood fellowship to which he was never beholden? You are blinded by your insular, ignorant tribal ways, hoof-orc. Fortunately, Uhad is not so small-minded. Again he came to your leaders with an offer of aid and he is spurned as some viperous oath-breaker. He accepts your scorn, but that does not mean that I must!"

Oats let out a breath. "Shit. You fucking care a heap for him."

Fuqtus relaxed the tension in his quivering jaw. "How can I not? Uhad strives to make safe the land of his kindred even when he knows he will not be welcome among them. That is more worthy of love than the deeds of any god."

"Is that what he's trying to do?" Oats asked, feeling a fool-ass for wanting to believe. "Make the Lots safe?"

"He has never given me cause to doubt it."

"And the Black Womb? Don't imagine that's what they care about."

Fuqtus shook his head, the motion weighted by his horns. "The High Conciliatrix, the Crown of Hispartha, the Black Womb. They are all powers in this world that existed before any of us drew breath. Some will survive long after we are dead. Many souls are mastered by them, yet some make a choice to flee from them, to fight them . . . to *use* them, all in the hope of one day being free from them. Uhad has not confided in me what he wishes his future to be, but I dream of a day he asks my help in escaping the bonds of sultans and sorcerers. I know what my ready answer will be."

Fuqtus hefted the Sixth Thunder and returned through the gate, leaving Oats with a hornet's nest of thoughts.

Thresh relieved him at midday, bringing bread, raisins, cheese, and a jar of wine. No meat had been offered since they came to the compound.

"They look . . . docile," Thresh said, peering at the dwarves.

Oats grunted an agreement. He tore the cheese in halves and handed them down to the mouros. Their eyes darted up, wary and sharp, but they took the morsels.

"Pleasant spot you've got here," he told them, and went through the gate. The monkeys leaped to the ropes fronting their cage as he passed.

Oats ate as he walked, devouring the bread and guzzling the wine. He could hear his mother's voice in his head, telling him not to eat so fast, as he did every time food went into his mouth. He wondered if she knew about Warbler, about him being free of Dog Fall, free of the plague. Likely not. What news reached Father from Fetching was unlikely to be passed to Beryl. Once, she would have demanded to know. Now, was she even leaving that little house in Salduba? Thistle would see that she did. Oats reckoned the woman hated him, saddling her with all his burdens as he'd done. The last swallow of wine went down bitter.

Oats heard laughter behind the rabbit hutch.

Stepping around, he found Mannrique tussling in the dirt with the bear cubs. Their rolling, their playful biting and raspy little yowls drew a string of throaty giggles from the man. Oats huffed a laugh of his own at the sight. Mannrique looked up to see him staring and the glee fell from his face, replaced by a deep embarrassment. He untangled himself from the bears and lurched to his feet, hurrying away with his head tucked low, the ass of his shoddy breeches shedding dust. The cubs bounded along after him.

Oats didn't purposefully follow, but the prince retreated to the stables, where Oats was bound to give Ugfuck the raisins. Unwilling to let the strangeness of some blue-blood frail hamper the care of his hog, Oats kept his course. The bear cubs had been scooped up by vigilant grooms before they entered the stables, but none said a word to prevent Oats. Mannrique leaned over the fence of the central paddock, scratching the giant ram. He tensed as Oats moved behind him to Ugfuck's stall, but did not turn.

Ug snuffled, smelling the raisins, and nearly knocked Oats over in his eagerness.

"Hells," Oats chuckled, offering his cupped palm to the sopping, searching snout. "I know you ain't starving." He noticed Mannrique's head had turned just slightly at his laughter. "They got names? Them cubs?"

The man turned away again. "No."

"My chief does that," Oats said. "Doesn't name her mounts. 'Course, the rest of us name them for her. Don't be surprised if you hear those cubs being called Dangleberry, Cunnylicker, and Small Rug one day here soon."

Mannrique did not reply.

"Speaking of names," Oats said, fishing into the hemp sack for more raisins. "Which of them dwarves is Biru?"

The prince's hand paused in its scratching. "Beiru. With the beard."

The way Mannrique said it gave Oats a realization. "That's what his name means? With the Beard?"

"In Old Kartani. Yes."

"Please tell me Britu means Without the Beard."

"With the Teeth."

"Ah . . ." Oats was out of raisins and began idly rubbing Ug's back. It took a moment for his hand and eyes to reconcile the change in the hog's flesh. It was smoother, the angry patches of moist rash had dried out and begun to fade. Robledondo's stables were the best kept Oats had ever seen, but he realized it wasn't simply the stall emitting a fresh aroma. It was Ugfuck.

"My hog smells like flowers," Oats said, stooping to inspect closer. "And his sweat scale is nearly gone! I ain't ever been able to clear that up."

Oats straightened to find Mannrique coming over. His steps were hesitant, but an excited expression had taken over his flat-nosed face.

"*Calendula*," the prince said. "A blossom from Traedria. I had some here, dried. Ground up and revivified with honey it makes a promising salve. It was difficult to apply because he kept trying to eat it."

"I just wager he did!" Oats said, looking again with awe at Ug's healthy hide. "I'm damn grateful!"

"I'm afraid it's not a cure," Mannrique said, stopping just shy of entering the stall. "The affliction will always be with him, yet it can be relieved in this way."

"Afraid there ain't many Traedrian flowers in the Lots."

The prince slumped, crestfallen. "Of course."

"But hells if we won't be glad of them while we're here, eh Ug?"

"That's his name? Ug?" the prince asked, a smile twitching his lip. "I had wondered."

"Ugfuck," Oats nodded.

Mannrique flinched and sputtered. "Pardon?"

Oats gestured at the entire hog. "Because he's ugly as fuck."

"Yes . . . I see . . ."

"Reckoned everyone else was going to be calling him that. That's the way mongrels are in the hoofs. So, I just went ahead and gave it to him proper. Rob their quivers, I reckon was what I meant to do."

"Did it work?" Mannrique asked.

Oats thought about it. "Mostly. Them that tried to insult him worse I just threatened to punch. Or did punch."

The prince shuffled away a step. "Well, I think he is wonderful."

"Me too," Oats said, smiling and knuckling Ug between the eyes. He stepped out of the stall and pointed to the barbarians penned just outside the stables. "Of course, you got some of the best pigs I ever seen."

Mannrique straightened. "Oh! Thank you."

Mention of the animals sent the prince moving toward their pen. Oats walked along beside him.

"They ever been ridden?" he asked as they reached the rail. Frails did not often possess the strength to master a hog.

"Not since coming to Robledondo," the prince replied. "They were broken to the saddle in Korpelanos. I bought them after the races two . . . or is it three? Madre, yes, three years ago now."

Oats leaned on the fence to look at the hogs. "Races?"

"The hippodrome built by Emperor Tauraxiphos is still used for such things," Mannrique replied, as if that answered it. "These four were injured, fated to be slaughtered, so I bought them."

"Wouldn't know they were ever hurt to look at them," Oats said truthfully. "You got a gift, Mannrique." From the corner of his eye, Oats saw the man shift uncomfortably. "Three years, though, spoiled as they've been, they'll either be easy as a lamb to saddle or they'll murder you to keep it off, depending on the animal. Each will be different. Best not to try, being earnest."

"Crafty says he will need one for his use soon," Mannrique said. "Perhaps I should try to . . . dissuade him."

Just saying the word was a struggle for the prince. The notion seemed to make him sick.

"He'll be fine," Oats muttered, remembering that Crafty had come to the Lots having never ridden a hog. Fat fuck had even refused a saddle. Jackal had thought he would be dumped on his lard-laden ass, but the wizard had ridden all the way to the Old Maiden without trouble. "He's got a gift too."

"Do you know him well?"

"We don't know anyone well outside our hoof," Oats said, for lack of a better answer. "Just the way of things in the Lots."

Mannrique stared into the hog pen and gave a shallow nod.

A thought struck Oats. "You called him Crafty."

Mannrique grew nervous. "Should I not? That is what he insisted I call him when we met, since we were kin. He said, though my nephew, we were near enough in years to be brothers. And his brothers call him Crafty."

Oats looked down to scrape his boot on the fence railing, hoping he hid his grimace in time. Brothers? Hells. No matter what Fuqtus claimed about Crafty, Oats felt a powerful urge to go break the wizard's smiling face that very instant.

"It's the best name for him," Oats muttered. He looked up and forced a smile. "Like Ugfuck. It don't leave anything for folk to guess at."

"And your name?" Mannrique asked. "I was told when you arrived, but forgive me, I was . . . distracted."

Oats huffed. "Reckon that can happen when a gaggle of half-orcs arrives at your door uninvited." He hooked a thumb at himself. "Oats."

"Oats, yes. Thank you. And you are welcome here. You were not uninvited. Crafty told me to expect the arrival of the Lot Lands' emissaries."

Oats noticed the choice of words. Crafty *told* him. Not asked.

"Never reckoned we'd be getting help from a blue blood," he said. "Not to sound an ingrate, but why you doing it?"

Mannrique did not look at him. His big hands grasped the fence railing, twisting slightly forward and back. "My father used to speak of Ul-wundulas. The land he relinquished. It nearly cost him his crown. He was embittered by that failure. It would have been the largest of his reign if not for . . ."

The prince trailed off.

"Not for what?" Oats asked.

"His sons." Mannrique shook his unkempt head, pushing out a nervous chuckle.

"Not sure I follow. How does aiding my chief fix that?"

"Oh. Oh, it doesn't." The prince lifted a knuckle to brush his flattened nose. "My father wanted to subdue the Lots from the moment of their creation, to bring them back into the kingdom. But he lacked the strength. His hope was that my brother would, but Girón was . . ."

"Mad-fuck crazy."

Mannrique ducked his head, "Not enough to fight a war with your kind. My father kept trying to turn his viciousness south, but battle did not interest Girón. He relished . . . smaller horrors. And I was, I am, lacking in every way for such a venture. But I've always wanted to see Ul-wundulas."

"What you've got here is a far sight better, believe me," Oats said.

"I know what Robledondo is," Mannrique said softly, though there was an ember in his voice.

Oats waited for more, but the man merely gazed morosely at the hogs.

What was this frail doing? Why was he allowing Crafty to wield him against the Crown? Was Mannrique as mad as his brother? Far as Oats could see the man gained nothing throwing in with the hoofs and conspiring with Tyrkania. Did he even know about Crafty's sorcery? About the Black Womb? Did he truly believe he was Crafty's uncle, or was he just too craven to challenge the sham? Knowing he should leave it alone, that he should allow Ahlamra to deal with the infuriating threads of the wizard's plots, Oats told himself to walk away. Yet all the questions, all the warnings, were cooking on his tongue, a heartbeat from being served steaming to the prince.

He was spared from that fool-ass urge by the arrival of Britu.

The dwarf sauntered toward the prince with a rolling gait, Thresher a few paces behind. Britu looked up at Mannrique, pinching his own throat with two fingers and a thumb before making a wiggling motion.

"Here?" the man said, voice strained as his eyes jerked across the compound toward the gate. Without another word, he ducked his head and hurried away, his heavy stride directed at the lodge.

Oats shot a questioning look at Thresher.

"Some chinless frail on a spavined horse at the gate," she explained. "Got the Crown's banner, plus his own. Four men with him."

"Gather the hoof."

It didn't take long. Most of the Bastards had seen Thresh come through with the dwarf and realized something was brewing. They met near the bull's pen in the rough center of the compound, all save Sluggard, who was taking a turn as Crafty's shadow.

"Anyone seen them?" Oats asked.

Culprit pointed. "There."

Crafty and Sluggard came around from behind the caretakers' bunkhouse.

"I understand we have visitors!" the wizard proclaimed as he drew closer. "And sooner than expected."

Britu passed by on his way back to the gate.

"Go with him, Fuqtus," Crafty said. "Make sure Volador's men remain outside."

The demon moved off to catch up with the dwarf, his fleshy azure tail giving Oats gooseflesh.

Soon, a lone rider came into the compound. Thresh was right about the horse. It was a miserable beast, clomping along on swollen joints. The man upon the aged mare's back was deeply tanned, his mustachios forming a lintel over a small mouth. Thresh was right about his chin too. This frail's neck began after his lower lip. He wore no armor, only the doublet and tight-fitting hose of a noble. An empty scabbard hung from his belt, the absent sword no doubt in the hands of Fuqtus or the mouros outside the gate.

"Anselmo Volador," Crafty told the hoof quietly. "Tax collector for Her Majesty. A hand of ice in a glove of velvet."

"The horse is a cruel touch," Ahlamra said.

Crafty gave her a knowing look.

"What about the horse?" Culprit whispered.

"Mannrique loves animals," Ahlamra replied. "The ailing horse will unsteady him."

Volador reined up, but did not dismount. He cast a placid look at the mongrels and turned back to await the prince, coming now with a small coffer cradled to his belly.

"Highness," Volador said, coughing slightly as he dismounted. He doffed his burgundy cap to reveal thinning hair. A groom stepped forward to take his horse in hand.

Mannrique halted, leaving a conspicuously long distance between himself and the other man.

"The mayordomo keeps our collection at the castle," Mannrique said, sounding peevish.

"I come on other business, Highness," Volador replied, his voice quavering as he held back another cough.

Mannrique's large hands fidgeted with the box. "What business?"

"Let us speak in private, Highness."

Mannrique hesitated.

"And now we see . . ." Crafty whispered.

The prince began to turn toward the lodge, but as his body swung to face the hoof he paused. His eyes darted up, glanced off the Bastards, and retreated again to the ground. But not before looking Oats in the eye for the barest of moments.

"I am more comfortable out of doors," Mannrique muttered. "We will speak here."

Volador rose slightly on his toes and cleared his throat. "As you will, Highness. Her Majesty is concerned for you. Distressing news has come to her ear. She fears you have been preyed upon by foreign culls and half-breed ruffians. She wonders if perhaps your good nature does not allow you to extricate yourself from their clutches. In this, she would help you, if you desire. You have but to say the word and you will be rid of these . . . uncouth influences."

"That is kind of her," Mannrique replied, still unable to address the tax collector directly. "However, I am in no such need. Nor danger. Envoys of Tyrkania and the Lot Lands have requested my patronage. I have given it."

Volador's head cocked a bit to the side. "Why, Highness?"

Mannrique opened the coffer and looked at its contents. He drew out a ring, forced it down the length of a prodigious finger and snapped the box closed. At last he looked at Volador squarely.

"My intention is to introduce them at court, as is my right as Prince of the Royal House of Trastorias. You can tell Her Majesty . . . you can tell Ursaria, that we will await her invitation."

Crafty spun fluidly around, brimming with triumph. He offered a hand to Ahlamra. "Come. Let us make our introductions." The gold in his smile flashed. "I hope you are rested, my friend Bastards. For we are soon to duel with monarchs."

TWENTY-NINE

MAGERIT. CITY OF THE QUEEN. Heart of Hispartha.

And the biggest fucking place Oats had ever seen.

"Hells overburdened," Culprit said, wrinkling his nose. "You can smell it from here."

He wasn't wrong. The hoof viewed the city from the west, their vantage provided by the final puckers of the Sierra Drakós behind them. The wind was laden with odors, too muddled to discern, but it was a long trot from pleasant.

The walls surrounding Magerit stood upon broken hills footed by the Chorismano River, a thin thread of silver shining through gaunt tableland. Two bridges bore the road across the water on their backs. The more central was a flat, elegant span supported by marching arches, inherited from the Imperium. It was filled with travelers coming and going. The other bridge was humpbacked, and shorter due to the river narrowing as it bent around the flank of the hills. It stood empty beneath the western end of the city, where the hills were highest and crowned by a squat fortress. The bridge itself was guarded by straddling towers at both ends. The road beyond wound steeply up to a fortified gate bulging from the shadow of the citadel.

"The Furiosa is the Queen's private access to the city," Sluggard said. "Any who attempt to cross it without dispensation are killed."

"Don't suppose Plucker's got that," Polecat said with a smirk, casting an eye back to Mannrique, still traversing the rough terrain behind the hoof with Crafty and Fuqtus.

Their journey from Vokastria had brought them through the mountains, their guide the prince himself. In truth, the man was a skilled rider, but no frail on a foal would ever outpace a hoof-rider on a long trek across unforgiving ground and, with the end in sight, the Bastards had pulled ahead.

The past days had revealed a different Mannrique. His habitual reluctance vanished in the saddle. He led them through the passes with unfaltering surety, keeping to himself at the front. He brought no one from Robledondo to serve him and saw not only to the care of his horse but those ridden by Ahlamra and Fuqtus, as well. The demon had been given use of a hardy, grey draft animal to bear his large frame. No stirrup would accommodate his cloven feet, but their lack did not hamper him, neither did the need to carry his axe, which was too large to strap to his tack. Crafty had indeed taken one of the prince's hogs as mount and, as Oats wagered, had no trouble with the beast. The Bastards quickly named the pig Muck Shovel.

"Because it's used to moving a heap of shit," Polecat delighted in informing Crafty.

The Sierra Drakós contained no settlements that the hoof saw, though they only slept beneath the open sky once. Caves used by highland shepherds and known to Mannrique sheltered them the other three nights. He spoke little during their rests, contenting himself with the playing of a lute.

Music wasn't commonly heard in the Lots. Oats had only ever encountered a few wandering minstrels at Sancho's, the sort of scoundrels with nowhere else to go and not enough grit to survive once they were there. None played or sang with Mannrique's skill. Unlike the desperate rakes at Sancho's grasping for coin or cunt or a free meal, the prince played deftly, humbly. If it were possible to pluck the strings silently, Oats had no doubt Mannrique would have.

The rapt attention he received made him uncomfortable. Crafty's clapping, Ahlamra's gentle and earnest praise, Sluggard's requests for certain ballads, Culprit's questions about the songs and the instrument, all of it made him squirm, duck his head. But none of it stopped him. The balm of the music was a greater necessity than his need to hide. A man dying of thirst would crawl through a pit of scorpions and serpents to reach water.

By the fourth day, Mannrique wasn't riding so far ahead.

They'd left Robledondo a day after Anselmo Volador. The tax collector would be taking the roads, but Mannrique set off over the mountains. It was a shorter route, and faster for one who knew the passes as well as the prince.

"Arriving ahead of the messenger bearing word that we're coming," Thresher had said. "That's either really damn clever or it's going to get us killed."

"Crafty's notion, sure as shit," Polecat said.

Oats agreed. Mannrique and the wizard had shut themselves up in the lodge after Volador departed and not emerged until the next morning, proclaiming the start of their own journey. The Bastards were already in the saddle thanks to Ahlamra's intuition.

Now with Magerit before them, she took in the city as if studying a battlefield.

"What are you thinking, Rue?" Thresher asked.

"Small," Ahlamra replied.

Culprit stared at her, astounded, and pointed at the flood of rooftops, spires, and smoke plumes sprouting behind the walls. "Small? That?"

Ahlamra raised her eyebrows, shrugged. "Compared to Sardiz. Yes."

Sluggard smiled. "It contains wonders enough, Cul, don't fret."

"Bring me all the whores," Polecat said, lifting his nose to the wind.

Crafty and Fuqtus caught up and rode by without a word, continuing across the stretch of low hills cascading down to meet the road. The bend of his course suggested they were not going to the queen's bridge. Farther back, Mannrique had slowed to a halt. He sat his horse and gazed at Magerit, the sight of the city further weighing down his already slumping shoulders.

"Who wants to wager he'll turn around?" Polecat said.

"What will that mean for us if he does?" Sluggard asked.

No one answered.

"Ay!" Culprit called out so suddenly it made the rest of them jump. The young mongrel made a coaxing gesture at the prince. "Plucker! Come ride with us. Likely to get lost down there without you."

"Hells," Thresher whispered. "He's sure to tuck tail n—"

Mannrique nudged his horse forward.

Culprit gloated in the face of his brethren's stares.

"A smile worked the first time," he told them. "Figured just fucking asking is an even better invitation."

The prince rode up to them, looking for all the earth like the city was about to eat him.

Ahlamra dipped her chin at Crafty's back. "Despite Uhad's unceremonious approach, I think it would be best, my prince, if we entered the city together."

Mannrique only gave a doleful nod.

"True Bastards," Oats said. "Let's show these civilized frails a mongrel hoof."

They took his meaning, forming up around Ahlamra and Mannrique. Cat and Culprit took the front, Oats and Sluggard the wings, Thresher and Hood the flanks. Mannrique produced the small coffer from his saddlebag and retrieved from it a thick gold chain bearing a medallion. The bull of Hispartha stood embossed upon the face. The prince draped the chain over his shoulders, mouth turning down further as it settled.

Culprit turned in the saddle. "Which bridge?"

"The Emperor's," Mannrique murmured.

"That's the long one, right?" Culprit asked. "Not the death-if-we-ain't-welcome one."

"Let us hope so," the prince said.

They spurred toward the city, hogs surrounding horses. They

caught up to Crafty just before striking the road, and the wizard eased his hog until he rode beside Mannrique. Fuqtus stayed out front on his sturdy horse. They had no banner, but a mighty-thewed, half-naked, brazen-horned, blue-skinned demon holding a giant, gilded axe preceded them better than any colorful rag. They kept their mounts at a walk, passing wains and oxcarts and footsore peddlers. The folk on the road made way with curses and breathy oaths, those that weren't rooted and dumbstruck. One merchant saw them coming and forced his line of porters carrying hods of charcoal off the road. As the hoof passed, Oats looked at the soot-covered laborers and met the wide eyes of a half-orc.

The words boiled up in Oats, unbidden, but he let them free.

"Live in the saddle!"

"Die on the hog!" the True Bastards answered without pause, announcing the arrival of the Lot Lands to the queen's city.

They crossed the bridge without challenge, but their presence stirred all those they passed. Many going away from the city turned around. Boys sitting on the bridge's rails abandoned their fishing rods to run beside them. Fuqtus kept an unhurried pace, allowing the spark of their appearance to send a blaze racing ahead. The city gates, larger than the castile's, were a clogged morass of the curious and confused by the time they reached them at the top of the hill. Mule teams and wine carts were beleaguered islands in a flood of folk, all shouting questions, yelling abuses, thrown amok by the wildfire of fresh rumor.

Fuqtus pressed on, his fearsome appearance and the size of his horse acting as a plow. The throng stumbled and shambled out of the way, the heat in their raised voices intensifying. Armed men pushed through from the other side, emerging from the shadows beneath the gate, the hafts of their spears shoving and butting the more stubborn aside. Breaking through, their scowls melted as they beheld the *jhevadi*.

"Move this rabble from our path," Fuqtus rumbled. "They impede the entrance of their prince."

The men-at-arms gawked, eyes moving swiftly but seeing nothing as they struggled to understand. The jostling crowd snapped one frail out of his stupor. He spun and pushed a furious merchant on his ass, turning back to the hoof with a set jaw and new resolve. His stare settled on Mannrique, a man on a horse, something he could reconcile. The next instant, he saw the medallion.

"Clear the way!" he shouted at his fellows.

Oats didn't relish seeing people battered and bullied aside just so he could pass. By the look of him, neither did Mannrique. It took some doing, but a path was forced through the crowd and the riders entered Magerit.

"I'll summon a proper escort," the guard said.

"He has one," Crafty replied.

"But those arbalests—"

Fuqtus did not slow. Leaving the men and the gate behind, they proceeded into the pungent, bustling embrace behind the walls. The invading swell of tradesmen and merchants were met with a counter-skirmish of beggars, buskers, and urchins. But the presence of the hoof blunted the fervor of the assault, the pleas for coin and offers to act as guide stalled by the spectacle of hogs and foreigners. Still, they were at the mercy of the city's inbound current. Slow-moving carters and their jostling wares frustrated the drovers, splitting the streams of livestock destined for the slaughter yards not far from the gate. Finally, they pushed into a plaza where ragpickers and soap sellers hawked their goods, decrying the stock of their competitors in the same breath.

"The hells . . ." Culprit marveled, spying a woman, stripped to the waist—with an ill-butchered piece of meat tied around her neck—being driven through the plaza and lashed by a pair of men. As they passed, Oats thought he saw a pair of testicles sewn onto the cut.

"Caught trying to pass ewe for beef!" one of the men kept calling between licks with his switch. "Caught trying to pass ewe for beef!"

Oats and Culprit shared a look, a laugh, and a shake of the head.

"I love it here already!" Polecat declared.

The twisting streets had no end. They passed through an entire section of the city devoted to the making of pottery, its inhabitants rendered ghosts by the clay dust. Oats spied a mongrel working hard at a kiln and couldn't help but wonder if this was the place the Claymaster had first been in servitude in some dim past when he was known by another name and had yet to mount a hog, fight a war, and endure the torture of the plague's creation.

Beyond the earthenware district, Oats had a moment's alarm when he caught sight of a group of Steel Friars coming down the lane. With their long beards, plain cassocks, and baldrics bearing sword and buckler, they were indistinguishable from the goats he'd fought in Ellerina. No chance they could be, though, this far from the Outmarches. There were more temples bordering the city's plazas venerating more gods than even Knuckle Child could name. Still, Oats kept waiting for one of the Steel Friars to point an accusing finger and proclaim him the merciless cunt who had set fire to their brother. They gave him a look, but it was no different from the one the hoof received from every frail in Magerit.

Their mounted band dragged a spell of bewilderment everywhere they went, stuttering the shouted enticements of merchants, slowing the swaggering steps of richly dressed men, muting the laughter and singing coming from dozens of taverna patios. Twice they were stopped by patrols of city guard, but the sight of Mannrique's medallion quashed any further hindrance to their passage.

The streets leading westward took them higher. As the cobbles climbed the hills, the air became cleaner, the bustling plazas yielding to gardens. The street sellers vanished and the houses of the gods bowed to dwellings of the nobility.

At last they halted at a low wall fronted by fruiting lemon trees. Mannrique came down from his horse and made to knock upon the door set into the wall, but paused, leveling his raised fist to push the door inward without resistance. His face settled into a sad resignation as he led his horse through. Oats and the others dismounted and led their animals into a yard littered with discarded wine jugs. A three-story house stood before them, the first floor comprised of a columned gallery with an open inner courtyard beyond. A small stable sat to the right of the yard, its thatching in dire need of replacing.

"The animals will need to share stalls," Mannrique said, taking Ahlamra's horse and his own.

What fodder remained in the empty stable was rotted and the troughs were dry.

"I'll sort this," Mannrique mumbled.

The Bastards untacked their hogs and got them sorted into the four stalls. It was cramped, forcing Ugfuck and the draft horse to be tied up outside.

"We'll see to them better shortly," Mannrique promised, gesturing toward the house.

They went through the arch into the court. Laughter drew their attention up to the veranda on the second floor. Someone ran by, a woman from the sound of the giggling. Next came the slight tinkling of bells. More laughter. Across the court, a naked woman scampered briefly into view, casting looks over her shoulder as she darted from one open room off the gallery to another. She failed to notice the perplexed half-orcs, scowling demon, and dispirited prince. Oats reckoned the mask on her face—fashioned into the likeness of a rabbit—may have impeded her vision.

A grinning Polecat moved to pursue, but was stopped by Thresher grabbing his ear.

They heard the tinkling again as a man wearing nothing but a blindfold ran down the gallery just to their left. The bells were dangling from his cods. Culprit had to dodge out of the naked frail's eagerly rushing path, but the man sensed the motion and changed course, laughing as he darted to give chase. His widely flailing and groping hands slapped Fuqtus's bare midriff. The demon swatted the man to the ground with a lazy backhand.

Oats didn't think he'd ever seen anything move as gracelessly as a naked man with bells tied to his nut basket trying to remove a blindfold after being knocked on his bare ass. Eventually he worked the rag up to his forehead. Seeing the assembled intruders, he gave a constricted little cry and tried to crab-crawl away, bells clinking.

"Loukas." Mannrique sighed, drawing the man's attention.

"'Rique?" came the squeaking reply. The naked frail shot to his feet. He was of an age with Mannrique, but there the similarities ended. Loukas was lithe, handsome, and dark-haired, a stark contrast to the cumbersome, homely, towheaded prince. "I . . . I didn't, didn't expect you back! When did . . . when did you arrive? Just now, of course! I hope. Oh, if only you'd sent word. I'd have had a feast laid. And half-orcs! Madre, you do surprise! How . . . how long will you be staying?"

The babbling drew no fewer than five curious unclad women, all wearing masks, peeking around corners and over the upper verandas. And those were just the ones Oats could see.

"Loukas, where are the grooms?" Mannrique asked.

"I haven't owned a horse in years," Loukas replied, smiling as he shrugged with overwrought contrition. "I dismissed the stable hands."

Mannrique's head lowered. "And how many of these women serve here?"

Loukas's face scrunched. "Two?"

"Is my house now a brothel?"

"I see time has not made you less a bloodless moralist, 'Rique," Loukas said, slipping the blindfold off his head and letting it drop to the floor. His smile was still in place, but his tongue had sharpened. "Do I get no thanks? No gratitude for keeping affairs here in your stead? For preventing greedy hands from taking what little is still yours?"

Mannrique shrank. "No, of course you do. I am grateful, Loukas. Truly."

"Then all is well!" the naked man exclaimed, throwing both arms high as his smile waxed full of bright teeth. "I will dress and then you shall tell me everything. There is certainly a tale here I am anxious to hear. I wager not even the lovely forests of Balsain have given you a taste for wine, eh? No matter! Come. I'll drink and you can talk."

"Later, Loukas, please," the prince replied, stepping away from the man's outstretched arm. "I am tired. I want solitude. Please see to the comfort of our guests."

"Guests?" Loukas gave a small scoffing laugh. "The half-breeds? Have you learned to jest at last? Surely these are only your newest exotic pets?"

Oats felt his brethren stiffen, but none uttered a vexed word or made an aggressive move.

"Guests, Loukas," Mannrique insisted. "I'll be in my chambers."

"Ahhhh..." Loukas said, taking a sliding step after the prince on his bare feet. "Your chambers are not suitable just now."

Mannrique's sullen stare darkened.

Loukas drew back, affronted. "You'd have me sleep in the servant's cottage? You may prefer to live as a rustic, my friend, but not I! This could have been avoided if only you'd sent word."

Mannrique held up his large hands to ward off further harsh words. "You're right. All is well. Do not be angry. I'm tired, Loukas."

"This city has ever taxed you, 'Rique," Loukas said, his bitterness switching to sympathy quicker than a snake strike. "Truly, I can't fathom what would cause you to come back. You know it's better when you stay away."

Crafty swept in. "After a cave for a chamber and pine cones for a bed, any room is a welcome comfort. Find you a place, uncle. When you emerge, all will be restored. Go, seek your repose."

Mannrique let out a grateful breath and slouched off.

"Uncle?" Loukas said, face curdled with confusion. "'Rique—"

He tried to go after the prince, but Crafty caught him in a one-armed scooping embrace, turning him around.

"We will let him rest, yes?"

Loukas tried to resist, but for all his suet Crafty was still a half-orc and he manhandled the naked frail with ease, ushering him back to the hoof. The wizard reached into his robes, produced a coin purse, and slapped it into Loukas's chest.

"We require feed for the animals. No grooms. I am certain my hoof-rider friends prefer to tend their own hogs. You do not look starved or filthy, so I assume a cook, scullion, and chamber maid remain in service. We will need provender for all you see here, however, and for a week at the least."

Loukas paled. "A week...?"

"Yes. The purse contains sufficient coin. I trust you are long-practiced in extracting the worth of your services from what remains. It would be best if you were swift."

Crafty released Loukas with a push toward the outer yard. The man spun, cradling the purse, slack-jawed.

"You'd have me go now?" He looked down at his nudity. "As I am?"

"Loukas," Crafty chuckled. "Since the day you left your swineherd father and embedded yourself in the prince's graces, I doubt you have ever shied from a reason to purchase new clothes."

"How do you kno—"

"Fuqtus. Please accompany our friend. For his safety."

The demon stepped forward.

Loukas scrambled back, pointing a trembling finger. "I'll not go anywhere with tha—"

Fuqtus seized the outstretched hand, wrenched the whining man around, and grabbed the back of his neck. Holding firm, he walked Loukas outside and across the outer court. The bells continued to tinkle.

"Shameless leech," Crafty said with distaste. "Suckling at a trusting breast."

"Yes," Ahlamra said. "Who would use the prince so?"

Ignoring the barb, Crafty walked to the stairs at the end of the gallery and ascended.

Polecat swaggered into the center of the inner court and put the blindfold on.

"My turn, ladies! Got another pair of bells?"

THE WHORES WERE SWEPT FROM the house. Three of the seven women claimed to serve there, but Ahlamra named two liars after a single glance.

"Those weren't the hands of a laundress," she told a curious Thresh.

"And the other?"

"Her eyes were too bold for a servant."

The third proved to be the scullery maid, as evident not only by her cracked hands and downcast eyes, but by the fact that they found her clothed and hidden away in the kitchen. She gave her name as Guiomar and was still a girl, but adept at keeping the house's plate from being pilfered when Loukas was distracted by his debaucheries. The cook was her father, away at the market fair in Anitorgis, to barter for Anvillese cheese. His name, she said, was Sancho.

"What do you wager he's a greasy, coin-biting ass-peddler?" Oats told Polecat, but his jest was met with little more than a huff. Cat was in a sour mood after the whores left untouched.

It wasn't long before others were filled with the same piss.

They were days in that house. Once the stables were put right, there was little to do but wander the verandas and languish in the courtyards. Oats had to keep reminding his brethren not to get drunk, for Loukas kept an ample store of wines. Hells, it was all Oats could do not to drown in a jug or three. There were rooms aplenty, more than he had ever seen outside the Kiln's hoof barracks. But those had been tiny cells compared to the bedchambers on the second floor of the city house. Still, there weren't enough for everyone to sleep alone, so the Bastards doubled up. The third floor was devoted to the prince's chambers. Loukas was ousted and Crafty installed. The wizard came down far more often than Mannrique, though the man did visit the stables to care for the horses. If Loukas bore a grudge, he hid it well. He was jovial, especially when in Ahlamra's presence.

"His quick and flippant acceptance of our presence is the mask of a seasoned sycophant," she confided in Oats. "He is long-acquainted with Mannrique's peculiarities and knows how best to weather them."

"So, he ain't a danger?" Oats asked.

"Not as long as his position isn't permanently threatened. He will abide, hoping our stay will be short. In many ways he moors the prince. A friend from boyhood, trusted, though entirely selfish. Mannrique would be hard-pressed to remain here without him. Crafty knows this or else I suspect Loukas would have been dealt with before we arrived."

"Is our stay going to be short? Been days, Rue. Polecat is a hair away from needing to be chained up. The damn forest was one thing, but trapped in this place is another. Sluggard is starting to crawl the walls too. And I can't say I blame them."

"This is the game as it is played. If Crafty saw some advantage to our being seen in the city, he would be parading us around without hesitation. Yet he knows when to be patient. Make no mistake, he eluded Jackal not by his ability to run but by knowing when to stay put. And Mannrique is a potent yet fragile pennant. Unfurl him in too strong a wind and he will tear free from the pole and fly away. Crafty is, wisely, waiting for the queen to make the next move."

Their eighth day in Magerit, she did.

A herald arrived at the gate. Loukas admitted him into the house and Mannrique came down to the courtyard. The herald handed Loukas the thickest parchment Oats had ever seen, weighted by a heavy wax seal. Loukas presented it to the prince. Mannrique broke the seal and hunched over the parchment as he read. Without a word, he gave it to Crafty, causing both Loukas and the herald to stiffen.

Crafty's eyes danced over the missive. Looking up, he nodded at the prince.

"We will attend," Mannrique told the herald. The man cut a swift exit. Mannrique's was even quicker. He vanished upstairs.

"We have been summoned," Ahlamra said. It wasn't a question.

"Oh, yes," Crafty replied, giving her the message.

"To the castle?" Sluggard asked with a mixture of eagerness and worry.

Ahlamra's brow gave the barest twitch as she read. "To a tournament."

THIRTY

OATS COULD STILL SMELL THE soap in his beard.

A late-morning breeze played across his face as the True Bastards rode northward through the city, sending cool wafts of lavender up his nostrils. The hoof all but shone. Their saddles were oiled, tack repaired, boots, brigands, and breeches rid of dust. Their swords were freshly whetted. But none carried a thrum. Stockbows were forbidden in the presence of the queen. There had been more than a little grousing, but Ahlamra was deaf to it. She insisted the thrums were left behind with the same calm fervor she used when ordering her brethren to bathe.

Loukas arranged for a trio of tubs to be delivered to the foreyard. Hired men hauled water from a fountain in a nearby plaza none of the Bastards had yet seen. Ahlamra and Thresher washed first while the brothers waited in the inner court.

"Which tub you use?" Polecat asked Thresh when she returned to the house damp and flush from scrubbing. "That's where I want to soak myself."

"See if you can tell from smelling the water," Thresher replied.

Cat raced outside.

"Let's go," Oats told Culprit, waving him along.

That left Sluggard and Hoodwink for last. A good match. No chance Hood would say anything about Slug's mutilation. In earnest, neither would any of the rest. But Cul and Cat—Oats himself—would be hard-pressed not to look. Grievous wounds always held a grim fascination. A mongrel hoped never to suffer them, but those who did, and survived, became something of a talisman, as if beholding them offered some manner of protection or, at the least, some assurance that such horrors could be borne. Fool-ass hogshit, really, and not something Hood would succumb to. His were the only scars that could rival Slug's. Truth was, Sluggard was so eager to be free of the confines of the house, he didn't balk at all. The tournament had put a fire in him Oats hadn't seen since before Winsome fell.

Two days after the summons, the time had come.

Loukas led, his velvet clothes as new and glossy as his horse. The faded and threadbare banner held in his gloved hand was an insult to his immaculate appearance, but the man carried it with convincing pride. Mannrique rode beside, drab and ratty as his flag, though the rearing bull and dragon on the banner showed a heap more vigor. Ahlamra had no power to make him bathe and the prince offered no chance, remaining hidden away since the summons. If Crafty made any attempt to improve his uncle's appearance, he failed. Mannrique did not even wear the medallion he'd donned to enter the city.

Behind the blue bloods came Crafty and Fuqtus. The wizard was a gem mine turned inside out and made flesh, the jewels sparkling against a sky of garish silks. His thin braid of a beard was freshly oiled, a garnet anchoring the end. Fuqtus was clad in nothing more than his waist wrap, though the plain white linen had been replaced with embroidered purple. Fresh plaits hung within his inky mane, the bronze bangles swapped for gold.

The Bastards formed a spearpoint with Ahlamra at the tip. Her loose-fitting eastern garments were fine linen, but she had added no ornaments save a headscarf of deep green. Loukas had tried to gift her with jewelry, but was refused.

"My home is not a rich land," Ahlamra told him.

Loukas had grinned, some gaudy web of precious metal hanging limply between his hands. "But Sardiz is said to be the wealthiest place in the world."

"The Lots are not," she said. "And they are the home I speak of. The home I am here to speak for."

Her hoof now sat tall in their saddles behind her.

Their progress through the city was again marked by hundreds of eyes, but where they first entered unexpected, transfixing Magerit's daily roiling with their oddity, they now found the folk already stilled, awaiting their second appearance. People clustered at the edges of the lanes, loitered in alleys, leaned out from windows and over balustrades. They began as colorfully bedecked nobles in brocaded cloth, the men with mustachios and swords, the women with pearls and monstrous headwear. They tracked Mannrique's passage with indifference, acting as if they had not stirred from their homes to watch him. The Tyrkanian mongrel and his demon startled and amused. The half-breeds on their swine drew nothing but scorn. The number of blue-blood frails who wrinkled their noses upon seeing the Bastards made Oats smile.

"We've never smelled better," he told Ugfuck, rubbing the hog's meaty shoulder.

The walled stone houses on the heights of the hills were left behind. Steadily, the people increased in number even as they diminished in wealth. The roofs of the guildhalls were packed, the workshops and storefronts suckling at their teats trading only in ogling this morning. The first of the jeers and shouted abuses began.

"Murdering mongrels!"

"Ravagers! Rapers!"

"Filthy, ash-colored animals!"

By the time the poorer reaches of Magerit surrounded them, the cries had become a humming hive, savage and rendered wordless by a horde of throats. Oats could see Mannrique at the head of their little column, a big man on his small favored mare, riding through the hot hatred stoked by the sootskins he kept as company. The prince's head lifted for the first time since they set out from his house.

He had cowered from the silent nobles, but in the face of the baying peasants, he straightened.

They came to the walls.

A gate yawned ahead, the mob kept away by a crescent of halberdiers, backed by mounted cavaleros. One rider nudged his horse forward and exchanged words with Loukas, swallowed by the tumult from the crowd. They moved on, the cavaleros falling in around them as they proceeded under the gate, exiting the city.

They emerged on the north side of the walls. The slope of the hills was shallower here, giving way to endless plain. The tournament grounds were evident below, a swath of field to the west. Oats could spy pavilions and paddocks and wagons and stalls, all arrayed on the short side of the grounds at the eastern end. A patch of forest bordered the field to the west, the northward course of the river beyond. There was a break between the wood and the banks that kept drawing Oats's eye. He couldn't quite grasp why, but there was something queer about the trees. Queerer still was the verdant little rise stretching across the entire long north end of the field. The surrounding plains were the dun grass that fleshed most of Hispartha, yet this fold was a lush green. Like the trees, the shape of the hill was unnatural. Both were too . . . square.

The cavaleros took them down the slopes on the slithering road. Reaching flat ground, they left the paving stones, striking west across the plain. Oats began to hear music. The pavilions grew closer. They were larger and more colorful than those he had seen camped outside the castile, guarded by a long cordon of spearmen. A pair of platforms had been erected at either side of the trodden lane running between the pavilions. Minstrels stood upon them, coaxing sound from all manner of instruments that Oats couldn't name. He saw a lute or two. The rest were as mystifying as the foreign tongue of the singers.

Anselmo Volador waited between the platforms, an army of servants arrayed behind him.

"Welcome, Highness," he said in his quivering voice. It hardly carried over the music. "Her Majesty wished me to convey her joy at your return to court. It is her hope that this celebration displays her affection. Our queen has tasked me with seeing to your every comfort. In this I am fervently committed. Indeed, I descended at dawn to ensure you did not arrive ahead of me."

Polecat stifled a snort.

"If you would care to dismount," Volador continued, "I will show you and your guests all Her Majesty has prepared in your honor."

Mannrique came down from his mare with all the enthusiasm of a slophead ordered to deepen a latrine pit. Loukas dismounted smoothly beside the prince. The Bastards waited for Ahlamra to give them a nod. The servants behind Volador leapt to the task of taking the animals in hand. Oats opened his mouth to say that frails couldn't handle hogs when he saw half-orcs among the grooms. They kept their heads bowed as they moved forward to take hold of the barbarians' swine-yankers.

"A paddock has been put aside for the mongrels' steeds," Volador said. "You may plant your banner there, Highness. None will disturb them, you have the queen's promise."

"A kindness, Lord Volador," Ahlamra said. "It is best, however, that one of our own remain close. Lot-born hogs are spirited and require a familiar hand. We would not wish anyone to suffer injury. Our brother Hoodwink will accompany them."

"As you will," Volador said.

The grooms began to move off.

"Go on, now," Oats told Ug, patting his rump. With a grunt the big pig allowed the mongrel servant to lead him away. Hood followed behind, along with Loukas and the prince's banner.

Volador extended an arm down the lane. "At your pleasure, Highness."

Mannrique stood a moment longer, gazing at the musicians, before striding past the chinless tax collector.

"Plucker looks like he's been told to shovel the shit pit," Polecat muttered.

"Just thinking that," Oats replied.

It was far from a shit pit. The pavilions sheltered trestles laden with food. Just one would have made a feast the hoof could not conquer, and there were ten such bounties, each beneath its own house of gay canvas, each manned by liveried servants. The next dozen pavilions contained the drink. Casks of wine, tuns of ale, with more waiting in the wagons behind. Even as the hoof walked, serving men came out bearing flagons. Mannrique shuffled by, but Crafty accepted a pair of sloshing tankards, passing one to Fuqtus. The wizard took a healthy pull. The demon drained his in a gulp and tossed the vessel. When Ahlamra reached for a proffered goblet, Sluggard, Polecat, and Culprit jumped to follow.

"Go easy, you fucks," Oats warned.

Ahlamra had forewarned the hoof not to imbibe more than she. Culprit took that a bit too baldly, and was now watching her close, matching her every sip like a fool-ass reflection.

"Today is restricted to the court," Volador said as they reached the end of the lane. He slowed a bit, gesturing to the empty expanse abutting the southern end of the tourney field, where men with mauls were busy driving posts into the ground, the beginnings of a fence. "The rabble will be permitted at noon tomorrow in time for the first tilt."

"Tomorrow?" Thresher groused. "How long does this fucking thing last?"

Volador led them around the eastern side of the field, bringing them closer to the mysterious green ridge. As the distance waned, Oats saw it wasn't a hill at all but a terraced ramp covered in sod. There were twenty steps in all, each hosting a row of long tables bedecked with garlands.

"Your Highness and his guests will join Her Majesty to watch the champion's tourney," Volador said, turning the corner to lead them in front of the grassy stage. They walked the length of the field toward the forest.

"Truly impressive," Crafty said as they neared the edge of the trees.

Oats couldn't see what the hells the tubby fuck was gushing about. It was only a decent-sized wood. And then he saw it. The trees stood in a perfect line, so close their branches interlaced. Latticed screens threaded with ivy filled the scant gaps, creating a lush, hardy wall. The ground at the base of the trunks was moist, dark, and churned. Oats realized why the forest had looked so strange from the hill, why it was so square. It hadn't grown here, but been placed here. A tunnel of flowering vines led through the wall, flanked by guards. Volador stepped aside, allowing Mannrique to proceed. The prince had to stoop through the tunnel. Moments later, Oats hunched over and entered the fragrant passage, patrolled by fat bees. His boots crunched on a path of crushed stone. He reached the tunnel's end and nearly collided with Polecat's rigid back.

"Fuck. My. Mouth," the hatchet-faced mongrel said, jaw hanging open to receive the requested cock.

They stood in a shaded haven provided by countless trees. Gone was the regimented placement of the forest wall. The trees stood thick and scattered in imitation of a natural wood. Only it weren't natural. The evidence of the fakery could be seen in the piles of woodchips at the base of each truck, the lack of leaf litter and fallen branches upon the grass. The Lots weren't known for woodlands, but Oats was fair certain no forest was home to bears, boars, and deer all wandering about looking puzzled without fleeing or attacking the gaggle of men and mongrels walking wide-eyed in their midst.

Volador led them deeper down the path. Soon, the entrance tunnel was lost from sight. The path ended at a small lake beneath the sheltering boughs. Not some muddy hole, the clear water revealed a basin of set stone, pike gliding and darting within. A ring of stone benches sat back from the lake, small tables placed between bearing ewers and goblets. Strutting peacocks and waddling geese made lazy progress through the surrounding trees.

"Her Majesty gathered her best wizards for this wonder, Highness," Volador told the prince, his quavering voice offering little weight to the claim. "She knows you are most comfortable keeping the company of beasts."

"This is all sorcery?" Culprit asked, moving slowly toward a nearby stag, expecting it to flee at any moment. The animal stood tense, its muscles tremoring beneath its hide. It watched Culprit approach, head drawing back, but it did not run.

"This is more the work of many hands and strong backs than magic," Crafty said, taking in his surroundings with a languid turn. "Though the art of the communers is commendable. Doubly so since they are not present to maintain the bewitching of these creatures. However, I would not risk *that*, young Culprit."

Culprit's hand paused halfway to touching the stag's neck.

"Best to think upon them as delightful decoration, I am thinking," the wizard said.

Volador coughed into his fist. "Highness, Her Majesty would not risk your safety. This is the work of court magicians, not gully wizards. Or foreign charlatans."

If Crafty noticed the slight, he hid it well.

Mannrique did look more content than he'd been since leaving Robledondo, but Oats could see the prince warring with himself, the momentary marvel of the forest grappling with his bone-deep qualms.

"You may be at ease here, Highness," Volador continued. "The entire court will soon come to revel, to receive you warmly and bask in this triumph of Her Majesty's fondness for you. Now, if you will permit my brief absence, there are some final preparations I must attend. Do you want for anything, Highness? I can have your heart's desires sent with all haste."

Mannrique shook his head and turned away to study the passel of brindled boar foraging impotently across the false forest floor.

"Lemons," Crafty told Volador.

The man raised an eyebrow. "Lemons?"

"A goodly number," Crafty said.

Bowing crisply, Anselmo Volador turned and walked back down the path.

"Perhaps we should not have cleaned ourselves," Ahlamra said when he was gone, an edge to her voice. "I would be loath to ruin the queen's wild tableau."

Crafty chuckled, but Oats was confused and his wasn't the only brow that wrinkled.

"What are you saying?" Thresh asked.

"Nothing."

"Rue . . ."

"Tell us, Ahlamra," Oats urged.

She swept a raised a hand to encompass their surroundings. "We are the final decoration. The prized spectacle at the heart of the enchanted wood. Why else are we here when others are not? With no attendants to spoil the effect? The queen wishes her court to behold the savage half-orcs come from the Lot Lands in the proper setting."

"Along with the exotic monsters from Tyrkania," Crafty said with a wink to Fuqtus.

And the peculiar rustic prince who keeps such companions, Oats realized. Mannrique was barely listening, slumped now on a bench and staring vacantly at the fish. Oats felt a simmering anger in his chest. Thresh was already boiling.

"Fuck them, then!" she declared, making for the path.

"Dacia," Ahlamra said, but it did no good. She cocked her head at Sluggard and he jumped to cut Thresher off.

"Out of my way," Thresh warned, and cut around him.

"Thresher!" Oats barked, putting enough punch in his voice to make her stop. "Stand with your hoof, Bastard."

Thresh spun. "I ain't a curiosity for blue bloods to snigger at. None of us should be!"

"I warned this would be the way of it," Ahlamra told her. "You were to steel yourself against all affronts."

Thresher took a long breath. "Tougher than I reckoned."

"Yes," Ahlamra said. "My own patience was flayed by this, I admit. I erred, speaking with such venom. So I shall remind myself, and you, that now is not the time for impatience or chafed pride. We approach the verge of our purpose in coming here, to further our chief's aim of freeing the Lots. Yet it will not be a swift conclusion, brethren. Nothing will be decided this day save our failure if we succumb to rage."

"And when it comes time to kneel?" Sluggard asked.

"Kneel?" Polecat said. "The fuck you mean, kneel?"

"The queen is coming," Sluggard replied. "Here. So . . ."

"I ain't fucking kneeling," Polecat declared.

Culprit shook his head. "Me either."

"Brothers—" Ahlamra began, but Oats cut her off.

"Pardons, Rue, but they're right. The mongrel hoofs don't kneel. Not to our own chiefs and certainly not to no frail with a crown. The Claymaster may have died a twisted, mad fuck, but before that he carved the Lots out of Hispartha's fist. I won't piss on that by kneeling. Fetch wouldn't suffer it either."

"Then she may very well have sent us here in vain," Ahlamra said.

"Oh, I do not think so," Crafty said. His eyes lit upon a man coming down the path bearing a bushel of lemons. "Ah! Wonderful. You may set those down. We require nothing else."

The man did as he was bid and hurried off, unable to hide his relief at not being asked to remain alone with the frowning half-breeds and looming devil.

Crafty went to the bushel and plucked a lemon.

"You shall be far too busy to kneel, my friends," he said, bringing the fruit to his nose. "And Ursaria too dazzled by our Ahlamra and myself to insist."

"Busy?" Oats asked. "With what?"

Crafty reached into his robes and, when it withdrew, flung a handful of chalky powder into the lake.

"Cooking," he said. "Fuqtus, I believe I saw a fine Humbameshi cedar down the path. It should serve our needs well, I am thinking."

The demon curled his lip. "You would have me use the Sixth Thunder to . . . chop wood?"

"A weapon so ancient has been used for far baser tasks. How many centuries did it hang above Bhadra's altar in Ul-Kadim doing nothing?" Crafty smirked. "Are you truly going to refuse the chance to hit something with it?"

Fuqtus shrugged. "No."

Shouldering his golden axe, the demon strode off.

The pike in the lake had grown listless.

Crafty looked at the hoof. "Now, if some of you would not mind doffing your boots, I believe you will find these fish can be caught by hand."

"The hells are you about, Lard Guts?" Polecat asked, though he was already standing on one foot to pull a boot off.

"I am merely eager to show the court the tradition of the hoofs to, when guests, prepare a meal for their host."

"We don't do that," Culprit said, his face becoming unsure the next instant as he looked to Oats. "Do we?"

"No," Oats replied.

"True," Crafty said, tossing him the lemon. "But these noble frails do not know that."

THIRTY-ONE

THE FAVORED BLUE BLOODS OF Magerit came in a long line already babbling about the succulent smells drawing them toward the lake. The coos and compliments were far too exaggerated. The sizzling fish, smoked over cedar coals and seasoned with lemon was pleasant, but to hear the nobles carry on it was an aroma sent by their countless gods.

"They think it's something the queen's prepared," Sluggard said with a grin, keeping his attention on turning the skewers. "Asslickers."

The Bastards had set their fire on the far side of the lake, beyond the benches, but the gasping frails were loud with their praise, each trying to outdo the next. Kissing the queen's cunt and she weren't even among them. Ahlamra had said she would come only after the court. It was likely to be a span. There didn't seem to be an end to the flow of swishing skirts and jaunty capes.

"Those are some backy hats," Culprit said, whittling branches into skewers.

"Hells, that fucker's fatter than Crafty," Polecat marveled at one tumescent man.

The wizard stood with Ahlamra at the path's end, bowing as they greeted every last frail. The boundaries of the lake steadily filled with larger peacocks that honked louder than the geese. The hoof stuck to their fire, gutting and scaling the pile of pike pulled from the well-stocked lake. Mannrique squatted among the Bastards, cutting lemons. He'd seem relieved to have a task to perform. Loukas had arrived between the lemons and the court, and now waited a quarter turn around the lake with Fuqtus, both carefully placed by Crafty. The demon drew the nobles' fascination while the handsome man invited them to share the hoof's catch with all the right manners and gentle words.

The hoof's instructions were simple.

"Be only who you are," Ahlamra told them. "Many will hate you. Most will fear you. Few will speak to you. But all will approach you on our terms."

"So we can serve them?" Thresher challenged.

Ahlamra placed a tender hand on her sister's face. "Imagine we were all in the Lots. Would these humans know how to fend for themselves? Would they survive a day in our Ul-wundulas? You have lived in their world, Dacia. You survived. They can never boast the same. If this were the Lots and you gave them food, you would not be serving them. You would be saving them. They will think of you, of us, how they will. Yet we know our power. Do not give that up by continuing to believe the falsehood that they are better than you."

And now they came, the boldest giving Fuqtus a final goggle and a nod to Loukas before approaching the half-orcs' cookfire.

Oats stood waiting. It was his duty to hand the fish over. He'd tried to tell Ahlamra that Sluggard would be a better choice, but she had smiled at him and given a shake of her head.

"It should be you."

He reckoned she had reasons, but he hadn't pressed to know them. He could give a fish to a blue blood without looking like a slave. And if any treated him like one, he'd give a glower that would make them shit their silken hose or piss their skirts. A thrice-blood didn't need to raise a hand or say a word to make a frail think twice about being a haughty cunt.

Hells. Oats reckoned he'd just worked out Ahlamra's reasons.

The first to come were a couple with locked arms. He had some grey in his hair, she looked barely out of girlhood. Father and daughter or wed, Oats couldn't say. They each took a skewer wordlessly, the woman casting skittish eyes at Oats while the man seemed intent on Mannrique. The prince kept to his lemons. The couple moved off. Oats watched them, curious to see if they would actually eat. He snorted when the man took both skewers and flicked them into the trees. Perhaps they feared poison. Oats couldn't fault them that caution. Or perhaps they had simply gorged themselves in the pavilions during their procession to the forest and had no stomach left. Either way, they were only the beginning of mute nobles tossing good food.

Duke Hernan of Baxscedures was the first to speak. He looked smaller out of his armor, but only by a cunt hair, the heavy layers of his court attire serving well enough in place of the plate. His bearded face was no less grim as he took the skewer from Oats, looking him square.

"I've a hunger," he said.

Oats gave him a second skewer. "You need more just hunt a few paces into the trees."

Hernan gave a fierce smile and walked away.

The last man to approach was the duke's opposite. Small, narrow-shouldered and potbellied, his clean-shaven face shot through with the tiny, webbed veins of a drunkard. He greeted Oats with an easy nod and took the fish, but did not hurry off as the others had. Instead, he remained where he was. And ate. He hummed appreciably with the first bite, pinched a smaller morsel, pushed it into his mouth and sucked the juices from his thumb. All the while he looked at Sluggard, who seemed careful to keep his back turned as he tended to the fish on the fire.

"This is good," the man said, smiling as he lifted the skewer. "Simple. It's been a span since I've had aught but rich food. The spices, the sauces, they can be too much for me. But this. This is good."

Sluggard had tensed as the man spoke.

"You are the Grey Bastards?" the man asked easily, continuing to eat.

"True Bastards," Oats replied.

"I saw your hogs. They were quite the diversion for the court. Most don't know what they're looking at. Just great, tusked swine. But I have an eye for bearded deer-hogs. I used to run them, in another life. And you have some impressive animals. One reminded me of the best hog I ever owned. Looks exactly like him, in truth. So much so that out of reflex I called out to him. Palla, I said. And do you know, the hog's ears twitched and he looked up to me. Odd fucking thing to happen."

Sluggard stood and turned around. "Enough, Barrasa."

The man made a mummery of surprise, taking it so far he dropped what was left of his fish.

"Sivastian?" he said with unconvincing shock. "Could it be you? Martyred Madre, look at us! Reunited. And here, in the midst of the queen's court, in her very city. Our dreams rendered true. Why do you just stand there? First no farewell and now no embrace?"

Barrasa spread his arms, but the gesture was far from affectionate.

Sluggard didn't move. His jaw was tight. "How did you find me?"

"Find you?" Barrasa said, his puzzled expression shedding all sham. He dropped his arms. "Herathos's Cock, Sivastian, I abandoned the search for you long ago. What need had I for a runaway carnavale rider—even the best carnavale rider—when I no longer owned a troupe. I gave it up when Her Majesty made me Master of Victuallers, thank all the gods that smiled on me."

"A place at court," Sluggard said dully. "You did get all you wanted. More, it seems."

Barrasa's moist eyes danced. "Perhaps I should thank you. It is as if your flight south lifted me up. I never thought a runaway mongrel on a stolen hog would bring me to such fortune, not after their disappearance brought me damn near to ruination. But I found that a desperate Barrasa is a fearless Barrasa. And a fearless Barrasa prospers."

"I wager he does," Sluggard replied.

The crowd around the lake began to stir, their attention drawn to the path. A pair of massive armor-clad men in umber tabards walked side by side, each bearing a pollaxe. Their helms were fashioned into the likeness of a fearsome bull, complete with sweeping horns. Hells, they were bigger than the duke.

Another pair followed, and a third.

"The Order of the Minotaur," Barrasa said. He turned back to the Bastards and winked. "Affectionately called the Queen's Bulls."

"They actually fucking minotaurs?" Culprit asked, causing Barrasa to laugh.

"No. No, of course not! Just Her Majesty's most loyal and deadly cavaleros. She arrives."

She chilled Oats to the bone. She came in plate similar to the Bulls, though she wore no helm and her tabard was white, decorated with a red heart pierced by a golden banner. Oats had seen that decoration before, on the shield of the woman atop the Heap. The woman who nearly killed him.

"The queen's a Maiden Spear?" he said, giving voice to his surprise. The sight of the weapon in her gauntleted hand caused the scar in his chest to ache.

Barrasa's laughter fermented into a chuckle. "Engraçia Bracara is the *Matron* Spear, head of the Blessed Sisters of Magritta. And Her Majesty's constant protector."

The Queen's Bulls split and fanned out around the lake as the Matron Spear strode forth. The gathered nobles made room for her, shrinking back from the sharp, vigilant motions of her head. Oats couldn't discern much of her face from across the lake, but her hair was dark and cut short.

Engraçia Bracara lifted a strong voice.

"Her Royal Majesty Ursaria Trastorias, Queen of Hispartha and the Stripped Isles, Countess of Ul-wundulas, Lady of the Upper and Lower Marches, Sovereign Grandmaster of the Ancient Order of the Minotaur, Devoted of Blessed Magritta, Favored Daughter of the Gods."

The woman who came down the path didn't look much different

from the dozens of others who had filed past Oats to get fish and give bland looks. There weren't even a crown on her head, though her cape was trimmed with miniver. If Mannrique and Ursaria shared blood, his height must have come from his mother, for the queen was stocky.

Engraçia knelt and the nobles followed. Crafty and Ahlamra did, as well. Likely a precaution against attack, the Queen's Bulls remained standing. Fuqtus too, Oats noticed. There was something defiant in the set of the demon's corded back.

The Bastards did not kneel. Those still squatting by the fire got to their feet, instead.

Mannrique offered neither deference nor defiance. He stayed sitting, cutting the lemons. But his hands were trembling with such violence Oats feared his knife would slip.

The queen stood for a small span. Oats couldn't see her eyes, but he suspected they moved over the crowd. They might have settled on him, his brethren, noting their lack of obedience. He couldn't be certain. At last, she stepped to Engraçia and the Matron Spear rose. This must have been some signal the court was trained to follow, for the nobles stood in a rustle of heavy cloth.

Ursaria gestured to Crafty and Ahlamra. They approached, and it was hard to say which did it with more fluid ease. Oats didn't catch what was said. Only Crafty's voice carried enough to reach him, but was little more than a garble of good-natured sounds.

The queen laughed. It wasn't a boisterous thing, but her head tilted back with merriment, her mouth smiling and open.

"Fucking Crafty," Polecat said.

"No," Thresh said. "That was Rue's doing."

The queen turned and walked to one of the benches. She sat, inviting the mongrel envoys to join her. The gathered nobles made it difficult for Oats to see them.

"I must go," Barrasa said as he began to move off. "It gladdens me to set eyes upon you again, Sivastian. A pleasure I'd not thought I'd ever get."

"Shit," Culprit said when the man was gone. "He doesn't like you at all."

"That a worry, Slug?" Oats asked.

"No."

Thresher looked concerned. "Sluggard . . ."

Sluggard turned to her and smiled, hunkering back down. "All's well."

Oats had a mind to pull him aside, but decided against it so he could focus on Ahlamra. Her palaver with the queen went on for a long time.

"Reckon we can eat," Oats said at last.

There was nothing else to do. None so much as spared the hoof a glance now that the queen was here to draw every boot-licking eye.

The ensorcelled animals continued their dull-witted meanderings as the day wore on. The nobles appeared under the same spell. Oats began to see the strain in their smiles. In ones and twos they all made their way over to the queen, kneeling once more before her bench and rising to share a brief exchange of words. Only Duke Hernan was invited to sit, his bulk blocking the queen from Oats's view. Ahlamra sat on Ursaria's other side and was also eclipsed, making Oats a little nervy. He wasn't alone in his agitation. Loukas kept casting vexed looks at Mannrique, but the prince never met his eye. Finally, Loukas came to the fire in a poorly hidden fume. He leaned down by Mannrique's ear.

"You must go over!" he hissed. "How long do you intend to malinger here?"

The prince said nothing. The lemons had long been exhausted, leaving him to poke at the coals.

Loukas steamed. "Dammit, 'Rique! Why do you do this to yourself? To me?"

Mannrique continued to sulk. With a silent snarl, Loukas seized the front of the prince's shirt and shook him. Mannrique looked up, startled by the sudden roughness, his unfortunate features twisted by injured alarm. Oats and the others tensed as Loukas berated the prince in a furious whisper.

"You'll not do this! Do you hear? You came back. *You*. You brought this. Now, rouse yourself, damn you!"

Loukas released Mannrique as quickly as he'd grabbed him and straightened, casting a swift look around to see if his temper had been witnessed. Oats was fair certain it had. These nobles were skilled at spying over their cups.

Mannrique kept his pained gaze on Loukas. "Will you go with me?"

"You know I can't," Loukas said, refusing to look at Mannrique.

The prince looked back to the fire, gave a small, forlorn nod, and stood. Slowly, he shuffled off, eyes downcast.

"Why can't you go with him?" Culprit asked, giving Loukas a sour glare.

"I'm a commoner," the man replied. "The only ones with less of a place here are you half-breeds."

Mannrique was now winding his way through the crowd. Most of the nobles didn't bother to budge, forcing him to thread his large, awkward frame between their little groupings. His back drew mocking smiles and whispered japes.

"Fuck this," Oats said, and moved to catch up.

His bulk and swift pace caused a few gasps, and one frail dumped wine down the front of his jerkin in his hurry to get out of the way, though Oats was nowhere near to knocking into him. He saw the Queen's Bulls begin to move, but he reached Mannrique's side the next heartbeat.

The prince shot him a startled look, his mouth opening, but any words were trapped along with Mannrique's feet. Oats halted next to him and the Bulls paused in unison. They were less than a stone's toss from the queen, but she continued her conversation with Crafty and Ahlamra. Behind her, the Matron Spear stood watchful. It was her raised hand that had stopped the Bulls, Oats saw now.

Oats gave Mannrique what he hoped was an encouraging look. Swallowing hard, the prince took a pair of steps forward and it was as if he crossed some unseen line that made him visible.

"Mannrique," the queen said, breaking off her conversation seamlessly. Oats was close enough now to see her mouth was a little crooked, but it lent a charm to her earnest smile. "I am joyed to see you."

The prince began to kneel.

"Oh, no. Stop that!" Ursaria said, standing. "It pains me to watch big men try to stoop so. Unless it is our treasured duke of Baxscedures, for it keeps him nimble." She cut a coy look at Duke Hernan, who dipped his head with a smile. Ursaria stepped to Mannrique and took his hands in hers. He towered over her, a bashful oaf faced with a bold and bright-eyed woman. What Oats could see of her hair through the strung pearls and complicated twists was deep chestnut. "Tell me, Mannrique, how fares your bull? And the lions? I have longed to see them."

"They . . . they flourish, Majesty. Thank you."

"Ursaria," she told him, pointing a scolding finger. "Or dear sister. I'll have no other from you." She stood on her toes to whisper, though it was clear she still wished for all nearby to hear. "Unless that dry old fulminator Barrientos can hear. Then you must drown me in titles, for both our sakes." She gave a tickling laugh, returning to her heels and her confident tone. "Thankfully our Lord Consult loathes celebration, so he will not darken our day. Do you enjoy yourself, Mannrique?"

"Yes," Mannrique replied, the word flat and meek.

Ursaria's mouth turned down in sympathy. "I know this puts you ill at ease. I did try to make it tolerable. There is nothing to be done about the court, I fear. They are like children. Always underfoot and demanding fresh distraction. They will tire of this wood soon, do not fret, and then it shall be yours entirely. You may retreat here whenever you wish. I know how you hate the lists. Oh, and the bullfights! More unavoidable trappings of your return. The people wish to celebrate and they are unimaginative in their tastes."

"I understand," Mannrique said. "It is a kindness. I am grateful."

The queen placed a hand on his face, lips pursing with affection. Her eyes moved now to Oats.

"Another man that would be tortured by kneeling," she said, detaching from the prince. "Or does my use of 'man' offend?"

"Mongrel sits well with us, Your Majesty," Ahlamra said. "It is how we name ourselves and each other."

"You are a thrice-blood?" Ursaria asked Oats.

"Yes."

"He is called Oats," Mannrique put in. "He leads the True Bastards."

"No," Oats said. "Our chief leads the hoof. And Ahlamra speaks for her."

"Yes," the queen said. "And well too. Though I will confess I have been slightly deafened by envy. I have never seen such beauty, and that is to say nothing of her skin." Ursaria cut a playful smile at Ahlamra.

"Your Majesty flatters me and is too kind."

"A blind man would be enthralled by you, girl," Ursaria said, though there was little difference in their age. Somehow it wasn't a slight. "Now, Oats. Ahlamra has told me some of Ul-wundulas, but she admits to being a newcomer. Am I right to assume you were born there?"

"I was."

"Will you sit and tell me of it," the queen said, returning to the bench. "Duke, make room for them. Mannrique . . ." She patted the bench to her right. "Oats, sit beside him there. Would you take wine?"

Oats saw a cup in Ahlamra's hand so he nodded. A servant brought him a brimming goblet.

The queen proceeded to ask questions—small, captivated questions. She looked him squarely and never interrupted nor grew restless as he answered. He tried to do what Ahlamra said, and be what he was, nothing more. The first time he said "fuck" the duke bristled, but the queen did not so much as blink.

As she guessed, Oats had spent his entire life in the Lots. An entire life spent hating the Crown, the frails, the boot of Hispartha. He never reckoned he'd ever set eyes on those who wore that crown, that boot. In his youth, the words "king" and "queen" were little more than curses uttered by the old riders like Creep and Warbler and the Claymaster. The orcs were the enemy, the true threat. Hispartha was more of an annoyance. Frails on foals. That had changed in recent days. The Bastards shedding the Grey to become True had also changed the notion of the hoof's enemies. Hells, they were fighting a war with Hispartha now, not simply grousing about the kingdom and the near useless presence of its cavaleros. Oats had led raids into this land, killed its soldiers, and still he'd never given a thought to those who ruled them. Not a solid thought, one that considered their manner, their minds. He'd never pondered what the queen would be like.

But if he had, he'd never have expected her to be kind.

THIRTY-TWO

OATS KNEW HE WAS DREAMING.

It was unlikely the queen of Hispartha would be astride his cock, her back leaning against him as she pushed herself up and down. And it was a far shot from probable that Ahlamra would have her head between both his legs and Ursaria's, doing all manner of delight with her tongue. Even if those acts could happen, the three of them wouldn't be in the Bastards' bunkhouse in Winsome, a place Oats hadn't seen in a year and was abandoned besides.

So, a dream. One of them rare ones where he could recognize it, but not wake, and had almost as much control of himself as he would were this real. It was a trap, luring him with the pleasure before seizing him with the strange. Suddenly, Ahlamra was commanding the queen away, saying it was time to change Oats's bedclothes. His bunk became Bermudo's huge bed in the castile and he was hurt again, bandaged and soiling himself. Thistle was angry with him, but he couldn't tell if it was because he was fucking the other women—both vanished—or because he'd pissed the linens.

He got up and it was a moment before he realized he was awake, the bed he'd risen from the one next to Hood's in their shared room in the prince's city house.

"Bad dream," the thin voice slid through the small span of murk between them.

"All them nobles dishes," Oats muttered, thankful he hadn't pissed the bed in the waking world.

In truth, he wasn't certain it was the food, though it had been excessive and exotic. The Bastards hadn't known much of what they were eating during the feast that closed the day.

They had all sat at the tables on the terraced hill. The queen occupied the highest step, inviting Ahlamra, Crafty, and Oats to dine with her, along with Mannrique. The Queen's Bulls took up places on the sides of the upper rows while the Matron Spear stood behind Ursaria. Having the woman at his back made Oats more than uneasy. Oddly, he felt better for having Fuqtus there, standing sentry behind Crafty. The rest of the Bastards were given the bottom step and Oats noted none of the court was sat with them.

During the lavish and lengthy meal, minstrels and jugglers and mummers had provided a never-ending parade of diversions on the tourney field below. Oats had been careful with the wine, but Rue had given no instructions about the food. The strong spices and heavy sauces must have conspired with the long span in the queen's company to concoct the dream. Had to be the answer, for he'd not felt one pang of desire for her during the night. Hells, he'd hardly spoken to her and couldn't even look her way without craning his neck fully to the left. As for Ahlamra, a mongrel would have to be dead not to want her, but it weren't something Oats had dwelled on overmuch, especially lately.

Fucking dreams.

Fucking *fucking* dreams. No sense trying to unknot them. The only certainty with this one was it had woken him fully. Sleep wouldn't be returning. Times like these it was best to flee the bed lest it become a pitiless altar for a tossing body.

Moonlight distilled through the shuttered windows gave his mongrel eyes enough detail to grab his breeches. His cock was still more erect than not, that vexing middle ground of swollen where it won't fit comfortable in the breeches' crotch nor down a leg. Grimacing, he tucked it away best he could and left the room. The door opened out onto the veranda on the second floor. Oats stood for a long while, leaning against the smooth, cool stone of the railing, looking up at the square of night sky above the inner courtyard.

A pair of strong desires struck him at the same moment. The first was a need to piss. The second, to see Ugfuck.

He went barefoot and shirtless down the stairs.

The forecourt was silent, cleared of the tubs. Oats crossed to the trees standing near the wall fronting the street and loosed his water. The house had a pair of fancy garderobes, but pissing in the open and better-smelling air felt more like home.

With the stable's few stalls full, Ugfuck was too big to fit inside, so he'd been left next to the building outside. The hog had been asleep, but roused himself and was nudging Oats's leg before his stream was done.

Oats laughed. "Gonna make me wet my feet, Ug, dammit."

He finished and laced his breeches, turning to rub Ug between the eyes. They ambled back toward the stable, nothing but a dozen strides. A thick pile of straw had been put over the cobbles for Ug to bed down on. The big pig flopped on his side and loosed a heavy breath. Oats sat next to his head and scratched his jowl.

"How in all the hells did we end up here, Ug?" he said at last. The hog didn't even grunt. "I got no answer either. Tonight I saw a man in a mask, looked like some kind of marsh bird with a long, curved beak, and he was juggling torches. Another—he didn't wear a mask—just talked loudly in a foreign tongue for a long span, kept doing all these big gestures with his arms. No notion what he was saying, but some of the noble frails on the tables below us were crying. Rue said it was Anvillese poetry. Bunch of mummers ran about with puppets after, made them fuck and kill each other. At least with that I understood why the frails were laughing. You reckon that's what it is up here? Blue bloods gorging themselves, crying and laughing at jesters. Hells . . . to think how many nights my mother struggled to feed us all."

A hot smell struck Oats's nostrils, one he knew well.

"You ain't been starving, you farting fuck," he told Ug, leaning to pat the hog's belly.

The gate from the street rattled and opened.

Oats tensed, but relaxed when he saw Loukas stumble through. He'd not returned to the house after the feast, where he'd sat on the lowest tier with the hoof, but gone off alone once they were within the city walls, pushing the banner at Mannrique and spurring his horse into a side street. The prince had offered no protest and merely watched him ride away. Polecat had reckoned Loukas was off to the brothels and suggested to Ahlamra he go along to make sure the man didn't find too much trouble. Ahlamra had said any trouble he found he could handle alone. If Cat had pouted any harder, his lower lip would have tripped his hog.

Oats couldn't say if Loukas had gone whoring, but he had certainly been drinking.

He shambled into the foreyard, leading with his head and concentrating to keep his feet moving forward while also remaining beneath him. He almost passed Oats by, but noticed him at the last moment. His brain was too slowed by wine to be startled, though he did halt. Oats said nothing, feeling suddenly foolish. A big mongrel in nothing but his breeches sitting in the straw beside his hog in the middle of the night. Hardly a sight to diminish the notion of half-orcs as swine-loving savages.

Loukas gave a bubbling chuckle and moved on, but turned back after a few reeling steps.

"Wha'tyou want withhim?" he asked.

"You want to slur that again?" Oats said.

"'Rique," Loukas said, plodding closer. "What. D'you want. With him?"

Oats hesitated, but Loukas didn't wait for an answer. He raised an arm, tried and failed to aim an accusing finger.

"You won't use 'im!"

Oats couldn't deny Mannrique was being used, but to have it thrown at him by this frail set his teeth to clenching.

"Worried we'll do it better than you, fucker?"

Loukas gawked at him. "Better? I fear you'll be worse, sootskin. Y'already are! He's no place here. Never wanted one. An'now you uprooted him, tossed him inta the cookpot. T'be devoured!"

"And it's his hide you're looking after, is it?"

It took a moment for the jibe to penetrate the fog of wine. Loukas gave a hard blink. "The hells with you! He's a brother to me."

"I stand with my brothers. Don't leave them to face shit alone."

"Oh, yes. The fearsome thrife . . . *thrice*-blood. Well, imagine, thrice-blood, if you were one ov'your lesser brothers. Smaller, weaker. And the powerful thrice-blood refused to fight. Always. Not for hisself, not f'you. For his entire life . . . your entire life. But you can't imagine it. Not you. Always strong. Always fighting."

The fatigue in Loukas's voice spread over Oats.

"You're wrong, frail. I know what it is to be weak. I ain't been the strongest of my brethren in a long time."

Loukas swayed, sneered unhappily. He didn't seem to have heard.

"You want help inside?" Oats asked.

The sneer turned into a snarl, the drunk's sudden flare of anger. Loukas rushed forward. Oats didn't bother to move. No way Loukas would cover the distance, not without . . .

He tripped and fell, hard, reflexes too slow to catch himself. His face hit the stones with a sound that made Oats wince. Besotted as he was, Loukas suffered more confusion than pain. He scrabbled face-down for a moment before managing to roll over. His nose was gushing, making him cough. Oats hunched forward, grabbed the neck of the man's doublet, and dragged him closer. He lifted him to sitting. Loukas probed tenderly at his nose, slumped beside Oats and a little in front. Raising his fingers, he squinted at the blood.

"It was a fall," he mumbled at last.

"What it was," Oats agreed.

Loukas craned to look at him, eyes unfocused. "What happened to 'Rique. His face. It was a fall. Girón threw him off a balcony. His own brother. 'Rique wasn't yet two."

Oats had a horrible image of Muro tossing Wily off some height. He shuddered, shook his head to rid himself of the thought. "Fucking hells."

"He says he doesn't remember," Loukas went on. "I hope that's true. Girón was sent away. Never allowed near him again. Though . . . that proved . . ." He blew a hiss from behind his teeth. "All 'fore I knew him. By then, 'Rique's father had taken Girón's place as his tormentor. Giving him up for dead was the greatest kindness the Old King ever did him."

"For dead?" Oats asked.

Loukas nodded, turned away again. "'Rique ran off when he was six. Escaped his nurses and tutors. He reached a farm. Don't know how long it took him, but if you and me, if we set out on foot from here right now it would be nine days before we arrived. My father found him in the pigs' sty, starving, nearly dead. Didn't know who he was. A filthy, big-boned boy with a squashed face didn't look to be a prince of the blood. I yearned for a brother, begged my parents not t'take him to the Steel Friars. We didn't have much, so they feared to feed another. But 'Rique proved a help and, big as he was, he didn't eat much. No matter how much my mother pressed, he never spoke of where he'd come from. Soon she gave up an'fer two years we lived . . . the four of us together."

Oats stayed quiet. The wine had become a river, powering the wheel of Loukas's tongue.

"It was chance that he was found. Cruel chance, since it was Girón that found 'im. To this day I d'know what he was doing at the market fair, but he knew his brother, the face he'd created. 'Rique didn't know him, though, and Girón was canny enough not to reveal his true self. But he looked a noble. Presented himself to my parents as a favorite of the king, thanked them with words for their care of the prince. Words, and coin." Loukas's mouth twisted in a way that made Oats fear he was about to vomit, but it was only bitter words that came spewing out. "The speed with which they gave him up! *Now* I see they were relieved not to be punished, but then it felt as if they sold him. My love for them withered in that moment an'I refused to let 'Rique go without me. Girón could have done anything in that moment. Refused. Accepted and murdered me on the road. But he offered to bring me t'court as the prince's companion. A better life.

"My father accepted with the same readiness. My mother? Asked for more coin. Perhaps she sought to offend, to force the withdrawal of the offer. I think so. And I think Girón saw it too. But why take offense when you can make a mother's heart bleed? He gave them more for me than 'Rique. With a smile. As for 'Rique, he didn't protest, didn't try to run. He did what he has done since. Nothing. Fortunate for us Girón was exiled from court and hunted by the Queen's Bulls . . . well, *King's*, then. Had it not been so, I suspect he might have slain us both for pleasure. Or worse. But he used Mannrique to buy back their father's favor."

Loukas looked at Oats once more. "And now he's being used again. Tell me, for what?"

"Peace in the Lots," Oats said, and hoped he wasn't lying.

Loukas huffed. "Ushered by Girón's mongrel son. Forgive me if that doesn't lull me with comfort." The man battled to his feet. "I wish I could make some oath, tell you if anything befalls Mannrique I will see you pay. But they'd be empty words. I can't voice them to you any more than I could to the queen herself. He was only safe so long as he stayed far from here. Now . . ."

Oats wanted to promise that no harm would come to the prince, but he didn't have the stomach for empty words either.

"What would you have done?" Loukas asked. "If I'd reached you before?"

"These flagstones hit you a heap harder than I would have," Oats replied.

Loukas touched his nose once more and dragged himself into the house.

Oats was still sitting beside a snoring Ugfuck when the sun rose.

THE TOURNEY BEGAN IN EARNEST on the second day. Magerit's people flowed from the city and down the hill, coming in droves. They flooded the grounds south of the field, pressing against the completed fence. Ale wagons provided by the Crown dotted the crowd, islands in threat of being swallowed by the heaving tides of eager folk.

The Bastards were again given a place of honor with the queen on the viewing hill, servants moving about at their backs, refilling goblets. The morning was cloudless, promising heat before noon. There were already men on horseback down on the field when Oats and the others arrived. They proved to be youths, jousting with thin, hollow lances. The nobles cheered and waved silk ribbons for their sons, but the commoners across the field were far more diverted by the ale. Oats couldn't blame them. Blue bloods with a few pubic hairs between them timidly charging each other with reeds wasn't much of a spectacle.

"They care more for the bullfights," Queen Ursaria said. She reached over to her right and placed a hand on Mannrique's wrist. "I set those for the final day, knowing you detest them. And they make a morass of the field."

Oats, sitting on Mannrique's other side, saw the man nod and give a weak smile, trying not to squirm at the queen's touch. She released him to cast a gentle, sweeping gesture at the field.

"Today we shall have the races, javelin hurl, and, if there is light remaining, the first tilts." Ursaria's face brightened. She cast a look at Ahlamra and then to Oats. Anyone else might have seemed a foolass looking from side to side in such a manner, but for the queen the motion was practiced and supple. "I have heard that one of your brothers was once a famed rider in the carnavales. Sivastian the Swain?"

"He is called Sluggard now, Majesty," Ahlamra answered.

Ursaria produced the smallest pout. "Hardly fitting for one who never lost a pàreo. My Master of Victuallers tells me I saw him perform once, but I admit I do not recall. It did make me wonder if your brothers would agree to ride in some of the games?"

"Majesty?"

"The bloodless ones, of course! It would be a shame for the Lot Lands not to take a part. There are knights from Guabia, Anville. And it would do much to win the admiration of the people. Allow them to see the half-orcs of the Lots as more than frightening marauders."

"What a delight!" Crafty exclaimed from beyond Ahlamra.

Oats nearly barked at him to keep his mouth closed, but Rue spoke first.

"We would have to vote on this as a hoof, Majesty."

"Oh, do. Do! But best be quick. These little lords will soon finish playing at war."

Ahlamra nodded and stood. Oats got up too, and they went to the side of the rise to descend. They said nothing as they turned to cross in front of the bottom tier. Thresh was the first to see them coming and alerted the rest. The Bastards stood.

"Come," Ahlamra told them.

The hoof went to the paddocks set back behind the north side of the row of pavilions, where Hood stood watch over their hogs.

"The queen wishes us to take part in the games," Ahlamra said when they were all gathered.

Culprit's face scrunched. "She wants us to knock them brats from the saddle?"

Polecat laughed. "Oh, that'll be fun!"

"No," Ahlamra said. "The events to come."

"We ain't considering that," Thresher said, her voice so heated Oats couldn't tell if it was a question or a pronouncement.

"I told her we had to vote," Ahlamra replied.

Polecat's hand shot up. "In."

"Hold your fucking hog," Oats said. "Rue, what's she about? The queen?"

"The reasons she voiced were earnest," Ahlamra said. "We are here under the patronage of the prince, and these festivities are held in his honor. Refusing to participate would weaken the Lots in the eyes of the court and the commoners. As for what a refusal will do to Ursaria herself, I cannot say."

"Then we have to do it," Culprit said. "Chief didn't send us here to be milksops."

"She sent us to stop a fucking war," Thresh said. "Not entertain the frails."

"I'm afraid the two are not riven," Ahlamra said. "I cannot say for certain the queen lacks other motivations. In truth it would be strange if she did not. As ruler, her concerns will be myriad. It bears mention that she did broach the matter by way of Sluggard and his past with the man Barrasa."

All eyes went to Sluggard, who had been as silent and still as Hoodwink.

"Slug?" Oats prodded. "You got any arguments?"

Sluggard shook his head, ridding himself of a pensive stare. "No. No, I say we do it."

"That's two," Polecat said, smiling.

"It's a fucking no from me and Anvil," Thresher declared.

"Oh, right." Culprit rubbed his head. "I have Warbler's vote. Shit. Well . . . he hates fun, so no for him. Me, yes."

Oats grunted. "This is just the sort of hogshit Jackal would rush to do, but Crafty was in favor so that would flip his mind. No for Jack. As for the chief, I reckon she'd follow Ahlamra on this."

"I would tell her we should."

"Hood," Polecat said. "Time to move your head in one of two ways."

Hoodwink did. It was a no, leaving Oats the deciding vote.

Hells. Why hadn't he just voiced his preference along with Fetching's and Jackal's? Because he didn't damn know then. Or now. The minds of queens, the intrigues of court, what did he know about any of it? Precisely nothing. He was a Lot-born mongrel. A Bastard. A hoof-rider. That's what he knew, how he thought. No sense in doubting that now.

Oats took a long breath.

"Saddle up."

THIRTY-THREE

A VOLLEY OF HISSES GREETED the True Bastards as they took the tourney field. The jeers intensified as they rode a circuit around the edge, following the riders from Majeth. Numbering only ten men, the Majethi had been delighted to find they were no longer the smallest in number and, therefore, no longer the rear of the procession. Theirs were the only smiles among the competing frails when the hoof arrived in the marshalling field behind the nobles' terrace. The Hisparthans wore scowls and mustachios, the Anvillese sneers and long locks, the Guabians stone faces behind aggressively styled beards.

The Crown's cavaleros caused a roar when they trotted onto the field, eighty men in scale coats lifting their javelins in salute to the queen. And these were the lesser houses, the men without land, coin, and title enough to merit a place in the joust. Sluggard had explained it all while they waited to enter the field.

"And so they try to garner attention in the tavolado," he said.

"Which is throwing a javelin at a wooden target?" Culprit asked, still convinced there had to be more to it.

There wasn't.

Portable palisades made of boards were already standing at staggered intervals in the field's center when the procession emerged. Each rider was to charge one at a gallop, fling a javelin, and knock the target down. Any that failed were removed from the contest. There were only twenty targets, so the tavolado was held in rounds, servants running out to reset the fallen palisades after each run and to retrieve the javelins. Half the targets were reserved for Hispartha's men at each run. The Bastards were given a single spot at the end nearest the queen's terrace. Thresher demanded to go first.

"Get this over with," she muttered.

The hoof was also given the shortest run up to the target, robbing their mounts a chance to build up speed to aid with the cast.

It didn't matter.

When a horn blast signaled the first run, Thresh kicked her hog forward, barely left a trot and threw with an almost languid motion, striking her target true and sending it flopping over.

Culprit blew air from between his lips. "The hells? This ain't shit."

But Sluggard pointed out several targets across the field still standing. Two Hisparthans and the first Majethi had failed. All those who succeeded their run were supposed to ride in front of the terraced steps and salute the queen, but Thresher turned her hog in a tight loop and rode directly back to the hoof. The crowd was not pleased.

"Can I go now?" Thresh asked over the harsh din.

Oats didn't bother to answer. She knew she had to keep with her brothers.

True to Culprit's derision, the tavolado proved simple for the Bastards. The javelins used were lighter than those they wielded in the Lots, something they had all noted when given the weapons. A few quick words of advice from Thresh while the targets were being reset helped prepare the rest of them. Oats was the only one to nearly fail the first run, throwing his javelin clear through the target with such force it almost didn't fall. He couldn't be certain, but he thought he heard a change in the crowd's voice as he rode by the nobles, lifting his fist at Ahlamra.

It was Sluggard's run that won them in earnest. He waited a moment after the horn and seemed to be watching the Majethi rider to his left, already spurring forward. Sluggard spurred Palla, made his cast, and knocked the target down. He immediately drew a second javelin and threw crosswise, striking the target the Majethi had failed to bring down, correcting the man's mistake.

The common folk erupted with cheers and laughter.

The blue bloods couldn't help but do the same when Sluggard made his ride before the terrace reclining on Palla's back, head nestled behind his hands in the pig's mane.

Even Thresher's foul mood was lightened by that display of balance and assery.

After all had taken a run, the targets were rearranged and the number to be struck increased. The second run demanded the riders fell two, then three in the third, the positioning and distance adding to the challenge. The frails were culled deeply in the second run, and by the third the Bastards began to falter. Polecat missed once on his three-target run. Thresh struck all three, but one remained stubbornly upright. Oats and Culprit failed at four.

Only three men reached the five-target run; two Hisparthans and one of the Guabians. Sluggard and Hoodwink remained for the Lots.

"This will decide it," Polecat said, shielding his brow from the sun.

The targets were arranged in a tight cluster, three forward and a pair flanking. The approach was almost the length of the field.

"Your first cast needs to be made midfield at the latest," Cat went on. "Else you won't have time for the rest. Even then . . ." He clicked his tongue.

"Ever hit five?" Culprit asked Sluggard.

"Hit?" Slug replied, stretching his shoulder. "Yes. Knocked over? No."

"What about you, Hood?"

"It is one less than an *ulyud*," Hoodwink stated.

The horn blared, sending the first cavalero into a gallop. He waited too long to cast and struck only three targets down before reaching the end of the run. The Guabian struck four, but only a pair fell. Sluggard was next.

He sent Palla surging forth. His first cast came just before midfield and cut a perfect arc, landing on the upper half of the middle target, slamming it down. The next javelin was in the air before the first struck. Oats cheered with the others as another target fell. Sluggard was nearly even with the third palisade when he threw. At that distance there was little chance of missing. The force splintered the boards. Just the pair sitting beyond remained. Palla's speed brought Sluggard to them swiftly. Too swiftly. He managed to get a fourth javelin off, knocking the target down, but he wasn't quick enough for the fifth. Still, he nudged Palla deftly at the last moment, and the hog knocked it over with a sweep of his tusk as he passed. Another burst of laughter and roar of approval went up from the rabble.

Sluggard returned to the hoof with a bright grin.

"Doesn't count," he said, weathering the backslaps. "But I was inspired by Hood's vision of them as orcs."

The Hisparthans wanted one of their own for last, so that put Hoodwink up.

"Good luck," Culprit told him as he guided his hog to the start of the run.

One of the Majethi riders spurred closer.

"Six drachmae he fail," the man called in accented Hisparthan.

The True Bastards all answered at the same time.

"Done!"

"Agreed!"

"Take that wager!"

"Get ready to pay!"

"Like poverty, fucker?"

Oats found he was holding his breath as Hood waited for the horn. It sounded.

Hood kicked his hog, but held it back from the speed Slug had goaded from Palla. His first cast was a mirror of Sluggard's. The next two targets fell so quickly Oats barely saw the javelins fly. The front three were down and the back pair closing. Hoodwink put a javelin in each hand and threw both in perfect unison. The targets slapped to the ground and the field erupted with hearty shouts. Hells, he'd made it look easy.

Face twisted with rancor the Majethi returned to his companions to gather the coin and receive several slaps to the face.

Hoodwink made the customary ride by the terrace, but followed his own custom of offering nothing more, keeping his gaze ahead and his hands on his hog.

Polecat was already distributing the coins among the hoof when Hood rode up.

"Reckon you get one too," Cat told him with a pleased grin, tossing the silver disc.

Hood snatched it out of the air.

The last Hisparthan was up.

"Seven drachmae *he* fail!" the Majethi called.

"No chance!"

"Fuck off!"

"Eat an entire cock!"

"Nice try!"

"How's my ass taste?"

"No."

The cavalero made his run. And the hostility he earned from the crowd after bringing down only three targets was louder than the Bastards received when they entered the field.

With a wide smile, Sluggard dipped his head at the coin still in Hoodwink's hand.

"You just earned a heap more than that."

"How much?" Culprit asked, breathless and beaming.

Sluggard shrugged. "We'll have to wait until tonight. The queen grants all prizes herself. And you'll have to sit up on the top and dine with her. Don't worry, Hood. I'll be up there with you after I win the pàreo. Though I suggest you forgo the race. These frails will be looking for a little comeuppance. They'll be eager to keep you from collecting."

"They can try," Hoodwink said.

"Yes, but we don't need any of *them* dead," Oats said. "No race for you, Hood. And none for me either. Ugfuck wouldn't thank me for putting him in something like that. The rest of you can make your own choice."

Polecat swatted Culprit on the chest. "What do you say, youngblood?"

"Try and stop me."

Thresher dismounted and started leading her hog back to the paddocks. "Try not to die, fool-asses."

OATS RETOOK HIS SEAT AT the queen's table. The looks he'd received from the court during his ascent ranged from open contempt to grudging respect. One woman had raised her goblet to him with a coy smile and appraising eyes. After that, he kept his eyes ahead.

"A fine showing, strong Oats," Crafty proclaimed, clapping his ring-laden hands.

Oats shuffled behind the wizard's chair without a word.

"I am so happy you chose to compete," the queen said as he sat. "Wonderful. That pale rider is a marvel." She looked to Ahlamra. "Hoodwink, was it?"

"Yes, Your Majesty."

"Wonderful," Ursaria repeated. She returned her attention to Oats, leaning forward to see past Mannrique. "You and your brothers did so well. Do you have a similar sport in the Lots?"

"We hunt orcs," Oats said.

Ursaria laughed. "Of course! Wine so early makes me a fool. Perhaps it should also be obvious to me why you are not entering the race?"

"My hog is lazy." He was only speaking in earnest, but received another laugh. "And barbarians don't mix well with horses. Reckoned it best to keep our numbers small."

"Yes, Volador and some others expressed alarm. They advised against allowing your hogs in the pàreo, but that is silliness. If we can contest each other in Ul-wundulas surely we can risk doing so here. Would you not agree?"

"Reckon so," Oats answered. If the queen caught his focus shifting to Ahlamra she gave no sign. Rue's calm mask held the smallest mote of apprehension.

Wooden poles affixed to stands were now being set up below.

Coils of rope festooned with bright ribbons were tied between the poles to create a circuit around the field.

The queen brushed Mannrique lightly with the back of her hand. "Who do you favor to win?"

"I have no favorite," the prince replied, his glance weighing less than her touch.

"Oh, come. No wager on one of the True Bastards? Does your patronage not extend to confidence in their prowess?"

"I've no taste for betting."

Letting the matter go, Ursaria shifted her smile to Crafty, who was all too ready to reflect it with his own.

"Surely you are not so demure, Emir Ultani."

"I take pride in never being so, gentle queen."

"So then, for whom shall we cheer?"

"I would not dare suggest Her Majesty lift her voice for any but a son of Hispartha," Crafty replied with exuberant playfulness.

The preparations upon the field were nearing completion and the riders began to assemble at the left end of the field closest to the terrace. Oats noticed that few of the Anvillese and none of the Guabians were present, though all ten of the Majethi were there. It appeared most of the cavaleros from the tavolado were eager to regain some honor. The lane denoted by the hastily erected ropes wasn't wide enough for every rider to race abreast, but unlike the last contest, it looked as if all would compete at the same time. Oats wasn't certain how the positions were determined, but his brothers sat their hogs at the front and upon the outward edge. Sluggard spoke to Cat and Culprit, making gestures with his hands to illustrate whatever advice he was intent on providing.

"But what of you?" the queen pressed Crafty. "What demands your own acclamations? Do you cheer for Majeth, an island ruled by the empire you serve? Or the mongrels? For you are one yourself."

"Or Hispartha," Crafty added with good cheer. "Home of my father and source of my human blood."

The queen made no reply, though her silence displayed no discomfort, only a confident patience.

"I need not choose," Crafty said. "To cheer for Majeth is to cheer for Hispartha, for the sultans have empowered me to make you a gift of the island, most glorious queen. As for the Lot Lands, I have come with no other purpose but to employ my voice on their behalf. And so I shall, knowing that to bellow heartily for their success does nothing to decry your great kingdom, for we are here to make peace. By inviting our friend hoof-riders to take part you have provided the spirit of this contest, Majesty. As you predicted, the cheers of the people begin to knit. All of us, I am thinking, shall be impressed and enlivened by the winner, whoever it may be."

Ursaria plucked her goblet from the table and raised it toward Crafty. "Well said."

"Majesty," the wizard replied, lifting his own cup.

The signal horn took Oats by surprise. Flinging his attention back to the field he found the riders thundering forward, those at the fore breaking swiftly away while the dense pack behind jostled for position, some struggling to get moving. Sluggard, Culprit, and Polecat had nothing but open ground before them and made a good start, but horses were faster from the kick, and several frails dashed ahead. Sluggard had said the race was eight circuits. And a hog could outpace any horse, given time.

Speed, it turned out, wasn't the only consideration.

While no weapons were allowed in the pàreo, there was nothing to prevent the riders from shoving and punching, methods playing out in a fury among the tight press fighting to break loose. Oats saw several riders knocked from bucking horses, creating a clog among the racers. Across the field, the commoners were building to a furor, fed by the conflict playing out under the nobles' noses. The cries of the blue bloods were only lesser due to their smaller numbers, but from where Oats sat their outpour of excitement was close to ear-splitting. The noise caused Mannrique to cringe. Chin tucked, he watched only from the corner of one eye.

The queen looked on with fixed concentration and raised her voice, but it wasn't to shout or cheer.

"Tell me of your chieftain. The fabled she-devil. Fletching, is it?"

Oats wasn't sure whom she was asking, but it was Ahlamra who answered, her response almost swallowed by the howling court.

"Fetching, Your Majesty."

"Oh! She is comely, then?"

"She is magnificent, Majesty."

"High praise coming from one who looks as you. Careful, you will make me hate this Fetching. The first are coming around!"

Down on the field the lead horsemen were a turn away from completing their first circuit, barreling toward the clot that had not yet cleared from the start. Some unhorsed men were foolish enough to remain on the track, attempting to wrangle their spooked animals. Others were sprawled in the sparse grass, hardly visible through the haze of dust. It would take a keen rider to pass through the ever-changing gaps without incident. Oats saw the boon of the starting position turn into a detriment as the lead man—one of the Majethi on a mare—collided with a rearing stallion. Both horses toppled in a flailing of legs and screams.

Oats heard Mannrique's pained gasp through the baying nobles.

"Is it true she is a sorceress?" Ursaria asked, stretching forward in her seat to witness the Majethi crawl free from the fallen horses and scurry to flee the track.

It was a moment before Ahlamra answered. Oats reckoned that her attention, like his own, was seized by their brethren coming around the first turn. They had stuck together, Polecat and Sluggard acting as flank guards for Culprit. They formed a stout arrowhead, but split up as they came around. The hogs could have cut an easy swath through the splintered obstacles of men and horses, but this was no band of thicks to slay. Avoiding bloodshed, the Bastards threaded through the turmoil and won free, gaining the straight fronting the terrace once more.

"The hogs are nimbler than one would expect!" the queen exclaimed. "Well? Is she?"

"Of a kind," Ahlamra replied. "She has the blood of elves."

"It is said she rides a great raptor, and cannot be pierced by steel."

"That is so, yet she was formidable long before she came to such power. Tempered by suffering and the harshness of the Lots. She was not welcome among the hoofs yet she earned her place and now all mongrel riders call her chief."

"War chief, I believe you mean."

"We hope that title may be soon set aside."

"That will be difficult if she continues to attack our castles and cities without provocation. Ah, the pàreo now truly begins. The start is always little more than a brawl."

A brawl that knocked close to a score from the race. Servants in the center of the track now risked ducking the ropes to help men and horses get clear. The fallen Majethi horse lay with a broken leg. A man hurried out with a stockbow to end its suffering. Mannrique lurched to his feet and fled the terrace. Oats saw Crafty give Fuqtus a small signal and the demon followed the prince down the steps.

"Majesty," Ahlamra said, "half-orcs were being hunted and slain by cavaleros without cause."

The queen made no reply, her rapt attention on the race.

Oats could no longer tell which of the frails led, the fastest now intermingled with the slowest. Some were in their second circuit, others still the first. A rider could not claim victory until the seventh, but Oats was fucked if he'd know when that was. His brothers were on the second, he knew that much. And the way the nobles carried on, shouting encouragement and insults at various men by name, they knew where their favorites stood.

Of the Bastards, Culprit was farthest ahead, but he was pushing his hog too hard, saving none of the sow's fire for the final stretches. It looked as if Polecat was shouting at the younger mongrel, trying to caution him, but Culprit was heedless. Sluggard had fallen back so Palla could hug the inner ropes. It would make the turns tighter, but reduce the lengths.

"There was cause, surely," the queen said over the tumult of pounding hooves and lusty voices. "As you said, the Lot Lands are harsh, lawless. I need not tell you that all who dwell there are surrounded by peril. Orcs and centaurs and elves. Killers and savages are the crop of Ul-wundulas. It takes brave men to endure there. I cannot imagine you would fault them for doing what they must to protect themselves. To survive."

A cavalero caught up to Polecat on his left and lashed out with an arm. Cat warded the blow with his own arm and his return strike almost knocked the man from the saddle. The cavalero scrambled to stay ahorse and fell behind once more. Cat continued to gain ground. The mongrels entered the third circuit within heartbeats of one another.

Ahlamra was silent. Oats reckoned she knew better than he, but he chewed on the gristle of angry words. Brave men! The cavaleros were exiles led by criminals and madmen. Ignacio was a slaver, Bermudo a haughty fuck blinded by hate. And then there was whatever stripe of loon Maneto had been. The Lots were well served with them in the dust. Hard to fathom Hispartha wasn't better off being rid of them in the bargain.

The crowd roared as an Anvillese rider fell from the saddle during a turn.

Sluggard, on the inside, was now even with Culprit, who occupied the middle of the track. Four horsemen separated Polecat from his brothers, but he was on the verge of passing one, staying out of arm's reach.

Crafty spoke up. "A war between your kingdom and the Lots is a boon for none but Dhar'gest, good queen."

"It could be argued Tyrkania, as well," Ursaria said, smiling at the spectacle below. "East of Traedria only the Halyxians remain to oppose the empire, and I am told their resistance will soon crumble."

"The sultans only wish to—"

"Claim the world," Ursaria cut him off pleasantly. "A lion devours, it rests. That is its nature. My half-brother may believe such a beast can be kept and tamed, but I am not so callow, Emir Ultani. Tyrkania may be resting now, but that does not mean it will not soon slaver for Hispartha."

"My masters dared hope the gift of Majeth would help convince Your Majesty the empire is not the ravenous monster it appears."

Ursaria laughed, a throaty, genial sound. "One tiny island passed between kings and conquerors since before the Imperium. Far from a tempting gift. I would have preferred they send you with a lime."

"I am grieved to have offended you, Queen Ursaria."

Crafty received an indifferent wave. "I am rarely offended, and then only when I have failed to find a better use for my energies. The sultans hold great power. What good does it do my kingdom to deny it? I am also powerful, named for the she-bear. And such a beast is nowhere more dangerous than where she lairs. Especially when the audacious hunter mistakes that she slumbers."

It made Oats uneasy when neither Crafty nor Ahlamra tried to convince the queen she wasn't being hunted. Though he watched the race, his ears were witness to a different contest. And he couldn't tell who was fucking winning.

The Bastards were midway through their fifth circuit. Culprit had fallen behind several places, his hog nearly blown. He'd done well, but inexperience had cost him. Still, Oats was proud of him. The chief would have been too, were she here to see. Though if she were, he reckoned this palaver with the queen would be going very differently.

"The Lots see that you have been roused, Majesty," Ahlamra said. "The blood spilled cannot be undone. It is the hope of our chieftain that further war can be prevented."

"By placing Mannrique on the throne," the queen said, amused. "The Lots allowed to descend further into barbarity, weakening our bulwark against the orcs, all while miserable 'Rique has a crown on his head and a Tyrkanian hand up his ass. It is everything my father warned against. Indeed, it could be said I exist solely to prevent that very outcome. Yes, I am roused. And will not be lulled by well-mannered mongrels, no matter how pretty or charming."

Oats fought the urge to look to his left. However Ahlamra and Crafty reacted, they were silent.

Sluggard entered the final circuit with two other riders in contention for the prize, both Hisparthan. Another cavalero and a rider from Anville weren't far behind, with Polecat, a cavalero, and a Majethi on their heels. Cat looked determined to catch Sluggard, but Oats didn't think he had the time, even without the other racers aggravating his pursuit. The riders seasoned enough to pace their mounts now pushed them to unleash their last bouts of speed.

"There is a saying I am certain you know," the queen said. "'The orcs have the strength to conquer the world. But to do so they will have to walk.'"

The Hisparthans dogging Sluggard converged upon him, one to his right, the other behind. The man beside him reached, attempting to wrest him from the saddle. Sluggard fended him off, but they were coming into the final turn and a gap formed while his concentration shifted. The cavalero at the rear bulled to occupy the inside, leaving Sluggard pinched between the horsemen. They struck at him, keeping pace, trying to make him slow to escape their blows. He held firm, taking the beating. The crowds on either side of the field were near to frenzy as the trio of battling riders came to the final straight.

"My father oft spoke another piece of wisdom."

The dead Majethi horse lay upon the track, a javelin's throw from the finish and directly in Palla's path. Hemmed by the cavaleros, Sluggard could not avoid it. His hog could jump the corpse, but he risked being unseated by the frails. He *had* to slow.

Instead, he leaped from his hog to the horse on his left, landing behind the rider. To the crowd's astonishment, Sluggard heaved the cavalero off the animal's back, sending him flying over the rope to land in the center of the track.

"He said it was fortunate male mongrels were sterile."

Sluggard hopped forward into the vacant saddle and remained on the galloping animal until Palla jumped the dead horse. As soon as his hog was over, Sluggard sprang back to his razor, using the motion to kick the last cavalero off his mount.

"For if half-orcs could breed true . . ."

Palla burst over the finish and Sluggard's arm struck the air to the feverish adulation of hundreds.

"They would rule all the lands of the earth."

THIRTY-FOUR

THE MAJETHI HORSE PROVED TO be the only casualty of the race. Some of the riders suffered broken bones, including the man Sluggard kicked, but thankfully he rolled clear of the track before the horses coming up behind trampled him.

With dusk fast approaching, the queen called a halt to the games. The court retired to the pavilions, where the day's competitors were invited to receive their fawning. Fearing reprisal, Oats gathered the hoof at the paddock.

"You can't mean for us to hide back here," Sluggard said, bemused. He raised a frustrated arm at the rear of the pavilions, less than a thrumshot away, where the sounds of merriment pulsed through the silk and canvas.

Oats didn't answer, and Sluggard paced with increasing vexation, though he uttered no further protest.

Anselmo Volador came to his rescue.

"Your presence is sorely missed," the weak-voiced tax collector said after crossing the stretch of plain with a pair of men-at-arms.

"Reckon the only thing sore is the pride of all them cavaleros,"

Oats replied. "I don't think your queen would take kindly to her festival being spoiled by a knife fight."

"Do you intend to start stabbing?" Volador asked with an arched brow.

"No."

"Then I doubt such will occur."

Oats hesitated. He wished Ahlamra were here to guide him, but she and Crafty had gone with the queen to the constructed wood.

Volador cleared his throat. "At least allow me to take the day's champions. It would be unseemly for them to deny those they have bested a chance to raise a cup to their victories."

Oats found Sluggard giving him an imploring look. Hoodwink's expression was blank.

"If it is for your hogs you fear I have brought these men to stand guard in your absence," Volador said. "I will vouch for their safety."

"I'll stay anyway," Thresh said, giving the men-at-arms a hard stare, "if the rest of you want to go."

Oats could see Culprit trying to hide his desire. Polecat was all but shivering with anticipation.

"Very well," Oats said. "We'll go."

Sluggard's smile threatened to sever his ears. Volador dipped a nod and turned, leaving the men-at-arms. Oats waved his brothers on, but tarried a moment with Thresher.

"I don't like the notion of you here alone," he whispered.

"Oh, I ain't," she replied without lowering her voice. "Got the hogs here with me. Nothing gonna hurt any of us."

"Stay alert."

"I will, but you best heed your own words, Big Bastard."

Oats grunted with agreement and moved to follow the others, making sure to stride between the men-at-arms on the way.

Full dark hadn't yet descended, but the lane between the pavilions was now lit with braziers. The feasting tents were filled with people and the glow of lanterns. Clusters of cavaleros loitered in the lane, often with a member of court simpering in their midst. As ever, the Bastards drew stares and brought silence. Oats saw the shit-eyes he expected, but also curt, manful nods and lifted cups.

"Well-ridden, half-orcs," one Anvillese rider said, his four companions babbling what sounded like agreement in their own tongue.

A broad-shouldered man stepped in their path. He was deep browed, his face half-eclipsed by the thick, flaxen beard of the Guabic. Though he was shorter than all but Volador he stood without apprehension, pale eyes searching the hoof until they alighted on Hoodwink. He stepped up to the pale mongrel.

"You," he said. "You did greatness. I wish know how." The man lifted a tankard in front of Hood's dead stare. "Drink with us."

Oats had never seen anyone put a companionable arm around Hoodwink before. He tensed, waiting for the Guabian to spit blood as a knife entered his lung. But Hood allowed himself to be guided into a pavilion, where he was greeted with a boisterous yell. The Guabian turned and made a coaxing gesture at the hoof.

"Come. Drink, yes?"

Polecat looked to Oats.

"Yes?" he asked, mimicking the frail's accent.

Oats nodded.

With broad grins, the Bastards entered the pavilion and were soon carousing with the Guabic knights and their women. Most didn't speak Hisparthan, but Sluggard knew their tongue. The Guabians had not entered the pàreo and were more interested in his skills as a translator than in his victory. Oats learned they didn't race because all were entering the joust tomorrow and did not want to risk their horses. Hoodwink was the center of their admiration and curiosity. The men plied him with ale and questions, and didn't seem to mind that both his answers and his drinking were sparing. Polecat and Culprit weren't so tempered. Oats tried to put a bridle on their quaffing and managed to keep them upright, but the celebration with the Guabians was only the first.

Volador escorted the hoof to gathering after gathering. Each pavilion contained a knot of nobles and cavaleros, constricting as the Bastards entered, and loosening as the boldest frail ventured forward to offer their compliments. A swaggering dandy, a cavalero making an overblown display of honor, a flushed lady looking to impress with her courage. There was always one ready to charge forward and be the first to welcome the half-orcs, their face changing with each pavilion. Oats and his brothers waded into each new fray, led by Sluggard, who charmed the forward assault within moments. He had men laughing and women blushing. Hells, he had women laughing and men blushing. He wore the skin of a champion well, never falling to boasting, but neither was he humble to the point of bootlicking. Oats was impressed with the way he kept close to Hood, often speaking for the silent mongrel yet somehow preventing him from appearing hostile or simple-minded. It was a kind of magic, being earnest. It left Oats to focus on preventing Polecat from whipping his cod out at a baroness or some shit. But the former Rutter was almost as easy in this company as Sluggard. His manner was less refined, but no less capable of treading these waters without drowning. And he kept Culprit afloat to boot, the younger mongrel at his elbow as they reveled with blue-blood frails.

There was still hatred in those tents, lingering at the edges with hard eyes and tight lips, but none were quarrelsome, as Oats feared. Still, he kept a sharp eye on his brothers and only nursed his wine.

"Nothing will befall them here."

Oats turned at the voice to find a woman beside him. She was less gaudily adorned than most, eschewing the towering, veiled headdresses swathing the heads of the other court women. Still, her hair—a pristine silver—was arranged in a fashion that Oats reckoned took several servants to accomplish. She wasn't looking at him, but the wry set of her lips suggested it was to him she spoke. That and, though they were in the company of many, no one else was engaged with her.

"Pardon?" Oats said.

The woman raised a finger away from her goblet and wagged it at the gathering. "They're all too well heeled. Their fear of the queen suppresses any malice toward you. She's made it known her mongrel guests are not to be mistreated."

"Huh."

The woman looked up at his grunt, eyes bright. Oats now recognized that bold stare. It was the same stare he'd spied on his way down the terrace. He'd been so quick to turn away he'd not noticed the silver hair. It was the most obvious testament to her age. There were wrinkles upon her brow and framing her lips, but they were etched by good humor. Her skin was a touch darker than what was common among the court, showing some time in the sun over the years, but was otherwise flawless. Older, certainly, but far, *far* from a crone.

"It's just that you looked like a worried mother goose," she said with a teasing smile.

"Oh." Oats drank from his goblet for lack of anything else to say.

The woman leaned toward him a hair and made a short, sharp hiss.

Oats couldn't help but shoot her a confused look. "The hells?"

"Oh-*tss*. I believe you meant. Your name."

"Right," he said, feeling a smile forming. "Oats. Yes. Queer when folk already know that."

"Why? I can't imagine you often need to introduce yourself among the hoofs. Surely most in the Lots know you by sight."

"Sure, but this ain't the Lots."

"No." The woman sipped from her goblet. "No, it is not. Sometimes I find it is far more dangerous."

Something in her tone gave Oats pause. "You've been to the Lots?"

"I was born there," the woman answered, her smile taking on a measure of pride. "My father's holding was near Xeret."

"That ruin on the Skull Sowers' land?" Oats said, taken aback.

"It was not so in my girlhood," the woman replied.

"Shit. Pardon. I didn't mean to—"

She waved his words off. "Please. My loss shed its power to be renewed long ago."

Oats was relieved he had not caused her harm. "We were born within a few days' ride of each other."

"Plus three decades, I'd say." That put this woman in her fifties. Hard to fathom, the way she looked. "The Bastards' lot lies between the Lucia and Batayat Hill, yes?"

"That's right."

"There was nothing there when I was a child."

Oats found himself staring into his cup. "Nothing there now."

The woman placed a hand on his arm. "Forgive me. You're young enough that your pain can still be further bruised. Was it orcs?"

Oats nodded. It had been the Orc Stains, in truth, but he wasn't about to speak about the hoofs warring on one another with a member of Ursaria's court.

"I am Xana," the woman said suddenly. She rolled her eyes. "I know. It sounds like a whore's name."

"I wasn't thinking that," Oats replied, laughing and lying. "But I reckon I was expecting some sort of contessa or something in the front."

"Well, I have a title. Though not, I'm afraid, one so lofty. I am a ricahembra."

"I . . . got no fucking notion what that is."

Xana tossed back her head and laughed. "No. No, I imagine not. It means my family is old and once held more than we do now. It means I was not worthy of a place at court until recently. But Her Majesty wished to surround herself with those with knowledge of Ul-wundulas, so I found myself summoned. I swear I heard my father gasp in his grave when the herald arrived and I broke the queen's seal."

Oats was coming to realize that Xana was more than a little drunk, but she hid it so well he'd missed the signs until now.

"So tell me, Oats, is this your first time in Hispartha?"

"Yes."

Xana narrowed her eyes a bit, but there was no scorn in her look. She knew he was lying, he was certain of it, but it seemed to amuse rather than anger her. "And?"

"I'll be glad when our task here is done."

Xana nodded, drawing in a long, silent breath. "It has been forty years since I fled Ul-wundulas. And do you know what I still miss?"

"What?"

"Absolutely nothing."

Oats's laughter drew every eye in the pavilion.

"You truly are from there," he said when he caught his breath. "Hells . . ."

A man in livery stepped into the pavilion and lifted his voice.

"Her Majesty the queen wishes her guests to attend her in the Prince's Wood!"

Xana's stare flashed at Oats. "Time to award the champions. It was pleasant speaking with you, Oats."

With that she turned and folded gracefully into the flow of nobles exiting the pavilion.

HUNDREDS OF CANDLES NOW FLOATED upon the lake in the constructed forest, bobbing in wide, shallow wooden bowls. The court and cavaleros gathered beneath the trees at the northern edge of the water, jostling for view of the queen. It seemed the common folk were not to witness the rewarding of the day's victors. Oats stood with the Bastards at the rear of the crowd upon its left edge.

Queen Ursaria, backed by torch-bearing Bulls and the fire-eyed Matron Spear, lifted her voice.

"Such a day! Worthy, I hope you all agree, of our beloved prince."

The court replied with a lusty cheer of agreement. Mannrique stood to his half-sister's left, and visibly shrank from the praise. Here and there, cavaleros added their voices, but most merely stood. They seemed eager for the night to be over. Oats didn't blame them. He longed to lie down. It wasn't fatigue so much as a desire to be in the quiet, away from so many. His every sinew had been drawn tighter than a thrumstring all day.

"And now I bid the champion of the tavolado come forward!"

Hoodwink slid from the hoof. Had it been any other brother the Bastards might have thrown some jests at his back and Polecat a swat at his ass, but they let Hood go unmolested. As he made his way around the crowd, a servant brought something to the queen. Oats couldn't quite make out what it was, but it was flat and pliable.

It was a queer sight, Hoodwink standing before the ruler of Hispartha. The scarred, hairless, bone-white mongrel had killed hells-only-knew how many. Orcs and thrice-bloods, cavaleros and god-blessed champions—all more formidable than the woman now in front of him—yet she was the most dangerous of them all. Oats wondered if Ursaria knew she faced a serpent, a cold-blooded creature that could strike quicker than an eye could blink. She would be dead before the Bulls could react. Oats doubted even Engraçia Bracara, standing nearer the queen than any, could oppose Hood if he'd a mind to murder.

A cold fear gripped Oats's heart. Hells, was this Crafty's plan? To cut the queen down in front of her own court? Hoodwink had been trained by the Black Womb. He claimed loyalty to Fetch and the hoof, but . . .

Hood's hands came up and accepted what the queen held forth. He turned to go and Ursaria laughed, high and clear, though without mockery.

"Wait, hoof-rider. Put it on."

Hood paused. He worked his hand into what Oats now saw was a heavy glove.

"Hold your arm up," the queen said.

Hood did as she said. The court gasped with delight as a falcon swooped from the shadowed trees to land on Hood's wrist.

"Suddenly glad it was him that won," Polecat muttered. "I'd have shat my breeches if that buzzard came flying at me unexpected."

Thresher huffed. "I might have slapped it out of the sky."

Culprit sniggered.

Of course, Hoodwink hadn't stirred. He stood a moment, staring at the falcon. When it was obvious nothing further was to happen, he walked away, bearing his gift. He retook his place among the hoof without meeting any eyes.

"What are you going to name it?" Culprit asked.

Hood and his new falcon killed the young mongrel's smile with identical glances.

"And now to offer the reward for the most thrilling pàreo I have ever beheld!" the queen announced. She tilted her head and grinned. "Though perhaps I should punish him for leaving me breathless."

There was laughter at this, including a chuckle from Sluggard, boots pawing the ground with eagerness.

The servant who brought the glove now approached with a gilded saddle slung over his forearms. The gems upon the cantle flashed as they caught the torchlight.

"Hells overburdened," Thresher gasped.

"Too bad it's for a horse," Culprit said.

Polecat cuffed him across the back of the head. "It ain't for riding, fool-ass."

No. But Oats didn't know what it *was* for. It had to be worth . . . hells, he'd no notion. The damn thing was too heavy to pass to the queen, so the servant stood beside her.

"I call forward the champion of the race, our very own Master of Victuallers, Barrasa de Oredal!"

The court cheered and applauded, mercifully covering Culprit's outburst.

"The fuck?!"

Oats was taken aback, but he managed not to expel any curses. He looked to Sluggard, now standing very straight and very still. His head was held carefully high.

Barrasa emerged from the crowd, flushed face bunched in a pleased smile. He knelt before the queen and, when bidden to rise, he went over and made a mummery of trying, and failing, to take the weighty saddle from the servant. The court laughed with appreciation.

Polecat stepped to Sluggard's side. "The hells is this?"

"The law," Sluggard replied. His voice was tight, eyes never leaving Barrasa. "The owner of the champion mount receives the prize. Not the rider."

"And you get nothing?"

Sluggard didn't answer right away, but when his words came they were flat. "I'd forgotten."

THERE WAS NO FEAST HELD that night. None dined with the queen. Sluggard had been wrong about that too. Instead, musicians invaded the wood and the nobles set to dancing. The court became a living wheel, the members moving with a unified precision as they circled and bowed, changing directions with the music. The cavaleros participated in some of the dances, but seemed to know when they should refrain. At times only women indulged, at others only men. It was a fluid beast of bodies, rippling and rolling in complicated patterns with practiced ease. After a time, Oats came to see it as a surging wall of silk and ritual the Bastards could not penetrate. Only Ahlamra held the secrets to join, but for all her grace she still appeared an outsider.

"Think I prefer the way the whores do it," Polecat said, his expression sour as he watched the latest crop of dancers. He leaned against a tree, Culprit asleep at its base. Sluggard and Hood had once again been drawn into the midst of the Guabians now gambling with dice against the Majethi in a hunkered clump across the lake. The game had finally drawn Thresher into the revels and from the sound of it, she was causing the humans to lose to a half-orc for the third time today.

Polecat rolled his cup around and pushed himself away from the tree. "I'm going to find one of them flagon boys. Get this filled. You want more wine?"

Oats shook his head. "And neither do you."

"No," Cat agreed, tossing the cup. "How much longer you wager these frails will go?"

"Till the queen says, I reckon."

Ursaria had joined in the dance only once at the start and spent the rest of the evening conversing with a steady rotation of nobles. Duke Hernan brought a handful of cavaleros into the queen's presence, and Oats saw the noblewoman Xana have a brief exchange with her. Mannrique sat beside the queen, receiving all with a forlorn resignation.

"Plucker's going to run back up to his mountain first chance he gets," Polecat said.

Oats didn't respond, but inwardly he agreed. If the queen was right and Crafty aimed to put Mannrique on the throne, the wizard would be hard-pressed to succeed. Oats didn't know much about court life, but it was clear the prince could hardly bear it. Another day of this and he was like to go mad. He looked ready to crack even now, as if the music and dancers were grinding the grist of his feeble stores of resolve. Ursaria didn't need swords to thwart Mannrique's claim, not when tourneys and minstrels would send him fleeing.

The commotion from the dice game stilled, yet one voice continued to rise. Oats looked over to see Sluggard and Thresher walking away from the group, pursued by a man shouting and pointing, a woman a step behind him.

Oats nudged Culprit awake with his boot. "Get up. We might have some trouble."

"Just a frail angry that he lost coin to mongrels," Polecat said.

"I don't think so. Come on."

Oats started walking. The unease in his gut swelled as he closed with Slug and Thresh. The man coming after them was Hisparthan, a member of court from his clothes. His words were now reaching Oats's ears through the music.

". . . demand an apology! You'll not slight us and walk away!"

Thresh had her hand on Sluggard's arm, encouraging him to keep walking.

The nobleman was undaunted in his steps and in his words. "I'll not suffer your half-breed backs another moment! Turn! We will have your pardon! Uncouth, impudent sootskins!"

Teeth bared, Sluggard tore from Thresh's grip, whirling on the man.

Oats reached him just in time, seizing his arm in a hold he couldn't break. Sluggard turned, his face enraged.

"Walk away," Oats said. "Whatever this is, we need to walk away."

Oats turned his eyes on the frails. Both were drunk, their expressions a hideous mix of haughty disdain and forced bravery. They were scared, Oats saw.

"Walk away," he growled.

The man hesitated a moment, but the woman reached forward to tug at his sleeve. He blinked, sneered, spat at Oats's feet, and turned. The woman took his arm and they retreated toward the dancing.

Oats let Sluggard go. "What happened?"

Fuming, Sluggard strode off without answering.

Oats put the question to Thresher with a look. She waited a moment, the tilt of her eyes making it known she wanted Sluggard out of earshot.

"They wanted him," she said. "For their bed."

"Oh, shit," Culprit said.

Thresher expelled a breath. "They said that fucker Barrasa told them he could be had. And . . . they'd already paid. Sluggard shoved the man away, said he should learn to pleasure his wife his own self."

Oats kept an eye on Sluggard, making sure he wasn't going to find Barrasa, but he'd stopped a short distance away. Hells, Fetch used to jest that his hoof name be Whore. He'd come to the Lots a gritter, a mongrel looking to get enough time in the badlands to gain a story or three, maybe a scar. After, he'd professed no other wish than to come back to the kingdom and be a paid plaything for noblewomen. The Orc Stains had robbed him of that chance, and yet here it was anyway.

Seeing him standing in that false wood now, Oats didn't think he'd ever seen a mongrel look more lost.

"We need to get him out of here," Thresher said.

Oats nodded in agreement. "You three take him back to the house. I'll stay here with Hood, watch out for Ahlamra."

Polecat, Thresh, and Culprit moved off without hesitation. Hoodwink stepped from the trees, where he'd been waiting, unseen, during the confrontation with the nobles.

"Where's your bird?" Oats asked.

"Set free."

"A trained falcon?" Oats said, thinking of Tarif's eagle. "Won't it just come back?"

"It needs no master to hunt."

"You know they wear hoods? Them hunting birds."

Hoodwink met his eye, one brow raised.

Oats sighed. "Yeah . . . not sure why I said that either."

They stood in silence, watching the dancing, for a long while.

"While we're waiting, you want to tell me where Xhreka is?" Oats muttered.

"No."

"Worth a try."

It was another three lengthy dances before the queen finally bade the musicians cease. The Bulls gathered around her as she took her leave, Engraçia Bracara leading the way down the path. The court waited until their queen was gone before shuffling away from the lake, many moving sore-footed. The drunkest were helped along by a friendly arm. Ahlamra and Crafty waited for the crowd to disperse, Fuqtus towering behind them. Several strides away Mannrique leaned over, his back turned. For a moment Oats thought he was being sick, but the prince was only lifting a besotted Loukas from one of the stone benches.

"Glad that's fucking over," Oats said when he and Hood approached.

"Yes," Ahlamra agreed. Her voice was tired, and her normally limpid eyes had dulled.

Oats stepped over to Mannrique and pointed at the swaying sack that was Loukas. "Better if I carry him."

"Thank you, but I have him." The prince squatted and hoisted his senseless friend across his shoulders like you would a calf.

"Perhaps I should have you do the same to me," Crafty jested at Fuqtus, but turned his smiling face away from the demon before getting an answer. The wizard motioned at the path. "Shall we?"

They left the wood. Mannrique carried Loukas all the way to the paddock, but accepted Oats's help when it came time to sling the man over the back of his horse. Dozens of servants worked beneath the night sky, clearing the pavilions, scurrying over the terrace to prepare it for the next day, all under the watchful eyes of sentries wearing the queen's tabard. The air was cool, the stars undimmed by clouds. Tired as he was, Oats felt enlivened as he climbed atop Ugfuck. The pleasant ride up to the city was a balm to the boisterous day. Even within the walls, where the smells and buildings were thick, he found a welcome retreat from the pageantry. They overtook several of the slower-moving nobles and Oats witnessed more than one coaxed off the street by the brazen calls of whores. There wasn't much of the night left, but some were willing to delay their rest to milk the last of its delights.

Oats dreaded the coming day. The return of cheering voices, sumptuous food, endless talk, the thought made him want to keep riding, to delay his own sleep and forestall the dawn. Try as he might, he could not fathom a life here. What he'd seen of Hispartha was a lie. Had Beryl brought him into the world in these lands, he wouldn't be attending this spectacle from behind a feasting table with the queen not a spit to his left. He wouldn't even be across the field with the common folk. Maybe he'd have driven the stakes for the tourney field, or loaded the barrels into the wine wagons. Or he'd have been like Incus and Sluggard, made to fight or ride for the joy of the blue bloods. Or perhaps he'd be leagues away, working a lord's fields, so distant and ignorant of the kingdom's rulers he would not even know their names, like Thresh once was. Beryl might have plied a trade, one he was meant to learn and continue, like Rant and Roar. No. Their father had been a frail, a thin shield of flesh able to protect his mongrel children for only so long as he lived. There'd have been no such father for him, a thrice-blood without a human parent to defy the world's hatred. Beryl's life, his life, would have been one of sweat and servitude.

Ul-wundulas squeezed plenty of sweat, but there was a reason that Slug and Thresh, Anvil, Rant and Roar, and countless other mongrels had come south. Oats wondered if he'd been fortunate to be Lot-born, to never have had to endure life among powerful frails. Or had it merely made him blind to the heart of all the hoofs stood against? Warbler knew. And the Claymaster. But did Oats himself? Did Jackal? Fetch? They knew that cavaleros were cunts and the Crown was to be defied, but the source of that defiance was little more than an inherited spite. Was there enough potency in such handed-down ire to stop Hispartha from returning? If so, what would the Lots look like, after? Oats could not imagine Kalbarca rebuilt to mirror Magerit. He could not picture windmills in the badlands. Mead and Sluggard had once dreamed of building an aqueduct, something Oats could hardly comprehend at the time. Now he'd seen them, along with the fountains they fed. Such sights were marvelous and yet still he could not find a place for them in the Ul-wundulas he knew.

Oats waited for the pang of restlessness to strike, the stirring in his blood that told him he needed to spur Ug south and return to the Lots, to the chief, to the fight. It did not come. He was disturbed to discover the thought of going home filled him with the same lack of fervor as another day at the tourney.

Hells, weariness was making him a maudlin fool.

Inside the foreyard to the prince's house, they got Loukas situated once more on Mannrique's shoulders.

"I'll see to your horse," Oats told the man. "Yours too, Rue."

Ahlamra handed him the reins with a grateful nod and followed Mannrique inside.

Crafty moved to lead Muck Shovel into the stable, but Fuqtus stepped in his path.

"Go," the demon said. "You need sleep."

Crafty said nothing, but he reached and placed a hand on Fuqtus's arm, letting it slide off as he walked away.

"Be back to untack you," Oats told Ugfuck, leaving him in the yard as he took the horses into the stable. Hood saw to his sow and came to help. Together, they got the horses stalled quickly. Hood drifted inside while Oats unsaddled Ug and made sure his bed of straw was thick enough.

Sleep, at last.

Oats went into the house, turning for the stairs. A wailing scream brought his steps to a startled halt. A shape ran from the gallery across the inner court and entered the moonlight. It was Guiomar, the scullery girl. Her face was contorted with despair and she stumbled in her flight, nearly blind with tears. Oats darted and caught the child in his hands.

"What is it?" he said, kneeling to try and get a look at her face. She did not appear harmed.

Guiomar sunk down, shaking. Her voice was stolen by sobs, but she pointed back the way she'd come.

Oats heard others moving on the floor above. Fuqtus was in the doorway behind.

"Watch her," Oats said, and ran for the back of the house, entering the room Guiomar fled to find a dark kitchen.

Nothing.

Oats moved past the cold hearth to the stairs at the rear of the room leading down into the scullery. He could smell the smoke from a snuffed candle as he descended.

He'd seen the awful suspended silhouette that greeted him once before. The same sick shock gripped his guts as it had all those years ago. The same disbelief, followed in the next heartbeat by the cold truth of the act before his eyes. Then, he'd been a young slop and rushed forward, gripping the mongrel's legs, lifting him to take the slack out of the rope, calling for help as he fumbled for his knife. Now he didn't move. He was older. And he knew. From the lack of swing in the body, from the horrible elongation in the neck, just enough to be unnatural, he knew it was too late.

Sluggard had made a choice. And there was nothing Oats could do to help him now.

Questions filled the numb cavity of Oats's mind, insistent and useless as he plodded up from the scullery. Questions that soon fled his skull to seek new life upon the tongues of his brethren, rushing into the kitchen. Thresh, Cat, Culprit. They all had weapons but no boots, no brigands. They relaxed, seeing Oats, but while his slow steps eased the tension in their bodies, his face planted worry in their eyes.

"It's Sluggard."

It was all he could say as he moved past them.

Out in the courtyard, Ahlamra sat on the ground, holding Guiomar. Fuqtus had come farther in, his axe drinking the cold moonlight.

"What has happened?" the demon demanded.

The same question was in Ahlamra's stare.

An anguished curse echoed from the scullery. Polecat.

Oats let that be the only answer. He looked up to the third story. Crafty stood at the railing of the veranda. Questions.

Sluggard's act had spawned a host that would never be answered. The hoof would ask them again and again in the coming days. Oats had breath for only one. The one that could, perhaps, be answered. He lifted his voice at the wizard.

"Why are we here?"

It was too far to see Crafty's expression.

"WHY ARE WE HERE!?"

His unanswered bellow fled the courtyard and perished beneath the small, remorseless square of fading night.

THIRTY-FIVE

SLUGGARD WAS CREMATED IN A roofless temple sitting at the base of the hills among the farms outside the city walls. Oats heard and immediately forgot the name of the goddess that was said to dwell there. If the state of her temple was any sign, she was ancient and poor.

Mannrique had known of the place, leading the hoof down not long after dawn. Three men and three women were already at work outside, cutting Hispartha's ever-encroaching wild grass away from the bleached stones with sickles. Seeing the riders, they ceased their labor. Sluggard's covered body rested on a wicker cart the prince had sent Loukas to purchase before the sun was up. That and a purse of coin were all the goddesses' servants needed to see.

There were preparations required. Washing and anointing and whatever else these folk believed necessary to complicate the burning of a corpse. Thresh accompanied them through the entrance columns with the cart. The rest of the Bastards waited among the dewy grass, fragrant from the fresh reaping. Mannrique chose to linger with them. The court was to be entertained with a hunt this morning and his absence would not be marked. Oats could sense Ahlamra was uneasy about the prospect of Crafty being alone with the queen, but she refused to leave. The girl Guiomar was also with them, too frightened to be left alone in the house.

Oats was angry at Sluggard for that. Poor child had risen and gone down to the scullery to begin preparations for the morning meal. She didn't deserve to find him hanging there.

Cat and Culprit were blaming themselves. Polecat hadn't even heard Slug leave the bedchamber they all shared, and Culprit thought he was merely going for a piss.

"What were you to do?" Thresher had barked at them in the house before the cart arrived. "Watch him his every waking moment? Selfish ass had made his mind."

"Dacia..." Ahlamra said, reaching out, but Thresh jerked away.

"He should have come to me!" she shouted, stabbing at her own chest with a vicious finger. "Why didn't he come to me?"

She'd said nothing since.

They were all quiet, worn out by grief, standing near one another yet isolated in their own heads. Mannrique and Guiomar waited a little removed from the hoof, the prince standing beneath a stand of pine where the horses were tethered, the girl sitting on a rock across the dirt track leading to the temple, her hands clasped upon her lap. Oats went to Mannrique.

"Thank you for this," he said, gesturing at the temple. "And for the coin it required."

"I regret it happened," the prince replied, rubbing his mare's nose. "The injustice done him at the race, as well."

Oats nodded.

"If there is more I can do, I will," Mannrique said.

"We're grateful."

The hogs were hobbled a short distance away from the horses. Oats cut Ugfuck out and led him into the partially cut field. He called to Guiomar. When the girl looked up he beckoned her over. She came at a dutiful walk, but could not entirely hide the trepidation in her eyes.

"Need a favor," Oats told her. He pointed at Ugfuck. "He was under them trees where there's gilt chain growing. It's poisonous and I don't need him eating it. So I'm going to walk him around. He does best with some weight in the saddle. Will you help?"

Guiomar cast a look back at the tree. "Aren't you worried about the other pigs?"

Oats shook his head. "They know what's good for them and what ain't. Ug here never quite learned that."

"What do you need me to do?"

Oats patted the saddle. "Just sit up here while I lead him around. He won't buck or nothing."

The girl squinted at the hog. "I don't think I can get up there."

"Well, I was going to offer to lift you up."

Guiomar thought a moment. She nodded.

Oats scooped her up under the arms and set her on Ug's back. She didn't weigh half what Muro did, though she was a finger taller.

"Now you can hold on here," Oats said, gripping the saddle pommel. "Or his mane. You won't hurt him if you do. We ain't gonna go fast."

Guiomar gripped the pommel with both hands.

Oats started walking, keeping his hand on Ug's left swine-yanker, but it was just to keep Guiomar from getting nervous. Ug would walk beside Oats all day without goading and there was no danger he'd throw the child. A snake could strike out of the grass and Ug would keep his calm.

"Good up there?" Oats asked after a span.

"Yes. He smells a little."

Oats chuckled. "A little." He remained quiet for several slow circuits of the field. "I'm sorry for what my friend did."

"It . . . I shouldn't have dropped the candle."

"Don't reckon anyone is sore at you for that."

"A room in the house down the lane burned because the serving boy placed a candle beneath a shelf. His master whipped him, notched his ear, and sold him. He was lucky not to be branded on the face with the mark of a firestarter."

"Shit," Oats said before he could stop himself. He cleared his throat. "Mannrique don't seem the sort to do that, even if the whole place was razed to the ground."

"This is the first time I've seen the prince. It's Master Loukas that lords the house."

"He mistreat you?" Oats tried to make the question light, but there was some tension in his voice he couldn't prevent.

"He's struck me a time or two," Guiomar replied with all the ease Oats had lacked. "Open-handed. Only once to the face. He's merry when he's in his cups and hosting whores, which is most days."

Hells, this girl had barely seen a decade yet sounded full grown. No. She'd have more bitterness in adulthood. For now, there was still no small amount of spirit in her.

"Sancho used to hit me much harder and more often."

It took Oats a moment to remember she meant her father, though his mind still conjured the long-dead whoremaster. He looked up at the girl. "What do you mean, used to?"

Guiomar's eyes flashed wide for a moment and her mouth drew tight. "No . . . of course he still does. When I've erred or talked willful. But . . . I'm older now, so I make less mistakes. And he stays away more. But I'm sure he'll be in a fury when he hears I've dropped a candle. Once he's back from Virovescos."

"Buying Traedrian wine?"

"That's right. It's a long journey."

Oats stopped walking and Ugfuck halted. "Guiomar. It was Anvillese cheese in Anitorgis when you first told it. I ain't as big a fool-ass as some say I look."

Guiomar began to squirm, throwing a less-than-artful look back toward the prince.

"You mustn't tell!" she hissed, jerking back to face Oats. "If Master Loukas finds out, he's likely to put me out in the street."

"Loukas ain't going to hear nothing from me," Oats said.

"Swear?" Guiomar asked, holding her breath.

"Swear."

The girl exhaled.

Oats set Ug to walking once more. "When did he run off?"

"Just after winter," Guiomar replied, her voice an old bruise, more ugly than pained. "Isn't much I can't cook as well as he did, so Master Loukas hasn't noticed. He's more for drink than food, anyway. He might have discovered it before much longer, but you all arriving has him distracted. I can say Sancho returned and went again, and perhaps fool him another month or two once you've gone."

"What happens when you don't serve all this foreign wine and cheese your father's been wandering the kingdom to purchase?"

"Master Loukas rarely listens. And never remembers when he does. I'm wagering that so long as he doesn't starve or have to launder his own clothes, he won't get wise. I'll have to leave when I grow tits anyway, lest he try to make me some hearth whore, which I'll not be."

"Then where will you go?"

Guiomar's cheek met her shoulder when she shrugged.

Oats didn't press it. Last thing this child needed was some Lotborn thrice-blood, ignorant of most of Hispartha's ways, offering advice. All he knew was Ul-wundulas, and there was nothing there that would benefit her. She was likely safer in the alleys of Magerit, should it come to that.

They walked a while longer in silence.

"Why'd he do it?" Guiomar asked.

"I couldn't say, girl. I ain't met a Sancho yet that was worth a heap of hogshit."

"No. Not my father. Your friend?"

Oats took a deep breath. He almost said he didn't know. It would have been simpler, and perhaps even the truth. But he'd been gnawing on it all morning. Hells, he'd thought about it often since he was a youth and found that fellow slop. He stopped once again and held up his left hand, showing Guiomar his shortened fingers.

"Lost these in a battle," he said. "The middle one here, that was gone when it happened. The other was still attached, but it was too crushed, too badly hurt. Best to cut it away. Might rot elsewise, and I'd lose the finger entire anyway. Or my hand. My life, even. Small wounds can do that, force you to suffer a worse injury to save your life. You can live without fingers, limbs. You likely knew that already."

Guiomar nodded. Oats went on.

"Sluggard. My friend? He suffered and survived some grievous shit. But there were other wounds, ones we couldn't see. They were in his head, his heart. And . . . they were rotting. They hurt, worse as time goes on. We didn't know it, maybe even Sluggard didn't know, but those wounds were killing him. Problem is, you can't cut those away and live, Guiomar."

"Do you have wounds like that?"

And there it was. The chance to unburden the truth. Oats wondered how many times Sluggard had been given that chance, how many times an earnest offer to lay his pain bare was put before him. Not often enough, Oats knew from his own relationship with the mongrel. Thresher had raged that Sluggard hadn't confessed his torments to her, but what hoof-rider admitted such to another? That fellow slophead hadn't, no doubt because he feared that revealing some inner weakness would surely have spelled an end to his bid for a brigand. It wasn't a thing you just came out and said, not to a sworn brother and especially not to a young, fatherless girl.

"*I*," Oats told her with a smile, "have a giant hog that smells a little. And sometimes a lot."

Guiomar laughed and Oats realized there was always a reason to spare another discomfort. Sluggard must have spared them all countless times. Oats wished for all the hells he hadn't.

THE CART PROVED TO BE more than a means of transporting the body. When it was time, they went into the temple and found the conveyance was part of the rite. Draped in linen, it rested now in a broad stone basin at the center of the temple. Sluggard was barely discernible beneath the layers of cloth until the priests and priestesses began to pour oil from amphorae over him, and the sodden linen sunk to reveal his features.

"You may speak now for the dead," one of the priests told the assembled hoof.

They all looked to Thresher.

She took a deep breath.

"So much should have killed Sluggard," she began. "He was, in some ways, the softest mongrel I ever knew. In others, the toughest. And those were the ways that mattered."

She stopped speaking and Oats thought she was through, but Thresh cleared her throat, started again.

"I've endured pain. Cruelty. More than most, I reckon. More than most men, for certain. And I bear the scars, out . . . and in. I'm alive, but joy for this life was murdered in me a long time ago. With all that was taken from Sluggard, he never let them take that. At least, that's what I thought. What his easy smiles convinced me to believe. Hells, he had a pretty smile." Thresh's words were coming in throbs now, but she pressed on. "Can't help but wonder now if it was a pretty lie, that smile. Wish I could see it again, have another chance to know. But I ain't ever gonna. Here's what I know. We rode together through this fucking kingdom, wanted and hiding, gathering up mongrels for months. He had courage. That was no lie. Neither was his friendship. Nor his grit. I don't ever got to wonder about that. Goodbye, Slug. Fuck this world for taking you from us."

The devoted of the goddess put flame to the linen.

As Sluggard burned, Oats thought of killing Crafty.

Fetch had said the wizard should die the moment he became a danger. He'd done nothing to hurt Sluggard, but . . . he'd *done* nothing. Where were the schemes to weaken Hispartha? They'd trusted only that he would be a serpent and, once again, he'd made them fools to trust. And once again, Bastards were starting to die. Could very well be time to give Hood the order.

And then?

Hoodwink had said Fuqtus could not be bested. Oats reasoned that was true. Horned fucker had fought the chief to a standstill. What could any of the mongrels here do against him? Was killing the wizard worth all their lives? Even if they ran, they'd never make it back to the Lots, not without the protection of Tyrkania's envoy. And on the miracle they did, they would have accomplished nothing. They couldn't flee, they couldn't fight. They'd come willingly into Hispartha and now it held them trapped.

Sluggard had been so eager to return. Through their tears his brethren watched him leave as smoke.

FROM HIS PLACE ON THE top tier of the queen's terrace, Oats viewed the joust in a fog of heartsick exhaustion. Were it not for the shrieking of the nobles he might have fallen asleep where he sat. Dimly, he'd witnessed the tide of commoners swell to the brink of bursting the fence, raising a clamor as every man to participate in the lists rode in a parade around the field. Seeing them, it appeared the contest was for the most elaborate armor. Their plate was enameled in every color where it wasn't bare metal chased with bronze or gold. Many wore helms fashioned to resemble beasts and monsters; others had the skins of actual animals affixed. Ribbons of silk, tied everywhere on man and horse, streamed behind the riders.

The field cleared and endless pairs of men were called forward by a herald to begin charging each other, again and again, their hollow lances breaking upon shields or knocking a man from the saddle. Packed shoulder to shoulder upon the terraces below, the members of court shouted themselves hoarse at every match, the women often waving lengths of scarf. The noise made talk impossible, leaving Ahlamra and Crafty nothing to do but add two more pairs of eyeballs to the spectacle. It didn't look to Oats like Queen Ursaria would allow anything to distract her from the joust even if it had been quieter. She stood for several of the cavaleros when they took their turns, a gesture that always renewed the din of voices.

Oats ate but little and drank even less, knowing a belly heavy with food swimming in wine would put him in a slumber despite the raucousness. Guiomar stood behind Ahlamra, allowed on the terrace as her servant. The girl was enraptured by the contests. Oats was glad to see her shed the horror of this morning. He envied her a little.

But the child saw more death before noon.

A cavalero unhorsed one of the Anvillese and the man took a hard fall. Oats knew he was doomed before he hit the ground. No helmet could save a neck from being snapped when falling at that angle.

It didn't end there.

The Guabic knights offered a fresh challenge, claiming that none were brave enough to throw down the hollow cañas and face them with war lances. The first cavalero to accept had his forearm snapped in two by the weapon before it carried through to pierce his pelvis. Rather than sober the crowd, the grim outcome stoked their howling. A Majethi had his shield arm torn off at the shoulder. He pitched from the saddle and died wallowing in his own blood. One unlucky Hisparthan took the head of his opponent's lance through the eye slit of his helm. Oats heard his skull split over the roar of the crowd.

It was only then that the queen called an end to the war lances and a respite for the joust. The commoners were not pleased and let her hear it, but she did not relent. Grateful for the chance to get out from behind the banquet table and stretch his legs, Oats followed the members of court down the steps. The hoof met him at the bottom of the terrace. The queen had not moved from her seat and was now speaking with Ahlamra and Crafty. Oats had thought she'd go to the wood, but perhaps she wanted to avoid Mannrique, who had fled there shortly after the joust began. The thought of returning to the upper terrace forced a sigh from Oats.

"Hood, keep an eye on Ahlamra," he said. "I'm about to crawl out of my skin up there. Culprit, go to the paddock. See if Thresher needs relieving. Cat, look to the prince."

"Fuck You is with him," Polecat replied.

"Is that blue devil a Bastard?" Oats growled.

Taking the point, Polecat raised his palms in pardon and ambled toward the wood.

Oats meandered among the pavilions. His mood was sour and he allowed it to show, keeping the more exuberant nobles at bay with a rigid scowl. He found a pavilion occupied by none but the attendant servant and loitered there, staring at the overflowing platters upon the trestles. He didn't eat, wasn't even tempted, and the knowledge caused him to huff a breath.

As a child, he dreamed of food, though the meager offerings of his mother's table had not stocked his imagination with what he now gazed upon. Fruits of every size and hue, piles of glistening game fowl, stout wheels of cheese. And this was but one table in one tent on a single day of this seemingly endless tourney. A few extra loaves of bread, an extra portion of beans, those would have been a hoard at the orphanage. His own time under that roof was bountiful compared to what the last crop of foundlings endured in the final days of Winsome.

"Strange to revile what you once coveted, isn't it?"

Oats turned to find Barrasa smiling at him from the pavilion's entrance. The man stepped farther in to approach the trestles. He surveyed their contents with a cocked head.

"I gorged for a month when I first gained Her Majesty's favor," he said without looking up at Oats. "Now I can hardly abide the smell of saffron and clove."

Barrasa picked up a peach. His lip wrinkled as he turned it over, fingers clenching in pulses. He tossed it back down.

"Take these away," he said to the servant. "They're running to soft. Go fetch something suitable to replace them."

The boy jumped to the task, fleeing the pavilion with a basket of fruit Oats would have killed for in his boyhood. Hells, he would have killed for it last year. Barrasa circled the provender, the sharp motions of his neck reminding Oats of a buzzard newly landed next to a carcass. Satisfied, the Master of Victuallers looked up.

"Most nights I sup on cinder bread and salted mullet," he said with a wry grin. "The repast of a carnavale master. My shits are easier, I've found."

Oats turned to go.

"Where might I find Sivastian?"

The question stopped him cold.

"Sluggard, I suppose I should say, though the name is horrid. Did he choose it to spite me?"

Slowly, Oats faced Barrasa once more. "I got no fucking notion, frail."

"About the name or where I can find him?"

"Pick one."

"His hog wasn't among your other swine," Barrasa said. "Has he run off from you as he did me? The boy never had a measure of loyalty."

"Shut your cunt mouth."

Barrasa rolled his eyes upward and loosed a sighing, humorless laugh. "Madre, he has. Why does he turn tail whenever his fortune is within reach?"

"Fortune? The one you fucking stole from him?"

Barrasa waved that off. "A gaudy saddle. Useless for a lifetime or sold for a year's comfort. And none in Magerit would give a mongrel a good price. The hog is mine, so the prize was mine. I offered him something far more valuable. A second chance at what he desired, what we'd nearly accomplished before he ran off. Fool that I am."

Outside, the queen's heralds were calling for the joust to continue. Oats heard the nobles moving through the lane at his back.

"Reckon you overestimated his desire to have you as his bawd," Oats said.

Barrasa blew a disgusted noise from his lips and came around the table. He lowered his voice. "These fucking blue bloods are slaves to tradition. Everything, everyone, has a place in their world. And they brand it with their court-speak. Every cortejo needs a pandarus. They won't stoop to solicit Sivastian directly. He knows that! I'd have given him the coin. He's no reason not to trust me."

"His former slaver," Oats muttered. "Wager he'd more than enough."

Barrasa came closer, his splotchy face darkening. "I'd no position when I found him. You think I was a lord, to own a mongrel? I was the wagon-born son of a gailliard. My inheritance was a keen eye for the knack. And that young half-orc had it. I took him into my carnavale and trained him, fed him, spent the coin to get him the swiftest hog to be found in the kingdom. I owned Palla, not him. And he owed me more than the betrayal I got when he stole from me and ruined my carnavale."

"You seem to have survived."

"And bore no grudges in the bargain. Yet he spit in my eye again. Humiliated a backy baron and his marinating wife, for what? To show he's too proud now that he's a Lots rider? No, can't be that, else he'd not have spurred away from you too. So, what I'm coming to understand is, Sivastian—for all his gifts—delights in nothing so much as he does to repay affection with abandonment. Will you send your brethren after him? From what I understand the mongrel hoofs don't brook desertion."

"You know nothing of us. Or him."

"I know he was ungrateful. I know he was comely when he left, finely shaped, but he came back fleshy. And with the scars of that hideous scalped pate, there was no chance of him catching lusty eyes the way he once did. If he'd not won the pàreo, I'd have been hard-pressed to tempt any with him. But I saw the chance, tried to take the sting out of him losing the saddle. And I know he ran rather than show me a fig of gratitude."

"He didn't fucking run."

Barrasa drew his head back in a mocking way. "No? Than why do your bloodshot eyes blaze as we speak of him? Why does your jaw threaten to snap beneath that beard? I may have risen to the queen's court, but I have not lost my eye. You don't have the knack for mummery, thrice. Your anger is not feigned. Sivastian has caused you grief, I can see it. He's put heel to hog . . ."

"No."

"He's broken faith again . . ."

"No."

"It's said you take on oaths when your flesh is inked. He's likely broken every vow he ever took—"

Oats seized Barrasa's doublet and snatched him close. The man's eyes went wide and he squirmed, but there was no chance of him breaking free.

"You listen to me," Oats said, pouring the soft, slow threat of his words down upon the little man. "Sluggard didn't run. He's dead. That grief you see is for my brother Bastard, so you best think about how you next speak of him."

Barrasa's struggles ceased. "Dead?"

Oats let him go with a slight shove.

Barrasa straightened his rumpled clothing. "May I ask how?"

"Killed himself," Oats replied, unwilling to place shame on the act by hiding it.

"Martyred Madre," Barrasa swore, jaw slack. It was quiet outside the pavilion now, though the cheers from the crowd were beginning to build from the direction of the tourney field. "Poor lad. But when you've suffered as he did . . . what man wouldn't?"

Oats went cold. "What?"

Barrasa held up his hand. "I only mean it is a tragedy. He always revered the Lots. To go down there, only to be so savagely mutilated . . ." The man shook his head with regret.

"How do you know about that? He wouldn't have told you."

"A scalping?" Barrasa gave Oats an incredulous stare. "I saw. He couldn't hide the scars, try as he might beneath that kerchief."

"No. That ain't what you meant. And you didn't see his scalp neither, now that I think on it."

"It fell off during the race."

"The same race I watched where it didn't? Try again."

"Must have been during the tavolado."

Oats shook his head. "He was careful with that kerchief. Didn't even take it off to . . . bathe." Realization made him bare his teeth. "Who fucking told you?"

"Calm yourself," Barrasa said, holding up a wary hand. "It was the prince's man."

"Loukas . . ." Oats snarled.

"I was merely curious about Sivastian. He looked so changed. The Lots aren't known as a land of largesse. It was strange to see him softer in the middle than when he left. When I learned he'd been made a eunuch, I felt nothing but pity. I wouldn't wish that upon him, no matter what transpired between us. I don't relish that he is dead. I'll risk your anger to admit it pains me to hear it."

"You knew," Oats said, teeth grinding. "You knew and yet still you conspired to peddle his fucking flesh?"

Barrasa hesitated. "The baron . . . has strange tastes."

Oats took a step forward. "Hogshit."

Barrasa held his ground. "I only wanted a small redress. A dose of retribution. I didn't know he would take his own life. How could I?"

"How could you," Oats repeated.

"Harm me and he won't be the only mongrel to die here," Barrasa said, calm in his certainty.

The truth of it brought Oats to a halt. Her Majesty's Master of Victuallers, unarmed, murdered by the thrice-blood Bastard in a rage. It was everything Ahlamra had cautioned them against.

Oats took a breath and backed off.

With a gloating grin, Barrasa nodded. He moved to leave, but paused next to Oats.

"Palla is stabled at the prince's house?" he asked.

Swallowing, Oats nodded.

"Good. I'll send a servant to fetch him."

Barrasa's head snapped to the side, flinging bloody spittle over Oats's fist. Like the jouster from Anville, Oats knew the man was dead before he hit the ground. He stood, staring down at the crumpled form, unable to move.

The serving boy returned to the pavilion and the basket of peaches tumbled from his grasp.

THIRTY-SIX

OATS STOOD CHAINED NEXT TO the lake in the middle of the queen's fool-ass forest, guarded by no fewer than sixty men-at-arms. He was certain of the number. He'd counted them several times now.

He hadn't considered fleeing. There'd been time when the boy ran off, raising a cry. Oats could have made it to the paddock, to Ug, but that would only have dragged Thresh and Culprit into the shit. They'd have insisted on riding with him. It wouldn't have been right. So, he'd stood firm, as he stood now. He was fortunate the cavaleros who came rushing into the pavilion hadn't slain him on the spot. Perhaps if they'd found him with a sword in his hand rather than a half-eaten peach . . .

It was something Jackal might have done, chewing on that fruit, but Oats wasn't trying to be cocky. He wasn't celebrating killing Barrasa, though the fucker deserved it. He simply, suddenly, wanted to taste something good, to find a grain of pleasure in the barren desert he'd blinked to find himself wandering.

Anselmo Volador had arrived at the pavilion not long after the cavaleros. In his quivering voice, the man actually asked if Oats would allow himself to be chained. A cautious question and, Oats had to admit, a wise one. To Volador's visible relief, Oats held his wrists out. He hadn't expected to be taken to the wood, but the path his guards took there—behind the pavilions and the Queen's terrace—revealed the reason. It was close, out of sight, giving the Queen a place to render judgment without alerting the commoners that anything was amiss.

The court, however, was gifted with fresh entertainment.

The nobles gathered around, listening in hungry silence as the serving boy told Ursaria what he saw. Oats kept his eyes on Ahlamra, her presence providing him a mixture of relief and shame. He hadn't seen the rest of the hoof. Likely they were barred from entering. The wood had been empty when Oats got there, so he'd no notion if Polecat had caught wind of what happened. If he had, the others would know by now. Hells, Oats hoped they knew better than to try a rescue.

"The half-orc is to die."

The queen's proclamation fell with the same swiftness, the same lack of thought or feeling Oats had used to kill Barrasa. He reckoned there was some poetry to that. But the judgment had come quicker than he expected. He hadn't even been asked to speak for himself.

"Your Majesty, I would beg mercy," Ahlamra said. She didn't grovel, but the soft plea within her face and voice was earnest.

The nobles stirred with aggravated murmurs.

"I cannot grant it," Ursaria said. "The base and dishonorable slaying of a member of my court will not be suffered."

"Majesty," Ahlamra said, quieter, but Oats was close enough to hear. "Among our hoof we call each other brother and sister. Yet Oats shares a true sibling's bond with our chief. Theirs is a companionship from birth. His execution here will end all hope of peace. I must risk Your Majesty's displeasure out of duty when I assure you, both our lands will bleed and burn should you do this. Fetching's thirst for vengeance will be unquenchable."

Ursaria's face went cold even as her eyes began to burn. She fixed Ahlamra with that conflicted fury, but mastered herself after a heartbeat. She turned to Crafty and voiced a steady question.

"And would the Tyrkanian Empire feel compelled to support the mongrels' war knowing it was a mongrel's mindless savagery that broke the peace?"

Crafty sighed, and damn him if his distress wasn't as earnest as Ahlamra's. He considered a moment.

"No, Righteous Queen," he replied, at last. "The sultans value honor above all. If dread Fetching cannot accept the just sentence brought down upon her rider for his red-handed deed, she will pursue any retribution without the empire."

"Retribution?" Ursaria said, her voice nettled. "Rebellion, surely, is what you mean."

"As you say," Crafty said, with a bow.

Queen Ursaria looked to Oats, stone-faced, and gathered a breath.

"However," Crafty said, taking a half step toward the queen. "I fear I would be remiss if I did not attempt to lessen the bloodshed. May I, Patient Queen, offer a cautery?"

Ursaria swallowed a rising vexation. "Speak."

Crafty spread his hands. "A murder demands execution. Yet, the gallows, the headsman's scaffold, they are . . . docile methods. Perhaps Her Majesty can seize the chance to end this festival with an amusement to rival all. One that will see justice done, but assuage the warlord Fetching's pride. You see, the mongrel hoofs hold dear a certain oath . . ."

The words came boiling from Oats's gut.

"Live in the saddle. Die on the hog."

He held Ahlamra's eyes as he said them. It was a plea of his own. Her face was softened by sorrow as she gave him the barest nod.

"Allow Oats to fulfill it and he meets the deserved punishment, Your Majesty," Crafty said. "Your tourney field stands perfectly prepared."

"A mounted duel," the queen mused, and Oats realized she was weighing the response of her court. He did not turn, but could feel the flutters of their enthusiasm.

"And should he prove victorious?" the queen challenged Crafty.

The wizard unveiled his smile. "Wise Queen, there is nothing to dictate the contest be something he can win."

IT WAS POLECAT WHO BROUGHT Ugfuck to the marshalling field behind the queen's terrace, eyeing the guards with crossbows as he came.

"We drew straws," the hatchet-faced mongrel said when he reached Oats. "Thresh won, but I told her I wanted to come."

"I owe you some coin I don't recall?" Oats asked.

Polecat did not so much as smile. His pained stare was held captive by Oats's chains.

"This ain't right," he whispered.

"It's as wrong as I've made it, Cat."

"Give the word," Polecat said in orcish. "And we'll come."

"None of that thick-speak!" one of the guards growled. "You've brought the pig, now get you gone."

Polecat gave the man a shit-eye, but bit back any reply. He turned to Oats.

"Brother, we—"

"Get gone, sootskin!"

The guard stepped and shoved Polecat. The mongrel's eyes ignited, but Oats caught them, returned a hard stare of his own, and shook his head. Polecat plodded backward a few steps, bullied by the guards.

"I ain't gonna wish you luck," Polecat called over the men hurrying him along. "I wish it to these frails! They don't know who you are. You're the Big Bastard! Champion of the Pit of Homage! Orcs. Giants. Centaurs. You put them all in the ground! You're a Bastard, Grey and True! YOU'RE FUCKING OATS! And we will see you again, brother! We will see you again!"

Oats stood beside Ugfuck and did not look away until Cat was out of sight. Wanting no interference, the queen had forbidden the hoof from viewing what was to come. Only Ahlamra was permitted. She was already sat up near the queen. He'd told her to make certain the others did not rile at the queen's order, and also to send Guiomar back to the city with Loukas. The girl should not be forced to witness any more horrors on the Bastards' account. Mannrique had no desire to be present, but the queen insisted.

Before they parted, Oats made a final request to Ahlamra. No reprisals. And no sending word to Fetch. He didn't know how possible peace with Hispartha was—and any chance had certainly been hobbled by his stupidity—but he wanted to give Ahlamra time to mend what he'd broken. Time she wouldn't get if the chief came.

Queer to think he wouldn't be here to see whatever happened.

He wondered if Warbler would do what he asked, what Ahlamra swore to tell him. The old thrice had left the hoof twice before. Unwillingly the first time, of his own notion the second. Would he leave a third? Shed the brigand and look after Beryl, take her back to Dog Fall with Wily and find her lost happiness? Would he honor the final wish of a son?

Again, Oats would be gone. He'd never know. Perhaps it should have angered him, but he was too damn tired.

"Wish they'd hurry this along," he told Ugfuck.

For all the lush beauty of the stepped terrace from the front, the back was nothing but a high slope of dirt, shored up with wooden framing. Standing in its shadow, Oats could see the backs of the Queen's Bulls just beyond the upper railing. The blare of unseen trumpets rose from the other side. Silence followed, but soon Oats caught the weakest slivers of a man's raised voice. A herald, he knew, proclaiming to the commoners what they were about to see.

Oats didn't need to hear the words to know what was said.

A mongrel. A murderer. A monster from Ul-wundulas, that untamed land from which rebellious half-orcs cast ravenous and jealous eyes northward, intent on slaughter and rape. Good Queen Ursaria was now to prove such creatures were not to be feared, to show her people they could be vanquished.

Ugfuck jerked a little when the terrace erupted with cheers. Whoever stood for the queen must have taken the field.

"Easy," Oats told Ug, placing the heels of his bound hands on the hog's withers.

As the cries intensified, his chains were removed and the guards commanded him to the field's northern entrance, a gap between the terrace and the Prince's Wood. The crossbowmen aimed their weapons and warned what would happen if Oats tried to run. He'd no intention of running. He didn't even mount, but walked Ug to the gap.

What he saw down the length of the field made him grunt. Crafty had been right, it wasn't a contest he could win.

Six cavaleros in full armor sat barded stallions, lances pointing skyward. And it wasn't the demi-lances, steel caps, and scale coats of the cavaleros Oats was used to fighting in the Lots but plate harness, full helms, and heavy war lances. Even with a thrum, a full quiver, and a brace of javelins, he would have stood little chance.

One of the guards handed him his tulwar.

"Ride out," the man said.

Oats didn't climb into the saddle. He stepped around in front of Ugfuck, instead, and knuckled him between the eyes.

"There ain't no oath worth you dying too," he said. "Not when you don't need to."

Ugfuck grunted and butted Oats in the cods with his snout.

"No. You're staying here. When you get back home, Anvil will need you. You look after her now." Ug complained again. Oats leaned down and placed his forehead on the broad, flat expanse of the hog's skull. "You ain't paying for my mistake, you beautiful ugly fuck."

The mouthy guard lost patience. "Mount up and ride out!"

"I'm walking out," Oats told him, straightening. "There's eight of you. More than enough to kill me with them thrums, but one volley ain't gonna drop this hog, which means he'll get mad. You'll all die uglier than him before you can reload. So leave him be and live. And let me go to the hells the way I want."

Oats gave Ugfuck the sign to stay and strode out onto the field.

The ugly noises from the crowd brought him back to his first fight in the Pit. They'd hated him then too. That changed after a few victories. The sickness he'd felt in his guts never did. Still, he was grateful to Crafty, sparing him the impotence of a death on the gallows, hands tied behind his back while some fucker put a noose around his neck. He would die today, but he didn't know which of the men before him would land the blow. He wouldn't endure that torturous trickle of collapsing time before the end, that evil wait before the drop. Sparing Ug had cost him the Bastards oath, but there was another he could fulfill, the words of the Fangs of Our Fathers.

Live in the battle. Die in a fury.

All fatigue fled Oats as he started running, fed by that building fury.

The cavaleros hesitated. They'd expected him to be ahog. Ug would have been his only real weapon in this fight and now he charged on foot, slower, smaller. It wouldn't take six horsemen to deal with him now. Oats sprinted on, desperate to rob them of the chance to declare he must be mounted, to keep Ug from being condemned. He saw the herald skirt the edge of the field, riding for the front of the terrace. If the queen decreed this was not the contest she desired ...

Oats changed direction, darting left, toward the herald. Toward the court. Let them think he intended to leap into the midst of the nobles.

Five of the cavaleros spurred their mounts to cut an angled course across the width of the field. They would reach the terrace ahead of Oats, to place themselves between him and their precious blue bloods. Didn't matter. They'd taken the bait. The remaining rider came straight for Oats, lowering his lance. Good. The battle would be joined and there would be no stopping it.

Oats again changed direction, to meet the lone cavalero.

The size of the man, his horse, that cobalt armor, that red hand painted on the shield.

It was Duke Hernan.

He'd admitted to being eager to lead the war against the Lots. Perhaps Oats could deprive him the chance before he went to the dust.

Hoping Mannrique wasn't watching—and silently asking for his forgiveness if he was—Oats flung his tulwar overhand at the horse's face. The spinning blade smote the plate strapped to the animal's forehead. Metal rang against metal, melded with the horse's scream as it reared. Oats kept coming, ducking beneath the kicking forelegs on the run. His neck, shoulders and palms slapped the belly of the beast. He'd never met such a weight. But he wagered the duke had never met a fucking thrice-blood. Screaming, straightening with all the power his legs contained, pushing with every grain of grit he possessed, Oats lifted the horse higher into the air. Its piercing shrieks reached their peak as Oats felt the tipping point. The horse toppled backward with a brutal clamor, but the duke was not crushed beneath. He must have leapt clear, for Oats caught a glimpse of his armored bulk lying in the grass. There wasn't time to finish him. The other cavaleros were coming.

Oats dove for Hernan's fallen lance, snatched it up, and planted its butt in the dirt, lifting the killing end without a moment to spare. In his haste to reach the duke, the lead rider charged full into the set lance. Oats grunted against the impact as the steel point and an arm's length of wooden shaft sank into the horse's chest. The lance began to bend as the doomed animal screamed and threw its rider.

A cavalero tried to bull through the gap between the lanced horse and the duke's fallen steed, but his mount shied at the mouth of all that kicking and screaming. The remaining three came hard around the other side, lances lowered.

Releasing the lance, Oats hunched and shouldered through the gap toward the stalled cavalero. He was buffeted by the flailing hooves of the dying horse and battered by the flank of the duke's as it lurched upright in a panic. He reeled against the blows, struggling to keep his balance as he came to grips with the lone cavalero. The man was still wrestling with his mount. His charge arrested, his lance was useless, and he let it fall, trying to draw a sword as Oats reached and tore him from the saddle. Oats tried to mount, but the damned horse balked, pivoting away. He held firm to the saddle horn, using the animal's body to shield him from the other three cavaleros still ahorse. Only . . . there was just the one. Oats snatched a glance to his left, found the other two had broken off to ride away from the tangle and were now wheeling to come at him from the side.

In trying to find an easier path to kill him, they saved his life, for Oats's eye fell upon Duke Hernan rushing him on foot, sword raised.

Fuck him.

Abandoning the disagreeable stallion, Oats ran to meet the duke bare-handed.

The man was big. He'd nearly the same reach Oats had even

without a blade. But that was reach with an arm. Oats turned his run into a leap, twisting to kick the oncoming duke with both feet. His boots hit a mass of man and metal, knocking them both to the earth.

Oats was up first, cast a look around. Behind, a cavalero coming on foot, another trying to calm and remount his horse, the third spurring his horse. To his right, the pair of flanking horsemen had thrown down their lances in favor of sword and mace, and were now coming at a cautious pace, no doubt fearing to trample the duke, who was picking himself up, breath echoing hotly inside his closed helm. The rider behind had no such qualms, and came with lance lowered at full-tilt.

Oats grabbed Hernan before the duke had found his footing and slung him at the hotfoot cavalero. The man dropped his lance to spare his lord a skewering and pulled his horse hard to the side, but the duke was still struck by the barrel of the animal and slammed to the ground once more. Oats scrambled for the fallen lance and, taking it two-handed, whirled the great length of wood and metal over his head, turning in place as he forced the weapon into rushing revolutions. He caught the dismounted cavalero with a blow to the head before coming around to fend off the pair of riders. They reined up hard to avoid the flying shaft. Hernan crawled away, fleeing the perilous whirlwind Oats wove. The cavalero whose lance Oats now wielded risked coming within reach. Sick of men on horses, Oats whipped the lance into the legs of his mount and heard the crack of bone. The screaming animal toppled, taking its rider down. The metal head and a span of wood had snapped off too, but there was more than enough lance left for Oats to heave crosswise over his head at the two dithering cavaleros. Both ducked behind their shields. Oats used the chance to spring at them, darting between their horses to seize a leg on each man. Jerking his arms upward he sent them tumbling from their saddles as he continued to run, spinning to swat both horses on the rump. The animals bolted. One cavalero fell clean. The other's foot caught in a stirrup. He was dragged away at a gallop, his armor-clad body jolting against the ground.

Oats stamped to a halt, spun about, and snatched a mace from the grass, moved to bash the fallen man's head in. No time. The last rider was bearing down on him.

Oats dove out of the horse's path, but the cavalero caught him with a slash to the shoulder blade. His brigand took some of the bite, but he was cut. The crowd must have known too, for he was suddenly aware of its conjoined voice once more.

Until now it hadn't gone their way, though Oats had only killed one horse, maimed a second, and sent the duke's fleeing. One cavalero was pinned beneath his mount, another was dragged off by his, but none were dead. Not yet.

Hernan was moving on him again, an unhorsed cavalero accompanying him on his left. They both held swords, but only the duke retained a shield. Not even his own, Oats noticed, from the colors. So the other man had handed it over. Oats grunted. These fucks had been tasked to kill him, but if Hernan was the cunt Oats suspected, the duke wanted to be the one to do it, which meant the others were more focused on keeping their lord alive.

Oats could use that.

The cavalero he'd dumped from the saddle had risen, but must have injured his sword arm in the fall, for he was shuffling backward to join the duke with nothing but a shield. The three men formed up. Oats couldn't see their faces through their helms, but their postures betrayed they looked beyond him to the last cavalero still ahorse. Oats glanced back. The horseman was a javelin's throw away, waiting, giving the duke and his companions a chance to gather themselves.

Fuck them and their need for a respite.

Oats took a step forward and his boot touched something hard. It was his tulwar. Luck and his own weapon, he could use those too. Switching the mace to his left hand, he took up the slicer and proceeded toward the duke. The man with only a shield was now to Hernan's right. They were all clad in strong armor and outnumbered their opponent, but if Oats knew anything, it was that warriors with no weapon felt naked no matter how well girded, no matter how many friends were beside them on the field.

He charged. Straight at the man with just the shield. He was supposed to protect his duke. But did he trust his duke to protect him against a rushing, bellowing thrice?

Shield Boy faltered, taking a pair of retreating steps, leaving Hernan's right side exposed.

Reckon not...

Oats sent his tulwar to fend the duke's cut and hammered the mace into the shield bearer, encouraging him to commit to his retreat. The force of the blow sent the man sprawling. Oats whirled full upon the duke, coming around with the mace. Hernan leaned into the stroke, blunting it with his weight behind his shield. Oats cut at his shoulder, but the edge of the tulwar only knocked against the metal plate. Sword Boy stepped around and lunged. Oats leaned away and swatted at the incoming blade with his own, turning it aside. The duke barreled forward, slamming with his shield. He might have been accustomed to knocking smaller men down, but Oats wasn't smaller. And he weren't no fucking man. He pillared himself with a back-flung leg, encircled the duke in a crushing embrace, and threw him into Sword Boy, giving Hernan the satisfaction of knocking a lighter frail down.

The duke kept his feet, sent a warding slash at Oats to prevent him from pressing. Oats pressed anyway, parrying the cut with his tulwar, countering with the mace to strike the duke's damned shield. The next instant, the fucker had two, Shield Boy returning to his lord's side. Oats ignored him, knowing Hernan's blade was the true foe, the one that had demanded the right to spill his blood, take his life. He chopped and hammered, driving forward, pushing both men back. Had they been men of meat and not metal, each would have died a dozen times, but their armor withstood every stroke of his blade, their shields turning every fall of the mace into a hand-numbing shock of futile effort. His shortened fingers turned the heavy weapon into a torture, the haft yearning to jump from his grasp. Teeth grit against an assault of pained panting, Oats cursed all weakness to the hells, delving deep into the grit that formed him, knowing that when it was exhausted, so too would he be, and then he would die. He fought, he strove, he grunted, growled, and spat at the men before him, at the black pit rising to claim his strength.

Oats reached the bottom, but what awaited him there wasn't death.

He found the orc.

It laughed, throaty and savage. Hating all that he was, all that he was not, Oats damned the orc as he set it free. Caged since the night he butchered Lucon, trapped in the memory of the brothel cellar, it emerged, ravenous and enraged.

It killed Shield Boy first, chopping down upon his helm with such savagery it broke his skull and the tulwar's blade. The third man had joined the fight. Oats couldn't say when. He'd seen only red before the black. The orc flung the broken hilt at him, the mace fast behind at the end of a bulging arm. The frail's parry was too slow, too weak. The mace crumpled his gauntlet; the sword fell from his hand. The next instant, the face of his helm was caved in, the flanges of the mace screeching as they burrowed into the steel.

The orc took a cut across the thigh. Hernan, acting too late to save his man. The wound was deep. The wound was nothing. Pain was the song of slaughter. The orc struck again, buckling the duke's shield, sending the mace spinning from its grip. More pain, the sword piercing the orc's gut low to the side. It stepped forward as the frail withdrew for another thrust and took hold of his shield in both hands, tearing it from his grasp. Disdaining the strength of steel, the orc struck the duke with its bare fists. Flesh and bone resounded against metal. Once. Twice.

Thri—

The orc heard hoofbeats and spun, sidestepping to seize the rider's descending arm and tear him from the pitiful animal's back. Wrenching the arm aloft behind the screaming frail's back, the orc stomped upon his spine until the shoulder broke.

The pummeled duke had lost his sword, but not his feet. He waded forward on unsteady limbs, a long spike of a dagger in his fist. The orc caught the man's wrist, took the weapon from him as if he were a child, and rammed it into his head. The spike burst through metal, bone, and brain, burying to the disc of the guard. Using the handle of the dagger, the orc twisted the duke's head around until the neck bones offered no more resistance.

The orc let the limp carcass flop to the grass and basked in the whimpering of the frail with the broken shoulder. His moist mewling was swallowed by the seething mob of onlookers, threatening to crack the sky with their adulation.

No. The orc now saw it was not for its victory they cheered. It was for the ten fresh cavaleros entering the field.

Oats fell to his knees.

His legs were gone. So was Hernan. He'd done that, at least. Perhaps it would matter.

The cavaleros did not hurry. They fanned out as they came, forming a crescent in front of him. Oats reckoned they'd send one man galloping forward to test him, see if he had any fight left. He didn't. He wouldn't budge. The elected rider would find him an easy target for the lance. It'd be quick as long as the man had any skill. Still, Oats wished they'd just sent the crossbowmen, but he reckoned that would stain the honor of the blue bloods. Heap of hogshit.

Oats tried not to, but the wait got the better of him, and he looked to the terrace. Ahlamra was there, at the top. As if waiting for his gaze to find her, she stood, her small, distant figure a calm comfort above the exulting nobles.

Less than a spit away from Oats, the man with the broken shoulder had gone quiet and unmoving. Whether he'd passed out or died, Oats couldn't say. The horsemen stood spread across half the field. Each looked to the queen. Oats closed his eyes. He didn't want to see her give the signal, didn't want to be tempted to make another stand. He wanted this over, an end to the pain, to the anger, to the regret. To the fruitless yearning to survive.

The howling of the peasantry reached a new height. Oats felt his heart race, his guts sour. Hells, the time had come. He felt a sudden, foolish hope that his brethren would remember him. Oats opened his eyes, but none of the riders were moving. The commoners and the nobles were no longer looking at him as they gestured and gawked down the field.

Oats craned around to look behind.

No.

Ugfuck was coming.

Oats shook his head, despair giving him the strength to stand. "No."

The crowd began to roar with alarm and outrage and elation.

"No!" Oats cried. "Ug, no! Go back!"

He stumbled forward a single step as the hog sped toward him. The cavaleros on both ends of the crescent spurred their mounts. They weren't coming for Oats.

"No!" Oats threw his arms up and fell once more to his knees. "I won't! I won't fight! Ug, go back! I don't want him! Please, I'm here! Kill me! Ug, don't!"

The cavaleros knew not to charge a barbarian from the front. They swept in from the flanks. Ugfuck came undeterred for Oats.

The lances lowered.

"UG!"

The first slammed in from the right, taking Ug in the flank. The hog screamed, half spun by the impact. Legs churning, he tried to keep coming, but the second lance struck from the other side, plunging into his shoulder, forcing him to the ground. His squeals were hideous agony. They filled Oats's ears, hollowed his heart. His own screams erupted to scour his throat, melding with the sound of Ugfuck's pain, unable to drown it.

Oats plummeted into the blackness of the pit once more. There was no bottom for the orc to lair, only a deepening chasm, rotten with grief. It was the festering wound Thoon had seen within him, where his heart should be. Oats had denied its existence. How could he be heartless when he held so much there? Yet the giant had seen true with his lone eye. Oats had thought his heart full, but it was only an abandoned storehouse stacked with doomed affections.

His hoof. Scraped away by war, now thin as old leather and destined to snap.

His mother. Broken by sorrow.

Jackal. Fetching. The faces of friends now little more than masks worn by the champions of gods and sorcery.

Xhreka. Gone and hidden, with no desire to be found.

Thistle and Muro. Offers of love he would be selfish to accept.

Ugfuck. Dying before his eyes, murdered by Hispartha.

The frails' hatred would take it all in the end. In death, Oats would have been spared the sight, tricked himself with a vain, false hope that it might be different in a world he would never know.

Ug's cries ripped the wound wide. Oats let everything he loved slide into that inevitable gulf and, using his anger as a torch, set fire to what was left clinging to the sticky, ragged edges. He burned away all that he feared to lose with the rage born of certainty that all was already lost. And there, in the blackened, gutted cavity left behind, he felt a distant pulse, a heartbeat not his own. It was small, weak, needlessly smothered by a burden that belonged to Oats. He should never have allowed another to bear it, this curse, the Claymaster's legacy. It had been created here in Hispartha, forced upon the half-orcs. It was time it was returned.

Oats rose from knees flooding with fluid.

These frails had wanted his life. They should have taken it. But they had robbed him of far more. Always, they wanted more. Had they but been content with slaying him . . .

His flesh flushed with fever, bubbled with sores.

The tiny heartbeat strengthened as his own breathing became labored, crackling in his lungs.

He would meet his end today, but his grave would be filled to bursting with those he took with him to the hells. The queen had at last forced a hoof-rider to kneel. She would suffer for not leaving him there.

Somewhere, far away, a little thrice-blood boy was freed from the grip of horrid magic. It was the last good act Oats could perform, though it was much, much too late. Ursaria had thought to show her people justice done to a murdering, ash-colored mongrel. It was time she saw there were worse things than a Bastard, a thrice-blood, an orc.

Offering Wily a silent pardon for taking so long, Oats showed these pitiless frails the face of the true plague-bearer.

THIRTY-SEVEN

THE MEN WHO LANCED UG were the first to die. Tendrils of the plague lashed out from Oats, snakes of living vapor that engulfed the cavaleros, pouring into the slits of their helms. They fell from panicked and blistering horses to cough and writhe upon the ground, clawing at their armored faces. One managed to cast his helm off and granted Oats a look at his frothing lips and pustule-ridden face.

It would be a slow, agonizing death. The man would be terrified to his last, thin breath.

The tourney field was surrounded by teeming waters of humanity. The commoners were shouting, those at the fence trying to flee but hampered by the rooted confusion of their fellows behind them.

Oats turned his back on them and limped toward the queen's terrace. The nobles had risen with alarm, but none were attempting to run. Well-trained hounds, they waited for their precious monarch to descend the steps, surrounded by her guard. The Matron Spear held Ursaria's hand as they hurried down, followed by Mannrique, Crafty, and Fuqtus. They were led and trailed by the Queen's Bulls. One of the cavaleros had Ahlamra by the arm, dragging her along, unhindered by her struggles.

Oats felt the rumble of hoofbeats and glanced down the field to see the remaining cavaleros coming. He need not run. He need not fight. Their charge was met by a thickening fog of sorcery. They came undaunted, courageous and dutiful. And paid the price. The horses that reached Oats galloped past him wearing empty saddles, blood streaming from their nostrils. Their riders were nothing but phantoms of agonized choking rising from the depths of the noxious cloud.

With ponderous steps, Oats proceeded on. It wasn't only the gash in his leg that slowed him. His joints were swollen, his back stiffened. Each plod forward sent a gurgling exhalation crawling past his lips. His body was a heavy, ungainly mass struggling within the eye of the plague, its beleaguered and straining heart. The magic flowed from him and through him. He suffered its corrosive caress, wracked by chills even as the dreadful spell boiled at his core, expelling fat drops of sweat and weeping pustules.

He'd forgotten the pain of this foul shit, for he'd held it only briefly before he was rescued by Jackal and the mercy of unconsciousness. He despaired that Wily had ever had to live a single day in such torment. The Claymaster had endured it for decades.

Oats needed only a few more moments.

The plague flooded the terrace long before he arrived. His every step brought it closer, yet it blossomed with the violent beating inside his constricted chest, growing as it consumed. The courageous resolve the court displayed while ensuring the queen's safety was now broken. They fell over one another in their rush to escape, several of the men shoving their wives out of the way in their dash to escape the cloud's grip. It was too late. They were spitting bile.

Oats stooped beneath the rail separating the terrace from the field, mouth dribbling some vile ichor as he bent. Straightening on the other side, he paused to cast rheumy eyes over the convulsing forms of Ursaria's court, their silk and brocade clad bodies lying in pools of bloody vomit on every level of the terrace. Housed in a thrice-blood, Crafty claimed the plague was now more deadly to orcs than frails. Still, it was a fucking plague. The court would be a long time dying. At his feet, Oats recognized the silver hair of Xana, fouled and dangling from the crawling woman's head. She retched and collapsed, rolling to her back to stare up at him with yellow, feverish eyes. Dimly, Oats recalled she'd been kind to him. He stepped over her and trudged on. He cared only for the Prince's Wood, where the queen had fled.

The crossbowmen who'd ushered him to the tourney field made a stand, but the plague preceded Oats by a javelin's toss now and their volley was rushed. They loosed their bolts into the occluding cloud, none hitting their mark, and tried to flee before the magic reached them. They weren't swift enough.

No others opposed him.

His onerous gait brought him to the forest path and, at last, to the lake.

Across the water, Ursaria stood resolute beside Engraçia Bracara, screened by the Order of the Minotaur. The six cavaleros held their pollaxes ready, the steel-wrought bull faces of their helms offering Oats mute and dispassionate challenge. Crafty too waited beyond their armored cordon, flanked by Fuqtus. The *jhevadi* held his axe in one hand and the back of Mannrique's neck with the other. Oats paused, seeing the restrained and quailing prince. Ahlamra was next to them. None had a hand upon her, but apprehension was writ in her rigid posture.

The plague cloud pushed forward, though Oats was now still, its edge lapping over the opposite bank. He drew it back, finding a control he had not cared to impose against the court. The vapors were subsumed into his body as he made his way around the shoreline.

"I trust you do not think this makes you the victor," Queen Ursaria declared.

"Shouldn't have killed my hog," Oats said, his voice a morass of hatred forced out by a tongue now tumid and sore-ridden.

"Such a faithful creature!" Ursaria said to Crafty, amused. "You owe it immense gratitude, Uhad. The tourney was unending! I feared my frivolous court would grow weary of the entertainments. I began to doubt you could deliver on your promise."

Crafty spread his hands. "For all my talents, Forbearing Queen, I cannot see the future. I could swear only to the assurance of the plague's return. Not the timing."

"I almost insisted you reveal which of them was the bearer," Ursaria chided. "I was certain it was either the ghastly white male or that female with the unbearable scars. Never the thrice-blood." She eyed Oats up and down. "He appeared so very hale. It's almost a pity I cannot reward you, Oats, but the slayer of Hispartha's court cannot be given land and title, even if he were not a vicious sootskin. I'll grant you a quick death when the time comes. You deserve that for giving me the joy of seeing that lout Hernan's head turned around on his brutish neck alone, to say nothing of all the other schemers and suitors. I do hope that rancid old dowager Saabedra didn't escape you."

"None of them escaped," Oats replied, guilt threatening to crush him as he thought of Xana. No doubt he'd slain a pile of evil fucks, but not all had deserved such a terrible end. Perhaps not even most. But there were a few more who truly did. He swept the conspirators with a promise. "Neither will you."

"Neither will your Bastards," Ursaria said. "I had them put under heavy guard before you took the field. They are being taken to the Madrasta even now. What do you suppose their fate will be if you harm me?"

"She will hang us no matter what you do, Oats," Ahlamra said, her voice taut. "We are now—"

"The mongrels that tried to murder her," Oats said. "I see it. Got rid of all them fucks she didn't want to marry in the doing. More than a few rivals of different stripes too, I reckon. And Crafty helped her. Tourney was just to get them all together. I ain't stupid. Or fucking surprised."

He wasn't worried for his brethren either. There wasn't a prison that could hold Hoodwink, if he allowed himself to be taken there at all. He'd get the others free or die trying. Nothing Oats could do to help them or hurt them with what he did now. The only question was what Crafty had hidden in his quiver that could stop him. Fuqtus, sure as shit. Maybe the demon wouldn't be affected by the plague.

But Ursaria would. The Sixth Thunder could cut Oats down so long as he saw her retching out her royal innards first.

"Shouldn't have killed my hog."

He sent the plague at her in a torrent without his body needing to twitch a muscle. It shot forth in a twisting column of putrescence, caustic and ravenous. Engraçia Bracara stepped into the maelstrom, her spear igniting as she plunged the blade into the ground. The plague broke against the flaming spear. Hissing and smoking, the diverted fume split to flow around the queen. Oats sent it back in, coiling from behind and above. But the tongues peeled away, defying his will. Ursaria stood, untouched, wearing the barest of smiles as the sorcerous miasma splayed, separating into branches that swam against the current of Oats's command to strike the Queen's Bulls. Grunts echoed from within their bestial helms and the cavaleros staggered, the vapors slithering beneath the plates of their armor.

Oats ceased fighting the pull. If the queen wished for him to kill more of her people, he'd oblige. It wouldn't spare her for long. But long enough . . .

Fuqtus wasn't coming for him. Neither was the Matron Spear. All merely stood, tense and watchful. Why did they not try to kill him? Ursaria would be unprotected when the Bulls fell.

Only, they did not fall.

Their bodies drank the fumes. Too late, Oats felt the plague draining from him. He tried to call it back, but the magic no longer heeded his will. The sores, the pain, the swamp in his lungs, they were torn away. The relief of their loss, the despair, toppled him. He hit the bed of damp pebbles ringing the lake, the sudden cool of their touch a terrible bliss against his face.

He heard footfalls, the soft crunch of the queen's steps amid the grinding trod of the Bulls. Something heavy splashed into the lake. Oats caught a glimpse of a metal bull's head, rolling briefly on the water's surface before it sank.

Ursaria's voice cascaded down on him.

"Thirty years is too long to remain idle."

Oats raised his head.

The queen stood over him, Bulls at her sides. One stood bare-headed. A ribbon of pustules ran across the face that regarded him with an easy loathing. The face of a half-orc.

"You were never going to catch me unprepared for what would return," Ursaria said. "And now I have repossessed all the threat you ever posed."

Oats snatched at the hem of her dress, but she was just out of reach. His failure provoked a breath of mirth from the queen. And a kick from the armored mongrel. The metal-plated boot took him under the jaw. Oats found himself lying on his back when the blinding pain ebbed. A pair of Bulls hauled him up. They still wore their helms, but the ease with which they lifted him betrayed them for mongrels. Their breath resounded hollow within the steel snouts. Oats could hear the wet hitches in each inhalation. The same sound the Claymaster always made.

Hells. Hispartha had six plague-bearers. And unlike the Claymaster, Quicklime, Seeper, Thrum Lung, and all the rest of the original nine, these mongrels were loyal to the Crown.

"There ain't a word for you cunts," Oats growled.

The helmless mongrel slammed a fist into his gut so hard, Oats vomited.

"Not all half-breeds need be outcasts and rebels," Ursaria said. "This insistence on ruling yourselves is an aberration. It won't last another generation."

"You are wrong," Ahlamra said.

"It is you that errs if you believe your elf-blooded chieftain and her paramour will be enough to stand against me," Ursaria told her. "You may have trained in the finest brothel in Tyrkania, you pretty mongrel slattern, but since my girlhood I was taught it was my duty to guard against the return of the orcs. And your mongrel hoofs. To do otherwise would have been unwise and unforgivable. Yet that's what my half-brothers would have done. One too mad, the other too weak. Our father knew it. And so he took steps, steps I have continued."

"You murdered your court," Mannrique muttered, unable to look at the queen. "You are as mad as Girón ever was."

Ursaria moved toward him, making him shrink with each stalking step.

"That smatter of fools would have spent years trying to maneuver another useless cull into my marriage bed. I suffered it once. I was young and Father said it would strengthen my succession. Now? I need nothing to be strong. And I'll not be saddled with another weak and preening man to assuage the clucking fears of the baronage. There is a war to fight and they fret over an heir! I am queen of Hispartha, not a brood mare for the sons of simpering toads. Nor will I wed one with a will to fight, men like Duke Hernan, who would reap all the glory of battle and forge it into a weapon to supplant me. No, my mewling, lackwit half-brother, no. The court has been purged of its uselessness. The rotten vines have been cut. Those who died without issue, like that hag the Countess of Caristios, their lands will go to the Crown. The sons and daughters of the dead, too young to attend the festivities, they will know the grief and protection of their queen, with ministers and tutors to aid in the governance of their holdings. And those who were not here, too proud to attend, or too menial to merit invitation, they will be fixed in purpose on bringing a reckoning against the truculent mongrels that slew their peers with sorcery and attempted to murder their queen beneath a banner of truce. Any that do not heel to me will find the half-orc's dreaded plague escaped the tourney field and can lay waste to any land within the kingdom. Hispartha is made stronger by what I have done."

Mannrique was a head and a half taller than the queen, yet he recoiled from her words, her presence, choking back tears.

"You helped her to do this," Ahlamra accused Crafty.

"Truly, I did little," he replied. "The wizards left in Hispartha after the Incursion were able to craft the plague anew, but were unequal to the task of allowing its bearers to draw the magic out of another bearer. There, I was able to help. A secret, potent protection, surely, yet also a perfect tool to help Her Majesty shed her desultory grandees. But not if it were unleashed by her own personal guard. I humbly suggested a cat's-paw in the original plague. Truly, arranging its return was the greater challenge. Fortunate that stalwart Oats was so desirous of its removal from the boy that he would risk journey here in pursuit of peace."

"And what did you gain?" Ahlamra spat.

"Enough prattle," Ursaria said. "The tumult caused by the thrice-blood must be calmed. The peasants will have carried word to the city, but we dare not let the panic run rampant long. The tale must spread, but not chaos." She looked to her Bulls and gestured at Oats. "Bring him. And the frailing slut. The people will need to see these Bastards have been cowed. As for you"—she returned her attention to Mannrique, forcing a sobbing breath past his lips—"go back to your goats and your dwarves. Utter word of what transpired here and I'll skin every one of your animals and carpet the throne room with their hides."

Blubbering, Mannrique nodded. They left him there, alone, in that false wood.

The Bulls ushered Oats down the forest path, supporting his stumbling steps. He didn't have the fight left for six naked frails, much less these steel-clad mongrel fucks.

"I'm sorry, Rue," he said, though he could not look behind to see her.

"You have nothing to ask pardon for, Oats."

It was a kindness, but he didn't reckon that was true.

Leaving the wood, Oats caught a glimpse of the tourney field and the lonely, fallen lump near its center. Sorrow flooded his mouth, burst the banks of his eyes. He'd no more rage left. Only tears.

The Bulls led them around the top of the wood before turning west toward the river. Four horses awaited them near a humble wooden bridge, held by a dozen men-at-arms with poorly concealed bewilderment on their faces. The wood blocked their view of the tourney grounds, but they must have heard the commotion, wondered what was amiss yet kept to their duty of keeping the royal steeds. A trio of heralds were among the men, already sitting their mares. Ursaria bid them ride to the city to proclaim her safety and the capture of the Lot Lands mongrels. The heralds spurred away over the bridge, their course momentarily puzzling Oats until he remembered the Furiosa, the queen's private entrance into Magerit. The northern gate, though closer, would be mobbed with the folk fleeing the tourney. The messengers could cross the river here, ride quickly south, and cross again at the Furiosa with none to impede their progress.

Oats and Ahlamra were put in chains while the queen and Engraçia Bracara mounted. There were animals for Crafty and Fuqtus as well.

"Such foresight," Ahlamra said, her words cutting at the wizard.

They set off over the small bridge and turned south, following the messengers' path beside the Chorismano. Oats and Ahlamra walked surrounded by the Queen's Bulls. At the fore rode Ursaria and the Matron Spear, the men-at-arms marching at the rear. Crafty and Fuqtus were just outside the encircling Bulls to the left, closer to the river.

The going was slow. Oats could do little more than hobble. Open fields stood before them on both sides of the river, dotted here and there by stands of trees and the crofts of shepherds. Magerit sprawled upon its hills in the distance, the bulk of the queen's citadel bulging over the walls above the river.

"I cannot see it."

Ahlamra's soft words drew Oats's attention. He looked over to find her staring at the ground before her feet, brow creased.

"See what?" he asked.

"The gain," she whispered. "For Uhad."

"He fucked us. We knew he would. Not the how or when, but . . . we knew."

Ahlamra met his eyes. "And the why?"

Oats lifted his gaze to the wizard. "He's Crafty."

"I cannot see it," Ahlamra said again, her voice filled with vexation.

At last, the city loomed to their left. Ahead, the Furiosa spanned the river, its stone arch anchored at both ends by formidable square towers. Oats could see men moving atop the tower standing on the west bank. A trail led out of its brother on the opposing side, winding up to a barbican jutting from the walls. Oats wasn't looking forward to that climb, though he reckoned whatever awaited him within the queen's fortress would be a heap more unpleasant.

"You see any way of saving yourself, you take it," he told Ahlamra. "Do what they want. Say what they want. Chief'll need you alive."

The portcullis in the first tower was already raised. Four men with halberds stood guard at the entrance, kneeling as the queen passed. Oats limped through the cool shadows of the tower gate, finding another four men on the bridge side. The heavy grate lowered behind them. Oats grit his teeth against the steady slope of the arching bridge.

"Here, I think, Fuqtus," Crafty said, reining his horse to a stop at the crest.

Fuqtus dismounted.

The Bulls eyed him, but did not stop, herding Oats and Ahlamra on, the rearguard of halberdiers following. They had left the wizard and his demon behind several paces before the Matron Spear turned in the saddle to notice the Tyrkanian was no longer moving with the entourage. She spoke a word to her queen and Ursaria stopped, bringing the Bulls and the men-at-arms to a halt.

The queen half turned her horse. "We do not dally, Uhad Ulbadir."

"No, Trusting Queen, we do not," Crafty replied. It was not often the wizard's voice shed its silky tone. "We, as the hoof-riders say, must palaver."

"At my pleasure," Ursaria said. "Not yours."

"A royal prerogative. One which you have lost without knowing."

"Tread carefully, Tyrkanian."

Crafty's smile appeared, but it was not gloating or joyous. It was tired.

"I have. For long years. Which is why I can now say that today, Ursaria Trastorias, today is the end of your reign."

The queen's crooked mouth twisted with confusion. She transformed it into a sneer.

"Take them."

The twelve men of the rearguard leveled their halberds. Crafty and Fuqtus did not flinch. The men-at-arms moved toward them in two ranks, while the Queen's Bulls formed up to block the bridge. Fuqtus watched the men come, axe held low across his thighs.

Movement upon the tower at the *jhevadi*'s back drew Oats's eye. Stirred by the building confrontation below, the men stationed at the top trained their stockbows, the eight halberdiers guarding the portcullis taking slow steps to support their fellows on the bridge. Crafty and Fuqtus were unmindful of the danger, their attentions fixed on the queen and her retinue.

More movement pulled Oats's gaze higher, into the sky above.

He grunted, the grunt tumbling into a chuckle which grew again to laughter.

Ahlamra gave him a quizzical stare.

"I always offered to sneak ahead," he told her, and shook his head. "She tried to tell me . . . when we parted."

Ahlamra's eyes narrowed, not understanding.

"Stealing the persimmons from the orphanage larder," Oats said, his smile growing. "I'd offer to go first, in case my mother found us. But Jackal and Fetch would never hear of it."

Oats turned his smile on Crafty.

"We always went in together."

The wizard winked.

The rokh dove from the clouds, its shadow stretching over the bridge. The Bulls' horses reared, the men-at-arms recoiled, crying out in alarm. Several fell upon their asses. But the swooping beast wasn't coming for them. It struck the top of the tower behind Crafty, massive wings beating over the parapet as it slowed to unleash its talons upon the stockbowmen.

The queen mastered her horse.

"What is this?" she demanded, furious eyes fixed on the tower.

"This, Trusting Queen, is dread Fetching," Crafty said without alarm.

The chief appeared between the merlons atop the tower, kataras in hand, the rokh savaging the screaming garrison behind her. A man stumbled into the tower passage beneath, expelled from the inner door, trying to hold his guts in, followed by a familiar, swaggering silhouette.

"Oh, and friend Jackal," Crafty said.

Jack came charging out of the shadows as Fetching leaped from the tower. They struck the portcullis guards at the same instant, he cutting down two on the run, she landing on a third, knives plunging into the sides of his neck.

"At them!" the queen shouted at her guard.

The twelve men leveled their halberds. Fetch and Jackal did not slow. They tore through the portcullis guards, darting past Crafty and Fuqtus to meet the blanching dozen, every flash of their blades crippling or killing. The chief struck with enough force to send several men flying from the bridge.

While the lowly frails died, the Queen's Bulls strode forth. The plague steamed from their bodies, the vapors languid for a moment before coalescing and flooding over the bridge. The few men-at-arms remaining loosed shrieks as their flesh began to bubble, their weapons and bodies dropping to the stones. The fetid cloud washed over Jackal and Fetch, causing them both to expel snarls of pain. Jack's flesh began to erupt, the blessings of Attukhan banishing the sores only to have them return. Outwardly, Fetch was unaffected, but after three labored steps she stumbled, her breath a jagged wheeze. Jackal reached her side, helped her stand, and they kept coming. But they made it only another few steps before the vile magic left them gasping.

Oats gathered his chains. The Matron Spear could skewer him in the back, but he wouldn't stand by and watch. If they were to die, let them die together.

He took a step, intent on looping the iron links around the helmless plague-bearer's neck, but Ahlamra grabbed his arm.

"Oats, wait."

Unwilling to be deterred, he tore away from her hand, but his next step was also halted. Not by Rue's hand, or a spear in the back, but by what he beheld.

The Queen's Bulls were trembling, the fumes roiling back to them. The plates of their armor rattling with furious convulsions, they dropped their pollaxes and began to collapse. The helmless mongrel spun as he dropped, to reveal his blackened flesh sloughing away. Cursing, Oats took a step back, shielding Ahlamra with his body. The plague cloud dissipated before it touched them, leaving the bodies of the Bulls twitching upon the bridge, putrid humors leaking from beneath armor.

Ursaria's face was pale, incensed. She turned a wide and baleful stare upon Crafty.

"You!"

The wizard shrugged. "Me."

Engraçia Bracara hurled her spear without need of a command, the weapon igniting as it screamed toward Crafty. Fuqtus snatched an arm up, catching the blazing weapon just below the head.

Crafty glanced down at the white-hot point, a finger's length from his nose. "Thank you, beloved."

Fuqtus lowered the spear, unfazed by its flames. His words rumbled toward the Matron Spear.

"Come, Chosen of Magritta. Let us see whose goddess is stronger."

He opened his fist and the spear flew back to Engraçia's hand.

The confined, sloping bridge was no place for mounted combat. The Matron Spear came down from her horse.

"Go, my queen," she said. "I will hold them."

Oats shot a glance at Jackal and Fetching. Both were getting to their feet, shaky and muddled.

The wizard nodded at Fuqtus. The *jhevadi* hefted his axe.

"Martyred Madre keep me," Engraçia Bracara intoned.

Fuqtus bared his teeth. "Let Bhadra count the dead."

The armored woman lunged. Fuqtus twisted away from the fiery spear, spun, the Sixth Thunder coming around in a hurtling arc. Engraçia flung herself to the side, leaving the axe to crack the stones. The spear thrust again, this time for the demon's face. Fuqtus tilted his head, deflected the spear with a brazen horn, and bulled forward, hammering Engraçia with the bulk of his body. They slammed into the side of the bridge, the Matron Spear's plate grating against the stonework. They struggled there for a moment, both of their weapons useless in such a grapple. Fuqtus was taller, heavier, yet his size did not appear to provide him an advantage. Oats knew, from his fight with the Maiden on the Heap, Magritta's chosen were far stronger than they appeared.

Engraçia Bracara slipped free, tried to gain some distance, but the demon struck out, taking a single step to whip a vicious crosscut, his hand sliding to the end of the long-hafted axe. The Matron Spear's speed spared her that terrible reaping blow, but the Sixth Thunder had more than an edge. It had a voice. A booming clap resounded as the axe cleaved the air, blasting Engraçia off her feet. She rolled and came up jabbing with her flaming weapon. Fuqtus pursued, knocking aside the warding point of the spear with a swat from his axe.

Fetch and Jackal were on their feet now, both looking a little haggard, but free from signs of the plague. No one moved to intervene, their attentions captured by the combat. The witnesses were forced to the edges of the span lest they become an errant victim of the duel.

Spear and axe. Fire and thunder. Priestess and demon. They sparked and clashed, the bridge tremoring with every blow from the Sixth Thunder, but Engraçia Bracara weathered the unseen impacts. Whether it was an enchantment of her armor or some gift of the Madre that blunted the Thunder's force, Oats couldn't say, but he'd seen Fetching tossed by those claps.

The scorching spear licked out, again and again. Unable to ward them all, Fuqtus bled from a score of wounds. Yet his ferocity was undiminished. For all the Matron Spear's skill, she could not keep him at bay. The axe found its way through her defenses, rending and denting her resplendent plate. At last, they both began to tire. The blade of the Sixth Thunder swept in, slower than when the fight began. But faster than the Matron Spear. Engraçia Bracara doubled over as the axe struck her ribs, biting deep into the metal breastplate. The air left her in a rush and welter of spat blood.

Fuqtus ripped the axe free, breathing heavily, his stance unsteady. The Matron Spear staggered away, dying but not dead. She continued to move backward, away from her foe, until the backs of her legs met the bridge's parapet. Winded and weary, Fuqtus did not press her, confident he'd delivered a mortal wound.

Yet, for Magritta's chosen, death was just another path to power.

Panic sparked in Oats's mind. Shit. The demon needed to put her down before she—

Engraçia Bracara adjusted the grip on her spear, positioning the point at her breast.

By fortune or the fuckery of fate, Oats was closest.

"Hells no, you don't!" he growled, and lurched forward.

He didn't have the time or the strength for anything graceful. Weight was the only weapon left to him. Oats struck Engraçia Bracara with all of it, shoving her over the side. His torn leg refused to arrest the motion and his balance tipped. The violent tug of dizzying space sent his guts to throat-fuck his skull. Engraçia Bracara plummeted in his upended vision, her path a prophecy of Oats's end. Jarring pain wracked his spine and the Matron Spear outpaced him, her armored body breaking the dark surface of the Chorismano. There was an eruption of churning white as the waters swallowed the queen's champion. She did not resurface.

Oats dangled upside down. Lifting his sickened and pounding head, he found Fetch and Jackal leaning over the parapet, each holding half the loop of his ankle chain.

"Don't just stare at me all relieved," he said, voice choked by his craning neck. "Haul me up!"

In moments they had him back on the blessedly solid surface of the bridge.

Now on foot and alone, Ursaria swept them all with a wild stare. In her hand was Engraçia's spear. Oats had not realized it did not fall with its bearer. Fuqtus stood tensed, his posture and Crafty's raised hand showing the demon had moved to prevent Ursaria from arming herself and been restrained.

"Cornered and desperate queen—" Crafty began, but whatever entreaty he was about to make was cut short by Ursaria mounting swiftly and spurring her horse away.

Setting her jaw, Fetch broke Oats's chains with her bare hands before stepping to Ahlamra and snapping hers in turn.

"Come," she said, striding across the bridge.

At the other end, they found Ursaria's horse dead from a thrumshot, the queen picking herself up, bruised and shaking. The portcullis of the tower was closed, the slain forms of men-at-arms beyond. Thresher, Culprit, and Polecat stood over them with purloined weapons. Hood was atop the tower, reloading a stockbow.

As Oats and the others came near, Ursaria scrambled to her feet, brandishing the spear.

"I'll not beg for my life," she declared in tremulous tones.

"Be a waste of fucking breath," Fetch told her.

Ursaria paled. Swallowing, she began to pray.

"O Blessed Magritta, protect me, your faithful daughter. I submit to your mercy, Martyred Madre, I plead your forbearance, beg your protection. My heart is your heart. My flesh your flesh. And in my death you are made undying."

"Fetch . . ." Oats said.

"Let her," the chief replied.

Ursaria shoved the butt of the spear into the angle where the side of the bridge met its surface and gathered to throw herself upon the point. She hesitated a moment, then another. Oats could see her begin to tremble. At last with a sob of defeat, she stepped swiftly away from the blade, allowing the spear to fall with a clatter.

Ursaria turned and delivered a confession to her feet.

"I can't."

Fetch stepped toward her. Stooping, the chief picked up the spear.

"Because you've never killed but with words," she said. "Me? I've slain all manner of monsters."

Fetch's free hand shot forward and seized the queen by the throat. She lifted her bodily as Ursaria's eyes bulged, hands clawing feebly at the iron grasp. Fetch wedged the butt of the spear between the flagstones and with a contemptuous motion of her arm, tossed Ursaria upon its point. With a gurgling cry the queen sank upon the shaft, the back of her dress puckering until the blade tore through. Blood spattered the stones, falling from her lips. Her legs gave out and she slumped over, breath slowing with each gasp. She stilled.

Oats stared down at her, waiting, grateful that Fetch and Jackal were here to stand against what was about to come.

The moments stretched on. Oats's lungs burned with unreleased air. But Queen Ursaria did not rise again.

He risked looking away to cast an uncertain glance at his brethren. Fuqtus now stood among them, mouth turned down in a judging grimace.

"Crowns and kingdoms and royal blood," the *jhevadi* rumbled. "Such things cannot earn the favor of a goddess. Nor grant the power of true belief."

"Hells overburdened," Polecat exhaled from behind the portcullis.

Ahlamra tore her eyes from the dead queen to look at Fetching.

"Chief. How are you here?"

"I followed orders for a long time before I gave them, Rue. You think I wouldn't follow yours?"

Ahlamra's frown only deepened. "Mine?"

"Bring Wily to the Heap!" a cheery voice called out. "When the plague leaves him, fly to Magerit. Strike the west tower when you see Crafty upon the bridge. Not before. We are moving on the queen."

They all turned to find Crafty a stone's throw away, still sitting his horse.

"You sent it," Fetch said.

The wizard smiled as Fuqtus strode back to join him.

"And killed the plague-bearers," Oats muttered.

"Plague-bearers?" he heard Culprit say. "The hells?"

"No, strong Oats," Crafty said. "That was you."

"Me?"

"It is more accurate to say it was the magic those bovine-masked mongrels stole from you. Thankfully, you wanted wine on the night you asked me to help you into your breeches."

Oats recalled Crafty appearing in Bermudo's bedchamber in the castile, recalled the water that had suddenly been wine.

"You gave me something."

"A draught of my own making," Crafty said, quite pleased with himself. "A potion to ensure that once the plague returned to you it would be changed, becoming deadly to any other that tried to wield it after. It was an effort of some years to brew. Fuqtus was nearly killed several times gathering the ingredients."

"Once," the *jhevadi* corrected.

"Forgive me. Once."

"You asked Crafty to help you put on your breeches?" Polecat asked, still behind the tower grate.

Oats didn't respond.

"What were you two doing *immediately* before that?"

"Shut it, Cat," Fetch said. She was in no mood for japes.

Neither was Oats. There was a question he needed answered.

"You tell Loukas to go to Barrasa? You have a hand in what happened to Sluggard?"

Crafty's smile melted away. He shook his head. "No. No, truly that was his inner despairs at work."

"Sluggard?" It was Jackal's voice, but Oats didn't look at him.

He grit his teeth against the pain, the fury. "How . . . how did you know the plague would come back to me?"

Crafty sighed. "Hatred. Hatred was the lure to bring it back to you. The magic forced upon your Claymaster changed him, yet he also changed it. I asked him once, how he survived the horrors used to create the plague. How he lived when so many hundreds of others died in that dreadful mine. He said it was because he hated Hispartha, the frails. That he wanted to live so that he could one day destroy the kingdom that made him a slave, a slayer. A monster. Not even the ancient medicine of elves could remove the spite imbued in that plague, the desire to see the Crown destroyed. Only once you felt that same hatred would the plague know you as its rightful bearer."

"How did you know I'd feel it?" Oats asked. The only hate he felt now was for himself, for knowing he'd made the wizard right.

Crafty spread his hands. "I ask you, I ask *all* of you, what is in your heart for this place? What do you believe was in poor Sluggard's at the end? When a land and its people hate you so, how can you be anything but stained by that hatred and begin to reflect it?

The castle of the Crown sits above us now on that hill. And no matter who has ruled from that seat, their intention has ever been to enslave you. And to kill you if you dare rise. How can you feel ought but hate when confronted with such a truth?"

"But how did you know when?" Ahlamra asked.

Crafty spread his hands. "I didn't."

"You knew to send me a fucking message," Fetch said.

"Another gambit," Crafty admitted. "The tourney was nearing its end and the queen losing patience. I had promised a trap for her court, hoping she would fall into mine. If the nobles left the tourney alive I reasoned we would quickly feel Ursaria's ire and the spurious talks of peace would end. One way or another, dread Fetching, we needed you and Jackal close. I knew you would want the chance to rescue your brethren should they find themselves fortunate enough to be imprisoned. In such an instance, I advised Hoodwink to wait until they reached the Furiosa's far tower before slaying the guard. Which I am pleased to see he had no difficulty in doing."

"Then we did for the rest of the garrison," Thresher said. Like the rest of them she held a frail's stockbow and wore a Hisparthan sword. "So quick and quiet the fucks on the other side never knew."

Ahlamra turned to Crafty. "*This* is what you gained. The queen isolated and trapped."

The wizard only smiled.

"You used us," Polecat said, huffing bitterly. "Fucking *again*!"

"I did what I said I would. I have ended the war between Hispartha and the Lots, with your help."

"Ended?" Thresher scoffed. She gestured at Ursaria's corpse. "Think Queen Impaled here will inspire more than a little vengeance. Frails' armies will be marching south with a hunger for mongrel blood now."

"No," Ahlamra said. "They will not."

"Why?" Thresh demanded.

"Because," Ahlamra replied, "they will be too busy fighting their new king."

They all followed her gaze to a smirking Crafty.

A thought struck Oats. He whirled on the chief.

"Who's on the Heap with Wily? No way that damn buzzard of yours can carry three mongrels and a child."

"Two mongrels, a child, and one Jacintho," Fetch replied. "Greasy fucker weighs less than a fart."

"But he's better? Wily. He's not—"

Jackal stepped up and put a hand on his shoulder. "He's healthy, Oats. He's free of it."

A clamor of bells rose from city. The threads of shouted voices reached them from the barbican.

"Swift has your magnificent bird borne you here," Crafty said, "its presence has not gone unnoticed. The queen is dead and soon men from the castle will be down to discover what we have done. So, I must ask you now, True Bastards, will you trust me far enough to see the rest of this scheme to end Hispartha's grip on your lands through, or shall the frails rush down to witness us attempting to kill each other on this bridge?"

As the question hung in the air, Fuqtus adjusted his grip on his axe.

All eyes rested on the chief. She looked to Oats.

THIRTY-EIGHT

LORD CONSULT LONO BARRIENTOS RUBBED his liver-spotted head with long, steady fingers. For many scattered days the dry, ill-tempered old man had snapped and shouted, bit and rebutted. He'd fought hard with nothing but his voice, flung spittle and a horde of dusty scrolls. But on this morning, this final morning, he was out of arguments.

Oats tried not to clear his throat, to rub his face and pull at his beard. He'd long had his fill of this musty chamber and its endless, overstuffed shelves. In the chair next to him, Ahlamra waited with serene patience. Crafty looked prepared to have a nap, hands folded across his ample middle. During the entire length of the closeted little war with Barrientos, neither had raised their voice nor lowered their guard.

At last, the Lord Consult's fingers slid from his brow and took up the quill. With strong, practiced strokes, he signed the besieging vellum before him and surrendered.

Barrientos rolled the document and offered it out to Crafty, his aggravation buried beneath mounds of dignity.

"Deepest gratitude, my Lord Consult," Crafty said, taking the scroll as he rose.

Oats was eager to stand, but his wounded leg had stiffened. An unfortunate mixture of speed and clumsiness caused his sliding chair to produce a sound akin to an ornery donkey. Barrientos aimed a scowl at him. Oats swallowed the offer of pardon that nearly left his lips. He was meant to be the plague-bearer, the promise of death hanging over the proceedings. Reckon he wouldn't be all that threatening offering apologies for an annoyance of furniture. He returned the old frail's frown and followed the others out of the archives.

They passed through the abandoned scriptorium, the scratching hive of scribes sent scurrying by Barrientos every time the mongrels came with a mind of parleying.

"You will be seeing him before me," Crafty said, passing the scroll to Oats on the move. "And here is the other." A second, smaller scroll was produced from the wizard's robes and given to Ahlamra.

By the time they reached the door at the far end, his leg was more or less moving properly. Seven weeks since he took the wound and it still put a hitch in his stride after sitting a span. At least he hadn't had to fight again in that time. Or unleash the plague, which would have been a fucking miracle, since it was gone from him. Gone from the world entire, Crafty claimed. Oats wouldn't wager on that being true, but it was becoming difficult to hold on to the distrust.

Fuqtus and the Bastards awaited them in the corridor, falling into step as they passed.

Magerit's castle was vast, the keep alone larger than any fortress Oats had ever seen. He still second-guessed every turn and stairway, but Crafty guided them with certainty. Of course, their destination wasn't all that challenging. Go up long enough and even the most lost mongrel will find the roof.

Three score Tyrkanian archers manned the keep's battlements, only a portion of the army that arrived at the city on the third morning after Ursaria died. Oats still didn't know how Crafty had summoned them, but they'd made a long march west after coming to land at Valentia, defeating the port's defenders and leaving an occupying force behind. When they reached Magerit, the castle was already in Crafty's hands, taken without blood when Hood appeared in the castellan's quarters and convinced him to order the garrison's surrender. Using the discord from the tourney, Crafty had played upon the city's uncertainty, sending false reports to the mayordomo that the queen was alive and safely installed in the castle, the ruse succeeding long enough for the empire's army to cross the Furiosa and take possession of the castle, ending any hope of Magerit's resistance.

In the nearly two months since, Crafty had worked tirelessly to increase his grip on the city. Bribes and trade agreements with the east brought the merchant guilds under his thumb. Promises of restored or long-coveted holdings swayed the weaker nobles, those whose lack of standing spared them the fate of their betters at the tourney. The peasantry proved the greatest challenge, and uprisings for the Martyred Queen continued to flare in the poorer districts, the flames fanned by the temples of Magritta. The Salt of Amarsaphes too refused to bow to the new rule and their Steel Friars had managed to slay several Tyrkanian patrols, vanishing among the people after they struck. Apparently, the goats had even sacrificed their beards to help hide their identities.

Still, the staunchest holdout was Lono Barrientos. Until now . . .

The keep supported four great towers at the corners and a central hexagonal tower. It was here Crafty led them, passing through the arch at its base to ascend the interior stairs.

The chief waited at the top, backed by her rokh. She made the journey every few days, always arriving before dawn to keep the great bird from fomenting further fear and hatred among the people.

"He still won't sign," she said as they emerged into the morning wind. "Hells, we should just cut his he—"

Oats held up the hefty roll of vellum. "He signed."

Fetching blinked, her frown relaxing.

Ahlamra produced a smile and the second scroll. "Which makes *this* now a royal decree."

She gave it to Fetch, who turned it over in her hands.

"Read it, chief," Culprit said.

Fetching gave them all a quick glance and unfurled the scroll. Her eyes moved over it for a moment.

"The language is fucking overwrought . . ."

"Quick and dirty, then," Polecat said.

Fetch took a breath. "Hispartha . . . renounces all claim to Ul-wundulas. Every half-orc living within its borders is free. The Lot Lands are dissolved and will from this day be known as . . . the Hoof Lands."

"Fuck me . . ." Polecat said, laughing the next instant as Culprit threw his arms and a whoop toward the sky.

"The Hoof Lands," Fetching repeated, looking up from the parchment.

"Rue's suggestion," Oats told her.

Thresher put an arm around Ahlamra and pulled her close, tears welling.

The chief flicked the scroll in Crafty's direction. "This in earnest?"

"It is ink on a page," the wizard replied. "To test its veracity you need but look to what has transpired in your lands these past weeks."

They all knew what he meant. Fetch had brought steady reports of the frails' withdrawal. The men left at the castile, those at Thricehold and Urci, they had all returned north, recalled by their lords to bring arms against the Tyrkanians. Hispartha had left Ul-wundulas.

"And now I must make haste for the Great Hall," Crafty said. "The king of Anville's emissary waits to hear what his lord will be offered to remain out of the coming conflict. Ahlamra, I trust you know when to make your entrance."

"I do."

Crafty dipped his chin at the chief. "Until your next visit, dread Fetching."

"Still takes all I got not to open his guts," Fetch said when the wizard was gone.

"Do you wish to sit the Hisparthan throne?" Ahlamra asked, her brow arching. "Or would you rather the war be waged here, between your enemies, leaving our lands alone?" They were now ritual questions, ones the chief need no longer answer.

"I must go soon," Ahlamra said. She stepped and put her hands upon the chief's arms. "And so should you. You bear momentous tidings to our brethren."

"Jackal's going to want to fuck so hard when he hears!" Polecat declared.

"He ain't the only one," Thresher said, snagging Cat by the thrum strap and pulling him toward the stairs. "Come, bedwarmer. Let's find a nook and get shameful."

Polecat beamed as he was hauled off. "Bye, chief."

Fetch waved, her mouth twisting, trying not to smile.

"I am for a far more tedious duty," Ahlamra said, sighing.

"Reckon fucking Cat's pretty damn tedious," Oats said.

"Not the way Dacia describes it," Ahlamra told him.

"Oh shit!" Culprit exclaimed, pointing at Oats. "Told you! He's a sex wizard!"

"Hells . . ."

Ahlamra slipped away and descended the tower.

Fetch raised her chin at Hoodwink. "Stay on her. Keep her safe."

Hood glided off to obey.

"Chief," Culprit said, scratching the shaved side of his head. "Could I . . . could I go back with you? This time? I'd . . . I'd like to be the one that tells Shed Snake. About the Hoof Lands."

"You better not fall off," Fetch replied. "Or get a hard cod while riding behind me."

Culprit wrinkled his face. "*Ech*. Chief!"

"Like Jackal doesn't," Oats said.

Fetching's teeth grit. "Every. Fucking. Time." She hooked a thumb over her shoulder at the rokh. "Best go let it get used to you, Cul."

Culprit moved toward the beast with a skip in his steps.

"I got a request too," Oats told the chief. He reached beneath his brigand and removed a square of folded parchment, sealed with wax. "Would you give this to Thistle? Reckon you'll be back at the Cradle long before I will."

"Of course." Fetch nodded, reaching for the letter.

Oats pulled it back at the last moment.

"Not gonna read it, Oats," Fetch teased.

"It ain't that," he said. He hesitated. Once it left his hand . . .

He gave it up and watched Fetch tuck it beneath her own brigand, feeling an unpleasant flutter in his guts. He took a long breath. And it was gone.

"Ruin woke yet?" he asked, needing something to say. He knew the answer even before Fetch shook her head. The Fangs of Our Fathers had taken Ruin away from Kalbarca weeks ago. None were certain exactly where they had gone, but if her twin had roused Fetch would know. There was a . . . heaviness to her since he was struck down, a burden that refused to lessen. Oats could see it lurking just beneath the skin, unshakable.

"Starling will find a way to wake him," she said, but the confidence was forced. "Kul'huun and the Fangs are pawing the ground to help. I offered, but Starling . . ." Fetch looked off, swallowing the hurt of her mother's refusal. "She has N'keesos."

Before Oats could offer any words of comfort, Fetching held up the scroll and took a backward step.

"Well, I got a bit of scrawl to deliver!"

Oats fiddled with the smaller roll of parchment in his hands. "Reckon I do too."

Fetch turned away. "Hells fuck, Culprit, don't feed it *that*!"

IT WAS TOO DANGEROUS FOR the Bastards to move through Magerit's streets, especially alone. Thankfully, Oats didn't need to. He made his way down from the tower and used the keep to reach the castle wall. It was a short walk to the barbican. The Tyrkanians there were used to his daily excursion and allowed him through to the path down the hill, but an escort was required to go farther. Thirty spearmen with mail coats and crescent shields marched with Oats to the Furiosa. They waited for the portcullis of the first tower to be raised. As Oats crossed the bridge, he avoided looking at the spot where Ursaria died. Her blood had stained the stones and would not yield to scrubbing. At the far end, the men posted at the second tower let them all through.

Oats moved north along the river, protected by the disciplined Tyrkanians. The full lash of summer had fallen over Hispartha's back. The day was already hot. Oats didn't envy the men their helms and mail and padded robes, but he reckoned they were well accustomed to heat.

Across the Chorismano, the wood had been removed, the terrace dismantled. The pavilions were gone. All but one, its colorful canvas resting in the center of an ordered camp.

As happened every day, Oats found himself getting nervous with every step closer to the small wooden bridge. The Tyrkanians had fortified both sides with stakes and archers, the defenses growing thicker on the far side. The camp itself was ringed by a ditch and troupes of patrolling cavalry.

Once within the camp, Oats was able to shed his escort, leaving them at the bridge. There were more than enough men with spears among the tents. Barring the castle, this was the safest place a hoof-inked mongrel could be.

Guiomar sat on a stool outside the last Hisparthan pavilion, tending a boiling pot hung above a fire.

"Prince's asleep," the girl told Oats, and he felt the knots in his gut loosen. She would have said something more if things had turned worse.

"Got something he needs to wake up for," he replied, and stepped into the pavilion.

Mannrique was indeed asleep, sprawled in the straw. He did not so much as stir when Oats ducked inside.

But Ugfuck did.

Grunting, he did more than stir. He tried to stand up.

"Easy," Oats said, rushing over to try to keep the hog down, but Ug kept pushing on quivering legs, his heavy breath punctuating his efforts. Not wanting to fight him, risk opening his wounds, Oats could do little but try to steady him.

"He's been resolved to try all morning," Mannrique said, rolling from the straw next to the hog to offer his own hands. "I think, with you here, he might just . . ." The prince reeked, his hair was matted. He hadn't changed clothes in a month, ate only at Guiomar's insistence. His efforts to save Ug had been tireless. And today, Oats dared to hope, they may have succeeded.

"I got you, Ug," Oats said, one hand beneath the hog's neck, the other at his belly. "I got you."

For weeks he had come, for weeks fearing he would find Ug had finally given up. The lance wounds were deep and wide. Every instinct Oats possessed as a hoof-rider screamed at him to end the suffering with a thrumbolt. But Mannrique's pleas were louder. They had moved the pavilion over where Ug had fallen, where they had found Mannrique alone, tending him in a fury. Fuqtus and the hoof had guarded the prince until the Tyrkanians arrived, but fear of the tourney grounds, of the plague, kept the Hisparthans from coming close.

With a snuffling exhale, Ugfuck got fully to his feet.

"You beautiful wonder," Oats said, trying to keep his voice steady. He looked over the hog's back and shared a breathless smile with Mannrique.

His point proven, Ug resettled into the straw.

Oats sat down next to his head, stroked him between the eyes. In his haste to reach the hog, he'd dropped the scroll near the pavilion's flaps.

"Shit," he said. "Doubt that was supposed to get mucked up."

Mannrique ambled over and bent to retrieve the roll of vellum.

"Barrientos signed," he said, the joy from Ug's achievement falling away.

Oats grunted an affirmation.

The prince's large hands spread the vellum, his sorrowful, flat-nosed face taking in the wall of ink. He read aloud.

"'I, Lord Consult Lono Barrientos, do hereby declare that the legitimate succession of the realms of Queen Ursaria Trastorias belongs to Mannrique Trastorias, son of Anscaro the Good. His Majesty, Mannrique, the third of his name bestowed the Crown, is confirmed King of Hispartha and the Stripped Isles, Count of Majeth, Lord of the Upper and Lower Marches, Favored Son of the Gods.'"

The prince—the new king—lowered the document, his shoulders slumping further with its weight.

"It is done, then."

"Your first act was to free the Lots," Oats said, hoping it would help, knowing it wouldn't.

Mannrique managed a weak smile. "I've done some good, then, already."

He tossed the vellum down, not bothering to roll it. There was no malice in the act, no pettiness. There was no emotion in it at all.

"I suppose my second act will be to name my nephew as heir."

Oats finally asked the question. "You really think he is? Crafty. You think he's your brother's son?"

Mannrique was a long time answering.

"I wanted him to be."

And that was all.

"At least you'll be able to abdicate soon." It wasn't a word Oats had known a fortnight ago, but the long hours in the Lord Consult's chamber had taught him all manner of royal hogshit.

Mannrique hummed. "Yes."

He didn't believe it and yet still he agreed. Oats didn't think the man capable of dissent or denial.

"Perhaps my nephew will allow me to winter in the mountains," Mannrique said, gazing beyond the walls of canvas, gazing to the northwest.

It was Oats's turn to utter agreement for something he didn't believe. Mannrique was too valuable for Crafty to let wander. The lengths taken to protect him down here in this fucking field were proof of that. Maybe he could return to Vokastria one day, when Crafty's hold on the kingdom was stronger. He might be safe in the castle there with enough loyal men to stand the walls. But Robledondo, his beloved lodge in those silent woods? How could he ever hide there again with nothing but dwarves and stable hands to guard him? Maybe he could go back, but Oats feared the peace his haven once brought him would be forever banished.

Guiomar brought in bowls of stew and they all three sat in the straw to eat in silence. Oats tried to feed some to Ug, but received a gentle reproach from Mannrique. When they were done, the girl took the bowls away, returning to the fresher air outside the pavilion. Oats was glad Rue had suggested she be asked to help here. He didn't know if Loukas missed her and didn't care. Guiomar would be better off with a king, even a morose king, than with that whoring drunk.

Oats stayed the meat of the day, helping to change Ug's dressings and apply fresh poultices. He insisted Mannrique go to the river and wash while he mucked the pavilion and changed the straw. Ugfuck stood twice more while he was there. He attempted a step the second time, but it was little more than an aborted hop accompanied by a pained squeal. Oats made sure to tell Mannrique when he returned.

"It's a good sign," the man said, scrutinizing the pig. "I'll watch him close. See he doesn't overexert."

Oats knew Mannrique wasn't comfortable with being touched, so he refrained from clapping him on the shoulder, but the desire was strong.

"There ain't no amount of gratitude I can express, Plucker," he said.

Mannrique looked away, the name giving him pleasure, which made him awkward.

"I'll be back tomorrow if not tonight," Oats told him.

"Oats," Mannrique said, stopping him at the flap. "There is something you should hear. About Ug."

Oats felt his mouth go dry. "Shit. We're still going to have to put him down, aren't we?"

"No," Mannrique said, holding up calming and apologetic hands. "No, he'll live, Oats. He's determined to. But his injuries . . . they were grave. His strength will never be what it was. His legs . . . even once he's fully healed, they won't bear more weight than his own."

Oats swallowed. "I can never ride him again."

"I'm sorry."

Oats looked beyond Mannrique. Ugfuck lay in the straw, eyes half-lidded. He let out a deep breath, as if he'd heard, as if he knew. And was asking for a pardon.

"He's done a heap more than any rider could ever ask," Oats said, voice wobbling. "He's more than earned a rest from my heavy ass."

Mannrique cleared his throat. "When he can travel on his own, if you wish, I can arrange for him to live at Robledondo. He'd be well cared for."

"I know he would, Plucker," Oats said, and this time he did not stop himself from placing a hand on the king's arm. "I know he would. But when he can travel, we're both going where we belong."

IT WAS NEARING AUTUMN WHEN the day came. The Bastards left Magerit with eighty Tyrkanian horsemen and rode east to Valentia. Ugfuck set the pace, Oats beside him on Palla.

Ahlamra remained in the city to serve as the Hoof Lands' emissary. Tarif sent thirty of his best warriors to stand as her personal guard. The chief had wanted Hood to stay behind with her, but Ahlamra insisted he would be wasted at court. The Zahracenes needed a presence in the changing kingdom and could protect her well enough, she said. For the moment, it was best if the mongrels made infamous by the ill-fated tourney were not around to rouse bitter passions among the Hisparthans.

In truth, they'd stayed too long. But those who came north together wanted to return in the same company. Fetch brought Culprit back so he could take his hog home, though they could have led the animal easily enough, especially at the speed Ug could manage.

It was nearly as ponderous a journey as the one that brought them, but none complained. At least this time they knew where they were bound. They stayed to the Imperium's roads and camped with the Tyrkanians, avoiding placing the burden of sheltering them on the towns and villages, except when they needed to resupply. The settlements between Magerit and Valentia had quickly become resigned to the empire's presence, with a steady flow of goods and soldiers moving overland between the port and the royal city.

Still, they were watchful. Crafty had control of the Crown and a great eastern port city, but the kingdom was far from conquered. As yet, none had stood openly to oppose him, but the cauldron was heating and would boil over to war. Ahlamra suspected it would come before winter. And she had made it clear to Crafty, the Hoof Lands would take no part.

A ship awaited them at Valentia, crewed by the White Wrists, and captained by Roar.

"You named it the *Squealhaul*, didn't you?" Oats said, leading Ug carefully up the ramp.

"No," Roar grumbled, crossing his meaty arms. "It's the *Eat Shit and Get Aboard, Cunt*."

Oats laughed and bent to whisper in Ugfuck's ear. "*Squealhaul*."

Once they were under way, Oats realized that their course down the eastern shore would save them from having to pass through the Gut. He nearly voiced his relief to his brethren before remembering that only Sluggard had been with him during that first sickening voyage. Oats hadn't thought to look back on Hispartha, but he found himself turning to behold the dwindling land to offer a silent farewell.

MONGREL'S CRADLE WAS AS BEGUILING as ever.

"Hells, *fuck* the Sons!" Polecat declared, slapping the heel of his hand upon the ship railing. "Perdition my finger-fucked ass."

Roar and the Wrists guided the ship into the harbor.

Culprit leaped onto the wharf and ran down the planking, arms thrust into the air.

"Hoof Lands!" he screamed, drawing every eye on the docks. "HOOF LANDS!"

"Would you come back and help with your damn hog!" Thresher called after him. She blew out an exasperated breath. "Not like he ain't been back."

"Kalbarca ain't the Cradle," Polecat said.

Thresher took in the morning light on the beach, the palm trees, and the perfection of the distant, sheltering mountains. "You ain't wrong."

Fetch had gathered the rest of the hoof to meet them. Oats and the others had spotted her in the sky several times during the journey, even among the clouds over Hispartha. She stood among the bustle of the docks, Jackal beside her, Anvil at her back. Rant was already on the wharf, hustling to help with the mooring lines.

"It'll be a moment until we can offload the barbarians," Roar said. "You can go ahead and kiss land if you've a mind. Or whatever you want."

The surly mongrel gave Oats a loaded look and tilted his head toward the other group waiting on the docks.

"OADS!"

Muro broke away from Thistle and came running as soon as Oats's boots hit the planks. The child's unsteady gait was made more erratic by his excitement. He tripped on the uneven boards, but Oats had already covered the distance and caught him up, lifting the boy into an embrace. Muro's arms snatched around his neck, squeezing tight, and he laughed as Oats kissed him over and again, beard tickling his neck and cheek.

Muro leaned back, put his hands on Oats's face. "I sawn you! On the boat, I sawn you!"

"I saw you too!"

"Oads. I have a friend. A little friend. We play. I teached him things."

Oats set Muro down, but held on to his hand. "Let's go see him."

Only, there was no one to see.

Muro looked up at Thistle, puzzled. "Where is he? Mama, where is he?"

Thistle smiled and shrugged.

Warbler made a clicking sound until Muro looked up at him. The old thrice made a furtive gesture to some nearby barrels. A grin grew on Muro's face as he began a slow, sneaking approach.

"Wah!" Wily jumped out from behind the barrels, hands raised.

Muro stiffened and squealed and jumped in place, shocked and delighted. He proceeded to chase the little thrice around the barrels. Wily moved without care, reckless and whole and healthy. Heedless of the world, the boys played and hollered. Oats looked to Beryl.

His mother's lips were tight, but she spoke as he stepped toward her.

"I never should have said—"

Oats leaned down, cutting off her words as he drew her close. Looking over her he met Thistle's eye, returned the hopeful trepidation in her face.

Beryl's voice rose from the depths of his chest. "Still cross with you for going into Hispartha."

"Don't worry, Mother," Oats said. "I ain't ever going back."

The True Bastards reunited, embracing and sharing jests. The hogs were offloaded, Ug receiving a cheer from the hoof as he trundled down the wharf. They lingered a moment, gathering gear.

"Can we get somewhere with some damn wine?" Thresher said, at last, receiving lusty sounds of agreement.

NIGHT FOUND THE BEACH STREWN with Bastards.

Culprit lay passed-out beneath the brewer's cart, his snores not quite drowned by the roar of the surf. Thoon had wheeled the laden conveyance down from Salduba, bringing enough wine and ale to sink a hundred mongrels. None of it went to waste. The Sons of Perdition joined the revels in a steady string of small groups, as their duties—and Father—allowed. Many of the White Wrists too added their thirst to the task along with Jacintho and a score of his hillmen. The stretch of sand set aside for the revels teemed with songs and laughter, cheers for the chief and the Hoof Lands, gloating curses for the dead queen and chastened Hispartha. The merriment of the day birthed friendly races, afoot and ahog. Men and mongrels swam in the surf, splashing and cavorting with the women of Salduba brazen enough to join in the celebration.

Few were still upright by sunset.

Oats sat in the sand, Thistle dozing on his shoulder. Muro and Wily lay on a blanket before them. They'd fallen asleep holding hands.

"Moving them now would be a cruelty," Beryl said from the bench Warbler had made for them using two barrels and a board.

Oats nodded in contented agreement.

"Think we committed to spending the night here several casks back," Fetching said, nestling deeper into Jackal's supporting embrace.

Anvil and Thresher were on the other side of the driftwood fire, sharing a bottle and a soundless conversation. Thoon sat behind them, his large, hunched form providing a windbreak.

"I can walk you back to town, if you're ready," Warbler said.

Beryl clasped the back of his hand. "No. No, I'd rather stay."

Tuneless singing drew every eye to a pair of stumbling figures making indirect progress toward the fire.

"Hells, you made it back," Thresher called out. "Made me lose a wager."

Propped by a struggling Jacintho, Polecat gurgled a laugh and tossed something long and weighty into the sand.

"Bet it ain't worth more'n that," he proclaimed an instant before Jacintho let him fall. Cat went facedown in the grit while his deliverer bent over double, hands resting on his skinny legs.

"Don't you think about spewing, frail," Fetch warned.

Jacintho waved a hand without looking up, the motion causing his hat to fall off.

Thresh leaned and picked up the object, a tapered length of polished wood banded with brass and affixed with leather straps.

"Is that—?" Jackal began.

"The lazy-eyed Traedrian captain's fake leg!" Polecat said, rolling over to his back and thrusting a triumphant, wavering arm into the air.

As the chuckles boiled up from the besotted mongrel's gut, Thresh continued to hold the leg, stilled by puzzlement.

"Why?" she asked.

Polecat's answer sailed on a flood of increased laughter. "Because I . . . I just . . . I just fucking wanted it!"

His mirth was contagious and soon the entire hoof was, at the least, smiling.

"Weren't Rant and Roar with you?" the chief asked.

"Still throwing bones," Cat panted. "Think they wan' the capn's ship. All he's got left. 'Cause I got his leg!"

"If you fool-asses cost me a fleet, I swea—"

Jacintho tossed his guts.

"All's well." The bandit waved. "It's all in the hat."

Slowly, the man scooped up the unfortunate receptacle and ambled toward the surf.

Thresher poked Polecat with the wooden leg. "How many whores you fuck?"

"None," Cat replied, crawling forward to rest his head on her leg. "For none were named Dacia."

"Must not have paid them enough," Jackal muttered, and got an elbow in the ribs from Fetch.

Polecat didn't hear, his sawing breaths joining Culprit's. Thistle joined the boys on the blanket. One by one, they all succumbed, reclining on saddles and bedrolls. Oats remained awake.

Strange to see his brethren slumbering around him. The arrangement of their weapons, the remuda of hogs close by with Hood standing watch, in many ways it resembled a night on patrol, one of hundreds. Yet, it was a heap more. And a heap less. The boys, Beryl, a bellows-breathing cyclops. Those didn't fit, to say nothing of a gorgeous, moonlit beach. Maybe that was common for a Sons patrol, but the Bastards? Tranquility weren't exactly a tradition.

"More of us should be here."

Oats turned at Fetch's soft words to find her eyes open. She lay facing him on her side, Jackal asleep behind her.

"We lost too many, Oats."

His only answer was to take her hand.

They were still clasped when dawn came. Fetching had slept again, but Oats never did. He'd watched Roar return, carrying his sister over a shoulder. Hells, he'd even witnessed Hoodwink at last lay down, though he wouldn't wager the mongrel had ever closed his eyes. Oats passed the entirety of that night unwilling to relinquish a single moment of it to slumber. No dream could have offered a more pleasant vision.

Beryl was the first to rise, the boys following almost immediately. The rest roused with no small amount of coughing, grousing, and throat-clearing.

"Knock the sand from your crevices, Bastards," the chief said. "We got a heap to do. Roar, Rant. You best not have started a war with Traedria!"

The hoof climbed to their feet, gathered their gear, and began to move toward the remuda with grins and playful cuffs.

Oats remained where he was, watching them.

"Are you certain?" Thistle asked from beside him.

He looked at her, repeated the question in his heart. The answer flourished. "I'm certain."

It was Jackal who noticed he wasn't following.

"Oats?" he said, slowing as he turned.

"I'm not going, Jack."

Jackal's grin spread as he looked at Thistle. "Sure. We'll take the boys. You can join us later."

"No."

The word stopped the rest of the hoof.

Fetch peered at him, her face creased with concern. Oats swallowed, took a breath, and took a single step forward. He faced the Bastards and the words came, painful with the ease they were spoken.

"I'm sorry, brethren. But I can't. Not anymore."

"What, fucking drink?" Polecat said. "We all feel that the next mor—"

Thresh reached and silenced him with a touch.

"Oats . . ." Fetching took another step.

"Isa, I'm . . . I'm done." He fought the shake in his voice, but it came anyway. "I'm leaving. The Bastards, the Lots. I'm leaving."

Jackal's face fell. "Leaving?"

"Idris . . ." Beryl said.

He looked at her, at them all. "I can't stay. Hispartha may be gone, but Ul-wundulas will continue to bleed. The orcs, Strava. The hoofs haven't seen the end of war. I have to get away from it. I have to get Muro away from it. And Wily too, Mother, if you'll go."

Beryl blanched, but said nothing.

"You know what you're saying, son?" Warbler asked.

"I do." Oats steadied himself, trying not to allow the looks on the faces to sway him.

Culprit's earnest dismay.

Anvil's pensive glower.

Jackal's slack jaw hardening with hurt.

"Blood is like wine here," Oats said. "The first taste is bitter, turns your stomach, but you soon grow to crave it. I don't want to taste it again. I don't want these boys to ever taste it. Not if I can help it. I want them to know more than pain and hatred and the graves of friends. I want them to live in peace. And it can't be found here. Not yet."

"Oats," Jackal pleaded. "Think about this."

"He has, Jack," Fetch said quietly. "He has." She meant the letter she'd delivered to Thistle. She hadn't read it, Oats was certain of that, but she knew now what it had said, what it had put in motion. And she weren't wrong.

Oats forced himself to meet her eye. "Chief, I'm sorry, but before we went north you said that we each had a choice of where we would fight, where we would die." He shook his head, voice growing dull with restrained tears. "But . . . I don't want to fight anymore. I can't, I can't fight anymore. Reckon that makes me a craven—"

Fetching darted forward and took his face between her hands.

"None ever dare say it!" she hissed, her own eyes bright and wet. "None ever dare."

Their foreheads met and Oats gave himself to the grief, to the relief of the sobbing breaths and his sister's firm, accepting hands.

"You've done enough, Oats," she whispered.

Oats wept and nodded, grateful that it was done. Fetch released him. Jackal stood by.

"Oats. Leave the Bastards, leave the fighting. Hells, live here and never pick up a thrum or sword again. But please, brother, you don't have to leave the Lots."

Oats remained silent, letting the friendship of a lifetime answer for him. Slowly, the pain left Jackal's face, leaving nothing but understanding.

"Hells, I hate this," Jackal said.

They enfolded each other, neither relinquishing the hold for a long time.

When they parted, Oats found Beryl and Warbler had moved away. They stood removed, speaking where none could hear. Both kept looking to Wily, now traipsing about with Muro beneath a discarded fishing net. Beryl reached up and placed a hand on Warbler's face. The old thrice leaned into the touch, cupped the hand with his. Oats looked away as they kissed, not for discomfort, but because it felt an intrusion.

As his mother approached, Oats steeled himself for her rebuke. Her hands reached for his and he took them.

"Where are we going?" she asked, the sea wind taking away a scrim of tears.

Oats expelled a joyous breath. He hadn't thought she'd agree.

Warbler had gone and squatted by the wobbling fishing net. He coaxed Wily out from beneath. To say goodbye. Oats couldn't bear to watch.

"A ship to start," he told Beryl before looking to Thistle.

She nodded down the beach, toward the harbor. "It will be ready and waiting for us."

Oats nodded. "After that . . . well, we ain't decided."

"Somewhere green," Beryl said.

"We'll find it," he promised.

He turned back to the hoof.

"Reckon there's one thing left." Oats removed his brigand, his shirt. "Can we do it quick? While the boys are distracted?"

Jackal's mouth wrinkled with distaste. "Surely—"

Fetch plucked the shirt from the ground and handed it back to Oats. "We ain't taking knives to your ink, fool-ass. The old ways are dead. No sense in scarring a mongrel when he's done nothing but have the courage to live the way he wants. Besides, that salty sea air would sting any cuts something evil."

"Hells," Oats swore, fighting fresh emotion. "This might have been easier if you'd been a cunt."

Fetch reached up and smacked his cheek, just hard enough. "No chance."

The True Bastards escorted them to the wharf, where a ship with a familiar captain awaited.

"Thought you retired?" Oats called to Burgos.

The grizzled river pirate scratched at his branded cheek. "Reckon

I should see a pinch more of the world before I settle on where that is."

The ship was larger than the *Mariposa*, with a deeper hold and larger crew.

Oats drew Rant aside. "That thing fit for the open sea?"

Rant rolled her eyes and smiled. "Safe voyage."

"Don't drown," Roar said, passing by to help load the vessel.

"Thanks," Oats muttered.

The rest of the hoof stood before him. Thresh was the first to come forward.

"Luck to you, Big Bastard," she said, hugging his neck.

Soon as she stepped away, Culprit darted forward, almost knocking Oats over with a tackling embrace. Oats laughed and hugged him back.

"I'll watch over them," Anvil said, next. Even with one eye, Oats had no doubt she would.

"Thistle, eh?" Polecat said with a wink. "I get it."

He swatted Oats in the cods as he backed away.

Warbler stood removed. Oats went to him, but the old thrice thumped him on the chest with his knuckles, silencing any words before they were spoken.

"Had about all the farewells I can stand, Idris."

"You told me I had a choice, before Kalbarca." Oats cocked his head back toward the wharf. "Them or the hoof, remember?"

Warbler nodded. It was the first time Oats had ever known the mongrel to struggle to meet another's eye.

"It ain't too late, War-boar. So, what's it to be? The family you made, or the brotherhood you helped found?"

When Warbler answered, his deep voice quavered, but his face was resolved. "Them boys need to keep together. They'll need each other. And Beryl. You do what I couldn't, Idris . . . what I still can't."

Oats turned away, trying not to let his love for the old thrice die. He was surprised to find Hood waiting for him. Even more surprised when the eerie mongrel leaned in. But it wasn't to embrace. It was to whisper a word in his ear. The name of a place.

"I thought she didn't want me to know," Oats said, bewildered.

"Her words were 'Tell him when he comes to his hells-damned senses.'"

Oats had to smile and he thought he saw the corner of Hood's mouth give the barest twitch upward.

The ship was ready. All that was left was the passengers. Ugfuck lumbered aboard with little coaxing, gifting the hoof with a parting fart.

"I've tooken a ship," Muro told Wily as they stood at the bottom ramp, taking the smaller boy's hand. "You'll be sick, but I'll help you."

Thistle guided the children up the ramp. Oats gave Beryl a hand before returning to the wharf one last time.

"Dammit, Idris," Fetching said, neck tightening. "You don't go soon, I'm going to order you to stay."

He grabbed her and picked her up. "Love you, sister mine."

Her laugh couldn't quite cover the sob. "I love you."

Oats set her down, but kept her close, reaching out his other arm for Jackal and dragging him in.

"Love you both."

They huddled there the three of them, heads together, hands clasping at the backs of necks, sniffing and miserable and comfortable. Oats clenched his eyes, his fists. Quickly, he kissed them both and tore away, up the plank.

The ship moved off. There were shouts, and laughs, and rude gestures, as the Bastards shrank with the growing distance. Oats intended to keep vigil until he could see them no more.

"Bears and moundtans, Oads!"

Wily's shriller voice took up the call. "Bears and mountains!"

Without hesitation, without regret, Oats turned his back on Ulwundulas, on his brothers and sisters, to face the eager smiles of his sons. He hunkered down into a ball. Muro bounced in anticipation as Oats unfolded himself to his full height, arms raised.

"Bears! And! MOUNTAINS!"

ACKNOWLEDGMENTS

Well, here they are, yet another author's Acknowledgments in what I imagine will be a bumper crop of such end matter that makes at least some passing mention to the past year of pandemic and isolation. All I will say is this: writers tend to live anywhere and everywhere, but the hubs of Big 5 . . . 4 (what are we down to these days?) . . . anyway, the hubs of Big Publishing are New York and London. Just about everyone on the production side of this book, and many others, resided in one of these cities and did their jobs from apartments and flats, juggling the responsibilities of their profession and, I'm sure at times, a growing case of stir-craziness. I never do know everyone involved, but my ignorance does not dampen my appreciation. There are those I *can* name, however, and I ask that they pass on my gratitude to all the wonderful folk who are mysteries to me but colleagues to them.

In London at Orbit, an Ugfuck-sized thank you to Anna for shepherding this series into success in the UK with the help of James, Emily, Nadia (who I now know is not the same as Nazia), and crew.

In New York at Del Rey, I am forever grateful for the professional attention of Caroline, Kathleen, and Stacey. And to Rachelle, who I recently learned copyedited all three books, for catching every one of my abuses of the written word, and more than a few continuity errors and plot holes. Leading the charge, of course, is Julian. Thanks for inviting me and the Bastards to compete in a new arena, for reading every word (more than thrice!), for providing such clear insight into both the strengths and weaknesses of these books, and for always allowing me the time I needed.

At Penguin Random House Audio, I am indebted to Julianna for putting such incredible people on the audiobook team. Harry, Lisa, and Will, you guys are incredible at a process that is alchemy to me. I'd hazard it's a rare thing for an author to form a friendship with the narrator of one of their books, but am happy to say it happened to me. Will, so glad you and January have entered our lives.

Much awe and respect to the amazing translators Hana and Artem, who figured out how to wrestle the Bastards into Czech and Russian, respectively! Their questions about some of the word origins and naming conventions in the books are among the most fascinating correspondence I've ever had.

To Ian Leino, a generous artist whose talent is only exceeded by his kindness.

At Donald Maass, thanks to Patricia for always making sure the checks reached me!

To my friend Cameron, who also happens to be a great agent, thank you for being on the other end of the phone. The chats about parenting, home repair, home *schooling,* the book industry, dogs, katars for home defense, and many more, they were all a lifeline during the past very trying year. To say nothing of your unerring guidance in terms of the Bastards and the career of writing. You are, frankly, the best.

Mounds of love to my family. I am often my own worst enemy, which makes them nothing short of heroes. Rob, thank you for being a source of wisdom, much needed perspective, and commiseration. Liza, thank you for shouldering so much during quarantine. You make everything you do look effortless, but I am aware that is far from true. You are made of stars. And a Gojira-sized "Dank You!" to Wyatt, the ultimate playmate and an awe-inspiring son. For all the games of Smash, 40K, and Mordheim (even though you're positively *wrecking* me!), the sword fights and wrestling matches, the walks for ice cream, the bike rides, the shouted reading of signs (POLAR POP! FROZEN COW! BURMA SHAVE!), for all those and countless other daily joys, thank you.

To any deserving person I failed to mention, please forgive me. I am fried.

And finally I would like to offer my immense gratitude to all the readers that became fans. You all built quite a ferocious hoof over these three books. While we must leave the Lots for the time being, I hope we will ride together again in the future. Until then . . . well, I reckon I don't need to say it anymore. You all know what to do.

—Jonathan, May 10, 2021

ABOUT THE AUTHOR

JONATHAN FRENCH lives in Atlanta with his wife and son. He is a devoted reader of comic books, an expert thrower of oddly shaped dice, and a serial con attendee.

ABOUT THE TYPE

This book was set in Fournier, a typeface named for Pierre-Simon Fournier (1712–68), the youngest son of a French printing family. He started out engraving woodblocks and large capitals, then moved on to fonts of type. In 1736 he began his own foundry and made several important contributions in the field of type design; he is said to have cut 147 alphabets of his own creation. Fournier is probably best remembered as the designer of St. Augustine Ordinaire, a face that served as the model for the Monotype Corporation's Fournier, which was released in 1925.